Henning Mankell

SIDETRACKED

Translated by Steven T. Murray

HARVILL CRIME IN VINTAGE

Published by Vintage 2002

❡ 8 10 9 7

Copyright © Henning Mankell 1995
English Translation © Steven T. Murray 1999

Map by Reginald Piggot

Henning Mankell has asserted his right under the
Copyright, Designs and Patents Act 1988 to be
identified as the author of this work

First published as *Villospår* by Ordfronts Förlag,
Stockholm 1995

First published in the United States by The New Press,
New York

First published in Great Britain by The Harvill Press
2000

Vintage
Random House, 20 Vauxhall Bridge Road,
London SW1V 2SA

Random House Australia (Pty) Limited
20 Alfred Street, Milsons Point, Sydney,
New South Waled 2061, Australia

Random House New Zealand Limited
18 Poland Road, Glenfield
Auckland 10, New Zealand

Random House (Pty) Limited
Endulini, 5A Jubilee Road, Parktown 2193,
South Africa

The Random House Group Limited Reg. No. 954009

www.randomhouse.co.uk

A CIP catalogue record for this books
is available from the British Library

ISBN 0 09 944698 7

Papers used by Random House are natural, recyclable
products made from wood grown in sustainable
forests. The manufacturing processes conform to the
environmental regulations of the country of origin

Printed and bound in Great Britain by
Bookmarque Ltd, Croydon, Surrey

SIDETRACKED

Henning Mankell was born in Stockholm in 1948. He is the author of many works of fiction, among them the nine books in the Kurt Wallander series. His books have been translated into 19 languages. He has worked as an actor, theatre director and manager in Sweden and more recently in Mozambique, where he now lives and is the head of the Teatro Avenida in Maputo. He won the Swedish Academy of Crime Literature award for *Faceless Killers*, and the CWA Gold Dagger 2001 for *Sidetracked*.

Steven T. Murray has translated numerous works from the Scandinavian languages, including the Pelle the Conqueror series by Martin Andersen Nexø and three of Henning Mankell's Kurt Wallander novels. He is Editor-in-Chief of Fjord Press in Seattle.

ALSO BY HENNING MANKELL

TO JON

This is a novel. None of the characters in it are real people. However, not every similarity to real people is possible or even necessary to avoid. I am grateful to everyone who helped me with the work on this book.

Paderne,
July 1995

Shall I bend, in vain, shall I shake
the old, hard, immovable bars?
– they will not stretch, they will not break
for the bars are riveted and forged inside myself,
and the bars will not shatter until I shatter too

From "A Ghasel" by Gustaf Fröding

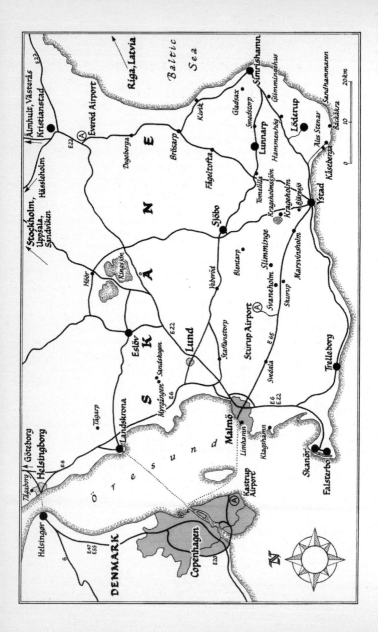

Dominican Republic

1978

PROLOGUE

Just before dawn, Pedro Santana woke. The kerosene lamp had started to smoke. When he opened his eyes he didn't know where he was. He had been roused from a dream in which he wandered through a peculiar, rocky landscape where the air was very thin, and he knew that all his memories were about to leave him. The smoking kerosene lamp had penetrated his consciousness like the distant smell of volcanic ash. But suddenly there was something else: a human sound, tormented, panting. And then the dream evaporated and he was forced to return to the dark room where he had now spent six days and six nights without sleeping more than a few minutes at a time.

The kerosene lamp had gone out. He lay completely still. The night was very warm. He smelt of sweat. It had been a long time since he had last managed to wash. He got up cautiously from the earthen floor and groped for the plastic jug of kerosene over by the door. It must have rained while he had slept. The floor was damp under his feet. Off in the distance he heard a rooster crow. Ramirez's rooster. It was always the first in the village to crow, before dawn. That rooster was like an impatient person. Like someone who lived in the city, someone who always seemed to have too much to do, but never did anything other than attend to his own haste. Life wasn't like that in the village: here everything moved as slowly as life itself. Why should people hurry when the plants that nourished them grew so slowly?

He found the jug of kerosene and pulled out the piece of cloth stuffed into the opening. The panting that filled the darkness grew more and more uneven. He found the lamp, pulled out the cork, and carefully poured in the kerosene. He struck a match, lifted the glass cover, and watched the wick start to burn.

Then he forced himself to turn around. He couldn't bear to see what was waiting for him. The woman lying in the bed next to the wall was going to die. He knew this now, even though for a long time he had tried to persuade himself that she would recover. His last attempt to flee had been in his dream. But a person could never escape death. Not his own, nor that of someone he loved.

He squatted down by the bed. The kerosene lamp threw restless shadows across the walls. He looked at her. She was still young. Even though her face was pale and sunken, she was beautiful. The last thing to leave my wife will be her beauty, he thought, as tears came to his eyes. He touched her forehead. The fever had risen again.

He glanced through the broken window patched with a piece of cardboard. Not dawn yet. If only it would come, he thought. Just let her have the strength to keep breathing until dawn. Then she won't leave me all alone in the night.

Suddenly her eyes flew open. He grasped her hand and tried to smile.

"Where is the child?" she asked in a voice so weak that he could hardly understand her.

"She's sleeping at my sister's house," he replied. "It's best that way."

She seemed reassured by his answer.

"How long have I been asleep?"

"For many hours."

"Have you been sitting here the whole time? You must rest. In a few days I won't need to lie here any longer."

"I've been sleeping," he replied. "Soon you're going to be well again."

He wondered whether she knew he was lying, whether she knew she would never get up again. Were both of them lying to each other in their despair? To make the inevitable easier?

"I'm so tired," she said.

"You must sleep so you'll get well," he answered, turning his head at the same time so she wouldn't see his face.

Soon the first light of dawn seeped in. She had slipped into unconsciousness again. He was so tired that he could no longer control his thoughts.

4

He had met Dolores when he was 21. He and his brother Juan walked the long road to Santiago de los Treinta Caballeros to see the carnival. Juan, who was older, had visited the city once before. But it was Pedro's first time. It took them three days to get there. Once in a while they got a ride for a few kilometres with an ox and cart. But they walked most of the way.

At last they reached their destination. It was a February day and the carnival was in full swing. Astonished, Pedro had stared at the garish costumes and the terrifying masks of devils and animals. The whole city was dancing to the beat of thousands of drums and guitars. Juan piloted him through the streets and alleys. At night they slept on benches in Parque Duarte. Pedro was afraid that Juan would disappear into the swirling crowds. He felt like a child frightened of losing his parents. But he didn't let on. He didn't want Juan to laugh at him.

On their last evening, Juan did suddenly vanish among the costumed, dancing people. They hadn't agreed on a place to meet if they were separated. Pedro searched for Juan all night. At daybreak he stopped by the fountain in the Plaza de Cultura.

A girl about his own age sat down beside him. She was the most beautiful girl he had ever seen. He watched as she took off her sandals and rubbed her sore feet. When she met his gaze, he lowered his eyes, embarrassed.

That was how he met Dolores. They sat by the fountain and started talking. Dolores had been looking for work as a housekeeper, going from house to house in the rich neighbourhood without success. She too was the child of a *campesino*, and her village was not far from Pedro's. They left the city together, plundered banana trees for food, and walked more and more slowly the closer they came to her village.

Two years later they were married, and moved into a little house in Pedro's village. Pedro worked on a sugar plantation while Dolores grew vegetables and sold them. They were poor, but they were happy.

Only one thing was not as it should be. After three years Dolores was not yet pregnant. They never talked about it, but Pedro sensed

Dolores's increasing anxiety. Without telling him, she had visited some *curiositas* on the Haitian border to seek help.

Eight years passed. And then one evening when Pedro was returning from the sugar plantation, Dolores met him on the road and told him she was pregnant. At the end of the eighth year of their marriage, she gave birth to a daughter. When Pedro saw his child for the first time, he could see at once that she had inherited her mother's beauty. That evening Pedro went to the village church and made an offering of some gold jewellery his mother had given him. Then he went home singing so loudly and fervently that the people he met thought he had drunk too much rum.

Dolores was asleep. She was breathing harder, and stirred restlessly.

"You can't die," whispered Pedro, no longer able to control his despair. "You can't die and leave me and our child."

Two hours later it was all over. For a brief moment her breathing grew completely calm. She opened her eyes and looked at him.

"You must baptise our daughter," she said. "You must baptise her and take care of her."

"You'll be well soon," he answered. "We'll baptise her together."

"I don't exist any more," she said and closed her eyes.

Then she was gone.

Two weeks later Pedro left the village, carrying his daughter in a basket on his back. His brother Juan followed him down the road.

"What are you doing?" he asked.

"What has to be done."

"Why must you go to the city to baptise your daughter? Why can't you have her baptised here in the village? That church has served us well. And our parents before us."

Pedro stopped and looked at his brother.

"For eight years we waited for a child. When our daughter finally came, Dolores died. She wasn't yet 30. She had to die. Because we are poor. Because of poverty's diseases. Now I will return to the big cathedral on the plaza where we met. My daughter will be baptised in the biggest church there is in this country. That's the least I can do for Dolores."

He didn't wait for Juan's reply. Late that evening, when he reached the village Dolores had come from, he stopped at her mother's house. Again he explained where he was going. The old woman shook her head sadly.

"Your sorrow will drive you crazy," she said.

Early the next morning Pedro resumed his journey. As he walked he told his daughter everything he could remember about Dolores. When he had no more to say, he started again.

Pedro reached the city one afternoon as heavy rain clouds gathered on the horizon. He sat down to wait on the steps of the cathedral, Santiago Apóstol, and watched the black-clad priests passing by. They seemed either too young, or in too much of a hurry to be worthy of baptising his daughter. He waited many hours. At last an old priest came slowing towards the cathedral. Pedro stood up, took off his straw hat, and held out his daughter. The old priest listened patiently to his story. Then he nodded.

"I will baptise her," he said. "You have walked a long way for something you believe in. In our day that is rare. People seldom walk long distances for their faith. That's why the world looks the way it does."

Pedro followed the priest into the dim cathedral. He felt that Dolores was near him as they made their way to the font.

"What will the girl be named?" he asked.

"She will be named Dolores, after her mother. And María. Dolores María Santana."

After the baptism Pedro went out to the plaza and sat down where he had met Dolores ten years before. His daughter was asleep in the basket. He sat completely still, deep in thought.

I, Pedro Santana, am a simple man. I have inherited nothing but poverty and relentless misery. I have not even been allowed to keep my wife. But I vow that our daughter will have a different life. I will do everything for her. I promise you, Dolores, that your daughter will live a long and happy and worthy life.

That evening Pedro left the city with his beloved daughter, Dolores María Santana. She was then eight months old.

Skåne

21–24 June 1994

CHAPTER 1

Before dawn he started his transformation.

He had planned everything meticulously so that nothing could go wrong. It would take him all day, and he didn't want to risk running out of time. He took up the first paintbrush and held it in front of him. From the cassette player on the floor he could hear the tape of drum music that he had recorded. He studied his face in the mirror. Then he drew the first black lines across his forehead. He noted that his hand was steady. So he wasn't nervous, at least. Even though this was the first time he had put on his war paint. Until this moment it had been merely an escape, his way of defending himself against the injustices he was continually subjected to. Now he went through the transformation in earnest. With each stroke that he painted on his face, he seemed to be leaving his old life behind. There was no turning back. This very evening the game would be over for good, he would go out into the war, and people were going to die.

The light in the room was very bright. He arranged the mirrors carefully, so that the glare didn't get in his eyes. When he had locked the door behind him, he had first checked that everything was where it was supposed to be: the well-cleaned brushes, the little porcelain cups of paint, the towels and water, next to the little lathe his weapons in rows on a black cloth – three axes, knives with blades of various lengths, and spray cans. This was the only decision still to be made. Before sundown he had to choose which to take with him. He couldn't take them all. But he knew that the choice would resolve itself once he had begun his transformation.

Before he sat down on the bench and started to paint his face, he tested the edges of his axes and knives. They were as sharp as could be. He couldn't resist the temptation to press a little harder on one of the knives. His finger started to bleed. He wiped it and the knife with a towel. Then he sat down in front of the mirrors.

The first strokes on his forehead had to be black. It was as if he were slicing two deep cuts, opening his brain, and emptying the memories and thoughts that had haunted him all his life, tormenting him and humiliating him. Then the red and white stripes, the circles, the squares, and at last the snake-like designs on his cheeks. None of his white skin should be visible. Then the transformation would be complete. What was inside him would be gone. He would be born again in the guise of an animal, and he would never speak as a human being again. He would cut out his tongue if he had to.

Just after 6 p.m. he was done. By then he had chosen the largest of the three axes. He stuck the shaft into his thick leather belt. Two knives were already there in their sheaths. He looked around the room. Nothing was forgotten. He stuffed the spray cans in the inside pockets of his jacket.

He looked at his face in the mirror one last time, and shuddered. Carefully he pulled his motorcycle helmet over his head, switched off the light, and left the room barefoot, just as he had come in.

At 9.05 p.m. Gustaf Wetterstedt turned down the sound on his TV and phoned his mother. It was a nightly ritual. Ever since he had retired as minister of justice more than 25 years earlier, leaving behind all his political dealings, he had watched the news with repugnance. He couldn't come to terms with the fact that he was no longer involved. During his years as minister, a man in the absolute centre of the public eye, he appeared on TV at least once a week. Each appearance had been meticulously copied from film to video by a secretary and the tapes now covered a whole wall of shelves in his study. Once in a while he watched them again. It was a great source of satisfaction to see that never once in all those years as minister of justice had he lost his composure when confronted by an unexpected question from a malicious reporter. He would recall with unbounded contempt how many of his colleagues had been terrified of TV reporters, how they would stammer and get entangled in contradictions. That had never happened to him. He was a man who couldn't be trapped. The reporters had never beaten him. Nor had they discovered his secret.

He had turned on his TV at 9 p.m. to see the top stories. Now he turned down the sound. He pulled over the telephone and called his mother. She was now 94, but with a clear mind and full of energy. She lived alone in a big flat in Stockholm's innercity. Each time he lifted the receiver and dialled the number he prayed she wouldn't answer. He was more than 70, and he had begun to be afraid that she would outlive him. There was nothing he wanted more than for her to die. Then he'd be left alone. He wouldn't have to call her any more, and soon he'd forget what she even looked like.

The telephone rang at the other end. He watched the silent anchorman. At the fourth ring he began to hope that she was dead. Then she answered. He softened his voice as he spoke. He asked how she was feeling, how had her day been, but now he knew that she was still alive, he wanted to make the conversation as brief as possible.

Finally he hung up and sat with his hand resting on the receiver. She's never going to die, he thought. She'll never die unless I kill her. All he could hear was the roar of the sea, and then a lone moped going past the house. He walked over to the big balcony window facing the sea. The twilight was beautiful. The beach below his huge estate was deserted. Everyone is sitting in front of their TVs, he thought. There was a time when they sat there and watched me make mincemeat of the reporters, back when I was minister of justice. I should have been made foreign minister. But I never was.

He drew the heavy curtains, making sure that there were no gaps. Even though he tried to live as discreetly as possible in this house located just east of Ystad, occasional curiosity-seekers spied on him. Although it had been 25 years since he left office, he had not yet been entirely forgotten. He went out to the kitchen and poured himself a cup of coffee from a thermos he had bought during an official visit to Italy in the late 1960s. He vaguely recalled that he'd gone to discuss efforts to prevent the spread of terrorism in Europe. All over his house there were reminders of the life he had lived. Sometimes he thought of throwing them away, but to make the effort seemed pointless.

He went back to the sofa with his coffee. He switched off the TV with the remote, and sat in the dark, thinking through the day's events. In the morning he'd had a visit from a journalist on one of the big monthly magazines. She was writing a series about famous people in retirement, but he couldn't really see why she had decided upon him. She had brought a photographer with her and they took pictures on the beach and inside the house. He had decided in advance that he would present the image of a kindly old man, reconciled with his past. He described his present life as very happy. He lived in seclusion so that he could meditate, he said, and he let slip with feigned embarrassment that he was thinking of writing his memoirs. The journalist, who was in her 40s, had been impressed and clearly respectful. Afterwards he escorted her and the photographer to their car and waved as they drove off.

He hadn't said a single thing that was true during the entire interview, he thought with satisfaction. This was one of the few things that still held any interest for him. To deceive without being discovered. To continue with the pretence. After all his years as a politician he realised all that was left was the lie. The truth disguised as a lie or the lie dressed up as the truth.

Slowly he drank the rest of his coffee. His sense of well-being grew. The evenings and nights were his best time. That was when his thoughts of all that he had lost sank beneath the surface, and he remembered only what no-one could rob him of. The most important thing. The utmost secret.

Sometimes he imagined himself as an image in a mirror that was both concave and convex at the same time. No-one had ever seen anything but the surface: the eminent jurist, the respected minister of justice, the kindly retiree strolling along the beach in Skåne. No-one would have guessed at his double-sided self. He had greeted kings and presidents, he had bowed with a smile, but in his head he was thinking, *if you only knew who I really am and what I think of you.* When he stood in front of the TV cameras he always held that thought – *if you only knew who I really am and what I think of you* – foremost in his mind. His secret. That he hated and despised the party he represented, the policies that he defended, and most of the people he met. His secret would stay hidden until he died. He had seen through the world, identified all its frailties, understood the meaninglessness of existence. But no-one knew about his insight, and that was the way it would stay.

He felt a growing pleasure at what was to come. Tomorrow evening his friends would arrive at the house just after 9 p.m., in the black Mercedes with tinted windows. They would drive straight into his garage and he would wait for them in the living-room with the curtains drawn, just as now. He could feel his expectation swell as he started to fantasise about what the girl they delivered to him this time would look like. He had told them there had been far too many blondes lately. Some of them had also been much too old, over 20. This time he wanted a younger one, preferably of mixed race. His friends would wait in the basement where he had installed a TV; he would take the girl with him to his bedroom. Before dawn they would be gone, and he would already be daydreaming about the girl they would bring the following week.

The thought of the next evening made him so excited that he got up from the sofa and went into his study. Before he turned on the light he drew the curtains. For a moment he thought he saw the shadow of someone down on the beach. He took off his glasses and squinted. Sometimes late-night strollers would stop on the edge of his property. On several occasions he had had to call the police in Ystad to complain of young people lighting bonfires on the beach and making noise.

He had a good relationship with the Ystad police. They came right away and moved anyone disturbing him. He never could have imagined the knowledge and contacts he had gained as minister of justice. Not only had he learned to understand the special mentality that prevails inside the police force, but he had methodically acquired friends in strategic places in the Swedish machinery of justice. As important were all the contacts he had made in the criminal world. There were intelligent criminals, individuals who worked alone as well as leaders of great crime syndicates, whom he had made his friends. Even though much had changed since he left office, he still enjoyed his old contacts. Especially the friends who saw to it that each week he had a visit from a girl of a suitable age.

He had imagined the shadow on the beach. He straightened the curtains and unlocked one of the cabinets in the desk he had inherited from his father, a distinguished professor of jurisprudence. He took out an expensive and beautifully decorated portfolio and opened it before him on the desk. Slowly, reverently, he leafed through his collection of pornographic pictures from the earliest days of photography. His oldest picture was a rarity, a daguerreotype from 1855 that he had acquired in Paris, of a naked woman embracing a dog. His collection was renowned in the discreet circle of men who shared his interest. His collection of pictures from the 1890s by Lecadre was surpassed only by the collection owned by an elderly steel magnate in the Ruhr. Slowly he turned the plastic-covered pages of the album. He lingered longest over the pages where the models were very young and one could see by their eyes that they were under the influence of drugs. He had often regretted that he himself had not begun to devote himself to photography earlier. Had he done so, he would today be in possession of an unrivalled collection.

When he had finished, he locked the album in the desk again. He had extracted a promise from his friends that upon his death they would offer the pictures to an antiquities dealer in Paris who specialised in the sale of such items. The money would be donated to a scholarship fund he had already established for young law students, which would be announced after his death. He switched off the desk lamp and remained sitting in the dark room. The sound of the surf was very faint. Once again he thought he heard a moped passing.

In spite of his age, he still found it difficult to imagine his own death. During trips to the United States, he had managed twice to be present anonymously at executions, the first by electric chair, the second in the gas chamber, which even then was rather rare. It had been a curiously pleasurable experience to watch people being killed. But his own death he could not contemplate. He left the study and poured a little glass of liqueur from the bar in the living-room. It was already approaching midnight. A short walk down to the sea was all that remained for him to do before he went to bed. He put on a jacket out in the hall, slipped his feet into a pair of worn clogs, and left the house.

Outside it was dead calm. His house was so isolated that he could not see the lights of any of his neighbours. The cars on the road to Kåseberga roared by in the distance. He followed the path that led through the garden and down to the locked gate to the beach. To his annoyance he discovered that the light on a pole next to the gate was out. The beach awaited him. He fished out his keys and unlocked the gate. He walked the short distance onto the sand and stopped at the water's edge. The sea was still. Far out on the horizon he saw the lights of a boat heading west. He unbuttoned his fly and peed into the water as he continued to fantasise about the visit he would have the next day.

Although he heard nothing, suddenly he knew that someone was standing behind him. He stiffened, seized with terror. Then he spun round.

The man standing there looked like an animal. Apart from a pair of shorts he was naked. The old man looked into his face with dread. He couldn't see if it was deformed or hidden behind a mask. In one hand the man held an axe. In his confusion the old man noticed that the hand around the shaft of the axe was very small, that the man was like a dwarf.

He screamed and started to run, back towards the garden gate.

He died the instant the edge of the axe severed his spine, just below the shoulder blades. And he knew no pain as the man, who was perhaps an animal, knelt down and slit an opening in his forehead and then with one violent wrench ripped most of the scalp from his skull.

It was a little after midnight. It was Tuesday, 21 June.

The motor of a moped started up somewhere nearby, and moments later died away.

Everything was once again very still.

CHAPTER 2

Around noon on 21 June, Kurt Wallander left the police station in Ystad. So that no-one would notice his going, he walked out through the garage entrance, got into his car, and drove down to the harbour. Since the day was warm he had left his sports jacket hanging over his chair at his desk. Anyone looking for him in the next few hours would assume he must be somewhere in the building. Wallander parked by the theatre, walked out on the inner pier and sat down on the bench next to the red hut belonging to the sea rescue service. He had brought along one of his notebooks, but realised that he hadn't brought a pen. Annoyed, he nearly tossed the notebook into the harbour. But this was impossible. His colleagues would never forgive him.

Despite his protests, they had appointed him to make a speech on their behalf at 3 p.m. that day for Björk, who was resigning his post as Ystad chief of police.

Wallander had never made a formal speech in his life. The closest he had come were the innumerable press conferences he had been obliged to hold during criminal investigations.

But how to thank a retiring chief of police? What did one actually thank him for? Did they have any reason to be thankful? Wallander would have preferred to voice his uneasiness and anxiety at the vast, apparently unthought-out reorganisations and cutbacks to which the force was increasingly subjected. He had left the station so he could think through what he was going to say in peace. He'd sat at his kitchen table until late the night before without getting anywhere. But now he had no choice. In less than three hours they would gather and present their farewell gift to Björk, who was to start work the next day in Malmö as head of the district board of immigration affairs.

Wallander got up from the bench and walked along the pier to the harbour café. The fishing boats rocked slowly in their moorings. He remembered idly that once, seven years ago, he had been involved in fishing a body out of this harbour. But he pushed away the memory. Right now, the speech he had to make for Björk was more important. One of the waitresses lent him a pen. He sat down at a table outside with a cup of coffee and forced himself to write a few sentences. By 1 p.m. he had put together half a page. He looked at it gloomily, knowing that it was the best that he could do. He motioned to the waitress, who came and refilled his cup.

"Summer seems to be taking its time," Wallander said to her.

"Maybe it won't get here at all," replied the waitress.

Apart from the difficulty of Björk's speech, Wallander was in a good mood. He would be going on holiday in a few weeks. He had a lot to be happy about. It had been a long, gruelling winter. He knew that he was in great need of a rest.

At 3 p.m. they gathered in the canteen of the station and Wallander made his speech to Björk. Svedberg gave him a fishing rod as a present, and Ann-Britt Höglund gave him flowers. Wallander managed to embellish his scanty speech on the spur of the moment by recounting a few of his escapades with Björk. There was great amusement as he recalled the time when they had both fallen into a pool of liquid manure after some scaffolding they were climbing collapsed. In his reply Björk wished his successor, a woman named Lisa Holgersson, good luck. She was from one of the bigger police districts in Småland and would take over at the end of the summer. For the time being Hansson would be the acting chief in Ystad. When the ceremony was over and Wallander had returned to his office, Martinsson knocked on his half-open door, and came in.

"That was a great speech," he said. "I didn't know you could do that sort of thing."

"I can't," said Wallander. "It was a lousy speech. You know it as well as I do."

Martinsson sat down cautiously in the broken visitor's chair.

"I wonder how it'll go with a woman chief," he said.

"Why wouldn't it go well?" replied Wallander. "You should be worrying instead about what's going to happen with all these cutbacks."

"That's exactly why I came to see you," said Martinsson. "There's a rumour going round that staff numbers are going to be cut back on Saturday and Sunday nights."

Wallander looked at Martinsson sceptically.

"That won't work," he said. "Who's going to deal with the people we've got in the cells?"

"Rumour has it that they're going to take tenders for that job from private security companies."

Wallander gave Martinsson a quizzical look.

"Security companies?"

"That's what I heard."

Wallander shook his head. Martinsson got up.

"I thought you ought to know about it," he said. "Do you have any idea what's going to happen within the force?"

"No," said Wallander. "Cross my heart."

Martinsson lingered in the office.

"Was there something else?"

Martinsson took a piece of paper out of his pocket.

"As you know, the World Cup has started. Sweden was 2–2 in the game against Cameroon. You bet 5–0 in favour of Cameroon. With this score, you came in last."

"How could I come in last? Either I bet right or wrong, didn't I?"

"We run statistics that show where we are in relation to everyone else."

"Good Lord! What's the point of that?"

"An officer was the only one who picked 2–2," said Martinsson, ignoring Wallander's question. "Now for the next match. Sweden against Russia."

Wallander was totally uninterested in football, although he had occasionally gone to watch Ystad's handball team, which had several times been ranked as one of the best in Sweden. But lately the entire country seemed to be obsessed by the World Cup. He couldn't turn on the TV or open a newspaper without being bombarded with speculation as to how the Swedish team would fare. He knew that he had no choice but to take part in the football pool. If he didn't, his colleagues would think he was arrogant. He took his wallet out of his back pocket.

"How much?"

"A hundred kronor. Same as last time."

He handed the note to Martinsson, who checked him off on his list.

"Don't I have to guess the score?"

"Sweden against Russia. What do you think?"

"4–4," said Wallander.

"It's pretty rare to have that many goals scored in football," Martinsson said, surprised. "That sounds more like ice hockey."

"All right, let's say 3–1 to Russia," said Wallander. "Will that do?"

Martinsson wrote it down.

"Maybe we can take the Brazil match while we're at it," Martinsson went on.

"3–0 to Brazil," said Wallander quickly.

"You don't have very high expectations for Sweden," said Martinsson.

"Not when it comes to football, anyway," replied Wallander, handing him another 100-krona note.

Martinsson left and Wallander began to mull over what he had been told, but then he dismissed the rumours with irritation. He would find out soon enough what was true and what wasn't. It was already 4.30 p.m. He pulled over a folder of material about an organised crime ring exporting stolen cars to the former Eastern-bloc countries. He had been working on the investigation for several months. So far the police had only succeeded in tracking down parts of the operation. He knew that this case would haunt him for many more months yet. During his leave, Svedberg would take over, but he suspected that very little would happen while he was gone.

There was a knock on the door, and Ann-Britt Höglund walked in. She had a black baseball cap on her head.

"How do I look?" she asked.

"Like a tourist," replied Wallander.

"This is what the new caps are going to look like," she said. "Just imagine the word POLICE above the peak. I've seen pictures of it."

"They'll never get one of those on my head," said Wallander. "I suppose that I should be glad I'm not in uniform any more."

"Someday we might discover that Björk was a really good chief," she said. "I think what you said in there was great."

"I know the speech wasn't any good," said Wallander, starting to feel annoyed. "But you are all responsible for having picked me."

Höglund stood up and looked out of the window. She had managed to live up to the reputation that preceded her when she came to Ystad the year before. At the police academy she had shown great aptitude for police work, and had developed even more since. She had filled part of the void left by Rydberg's death a few years ago. Rydberg was the detective who had taught Wallander most of what he knew, and sometimes Wallander felt that it was his task to guide Höglund in the same way.

"How's it going with the cars?" she asked.

"They keep on being stolen," said Wallander. "The organisation seems to have an incredible number of branches."

"Can we punch a hole in it?" she asked.

"We'll crack it," replied Wallander. "Sooner or later. There'll be a lull for a few months. Then it'll start up again."

"But it'll never end?"

"No, it'll never end. Because of Ystad's location. Just 200 kilometres from here, across the Baltic, there's an unlimited number of people who want what we've got. The only problem is they don't have the money to pay for it."

"I wonder how much stolen property is shipped with every ferry," she mused.

"You don't want to know," said Wallander.

Together they went and got some coffee. Höglund was supposed to go on holiday that week. Wallander knew that she was going to spend it in Ystad, since her husband, a machinery installer with the whole world as his market, was currently in Saudi Arabia.

"What are you going to do?" she asked when they started talking about their upcoming breaks.

"I'm going to Denmark, to Skagen," said Wallander.

"With the woman from Riga?" Höglund wondered with a smile.

Wallander was taken aback.

"How do you know about her?"

"Oh, everybody does," she said. "Didn't you realise? You might call it the result of an ongoing internal investigation."

Wallander had never told anyone about Baiba, whom he had met during a criminal investigation. She was the widow of a murdered Latvian policeman. She had been in Ystad over Christmas almost six months ago. During the Easter holiday Wallander had visited her in Riga. But he had never spoken about her or introduced her to any of his colleagues. Now he wondered why not. Even though their relationship was new, she had pulled him out of the melancholy that had marked his life since his divorce from Mona.

"All right," he said. "Yes, we'll be in Denmark together. Then I'm going to spend the rest of the summer with my father."

"And Linda?"

"She called a week ago and said she was taking a theatre class in Visby."

"I thought she was going to be a furniture upholsterer?"

"So did I. But now she's got it into her head that she's going to do some sort of stage performance with a girlfriend of hers."

"That sounds exciting, don't you think?"

Wallander nodded dubiously.

"I hope she comes here in July," he said. "I haven't seen her in a long time." They parted outside Wallander's door.

"Drop in and say hello this summer," she said. "With or without the woman from Riga. With or without your daughter."

"Her name is Baiba," said Wallander.

He promised he'd come by and visit.

After Ann-Britt left he worked on the file for a good hour. Twice he called the police in Göteborg, trying without success to reach a detective who was working on the same investigation. At 5.45 p.m. he decided to go out to eat. He pinched his stomach and noted that he was still losing weight. Baiba had complained that he was too fat. After that, he had no problem eating less. He had even squeezed into a tracksuit a few times and gone jogging, boring though he found it.

He put on his jacket. He would write to Baiba that evening. The telephone rang just as he was about to leave the office. For a moment he wondered whether to let it ring. But he went back to his desk and picked up the receiver.

It was Martinsson.

"Nice speech you made," said Martinsson. "Björk seemed genuinely moved."

"You said that already," said Wallander. "What is it? I'm on my way home."

"I just got a call that was a little odd," said Martinsson. "I thought I ought to check with you."

Wallander waited impatiently for him to go on.

"It was a farmer calling from out near Marsvinsholm. He claimed that there was a woman acting strangely in his rape field."

"Is that all?"

"Yes."

"A woman acting strangely out in a rape field? What was she doing?"

"If I understood him correctly, she wasn't doing anything. The peculiar thing was that she was out in the field."

Wallander thought for a moment before he replied.

"Send out a squad car. It sounds like something for them."

"The problem is that all the units seem to be busy right now. There were two car accidents almost simultaneously. One by the road into Svarte, the other outside the Hotel Continental."

"Serious?"

"No major injuries. But there seems to be quite a mess."

"They can drive out to Marsvinsholm when they have time, can't they?"

"That farmer seemed pretty upset. I can't quite explain it. If I didn't have to pick up my children, I'd go myself."

"All right, I can do it," said Wallander. "I'll meet you in the hall and get the name and directions."

A few minutes later Wallander drove off from the station. He turned left at the roundabout and took the road towards Malmö. On the seat next to him was a note Martinsson had written. The farmer's name was Salomonsson, and Wallander knew the road to take. When he got out onto the E65 he rolled down the window. The yellow rape fields stretched out on both sides of the road. He couldn't remember the last time he had felt as good as he did now. He stuck in a cassette of *The Marriage of Figaro* with Barbara Hendricks singing Susanna, and he thought about meeting Baiba in Copenhagen. When he reached the side road to Marsvinsholm he turned left, past the castle and the castle church, and turned left again. He glanced at Martinsson's directions and swung onto a narrow road that led across the fields. In the distance he caught a glimpse of the sea.

Salomonsson's house was an old, well-preserved Skåne farmhouse. Wallander got out of the car and looked around. Everywhere he looked were yellow rape fields. The man standing on the front steps was very old. He had a pair of binoculars in his hand. Wallander thought that he must have been imagining the whole thing. All too often, lonely old people out in the country let their imaginations run riot. He walked over to the steps and nodded.

"Kurt Wallander from the Ystad police," he said.

The man on the steps was unshaven and his feet were stuck into a pair of worn clogs.

"Edvin Salomonsson," said the man, stretching out a skinny hand.

"Tell me what happened," said Wallander.

The man pointed out at the rape field that lay to the right of the

25

house. "I discovered her this morning," he began. "I get up early. She was already there at five. At first I thought it was a deer. Then I looked through the binoculars and saw that it was a woman."

"What was she doing?" asked Wallander.

"She was standing there."

"That's all?"

"She was standing and staring."

"Staring at what?"

"How should I know?"

Wallander sighed. Probably the old man *had* seen a deer. Then his imagination had taken over.

"Do you know who she is?" he asked.

"I've never seen her before," replied the man. "If I knew who she was, why would I call the police?"

"You saw her the first time early this morning," he went on, "but you didn't call the police until late this afternoon?"

"I wouldn't want to put you out for no reason," the man answered simply. "I assume the police have plenty to do."

"You saw her through your binoculars," said Wallander. "She was out in the field and you had never seen her before. What did you do?"

"I got dressed and went out to tell her to leave. She was trampling down the rape."

"Then what happened?"

"She ran."

"Ran?"

"She hid in the field. Crouched down so I couldn't see her. First I thought she was gone. Then I discovered her again through the binoculars. It happened over and over. Finally I got tired of it and called you."

"When did you see her last?"

"Just before I called."

"What was she doing then?"

"Standing there staring."

Wallander glanced out at the field. All he could see was the billowing rape.

"The officer you spoke with said that you seemed uneasy," said Wallander.

"Well, what's somebody doing standing in a rape field? There's got to be something odd about that."

Wallander decided he ought to end the conversation as rapidly as possible. It was clear to him now that the old man had imagined the whole thing. He would contact social services the next day.

"There's not really much I can do," said Wallander. "She's probably gone by now. And in that case, there's nothing to worry about."

"She's not gone at all," said Salomonsson. "I can see her right now."

Wallander spun around. He followed Salomonsson's pointing finger.

The woman was about 50 metres out in the rape field. Wallander could see that her hair was very dark. It stood out sharply against the yellow crop.

"I'll go and talk to her," said Wallander. "Wait here."

He took a pair of boots from his car, and put them on. Then he walked towards the field, feeling as though he were caught in something surreal. The woman was standing completely still, watching him. When he got closer he saw that not only did she have long black hair, but her skin was dark too. He stopped when he reached the edge of the crop. He raised one hand and tried to wave her over. She continued to stand motionless. Even though she was still quite far from him and the billowing rape hid her face every so often, he had the impression that she was rather beautiful. He shouted to her to come towards him. When she still didn't move he took a step into the field. At once she vanished. It happened so fast that she seemed like a frightened animal. He could feel himself getting angry. He went on walking out into the field, looking in every direction. When he caught sight of her again she had moved to the eastern corner of the field. So that she wouldn't get away, he started running. She moved swiftly, and Wallander was soon out of breath. When he got as close as 20 metres or so from her, they were out in the middle of the field. He shouted to her.

"Police!" he yelled. "Stop where you are!"

He started walking towards her. Then he pulled up short.

Everything happened very fast. She raised a plastic container over her head and started pouring a colourless liquid over her hair, her face, and her body. He thought fleetingly that she must have been carrying it the whole time. He could see that she was terrified. Her eyes were wide open and she was staring straight at him.

"Police!" he shouted again. "I just want to talk to you."

At the same moment a smell of petrol wafted towards him. Suddenly she had a flickering cigarette lighter in one hand, which she touched to her hair. Wallander cried out as she burst into flame. Paralysed, he watched her lurch around the field as the fire sizzled and blazed over her body. Wallander could hear himself screaming. But the woman on fire was silent. Afterwards he couldn't remember hearing her scream at all.

When he tried to run up to her the field exploded in flames. He was suddenly surrounded by smoke and fire. He held his hands in front of his face and ran, without knowing which direction he was heading. When he reached the edge of the field he tripped and tumbled into the ditch. He turned around and saw her one last time before she fell over and disappeared from his sight. She was holding her arms up as if appealing for mercy. The entire field was aflame.

Somewhere behind him he could hear Salomonsson wailing. Wallander got to his feet. His legs were shaking. Then he turned away and threw up.

CHAPTER 3

Afterwards Wallander would remember the burning girl in the rape field the way you remember, with the greatest reluctance, a distant nightmare sooner forgotten. If he appeared to maintain at least an outward sense of calm for the rest of that evening and far into the night, later he could recall nothing but trivial details. Martinsson, Hansson and especially Ann-Britt Höglund had been astonished by his calm. But they couldn't see through the shield he had set up to protect himself. Inside him there was devastation, like a house that had collapsed.

He got back to his flat just after 2 a.m. Only then, when he sat down on his sofa, still in his filthy clothes and muddy boots, did the shield crumble. He poured himself a glass of whisky. The doors of his balcony stood open and let in the balmy night, and he cried like a baby.

The girl had been a child. She reminded him of his own daughter Linda. During his years as a policeman he had learned to be prepared for whatever might await him when he arrived at a place where someone had met a violent or sudden death. He had seen people who had hanged themselves, stuck a shotgun in their mouth, or blown themselves to bits. Somehow he had learned to endure what he saw and push it aside. But he couldn't when there were children or young people involved. Then he was as vulnerable as when he was first a policeman. He knew that many of his colleagues reacted the same way. When children or young people died violently, for no reason, the defences erected out of habit collapsed. And that's how it would be for Wallander as long as he continued working as a policeman.

He had completed the initial phase of the investigation in an exemplary manner. With traces of vomit still clinging to his mouth he had run up to Salomonsson, who was watching his crop burn with astonishment, and asked where the telephone was. Since Salomonsson didn't seem to understand the question, maybe didn't even hear it, he dashed past him into the house. He was assailed by the acrid smell of the unwashed old man. In the hall he found the telephone. He dialled 90–000, and the operator said later that Wallander had sounded quite calm when he described what had happened and asked for a full team to be sent out.

The flames from the field were shining through the windows like floodlights lighting up the summer evening. He called Martinsson at home, talking first with his daughter and then his wife before Martinsson was called in from the back yard. As succinctly as possible he described what had happened and asked Martinsson to call Hansson and Höglund too. Then he went out to the kitchen and washed his face under the tap. When he came back outside, Salomonsson was still rooted to the same spot, as if mesmerised. A car arrived with some of his closest neighbours in it. But Wallander shouted to them to stay back, not allowing them to approach Salomonsson. In the distance he heard sirens from the fire engines, which almost always arrived first. Soon afterwards, two squad cars of uniformed officers and an ambulance arrived. Peter Edler was directing the firefighting, a man in whom Wallander had total confidence.

"What's going on?" he asked.

"I'll explain later," said Wallander. "But don't stamp around in the field. There's a body out there."

"The house isn't threatened," said Edler. "We'll work on containing the fire."

Edler turned to Salomonsson and asked how wide the tractor paths and the ditches between the fields were. One of the ambulance crew came over. Wallander had met him before but couldn't remember his name.

"Is anyone hurt?" he asked.

Wallander shook his head.

"One person dead," he replied. "She's lying out in the field."

"Then we'll need a hearse," said the ambulance driver. "What happened?"

Wallander didn't feel like answering. Instead he turned to Norén, who was the officer he knew best.

"There's a dead woman in the field," he said. "Until the fire is put out we can't do anything but block it off."

Norén nodded.

"Was it an accident?" he asked.

"More like a suicide," said Wallander.

A few minutes later, as Martinsson arrived, Norén handed him a paper cup of coffee. He stared at his hand and wondered why it wasn't shaking. Hansson and Ann-Britt Höglund arrived in Hansson's car, and he told his colleagues what had happened.

Again and again he used the same phrase: *She burned like a flare.*

"This is just terrible," said Höglund.

"It was worse than you can imagine," said Wallander. "Not to be able to do anything. I hope none of you ever has to experience anything like this."

Silently they watched the firefighters work. A large group of bystanders had gathered, but the police kept them back.

"What did she look like?" asked Martinsson. "Did you see her?"

Wallander nodded.

"Someone ought to talk to the old man," he said. "His name is Salomonsson."

Hansson took Salomonsson into his kitchen. Höglund went over and talked to Peter Edler. The fire had begun to die down. When she returned she told them it would be all over shortly.

"Rape burns fast," she said. "And the field is wet. It rained yesterday."

"She was young," said Wallander, "with black hair and dark skin. She was dressed in a yellow windcheater. I think she had jeans on. I don't know about her feet. And she was frightened."

"What of?" asked Martinsson.

Wallander thought a moment.

"She was frightened of me," he replied. "I'm not absolutely sure, but I think she was even more terrified when I called out that I was a policeman and told her to stop. But beyond that, I have no idea."

"She understood everything you said?"

"She understood the word 'police' at least. I'm certain of that."

All that remained of the fire was a thick pall of smoke.

"There was no-one else out there in the field?" asked Höglund. "You're sure she was alone?"

"No," said Wallander. "I'm not sure at all. But I didn't see anyone but her."

They stood in silence. *Who was she?* Wallander asked himself. *Where did she come from? Why did she set herself on fire? If she wanted to die, why did she choose to torture herself?*

Hansson came back from the house, where he had been talking with Salomonsson.

"We should do what they do in the States," he said. "We should have menthol to smear under our noses. Damn, the smell in there. Old men shouldn't be allowed to outlive their wives."

"Get one of the ambulance crew to ask him how he's feeling," said Wallander. "He must be suffering from shock."

Martinsson went to deliver the message. Peter Edler took off his helmet and stood next to Wallander.

"It's nearly out," he said. "But I'll leave a truck here tonight."

"When can we go out in the field?" asked Wallander.

"Within an hour. The smoke will hang around for a while yet. But the field has already started to cool off."

Wallander took Peter Edler aside.

"What am I going to see?" he asked. "She poured a five-litre container of petrol over herself. And the way everything exploded around her, she must have already poured more on the ground."

"It won't be pretty," Edler replied candidly. "There won't be a lot left."

Wallander said nothing. He turned to Hansson.

"No matter how we look at it, we know that it was suicide," said

Hansson. "We have the best witness we can get: a policeman."

"What did Salomonsson say?"

"That he'd never seen her before she appeared at 5 a.m. this morning. There's no reason to think he's not telling the truth."

"So we don't know who she is," said Wallander, "and we don't know what she was running from either."

Hansson looked at him in surprise.

"Why should she be running from something?" he asked.

"She was frightened," said Wallander. "She was hiding. And when a policeman arrived she set herself on fire."

"We don't know what she was thinking," said Hansson. "You may be imagining that she was frightened."

"No," said Wallander. "I've seen enough fear in my time to know what it looks like."

One of the ambulance crew came walking towards them.

"We're taking the old boy with us to the hospital," he said. "He looks in pretty bad shape."

Wallander nodded.

Soon the forensic team arrived. Wallander tried to point out where in the smoke the body might be located.

"Maybe you should go home," said Höglund. "You've seen enough this evening."

"No," said Wallander. "I'll stay."

Eventually the smoke had cleared, and Peter Edler said they could start their examination. Even though the summer evening was still light, Wallander had ordered floodlights to be brought in.

"There might be something out there apart from a body," said Wallander. "Watch your step, and everyone who doesn't have work to do out there should stay back."

He realised then that he really didn't want to do what had to be done. He would far rather have driven away and left the responsibility to the others. He walked out into the field alone. The others watched. He was afraid of what he would see, afraid that the knot he had in his stomach would burst.

He reached her. Her arms had stiffened in the upstretched motion he had seen her make before she died, surrounded by the raging flames. Her hair and face, along with her clothes, were burned off. All that was left was a blackened body that still radiated terror and desolation. Wallander turned around and walked back across the charred ground. For a moment he was afraid he was going to faint.

The forensic technicians started to work in the harsh glare of the floodlights, where moths swarmed. Hansson had opened Salomonsson's kitchen window to drive out the smell. They pulled out the chairs and sat around the kitchen table. At Höglund's suggestion they made coffee on Salomonsson's ancient stove.

"All he has is ground coffee," she said after searching through the drawers and cupboards. "Is that all right?"

"That's fine," said Wallander. "Just as long as it's strong."

Hanging on the wall beside the ancient cupboards with sliding doors was an old-fashioned clock. Wallander noticed that it had stopped. He had seen a clock like that once before, at Baiba's flat in Riga, and it too had had a pair of immobile hands. As though they were trying to ward off events that had not yet happened by stopping time, he thought. Baiba's husband was killed execution-style on a frozen night in Riga's harbour. A lone girl appears as if shipwrecked in a sea of rape and takes her life by inflicting the worst pain imaginable.

She had set herself on fire as though she were her own enemy, he thought. It wasn't him, the policeman with the waving arms, she had wanted to escape. It was herself.

He was jolted out of his reverie by the silence around the table. They were looking at him and waiting for him to take the initiative. Through the window he could see the technicians moving slowly about in the glare of the floodlights. A camera flash went off, then another.

"Did somebody call for the hearse?" asked Hansson.

For Wallander it was as if someone had struck him with a sledge-hammer. The simple, matter-of-fact question from Hansson brought him back to painful reality.

The images flickered inside his head. He imagined driving through the beautiful Swedish summertime, Barbara Hendricks's voice strong and clear. Then a girl skitters away like a frightened animal in the field of tall rape. The catastrophe strikes. Something happens that shouldn't. The hearse on its way to carry off the summer itself.

"Prytz knows what to do," said Martinsson, and Wallander recognised the ambulance driver whose name he'd forgotten earlier.

He knew he had to say something.

"What do we know?" he began tentatively, as if each word were offering resistance. "An elderly farmer, living alone, rises early and discovers a strange woman in his rape field. He tries calling to her, to get her to leave, since he doesn't want his crop destroyed. She hides and then reappears, again and again. He calls us late in the afternoon. I drive out here, since the regular officers are all busy. To be honest, I have trouble taking him seriously. I decide to leave and contact social services, since he seems so confused. But the woman suddenly pops up in the field again. So I try to reach her, but she moves away. She lifts a plastic container over her head, drenches herself in petrol, and sets fire to herself with a cigarette lighter. The rest you know. She was alone, she had a container of petrol, and she took her own life."

He broke off abruptly, as if he no longer knew what to say. A moment later he went on.

"We don't know who she is," he said. "We don't know why she killed herself. I can give a fairly good description of her. But that's all."

Ann-Britt Höglund got some cracked coffee cups out of a cupboard. Martinsson went out into the yard to have a pee. When he returned, Wallander continued his cautious summary.

"The most important thing is to find out who she was. We'll search through all missing persons. Since I think she was dark-skinned, we can start by putting a little extra focus on checking on refugees and the refugee camps. Then we'll have to wait for what the forensic technicians come up with."

"At any rate, we know there was no crime committed," said Hansson. "So our job is to determine who she was."

"She must have come from somewhere," said Höglund. "Did she walk here? Did she ride a bike? Did she drive? Where did she get the petrol?"

"And why here, of all places?" said Martinsson. "Why Salomonsson's place? This farm is way off the beaten track."

The questions hung in the air. Norén came into the kitchen and said that some reporters had arrived who wanted to know what happened. Wallander, who knew that he had to get moving, stood up.

"I'll talk to them," he said.

"Tell them the truth," said Hansson.

"What else?" Wallander replied in surprise.

He went out into the yard and recognised the two newspaper reporters. One was a young woman who worked for *Ystad Recorder*, the other an older man from *Labour News*.

"It looks like a film shoot," said the woman, pointing at the floodlights in the charred field.

"It's not," said Wallander.

He told them what had happened. A woman had died in a fire. There was no suspicion of criminal activity. Since they still didn't know who she was, he didn't want to say anything more at this time.

"Can we take some pictures?" asked the man from *Labour News*.

"You can take as many pictures as you like," replied Wallander. "But you'll have to take them from here. No-one is allowed to go into the field."

The reporters drove off in their cars. Wallander was about to return to the kitchen when he saw one of the technicians working out in the field waving to him. Wallander went over. It was Sven Nyberg, the surly but brilliant head of forensics. They stopped at the edge of the area covered by the floodlights. A slight breeze came wafting from the sea across the field. Wallander tried to avoid looking at the body, with its upstretched arms.

"I think we've found something," said Nyberg.

In his hand he had a little plastic bag. He handed it to Wallander, who moved under one of the floodlights. In the bag was a gold necklace with a tiny pendant.

"It has an inscription," said Nyberg. "The letters 'D.M.S.' and it's a picture of the Madonna."

"Why didn't it melt?" asked Wallander.

"A fire in a field doesn't generate enough heat to melt jewellery," Nyberg replied. He sounded tired.

"This is exactly what we needed," said Wallander.

"We'll be ready to take her away soon," said Nyberg, nodding towards the black hearse waiting at the edge of the field.

"How does it look?" Wallander asked cautiously.

Nyberg shrugged.

"The teeth should tell us something. The pathologists are excellent. They can find out how old she was. With DNA technology they can also tell you whether she was born in this country of Swedish parents or if she came from somewhere else."

"There's coffee in the kitchen," said Wallander.

"No thanks," said Nyberg. "I'll be done here pretty soon. In the morning we'll go over the entire field. Since there was no crime it can wait until then."

Wallander went back to the house. He laid the plastic bag containing the necklace on the kitchen table.

"Now we have something to go on," he said. "A pendant, a Madonna. Inscribed with the initials 'D.M.S.' I suggest you all go home now. I'll stay here a while longer."

"We'll meet at nine o'clock tomorrow morning," said Hansson, getting up.

"I wonder who she was," said Martinsson. "The Swedish summertime is too beautiful and too brief for something like this to happen."

They parted in the yard. Höglund lingered behind.

"I'm thankful I didn't have to see it," she said. "I think I understand what you're going through."

"I'll see you tomorrow," he said.

When the cars had gone he sat down on the steps of the house. The floodlights shone as if over a bleak stage on which a play was being performed, with him the only spectator.

The wind had started to blow. They were still waiting for the warmth of summer. The night air was cold, and Wallander realised that he was freezing sitting there on the steps. How intensely he longed for the summer heat. He hoped it would come soon.

After a while he got up and went inside the house and washed the coffee cups.

CHAPTER 4

Wallander gave a start. Someone was trying to tear off one of his feet. When he opened his eyes he saw that his foot was caught in the broken bed frame. He turned over onto his side to free it. Then he lay still. The dawn light filtered through the crookedly drawn shade. He looked at the clock on the beside table. It was 4.30 a.m. He had hardly slept, and he was very tired. He found himself back out in the field again. He could see the girl much more clearly now. It wasn't me she was afraid of, he thought. She wasn't hiding from me or Salomonsson. There was someone else.

He got up and shuffled out to the kitchen. While he waited for the coffee to brew he went into his messy living-room and checked the answer machine. The red light was flashing. He pushed the replay button. First was his sister Kristina. "I need you to call me. Preferably in the next couple of days." It must be something to do with their father. Although he had married his care worker and no longer lived alone, he was still moody and unpredictable.

There was a scratchy, faint message from *Skåne Daily*, asking if he was interested in a subscription. He was just on his way back to the kitchen when he heard the next message. "It's Baiba. I'm going to Tallinn. I'll be back on Saturday."

He was seized with jealousy. Why was she going to Tallinn? She had said nothing about it the last time they spoke. He poured a cup of coffee, and called her number in Riga, but there was no answer. He dialled again. His unease was growing. She could hardly have left for Tallinn at 5 a.m. Why wasn't she home? Or if she was home, why didn't she answer?

He picked up his coffee cup, opened the balcony door facing

Mariagatan, and sat down. Once again he saw the girl running through the rape. For an instant she looked like Baiba. He forced himself to accept that his jealousy was unwarranted. They had agreed not to encumber their new relationship with promises of fidelity. He remembered how they had sat up on Christmas Eve and talked about what they wanted from one another. Most of all, Wallander wanted them to get married. But when Baiba spoke of her need for freedom, he had agreed with her. Rather than lose her, he would accept her terms.

The sky was clear blue and the air was already warm. He drank his coffee in slow sips and tried to keep from thinking of the girl. When he had finished he went into the bedroom and searched for a long time before finding a clean shirt. Next he gathered all the clothes strewn around the flat. He made a big pile in the middle of the living-room floor. He would have to go to the launderette today.

At 5.45 a.m. he left his flat and went down to the street. He got into his car and remembered that it was due for its M.O.T. by the end of June. He drove off down Regementsgatan and then out along Österleden. On the spur of the moment, he turned onto the road heading out of town and stopped at the new cemetery at Kronoholmsvägen. He left the car and strolled along the rows of gravestones. Now and then he would catch sight of a name he vaguely recognised. When he saw a year of birth the same as his own he averted his eyes. Some young men in blue overalls were unloading a mower from a trailer. When he reached the memorial grove, he sat on one of the benches. He hadn't been here since the windy autumn day four years ago when they had scattered Rydberg's ashes. Björk had been there, and Rydberg's distant and anonymous relatives. Wallander had often meant to come back. A gravestone with Rydberg's name on it would have been simpler, he thought. A focal point for my memories of him. In this grove, full of the spirits of the dead, I can find no trace of him.

He realised that he had difficulty remembering what Rydberg looked like. He's dying away inside me, he thought. Soon even my memories of him will be gone.

He stood up, suddenly distressed. He kept seeing the burning girl.

He drove straight to the station, went into his office, and closed the door, forcing himself to prepare a summary of the car theft investigation that he had to turn over to Svedberg. He moved folders onto the floor so that his desk would be completely clear.

He lifted up his desk blotter to see whether there were any items there that he'd forgotten about. He found a scratch-off lottery ticket he had bought several months before. He rubbed it with a ruler until the numbers appeared, and saw that he had won 25 kronor. From the hall he could hear Martinsson's voice, then Ann-Britt Höglund's. He leaned back in his chair, put his feet up on the desk, and closed his eyes. When he woke up he had a cramp in one of his calf muscles, but he'd slept for no more than ten minutes. The telephone rang. It was Per Åkeson from the prosecutors' office. They exchanged greetings, and some words about the weather. They had worked together for many years, and had slowly developed a rapport that had become like a friendship. They often disagreed about whether an arrest was justified or whether remanding an offender in custody was reasonable. But there was also a trust that went deep, although they almost never spent time together off duty.

"I read in the paper about the girl who burned to death in a field by Marsvinsholm," said Åkeson. "Is that something for me?"

"It was suicide," replied Wallander. "Other than a farmer named Salomonsson, I was the only witness."

"What in heaven's name were you doing there?"

"Salomonsson called. Normally a squad car would have dealt with it. But they were busy."

"The girl can't have been a pretty sight."

"It was worse than you could imagine. We have to find out who she was. The switchboard has already started taking calls from people worried about missing relatives."

"So you don't suspect foul play?"

Without understanding why, Wallander hesitated before answering.

"No," he said then. "I can't think of a more blatant way to take your own life."

"You don't sound entirely convinced."

"I had a bad night. It was as you say – a pretty horrible experience."

They fell silent. Wallander could tell that Åkeson had something else he wanted to talk about.

"There's another reason why I'm calling," he said finally. "But keep it between us."

"I usually know how to keep my mouth shut."

"Do you remember I told you a few years ago that I was thinking of doing something else? Before it's too late, before I get too old."

"I remember you talked about refugees and the UN. Was it the Sudan?"

"Uganda. And I've actually got an offer. Which I've decided to accept. In September I'm going to take a year's sabbatical."

"What does your wife think about this?"

"That's why I'm calling. For moral support. I haven't discussed it with her yet."

"Is she supposed to go with you?"

"No."

"Then I suspect she'll be a little surprised."

"Have you any idea how I should break it to her?"

"Unfortunately not. But I think you're doing the right thing. There has to be more to life than putting people in jail."

"I'll let you know how it goes."

They were just about to hang up when Wallander remembered that he had a question.

"Does this mean that Anette Brolin is coming back as your replacement?"

"She's changed sides; she's working as a criminal barrister in Stockholm now," said Åkeson. "Weren't you a little in love with her?"

"No," Wallander said. "I was just curious."

He hung up. He felt a pang of jealousy. He would have liked to travel to Uganda himself, to have a complete change. Nothing could undo the horror of seeing a young person set herself alight. He envied Per Åkeson, who wasn't going to let his desire to escape stop at mere dreams.

The joy he had felt yesterday was gone. He stood at the window and gazed out at the street. The grass by the old water tower was still green. Wallander thought about the year before, when he had been on sick leave for a long time after he had killed a man. Now he wondered whether he had ever really recovered from that depression. I ought to do something like Åkeson, he thought. There must be a Uganda for me somewhere. For Baiba and me.

He stood by the window for a long time, then went back to his desk and tried to reach his sister. Several times he got a busy signal. He spent the next half hour writing up a report of the events of the night before. Then he called the pathology department in Malmö but couldn't find a doctor who could tell him anything about the burned corpse.

Just before 9 a.m. he got a cup of coffee and went into one of the conference rooms. Höglund was on the phone, and Martinsson was leafing through a catalogue of garden equipment. Svedberg was in his usual spot, scratching the back of his neck with a pencil. One of the windows was open. Wallander stopped just inside the door with a strong feeling of déjà vu. Martinsson looked up from his catalogue and nodded, Svedberg muttered something unintelligible, while Höglund patiently explained something to one of her children. Hansson came into the room. He had a coffee cup in one hand and a plastic bag with the necklace that had been found in the field in the other.

"Don't you ever sleep?" asked Hansson.

Wallander felt himself bristle at the question.

"Why do you ask?"

"Have you taken a look in the mirror lately?"

"I didn't get home until early this morning. I sleep as much as I need to."

"It's those football matches," said Hansson. "They're on in the middle of the night."

"I don't watch them," said Wallander.

"I thought everyone stayed up to watch."

"I'm not that interested," Wallander admitted. "I know it's unusual, but as far as I know, the chief of the national police hasn't sent out any instruction that it's a dereliction of duty not to watch the games."

"This might be the last time we'll have a chance to see it," Hansson said sombrely.

"See what?"

"Sweden playing in the World Cup. I just hope our defence doesn't go pear-shaped."

"I see," Wallander said politely. Höglund was still talking on the phone.

"Ravelli," Hansson went on, referring to Sweden's goalkeeper.

Wallander waited for him to continue, but he didn't.

"What about him?"

"I'm worried about him."

"Why? Is he sick?"

"I think he's erratic. He didn't play well against Cameroon. Kicking the ball out at strange times, odd behaviour in the goal area."

"Policemen can also be erratic," said Wallander.

"You can't really compare them," said Hansson. "At least we don't have to make lightning-fast decisions about whether to rush out or stay back on the goal line."

"Hell, who knows?" said Wallander. "Maybe there's a similarity between the policeman who rushes to the scene of a crime and the goalie who rushes out on the field."

Hansson gave him a baffled look. The conversation died. They sat around the table and waited for Höglund to finish her call. Svedberg, who had a hard time accepting female police officers, drummed his pencil on the table in annoyance to let her know they were waiting for her. Soon Wallander would have to tell Svedberg to put a stop to these tiresome protests. Höglund was a good policewoman, in many ways much more talented than Svedberg.

A fly buzzed around his coffee cup. They waited.

Finally Höglund hung up and sat down at the table.

"A bike chain," she said. "Children have a hard time understanding

44

that their mothers might have something more important to do than come straight home and fix it."

"Go ahead," said Wallander on impulse. "We can do this run-through without you."

She shook her head. "They'd come to expect it", she said.

Hansson put the necklace in its plastic bag on the table in front of him.

"A woman commits suicide," he said. "No crime has been committed. All we have to do is work out who she was."

Hansson was starting to act like Björk, thought Wallander, just managing not to burst out laughing. He caught Ann-Britt's eye. She seemed to be thinking the same thing.

"Calls have started coming in," said Martinsson. "I've put a man on it."

"I'll give him my description of her," said Wallander. "Otherwise we have to concentrate on people who've been reported missing. She might be one of them. If she's not on that list, someone is going to miss her soon."

"I'll take care of it," said Martinsson.

"The necklace," said Hansson, opening the plastic bag. "A Madonna and the letters D.M.S. I think it's solid gold."

"There's a database of abbreviations and acronyms," said Martinsson, who knew the most about computers. "We can put in the letters and see if we get anything."

Wallander reached for the necklace. It was still soot-marked.

"It's beautiful," he said. "But people in Sweden mostly wear a cross, don't they? Madonnas are more common in Catholic countries."

"It sounds as though you're talking about a refugee or immigrant," said Hansson.

"I'm talking about what the medallion represents," replied Wallander. "In any case, it has to be included in the description of the girl, and the person taking the calls has to know what it looks like."

"Shall we release a description?" Hansson asked.

Wallander shook his head.

"Not yet."

He was thinking about the night before. He knew he wouldn't give up until he knew what it was that had made the girl burn herself to death alone in the rape field. I'm living in a world where young people take their own lives because they can't stand it any more, he thought. I have to understand why, if I'm going to keep on being a policeman.

He gave a start. Hansson had spoken.

"Do we have anything more to discuss right now?" Hansson asked again.

"I'll take care of the pathologist in Malmö," Wallander said. "Has anyone been in touch with Sven Nyberg? If not, I'll drive over and talk to both of them."

The meeting was over. Wallander went to his office and got his jacket. He hesitated a moment, wondering whether he ought to make another attempt to get hold of his sister. Or Baiba in Riga. But he decided against doing either.

He drove first to Salomonsson's farm. Policemen were taking down the floodlights and rolling up the cables. The house was locked up, and he remembered that he must check and see how Salomonsson was doing. Maybe he had remembered something that would be of help.

He walked out into the field. The fire-blackened ground stood out sharply against the surrounding yellow crops. Nyberg was kneeling in the mud. In the distance he saw two other technicians who seemed to be searching along the edges of the burned area. Nyberg nodded curtly to Wallander. The sweat was running down his face.

"How's it going?" asked Wallander. "Have you found anything?"

"She must have had a lot of petrol with her," said Nyberg, getting up. "We found five half-melted containers. They were apparently empty when the fire broke out. If you draw a line through the spots where we found them, you can see that she had surrounded herself."

"What do you mean?" Wallander asked.

Nyberg threw out one arm in a sweeping gesture.

"I mean that she built a fortress around herself. She poured petrol

46

in a wide circle. It was a moat, and there was no way into her fortress. She was standing right in the middle, with the last container, which she had saved for herself. Maybe she was hysterical and depressed. Maybe she was mad or seriously ill. I don't know. But that's what she did. She knew full well what she was going to do."

"Can you tell me anything about how she got here?"

"I've sent for a dog unit," said Nyberg. "But they probably won't be able to pick up her trail. The smell of petrol has permeated the ground. The dogs will just be confused. We haven't found a bicycle. The tractor paths that lead down towards the E65 didn't have anything either. She could have landed in this field by parachute."

Nyberg took a roll of toilet paper out of one of his bags of equipment and wiped the sweat from his face.

"What do the doctors say?" he asked.

"Nothing yet," said Wallander. "I think they've got a difficult job ahead of them."

"Why would anyone do something like this?" Nyberg asked. "Could someone really have such strong reasons for dying that she'd end her life by torturing herself as much as she possibly could?"

"I've asked myself the same question," said Wallander.

Nyberg shook his head.

"What's happening?" he asked.

Wallander had no answer.

He went back to the car and called the station. Ebba answered. To avoid her concern, he pretended to be in a hurry.

"I'm going to see the farmer," he said. "I'll be in this afternoon."

He drove back to Ystad. In the cafeteria at the hospital he had some coffee and a sandwich. Then he looked for the ward where Salomonsson was. He stopped a nurse, introduced himself, and stated his business. She gave him a quizzical look.

"Edvin Salomonsson?"

"I don't remember whether his name was Edvin," Wallander said. "Did he come in last night after the fire outside Marsvinsholm?"

The nurse nodded.

"I'd like to speak with him," said Wallander. "If he's not too sick, that is."

"He's not sick," replied the nurse. "He's dead."

Wallander gave her an astonished look.

"Dead?"

"He died this morning in his sleep. Apparently it was a heart attack. It would probably be best if you spoke to one of the doctors."

"I just came by to see how he was doing," said Wallander. "Now I have my answer."

He left the hospital and walked out into the bright sunshine. He had no idea what to do next.

CHAPTER 5

Wallander drove home knowing that he must sleep if he were ever going to be able to think clearly again. No-one could be blamed for the old farmer's death. The person who might have been held responsible, the one who had set fire to his rape field, was already dead herself. It was the events themselves, the fact that any of this had happened, that made him feel sick at heart. He unplugged the phone and lay down on the sofa in the living-room with a flannel over his eyes. But sleep wouldn't come. After half an hour he gave up. He plugged in the telephone, lifted the receiver, and dialled Linda's number in Stockholm. On a sheet of paper by the phone he had a long list of numbers, each crossed out. Linda moved often, and her number was forever changing. He let it ring a long time. Then he dialled his sister's number. She answered almost at once. They didn't speak very often, and hardly ever about anything but their father. Sometimes Wallander thought that their contact would cease altogether when their father died.

They exchanged the usual pleasantries, without really being interested in the answers.

"You called," Wallander said.

"I'm worried about Dad," she said.

"Has something happened? Is he sick?"

"I don't know. When did you visit him last?"

Wallander tried to remember.

"About a week ago," he said, feeling guilty.

"Can you really not manage to see him more often?"

"I'm working almost round the clock. The department is hopelessly understaffed. I visit him as often as I can."

"I talked to Gertrud yesterday," she went on, without commenting on what Wallander had said. "I thought she gave an evasive answer when I asked how Dad was doing."

"Why would she?" said Wallander, surprised.

"I have no idea. That's why I'm calling."

"He was the same as always," Wallander said. "Cross that I was in a hurry and couldn't stay very long. But the whole time I was there he sat painting his picture and made out as though he didn't have time to talk to me. Gertrud was happy, as usual. I have to admit I don't understand how she puts up with him."

"Gertrud likes him," she said. "It's a question of love. Then you can put up with a lot."

Wallander wanted to end the conversation as quickly as possible. As she got older, his sister reminded him more and more of their mother. Wallander had never had a very happy relationship with his mother. When he was growing up it was as though the family had been divided into two camps – his sister and his mother against him and his father. Wallander had been very close to his father until his late teens, when he decided to become a policeman. Then a rift had developed. His father had never accepted Wallander's decision, but he couldn't explain to his son why he was so opposed to this career, or what he wanted him to do instead. After Wallander finished his training and started on the beat in Malmö, the rift had widened to a chasm. Some years later his mother was stricken with cancer. She was diagnosed at New Year and died in May. His sister Kristina left the house the same summer and moved to Stockholm, where she got a job in a company then known as L. M. Ericsson. She married, divorced, and married again. Wallander had met her first husband once, but he had no idea what her present husband even looked like. He knew that Linda had visited their home in Kärrtorp a few times, but he got the impression that the visits were never very successful. Wallander knew that the rift from their childhood and teenage years was still there, and that the day their father died it would widen for good.

"I'm going to see him tonight," said Wallander, thinking about the pile of dirty laundry on his floor.

"I'd appreciate it if you called me," she said.

Wallander promised he would. Then he called Riga. When the phone was picked up he thought it was Baiba at first. Then he realised that it was her housekeeper, who spoke nothing but Latvian. He hung up quickly. At the same moment his phone rang and he jumped.

He picked up the phone and heard Martinsson's voice.

"I hope I'm not bothering you," said Martinsson.

"I just stopped by to change my shirt," said Wallander, wondering why he always felt it necessary to excuse himself for being at home. "Has something happened?"

"A few calls have come in about missing persons," said Martinsson. "Ann-Britt is busy going through them."

"I was thinking more of what you had come up with on the computer."

"The mainframe has been down all morning," Martinsson replied glumly. "I called Stockholm a while ago. Somebody there thought it might be up and running again in an hour, but he wasn't sure."

"We're not chasing crooks," Wallander said. "We can wait."

"A doctor called from Malmö," Martinsson continued. "A woman. Her name was Malmström. I promised her you'd call."

"Why couldn't she talk to you?"

"She wanted to talk to *you*. I suppose it's because you were the last one to see the woman alive."

Wallander wrote down the number. "I was out there today," he said. "Nyberg was on his knees in the filth, sweating. He was waiting for a police dog."

"He's like a dog himself," said Martinsson, not disguising his dislike of Nyberg.

"He can be grumpy," Wallander protested. "But he knows his stuff."

He was about to hang up when he remembered Salomonsson.

"The farmer died," he said.

"Who?"

"The man whose kitchen we were drinking coffee in last night. He had a heart attack."

After he hung up, Wallander went to the kitchen and drank some water. For a long time he sat at the kitchen table doing nothing. Eventually he called Malmö. He had to wait while the doctor named Malmström was called to the phone. From her voice he could hear that she was very young. Wallander introduced himself and apologised for the delay in returning her call.

"Has any new information come to light that indicates that a crime was committed?" she asked.

"No."

"In that case we won't have to do an autopsy," she replied. "That will make it easier. She burned herself to death using petrol – leaded."

Wallander felt that he was about to be sick. He imagined her blackened body, as if it were lying right next to the woman he was speaking to.

"We don't know who she was," he said. "We need to know as much as possible about her in order to be able to give a clear description."

"It's always hard with a burned body," she said, without emotion. "All the skin is burned away. The dental examination isn't ready yet. But she had good teeth. No fillings. She was 163 centimetres tall. She had never broken a bone."

"I need her age," said Wallander. "That's almost the most important thing."

"That'll take a few more days. We can base it on her teeth."

"What would you guess?"

"I'd rather not."

"I saw her from 20 metres away," said Wallander. "I think she was about 17. Am I wrong?"

The female doctor thought a moment before she replied.

"I don't like to guess," she said at last. "But I think she was younger."

"What makes you think so?"

"I'll tell you when I know. But I wouldn't be surprised if it turned out she was only 15."

"Could a 15-year-old really kill herself in that way?" Wallander asked. "I have a hard time believing that."

"Last week I put together the pieces of a seven-year-old girl who blew herself up," replied the doctor. "She had planned it very carefully. She made certain that no-one else would be hurt. Since she could barely write, she left behind a drawing as her farewell letter. And recently I heard of a four-year-old who tried to poke his own eyes out because he was afraid of his father."

"That just isn't possible," said Wallander. "Not here in Sweden."

"It was here, all right," she said. "In Sweden. In the centre of the universe. In the middle of summer."

Wallander's eyes filled with tears.

"As we don't know who she was, we'll keep her here," the doctor said.

"I have a question," said Wallander. "Is it incredibly painful to burn to death?"

"People have known that through the ages," she replied. "That's why they used fire as one of the worst punishments or tortures that someone could be subjected to. They burned Joan of Arc, they burned witches. In every era people have been tortured by fire. The pain is beyond imagining. And, you don't lose consciousness as fast as you would hope. There's an instinct to run from the flames that's stronger than the desire to escape the pain. That's why your mind forces you not to pass out. Then you reach a limit. For a while the burned nerves become numbed. There are examples of people with 90 per cent of their body burned who for a brief time felt uninjured. But when the numbness wears off . . ."

She didn't finish her sentence.

"She burned like a flare," said Wallander.

"The best thing you can do is stop thinking about it," she said. "Death can actually be a liberator. No matter how reluctant we are to accept that."

When the conversation was over, Wallander got up, grabbed his jacket, and left the flat. The wind had started blowing outside. Cloud cover had moved in from the north. On the way to the station he pulled in to the M.O.T. garage and made an appointment. When he arrived at the garage, he stopped at the reception desk. Ebba had recently slipped and broken her hand. He asked how she was feeling.

"It reminds me that I'm getting old," she said.

"You'll never get old," said Wallander.

"That's a nice thing to say," she said. "But it's not true."

On the way to his office Wallander stopped to see Martinsson, who was sitting in front of his computer.

"They got it up and running 20 minutes ago," he said. "I'm just checking the description to see whether there are any missing persons who fit."

"Add that she was 163 centimetres tall," said Wallander. "And that she was between 15 and 17 years old."

Martinsson gave him a baffled look.

"Only 15? That can't be possible, can it?"

"I wish it weren't true," said Wallander. "But for now we have to consider it a possibility. How's it going with the initials?"

"I haven't got that far yet," said Martinsson. "But I was planning to stay late this evening."

"We're trying to make an identification," said Wallander. "We're not searching for a fugitive."

"There's no-one at home tonight anyway," said Martinsson. "I don't like going back to an empty house."

Wallander left Martinsson and looked in on Höglund's room, which was empty. He went back down the hall to the operations centre, where the emergency alerts and phone calls were received. Höglund was sitting at a table with a senior officer, going through a pile of papers.

"Any leads?" he asked.

"We've got a couple of tip-offs we have to look into more closely," she said. "One is a girl from Tomelilla Folk College who's been missing for two days."

"Our girl was 163 centimetres tall," said Wallander. "She had perfect teeth. She was between 15 and 17 years old."

"That young?" she asked in amazement.

"Yep," said Wallander. "That young."

"Then it's not the girl from Tomelilla, anyway," said Höglund, putting down the paper in her hand. "She's 23 and tall."

She searched through the stack of papers for a moment.

"Here's another one," she said. "A 16-year-old girl named Mari Lippmansson. She lives here in Ystad and works in a bakery. She's been missing from her job for three days. It was the baker who called. He was furious. Her parents evidently don't care about her at all."

"Take a look at her," Wallander said encouragingly. But he knew she wasn't the one.

He got a cup of coffee and went to his room. The folder on the car thefts was still lying on the floor. He'd better turn the case over to Svedberg now. He hoped no serious crimes would be committed before he started his holiday.

Later that afternoon they met in the conference room. Nyberg was back from the farm, where he had finished his search. It was a short meeting. Hansson had excused himself because he had to read an urgent memo from national headquarters.

"Let's be brief," said Wallander. "Tomorrow we'll go over all the cases that can't wait."

He turned to Nyberg, sitting at the end of the table.

"How'd it go with the dog?" he asked.

"He didn't find a thing," Nyberg replied. "If there was ever anything to give him a scent, it was covered up by the odour of petrol."

Wallander thought for a moment.

"You found five melted petrol containers," he said. "That means that she must have come to Salomonsson's field in some sort of vehicle. She couldn't have carried all that petrol by herself. Unless she walked there several times. There's one more possibility, of course. That she didn't come alone. But that doesn't seem reasonable, to say the least. Who would help a young girl commit suicide?"

"We could try to trace the petrol containers," said Nyberg dubiously. "But is it really necessary?"

"As long as we don't know who she was, we have to trace her by any leads we have," Wallander replied. "She must have come from somewhere, somehow."

"Did anyone look in Salomonsson's barn?" asked Höglund. "Maybe the petrol containers came from there."

Wallander nodded.

"Someone had better drive out there and check," he said.

Höglund volunteered.

"We'll have to wait for Martinsson's results," Wallander said, winding up the meeting. "And the pathologists' work in Malmö. They're going to give us an exact age tomorrow."

"And the gold medallion?" asked Svedberg.

"We'll wait until we have some idea of what the letters on it might mean," said Wallander.

He suddenly realised something he had completely overlooked earlier. Behind the dead girl there were other people. Who would mourn her. Who would forever see her running like a living flare in their heads, in a totally different way from him. The fire would stay with them like scars. It would gradually fade away from him like nightmare.

They went their separate ways. Svedberg went with Wallander to get the papers on the car thefts. Wallander gave him a brief run-down. When they were done, Svedberg didn't get up, and Wallander sensed that there was something he wanted to talk about.

"We ought to get together and talk," said Svedberg hesitantly. "About what's going on."

"You're thinking about the cuts? And security companies taking over the custody of suspects?"

Svedberg nodded glumly. "What use are new uniforms if we can't do our jobs?"

"I don't really think it'll help to talk about it," Wallander said warily. "We have a union that's paid to take care of these matters."

"We ought to protest, at least," said Svedberg. "We ought to talk to people on the street about what's going to happen."

"People have their own troubles," replied Wallander, and at the same time it occurred to him that Svedberg was quite right. The public was prepared to bend over backwards to save their police stations.

Svedberg stood up. "That's about it," he said.

"Set up a meeting," Wallander said. "I promise I'll come. But wait until summer's over."

"I'll think about it," said Svedberg and left the room with the files under his arm.

It was late afternoon. Through the window Wallander could see that it was about to rain. He decided to have a pizza before he drove out to see his father in Löderup. On the way out he stopped in on Martinsson.

"Don't stay there too long," he said.

"I haven't found anything yet," said Martinsson.

"See you tomorrow."

Wallander went out to his car, which was already spattered with raindrops. He was just about to drive away when Martinsson ran out waving his arms. We've got her, he thought, and felt a knot in his stomach. He rolled down the window.

"Did you find her?" he asked.

"No," said Martinsson.

Wallander realised something serious had happened. He got out of the car.

"What is it?" he asked.

"Someone phoned in," said Martinsson. "A body has been found on the beach out past Sandskogen."

Damn, thought Wallander. Not now. Not that.

"It sounds like a murder," Martinsson went on. "It was a man that called. He was unusually lucid, even though I think he was in shock."

"Get your jacket," said Wallander. "It's raining."

Martinsson didn't move.

"The man who called seemed to know who the victim was."

Wallander could tell by Martinsson's face that he ought to dread what would come next.

"He said it was Wetterstedt. The former minister of justice."

Wallander stared at Martinsson.

"What?"

"Gustaf Wetterstedt. The minister of justice. And he said it looked as if he'd been scalped."

It was Wednesday, 22 June.

CHAPTER 6

The rain was coming down harder by the time they got to the beach. On the way there they had spoken very little. Martinsson gave directions. They turned off onto a narrow road past the tennis courts. Wallander tried to picture what awaited them. What he wanted least of all had happened. If the man who called the station turned out to be right, his leave was in danger. Hansson would appeal to him to postpone it, and eventually he would have to give in. What he had been hoping for – that his desk would be cleared of pressing matters at the end of June – was not going to happen.

They saw the dunes ahead of them and stopped. A man came forward to meet them. To Wallander's surprise, he didn't seem older than 30. If it was Wetterstedt who had died, this man couldn't have been more than ten when the minister of justice had retired and vanished from public view. Wallander had been a young detective at the time. In the car he had tried to remember Wetterstedt's face. He wore his hair cropped short, and glasses without frames. Wallander vaguely recalled his voice: blaring, invariably self-confident, never willing to admit a mistake.

The young man introduced himself as Göran Lindgren. He was dressed in shorts and a thin sweater, and he seemed very agitated. They followed him down to the beach, deserted now that it had started to rain. Lindgren led them over to a big rowing boat turned upside down. On the far side there was a wide gap between the sand and the boat's gunwale.

"He's under there," said Lindgren in an unsteady voice.

Wallander and Martinsson looked at each other, still hoping the man had imagined it. They knelt down and peered in under the boat. In the dim light they could see a body lying there.

"We'll have to turn the boat over," said Martinsson in a low voice, as if afraid the dead man would hear him.

"No," said Wallander, "we're not turning anything over." He got up quickly and turned to Göran Lindgren.

"I assume you have a torch," he said. "Otherwise you couldn't have described the body in such detail."

The man nodded in surprise and pulled a torch out of a plastic bag near the boat. Wallander bent down again and shone the light inside.

"Holy shit," said Martinsson at his side.

The dead man's face was covered with blood. But they could see that the skin from the forehead up over his skull was torn off, and Lindgren had been right. It was Wetterstedt under the boat. They stood up. Wallander handed back the torch.

"How did you know it was Wetterstedt?" he asked.

"He lives here," said Lindgren, pointing up towards a villa to the left of the boat. "Besides, everyone knows him. You don't forget a politician who was on TV all the time."

Wallander nodded doubtfully.

"We'll need a full team out here," he said to Martinsson. "Go and call. I'll wait here."

Martinsson hurried off. It was raining harder now.

"When did you find him?" asked Wallander.

"I don't have a watch on me," said Lindgren. "But it couldn't have been more than half an hour ago."

"Where did you call from?"

Lindgren pointed to the plastic bag.

"I have a mobile phone."

Wallander regarded him with interest.

"He's lying under an overturned boat," he said. "He's invisible from outside. You must have bent down to be able to see him?"

"It's my boat," said Lindgren simply. "Or my father's, to be exact. I usually walk here on the beach when I finish work. Since it was starting to rain, I thought I'd put my things under the boat. When

I felt the bag bump into something I bent down. At first I thought it was a plank, but then I saw him."

"It's really none of my business," said Wallander, "but I wonder why you had a torch with you?"

"We have a summer cottage in the woods at Sandskogen," replied Lindgren. "Over by Myrgången. We're in the process of rewiring it, so it has no lights. My father and I are electricians."

Wallander nodded. "You'll have to wait here," he said. "We'll have to ask you these questions again in a while. Have you touched anything?"

Lindgren shook his head.

"Has anyone other than you seen him?"

"No."

"When did you or your father last turn over this boat?"

Lindgren thought for a moment.

"It was over a week ago," he said.

Wallander had no more questions. He stood there thinking for a moment and then left the boat and walked in a wide arc up towards the villa where Wetterstedt lived. He tried the gate. It was locked. He waved Lindgren over.

"Do you live nearby?" he asked.

"No," he said. "I live in Åkesholm. My car is parked on the road."

"But you knew that Wetterstedt lived in this house?"

"He used to walk along the beach here. Sometimes he stopped to watch while we were working on the boat, Dad and I. But he never spoke to us. He was rather arrogant."

"Was he married?"

"Dad said that he'd read in a magazine that he was divorced."

Wallander nodded.

"That's fine," he said. "Don't you have a raincoat in that bag?"

"It's up in the car."

"Go ahead and get it," Wallander said. "Did you call anyone besides the police and tell them about this?"

"I think I ought to call Dad. It's his boat, after all."

"Hold off for the time being," said Wallander. "Leave the phone here, and go and get your raincoat."

Lindgren did as he was told. Wallander went back to the boat. He stood looking at it and tried to imagine what had happened. He knew that the first impression of a crime scene was often crucial. During an investigation that was long and difficult, he would return to that first moment.

Some things he was already sure of. It was out of the question that Wetterstedt had been murdered underneath the boat. Someone had wanted to hide him. Since Wetterstedt's villa was so close, there was a good chance that he had died there. Besides, Wallander had a hunch that the killer couldn't have acted alone. The boat must have been lifted to get the body underneath. And it was the old-fashioned kind, clinker-built and heavy.

Wallander turned his mind to the torn-off scalp. What was it that Martinsson had said? Lindgren had told him on the phone that the man had been "scalped". Wallander tried to imagine what other reasons there might be for the wound to the head. They didn't know how Wetterstedt had died. It wasn't natural to think that someone would intentionally have torn off his hair. Wallander felt uneasy. The torn-off skin disturbed him.

Just then the police cars started to arrive. Martinsson had been smart enough to tell them not to turn on their sirens and lights. Wallander walked about ten metres away from the boat so that the others wouldn't trample the sand around it.

"There's a dead man underneath the boat," said Wallander when the police had gathered. "Apparently it's Gustaf Wetterstedt, who was once our top boss. Anyone as old as I am, at least, will remember the days when he was minister of justice. He was living here in retirement. And now he's dead. We have to assume that he was murdered. So we'll start by cordoning off the area."

"It's a good thing the game isn't on tonight," said Martinsson.

"No doubt the person who did this is a football fan too," said Wallander. He was getting annoyed at the constant references to the World Cup, but he hid his irritation from Martinsson.

"Nyberg is on his way," said Martinsson.

"We'll have to work on this all night," said Wallander. "We might as well get started."

Svedberg and Ann-Britt Höglund were in one of the first cars. Hansson showed up right after they did. Lindgren reappeared in a yellow raincoat. He explained again how he had found the dead man while Svedberg took notes. It was raining hard now, and they gathered under a tree at the top of one of the dunes. When Lindgren had finished, Wallander asked him to wait. Since he still didn't want to turn the boat over, the doctor had to dig out some sand to get far enough in under the boat to confirm that Wetterstedt was indeed dead.

"Apparently he was divorced," said Wallander. "But we'll have to get confirmation on that. Some of you will have to stay here. Ann-Britt and I will go up to his house."

"Keys," said Svedberg.

Martinsson went down to the boat, lay on his stomach, and reached in. After a minute or so he managed to find a key ring in Wetterstedt's jacket pocket. Covered in wet sand, Martinsson handed Wallander the keys.

"We've got to put up a canopy," Wallander said testily. "Where is Nyberg? Why the delay?"

"He's coming," said Svedberg. "Today is his sauna day."

Wallander and Höglund made their way up to Wetterstedt's villa.

"I remember him from the police academy," she said. "Somebody put up a photo of him on the wall and used it as a dartboard."

"He was never popular with the police," Wallander said. "It was during his administration that we noticed something new was coming, a change that snuck up on us. I remember it felt like someone had pulled a hood over our eyes. It was almost shameful to be a policeman then. People seemed to worry more about how the prisoners were doing than the fact that crime was steadily on the rise."

"There's a lot I can't recall," said Höglund. "But wasn't he mixed up in some sort of scandal?"

"There were a lot of rumours," said Wallander. "About one thing and another. But nothing was ever proven. A number of police officers in Stockholm were said to be quite upset."

"Maybe time caught up with him," she said.

Wallander looked at her in surprise. But he said nothing.

They had reached the gate.

"I've been here before, you know," she said suddenly. "He used to call the police and complain about young people sitting on the beach and singing on summer nights. One of those young people wrote a letter to the editor of *Ystad Recorder* to complain. Björk asked me to look into it."

"Look into what?"

"I'm not really sure," she answered. "But Björk was very sensitive to criticism."

"That was one of his best traits," said Wallander. "He always defended us and that isn't always the case."

They found the key and opened the gate. Wallander noticed that the light was burned out. The garden they stepped into was well tended. There were no fallen leaves on the lawn. There was a little fountain with two nude plaster children squirting water at each other from their mouths. A swing hung in the arbour. On a flagstone patio stood a marble-topped table and chairs.

"Well cared for and expensive," said Höglund. "What do you think a marble table like that costs?"

Wallander didn't answer, since he had no idea. They continued up towards the villa. He guessed that it had been built around the turn of the century. They followed the flagstone path around to the front of the house. Wallander rang the bell. He waited for over a minute before he rang again. Then he looked for the key and unlocked the door. They stepped into a lit hall. Wallander called out into the silence, but there was no-one there.

"Wetterstedt wasn't killed under the boat," said Wallander. "Of course he could have been attacked on the beach. But I think it happened here."

"Why's that?" she asked.

"I don't know," he said. "Just a hunch."

They went through the house slowly, from the basement to the attic, without touching anything but the light switches. It was a cursory examination. Yet for Wallander it was important. The man who now lay dead on the beach had lived in this house. They had to seek clues as to how his death had come about.

But they didn't find the slightest sign of disorder. Wallander looked in vain for the place where the crime might have taken place. At the front door he had looked for signs of a break-in. As they had stood in the hall listening to the silence, Wallander had told Höglund to take off her shoes. Now they padded soundlessly through the huge villa, which seemed to grow with each step they took. Wallander could feel his colleague looking as much at him as at the objects in the rooms they passed through. He remembered how he had done the same thing with Rydberg, when he was still a young, inexperienced detective. Instead of considering it flattering, it depressed him. The changing of the guard was under way already. She was the one on the way in, he was on the way out.

He remembered when they had first met, almost two years ago. She was a pale, plain young woman who had graduated from the police academy with top marks. But the first thing that she said to him was that he'd teach her everything that the academy couldn't about the unpredictability of the real world. But maybe it was the other way round, he thought, as he looked at a rather blurry lithograph. Imperceptibly, the transition had taken place.

They stopped by a window on the upper floor where they had a view of the beach. The floodlights were in place; Nyberg was gesticulating angrily as he supervised the arrangement of a plastic canopy over the rowing boat. The cordon was guarded by policemen in raincoats. Only a few people stood outside the cordon in the driving rain.

"I'm beginning to think I was wrong," Wallander said as he watched the canopy finally settle into place. "There are no signs that Wetterstedt was killed in here."

"The killer might have cleaned up," Höglund suggested.

"We'll find that out after Nyberg goes through the house with a fine-tooth comb," said Wallander. "But I'm sure it happened outside."

They went back downstairs in silence.

"There was no mail on the floor inside the front door," she said. "The property is walled off. There must be a letter box somewhere."

"We'll take that up later," said Wallander.

He walked into the living-room and stood in the middle. She watched from the doorway, as though expecting him to make an impromptu speech.

"I make a habit of asking myself what I'm missing," Wallander said. "But everything here seems in place. A man living alone in a house where everything is orderly, no bills are unpaid, and where loneliness lingers like old cigar smoke. The only thing that doesn't fit is that the man in question is now lying dead underneath a rowing boat down on the beach."

Then he corrected himself, "No, there's one other thing," he said. "The light by the garden gate isn't working."

"It may have just burned out," she said, surprised.

"Right," said Wallander, "but it still breaks the pattern."

There was a knock on the door. When Wallander opened it, Hansson was standing there, raindrops streaming down his face.

"Neither Nyberg nor the doctor are going to get anywhere unless we turn that boat over," he said.

"Turn it over," said Wallander. "I'll be right there."

Hansson disappeared into the rain.

"We have to start looking for his relatives," Wallander said. "He must have an address book somewhere."

"There's one thing that's odd," said Höglund. "This house is full of souvenirs from a long life with lots of travel and countless meetings with people. But there are no family photographs."

They were back in the living-room. Wallander looked around and saw that she was right. It bothered him that he hadn't thought of it himself.

"Maybe he didn't want to be reminded that he was old," Wallander said without conviction.

"A woman would never be able to live without pictures of her family," she said. "That's probably why I thought of it."

There was a telephone on a table next to the sofa.

"There's a phone in his study too," he said, pointing. "You look in there, and I'll start here."

Wallander squatted by the low telephone stand. Next to the phone was the remote control for the TV. Wetterstedt could talk on the phone and watch TV at the same time, he thought. Just like me. We live in a world where people can't bear not to be able to change channel and talk on the phone at the same time. He riffled through the phone books, but didn't find any private notes. Next he pulled out two drawers in a bureau behind the telephone stand. In one there was a stamp album, in the other some tubes of glue and a box of napkin rings.

As he was walking towards the study, the phone rang. He stopped. Höglund appeared at once in the doorway to the study. Wallander sat down carefully on the corner of the sofa and picked up the receiver.

"Hello," said a woman's voice. "Gustaf? Why haven't you called me?"

"Who's speaking, please?" asked Wallander.

The woman's voice suddenly turned formal. "This is Gustaf Wetterstedt's mother calling," she said. "With whom am I speaking?"

"My name is Kurt Wallander. I'm a police officer here in Ystad."

He could hear the woman breathing. He realised that she must be very old if she was Gustaf Wetterstedt's mother. He made a face at Höglund, who was standing looking at him.

"Has something happened?" asked the woman.

Wallander didn't know how to react. It went against all written and unwritten procedures to inform the next of kin of a sudden death over the telephone. But he had already told her his name, and that he was a police officer.

"Hello?" said the woman. "Are you still there?"

Wallander didn't answer. He stared helplessly at Höglund. Then he did something which he couldn't decide was justified. He hung up.

"Who was that?" she asked.

Wallander shook his head. He picked up the phone and called the headquarters of the Stockholm police.

CHAPTER 7

Later that evening, Gustaf Wetterstedt's telephone rang again. By that time Wallander had arranged for his colleagues in Stockholm to tell Wetterstedt's mother of his death. An inspector who introduced himself as Hans Vikander was calling from the Östermalm police. In a few days, 1 July, the old name would disappear and be replaced by "city police".

"She's been informed," Vikander said. "Because she was so old I took a clergyman along with me. I must say she took it calmly, even though she's 94."

"Maybe that's why," said Wallander.

"We're trying to track down Wetterstedt's two children," Vikander went on. "The older, a son, works at the UN in New York. The daughter lives in Uppsala. We hope to reach them this evening."

"What about his ex-wife?" asked Wallander.

"Which one?" Vikander asked. "He was married three times."

"All three of them," said Wallander. "We'll have to contact them ourselves later."

"I've got something that might interest you," Vikander went on. "When we spoke with the mother she said that her son called her every night, at precisely nine o'clock."

Wallander looked at his watch. It was just after 9 p.m. At once he understood the significance of what Vikander had said.

"He didn't call yesterday" Vikander continued. "She waited until 9.30 p.m. Then she tried to call him. No-one answered, although she claimed she let it ring at least 15 times."

"And the night before?"

"She couldn't remember too well. She's 94, after all. She said that her short-term memory was pretty bad."

"Did she say anything else?"

"It was a little hard to know what to ask."

"We'll have to talk to her again," Wallander said. "Since she's already met you, it would be good if you could take it on."

"I'm going on holiday the second week in July," said Vikander. "Until then, that's no problem."

Wallander hung up. Höglund came into the hall. She had been checking the letter box.

"Newspapers from today and yesterday," she said. "A phone bill. No personal letters. He can't have been under that boat for very long."

Wallander got up from the sofa.

"Go through the house one more time," he said. "See if you can find any sign that something is missing. I'll go down and take a look at him."

It was raining even harder now. As Wallander hurried through the garden he remembered that he was supposed to be visiting his father tonight. With a grimace he went back to the house.

"Do me a favour," he asked Höglund. "Call my father and tell him I'm tied up with an urgent investigation. If he asks who you are, tell him you're the new chief of police."

She nodded and smiled. Wallander gave her the number. Then he went out into the rain.

The cordoned area was a ghostly spectacle, lit up by the powerful floodlights. With a strong feeling of unease, Wallander walked in under the temporary canopy. Wetterstedt's body lay stretched out on a plastic sheet. The doctor was shining a torch down Wetterstedt's throat. He stopped when he realised that Wallander had arrived.

"How are you?" asked the doctor.

Wallander hadn't recognised him until that moment. It was the doctor who had treated him in hospital a few years earlier when he'd thought he was having a heart attack.

"Apart from this business, I'm doing fine," said Wallander. "I never had a recurrence."

"Did you take my advice?" asked the doctor.

"Of course not," Wallander muttered.

He looked at the dead man, who gave the same impression in death as he had on the TV screen. There was something obstinate and unsympathetic about his face, even when covered with dried blood. Wallander leaned forward and looked at the wound on his forehead, which extended up towards the top of his head, where the skin and hair had been ripped away.

"How did he die?" asked Wallander.

"From a powerful blow to the spine with an axe," the doctor replied. "It would have killed him instantly. The spine is severed just below the shoulder blades. He was probably dead before he hit the ground."

"Are you sure it happened outside?" Wallander asked.

"I think so. The blow to the spine must have come from someone standing behind him. It's most likely that the force of the blow made him fall forwards. He has grains of sand in his mouth and eyes. It probably happened right nearby."

"There must be traces of blood somewhere," said Wallander.

"The rain makes it difficult," said the doctor. "But with a little luck maybe you can scrape through the surface layer and find some blood that seeped deep enough that the rain hasn't washed it away."

Wallander pointed at Wetterstedt's butchered head.

"How do you explain this?" he asked.

The doctor shrugged.

"The incision in the forehead was made with a sharp knife," he said. "Or maybe a razor. The skin and hair seem to have been torn off. I can't tell yet if it was done before or after he received the blow to the spine. That will be a job for the pathologist in Malmö."

"Malmström will have a lot to do," said Wallander.

"Who?"

"Yesterday we sent in the remains of a girl who burned herself to death. And now we're sending over a man who's been scalped. The pathologist I talked to was named Malmström. A woman."

"There's more than one," said the doctor. "I don't know her."

Wallander squatted next to the corpse.

"Give me your interpretation," he said to the doctor. "What do you think happened?"

"Whoever struck him in the back knew what he was doing," said the doctor. "A sharpshooter couldn't have done better. But to scalp him! That's the work of a madman."

"Or an American Indian," said Wallander.

He got up and felt a twinge in his knees. The days when he could squat without pain were over.

"I'm finished here," said the doctor. "I've already told Malmö that we're bringing him in."

Wallander didn't reply. He had noticed that Wetterstedt's fly was open.

"Did you touch his clothes?" he asked.

"Just on the back, around the wound to his spine," said the doctor.

Wallander nodded. He could feel the nausea rising.

"Could I ask you one thing?" he said. "Could you check inside Wetterstedt's fly and see if he's still got what's supposed to be there?"

The doctor gave Wallander a questioning look.

"If someone cut off half his scalp, they might cut off other things too," Wallander explained.

The doctor nodded and pulled on a pair of latex gloves. Then he cautiously stuck his hand in and felt around.

"Everything that's supposed to be there seems to be there," he said when he pulled out his hand.

Wallander nodded.

Wetterstedt's corpse was taken away. Wallander turned to Nyberg, who was kneeling next to the boat, which had been turned right side up.

"How's it going?" asked Wallander.

"I don't know," said Nyberg. "With this rain, everything is washing away."

"We'll have to dig tomorrow," said Wallander and told him what the doctor said. Nyberg nodded.

"If there's any blood, we'll find it. Any special place you want us to start looking?"

"Around the boat," said Wallander. "Then in the area from the garden gate down to the water."

Nyberg pointed at a case with the lid open. There were plastic bags inside.

"All I found in his pockets was a box of matches," said Nyberg. "You've got his keys. The clothes are expensive. Except for the clogs."

"The house seems to be untouched," Wallander said. "But I'd appreciate it if you could take a look at it tonight."

"I can't be in two places at once," Nyberg grumbled. "If we're going to secure any evidence out here, we'll have to do it before it's all washed away by the rain."

Wallander was just about to return to Wetterstedt's house when he noticed that Lindgren was still there. He went over to him. He could see that the young man was freezing.

"You can go home now," Wallander said.

"Can I phone my father and tell him about it?"

"Go ahead."

"What happened?" Lindgren asked.

"It's too soon to say," Wallander replied.

There were still a handful of people outside the cordon, watching the police work. Some senior citizens, a younger man with a dog, a boy on a moped. Wallander thought about the days that lay ahead with dread. A former minister of justice who had been found scalped with his spine chopped in half was the sort of juicy titbit that would drive the media wild. The only positive thing that he could think of was that the girl who burned herself to death in Salomonsson's rape field would not end up on the front pages after all.

He had to have a pee. He went down to the water and unzipped his fly. Maybe it's that simple, he thought. Wetterstedt's fly was open because he was standing taking a pee when he was attacked.

He started to walk back up towards the house, then stopped. He was overlooking something. He went back to Nyberg.

"Do you know where Svedberg is?" he asked.

"I think he's trying to find some more plastic sheeting and a couple of big tarpaulins. We've got to cover up the sand."

"I'll talk to him when he gets back," said Wallander. "Where are Martinsson and Hansson?"

"I think Martinsson went to get something to eat," said Nyberg sourly. "Who the hell has time for food?"

"We can arrange to get you something," said Wallander. "Where's Hansson?"

"He was going to speak to the prosecutors' office. And I don't want anything."

Wallander walked back to the house. After he hung up his soaked jacket and pulled off his boots he realised he was hungry. He went to the kitchen and turned on the light. He remembered how they had sat in Salomonsson's kitchen drinking coffee. Now Salomonsson was dead. Compared with the old farmer's kitchen, this was another world. Shiny copper pots hung on the walls. An open grill with a smoke hood attached to an old oven chimney stood in the middle of the room. He opened the refrigerator and took out a piece of cheese and a beer. He found some crispbread in one of the cupboards, and sat down at the kitchen table and ate, his mind empty. By the time Svedberg came in the front door he had finished.

"Nyberg said you wanted to talk to me?"

"How'd it go with the tarpaulins?"

"We're still trying to cover up the sand as best we can. Martinsson called the weather office and asked how long the rain was going to last. It's supposed to keep raining all night. Then we'll have a few hours' break before the next storm arrives. That one's expected to be a real summer gale."

A puddle had formed on the kitchen floor around Svedberg's boots. But Wallander didn't feel like asking him to take them off. They were unlikely to find the clue to Wetterstedt's death in his kitchen.

Svedberg sat down and dried off his hair with a handkerchief.

"I vaguely remember that you once told me you were interested in the history of the American Indians," Wallander began. "Or am I wrong?"

Svedberg gave him a puzzled look.

"You're right," he said. "I've read a lot about American Indians. I never liked watching movies that didn't tell the truth about them. I corresponded with an expert named Uncas. He won a prize on a TV show once. I think that was before I was born. But he taught me a lot."

"I assume you're wondering why I ask," Wallander went on.

"Actually, no," said Svedberg. "Wetterstedt was scalped, after all."

Wallander looked at him intently.

"Was he?"

"If scalping is an art, then in this case it was done almost perfectly. A cut with a sharp knife across the forehead. Then some cuts up by the temples. To get a firm grip."

"He died from a blow to the spine," said Wallander. "Just below the shoulder blades."

Svedberg shrugged.

"Native American warriors struck at the head," he said. "It's hard to hit the spine. You have to hold the axe at an angle. It's particularly hard, of course, if the person you're trying to kill is in motion."

"What if he's standing still?"

"In any case, it's not very warrior-like," said Svedberg. "In fact, it's not like an American Indian to kill someone from behind. Or to kill anyone at all, for that matter."

Wallander rested his head in his hands.

"Why are you asking about this?" said Svedberg. "It's hardly likely that an American Indian murdered Wetterstedt."

"Who would take his scalp?" asked Wallander.

"A madman," said Svedberg. "Anyone who does something like this has to be nuts. We must catch him as fast as possible."

"I know," said Wallander.

Svedberg stood up and left. Wallander got a mop and cleaned the floor. Then he went in to see Höglund in the study.

"Your father didn't sound too happy," she said. "But I think the main

74

thing that was bothering him was that you hadn't called earlier."

"He's right about that," said Wallander. "What have you found?"

"Surprisingly little," she said. "On the surface nothing seems to have been stolen. No cabinets are broken open. I think he must have had a housekeeper to keep this big place clean."

"Why do you say that?"

"Two reasons. First, you can see the difference in the way a man and a woman clean. Don't ask me how. That's just the way it is."

"And the second reason?"

"There's a note in his diary that says 'charwoman' and then a time. The note comes up twice a month."

"Did he really write 'charwoman'?"

"A fine old contemptuous word."

"When was she here last?"

"Last Thursday."

"That explains why everything seems so clean and tidy."

Wallander sank down into a chair in front of the desk.

"How did it look down there?" she asked.

"An axe blow severed the spine. He died instantly. The killer cut off his scalp."

"Earlier you said there had to be at least two of them."

"I know I did. But now all I'm certain about is that I don't like this one bit. Why would someone murder an old man who's been living in seclusion for 20 years? And why take his scalp?"

They sat for a while in silence. Wallander thought about the burning girl. About the man with his hair torn off. And about the pouring rain. He tried to push these thoughts away by remembering himself and Baiba in a hollow behind a dune at Skagen in Denmark. But the girl kept running through the field with her hair on fire. And Wetterstedt lay scalped on a stretcher on the way to Malmö.

He forced himself to concentrate, and looked at Höglund.

"Give me a run-down," he said. "What do you think? What happened here? Describe it for me. Don't hold anything back."

"He went out," she said. "A walk down to the beach. To meet

someone. Or just to get some exercise. But he was only going for a short walk."

"Why?"

"The clogs. Old and worn out. Uncomfortable. But good enough if you're just going to be out for a short time."

"And then?"

"It happened at night. What did the doctor say about the time?"

"He's not sure yet. Keep going. Why at night?"

"The risk of being seen is too great in the daytime. At this time of year, the beach is never deserted."

"What else?"

"There's no obvious motive. But I think you can tell that the killer had a plan."

"Why?"

"He took time to hide the body."

"Why did he do that?"

"To delay its discovery. So he'd have time to get away."

"But nobody saw him, right? And why a man?"

"A woman would never sever someone's spine. A desperate woman might hit her husband with an axe. But she wouldn't scalp him. It's a man."

"What do we know about the killer?"

"Nothing. Unless you know something I don't."

Wallander shook his head.

"You've outlined everything we know," he said. "I think it's time for us to leave the house to Nyberg and his people."

"There's going to be a big commotion about this," she said.

"I know," said Wallander. "It'll start tomorrow. You can be glad you've got your holiday coming up."

"Hansson has already asked me whether I'd postpone it," she said. "I said yes."

"You should go home now," Wallander said. "I think I'll tell the others that we'll meet early tomorrow morning to plan the investigation."

Wallander knew that they had to form a picture of who Wetterstedt was. They knew that every evening at the same time he called his mother. But what about all the routines that they didn't know about? He went back to the kitchen and searched for some paper in one of the drawers. Then he made a list of things to remember for tomorrow morning's meeting. A few minutes later Nyberg came in. He took off his wet raincoat.

"What do you want us to look for?" he asked.

"I want to be able to rule out that he was killed inside. I want you to go over the house in your usual way," Wallander answered.

Nyberg nodded and left the kitchen. Wallander heard him reprimanding one of his crew. He knew he ought to drive home and sleep for a few hours, but instead he decided to go through the house one more time. He started with the basement. An hour later he was on the top floor. He went into Wetterstedt's spacious bedroom and opened his wardrobe. Pulling the suits back, he searched the bottom. Downstairs he could hear Nyberg's voice raised in anger. He was just about to close the wardrobe doors when he caught sight of a small case in one corner. He bent down and took it out, sat down on the edge of the bed, and opened it. Inside was a camera. Wallander guessed that it wasn't particularly expensive. He could see that it was more or less the same type as the one Linda had bought last year. There was film in it, and seven pictures out of 36 were exposed. He put it back in the bag. Then he went downstairs to Nyberg.

"There's a camera in this bag," he said. "I want you to get the photos developed as quickly as possible."

It was almost midnight when he left Wetterstedt's villa. It was still pouring outside. He drove straight home.

When he got to his flat he sat down at the kitchen table, wondering what the photographs would be of. The rain pounded against his windows, and he was aware of a feeling of foreboding. He sensed that what had happened was only the beginning of something much worse.

CHAPTER 8

On Thursday morning, 23 June, there was no Midsummer Eve mood in the Ystad station. Wallander had been woken at 3 a.m. by a reporter from *Daily News* in Stockholm who had heard about Wetterstedt's death from the Östermalm police. Just when Wallander finally managed to get back to sleep, the *Express* called. Hansson had also been woken during the night. They gathered in the conference room just after 7 a.m., everyone looking haggard and tired. Nyberg was there, even though he had been going through Wetterstedt's house until 5 a.m. Before the meeting, Hansson took Wallander aside and told him that he would have to run the investigation.

"I think Björk knew this would happen," said Hansson. "That's why he retired."

"He didn't retire," said Wallander. "He was promoted. Besides, seeing into the future was definitely not one of his talents. He worried enough about what was happening around him from day to day."

But Wallander knew that the responsibility for organising the hunt for Wetterstedt's killer would fall to him. The big difficulty was the fact that they would be short of staff all summer. He was grateful that Ann-Britt Höglund had agreed to postpone her holiday. But what was going to happen to his? He had counted on being on his way to Skagen with Baiba in two weeks.

He sat down at the table and took stock of the exhausted faces around him. It was still raining, but it was easing off. In front of him on the table he had a pile of messages that he had picked up at the reception desk. He pushed them aside and tapped on the table with a pencil.

"We have to get started," he said. "The worst thing possible has happened. We've had a murder during the summer holiday. We'll have to organise ourselves as best we can. We also have the Midsummer holiday coming up that will keep the uniformed officers busy. We'll have to plan our investigation with this in mind."

No-one spoke. Wallander turned to Nyberg and asked how the forensic investigation was going.

"If only it would stop raining for a few hours," said Nyberg. "To find the murder site we'll have to dig through the surface layer of the sand. That's almost impossible to do until it's dry. Otherwise we'll just end up with lumps of wet sand."

"I called the meteorologist at Sturup Airport a while ago," said Martinsson. "He's predicting that the rain will stop here just after 8 a.m. But a new storm will come in this afternoon, and we'll get more rain. After that it'll clear up."

"If it's not one thing it's another," said Wallander. "Usually it's easier for us if the weather's bad on Midsummer Eve."

"For once it looks like the football game will be a help," said Nyberg. "I don't think people will drink as much. They'll be glued to their TVs."

"What'll happen if Sweden loses to Russia?" asked Wallander.

"They won't," Nyberg proclaimed. "We're going to win."

Wallander hadn't realised that Nyberg was a football fan.

"I hope you're right," he said.

"Anyway, we haven't found anything of interest around the boat," Nyberg continued. "We also went over the part of the beach between Wetterstedt's gate, the boat, and down to the water. We picked up a number of items. But nothing that is likely to be of interest to us. With one possible exception."

Nyberg put one of his plastic bags on the table.

"One of the officers found this. It's a mace spray. The kind that women carry in their handbags to defend themselves if they're attacked."

"Aren't those illegal in Sweden?" asked Höglund.

"Yes, they are," said Nyberg. "But there it was, in the sand just outside the cordon. We're going to check it for prints. Maybe it'll turn up something."

Nyberg put the plastic bag back in his case.

"Could one man turn that boat over by himself?" asked Wallander.

"Not unless he's incredibly strong," said Nyberg.

"That means there were two of them," Wallander replied.

"The murderer could have dug out the sand under the boat," said Nyberg hesitantly. "And then pushed it back in after he shoved Wetterstedt underneath."

"That's a possibility," said Wallander. "But does it sound plausible?"

No-one at the table answered.

"There's nothing to indicate that the murder was committed inside the house," Nyberg continued. "We found no traces of blood or other signs of a crime. No-one broke in. We can't say whether anything was stolen, but it doesn't appear so."

"Did you find anything else that seemed unusual?" asked Wallander.

"I think the entire house is unusual," said Nyberg. "Wetterstedt must have had a lot of money."

They thought about that for a moment. Wallander realised he should sum up.

"It is important to find out when Wetterstedt was murdered," he began. "The doctor who examined the body thought that it probably happened on the beach. He found grains of sand in the mouth and eyes. But we'll have to wait to see what the doctors have to say. Since we don't have any clues to go on or any obvious motive, we'll have to proceed on a broad front. We have to find out what kind of man Wetterstedt was. Who did he associate with? What routines did he have? We have to understand his character, find out what his life was like. And we can't ignore the fact that 20 years ago he was very famous. He was the minister of justice. He was very popular with some people, and he was hated by others. There were rumours of scandals that he was involved in. Could revenge be part of the picture? He was cut down with an axe and had his hair ripped off. He was scalped. Has anything like this happened before? Can we find any similarities with previous murders? Martinsson will have to get his computer going. And Wetterstedt had a housekeeper we'll have to find and talk to, today."

"What about his political party?" asked Höglund.

"I was just getting to that. Did he have any unresolved political disputes? Did he continue to see old party allies? We have to clear this up too. Is there anything in his background that might point to a conceivable motive?"

"Since the news broke, two people have already called in to confess to the murder," said Svedberg. "One of them called from a phone booth in Malmö. He was so drunk it was hard to understand what he said. We asked our colleagues in Malmö to question him. The other one who called was a prisoner at Österåker. His last leave was in February. So it's quite clear that Gustaf Wetterstedt still arouses strong feelings."

"Those of us who have been around for a while know that the police hold a grudge too," said Wallander. "During his tenure as minister of justice, a lot of things happened that none of us can forget. Of all the ministers of justice and national police chiefs, in my time anyway, Wetterstedt was the one who did the least for us."

They went over the various assignments and divided them up. Wallander himself was going to question Wetterstedt's housekeeper. They agreed to meet again at 4 p.m.

"A few more items," said Wallander. "We're going to be invaded by reporters. We're going to be seeing headlines like 'The Scalp Murderer'. So we might as well hold a news conference today. I would prefer not to have to run it."

"You must," said Svedberg. "You have to take charge. Even if you don't want to, you're the one who does it best."

"All right, but I don't want to do it alone," said Wallander. "I want Hansson with me. And Ann-Britt. Shall we say 1 p.m.?"

They were all about to leave when Wallander asked them to wait.

"We can't stop the investigation into the girl who burned herself to death," he said.

"You think there's a connection?" Hansson asked in astonishment.

"Of course not," said Wallander. "But we still have to try and find out who she was, even though we're busy working on Wetterstedt."

"We've no positive leads on our database search," said Martinsson. "Not even on the combination of letters. But I promise to keep working on it."

"Someone must miss her," said Wallander. "A young girl. I think this is very odd."

"It's summer," said Svedberg. "A lot of young people are on the road. It could take a couple of weeks before someone is missed."

"You're right," Wallander admitted. "We'll have to be patient."

The meeting was over. Wallander had run it at a brisk pace since they all had a lot of work ahead of them. When he got to his office he went rapidly through his messages. Nothing looked urgent. He took a notebook out of a drawer, wrote "Gustaf Wetterstedt" at the top of the page, and leaned back in his chair and closed his eyes.

What does his death tell me? What kind of person would kill him with an axe and scalp him? Wallander leaned over his desk again. He wrote:

"Nothing indicates that Wetterstedt was murdered by a burglar, but of course that can't be excluded yet. It wasn't a murder of convenience either, unless it was committed by someone insane. The killer took the time to hide the body. So the revenge motive remains. Who would want to take revenge on Gustaf Wetterstedt, to see him dead?"

Wallander put down his pen and read through the page with dissatisfaction. It's too soon to draw conclusions, he thought. I have to know more. He got up and left the room. When he walked out of the station it had stopped raining. The meteorologist at Sturup was right. Wallander drove straight to Wetterstedt's villa.

The cordon on the beach was still there. Nyberg was already at work. Along with his crew he was busy removing the tarpaulins over a section of the beach. There were a lot of spectators standing at the edge the cordon this morning.

Wallander unlocked the front door with Wetterstedt's key and then went straight to the study. Methodically he continued the search that Höglund had begun the night before. It took him almost half an hour to find the name of the woman Wetterstedt had called the "charwoman". Her name was Sara Björklund. She lived on Styrbordsgången, which Wallander knew lay just past the big warehouses at the west end of town. He picked up the telephone on the desk and dialled the number. Eventually a harsh male voice answered.

"I'm looking for Sara Björklund," said Wallander.

"She's not home," said the man.

"Where can I get in touch with her?"

"Who's asking?" said the man evasively.

"Inspector Kurt Wallander from the Ystad police."

There was a long silence at the other end.

"Are you still there?" said Wallander, not bothering to conceal his impatience.

"Does this have something to do with Wetterstedt?" asked the man. "Sara Björklund is my wife."

"I have to speak with her."

"She's in Malmö. She won't be back till this afternoon."

"When can I get hold of her? What time? Try to be exact!"

"I'm sure she'll be home by 5 p.m."

"I'll come by your house then," said Wallander and hung up.

He left the house and went down to Nyberg on the beach.

"Find anything?" he asked.

Nyberg was standing with a bucket of sand in one hand.

"Nothing," he said. "But if he was killed here and fell into the sand, there has to be some blood. Maybe not from his back. But from his head. It must have spurted blood. There are some big veins in the scalp."

Wallander nodded.

"Where did you find the spray can?" he asked.

Nyberg pointed to a spot beyond the cordon.

"I doubt it has anything to do with this," said Wallander.

"Me neither," said Nyberg.

Wallander was just about to go back to his car when he remembered that he had one more question for Nyberg.

"The light by the gate to the garden is out," he said. "Can you take a look at it?"

"What do you want me to do?" Nyberg wondered. "Change the bulb?"

"I just want to know why it's not working," said Wallander. "That's all."

He drove back to the station. The sky was grey, but it wasn't raining.

"Reporters are calling constantly," said Ebba as he passed the reception desk.

"They're welcome to come to the press conference at one o'clock," said Wallander. "Where's Ann-Britt?"

"She left a while ago. She didn't say where she was going."

"What about Hansson?"

"I think he's in Per Åkeson's office. Should I find him for you?"

"We have to get ready for the press conference. Get someone to bring more chairs into the conference room. There are going to be lots of people."

Wallander went to his office and started to prepare what he was going to say to the press. After about half an hour Höglund knocked on the door.

"I was at Salomonsson's farm," she said. "I think I know where that girl got the petrol from."

"Salomonsson had petrol in his barn?"

She nodded.

"Well, that's something," said Wallander. "That means that she actually could have walked to the farm. She wouldn't have had to come by car or bicycle."

"Could Salomonsson have known her?" she asked.

Wallander thought for a moment before he answered.

"No, Salomonsson wasn't lying. He'd never seen her before."

"So the girl walks to the farm from somewhere. She goes into Salomonsson's barn and finds a number of containers of petrol.

She takes five of them with her out into the rape. Then she sets herself on fire."

"That's about it," said Wallander. "Even if we manage to find out who she was, we'll probably never know the whole story."

They got coffee and discussed what they were going to say at the press conference. It was mid-morning when Hansson joined them.

"I talked to Per Åkeson," he said. "He told me he would contact the chief public prosecutor."

Wallander looked up from his papers in surprise.

"Why?"

"Wetterstedt was an important person. Ten years ago the prime minister of this country was murdered. Now we have a minister of justice murdered. I assume that he wants to know whether the investigation should be handled in any special way."

"If he were still in office I could understand it," said Wallander. "But he was an old man who had left his public duties behind a long time ago."

"You'll have to talk to Åkeson yourself," said Hansson. "I'm just telling you what he said."

At 1 p.m. they took their seats on the little dais at one end of the conference room. They had agreed to keep the meeting with the press as brief as possible. The main thing was to head off too many wild, unfounded speculations. So they decided to be vague when it came to answering how Wetterstedt had actually been killed. They wouldn't say anything at all about his having been scalped.

The room was crowded with reporters. Just as Wallander had imagined, the national newspapers were regarding Wetterstedt's murder as a major event. Wallander counted cameras from three different TV stations when he looked in the crowd.

It went unusually well. They were as terse as possible with their answers, citing the requirements of the investigation for limiting candour and withholding detail. Eventually the press realised they weren't going to get anything more. When the newspaper reporters had gone, Wallander allowed himself to be interviewed by the local radio station while Höglund answered questions for one of the TV stations. He looked at her and was relieved that for once he didn't have to be the one on camera.

At the end of the press conference Åkeson had slipped in unnoticed to the back of the room. Now he stood waiting for Wallander.

"I heard you were going to call up the chief public prosecutor," said Wallander. "Did he give you any directives?"

"He wants to be kept informed," said Åkeson. "The same way you keep me informed."

"You'll get a daily summary," said Wallander. "And hear as soon as we make a breakthrough."

"Nothing conclusive yet?"

"No."

The investigative team had a quick meeting at 4 p.m. Wallander knew that this was the time for work, not reports. He went rapidly around the table before asking everyone to go back to their tasks. They agreed to meet again at 8 a.m. the next morning, provided nothing crucial happened before then.

Just before 5 p.m. Wallander left the station and drove to Styrbordsgången, where Sara Björklund lived. It was a part of town that Wallander almost never visited. He parked and went in through the gate. The door was opened before he reached the house. The woman standing there was younger than he had expected. He guessed her to be around 30. And to Wetterstedt she had been a "charwoman". He wondered fleetingly whether she knew what Wetterstedt had called her.

"Good afternoon," said Wallander. "I called earlier today. Are you Sara Björklund?"

"I recognised you," she said, nodding.

She invited him in. She had set out a tray of buns and coffee in a thermos in the living-room. Wallander could hear a man upstairs scolding some children for making a racket. Wallander sat down in an armchair and looked around. He half expected one of his father's paintings to be hanging on the wall. That's all that's missing, he thought. Here's the old fisherman, the gypsy woman, and the crying child. My father's landscape is all that's needed. With or without the grouse.

"Would you like coffee, sir?" she asked.

"No need to call me sir," said Wallander. "Yes, please."

"You had to be formal with Wetterstedt," she said suddenly. "You had to call him Mr Wetterstedt. He gave strict instructions about that when I started working there."

Wallander was thankful to start right away on the matter in hand. He took out a notebook and pen.

"So you know that Gustaf Wetterstedt has been murdered," he began.

"It's terrible," she said. "Who could have done it?"

"We're wondering the same thing," said Wallander.

"Was he really lying on the beach? Under that ugly boat? The one you could see from upstairs?"

"Yes, he was," said Wallander. "But let's begin at the beginning. You cleaned the house for Mr Wetterstedt?"

"Yes."

"How long have you been with him?"

"Almost three years. I wasn't working. This house costs money so I was forced to look for cleaning work. I found the job in the paper."

"How often did you go to his house?"

"Twice a month. Every other Thursday."

Wallander made a note.

"Always on Thursdays?"

"Always."

"Did you have your own keys?"

"No. He never would have given them to me."

"Why do you say that?"

"When I was in the house he watched every step I took. It was incredibly nerve-wracking. But he paid well."

"Did you ever come across anything odd?"

"Such as?"

"Was there ever anyone else there?"

"No, never."

"He didn't have people to dinner?"

"Not that I know of. There were never any dishes waiting for me when I came."

Wallander paused for a moment before continuing.

"How would you describe him as a person?"

Her reply was swift and firm.

"He was the type you'd call arrogant."

"What do you mean by that?"

"He patronised me. To him I was nothing more than a cleaning woman. Despite the fact that he once belonged to the party that supposedly represented our cause. The cleaning women's cause."

"Did you know that he referred to you as a charwoman in his diary?"

"That doesn't surprise me in the least."

"But you stayed on with him?"

"I told you, he paid well."

"Try to remember your last visit. You were there last week?"

"Everything was as usual. He was just the way he always was."

"Over the past three years, then, nothing out of the ordinary happened?"

She hesitated before she answered. He was immediately on the alert.

"There was one time last year," she began tentatively. "In November. I don't know why, but I forgot what day it was. I went there on a Friday morning instead of Thursday. As I arrived, a big black car drove out of the garage. The kind with windows you can't see through. Then I rang the bell at the front door as I always do. It took a long time before he came to open the door. When he saw me he was furious. He slammed the door. I thought I was going to get the sack. But when I came back the next time he said nothing about it, just pretended that nothing had happened."

Wallander waited for her to go on.

"Was that all?"

"Yes."

"A big black car leaving his house?"

"That's right."

Wallander knew that he wouldn't get any further. He finished his coffee and stood up.

"If you remember anything else that might be helpful to the enquiry, I'd appreciate it if you'd call me," he said as he left.

He drove back to Ystad.

A big black car had visited Wetterstedt's house. Who was in the car? A strong wind began to blow, and the rain started again.

CHAPTER 9

By the time Wallander returned to Wetterstedt's house, Nyberg and his crew had moved back inside. They had carted off tons of sand without finding what they were looking for. When it started raining again, Nyberg immediately decided to lay out the tarpaulins. They couldn't carry on until the weather improved. Wallander returned to the house feeling that what Sara Björklund had said about showing up on the wrong day and the big black car meant they had knocked a small hole in Wetterstedt's shell. She had seen something that no-one was supposed to see. Wallander couldn't interpret Wetterstedt's rage in any other way, or the fact that he didn't fire her and never spoke of it again. The anger and the silence were two sides of the same temperament.

Nyberg was in Wetterstedt's living-room drinking coffee from an old thermos that reminded Wallander of the 1950s. He was sitting on a newspaper to protect the chair.

"We haven't found the murder site yet," said Nyberg "And now there's no point in looking because of the rain."

"I hope the tarpaulins are securely fastened," Wallander said. "It's blowing harder all the time."

"They won't move," said Nyberg.

"I thought I'd finish going through his desk," said Wallander.

"Hansson called. He has spoken to Wetterstedt's children."

"It took him this long?" said Wallander. "I thought he'd done that a while ago."

"I don't know anything about it," said Nyberg. "I'm just telling you what he said."

Wallander went into the study and sat down at the desk. He adjusted the lamp so that it cast its light in as big a circle as possible.

Then he pulled out one of the drawers in the left-hand cabinet. In it lay a copy of this year's tax return. Wallander placed it on the desk. He could see that Wetterstedt had declared an income of almost 1,000,000 kronor, and that the income came primarily from Wetterstedt's private pension plan and share dividends. A summary from the securities register centre revealed that Wetterstedt held shares in traditional Swedish heavy industry; Ericsson, Asea Brown Boveri, Volvo, and Rottneros. Apart from this income, Wetterstedt had reported an honorarium from the foreign ministry and royalties from Tidens publishing company. Under the entry "Net Worth" he had declared 5,000,000 kronor. Wallander memorised this figure.

He put the tax return back. The next drawer contained something that looked like a photo album. Here are the family pictures Ann-Britt was missing, he thought. But he leafed through the pages with growing astonishment: old-fashioned pornographic pictures, some of them quite sophisticated. Wallander noted that some of the pages fell open more easily than others. Wetterstedt had a preference for young models. Martinsson walked in. Wallander nodded and pointed to the open album.

"Some people collect stamps," said Martinsson, "others evidently collect pictures like this."

Wallander closed the album and put it back in the desk drawer.

"A lawyer named Sjögren called from Malmö," said Martinsson. "He said he had Wetterstedt's will. There are rather large assets in the estate. I asked him whether there were any unexpected beneficiaries. But everything goes to the direct heirs. Wetterstedt had also set up a foundation to distribute scholarships to young law students. But he put the money into it long ago and paid tax on it."

"So, we know that Gustaf Wetterstedt was a wealthy man. But wasn't he born the son of a poor docker?"

"Svedberg is working on his background," said Martinsson. "I gather he's found an old party secretary with a good memory who had a lot to say about Wetterstedt. But I wanted to have a word about the girl who committed suicide."

"Did you find out who she was?"

"No. But through the computer I've found more than 2,000 possibilities for what the letter combination might mean. It was a pretty long print-out."

"We'll have to put it out on Interpol," said Wallander after a pause. "And what's the new one called? Europol?"

"That's right."

"Send out a query with her description. Tomorrow we'll take a photo of the medallion. Even if everything else is getting pushed aside in the wake of Wetterstedt's death, we have to try and get that picture in the papers."

"I had a jeweller look at it," said Martinsson. "He said it was solid gold."

"Surely somebody is missing her," said Wallander. "It's rare for someone to have no relatives at all."

Martinsson yawned and asked whether Wallander needed any help.

"Not tonight," he said, and Martinsson left the house. Wallander spent another hour going through the desk. Then he turned off the lamp and sat there in the dark. Who was Gustaf Wetterstedt? The picture he had of him was still unclear.

An idea came to him. He looked up a name in the telephone book. He dialled the number and got an answer almost at once. He explained who it was and asked whether he could come over. Then he hung up. He found Nyberg upstairs and told him he'd be back later that evening.

The wind and the rain lashed at him as he ran to his car. He drove into town, to a block of flats near Österport School. He rang the bell and the door was opened. When he reached the third floor Lars Magnusson was waiting for him in his stockinged feet. Beautiful piano music was playing.

"Long time no see," said Magnusson as they shook hands.

"You're right," said Wallander. "It must be more than five years."

Long ago Magnusson had been a journalist. After a number of years at the *Express* he had tired of city life and returned to his roots in

Ystad. He and Wallander met because their wives became friends. The two men discovered that they shared an interest in opera. It wasn't until many years later, after he and Mona had divorced, that Wallander found out Magnusson was an alcoholic. But when the truth finally did come out, it came out with a vengeance. By chance, Wallander had been at the station late one night when Magnusson was dragged in, so drunk that he couldn't stand up. He had been driving in that state, and had lost control and gone straight through the plate-glass window of a bank. He'd ended up spending six months in jail.

When he returned to Ystad he didn't go back to his job. His wife had left their childless marriage. He continued drinking but managed not to step too far over the line. He gave up his career in journalism and made a living setting chess problems for a number of newspapers. The only reason he hadn't drunk himself to death was that every day he forced himself to hold off on that first drink until he had devised at least one chess problem. Now that he had a fax machine, he didn't even have to go to the post office.

Wallander walked into the simple flat. He could smell that Magnusson had been drinking. A bottle of vodka stood on the coffee table, but Wallander didn't see a glass.

Magnusson was a good many years older than Wallander. He had a mane of grey hair falling over his dirty collar. His face was red and swollen, but his eyes were curiously clear. No-one doubted Magnusson's intelligence. Rumour had it that he once had a collection of poems accepted by Bonniers, but had withdrawn it at the last minute and repaid the small advance.

"This is unexpected," said Magnusson. "Have a seat. What can I get you?"

"Nothing, thanks," said Wallander, moving a pile of newspapers and making himself comfortable on a sofa.

Magnusson casually took a swig from the bottle of vodka and sat down opposite Wallander. He had turned down the piano music.

"It's been a long time," said Wallander. "I'm trying to remember when it was."

"At the state off licence," Magnusson replied quickly. "Almost exactly five years ago. You were buying wine and I was buying everything else."

Wallander nodded. He remembered now.

"There's nothing wrong with your memory," he said.

"I haven't ruined *that* yet," said Magnusson. "I'm saving it for last."

"Have you ever considered quitting?"

"Every day. But I doubt you came here to talk me into going on the wagon."

"You've probably read that Gustaf Wetterstedt was murdered, haven't you?"

"I saw it on the TV."

"I seem to remember that you told me something about him once. About the scandals that were hushed up."

"And that was the biggest scandal of them all," Magnusson interrupted him.

"I'm trying to get a fix on what sort of man he was," Wallander went on. "I hoped you might be able to help me."

"The question is whether you want to hear the unsubstantiated rumours or whether you want to know the truth," said Magnusson. "I'm not sure I can tell them apart."

"Rumours don't usually get started without reason," said Wallander.

Magnusson pushed away the vodka bottle as though it was too close to him.

"I started as a 15-year-old trainee at one of the Stockholm newspapers," he said. "That was in the spring of 1955. There was an old night editor there named Ture Svanberg. He was almost as big a drunk as I am now. But he was meticulous at his work. And he was a genius at writing headlines that sold papers. He wouldn't stand for anything sloppily written. Once he flew into such a rage over a story that he tore up the copy and ate the pieces, chewed the paper and swallowed it. Then he said: 'This isn't coming out as anything but shit.' It was Svanberg who taught me to be a journalist. He used to say that there were two kinds of reporters. 'The first kind digs in the ground for the truth. He stands down in the hole shovelling out dirt. But up on top there's another man, shovelling the dirt back in. There's always a duel going on between these two. The fourth estate's eternal test of strength for dominance. Some journalists want to expose and reveal things, others run errands for those in power and help conceal what's really happening.'

"And that's how it really was. I learned fast, even though I was only 15. Men in power always ally themselves with symbolic cleaning companies and undertakers. There are plenty of journalists who won't hesitate to sell their souls to run errands for those men. To shovel the dirt back into the hole. Paste over the scandals. Pile on the semblance of truth, maintain the illusion of the squeaky-clean society."

With a grimace he reached for the bottle again and took a swig. Wallander saw that he'd put on weight around the middle.

"Wetterstedt," Magnusson said. "So what was it that actually happened?" He fished a crumpled packet of cigarettes out of his shirt pocket. He lit one and blew out a cloud of smoke.

"Whores and art," he said. "For years it was common knowledge that the good Gustaf had a girl delivered to the block of flats in Vasastan every week, where he kept a small hideaway his wife didn't know about. He had a right-hand man who took care of the whole thing. The rumour was that this man was hooked on morphine, supplied by Wetterstedt. He had a lot of doctor friends. The fact that he went to bed with whores wasn't something the papers bothered with. He was neither the first nor the last Swedish minister to do that. Sometimes I wonder whether we're talking about the rule or the exception. But one day it went too far. One of the hookers got her courage up and reported him to the police for assault."

"When was that?" Wallander interrupted.

"Mid-60s. Her complaint said he'd beaten her with a leather belt and cut the soles of her feet with a razor. It was probably the stuff with the razor and her feet that made the difference. Perversion was newsworthy. The only problem was that the police had lodged a complaint against the highest defender of Swedish law and order next to the king. So the whole thing was hushed up, and the police report disappeared."

"Disappeared?"

"It literally went up in smoke."

"But the girl who reported him? What happened to her?"

"Overnight she became the proprietor of a lucrative boutique in Västerås."

Wallander shook his head.

"How do you know all this?"

"I knew a journalist called Sten Lundberg. He dug around in the whole mess. But when the rumours started that he was about to snoop his way to the truth, he was frozen out, blacklisted."

"And he accepted it?"

"He had no choice. Unfortunately *he* had a weakness that couldn't be covered up. He gambled. Had huge debts. There was a rumour that those gambling debts suddenly went poof. The same way the hooker's assault report did. So everything was back to square one. And Wetterstedt went on sending his morphine addict out after girls."

"You said there was one more thing," Wallander said.

"There was a story that he was mixed up in some of those art thefts carried out during his term as minister of justice. Paintings that were never recovered, and which now hang on the walls of collectors who will never show them to the public. The police arrested a fence once, a middleman. Unintentionally, I'm afraid. The fence swore that Wetterstedt was involved. But it couldn't be proved. It was buried. There were more people filling up the hole than there were people standing down in it and tossing the dirt out."

"Not a pretty picture," said Wallander.

"Remember what I asked? Do you want the truth or the rumours? Because the rumour about Wetterstedt was that he was a talented politician, a loyal party member, an amiable human being. Educated and competent. That's how his obituaries will read. As long as none of the girls he whipped talk."

"Why did he leave office?" asked Wallander.

"I don't think he got along so well with some of the younger ministers. Especially the women. There was a big shift between the generations in those days. I think he realised that his time was over. Mine was too. I quit being a journalist. After he came to Ystad I never wasted a thought on him. Until now."

"Can you think of anyone who would want to kill him, so many years later?"

Magnusson shrugged.

"That's impossible to answer."

Wallander had just one question left.

"Have you ever heard of a murder in this country where the victim was scalped?"

Magnusson's eyes narrowed. He looked at Wallander with a sudden, alert interest.

"Was he scalped? They didn't say that on TV. They would have, if they knew about it."

"Just between the two of us," Wallander said, looking at Magnusson, who nodded.

"We didn't want to release it just yet," he went on. "We can always say we can't reveal it 'for investigative reasons'. The excuse the police have for presenting half-truths. But this time it's actually true."

"I believe you," said Magnusson. "Or I don't believe you. It doesn't really matter, since I'm no longer a journalist. But I can't recall a murderer who scalped people. That would have made a great headline. Ture Svanberg would have loved it. Can you avoid leaks?"

"I don't know," Wallander answered frankly. "I've had a number of bad experiences over the years."

"I won't sell the story," said Magnusson.

Then he accompanied Wallander to the door.

"How the hell can you stand being a policeman?" he asked.

"I don't know," said Wallander. "I'll let you know when I work it out."

Wallander drove back to Wetterstedt's house. The wind was gusting up to gale force. Some of Nyberg's men were taking fingerprints upstairs. Looking out of the balcony window, he saw Nyberg perched on a wobbly ladder leaning against the light pole by the garden gate. He was clinging to the pole, so the wind wouldn't blow the ladder over. Wallander went to help him, but saw Nyberg begin to climb down. They met in the hall.

"That could have waited," said Wallander. "You might have been blown off the ladder."

"If I fell off I might have hurt myself," Nyberg said sullenly. "And of course checking the light could have waited, but it might have been forgotten. Since you were the one who wondered about it, and I have a certain respect for your ability to do your job, I decided to look at the light. I can assure you that it was only because you were the one who asked me."

Wallander was surprised, but he tried not to show it.

"What did you find?" he asked instead.

"The bulb wasn't burnt out," said Nyberg. "It was unscrewed."

"Hold on a minute," Wallander said, and went into the living-room to call Sara Björklund. She answered.

"Excuse me for disturbing you so late at night," he began. "But I have an urgent question. Who changed the light bulbs in Wetterstedt's house?"

"He did that himself."

"Outside also?"

"I think so. He did all of his own gardening, and I think I was the only other person who set foot inside his house."

Except for whoever was in the black car, thought Wallander.

"There's a light by the garden gate," he said. "Was it usually turned on?"

"In the winter, when it was dark, he always kept it lit."

"That's all I wanted to know," said Wallander. "Thanks for your help."

"Can you manage to climb up the ladder one more time?" he asked Nyberg when he came back to the hall. "I'd like you to screw in a new bulb."

"The spare bulbs are in the room next to the garage," said Nyberg and started to pull on his boots.

They went back out into the storm. Wallander held the ladder while Nyberg climbed up and screwed in the bulb. It went on at once. Nyberg climbed back down the ladder. They walked out onto the beach.

"There's a big difference," said Wallander. "Now it's light all the way down to the water."

"Tell me what you're thinking," said Nyberg.

"I think the place where he was murdered is somewhere within this circle of light," said Wallander. "If we're lucky we can get fingerprints from the light fixture."

"So you think the murderer planned the whole thing? Unscrewed the bulb because it was too bright?"

"Yes," said Wallander, "that's pretty much what I'm thinking."

Nyberg went back into the garden with the ladder. Wallander stayed behind, the rain pelting against his face.

The cordons were still there. A police car was parked just above the dunes. Except for a man on a moped there were no onlookers left.

Wallander turned around and went back inside the house.

CHAPTER 10

He stepped into the basement just after 7 a.m. The floor was cool under his bare feet. He stood still and listened. Then he closed the door behind him and locked it. He squatted to inspect the thin layer of flour he had dusted over the floor the last time he was here. No-one had intruded into his world. There were no footprints. Then he checked the traps. He had been lucky. He had a catch in all four cages. One of the cages held the biggest rat he had ever seen.

Once, towards the end of his life, Geronimo told the story of the Pawnee warrior he had vanquished in his youth. His name was Bear with Six Claws, since he had six fingers on his left hand. That had been his first enemy. Geronimo came close to dying that time, even though he was very young. He cut off his enemy's sixth finger and left it in the sun to dry. Then he carried it in a little leather pouch on his belt for many years.

He decided to try out one of his axes on the big rat. On the small ones he would test the effect of the can of mace.

But that would be much later. First he had to undergo the big transformation. He sat down before the mirrors, adjusted the light so that there was no glare, and then gazed at his face. He had made a small cut on his left cheek. The wound had already healed. It was the first step in his final transformation.

The blow had been perfect. It had been like chopping down a tree when he cut into the spine of the first monster. He had heard the jubilation of the spirit world from within him. He had flopped the monster over on his back and cut off his scalp, without hesitation. Now it lay where it belonged, buried in the earth, with one tuft of hair sticking up from the ground.

Soon another scalp would join it. He looked at his face and considered whether he ought to make the second cut next to the first one.

Or should the knife consecrate the other cheek? Really it made no difference. When he was finished, his face would be covered with cuts.

Carefully he began to prepare himself. From his backpack he pulled out his weapons, paints and brushes. Last of all he took out the red book in which the Revelations and the Mission were written. He set it down on the table between himself and the mirrors.

Last night he had buried the first scalp. There was a guard by the hospital grounds. But he knew where the fence had come down. The secure wing, where there were bars on the windows and doors, stood apart on the outskirts of the large grounds. When he had visited his sister he had established which window was hers. No light shone from it. A faint gleam from the hall light was all that escaped from the menacing building. He had buried the scalp and whispered to his sister that he had taken the first step. He would destroy the monsters, one by one. Then she would come out into the world again.

He pulled off his shirt. It was summer, but he shivered in the cool of the basement. He opened the red book and turned past what was written about the man named Wetterstedt, who had ceased to exist. On page 7 the second scalp was described. He read what his sister had written and decided that this time he would use the smallest axe.

He closed the book and looked at his face in the mirror. It was the same shape as his mother's, but he had his father's eyes. They were set deep, like two retracted cannon muzzles. Because of these eyes, he might have regretted that his father would have to be sacrificed too. But it was only a small doubt, one that he could easily conquer. Those eyes were his first childhood memory. They had stared at him, they had threatened him, and ever since then he could see his father only as a pair of enormous eyes with arms and legs and a bellowing voice.

He wiped his face with a towel. Then he dipped one of the wide brushes into the black paint and drew the first line across his brow, precisely where the knife had cut open the skin on Wetterstedt's forehead.

He had spent many hours outside the police cordon. It was exciting to see all these policemen expending their energy trying to find out what happened and who had killed the man lying under the boat. On several occasions he had felt a compulsion to call out that he was the one.

It was a weakness that he had still not completely mastered. What he was doing, the mission he had undertaken from his sister's book of revelations, was for her sake alone, not his. He must conquer this urge.

He drew the second line across his face. The transformation had barely begun, but he could feel his external identity starting to leave him.

He didn't know why he had been named Stefan. On one occasion, when his mother had been more or less sober, he had asked her. Why Stefan? Why that name and not something else? Her reply had been very vague. It's a fine name, she said. He remembered that. A fine name. A name that was popular. He would be spared from having a name that was different. He still remembered how upset he had been. He left her lying there on the sofa in their living-room, stormed from the house and rode his bike down to the sea. Walking along the beach, he chose himself a different name. He chose Hoover. After the head of the F.B.I. He had read a book about him. It was rumoured that Hoover had a drop of American Indian blood in his veins. He wondered whether there was some in his own blood. His grandfather had told him that many of their relatives had emigrated to America a long time ago. Maybe one of them had taken up with an American Indian. Even if the blood didn't run through his own veins, it might be in the family.

It wasn't until his sister had been locked up in the hospital that he decided to merge Geronimo and Hoover. He had remembered how his grandfather had shown him how to melt pewter and pour it into plaster moulds to make miniature soldiers. He had found the moulds and the pewter ladle when his grandfather died. He had changed the mould so that the molten pewter would make a figure that was both a policeman and an Indian. Late one evening when everyone was asleep and his father was in jail, so he wouldn't come storming into the flat, he locked himself in the kitchen and carried out the great ceremony. By melting Hoover and Geronimo together he created his own new identity. He was a feared policeman with the courage of an

American Indian warrior. He would be indestructible. Nothing would prevent him from seeking vengeance.

He continued drawing the curved black lines above his eyes. They made his eyes appear to sink even deeper into their sockets, where they lurked like beasts of prey. Two predators, watching. Methodically he rehearsed what awaited him. It was Midsummer Eve. It was rainy and windy, which would make the task more difficult, but it wouldn't stop him. He would have to dress warmly before the trip to Bjäresjö. He didn't know whether the party he was going to visit had been moved indoors because of the rain, but he would trust in his ability to wait. This was a virtue Hoover had always preached to his recruits. Just like Geronimo. There would always be a moment when the enemy's alertness flagged. That's when he had to strike, even if the party was moved indoors. Sooner or later the man he sought would have to leave the house. Then it would be time.

He had been there the day before. He had left his moped among some trees and made his way to the top of a hill where he could watch undisturbed. Arne Carlman's house was isolated, just like Wetterstedt's. There were no close neighbours. An avenue of trimmed willows led up to the old whitewashed Scanian farmhouse.

Preparations for the Midsummer festivities had already begun. He'd seen people unloading folding tables and stackable chairs from a van. In one corner of the garden they were putting up a serving tent.

Carlman was there too. Through his binoculars he could see the man he would visit the next day, directing the work. He was wearing a tracksuit and a beret.

He thought of his sister with this man, and nausea overwhelmed him. He hadn't needed to see any more after that, he'd known what his plan would be.

When he had finished painting his forehead and the shadows around his eyes, he drew two heavy white lines down each side of his nose. He could already feel Geronimo's heart pounding in his chest. He bent down and started the player on the basement floor. The drums were very loud. The spirits started talking inside him.

He didn't finish until late afternoon. He selected the weapons he would take with him. Then he released the four rats into a large box. In vain they tried to scramble up the sides. He aimed the axe he wanted to try at the biggest. It was so fast that the rat didn't even have time to squeak. The blow split it in two. The other rats scratched at the sides. He went to his leather jacket, and reached into the inside pocket for the spray can. But it was gone. He searched the other pockets. It wasn't there. For a moment he stood frozen. Had someone been here after all? That was impossible.

To collect his thoughts, he sat down in front of the mirrors again. The spray can must have fallen out of his jacket pocket. Slowly and methodically he went over the days since he had visited Gustaf Wetterstedt. He realised he must have dropped the can when he was watching the police from outside the cordon. He had taken off his jacket at one point so he could put on a sweater. That's how it had happened. He decided that it presented no danger. Anyone could have dropped a spray can. Even if his fingerprints were on it, the police didn't have them on file. Not even F.B.I. chief Hoover would have been able to trace that spray can.

He got up from his place in front of the mirrors and returned to the rats in the box. When they caught sight of him they began rushing back and forth. With three blows of his axe he killed them all. Then he tipped the bleeding bodies into a plastic bag, tied it carefully, and put it inside another. He wiped off the edge of the axe and then felt it with his fingertips.

By just after 6 p.m. he was ready. He had stuffed the weapons and the bag of rats into his backpack. He put on socks and running shoes with the pattern on the soles filed off. He turned off the light and left the basement. Before he went out on the street he pulled his helmet over his head.

Just past the turn off to Sturup he drove into a car park and stuffed the plastic bag containing the rats into a rubbish bin. Then he continued on towards Bjäresjö. The wind had died down. There had been a sudden change in the weather. The evening would be warm.

Midsummer Eve was one of art dealer Arne Carlman's biggest occasions of the year. For more than 15 years he had invited his friends to a party at the Scanian farm where he lived during the summer. In a certain circle of artists and gallery owners it was important to be invited to Carlman's party. He had a strong influence on everyone who bought and sold art in Sweden. He could create fame and fortune for any artist he decided to promote, and he could topple any who didn't follow his advice or do as he required. More than 30 years earlier he had travelled all over the country in an old car, peddling art. Those were lean years but they had taught him what kind of pictures he could sell to whom. He had learned the business, and divested himself of the notion that art was something above the control of market forces. He had saved enough to open a combined frame shop and gallery on Österlånggatan in Stockholm. With a ruthless mixture of flattery, alcohol and crisp banknotes he bought paintings from young artists and then built up their reputations. He bribed, threatened and lied his way to the top. Within ten years he owned 30 galleries all over Sweden, and had started selling art by mail order. By the mid-70s he was a wealthy man. He bought the farm in Skåne and began holding his summer parties a few years later. They had become famous for their extravagance. Each guest could expect a present that cost no less than 5,000 kronor. This year he had commissioned a limited edition fountain pen from an Italian designer.

When Arne Carlman woke up beside his wife early on Midsummer Eve morning, he went to the window and gazed over a landscape weighed down by rain and wind. He quickly quelled a wave of irritation and disappointment. He had learned to accept that he had no power over the weather. Five years before he had had a special collection of rainwear designed for his guests. Those who wanted to be in the garden could be, and those who preferred to be inside could be in the old barn, converted into a huge open space.

When the guests began arriving around 8 p.m, what had promised to be a wet, nasty Midsummer Eve had become a beautiful summer evening. Carlman appeared in a dinner jacket, one of his sons following him holding an umbrella. As always, he had invited 100 people, of whom half were first-time guests. Just after 10 p.m. he clinked a knife on his glass, and gave his traditional summer speech. He did so in the knowledge that many of his guests hated or despised him. But at the age of 66, he had stopped worrying about what people thought. His empire could speak for itself. Two of his sons were prepared to take over the business when he could no longer run it, although he wasn't ready to retire. This is what he said in his speech, which was devoted entirely to himself. They couldn't count him out yet. They could look forward to many more Midsummer parties – at which the weather, he hoped, would be better than this year. His words were met with half-hearted applause. Then an orchestra started playing in the barn. Most of the guests made their way inside. Carlman led off the dancing with his wife.

"What did you think of my little speech?" he asked her.

"You've never been more spiteful," she replied.

"Let them hate me," he said. "What do I care? What do *we* care? I still have a lot to do."

Just before midnight, Carlman strolled to an arbour at the edge of the huge garden with a young woman artist from Göteborg. One of his talent scouts had advised him to invite her to his summer party. He had seen a number of transparencies of her paintings and recognised at once that she had something. It was a new type of idyllic painting. Cold suburbs, stone deserts, lonely people, surrounded by Elysian fields of flowers. He already knew that he was going to promote the woman as the leading exponent of a new school of painting, which could be called New Illusionism. She was very young, he thought, as they walked towards the arbour. But she was neither beautiful nor mysterious. Carlman had learned that just as important as the painting was the image presented by the artist. He wondered what he was going to do with this skinny, pale young woman.

It was a magnificent evening. The dance was still in full swing. But many of the guests had started gathering around the TV sets. Sweden's football match against Russia would be starting shortly. He wanted to finish his conversation with her so that he could watch it too.

Carlman had a contract in his pocket. It would provide her with a large cash sum in exchange for his acquiring the exclusive right to sell her work for three years. On the surface it seemed a very advantageous contract. But the fine print, difficult to read in the pale light of the summer night, granted him certain rights to future paintings. He wiped off two chairs with a handkerchief and invited her to sit. It took him less than half an hour to persuade her to agree to the arrangement. Then he handed her one of the designer pens and she signed the contract.

She left the arbour and went back to the barn. Later she would claim with absolute certainty that it had been three minutes to midnight. For some reason she had looked at the time as she walked along the gravel path up towards the house. With equal conviction she told the police that Arne Carlman had given no impression that he was uneasy. Nor that he was waiting for anyone. He had said that he was going to sit there for a few minutes and enjoy the fresh air after the rain. She hadn't looked back. But she was certain that there was no-one else in that part of the garden.

Hoover had been hiding on top of the hill all evening. The damp ground made him cold. Now and then he got up to shake some life into his limbs. Just after 11 p.m. he had seen through his binoculars that the moment was approaching. There were fewer and fewer people in the garden. He took out his weapons and stuck them in his belt. He also took off his shoes and socks and put them in his backpack. Then, bent almost double, he slipped down the hill and ran along a tractor path in the cover of a rape field. When he reached the edge of the property, he sank onto the wet ground. Through the hedge he had a view of the garden.

It was not long before his wait was over. Carlman was walking straight towards him, accompanied by a young woman. They sat down in the arbour. Hoover couldn't hear what they were talking about. After about half an hour the woman got up, but Carlman remained seated. The garden was deserted. The music in the barn had stopped; instead he could hear the blare of TV sets. Hoover got up, drew his axe, and squeezed through the hedge right behind the arbour. Swiftly, he checked again that no-one was in the garden. Then all doubt vanished, and his sister's revelations exhorted him to carry out his task. He rushed into the arbour and buried the axe in Arne Carlman's face. The powerful blow split the skull all the way to the upper jaw. He was still sitting on the bench, with the two halves of his head pointing in opposite directions. Hoover pulled out his knife and cut off the hair on the part of Carlman's head that was closest. Then he left as quickly as he had come. He climbed up the hill, picked up his backpack, and ran down the other side to the little gravel road where he had left his moped leaning against one of the road workers' huts.

Two hours later he buried the scalp next to the other one, beneath his sister's window.

There wasn't a cloud in the sky, and the wind had died completely. Midsummer Day would be both fair and warm. Summer had arrived. More quickly than anyone could have imagined.

Skåne

25–28 June 1994

CHAPTER 11

The emergency call came in to the Ystad station just after 2 a.m.

Thomas Brolin had just scored for Sweden in the match against Russia. He rammed in a penalty kick. A cheer rose in the Swedish summer night. It had been an unusually calm Midsummer Eve. The officer who received the call did so standing, since he had leapt to his feet shouting. But he realised at once that the call was serious. The woman shrieking in his ear seemed sober. Her hysteria was real. The officer sent for Hansson, who had felt his temporary appointment as police chief to be such a responsibility that he hadn't risked leaving the station on Midsummer Eve. He'd been busy weighing how his limited resources could best be employed on each case. At 11 p.m. fights had broken out at two different parties. One was caused by jealousy. In the other the Swedish goalkeeper, Ravelli, was the cause of the tumult. In a report later drafted by Svedberg, he stated that it was Ravelli's action in the game against Cameroon, when Cameroon scored their second goal, that triggered a violent argument that left three people in hospital.

Hansson went out to the operations centre and spoke with the officer who had taken the call.

"Did she really say that a man had his head split in half?"

The officer nodded. Hansson pondered this.

"We'll have to ask Svedberg to drive out there," he said.

"But isn't he busy with that domestic violence case in Svarte?"

"Right, I forgot," said Hansson. "Call Wallander."

For the first time in over a week Wallander had managed to get to sleep before midnight. In a moment of weakness he considered joining the rest of the country watching the match against Russia. But he fell asleep while he was waiting for the players to take the field. When the telephone rang, he didn't know where he was for a moment. He fumbled on the table next to the bed.

"Did I wake you up?" asked Hansson.

"Yes," replied Wallander. "What is it?"

Wallander was surprised at himself. He usually claimed that he was awake when someone called, no matter what time it was.

Hansson told him about the call. Later Wallander would brood over why he hadn't immediately made the connection between what had happened in Bjäresjö and Wetterstedt's murder. Was it because he didn't want to believe that they had a serial killer on their hands? Or was he simply incapable of imagining that a murder like Wetterstedt's could be anything but an isolated event? The only thing he did now was to ask Hansson to dispatch a squad car to the scene ahead of him.

Just before 3 a.m. he pulled up outside the farm in Bjäresjö. On the car radio he heard Martin Dahlin score his second goal against Russia. He realised that Sweden was going to win and that he had lost another 100 kronor.

He saw Norén running over to him, and knew at once that it was serious. But it wasn't until he went into the garden and passed a number of people who were either hysterical or dumbstruck that he grasped the full extent of the horror. The man who had been sitting on the bench in the arbour had actually had his head split in half. On the left half of his head, someone had also sliced off a large piece of skin and hair.

Wallander stood there completely motionless for more than a minute. Norén said something, but it didn't register. He stared at the dead man and knew without doubt that it was the same killer who had axed Wetterstedt to death. Then for a brief moment he felt an indescribable sorrow.

Later, talking to Baiba, he tried to explain the unexpected and very un-policeman-like feeling that had struck him. It was as though a dam inside him had burst, and he knew that there were no longer invisible lines dividing Sweden. The violence of the large cities had

112

reached his own police district once and for all. The world had shrunk and expanded at the same time.

Then sorrow gave way to horror. He turned to Norén, who was very pale.

"It looks like the same offender," said Norén.

Wallander nodded.

"Who's the victim?" he asked.

"His name is Arne Carlman. He's the one who owns this farm. There was a Midsummer party going on."

"No-one must leave yet. Find out if anyone saw anything."

Wallander took out his phone, punched in the number of the station, and asked for Hansson.

"It looks bad," he said when Hansson came on.

"How bad?"

"I'm having a hard time thinking of anything worse. There's no doubt it's the same person who killed Wetterstedt. This one was scalped too."

Wallander could hear Hansson's breathing.

"You'll have to mobilise everything we've got," Wallander went on "And I want Åkeson to come out here."

Wallander hung up before Hansson could ask questions. What will I do now? he thought. Who am I looking for? A psychopath? An offender who acts in a precise and calculated way?

Deep inside he knew the answer. There must be a connection between Gustaf Wetterstedt and Arne Carlman. That was the first thing he had to discover.

After 20 minutes the emergency vehicles started arriving. When Wallander caught sight of Nyberg, he ushered him straight to the arbour.

"Not a pretty sight," was Nyberg's first comment.

"This has got to be the same man," said Wallander. "He has struck again."

"It doesn't look as though we'll have trouble identifying the scene of the crime this time," said Nyberg, pointing at the blood sprayed over the hedge and the table. He summoned his crew and set to work.

Norén had assembled all the guests in the barn. The garden was strangely deserted. He came over to Wallander and pointed up towards the farmhouse.

"He's got a wife and three children in there. They're in shock."

"Maybe we ought to call a doctor."

"She called one herself."

"I'll talk to them," said Wallander. "When Martinsson and Ann-Britt and the others get here, tell them to talk to anyone who might have seen something. The rest can go home. But write down every name. And don't forget to ask for identification. Were there any witnesses?"

"Nobody has come forward."

"Have you got a time frame?"

Norén took a notebook out of his pocket.

"At 11.30 Carlman was seen alive. At 2 a.m. he was found dead. So the murder took place sometime in between."

"It must be possible to shorten the time span," said Wallander. "Try and find out who was the last one to see him alive. And of course who found him."

Wallander went inside. The old Scanian farmhouse had been lovingly restored. Wallander stepped into a large room that served as living-room, kitchen, and dining area. Oil paintings covered the walls. In one corner of the room, the dead man's family sat on a sofa upholstered in black leather. A woman in her 50s stood up and came over to him.

"Mrs Carlman?"

"Yes."

She had been crying. Wallander looked for signs that she might break down. But she seemed surprisingly calm.

"I'm sorry," said Wallander.

"It's just terrible."

Wallander noted something a little rehearsed in her answer.

"Do you have any idea who might have done such a thing?"

"No."

The answer came too quickly. She had been prepared for that

question. That means there are plenty of people who might have considered killing him, he told himself.

"May I ask what was your husband's job?"

"He was an art dealer."

Wallander stiffened. She misconstrued his intense gaze and repeated her answer.

"I heard you," said Wallander. "Excuse me for a moment."

Wallander went back outside. He thought about what the woman inside had said, connecting it with what Lars Magnusson had told him about the rumours about Wetterstedt. Stories of stolen art. And now an art dealer was dead, murdered by the hand that took Wetterstedt's life. He was about to go back inside when Ann-Britt Höglund came around the corner of the house. She was paler than usual and very tense. Wallander remembered his early years as a detective, when he took every violent crime to heart. From the start, Rydberg had taught him that a policeman could never permit himself to identify with a victim of violence. That lesson had taken Wallander a long time to learn.

"Another one?" she asked.

"Same offender," said Wallander. "Or offenders."

"This one scalped too?"

"Yes."

He saw her flinch involuntarily.

"I think I've found something that ties these two men together," Wallander went on, and explained. In the meantime Svedberg and Martinsson arrived. Wallander quickly repeated what he had told Höglund.

"You'll have to interview the guests," said Wallander. "If I understood Norén correctly, there are at least a hundred. And they all have to show some identification before they leave."

Wallander went back into the house. He pulled up a chair and sat down near the sofa where the family was gathered. Besides Carlman's widow there were two boys in their 20s and a girl a couple of years older. All of them seemed oddly calm.

"I promise that I'll only ask questions that we absolutely must have answers to tonight," he said. "The rest can wait."

Silence. None of them said a word.

"Do you know who the murderer is?" Wallander asked. "Was it one of the guests?"

"Who else could it be?" replied one of the sons. He had short-cropped blond hair. Wallander had an uneasy feeling that he could see a resemblance to the mutilated face he had just examined out in the arbour.

"Is there anyone in particular that comes to mind?" Wallander continued.

The boy shook his head.

"It doesn't seem very likely that someone would have chosen to come here when a big party was going on," said Mrs Carlman.

Someone cold-blooded enough wouldn't have hesitated, thought Wallander. Or someone crazy enough. Someone who doesn't care whether he gets caught or not.

"Your husband was an art dealer," Wallander went on. "Can you describe for me what that involves?"

"My husband has 30 galleries around the country," she said. "He also has galleries in the other Nordic countries. He sells paintings by mail order. He rents paintings to companies. He's responsible for a large number of art auctions each year. And much more."

"Did he have any enemies?"

"A successful man is always disliked by those who have the same ambitions but lack the talent."

"Did your husband ever say he felt threatened?"

"No."

Wallander looked at the children sitting on the sofa. They shook their heads almost simultaneously.

"When did you see him last?" he continued.

"I danced with him at around 10.30 p.m.," she said. "Then I saw him a few more times. It might have been around 11 p.m. when I saw him last."

None of the children had seen him any later than that. Wallander knew that all the other questions could wait. He put his notebook back in his pocket and stood up. He wanted to offer some words of sympathy, but couldn't think what to say, so he just nodded and left the house.

Sweden had won the football game 3–1. Ravelli had been brilliant; Cameroon was forgotten, and Martin Dahlin's headed goal was a work of genius. Wallander picked up fragments of conversations going on around him, and pieced them together. Höglund and two other police officers had guessed the right score. Wallander sensed that he had solidified his position as the biggest loser. He couldn't decide whether this annoyed or pleased him.

They worked hard and efficiently. Wallander set up his temporary headquarters in a storeroom attached to the barn. Just after 4 a.m. Höglund came in with a young woman who spoke a distinct Göteborg dialect.

"She was the last one to see him alive," said Höglund. "She was with Carlman in the arbour just before midnight."

Wallander asked her to sit down. She told him her name was Madelaine Rhedin and she was an artist.

"What were you doing in the arbour?" asked Wallander.

"Arne wanted me to sign a contract."

"What sort of contract?"

"To sell my paintings."

"And you signed it?"

"Yes."

"Then what happened?"

"Nothing."

"Nothing?"

"I got up and left. I looked at my watch. It was 11.57 p.m."

"Why did you look at your watch?"

"I usually do when something important happens."

"The contract was important?"

"I was supposed to get 200,000 kronor on Monday. For a poor artist that's a big deal."

"Was there anyone nearby when you were sitting in the arbour?"

"Not that I saw."

"And when you left?"

"The garden was deserted."

"What did Carlman do when you left?"

"He stayed there."

"How do you know? Did you turn around?"

"He told me he was going to enjoy the fresh air. I didn't hear him get up."

"Did he seem uneasy?"

"No, he was cheerful."

"Think it over," Wallander said. "Maybe tomorrow you'll remember something else. Anything might be important. I want you to keep in touch."

When she left the room, Åkeson came in from the other direction. He was totally white. He sat down heavily on the chair Madelaine Rhedin had just vacated.

"That's the most disgusting thing I've ever seen," he said.

"You didn't have to look at him," said Wallander. "That's not why I wanted you to come."

"I don't know how you stand it," said Åkeson.

"Me neither," said Wallander.

Suddenly Åkeson was all business.

"Is it the same man who killed Wetterstedt?" he asked.

"Without a doubt."

"In other words, he may strike again?"

Wallander nodded. Åkeson grimaced.

"If there was ever a time to give priority to an investigation, this is it," he said. "I assume you need more personnel, don't you? I can pull some strings if necessary."

"Not yet," said Wallander. "A large number of policemen might aid the capture if we knew the killer's name and what he looked like. But we're not that far yet."

He told him what Magnusson had said, and that Arne Carlman was an art dealer.

"There's a connection," he concluded "And that will make the work easier."

Åkeson was doubtful.

"I hope you won't put all your eggs in one basket too early," he said.

"I'm not closing any doors," said Wallander. "But I have to explore every avenue I find."

Åkeson stayed for another hour before he drove back to Ystad. By 5 a.m. reporters had begun to show up at the farm. Furious, Wallander called the station and demanded that Hansson deal with them. He knew already that they wouldn't be able to conceal the fact that Carlman had been scalped. Hansson held an improvised and exceedingly chaotic press conference on the road outside the farm. Meanwhile Martinsson, Svedberg and Höglund herded out the guests, who all had to undergo a short interrogation. Wallander interviewed the sculptor who had discovered Carlman's body. He was extremely drunk.

"Why did you go out to the garden?" asked Wallander.

"To throw up."

"And did you?"

"Yes."

"Where did you throw up?"

"Behind one of the apple trees."

"Then what happened?"

"I thought I'd sit in the arbour to clear my head."

"And then?"

"I found him."

Wallander had been forced to stop there, because the sculptor started feeling sick again. He got up and went down to the arbour. The sky was clear, and the sun was already high. Midsummer Day would be warm and beautiful. When he reached the arbour he saw to his relief that Nyberg had covered Carlman's head with an opaque plastic sheet. Nyberg was on his knees next to the hedge that separated the garden from the adjacent rape field.

"How's it going?" asked Wallander encouragingly.

"There's a slight trace of blood on the hedge here," he said. "It couldn't have sprayed this far from the arbour."

"What does that mean?" asked Wallander.

"It's your job to answer that," replied Nyberg.

He pointed at the hedge.

"Right here it's quite sparse," he said. "It would have been possible for someone with a slight build to slip in and out of the garden this way. We'll have to see what we find on the other side. But I suggest you get a dog out here. A.S.A.P."

Wallander nodded.

The officer, named Eskilsson, arrived with his German shepherd shortly afterwards, as the last of the guests were leaving the garden. Wallander nodded to him. The dog was old and had been in service for a long time. His name was Shot.

The dog picked up a scent in the arbour at once and started towards the hedge. He wanted to push through the hedge exactly at the spot where Nyberg had found the blood. Eskilsson and Wallander found another spot where the hedge was thin and emerged onto the path that ran between Carlman's property and the field. The dog found the scent again, following it alongside the field towards a dirt road that led away from the farm. At Wallander's suggestion Eskilsson released the dog. Wallander felt a surge of excitement. The dog sniffed along the dirt road and came to the end of the field. Here he seemed to lose his bearings for a moment. Then he found the scent and kept following it towards a hill, where the trail seemed to end. Eskilsson searched in various directions, but the dog couldn't find the scent again.

Wallander looked around. A single tree bent over by the wind stood on top of the hill. An old bicycle frame lay half-buried in the ground. Wallander stood next to the tree and looked at the farm in the distance. The view of the garden was excellent. With binoculars it would have been possible to see who was outside the house at any given time.

He shuddered at the thought that someone else, someone unknown to him, had stood on the same spot earlier that night. He went back to the garden. Hansson and Svedberg were sitting on the steps of the farmhouse. Their faces were grey with fatigue.

"Where's Ann-Britt?" asked Wallander.

"She's getting rid of the last guest," said Svedberg.

"Martinsson? What's he doing?"

"He's on the phone."

Wallander sat down next to the others on the steps. The sun was already starting to feel hot.

"We've got to keep at it a little longer," he said. "When Ann-Britt is done, we'll go back to Ystad. We have to summarise what we know and decide what to do next."

No-one spoke. Höglund emerged from the barn. She crouched in front of the others.

"To think that so many people can see so little," she said wearily. "It's beyond me."

Eskilsson passed by with his dog. They heard Nyberg's grumpy voice near the arbour.

Martinsson came striding around the corner of the house. He had a telephone in his hand.

"This may be irrelevant right now," he said. "But we've received a message from Interpol. They have a positive identification of the girl who burned herself to death."

Wallander looked at him quizzically.

"The girl in Salomonsson's field?"

"Yes."

Wallander got up.

"Who is she?"

"I don't know. But there's a message waiting for you at the station."

They left Bjäresjö at once and headed back to Ystad.

CHAPTER 12

Dolores María Santana.

It was 5.45 a.m. on Midsummer morning. Martinsson read out the message from Interpol identifying the girl.

"Where's she from?" asked Höglund.

"The message is from the Dominican Republic," replied Martinsson. "It came via Madrid."

Puzzled, he looked around the room.

Höglund knew the answer.

"The Dominican Republic is one half of the island where Haiti is," she said. "In the West Indies. Isn't it called Hispaniola?"

"How the hell did she wind up here, in a rape field?" asked Wallander. "Who is she? What else did Interpol say?"

"I haven't had time to go through the message in detail," said Martinsson. "But it seems that her father has been looking for her, and she was reported missing in late November last year. The report was originally filed in a city called Santiago."

"Isn't that in Chile?" Wallander interrupted, surprised.

"This city is called Santiago de los Treinta Caballeros," said Martinsson. "Don't we have an atlas somewhere?"

"I'll get one," said Svedberg and left the room.

A few minutes later he returned, shaking his head.

"It must have been Björk's," he said. "I couldn't find it."

"Call our bookseller and wake him up," said Wallander. "I want an atlas here now."

"Are you aware that it's not even six in the morning and it's Midsummer Day?" Svedberg asked.

"It can't be helped. Call him. And send a car over to get it."

Wallander took a 100-krona note out of his wallet and gave it to Svedberg. A few minutes later Svedberg had roused the bookseller and the car was on its way.

They got coffee and went into the conference room. Hansson told them that they wouldn't be disturbed by anyone except Nyberg. Wallander took a look around the table. He met the gazes of the group of weary faces and wondered how he looked himself.

"We'll have to come back to the girl later," he began. "Right now we need to concentrate on what happened last night. And we might as well assume from the start that the same person who killed Gustaf Wetterstedt has struck again. The *modus operandi* is the same, even though Carlman was struck in the head and Wetterstedt had his spine severed. But both of them were scalped."

"I've never seen anything like it," said Svedberg. "The man who did this must be a complete animal."

Wallander held up his hand.

"Hold on a minute," he said. "There's something else we know too. Arne Carlman was an art dealer. And now I'm going to tell you something I learnt yesterday."

Wallander told them about his conversation with Lars Magnusson, and the rumours about Wetterstedt.

"So we have a conceivable link," he concluded. "Art: stolen art and fenced art. And somewhere, when we find the point that connects the two men, we'll find the offender."

No-one spoke. Everyone seemed to be considering what Wallander had said.

"We know where to concentrate our investigation," Wallander continued. "Finding the connection between Wetterstedt and Carlman. But we have another problem."

He looked around the table and could see that they understood.

"The killer could strike again," said Wallander. "We don't know why he killed either man. So we don't know whether he's after other people too. And we don't know who they might be. The only thing we can hope for is that the people threatened are aware of it."

"Another thing we don't know," said Martinsson. "Is the man insane? We don't know whether the motive is revenge or something else. We can't even be sure that he hasn't simply invented a motive. No-one can predict the workings of an insane mind."

"You're right, of course," replied Wallander. "We're dealing with many unknowns."

"Maybe this is just the beginning," Hansson said grimly. "Do you think we've got a serial killer on our hands?"

"It could be that bad," said Wallander firmly. "That's why I also think we should get some help from outside, from the criminal psychiatric division in Stockholm. Since this man's *modus operandi* is so remarkable, perhaps they can do a psychiatric profile of him."

"Has this offender killed before?" asked Svedberg. "Or is this the first time?"

"I don't know," said Wallander. "But he's cautious. I get a feeling that he plans what he does very carefully. When he strikes he does it without hesitation. There could be at least two reasons for this. First, he doesn't want to get caught. Second, he doesn't want to be interrupted before he finishes what he set out to do."

A shudder of revulsion passed through the group.

"This is where we have to start," he said. "Where is the connection between Wetterstedt and Carlman? Where do their paths cross? That's what we have to clarify. And we have to do it as quickly as possible."

"We should also realise that we won't be working in peace," said Hansson. "Reporters will be swarming around us. They know that Carlman was scalped. They have the story they've been longing for. For some strange reason Swedes love to read about crime when they're on holiday."

"That might not be such a bad thing," said Wallander. "At least it might send a warning to anyone who might be on the hit list."

"We ought to stress that we want clues from the public," said Höglund. "If we assume that you're right, that the murderer has a list he's working through, and that other people could realise that they're on it, then there may be a chance that some of them have an idea of who the killer is."

"You're right," said Wallander, turning to Hansson. "Call a press conference as soon as possible. We'll tell the press everything we know. That we're looking for a single killer. And that we need all the clues we can get."

Svedberg got up and opened a window. Martinsson yawned loudly.

"I know we're all tired," said Wallander. "But we have to carry on. Try to grab some sleep when you get a chance."

There was a knock on the door. An officer handed over an atlas. They set it on the table and found the Dominican Republic and the city of Santiago.

"We'll have to deal with this girl later," said Wallander. "We can't worry about it now."

"I'll send a reply," said Martinsson. "And ask for more information about her disappearance."

"How did she end up here?" muttered Wallander.

"The message from Interpol gives her age as 17," said Martinsson. "And her height as about 160 centimetres."

"Send them a description of the medallion," said Wallander. "If the father can identify it, the case is closed."

They left the conference room. Martinsson went home to talk to his family and cancel their holiday. Svedberg went down to the basement and took a shower. Hansson vanished down the hall to organise the press conference. Wallander followed Höglund into her office.

"Do you think we'll catch him?" she asked gravely.

"I don't know," said Wallander. "We have a lead that seems solid. This isn't an offender who simply kills anyone who gets in his way. He's after something. The scalps are his trophies."

She sat down in her chair as Wallander leaned against the door-frame.

"Why do people take trophies?" she asked.

"So they can brag about them."

"To themselves or to others?"

"Both."

Suddenly he realised why she had asked about the trophies.

"You think that he took these scalps so he could show them to somebody?"

"It can't be ruled out," she said.

"No," said Wallander, "it can't be ruled out. Nothing can."

He was just about to leave the room, but turned around.

"Will you call Stockholm?" he asked.

"It's Midsummer Day," she said. "I don't think they'll be on duty."

"You'll have to call someone at home," said Wallander. "Since we don't know whether he's going to strike again, we've got no time to lose."

Wallander went to his own office and sat down heavily in the visitor's chair. One of its legs creaked precariously. He leaned his head back and closed his eyes. Soon he was asleep.

He woke up with a start when someone entered the room. He glanced at his watch and saw that he'd been asleep for almost an hour. He still had a headache, but he wasn't quite so tired.

It was Nyberg. His eyes were bloodshot and his hair was standing on end.

"I didn't mean to wake you," he said apologetically.

"I was just dozing," said Wallander. "Have you got any news?"

Nyberg shook his head.

"All I can come up with is that the person who killed Carlman must have had his clothes drenched with blood. Subject to the forensic examination, I think we can assume that the blow came from directly overhead. That would mean that the person holding the axe was standing quite close."

"Are you sure it was an axe?"

"No," said Nyberg. "It could have been a heavy sabre. Or something else. But Carlman's head was split like a log."

Wallander felt sick.

"All right, then," he said. "So the killer got his clothes covered with blood. Someone might have seen him. And that clears all of the guests."

"We looked along the hedge," said Nyberg. "We searched all the way along the rape field and up towards that hill. The farmer who owns the fields around Carlman's farmhouse came and asked whether he could harvest the rape. I said that he could."

"A wise decision," said Wallander. "Isn't it late already?"

"I think so," said Nyberg. "It's Midsummer, after all."

"What about the hill?" asked Wallander.

"The grass was trampled down. At one spot it looked as if someone had been sitting there. We took samples of the grass and the soil."

"Anything else?"

"I don't think that old bicycle is of any interest to us," said Nyberg.

"The police dog lost the scent. Why?"

"You'll have to ask the officer about that," said Nyberg. "But it could be that another smell is so strong that the dog loses the scent he was originally following. There are plenty of reasons why trails suddenly stop."

"Go home and get some sleep," said Wallander. "You look exhausted."

"I am," said Nyberg.

After Nyberg left, Wallander went into the canteen and fixed himself a sandwich. A girl from the front desk came and gave him a pile of messages. He leafed through them and saw that reporters were calling. He knew he ought to go home and change his clothes, but instead he decided to do something entirely different. He knocked on the door of Hansson's office and told him he was driving out to Carlman's farm.

"I said we'd talk to the press at one o'clock," said Hansson.

"I'll be back by then," replied Wallander. "But unless something crucial happens, I don't want anyone to look for me. I need to think."

"And everybody needs to get some sleep," said Hansson. "I never imagined we'd wind up in such a nightmare."

"It always happens when you least expect it," said Wallander.

He drove out towards Bjäresjö in the beautiful summer morning, the windows rolled down. He ought to visit his father today. And call Linda too. Tomorrow Baiba would be back in Riga after her trip to Tallinn. In less than two weeks his holiday should be starting.

He parked the car by the cordon surrounding Carlman's farm. Small groups of people had gathered on the road. Wallander nodded to the officer guarding the cordon. Then he walked around the garden and followed the dirt road up towards the hill. He stood at the spot where the dog had lost the scent and looked around.

He had chosen the hill with care. From here he could see everything going on in the garden. He also must have been able to hear the music coming from inside the barn. Late in the evening the crowd in the garden thinned out. The guests had all said that everyone went indoors. At about 11.30 p.m. Carlman came walking towards the arbour with Madelaine Rhedin. Then what did you do?

Wallander didn't try to answer the question. Instead he turned around and looked down the other side of the hill. At the bottom there were tractor tracks. He followed the grassy slope until he reached the road. In one direction the tractor tracks led into a wood, and in the other down towards a road to the motorway to Malmö and Ystad. Wallander followed the tracks towards the woods. He walked under a clump of tall beech trees. The sunshine shimmered through the foliage. He could smell the earth. The tractor tracks stopped at a site where some newly felled trees were stacked.

Wallander searched in vain for a path. He tried to picture the roads. Anyone wanting to reach the motorway from the woods would have to pass two houses and several fields. The motorway was about two kilometres away. He retraced his steps and continued in the opposite direction. After almost a kilometre he came to the place where the road reached the E65.

By the side of the road was a road workers' hut, which was locked. He stood there and looked around. Then he went around to the back, finding a folded tarpaulin and a couple of iron pipes. Something was lying on the ground. He bent down and saw that it was a piece torn from a brown paper bag. It had some dark spots on it. Carefully he placed the piece of paper back on the ground. He looked underneath the hut, which was raised on four concrete blocks, and saw the rest of the paper bag. He reached in and pulled it out. There were no spots on the bag itself. He stood motionless, thinking. Then he put down the bag and called the station. He got hold of Martinsson, who had just got back.

"I need Eskilsson and his dog," said Wallander.

"Where are you? Did something happen?"

"I'm out by Carlman's farm," replied Wallander. "I just want to make sure of one thing."

After a short while Eskilsson arrived with his dog. Wallander explained what he wanted.

"Go over to the hill where the dog lost the scent," he said. "Then come back here."

Eskilsson left. After about ten minutes he returned. Wallander saw that the dog had stopped searching. But just as he reached the hut he reacted. Eskilsson gave Wallander a questioning look.

"Let him go," said Wallander.

The dog went straight for the piece of paper and halted. But when Eskilsson tried to get him to continue his search he quickly gave up. The scent had disappeared again.

"Is it blood?" asked Eskilsson, pointing at the piece of torn paper.

"I think so," said Wallander "At any rate, we've found something associated with the man who was up on the hill."

Eskilsson left with his dog. Wallander was just about to call Nyberg when he found that he had a plastic bag in one pocket. Carefully he deposited the piece of paper in it.

It couldn't have taken you more than a few minutes to get here from Carlman's farm. Presumably there was a bicycle here. You changed clothes since you had blood all over them. But you also wiped an object. Maybe a knife or an axe. Then you took off, either towards Malmö or Ystad. You probably crossed the motorway and chose one of the many small roads that criss-cross this area. I can follow you this far right now. But no further.

Wallander walked back to Carlman's farm. He asked the officer guarding the cordon whether the family was still there.

"I haven't seen anybody," he said. "But no-one has left the house."

Wallander nodded and walked to his car. There was a crowd of onlookers standing outside the cordon. Wallander glanced at them hastily and wondered what kind of people would give up a summer morning for the opportunity to smell blood.

He didn't realise until he drove off that he had seen something important. He slowed down and tried to remember what it was.

It had something to do with the people who were standing outside the cordon. What was it he had thought? Something about people sacrificing a summer morning?

He braked and made a U-turn in the middle of the road. When he got back to Carlman's house the onlookers were still there outside the cordon. Wallander looked around without finding any explanation for his reaction. He asked the officer whether anyone had just left.

"Maybe. People come and go all the time."

"Nobody special that you recall?"

The officer thought for a moment. "No."

Wallander went back to his car.

It was 9.10 a.m. on the morning of Midsummer Day.

CHAPTER 13

When Wallander got back to the station, the girl in reception told him he had a visitor waiting in his office. Wallander lost his temper and shouted at the girl, a summer intern, that no-one, no matter who it was, was to be allowed into his office. He stormed down the hall and threw open the door, coming face to face with his father, sitting in the visitor's chair.

"The way you tear open doors," said his father. "Somebody might think you were in a rage."

"All they told me was that someone was waiting in my office," said Wallander, astonished. "Not that it was you."

Wallander's father had never visited him at work. When he was a young officer, his father had even refused to let him into the house in uniform. But now here he was, wearing his best suit.

"I'm surprised," said Wallander. "Who drove you here?"

"My wife has both a driver's licence and a car," replied his father. "She went to see one of her relatives while I came here. Did you see the game last night?"

"No. I was working."

"It was great. I remember the way it was back in '58, when the World Cup was held in Sweden."

"But you were never interested in football, were you?"

"I've always liked football."

Wallander stared at him in surprise.

"I didn't know that."

"There's a lot of things you don't know. In 1958 Sweden had a defender named Sven Axbom. He was having big problems with one of Brazil's wingers, as I recall. Have you forgotten about that?"

"How old was I in 1958? I was a baby."

"You never were much for playing football. Maybe that's why you became a policeman."

"I bet that Russia would win," said Wallander.

"That's not hard to believe," said his father. "I bet 2–0 myself. Gertrud, on the other hand, was cautious. She thought it would be 1–1."

"Would you like some coffee?" asked Wallander.

"Yes, please."

In the hall Wallander ran into Hansson.

"Will you see to it that I'm not disturbed for the next half hour?" he said.

Hansson gave him a worried look.

"I absolutely must speak with you."

Hansson's formal manner irritated Wallander.

"In half an hour," he repeated. "Then we'll talk as much as you like."

He went back to his room and closed the door. His father took the plastic cup in both hands. Wallander sat down behind the desk.

"I never thought I'd see you in the station," he said.

"I wouldn't have come if I didn't have to," his father replied.

Wallander set his plastic cup on the desk. He should have known straight away that it must be something very important for his father to visit him here.

"What's happened?" Wallander asked.

"Nothing, except that I'm sick," replied his father simply.

Wallander felt a knot in his stomach.

"What do you mean?" he asked.

"I'm starting to lose my mind," his father went on calmly. "It's a disease with a name I can't remember. It's like getting senile. But it can make you angry at everything. And it can progress very fast."

Wallander knew what his father meant. Svedberg's mother was stricken with it. But he couldn't remember the name either.

"How do you know?" he asked. "Have you been to the doctor? Why didn't you say something before now?"

"I've even been to a specialist, in Lund," said his father. "Gertrud drove me there."

Wallander didn't know what to say.

"Actually, I came here to ask you something," his father said, looking at him.

The telephone rang. Wallander put the receiver on the desk.

"I've got time to wait," said his father.

"I told them I didn't want to be disturbed. So tell me what it is you want."

"I've always dreamed of going to Italy," his father said. "Before it's too late, I'd like to take a trip there. And I thought you might come with me. Gertrud doesn't have any interest in Italy. I don't think she wants to go. I'll pay for the whole thing. I've got the money."

Wallander looked at his father. He seemed small and shrunken sitting there in the chair. At that moment he suddenly looked his age. Almost 80.

"Of course, let's go to Italy," said Wallander. "When did you have in mind?"

"It's probably best that we don't wait too long. Apparently it's not too hot in September. But will you have time then?"

"I can take a week off any time. Or did you want longer than that?"

"A week would be fine."

His father leaned forward, put down the coffee cup, and stood up.

"Well, I won't bother you any longer," he said. "I'll wait for Gertrud outside."

"You can wait here," said Wallander.

His father waved his cane at him.

"You've got a lot to do," he said. "I'll wait outside."

Wallander accompanied him out to reception, where his father sat down on a sofa.

"I don't want you to wait with me," said his father. "Gertrud will be here soon."

Wallander nodded.

"We'll go to Italy together," he said. "And I'll come out and see you as soon as I can."

"The trip might be fun," said his father. "You never know."

Wallander left him and went over to the girl at the front desk.

"I'm sorry," he said. "It was quite right of you to let my father wait in my office."

He went back to his room, tears welling in his eyes. Even though his relationship with his father was strained, coloured by guilt, he felt a great sorrow. He stood by the window and looked out at the beautiful summer weather.

There was a time when we were so close that nothing could come between us, he thought. That was back when the silk knights, as we called them, used to come in their shiny American cars that we called land yachts and buy your paintings. Even then you talked about going to Italy. Another time, only a few years ago, you actually set off. I found you, dressed in pyjamas, with a suitcase in your hand in the middle of a field. And now we have to make that trip. I won't allow anything to stop us.

Wallander returned to his desk and called his sister in Stockholm. The answer machine informed him that she wouldn't be back until that evening.

It took him a long while to push aside his father's visit and collect his thoughts. He couldn't seem to accept that what his father had told him was true.

After talking to Hansson he made an extensive review of the investigation. Just before 11 a.m. he called Per Åkeson at home and gave him an update. Then he drove over to Mariagatan, took a shower, and changed his clothes. By midday he was back at the station. On the way to his room he stopped to see Ann-Britt Höglund. He told her about the paper he'd found behind the road workers' hut.

"Did you get hold of the psychologists in Stockholm?" he asked.

"I found a man named Roland Möller," she said. "He was at his summer house outside Vaxholm. But Hansson must make a formal request as acting chief."

"Did you talk to him?"

"He's done it."

"Good," said Wallander. "Now, something else. Do criminals return to the scene of the crime?"

"It's both a myth and a truth."

"In what sense is it a myth?"

"In that it's supposed to be something that always happens."

"And what's the reality?"

"That it actually does happen once in a while. The most classic example in our own legal history is probably from here in Skåne. The policeman who committed a series of murders in the early 1950s and was later on the team investigating what happened."

"That's not a good example," Wallander objected. "He was forced to return. I'm talking about the ones who return of their own accord. Why?"

"To taunt the police. To gloat. Or to find out how much the police actually know."

Wallander nodded thoughtfully.

"Why are you asking me this?"

"I had a peculiar experience," said Wallander. "I got a feeling that I saw someone out by Carlman's farm that I'd also seen outside the cordon near Wetterstedt's villa."

"Why couldn't it be the same person?" she asked, surprised.

"No reason. But there was something odd about this person. I just can't put my finger on what it was."

"I don't think I can help you."

"I know," said Wallander. "But in the future I want someone to photograph everyone standing outside the cordon, as discreetly as possible."

"In the future?"

Wallander knew that he had said too much. He tapped on the desk three times with his index finger.

"Naturally I hope nothing else will happen," he said. "But if it does."

Wallander accompanied Höglund back to her office. Then he continued out of the station. His father was gone. He drove to a restaurant on the edge of town and ate a hamburger. On a thermometer he saw that it was 26°C.

The press conference on Midsummer Day at the Ystad station was memorable because Wallander lost his temper and left the room before it was over. Afterwards he refused to apologise. Most of his colleagues thought he did the right thing. But the next day Wallander got a phone call from the director of the national police board, telling him that it was highly unsuitable for the police to make abusive comments to journalists. The relationship was strained enough as it was, and no additional aggravation could be tolerated.

Towards the end of the press conference, a journalist from an evening paper had stood up and started to question Wallander about the fact that the offender had taken the scalps of his victims. Wallander tried hard to avoid going into the gory details. He had replied that some of the hair of both Wetterstedt and Carlman had been torn off. But the reporter persisted, demanding details even when Wallander said that he couldn't give more information because of the forensic investigation. By then Wallander had developed a splitting headache. When the reporter accused him of hiding behind the requirements of the investigation, and said that it seemed like pure hypocrisy to withhold details when the police had called the press conference, Wallander had had enough. He banged his fist on the table and stood up.

"I will not let police policy be dictated by a journalist who doesn't know when to stop!" he shouted.

The flashbulbs went off in an explosion as he left the room. Afterwards, when he had calmed down, he asked Hansson to excuse his behaviour.

"I hardly think that it will change the way the headlines will read tomorrow morning," Hansson replied.

"I had to draw the line somewhere," said Wallander.

"I'm on your side, of course," said Hansson. "But I suspect there are others who won't be."

"They can suspend me," said Wallander. "They can fire me. But they can't ever make me apologise to that reporter."

"That apology will probably be discreetly given by the national police board to the editor-in-chief of the newspaper," said Hansson. "And we won't ever hear about it."

At 4 p.m. the investigative group shut themselves behind closed doors. Hansson had given strict instructions that they were not to be disturbed. At Wallander's request a squad car had gone to pick up Åkeson.

He knew that the decisions they made this afternoon would be crucial. They would be forced to go in so many directions at once. All options had to be explored. But at the same time Wallander knew that they had to concentrate on the main lead.

Wallander borrowed a couple of aspirin from Höglund and thought again about what Lars Magnusson had said, about the connection between Wetterstedt and Carlman. Was there something else he'd missed? He searched his weary mind without coming up with anything. They would concentrate their investigation on art sales and art thefts. They would have to dig deep into the rumours, some almost 30 years old, surrounding Wetterstedt, and they would have to move fast. Wallander knew they wouldn't get help along the way. Lars Magnusson had talked about the collaborators who cleaned up the mess left by those wielding power. Wallander would have to find a way of throwing light on these activities, but it would be very difficult.

The investigative meeting was one of the longest Wallander had ever attended. They sat for almost nine hours before Hansson blew the final whistle. By then everyone was exhausted. Höglund's bottle of aspirin was empty. Plastic coffee cups covered the table. Cartons of half-eaten pizza were piled in a corner of the room.

But this meeting was also one of the best Wallander had ever experienced. Concentration hadn't flagged, everyone contributed their opinions, and logical plans for the investigation had developed as a result.

Svedberg went over the telephone conversations he had had with

Wetterstedt's two children and his third ex-wife, but no-one could see a possible motive. Hansson had also managed to talk with the 80-year-old who had been party secretary during Wetterstedt's term as minister of justice. He had confirmed that Wetterstedt had often been the subject of rumours within the party. But no-one had been able to ignore his unflagging loyalty.

Martinsson reported on his interview with Carlman's widow. She was still very calm, leading Martinsson to think she must be on sedatives. Neither she nor any of the children was able to suggest a motive for the murder. Wallander outlined his talk with Sara Björklund, Wetterstedt's "charwoman". He also told them that the light bulb on the pole by the gate had been unscrewed. And finally, he told them about the bloody piece of paper he had found behind the road workers' hut.

None of his colleagues knew that his father was constantly on his mind. After the meeting he asked Höglund whether she had noticed how distracted he had been. She told him she hadn't noticed this, that he had seemed more dogged and focused than ever.

At 9 p.m. they took a break. Martinsson and Höglund called home, and Wallander finally got hold of his sister. She had wept when he told her about their father's visit and his illness. Wallander tried to console her as best he could, but he fought back tears himself. At last they agreed that she should talk to Gertrud the next day and that she would visit as soon as possible. She asked whether he really believed that their father would be able to manage a trip to Italy. Wallander answered honestly – he didn't know. But he reminded her that their father had dreamed of going to Italy since they were children.

During the break Wallander also tried to call Linda. After 15 rings he gave up. Annoyed, he decided he would have to give her the money to buy an answer machine.

When they returned to the meeting room Wallander started by discussing the connection between the two victims. That was what they had to seek, without ruling out other possibilities.

"Carlman's widow was sure that her husband had never had

anything to do with Wetterstedt," said Martinsson. "Her children said the same thing. They searched through all his address books without finding Wetterstedt's name."

"Carlman wasn't in Wetterstedt's address book either," said Höglund.

"So the link is invisible," said Wallander. "Or, more precisely, elusive. Somewhere we must be able to find it. If we do, we may also catch sight of the killer. Or at least a motive. We have to dig deep and fast."

"Before he strikes again," said Hansson. "There is no knowing whether that will happen."

"We also don't know who to warn," said Wallander. "The only thing we know about the killer or killers, is that they plan the murders."

"Do we know that?" Åkeson interjected. "It seems to me you're jumping to that conclusion prematurely."

"Well there's no indication that we're dealing with someone who kills on impulse, who has a spontaneous desire to rip the hair off his victims," replied Wallander, feeling his temper rise.

"It's the conclusion that I'm having trouble with," said Åkeson. "That's not the same thing as discrediting the evidence."

The mood in the room grew oppressive. No-one could miss the tension between the two men. Normally, Wallander wouldn't hesitate to argue with Åkeson in public. But this evening he chose to back down, mainly because he was exhausted and knew he would have to keep the meeting going for hours yet.

"I agree," was all he said. "We'll scrub that conclusion and settle for saying that the murders appear planned."

"A psychologist from Stockholm is coming down tomorrow," said Hansson. "I'm going to pick him up at Sturup Airport. Let's hope he can help us."

Wallander nodded. Then he threw out a question that he hadn't really prepared. But now seemed a suitable time.

"The murderer," he said. "For the sake of argument let's think of him for the time being as a man who acts alone. What do you see? What do you think?"

"Strong," said Nyberg. "The axe blows were delivered with tremendous force."

"I'm afraid he's collecting trophies," said Martinsson. "Only an insane person would do something like that."

"Or someone who intends to throw us off the track with the scalps," said Wallander.

"I have no idea," said Höglund. "But it must be someone who's profoundly disturbed."

In the end the character of the killer was left. Wallander summed up in one last run-through, in which they planned the investigative work to be done and divided up the tasks. At around midnight Åkeson left, saying that he would help out by arranging for reinforcements for the investigative team whenever they thought it necessary. Although they were all exhausted, Wallander went over the work one more time.

"None of us is going to get a lot of sleep for the next few days," he said in closing. "And I realise that this will throw many of your holiday plans into chaos. But we have to muster all our forces. We have no option."

"We'll need reinforcements," said Hansson.

"Let's decide about that on Monday," said Wallander. "Let's wait until then."

They decided to meet again the following afternoon. Before then Wallander and Hansson would present the case to the psychologist from Stockholm.

Then they broke up and went their separate ways. Wallander stood by his car and looked up at the pale night sky. He tried to think about his father. But something else kept intruding. Fear that the killer would strike again.

CHAPTER 14

Early on Sunday morning, 26 June, the doorbell rang at Wallander's flat on Mariagatan in central Ystad. He was wrenched out of a deep sleep and at first thought the telephone was ringing. When the doorbell rang again he got up quickly, found his dressing gown lying halfway under the bed, and went to the door. It was Linda with a friend Wallander hadn't met. He hardly recognised Linda either, since she had cropped her long blonde hair and dyed it red. But he was relieved and happy to see her.

He let them in and said hello to Linda's friend, who introduced herself as Kajsa. Wallander was full of questions. How did they come to be ringing his doorbell so early on a Sunday morning? Were there really train connections this early? Linda explained that they had arrived the night before, but they had stayed at the house of a girl she had gone to school with, whose parents were away. They would be staying there for the whole week. They came over so early because after reading the papers in the past few days, Linda knew it would be hard to get hold of her father.

Wallander made a breakfast of leftovers he dug out of his refrigerator. While they ate they told him they'd be spending the week rehearsing a play they had written. Then they were going to the island of Gotland to take part in a theatre seminar. Wallander listened, trying to disguise how disappointed he was that Linda had abandoned her dream to become a furniture upholsterer, settle down in Ystad, and open her own shop. He also yearned to talk to her about her grandfather. He knew how close she was to him.

"There's so much going on. I'd like to talk with you in peace and quiet, just you and me," he said, when Kajsa was out of the room.

"That's the best thing about you," she said. "You're always so glad to see me." She wrote down her phone number and promised to come over when he called.

"I saw the papers," she said. "Is it really as bad as they make out?"

"It's worse," Wallander said. "I've got so much to do that I don't know how I'm going to cope. It was pure luck that you caught me at home."

They sat and talked until Hansson called and said he was at Sturup Airport with the psychologist. They agreed to meet at the station at 9 a.m.

"I have to go now," he told Linda.

"We do, too," she said.

"Does this play you're putting on have a name?" Wallander wondered when they got out to the street.

"It's not a play," replied Linda. "It's a revue."

"I see," said Wallander, trying to remember what the difference was. "And does it have a name?"

"Not yet," said Kajsa.

"Can I see it?" Wallander asked tentatively.

"When it's ready," said Linda. "Not before."

Wallander asked whether he could drive them somewhere.

"I'm going to show her the town," said Linda.

"Where are you from?" he asked Kajsa.

"Sandviken, up north," she said. "I've never been to Skåne before."

"Then we're even," said Wallander. "I've never been to Sandviken."

He watched them disappear around the corner. The fine weather was holding. It would be even warmer today. He felt cheerful because of his daughter's unexpected visit, even though he couldn't adjust to the drastic way she had been experimenting with her looks the past few years. But when she'd stood in the doorway, he'd seen for the first time what many people had told him before. Linda looked like him. He had discovered his own face in hers.

He arrived at the station, feeling renewed vigour after Linda's unexpected visit. He strode down the hall, thinking that he clumped along like an overweight elephant, and threw off his jacket when he entered his room. He grabbed the telephone before he even sat down and asked the receptionist to get hold of Nyberg. Just as he'd fallen asleep the night before, an idea had come to him that he wanted to explore. It took five minutes before the girl at the front desk managed to locate Nyberg.

"It's Wallander," he said. "Do you remember telling me about a can of some sort of spray that you found outside the cordon on the beach?"

"Of course I remember," snapped Nyberg.

Wallander ignored the fact that Nyberg was obviously in a bad mood.

"I thought we ought to check it for fingerprints," he said. "And compare them to whatever you can find on that piece of paper I found near Carlman's house."

"Will do," said Nyberg. "But we would have done it anyway, even if you hadn't asked us to."

"I know," said Wallander. "But you know how it is."

"No, I don't," said Nyberg. "You'll have the results as soon as I've got something."

Wallander slammed down the receiver, full of energy. He stood by the window and looked out at the old water tower while he went through what he wanted to get done that day. He knew from experience that something almost always came along to spoil the plan. If he managed to get half the things done he'd be pleased.

At 9 a.m. he left his office, got some coffee, and went into one of the small meeting rooms, where Hansson was waiting with the psychologist from Stockholm. The man introduced himself as Mats Ekholm. He was around 60, with a firm handshake. Wallander had an immediately favourable impression of him. Like many police officers, Wallander had always felt sceptical about what psychologists could contribute in a criminal investigation. But from conversations with Ann-Britt Höglund he had begun to realise that this was wrong. He decided to give Ekholm a chance to show them what he could do.

The investigation files were set out on the table.

"I've read through them as best I could," said Ekholm. "I suggest that we start by talking about what isn't in the files."

"It's all there," said Hansson, surprised. "If there's one thing the police are forced to learn, it's how to write reports."

"I suppose you want to know what *we* think," interrupted Wallander. "Isn't that right?"

Ekholm nodded.

"There's a fundamental rule that says that the police are always searching for something specific," he answered. "If they don't know what an offender looks like they include an approximation. Quite often the phantom image turns out to have similarities with the offender who is finally apprehended."

Wallander recognised his own reactions in Ekholm's description. He always created an image of a criminal that he carried with him during an investigation.

"Two murders have been committed," Ekholm continued. "The *modus operandi* is the same, even though there are some interesting differences. Wetterstedt was killed from behind. The murderer struck him in the back, not in the head. He chose the more difficult alternative. Or could it be that he wanted to avoid smashing Wetterstedt's head? We don't know. After the blow he cut off his scalp and took the time to hide the body. If we look at Carlman's death, we can easily identify the similarities and differences. Carlman was also struck down with an axe. He too had a piece of his scalp torn off. But he was killed from directly in front. He must have seen his attacker. The offender chose a time when there were many people nearby, so the risk of discovery was high. He made no attempt to hide the body, realising that it would be virtually impossible. The first question we have to ask is: which are more important? The similarities or the differences?"

"He's a murderer," said Wallander. "He selected two people. He made plans. He must have visited the beach outside Wetterstedt's house several times. He even took the time to unscrew a bulb to obscure the area between the garden gate and the sea."

"Do we know whether Wetterstedt was in the habit of taking an evening walk on the beach?" Ekholm interjected.

"No," said Wallander. "But of course we ought to find out."

"Keep going," said Ekholm.

"On the surface the pattern looks completely different when it comes to Carlman," said Wallander. "Surrounded by people at a Midsummer party. But maybe the killer didn't see it that way. Maybe he thought he could make use of the fact that no-one sees anything at all at a party. Nothing is as difficult as obtaining a detailed impression of events from a large group of people."

"To answer that question we have to examine what alternatives he may have had," said Ekholm. "Carlman was a businessman who moved around a lot. Always surrounded by people. Maybe the party was the right choice after all."

"The similarity or the difference," said Wallander. "Which one is crucial?"

Ekholm threw out his hands.

"It's too early to say, of course. What we can be sure of is that he plans his crimes carefully and that he's extremely cold-blooded."

"He takes scalps," said Wallander. "He collects trophies. What does that mean?"

"He's exercising power," said Ekholm. "The trophies are the proof of his actions. For him it's no more peculiar than a hunter putting up a pair of horns on his wall."

"But the decision to scalp," Wallander went on. "Where does that come from?"

"It's not that strange," said Ekholm. "I don't want to seem cynical. But what part of a human being is more suitable to be taken as a trophy? A human body rots. A piece of skin with hair on it is easy to preserve."

"I guess I still can't stop thinking of American Indians," said Wallander.

"Naturally it can't be excluded that your killer has a fixation on an American Indian warrior," said Ekholm. "People who find themselves in a psychic borderland often choose to hide behind another person's identity. Or transform themselves into a mythological figure."

"Borderland?" said Wallander. "What does that involve?"

"Your killer has already committed two murders. We can't rule out that he intends to commit more, since we don't know his motive. This indicates he has probably passed a psychological boundary, that he has freed himself from our normal inhibitions. A person can commit murder or manslaughter without premeditation. A killer who repeats his actions is following completely different psychological laws. He finds himself in a twilight zone where all the boundaries that exist for him are of his own making. On the surface he can live a completely normal life. He can go to a job every morning. He can have a family and devote his evenings to playing golf or tending his garden. He can sit on his sofa with his children around him and watch the news reports on the murders he himself has committed. He can deplore the crimes, and wonder why such people are on the loose. He has two different identities that he controls utterly. He pulls his own strings. He is both marionette and puppet master."

Wallander thought about what Ekholm had said.

"Who is he?" he finally asked. "What does he look like? How old is he? I can't hunt someone who looks entirely normal on the surface. I must search for a specific person."

"I can't answer that yet," said Ekholm. "I need time to get into the material before I can create a profile of the killer."

"I hope you're not considering today a day of rest," said Wallander wearily. "We'll need that profile as soon as possible."

"I'll try to get something together by tomorrow," said Ekholm. "But you and your colleagues have to realise that the difficulties and the margins of error are daunting."

"I realise that," said Wallander. "We still need all the help you can give us."

When the meeting was over Wallander drove down to the harbour and walked out onto the pier, where he had sat a few days earlier trying to write his speech for Björk. He sat and watched a fishing boat on its way out to sea. He unbuttoned his shirt and closed his eyes, facing the sun. Somewhere close by he heard children laughing. He tried to empty his mind and enjoy the heat. But after a few minutes he stood up and left.

Your killer has already committed two murders. We can't rule out that he intends to commit more, since we don't know his motive.

Ekholm's words might have been his own. He would not relax until they had caught Wetterstedt and Carlman's killer. Wallander knew his strength was his determination. And sometimes he had moments of insight. But his weakness was also clear. He couldn't keep his job from becoming a personal matter. Your killer, Ekholm had said. There was no better description of his weakness. The man who killed Wetterstedt and Carlman was actually his own responsibility. Whether he liked it or not.

He went back to his car, deciding to follow the plan he had made that morning. He drove out to Wetterstedt's villa. The cordons on the beach were gone. Lindgren and an older man, who he assumed was Lindgren's father, were busy sanding the boat. He didn't feel like saying hello.

He still had Wetterstedt's keys, and he unlocked the front door. The silence was deafening. He sat down in one of the leather chairs in the living-room. He could just hear sounds from the beach. He looked around the room. What did it tell him? Had the killer ever been inside the house? He was having a hard time gathering his thoughts. He got up and went over to the big window facing the garden, the beach and the sea. Wetterstedt had stood here many times. He could see that the parquet floor was worn at this spot. He looked out of the window. Someone had shut off the water to the fountain in the garden. He let his gaze wander as he went over the thoughts he'd had earlier.

On the hill outside Carlman's house my killer stood and observed the party. He may have been there many times. From there he could see without being seen. Where is the hill from which you would have the same view of Wetterstedt? From what point could you see him without being seen?

He walked around the house, stopping at each window. From the kitchen he looked for a long time at a pair of trees growing just outside Wetterstedt's property. But they were young birches that wouldn't have held a person's weight.

Not until he came to the study and looked out of the window did he realise that he had found the answer. From the projecting garage roof it was possible to see straight into the room. He left the house and went around the garage. A younger, fit man could jump up, grab hold of the eaves and pull himself up. Wallander went and got a ladder he had seen on the other side of the house. He leaned it against the garage roof and climbed up. The roof was the old-fashioned tar-paper type. Since he wasn't sure how much weight it would hold, he crawled on all fours over to a spot where he could look straight into Wetterstedt's study. He searched until he found the point farthest away from the window that still had a good view inside. On his hands and knees he inspected the tar-paper. Almost at once he discovered some cuts in it criss-crossing each other. He ran his fingertips across the tar-paper. Someone had slashed it with a knife. He looked around. It was impossible to be seen either from the beach or from the road above Wetterstedt's house.

Wallander climbed down and put the ladder back. Carefully he inspected the ground next to the garage, but all he found were some tattered pages from a magazine that had blown onto the property. He went back into the house. The silence was oppressive. He went upstairs. Through the window in Wetterstedt's bedroom he could see Lindgren and his father turning their boat right side up. He could see that it took two people to turn it over.

And yet he now knew that the killer had been alone, both here and when he killed Carlman. Though there were few clues, his intuition told him that it had been one person sitting on Wetterstedt's roof and on the hill above Carlman's.

I'm dealing with a lone killer, he thought. A lone man who leaves his borderland and hacks people to death so he can then take their scalps as trophies.

He left Wetterstedt's house, emerging into the sunshine again with relief. He drove over to a café and ate lunch at the counter. A young woman at a table nearby nodded to him and said hello. He replied, unable to remember who she was. Not until he left did he recall that she was Britta-Lena Bodén, the bank teller whose excellent memory had been so important during an investigation.

By midday he was back at the station. Ann-Britt Höglund met him in the foyer.

"I saw you from my window," she said.

Wallander knew at once that something had happened. He waited, tense, for her to continue.

"There is a point of contact," she said. "In the late 1960s Carlman did some time in prison. At Långholmen. Wetterstedt was minister of justice at the time."

"That isn't enough," said Wallander.

"I'm not finished. Carlman wrote a letter to Wetterstedt. And when he got out of prison they met."

Wallander stood motionless.

"How do you know this?"

"Come to my office and I'll tell you."

Wallander knew what this meant. If there was a connection, they had broken through the hard, outermost shell of the investigation.

CHAPTER 15

It had started with a telephone call.

Ann-Britt Höglund had been on her way down the hall to talk to Martinsson when she was paged. She returned to her office and took the call. It was a man who spoke so softly that at first she thought he was sick or injured. But she understood that he wanted to talk to Wallander. No-one else would do, least of all a woman. She explained that Wallander had gone out and no-one could say when he was coming back. But the man was extremely persistent, although she didn't understand how a man who spoke so softly could seem so strong-willed. She considered transferring the call to Martinsson and having him pretend to be Wallander. But something told her that he might know Wallander's voice.

He said that he had important information. She asked him whether it had to do with Wetterstedt's death. Maybe, he replied. Then she asked whether it was about Carlman. Maybe, he said once again. She knew that somehow she had to keep him talking. He had refused to give his name or phone number.

He finally resolved the impasse. He had been silent for so long that Höglund thought he had hung up, but then he asked for the station fax number. Give the fax to Wallander, the man had said. Not to anyone else.

An hour later the fax had arrived. She handed it to Wallander. To his astonishment he saw that it was sent from Skoglund's Hardware in Stockholm.

"I looked up the number and called them," she said. "I also thought it was strange that a hardware shop would be open on Sunday. From a message on their answer machine I got hold of the owner via his mobile phone. He had no idea either how someone could have sent a fax from his office. He was on his way to play golf but promised to look into the matter. Half an hour later he called and reported that someone had broken into his office."

"How strange," said Wallander.

He read the fax. It was hand-written and hard to read. He must get reading glasses soon. He couldn't pretend any longer he was just tired or stressed. The fax seemed to have been written in great haste. Wallander read it silently. Then he read it aloud to make sure he hadn't misunderstood anything.

"'Arne Carlman was in Långholmen during the spring of 1969 for fraud and fencing stolen goods. At that time Gustaf Wetterstedt was minister of justice. Carlman wrote letters to him. He bragged about it. When he got out he met with Wetterstedt. What did they talk about? What did they do? We don't know. But things went well for Carlman. He never went to prison again. And now they're dead. Both of them.' Have I read this correctly?"

"I came up with the same thing," she said.

"No signature," said Wallander. "And what is he really getting at? Who is he? How does he know this stuff? Is any of it true?"

"I don't know," she said. "But I had a feeling that this man knew what he was talking about. Anyway, it's not hard to check whether Carlman was really at Långholmen in the spring of 1969. We know that Wetterstedt was minister of justice then."

"Wasn't Långholmen closed by then?" Wallander asked.

"That was a few years later, in 1975, I think. I can check on exactly when."

Wallander waved it off.

"Why did he only want to talk to me?" he asked. "Did he give any explanation?"

"I got a feeling he'd heard about you."

"So he wasn't claiming that he knew me?"

"No."

Wallander thought for a moment.

"Let's hope what he wrote is true," he said. "Then we've established the connection."

"It shouldn't be too hard to verify," said Höglund. "Even if it is Sunday."

"I'll go out and talk to Carlman's widow right now. She must know whether her husband was ever in prison," said Wallander.

"Do you want me to come along?"

"No."

Half an hour later Wallander parked his car outside the cordon in Bjäresjö. A bored-looking officer sat in a squad car reading the paper. He straightened up when he saw Wallander approaching.

"Is Nyberg still working here?" asked Wallander in surprise. "Isn't the forensic investigation finished?"

"I haven't seen any technicians around," said the officer.

"Call Ystad and ask them why the cordons haven't been removed," said Wallander. "Is the family home?"

"The widow is probably there," said the officer. "And the daughter. But the sons left in a car a few hours ago."

Wallander entered the grounds of the farm. The bench and the table in the arbour were gone. In the beautiful summer weather the events of the last few days seemed unbelievable. He knocked on the door. Carlman's widow opened it almost at once.

"I'm sorry to bother you," said Wallander. "But I have a few questions that I need answered as soon as possible."

She was very pale. As he stepped inside he smelled a faint whiff of alcohol. Somewhere inside, Carlman's daughter shouted, asking who was at the door. Wallander tried to remember the name of the woman leading the way. Had he ever heard it? Yes – it was Anita. He'd heard Svedberg use it during the long investigative meeting. He sat down on the sofa facing her. She lit a cigarette. She was wearing a flimsy summer dress. Wallander felt vaguely disapproving. Even if she didn't love her husband, he had been murdered. Didn't people believe in showing respect for the dead any more? Couldn't she have chosen more sombre attire? He had such conservative views sometimes that he surprised himself. Sorrow and respect didn't follow a colour scheme.

"Would the inspector like something to drink?" she asked.

"No thank you," said Wallander. "I'll be as brief as I can."

She shot a glance past his face. He turned around. Her daughter, Erika, had entered the room silently and was sitting in the background. She was smoking and seemed nervous.

"Do you mind if I listen?" she asked in a belligerent voice.

"Not at all," he said. "You're welcome to join us."

"I'm fine here," she said.

Her mother shook her head almost imperceptibly. She seemed resigned about her daughter's behaviour.

"Actually I came here because it's Sunday," Wallander began. "Which means that it's difficult to get information from archives. And since we need to have an answer as soon as possible, I came to you."

"You don't have to excuse yourself," said the woman. "What is it you want to know?"

"Was your husband in prison in the spring of 1969?"

Her reply was swift and resolute.

"He was in Långholmen between the 9th of February and the 19th of June. I drove him there and I picked him up. He was convicted of fraud and fencing stolen goods."

Her frankness made Wallander lose his train of thought. But what had he expected? That she would deny it?

"Was this the first time he was sentenced to a prison term?"

"The first and the last."

"Can you tell me any more about the convictions?"

"He denied having either received stolen paintings or forged any cheques. Other people did it in his name."

"So you think he was innocent?"

"It's not a matter of what I think. He was innocent."

Wallander decided to change tack.

"It has come to light that your husband knew Gustaf Wetterstedt, despite the fact that both you and your children claimed earlier that this was not the case."

"If he knew Gustaf Wetterstedt then I would have known about it."

"Could he have had contact with him without your knowledge?"

She thought for a moment before she replied.

"I would find that very difficult to believe," she said.

Wallander knew at once that she was lying. But he couldn't see why. Since he had no more questions he stood up.

"Perhaps you can find your own way out," said the woman on the sofa. She seemed very tired suddenly.

Wallander walked to the door. As he approached the daughter, who had been watching him intently, she stood up and blocked his way, holding her cigarette in her left hand.

Out of nowhere came a slap that struck Wallander hard on his left cheek. He was so surprised that he took a step back, tripped, and fell to the floor.

"Why did you let it happen?" she shrieked.

Then she started pummelling Wallander, who managed to fend her off as he tried to get up. Mrs Carlman came to his rescue. She did the same thing as the girl had just done to Wallander. She slapped her daughter hard in the face. When the girl calmed down, her mother led her over to the sofa. Then she returned to Wallander, who was standing there with his burning cheek, torn between rage and astonishment.

"Erika's been so depressed about what happened," said Anita Carlman. "She's lost control. The inspector must forgive her."

"Maybe she should see a doctor," said Wallander, noticing that his voice was shaking.

"She already has."

Wallander nodded and went out of the door. He tried to remember the last time he had been struck. It was more than ten years ago. He was interrogating a man suspected of burglary. Suddenly the man had jumped up from the table and slugged him in the mouth. That time Wallander struck back. His rage was so fierce that he broke the man's nose. Afterwards the man tried to sue Wallander for police brutality, but he was found innocent. The man later sent a complaint to the ombudsman about Wallander, but that too was dropped with no measures taken.

He had never been hit by a woman before. When his wife Mona had lost control, she had thrown things at him. But she had never tried to slap him. He often wondered what would have happened if she had. Would he have hit back? He knew there was a good chance he would.

He stood in the garden touching his stinging cheek. All the energy he had felt that morning had evaporated. He was so tired that he couldn't even manage to hold on to the feeling the girls' visit had given him.

He walked back to his car. The officer was slowly rolling up the yellow tape.

He put *The Marriage of Figaro* in the cassette deck. He turned up the volume so high that it thundered inside the car. His cheek stung. In the rear-view mirror he could see that it was red. When he got to Ystad he turned into the big car park by the furniture shop. Everything was closed, the car park deserted. He opened the car door and let the music flow. Barbara Hendricks made him forget about Wetterstedt and Carlman for a moment. But the girl in flames still ran through his mind. The field seemed endless. She kept running and running. And burning and burning.

He turned down the music and started pacing back and forth in the car park. As always when he was thinking, he walked along staring at the ground. And so Wallander didn't notice the photographer who saw him by chance, and took a picture of him through a telephoto lens as he paced around the empty car park. A few weeks later, when an astonished Wallander saw the picture, he'd even forgotten that he'd stopped there to try and clear his head.

The team met very briefly that afternoon. Mats Ekholm joined them and ran through what he had discussed earlier with Hansson and Wallander. Höglund told the team about the fax, and Wallander reported that Anita Carlman had confirmed the information it contained. He didn't mention being slapped. When Hansson asked tentatively whether he'd consider talking to the reporters camped out around the station who seemed to know when a meeting had taken place, he refused.

"We have to teach these reporters that we're working on a legal matter," Wallander said, and could hear how affected he sounded. "Ann-Britt can take care of them. I'm not interested."

"Is there anything I shouldn't say?" she asked.

"Don't say we have a suspect," said Wallander. "Because we don't."

After the meeting Wallander exchanged a few words with Martinsson.

"Has anything more been discovered about the girl?" he asked.

"Not yet," said Martinsson.

"Let me know as soon as something happens."

Wallander went to his room. The telephone rang immediately, making him jump. Every time it rang he expected to be told of another murder. But it was his sister. She told him that she had talked to Gertrud. There was no doubt that their father had Alzheimer's disease. Wallander could hear how upset she was.

"He's almost 80," he consoled her. "Sooner or later something had to happen."

"But even so," she said.

Wallander knew what she meant. He could have used the same words himself. All too often life was reduced to those powerless words of protest, *but even so*.

"He won't be able to handle a trip to Italy," she said.

"If he wants to, then he will," said Wallander. "Besides, I promised him."

"Maybe I should come with you."

"No. It's our trip."

He hung up, wondering whether she was offended that he didn't invite her to join them. But he put aside those thoughts and decided that he really had to go and visit his father. He located the scrap of paper on which he had written Linda's phone number and called her. He was surprised when Kajsa answered at once, expecting them to be outside on such a beautiful day. When Linda came on he asked whether she'd leave her rehearsal and drive out with him to see her grandfather.

"Can Kajsa come too?" she asked.

"Normally I'd say yes," replied Wallander. "But today I'd prefer it if it was just you and me. There's something I need to talk to you about."

He picked her up in Österport Square. On the way to Löderup he told her about his father's visit to the station, and that he was ill.

"No-one knows how fast it will progress," said Wallander. "But he will be leaving us. Sort of like a ship sailing farther and farther out towards the horizon. We'll still be able to see him clearly, but for him we'll seem more and more like shapes in the fog. Our faces, our words, our common memories, everything will become indistinct and finally disappear altogether. He might be cruel without realising he's doing it. He could turn into a totally different person."

Wallander could tell that she was upset.

"Can't anything be done?" she asked after sitting for a long time in silence.

"Only Gertrud can answer that," he said. "But I don't think there is a cure."

He also told her about the trip that he and his father wanted to take to Italy.

"It'll be just him and me," said Wallander. "Maybe we can work out all the problems we've had."

Gertrud met them on the steps when they pulled into the courtyard. Linda ran to see her grandfather, who was painting out in the studio he had made in the old barn. Wallander sat down in the kitchen and talked to Gertrud. It was just as he thought. There was nothing to be done but try to live a normal life and wait.

"Will he be able to travel to Italy?" asked Wallander.

"That's all he talks about," she said. "And if he should die while he's there, it wouldn't be the worst thing."

She told him that his father had taken the news of his illness calmly.

This surprised Wallander, who had known his father to fret about the slightest ailment.

"I think he's come to terms with old age," said Gertrud. "He probably thinks that by and large he would live the same life again if he had the chance."

"But in that life he would have stopped me from becoming a policeman," said Wallander.

"It's terrible, what I read in the papers," she said. "All the horrible things you have to deal with."

"Someone has to do it," said Wallander. "That's just the way it is."

They stayed and ate dinner in the garden. Wallander could see that his father was in an unusually good mood. He assumed that Linda was the reason. It was already 11 p.m. by the time they left.

"Adults can be so childlike," Linda said suddenly. "Sometimes because they're showing off, trying to act young. But Grandpa can seem childlike in a way that seems totally unaffected."

"Your grandpa is a very special person," said Wallander.

"Do you know you're starting to look like him?" she asked. "You two are becoming more alike every year."

"I know," said Wallander. "But I don't know if I like it."

He dropped her off where he'd picked her up. They decided that she would call in a few days. He watched her disappear past Österport School and realised to his astonishment that he hadn't thought about the investigation once the whole evening. He immediately felt guilty, then pushed the feeling away. He knew that he couldn't do any more than he had already done today.

He drove to the station. None of the detectives were in. There weren't any messages important enough to answer that evening. He drove home, parked his car, and went up to his flat.

Wallander stayed up for a long time that night. He had the windows open to the warm summer air. On his stereo he played some music by Puccini. He poured himself the last of the whisky. He felt some of the happiness he had felt the afternoon he was driving out to Salomonsson's farm, before the catastrophe had struck. Now he was in the middle of an investigation that was marked by two things. First, they had very little to help them identify the killer. Second, it was quite possible that he was busy carrying out his third murder at that very moment. Still, Wallander tried to put the case out of his mind. And for a short time the burning girl disappeared from his thoughts too. He had to admit that he couldn't single-handedly solve every violent crime that happened in Ystad. He could only do his best. That's all anyone could do.

He lay down on the sofa and dozed off to the music and the summer night with the whisky glass within reach.

But something drew him back to the surface again. It was something that Linda had said in the car. Some words that suddenly took on a whole new meaning. He sat up on the sofa, frowning. What was it she had said? *Adults can be so childlike.* There was something there that he couldn't grasp. *Adults can be so childlike.*

Then he realised what it was. And he couldn't understand how he could have been so sloppy. He put on his shoes, found a torch in one of the kitchen drawers, and left the flat. He drove out along Österleden, turned right, and stopped outside Wetterstedt's house, which lay in darkness. He opened the gate to the front yard. He gave a start when a cat vanished like a shadow among the bushes. He shone the torch along the base of the garage, and didn't have to search long before he found what he was looking for. He took the torn-out pages of the magazine between his thumb and forefinger and shone the light on them. They were from an issue of *The Phantom.* He searched in his pockets for a plastic bag and put the pages inside.

Then he drove home. He was still annoyed that he had been so sloppy.

Adults can be so childlike.

A grown man could very well have sat on the garage roof reading an issue of *The Phantom.*

CHAPTER 16

When Wallander awoke just before 5 a.m., on Monday 27 June, a cloud bank had drifted in from the west and reached Ystad, but there was still no rain. Wallander lay in bed and tried in vain to go back to sleep. At 6 a.m. he got up, showered and made coffee. The fatigue was like a dull pain. Ten or 15 years ago he'd almost never felt tired in the morning, no matter how little sleep he'd got, he thought with regret. But those days were gone forever.

Just before 7 a.m. he walked into the station. Ebba had already arrived, and she smiled at him as she handed him some phone messages.

"I thought you were on holiday," said Wallander in surprise.

"Hansson asked me to stay a few extra days," said Ebba. "Now that there's so much happening."

"How's your hand?"

"Like I said. It's no fun getting old. Everything just starts to fall apart."

Wallander couldn't recall ever having heard Ebba make such a dramatic statement. He wondered whether to tell her about his father and his illness, but decided against it. He got some coffee and sat down at his desk. After looking through the phone messages and stacking them on top of the pile from the night before, he called Riga, feeling a pang of guilt at making a personal call. He was still old-fashioned enough not to want to burden his employer. He remembered how a few years ago Hansson had been consumed by a passion for betting on the horses. He had spent half his working day calling racetracks all over the country for tips. Everyone had known about it, but no-one had complained. Wallander had been surprised that only he had thought someone should talk to Hansson. But then one day all the form guides and half-completed betting slips vanished from Hansson's desk. Through the grapevine Wallander heard that Hansson had decided to stop before he wound up in debt.

Baiba picked up the phone after the third ring. Wallander was nervous. Each time he called he was afraid that she'd tell him they shouldn't see each other again. He was as unsure of her feelings as he was sure of his own. But she sounded happy, and her happiness was infectious. Her decision to go to Tallinn had been made quite hastily, she explained. One of her friends was going and asked Baiba to go with her. She had no classes at the university that week, and the translation job she was working on didn't have a pressing deadline. She told him about the trip and then asked how he was. Wallander decided not to mention that their trip to Skagen might be jeopardised. He said that everything was fine. They agreed that he would call her that evening. Afterwards, Wallander sat worrying about how she'd react if he had to postpone their holiday.

Worry was a bad habit, which seemed to grow worse the older he got. He worried about everything. He worried when Baiba went to Tallinn, he worried that he was going to get sick, he worried that he might oversleep or that his car might break down. He wrapped himself in clouds of anxiety. With a grimace he wondered whether Mats Ekholm might be able to do a psychological profile of him and suggest how he could free himself from all the problems he created.

Svedberg knocked on his half-open door and walked in. He hadn't been careful in the sun the day before. The top of his head was completely sunburnt, as were his forehead and nose.

"I'll never learn," Svedberg complained. "It hurts like hell."

Wallander thought about the burning sensation he'd felt after being slapped the day before. But he didn't mention it.

"I spent yesterday talking to the people who live near Wetterstedt," Svedberg said. "He went for walks quite often. He was always polite and said hello to the people he met. But he didn't socialise with anyone in the neighbourhood."

"Did he also make a habit of taking walks at night?"

Svedberg checked his notes. "He used to go down to the beach."

"So this was a routine?"

"As far as I can tell, yes."

Wallander nodded. "Just as I thought," he said.

"Something else came up that might be of interest," Svedberg continued. "A retired civil servant named Lantz told me that a reporter had rung his doorbell on Monday 20 June, and asked for directions to Wetterstedt's house. Lantz understood that the reporter and a photographer were going there to do a story. That means someone was at his house on the last day of his life."

"And that there are photographs," said Wallander. "Which newspaper was it?"

"Lantz didn't know."

"You'll have to get someone to make some calls," said Wallander. "This could be important."

Svedberg nodded and left the room.

"And you ought to put some cream on that sunburn," Wallander called after him. "It doesn't look good."

Wallander called Nyberg. A few minutes later he came in.

"I don't think your man came on a bicycle," said Nyberg. "We found some tracks behind the hut from a moped or a motorcycle. And every worker on the road team drives a car."

An image flashed through Wallander's mind, but he couldn't hold on to it. He wrote down what Nyberg had said.

"What do you expect me to do with this?" asked Nyberg, holding up the bag with the pages from *The Phantom*.

"Check for fingerprints," said Wallander. "Which may match other prints."

"I thought only children read *The Phantom*," said Nyberg.

"No," replied Wallander. "There you're wrong."

When Nyberg had gone, Wallander hesitated. Rydberg had taught him that a policeman must always tackle what was most important at a given moment. But what was now? No one thing could yet be assumed to be more important than another. Wallander knew that what mattered now was to trust his patience.

He went out into the hall, knocked on the door of the office that had been assigned to Ekholm and opened the door. Ekholm was sitting with his feet on the desk, reading through some papers. He nodded towards the visitor's chair and tossed the papers on the desk.

"How's it going?" asked Wallander.

"Not so good," said Ekholm evenly. "It's hard to pin down this person. It's a shame we don't have a little more material to go on."

"He needs to have committed more murders?"

"To put it bluntly, that would make the case easier," said Ekholm. "In many investigations into serial murders conducted by the F.B.I., a breakthrough comes only after the third or fourth crime. Then it's possible to sift out the things that are particular to each killing, and start to see an overall pattern. And a pattern is what we're looking for, one that enables us to see the mind behind the crimes."

"What can you say about adults who read comic books?" asked Wallander.

Ekholm raised his eyebrows.

"Does this have something to do with the case?"

"Maybe."

Wallander told him about his discovery. Ekholm listened intently.

"Emotional immaturity or abnormality is almost always present in individuals who commit serial murders," said Ekholm. "They don't value other human beings. That's why they don't comprehend the suffering they cause."

"But all adults who read *The Phantom* aren't murderers," said Wallander.

"Just as there have been examples of serial killers who were experts on Dostoevsky," replied Ekholm. "You have to take a piece of the puzzle and see whether it fits anywhere."

Wallander was starting to get impatient. He didn't have time to get into a theoretical discussion with Ekholm.

"Now that you've read through our material," he said, "what sort of conclusions have you made?"

"Just one, actually," said Ekholm. "That he will strike again."

Wallander waited for something more, an explanation, but it didn't come.

"Why?"

"Something about the total picture tells me so. And I can't say why except that it's based on experience. From other cases with trophy hunters."

"What kind of image do you see?" asked Wallander. "Tell me what you're thinking right now. Anything at all. And I promise I won't hold you to it later."

"An adult," replied Ekholm. "Considering the age of the victims and his possible connection to them, I'd say he's at least 30, but maybe older. The possible identification with a myth, perhaps of an American Indian, makes me think that he's in very good physical condition. He's both cautious and cunning. Which means that he's the calculating type. I think he lives a regular, orderly life. He hides his inner life beneath a surface of normality."

"And he's going to strike again?"

Ekholm threw out his hands.

"Let's hope I'm wrong. But you asked me to tell you what I think."

"Wetterstedt and Carlman died three days apart," said Wallander. "If he keeps to that pattern, he'll kill someone today."

"That's not inevitable," said Ekholm. "Since he's cunning, the time factor won't be crucial. He strikes when he's sure of success. Something might happen today. But it could also take several weeks. Or years."

Wallander had no more questions. He asked Ekholm to attend the team meeting an hour later. He went back to his room feeling increasingly anxious. The man they were looking for, of whom they knew nothing, would strike again.

He took out the notebook in which he had written Nyberg's words, and tried to recapture the fleeting image that had passed through his mind. He was sure that this was important, and that it had something

164

to do with the road workers' hut. But he couldn't pin it down. He got up and went to the conference room. He missed Rydberg more than ever now.

Wallander sat in his usual seat at one end of the table. He looked around. Everyone was there. He sensed that the group hoped they were going to make a breakthrough. Wallander knew they'd be disappointed. But none of them would show it. The detectives gathered in this room were professionals.

"Let's start with a review of what's happened in the scalping case in the past 24 hours," he began.

He hadn't planned to say *the scalping case*. But from that moment on the investigation wasn't called anything else.

Wallander usually waited until last to give his report, since he was expected to sum up and provide further directions. It was natural for Höglund to speak first. She passed around the fax that had come from Skoglund's Hardware. What Anita Carlman had confirmed had also been checked in the national prison register. Höglund had just begun the most difficult task – to find evidence or even copies of the letters that Carlman was said to have written to Wetterstedt.

"It all happened so long ago," she concluded. "Although archives are generally well organised in this country, it takes a long time to find documents from more than 25 years ago. We're dealing with a time before computers were in use."

"We must keep looking, though," said Wallander. "The connection between Wetterstedt and Carlman is crucial."

"The man who rang," said Svedberg, rubbing his burnt nose. "Why wouldn't he say who he was? Who would break into a shop just to send a fax?"

"I've thought about that," said Höglund. "There could be a lot of reasons why he wants to protect his identity, perhaps because he's scared. And he obviously wanted to point us in a particular direction."

The room fell silent. Wallander could see that Höglund was on the right track. He nodded to her to continue.

"Naturally we're guessing. But if he feels threatened by the man who killed Wetterstedt and Carlman, he would be extremely eager for us to capture him. Without revealing his own identity."

"In that case he should have told us more," said Martinsson.

"Maybe he couldn't," Höglund objected. "If I'm right, that he contacted us because he's frightened, then he probably told us everything he knows."

Wallander lifted his hand.

"Let's take this even further," he said. "The man gave us information relating to Carlman. Not Wetterstedt. That's crucial. He claims that Carlman wrote to Wetterstedt and that they met after Carlman was released from prison. Who would know this?"

"Another inmate," said Höglund.

"That was exactly my thought," said Wallander. "But your theory is that he's contacting us out of fear. Would that fit if he was only Carlman's fellow prisoner?"

"There's more to it," said Höglund. "He knows that Carlman and Wetterstedt met after Carlman got out. So contact continued outside of prison."

"He could have witnessed something," said Hansson, who had been silent until now. "For some reason this has led to two murders 25 years later."

Wallander turned to Ekholm, who was sitting by himself at the end of the table.

"25 years is a long time," he said.

"The desire for revenge can go on indefinitely," said Ekholm. "There are no prescribed time limits. It's one of the oldest truths in criminology that an avenger can wait forever. If these are revenge killings, that is."

"What else could they be?" asked Wallander. "We can rule out crimes against property, probably with Wetterstedt, and with complete certainty in Carlman's case."

"A motive can have many components," said Ekholm. "A serial killer may choose his victims for reasons that seem inexplicable. Take the scalps, for instance: we might ask whether he's after a special kind of hair. Wetterstedt and Carlman had the same full head of grey hair. We can't exclude anything. But as a layman, I agree that right now the point of contact ought to be the most important thing to focus on."

"Is it possible that we're thinking along the wrong lines altogether?" asked Martinsson suddenly. "Maybe for the killer there's a *symbolic* link between Wetterstedt and Carlman. While we search for facts, maybe he sees a connection that's invisible to us. Something that's completely inconceivable to our rational minds."

Wallander knew that Martinsson had the ability to turn an investigation around on its axis and get it back on the right track.

"You're thinking of something," he said. "Keep going."

Martinsson shrugged his shoulders and seemed about to change his mind.

"Wetterstedt and Carlman were wealthy men," he said. "They both belonged to a certain social class. They were representatives of political and economic power."

"Are you suggesting a political motive?" Wallander asked, surprised.

"I'm not suggesting anything," said Martinsson. "I'm listening to you and trying to see the case clearly myself. I'm as afraid as everyone else in this room that he's going to strike again."

Wallander looked around the table. Pale, serious faces. Except for Svedberg with his sunburn. Only now did he see that they were all as frightened as he was. He wasn't the only one who dreaded the next ring of the telephone.

The meeting broke up before 10 a.m., but Wallander asked Martinsson to stay behind.

"What is happening with the girl?" he asked. "Dolores María Santana?"

"I'm still waiting to hear from Interpol."

"Give them a nudge," said Wallander.

Martinsson gave him a puzzled look.

"Do we really have time for her now?"

"No. But we can't just let it drop either."

Martinsson promised to send off another request. Wallander went in his office and called Lars Magnusson. He answered after a long time. Wallander could hear that he was drunk.

"I need to continue our conversation," he said.

"I don't conduct conversations at this time of day," said Magnusson.

"Make some coffee," said Wallander. "And put away the bottles. I'm coming over in half an hour." He hung up on Magnusson's protests.

Someone had placed two preliminary autopsy reports on his desk. Wallander had gradually learned to decipher the language used by pathologists and forensic doctors. Many years ago he had taken a course in Uppsala arranged by the national police board. Wallander remembered how unpleasant it was to visit an autopsy room.

There was nothing unexpected in the reports. He put them aside and looked out the window, trying to visualise the killer. What did he look like? What was he doing right now? But Wallander saw nothing but darkness before him. Depressed, he got up and left.

CHAPTER 17

When Wallander left Lars Magnusson's flat after more than two hours of trying to conduct a coherent conversation, all he wanted to do was go home and take a bath. He hadn't noticed the filth on his first visit, but this time it was obvious. The front door was ajar when Wallander arrived. Magnusson was lying on the sofa while a saucepan of coffee boiled over in the kitchen. He'd greeted Wallander by telling him to go to hell.

"Don't come around here, just get out and forget there's anyone called Lars Magnusson," he'd shouted.

But Wallander stood his ground. The coffee on the stove indicated that Magnusson had thought he might talk to someone in the daytime after all. Wallander searched in vain for clean cups. In the sink were plates on which the food and grease seemed have fossilised. Eventually he found two cups, which he washed and carried into the living-room.

Magnusson wore only a pair of dirty shorts. He was unshaven and clutched a bottle of dessert wine like a crucifix. Wallander was horrified at his dissipation. What he found most disgusting was that Lars Magnusson was losing his teeth. Wallander grew annoyed and then angry that the man on the sofa wasn't listening to him. He yanked the bottle away from him and demanded answers to his questions. He had no idea what authority he was acting on. But Magnusson did as he was told. He even hauled himself up to a sitting position. Wallander wanted to get more of a sense of the time when Wetterstedt was minister of justice, of the rumours and scandal. But Magnusson seemed to have forgotten everything. He couldn't even remember what he'd said on Wallander's last visit. Finally, Wallander gave him back the bottle and once he had taken a few more slugs, feeble memories begin to surface.

Wallander left the flat with one lead. In an unexpected moment of clarity, Magnusson remembered that there was a policeman on the Stockholm vice squad who had developed a particular interest in Wetterstedt. Rumour had it that this man, who Magnusson remembered was Hugo Sandin, had created a dossier on Wetterstedt. As far as Magnusson knew, nothing had ever come of it. He'd heard that Sandin had moved south when he retired and now lived with his son, who had a pottery workshop outside Hässleholm.

"If he's still alive," Magnusson said, smiling his toothless smile, as though he hoped that Hugo Sandin had died before him.

Wallander drove back to the station, feeling determined to locate Sandin. In reception he ran into Svedberg, whose burnt face was still troubling him.

"Wetterstedt was interviewed by a journalist from *MagaZenith*," said Svedberg.

Wallander had never heard of the magazine.

"Retirees get it," Svedberg told him. "The journalist's name was Anna-Lisa Blomgren, and she did take a photographer with her. Now that Wetterstedt is dead they aren't going to publish the article."

"Talk to her," said Wallander. "And ask for the pictures."

Wallander went to his office. He called the switchboard and asked them to find Nyberg, who called back 15 minutes later.

"Do you remember the camera from Wetterstedt's house?" Wallander asked.

"Of course I remember," said Nyberg grumpily.

"Has the film been developed yet? There were seven pictures exposed."

"Didn't you get them?" Nyberg asked, surprised.

"No."

"They should have been sent over to you last Saturday."

"I never got them."

"Are you sure?"

"Maybe they're lying around somewhere."

"I'll have to look into this," said Nyberg. "I'll get back to you."

Somebody would bear the brunt of Nyberg's wrath, and Wallander was glad that it wouldn't be him.

He found the number of the Hässleholm police and after some difficulty managed to get hold of Hugo Sandin's phone number. When Wallander asked about Sandin, he was told that he was about 85 years old but that his mind was still sharp.

"He usually stops by to visit a couple of times a year," said the officer Wallander spoke to, who introduced himself as Mörk.

Wallander wrote down the number and thanked him. Then he called Malmö and asked for the doctor who had done the autopsy on Wetterstedt.

"There's nothing in the report about the time of death," Wallander said to him. "That's very important for us."

The doctor asked him to wait a moment while he got his file. After a moment he returned and apologised.

"It was left out of the report. Sometimes my dictaphone acts up. But Wetterstedt died less than 24 hours before he was found. We're still waiting for some results from the laboratory that will enable us to narrow the time span further."

"I'll wait for those results," said Wallander and thanked him.

He went in to see Svedberg, who was at his computer.

"Did you talk to that journalist?"

"I'm just typing up a report."

"Did you get the time of their visit?"

Svedberg looked through his notes.

"They got to Wetterstedt's house at 10 a.m. and stayed until 1 p.m."

"After that, nobody else saw him alive?"

Svedberg thought for a moment. "Not that I know of."

"So, we know that much," said Wallander and left the room.

He was just about to call Hugo Sandin, when Martinsson came in.

"Have you got a minute?" he asked.

"Always," said Wallander. "What's up?"

Martinsson waved a letter.

"This came in the mail today," he said. "It's from someone who says he gave a girl a ride from Helsingborg to Tomelilla on Monday, 20 June. He's seen the description of the girl in the papers, and thinks it might have been her."

Martinsson handed the envelope to Wallander, who took out the letter and read it.

"No signature," he said.

"But the letterhead is interesting."

Wallander nodded. "Smedstorp Parish," he said. "Official church stationery."

"We'll have to look into it," said Martinsson.

"We certainly will," said Wallander. "If you take care of Interpol and the other things you're busy with, I'll look after this."

"I still don't see how we have time," said Martinsson.

"We'll make time," said Wallander.

After Martinsson left, Wallander realised that he'd been subtly criticised for not leaving the suicide case for the moment. Martinsson might be right, he thought. There was no space for anything but Wetterstedt and Carlman. But then he decided the criticism was unjustified. They must make time to handle every case.

As if to prove that he was right, Wallander left the station and drove out of town towards Tomelilla and Smedstorp. The drive gave him time to think about the murders. The summer landscape seemed a surreal backdrop to his thoughts. Two men are axed to death and scalped, he thought. A young girl walks into a rape field and sets herself on fire. And all around me it's summertime. Skåne couldn't be more beautiful than this. There's a paradise hidden in every corner of this countryside. To find it, all you have to do is keep your eyes open. But you might also glimpse hearses on the roads.

The parish offices were in Smedstorp. After he passed Lunnarp he turned left. He knew that the office kept irregular hours, but there were cars parked outside the whitewashed building. A man was mowing the lawn. Wallander tried the door. It was locked. He rang the bell, noting from the brass plate that the office wouldn't be open until Wednesday. He waited. Then he rang again and knocked on the door.

The lawnmower hummed in the background. Wallander was just about to leave when a window on the floor above opened. A woman stuck out her head.

"We're open on Wednesdays and Fridays," she shouted.

"I know," Wallander replied. "But this is urgent. I'm from the Ystad police."

Her head disappeared. Then the door opened. A blonde woman dressed in black stood before him, heavily made up and wearing high heels. What surprised Wallander was the white clerical collar set against all that black. He introduced himself.

"Gunnel Nilsson," she replied. "I'm the vicar of this parish."

Wallander followed her inside. If I were walking into a nightclub I could better understand it, he thought. The clergy don't look the way I'd imagine these days.

She opened the door to an office and asked him to have a seat. Gunnel Nilsson was a very attractive woman, although Wallander couldn't decide whether the fact that she was a vicar made her seem more so.

He saw a letter lying on her desk. He recognised the parish letterhead.

"The police received a letter on your letterhead. That's why I'm here."

He told her about the girl. The vicar seemed upset. When he asked her why, she explained that she had been sick for a few days and hadn't read the papers. Wallander showed her the letter.

"Do you have any idea who wrote it? Or who has access to your letterhead?"

She shook her head.

"Only women work here."

"It's not clear whether a man or a woman wrote the letter," Wallander pointed out.

"I don't know who it could be," she said.

"Does anyone in the office live in Helsingborg? Or drive there often?"

She shook her head again. Wallander could see that she was trying to be helpful.

"How many people work here?" he asked.

"There are four of us. And there's Andersson, who takes care of the garden. We also have a full-time watchman, Sture Rosell. But he mainly stays out at our churches. Any of them could have taken some letterhead from here, of course. Plus anyone who visited the vicar's office on business."

"You don't recognise the handwriting?"

"No."

"It's not illegal to pick up hitchhikers," said Wallander. "So why would someone write an anonymous letter? Because they wanted to hide the fact that they'd had been in Helsingborg? It's puzzling."

"I could ask whether anyone here was in Helsingborg that day," she said. "And try to match the handwriting."

"I'd appreciate your help," said Wallander, standing up. "You can reach me at the Ystad police station."

He wrote his phone number down for her. She followed him out.

"I've never met a female vicar before," he said.

"Many people are still surprised," she replied.

"In Ystad we have our first woman chief of police," he said. "Everything changes."

"For the better, I hope," she said and smiled.

Wallander looked at her, deciding she was quite beautiful. He didn't see a ring on her finger. He couldn't help thinking forbidden thoughts. She really was terribly attractive.

The man cutting the grass was now sitting on a bench smoking. Without really knowing why, Wallander sat down on the bench and started talking to him. He was about 60, and dressed in a blue work shirt, dirty corduroy trousers and a pair of ancient tennis shoes. Wallander noted that he was smoking unfiltered Chesterfields, the brand that his father had smoked when he was a child.

"She doesn't open the door when the office is closed," the man said thoughtfully. "This is the first time it's ever happened."

"The vicar is quite good-looking," said Wallander.

"She's nice too," said the man. "And she gives a good sermon. I don't know whether we've ever had such a good vicar. But many people would still rather have a man."

"They would?" said Wallander absentmindedly.

"Quite a few people would never think of having a woman. People in Skåne are conservative. For the most part."

The conversation died. It was as if both men had run out of steam. Wallander listened to the birds. He could smell the freshly mown grass. He remembered that he should contact Hans Vikander at the Östermalm police, and find out how the interview with Gustaf Wetterstedt's mother had gone. He had a lot to do. He certainly didn't have time to sit on a bench outside the parish offices in Smedstorp.

"Were you here to get a change of address certificate?" the man asked suddenly.

"I had a few questions to ask," he said, getting up.

The man squinted at him.

"I recognise you," he said. "Are you from Tomelilla?"

"No," said Wallander. "I'm originally from Malmö. But I've lived in Ystad for many years."

He was about to say goodbye when he noticed the white T-shirt showing under the man's unbuttoned work shirt. It advertised the ferry line between Helsingborg and Helsingør, in Denmark. He knew it could be a coincidence, but decided that it wasn't. He sat back down on the bench. The man stubbed out his cigarette in the grass, about to get up.

"Just a moment," said Wallander. "There's something I'd like to ask you about."

The man heard the change in Wallander's voice. He gave him a wary look.

"I'm a police officer," said Wallander. "I didn't come here to talk to the vicar. I came to talk to you. Why didn't you sign the letter you sent? About the girl you gave a lift from Helsingborg?"

It was a reckless move, he knew, in defiance of everything he had been taught. It was a punch below the belt – the police didn't have the right to lie to extract information, especially when no crime had been committed.

But it worked. The man jumped, caught off guard. Wallander could see him wondering how he could know about the letter.

"It's not against the law to write anonymous letters," he said. "Or to pick up hitchhikers. I just want to know why you did. And what time you picked her up and where you took her. The exact time. And whether she said anything during the journey."

"Now I recognise you," muttered the man. "You're the policeman who shot a man in the fog a few years ago. On the shooting range outside Ystad."

"You're right," said Wallander. "That was me. My name is Kurt Wallander."

"She was standing at the slip road of the southbound motorway," said the man suddenly. "It was 7 p.m. I had driven over to Helsingborg to buy a pair of shoes. My cousin has a shoe shop there. He gives me a discount. I don't usually pick up hitchhikers. But she looked so forlorn."

"What happened?"

"Nothing happened. What do you mean?"

"When you stopped the car. What language did she speak?"

"I have no idea what language it was, but it certainly wasn't Swedish. And I don't speak English. I said I was going to Tomelilla. She nodded. She nodded to everything I said."

"Did she have any luggage?"

"Not a thing."

"Not even a handbag?"

"Nothing."

"And then you drove off?"

"She sat in the back seat. She didn't speak. I thought there was something odd about the whole thing. I was sorry I'd picked her up."

"Why's that?"

"Maybe she wasn't going to Tomelilla at all. Who the hell goes to Tomelilla?"

"So she didn't say a word?"

"Not a word."

"What did she do?"

"Do?"

"Did she sleep? Look out the window? What?"

The man tried to remember.

"There was one thing I worried about afterwards. Every time a car passed us she crouched down. As if she didn't want to be seen."

"So she was frightened?"

"Definitely."

"What happened next?"

"I stopped at the roundabout on the outskirts of Tomelilla and let her out. To tell you the truth, I don't think she had any idea where she was."

"So she wasn't going to Tomelilla?"

"I think she just wanted to get out of Helsingborg. I drove off. But when I was almost home I thought, I can't just leave her there. So I drove back. But she was gone."

"How long did it take you to go back?"

"Not more than ten minutes."

Wallander thought for a moment.

"When you picked her up outside Helsingborg, she was standing at the slip road. Is it possible she'd had a lift to Helsingborg? Or was she coming from there?"

The man thought for a while.

"From Helsingborg," he said. "If she'd had a lift down from the north, she wouldn't have been standing where she was."

"And you never saw her again? You didn't look for her?"

"Why would I?"

"What time was this?"

"I let her off at 8 p.m. I remember the news came on the car radio just as she got out of the car."

Wallander thought about what he had heard. He knew he'd been lucky.

"Why did you write to the police?" he asked. "Why anonymously?"

"I read about the girl who'd burned herself to death," he said. "And I had a feeling that it might have been her. But I decided not to identify myself. I'm a married man. The fact that I picked up a female hitchhiker might have been misinterpreted."

Wallander could see that he was telling the truth.

"This conversation is off the record," he said. "But I will still have to ask you for your name and telephone number."

"My name is Sven Andersson," said the man. "I hope there won't be any trouble."

"Not if you've told me the truth," Wallander replied.

He wrote down the number.

"One more thing," he said. "Can you remember whether she was wearing a necklace?"

Andersson thought. Then he shook his head. Wallander got up and shook his hand.

"You've been a great help," he said.

"Was it her?" Andersson asked.

"Possibly," said Wallander. "The question we must answer is what she was doing in Helsingborg."

He left Andersson and walked to his car. Just as he opened the door his phone rang. His first thought was that the killer had struck again.

CHAPTER 18

Wallander answered the phone and spoke to Nyberg, who told him that the developed photos were on his desk. He felt great relief that it wasn't news of a third killing. As he drove away from Smedstorp, he realised he should learn to control his anxiety. There was no knowing whether the man had more victims on his list, but Wallander couldn't shake a sense of foreboding. They must continue the investigation as though nothing else was going to happen. Otherwise they'd waste their energy with fruitless worry. On the way back to Ystad, Wallander decided he would drive up to Hässleholm later that day to talk to Hugo Sandin.

He went straight to his office and wrote up a report of his conversation with Andersson. He tried to get hold of Martinsson, but all Ebba could tell him was that he had left the station without saying where he was going. Wallander tried to reach him on his mobile phone, but it was turned off. He was annoyed that Martinsson was often impossible to contact. At the next meeting, he would state that everyone must be contactable at all times. Then he remembered the photos. He had put his notebook on top of the envelope without noticing it. He turned on his desk lamp and looked at them one by one. Although he didn't really know what he had expected, he was disappointed. The photos showed nothing more than the view from Wetterstedt's house. They were taken from upstairs. He could see Lindgren's overturned boat and the sea, which was calm. There were no people in the pictures. The beach was deserted. Two of the pictures were blurry. He wondered why Wetterstedt had taken them – if, indeed, he had. He found a magnifying glass in a desk drawer, but still couldn't see anything of interest. He put them back in the envelope, deciding he'd ask someone else on the team to have a look, just to confirm he hadn't missed anything.

He was just about to call Hässleholm when a secretary knocked on the door with a fax from Hans Vikander in Stockholm. It was a report, five single-spaced pages, of the conversation he had had with Wetterstedt's mother. He read through it quickly. It was a precise report, but completely lacking in imagination. Every question was routine. An interview related to a criminal investigation should balance general enquiries with surprise questions. But perhaps he was being unfair to Hans Vikander. What was the chance that a woman in her 90s would say something unexpected about her son, whom she hardly ever saw and only exchanged brief phone calls with?

As he got some coffee, he thought idly about the female vicar in Smedstorp. Back in his room, he called the number in Hässleholm. A young man answered. Wallander introduced himself. It took several minutes for Hugo Sandin to come to the phone. He had a clear, resolute voice. Sandin told Wallander that he would meet him that same day. Wallander grabbed his notebook and wrote down the directions.

On the way to Hässleholm he stopped to eat. It was late afternoon when he turned off at the sign for the pottery shop and drove to the renovated mill. An old man was in the garden pulling up dandelions. When Wallander got out of the car the man came towards him, wiping his hands. Wallander couldn't believe that this vigorous man was over 80, that Sandin and his own father were almost the same age.

"I don't get many visitors," said Sandin. "All my friends are gone. I have one colleague from the old homicide squad who's still alive. But now he's in a home outside Stockholm and can't remember anything that happened after 1960. Old age really is shitty."

Sandin sounded just like Ebba. His own father almost never complained about his age. In an old coach house that had been converted into a showroom for the pottery there was a table with a thermos and cups set out. Out of courtesy, Wallander spent a few minutes admiring the ceramics on display. Sandin sat down at the table and served coffee.

"You're the first policeman I've met who's interested in ceramics," he said.

Wallander sat down. "Actually, I'm not," he admitted.

"Policemen usually like to fish," said Sandin. "In lonely, isolated mountain lakes. Or deep in the forests of Småland."

"I didn't know that," said Wallander. "I never go fishing."

Sandin looked at him intently.

"What do you do when you're not working?"

"I have a pretty hard time relaxing."

Sandin nodded in approval.

"Being a policeman is a calling," he said. "Just like being a doctor. We're always on duty. Whether we're in uniform or not."

Wallander said nothing, even though he disagreed. Once he might have believed that a policeman's job was his calling. But not any more. At least he didn't think so.

"So," Sandin prompted. "I read in the papers about what's going on in Ystad. Tell me what they left out."

Wallander recounted the circumstances surrounding the two murders. Now and then Sandin would interrupt with a question, always pertinent.

"So he may kill again," he said when Wallander had finished.

"We can't ignore that possibility."

Sandin shoved his chair back from the table and stretched out his legs.

"And you want me to tell you about Gustaf Wetterstedt," he said. "I'll be happy to. May I first ask you how you found out that a long time ago, I took a special interest in him?"

"A journalist in Ystad told me. Lars Magnusson. Unfortunately, quite an alcoholic."

"I don't recognise the name."

"Well, he's the one who knew about you."

Sandin sat silently, stroking his lips with one finger. Wallander sensed that he was looking for the right place to begin.

"The truth about Wetterstedt is straightforward," said Sandin. "He was a crook. He may have appeared to be a competent minister of justice. But he was totally unsuitable for the role."

"Why?"

"His activities were governed by attention to his career rather than the good of the country. That's the worst testimonial you can give a government minister."

"And yet he was in line to be leader of the party?"

Sandin shook his head vigorously.

"That's not true," he said. "That was media speculation. Within the party it was obvious that he could never be their leader. It's hard to see why he was even a member."

"But he was minister of justice for years. He couldn't have been totally unsuitable."

"You're too young to remember. But there was a change sometime in the 1950s. It was barely perceptible, but it happened. Sweden was sailing along on unbelievably fair winds. It seemed as though unlimited funds were available to obliterate poverty. At the same a change occurred in political life. Politicians were turning into professionals. Career politicians. Before, idealism had been a dominant part of political life. Now this idealism began to be diluted. People like Wetterstedt began their ascent. Youth associations became the hatcheries for the politicians of the future."

"Let's talk about the scandals," said Wallander, afraid that Sandin would get lost in political reminiscences.

"He used prostitutes," said Sandin. "He wasn't the only one, of course. But he had certain predilections that he subjected the girls to."

"I heard that one girl filed a complaint," said Wallander.

"Her name was Karin Bengtsson," said Sandin. "She came from an unhappy background in Eksjö. She ran away to Stockholm and came to our notice for the first time in 1954. A few years later she wound up with the group from which Wetterstedt picked his girls. In January 1957 she filed a complaint against him. He had slashed her feet with a razor blade. I met her myself at the time. She could hardly walk. Wetterstedt knew he'd gone too far. The complaint was dropped, and Bengtsson was paid off. She received money to invest in a clothing boutique in Västerås. In 1959, money magically appeared in her bank account, enough to buy a house. In 1960, she started holidaying in Mallorca every year."

"Who came up with the money?"

"Even then there were slush funds. The Swedish royal family had established a precedent by paying off women who had been intimate with the old king."

"Is Karin Bengtsson still alive?"

"She died in 1984. She never married. I didn't see her after she moved to Västerås. But she called once in a while, right until the last year of her life. She was usually drunk."

"Why did she call?"

"As soon as I heard that there was a prostitute who wanted to file a complaint against Wetterstedt, I got in touch with her. I wanted to help her. Her life had been destroyed. Her self-esteem wasn't very high."

"Why did you get involved?"

"I was pretty radical in those days. Too many policemen accepted the corruption. I didn't. No more than I do now."

"What happened later, when Karin Bengtsson was out of the picture?"

"Wetterstedt carried on as before. He slashed lots of girls. But none of them filed a complaint. Two of them did disappear."

"What do you mean?"

Sandin looked at Wallander in surprise.

"I mean they were never heard from again. We searched for them, tried to trace them. But they were gone."

"What do you think happened?"

"They were killed, of course. Dissolved in lime, dumped in the sea. How do I know?"

Wallander couldn't believe what he was hearing.

"Can this be true?" he said doubtfully. "It sounds incredible."

"What is the saying? Amazing but true?"

"You think Wetterstedt committed murder?"

Sandin shook his head.

"I'm not saying that. Actually I'm convinced he didn't. I don't know

183

exactly what happened, probably never will. But we can still draw conclusions, even if there's no real evidence."

"I'm having a hard time accepting this is true," said Wallander.

"It's absolutely true," said Sandin firmly. "Wetterstedt had no conscience. But nothing could be proved."

"There were many rumours about him."

"And they were all justified. Wetterstedt used his position and his power to satisfy his perverted sexual desires. But he was also mixed up in secret deals that made him rich."

"Art deals?"

"Art thefts, more likely. In my free time I tried to track down all the connections. I dreamed that one day I'd be able to slam such an airtight report down on the prosecutor's desk that Wetterstedt would not only be forced to resign, but would end up with a long prison sentence. Unfortunately I never got that far."

"You must have a great deal of material from those days, don't you?"

"I burnt it all a few years ago. In my son's kiln. At least ten kilos of paper."

Wallander swore under his breath. He hadn't dreamed that Sandin would get rid of the material he had gathered so laboriously.

"I still have a good memory," said Sandin. "I could probably remember everything I burned."

"Arne Carlman," said Wallander "Who was he?"

"A man who raised peddling art to a higher level," replied Sandin.

"In the spring of 1969 he was in Långholmen prison," said Wallander. "We got an anonymous tip-off that he had contacted Wetterstedt. And that they met after Carlman got out of jail."

"Carlman popped up now and then in reports. I think he wound up in Långholmen for something as simple as passing a bad cheque."

"Did you find links between him and Wetterstedt?"

"There was evidence that they had met as early as the late 1950s. Apparently they had a mutual interest in betting on the horses. Their names came up in connection with a raid on Täby racetrack around 1962. Wetterstedt's name was removed, since it wasn't considered wise to tell the public that the minister of justice had been frequenting a racetrack."

"What kind of dealings did they have?"

"Nothing we could pin down. They circled like planets in separate orbits which happened to cross now and then."

"I need to find that connection," said Wallander. "I'm convinced we have to find it to identify their killer."

"You can usually find what you're looking for if you look hard enough," said Sandin.

Wallander's mobile phone rang. He felt an icy fear. But he was wrong again. It was Hansson.

"I just wanted to know whether you'll be back today. Otherwise I'll set up a meeting for tomorrow."

"Has anything happened?"

"Nothing crucial. Everyone's up to their eyes in their own assignments."

"Tomorrow morning at 8 a.m.," said Wallander. "Not tonight."

"Svedberg went to the hospital to get his sunburn looked at," said Hansson.

"This happens every year," said Wallander. He hung up.

"You're in the papers a lot," said Sandin. "You seem to have gone your own way occasionally."

"Most of what they say isn't true," said Wallander.

"I often ask myself what it's like to be a policeman nowadays," said Sandin.

"So do I," said Wallander.

They got up and walked to Wallander's car. It was a beautiful evening.

"Can you think of anyone who might have wanted to kill Wetterstedt?" asked Wallander.

"There are probably quite a few," said Sandin.

Wallander stopped short.

"Maybe we're thinking about this the wrong way," he said. "Maybe we should separate the investigations. Not look for a common denominator, but for two separate solutions. And find the connection that way."

"The murders were committed by the same man," said Sandin, "so the investigations have to be interlinked. Otherwise you might end up on the wrong track."

Wallander nodded.

"Call me again sometime," said Sandin. "I have all the time in the world. Growing old means loneliness. A long wait for the inevitable."

"Did you ever regret joining the police?" asked Wallander.

"Never," said Sandin. "Why would I?"

"Just wondering," said Wallander. "Thanks for taking the time to talk to me."

"You'll catch him," said Sandin encouragingly. "Even if it takes a while."

Wallander nodded and got into the car. As he drove off he could see Sandin in the rear-view mirror, pulling dandelions from the lawn.

It was 7.45 p.m. by the time Wallander got back to Ystad. He parked the car outside his building and was just about to walk through the main door when he remembered that he hadn't any food in the house. And that he had forgotten to have the car inspected again. He swore out loud.

He walked into town and ate dinner at the Chinese restaurant on the square. He was the only customer. After dinner he strolled down to the harbour and walked out on the pier. As he watched the boats rocking in their moorings he thought about the two conversations he had had that day.

Dolores María Santana had stood at the motorway slip road from Helsingborg one evening, looking for a ride. She didn't speak Swedish and she was frightened. All they knew about her was that she was born in the Dominican Republic.

He stared at an old, well-kept wooden boat as he formulated his questions. Why and how did she come to Sweden? What was she running from? Why had she burned herself to death?

He walked farther out along the pier.

There was a party going on board a yacht. Someone raised a glass and said "*Skål*" to Wallander. He nodded back and raised an invisible glass.

At the end of the pier he sat down on a bollard and went over his conversation with Sandin. Everything was one big tangle. He couldn't see any openings, anything that might lead to a breakthrough.

At the same time he still felt a sense of dread. He couldn't get away from the possibility that it might happen again. He tossed a fistful of gravel into the water and got up. The party on the yacht was in full swing. He walked back through town. The heap of dirty clothes still lay in the middle of his floor. He wrote himself a note and put it on the kitchen table. *M.O.T., damn it!* Then he switched on the TV and lay down on the sofa.

A little later he phoned Baiba. Her voice was clear and close by.

"You sound tired," she said. "Have you got a lot to do?"

"It's not so bad," he lied. "But I miss you."

He heard her laugh.

"We'll see each other soon," she said.

"What were you really doing in Tallinn?"

She laughed again.

"Meeting another man. What did you think?"

"Just that."

"You need some sleep," she said. "I can hear that all the way from Riga. I hear Sweden's doing well in the World Cup."

"Are you interested in sports?" asked Wallander, surprised.

"Sometimes. Especially when Latvia is playing."

"People here are completely nuts about it."

"But not you?"

"I promise to improve. When Sweden plays Brazil I'll try to stay up and watch."

He heard her laugh again. He wanted to say something more, but he couldn't think of anything. After he hung up he went back to the TV. For a while he tried to watch a movie. Then he turned it off and went to bed. Before he fell asleep he thought about his father. This autumn they would take a trip to Italy.

CHAPTER 19

The fluorescent hands of the clock twisted like snakes and showed 7.10 p.m. on Tuesday 28 June. A few hours later Sweden would play Brazil. This was part of his plan. Everybody would be focused on their TV sets. No-one would think about what was happening outside in the summer night.

The basement floor was cool under his bare feet. He had been sitting in front of his mirrors since early morning. He had completed his great transformation several hours earlier, changing the pattern on his right cheek. He had painted the circular decoration with blue-black paint. Until now he had used blood-red paint. His face was even more frightening.

He put down the last brush and thought about the task awaiting him. It would be the greatest sacrifice for his sister yet, even though he had been forced to alter his plans. For a brief moment the evil forces surrounding him had got the upper hand. He had spent an entire night in the shadows below his sister's window planning his strategy. He'd sat between the two scalps and waited for the power from the earth to enter him. With his torch he had read from the holy book she had given him, and he realised that nothing prevented him from changing the order that he had prepared.

The last victim was to have been their evil father. But since the man who was supposed to meet his fate this evening had left the country suddenly, the sequence would have to be changed.

He had listened to Geronimo's heart beating in his chest. The beats were like signals from the past. His heart drummed a message: the most important thing was not to waver from his sacred task. The earth under his feet was already crying out for the third retribution.

He would wait until the third man returned from abroad. Their father would have to take his place.

As he'd sat in front of the mirrors, undergoing the great transformation, he'd looked forward to meeting his father with special anticipation. This mission required careful preparation. He'd begun by readying his tools. It had taken him more than two hours to attach a blade to the toy axe he had been given by his father as a birthday present. He was seven at the time. Even then he knew that one day he would use it against the man who had given it to him. Now the moment had finally arrived. He had reinforced the badly decorated plastic shaft with special tape used by ice hockey players.

You don't know what it's called. It's not for chopping wood. It's a tomahawk.

He felt violent contempt when he remembered how his father had given the toy to him so long ago. It was a plastic replica manufactured in an Asian country. Now, with a proper blade, he had transformed it into a real axe.

He waited until 8.30, going over the plan once more. He checked his hands, noting that they weren't shaking. Everything was under control. The arrangements he had made over the past two days would ensure that things would go well.

He packed up his weapons, a glass bottle wrapped in a handkerchief, and a rope in his backpack. Then he pulled on his helmet, turned out the light, and left the room. When he came out onto the street he looked up at the sky. It was cloudy. It could rain. He started up the moped he had stolen the day before and rode to the centre of Malmö. At the train station he entered a phone booth. He had selected one in advance that was out of the way. On one side of the window he had pasted up a fake poster for a concert at a youth club. There was no-one around. He pulled off his helmet and stood with his face pressed against the poster. Then he stuck in his phone card and dialled the number. With his left hand he held a rag over his mouth. It was just before 9 p.m. He waited as the phone rang. He was totally calm. His father answered. Hoover could hear his irritation.

That meant he had started drinking and didn't want to be disturbed.

He spoke into the rag, holding the receiver away from his mouth.

"This is Peter," he said. "I've got something that should interest you."

"What is it?" His father was still annoyed. But he believed it was Peter calling.

"Stamps. Worth almost half a million."

His father hesitated.

"Are you sure?"

"At least half a million. Maybe more."

"Speak up a little, will you?"

"We must have a bad connection."

"Where are they coming from?"

"A house in Limhamn."

His father sounded less irritable. His interest was caught. Hoover had chosen stamps because his father had once taken his own collection – which Hoover had worked on for a long time – and sold it.

"Can't it wait until tomorrow? The match against Brazil is starting soon."

"I'm leaving for Denmark tomorrow. Either you take them tonight, or someone else will."

Hoover knew his father would never let such a large sum of money fetch up in someone else's pocket. He waited, still completely calm.

"All right, I'll come," his father said. "Where are you?"

"At the boat club in Limhamn. The car park."

"Why aren't you in Malmö?"

"I told you it was a house in Limhamn, didn't I?"

"I'll be there," said his father.

Hoover hung up and put on his helmet.

He left the telephone card sitting in the phone. He had plenty of time to ride out to Limhamn. His father always got undressed before he started drinking. And he never did anything in a hurry. His laziness was as vast as his greed. He started up the moped and rode through the city until he came out on the road that led to Limhamn. There were only a few cars in the car park outside the boat club. He ditched the moped behind some bushes and threw away the keys. He pulled off his helmet and took out the axe. He put the helmet into his backpack carefully so he wouldn't damage the glass bottle.

Then he waited. His father usually parked his van in one corner of the car park when he was delivering stolen property. Hoover guessed that he would do so now. His father was a creature of habit. And he was already drunk, his judgement muddled and reactions dulled.

After 20 minutes Hoover heard the van. The headlights swept across the trees before his father turned into the car park. Just as Hoover had expected, he stopped in the corner. Hoover ran barefoot across the car park until he reached the van. When he heard his father open the driver's door, he moved quickly around to the other side. His father looked out towards the car park with his back to him. Hoover raised the axe and struck him on the back of the head with the blunt end. This was the most critical moment. He didn't want to hit him so hard that he'd die, but hard enough that his father, who was big and very strong, would be knocked out.

His father fell without a sound to the pavement. Hoover waited a moment with the axe raised, but he lay still. He reached for the car keys and unlocked the side doors of the van, dragging him over to it. It took Hoover several minutes to get the whole body inside. He got his backpack, climbed into the van, and shut the doors. He turned on the overhead light. His father was still unconscious. With the rope he tied his hands behind his back, and then his legs to a post supporting one of the seats. Next he taped his mouth shut and turned off the light. He climbed into the driver's seat and started the engine. His father had taught him to drive a few years earlier. He pulled out of the car park and headed towards the ring road that skirted Malmö. Since his face was painted he didn't want to drive where the streetlights could shine through the van's windows. He drove out onto the E65 and continued east. It was just before 10 p.m. The game was about to begin.

He had found the place by accident. He had been on his way back to Malmö after observing the police at work on the beach outside Ystad, the beach where he had carried out the first sacred task given

191

to him by his sister. He was driving along the coast when he discovered the dock, which was almost impossible to see from the road. He realised at once that he had found the right place.

An hour later he reached the place and turned off the road with his headlights off. His father was still unconscious but was moaning softly. He hurried to loosen the rope tied to the seat and pulled him out of the van. The man groaned as Hoover dragged his body down to the dock. He turned him over on his back and tied his arms and legs to its iron rings. His father looked like an animal skin stretched out to dry. He was dressed in a wrinkled suit, his shirt unbuttoned down to his belly. Hoover pulled off his shoes and socks. Then he got the backpack from the van. There was a light breeze. A few cars drove past up on the road, but their headlights missed the dock.

When he returned, his father was conscious. His eyes were wide. He jerked his head back and forth, thrashing his arms and legs. Hoover couldn't resist stopping in the shadows to watch him. He no longer saw a human being before him. His father had undergone the transformation he had planned for him. He was an animal.

Hoover came out of the shadows and went out on the dock. His father stared at him. Hoover realised he didn't recognise him. He thought about the fear he had felt when his father stared at him. Now the tables were turned. Terror had changed its shape. He leaned down close to his father's face, so that he could see through the paint and realise it was his own son. This would be the last thing he would see. This would be the image he would carry with him when he died.

Hoover had unscrewed the cap on the glass bottle and was holding it behind his back. Quickly he poured a few drops of hydrochloric acid into his father's left eye. Somewhere underneath the tape the man started screaming. He struggled with all his might. Hoover pulled open his other eyelid and poured acid into that eye. Then he stood up and threw the bottle into the sea. Before him was a beast thrashing back and forth in its death throes. Hoover looked down at his own hands again. His fingers were quivering a little. That was all. The beast lying on the dock in front of him was twitching spasmodically.

Hoover took his knife out of his backpack and cut off the skin from the top of the animal's head. He raised the scalp to the night sky. Then he took his axe and smashed it straight through the beast's forehead with such force that the blade stuck in the wood underneath.

It was over. Soon his sister would be brought back to life.

Just before 1 a.m. he drove into Ystad. The town was deserted. For a long time he had wondered whether he was doing the right thing. But Geronimo's beating heart had convinced him. He had seen the police fumbling on the beach, he had watched them move as if in a fog outside the farm he had visited. Geronimo had exhorted him to defy them.

He turned in at the railway station. He had already picked the spot. Work was under way to replace some old sewerage pipes. There was a tarpaulin covering the excavation. He turned off the headlights and rolled down the window. From a distance he could hear some men yelling drunkenly. He got out of the van and drew back part of the tarpaulin. Then he listened again. Silence. Quickly he opened the doors of the van, dragged his father's body out, and shoved him into the hole. He replaced the tarpaulin, started the engine and drove off. It was just before 2 a.m. when he parked the van in the outdoor car park at Sturup Airport. He checked carefully to see if he had forgotten anything. There was a lot of blood in the van. He had blood on his feet. He thought about all the confusion he was going to cause, how the police would fumble even more.

Suddenly he stopped and stood motionless.

The man who had left the country might not return. He'd need a replacement. He thought about the policemen he had seen on the beach by the overturned boat. He thought about the ones he had seen outside the farmhouse where the Midsummer party was held. One of them. One of them would be sacrificed so that his sister could come back to life. He would choose one. He would find out their names and then toss stones onto a grid, just as Geronimo had done, and he would kill the one that chance selected for him.

He pulled the helmet down over his head. Then he went over to his moped, which he had ridden there the day before and left parked under a lamppost, taking a bus back to Malmö. He started up the engine and rode off. It was already light when he buried his father's scalp underneath his sister's window.

Carefully he unlocked the door to the flat in Rosengård. He stood still and listened. Then he peeked into the room where his brother lay sleeping. Everything was quiet. His mother's bed was empty. She was lying on the sofa in the living-room, sleeping with her mouth open. Next to her on the table stood a half-empty wine bottle. He covered her gently with a blanket. Then he locked himself in the bathroom and wiped the paint from his face.

It was almost 6 a.m. before he undressed and went to bed. He could hear a man coughing outside on the street. His mind was completely blank. He fell asleep at once.

Skåne

29 June– 4 July 1994

CHAPTER 20

The man who lifted the tarpaulin screamed. Then he fled.

One of the ticket agents was standing outside the railway station smoking a cigarette. It was just before 7 a.m. on the morning of 29 June, and it was going to be a hot day. The agent was wrenched from his thoughts, which were focused less on selling tickets than on the trip he was about to take to Greece. He turned when he heard the scream. He saw the man drop the tarpaulin and run off towards the ferry terminal. The ticket agent flicked away his cigarette butt and walked over to the pit. He stared down at a bloody head for a moment, then dropped the tarpaulin as if it had burned him. He ran into the station, tripping over a couple of suitcases left in the middle of the floor, and grabbed one of the phones inside the stationmaster's office.

The call arrived at the Ystad station on the 90–000 line just after 7 a.m. Svedberg, who was in unusually early that morning, was summoned to take the call. When he heard the agent talking about a bloody head he froze. His hand shook as he wrote down a single word, *station*, and hung up. He dialled the wrong number twice before managing to get hold of Wallander.

"I think it's happened again," said Svedberg.

For a few brief seconds Wallander didn't understand what Svedberg meant, even though every time the phone rang he feared that very thing. But now he experienced a moment of shock, or perhaps a desperate attempt at denial.

He knew he would never forget this moment. Fleetingly he thought that it was like having a premonition of his own death, a moment when denial and escape were impossible. *I think it's happened again.* He felt as if he were a wind-up toy. Svedberg's stammered words were like hands twisting the key attached to his back. He was wrenched out of his sleep and his bed, out of dreams he couldn't remember but which might have been pleasant. He got dressed in a desperate frenzy, buttons popping off, and his shoelaces flopped untied as he raced down the stairs and outside.

When he came screeching to a stop in his car, which still needed its M.O.T., Svedberg was already there. Directed by Norén, some officers were busy rolling out the striped crime-scene tape. Svedberg was awkwardly patting the weeping ticket agent on the shoulder, while some men in blue overalls stared into the pit, now transformed into a nightmare. Wallander left his door open and ran over to Svedberg. Why he ran he didn't really know. Maybe his internal police mechanism had started to speed up. Or maybe he was so afraid of what he was going to see that he simply didn't dare approach it slowly.

Svedberg was white in the face. He nodded towards the pit. Wallander walked slowly over and took several deep breaths before looking into the hole.

It was worse than he could have imagined. He was looking straight into a dead man's brain. Ann-Britt Höglund arrived next to Wallander. She flinched and turned away. Her reaction made him start to think clearly.

"No doubt about it," he said to Höglund, turning back to the pit. "It's him again."

She was very pale. Wallander was afraid she was going to faint. He put his arm around her shoulders.

"Are you OK?" he asked.

She nodded.

Martinsson arrived with Hansson. Wallander saw them both give a start when they looked in the hole. He was overcome with rage. The man who had done this had to be stopped.

"It must be the same killer," said Hansson in an unsteady voice. "Isn't it ever going to end? I can't take responsibility for this any more. Did Björk know about this before he left? I'm going to ask for reinforcements from the National Criminal Bureau."

"Do that," said Wallander. "But first let's get him out of there and see whether we can solve this ourselves."

Hansson stared in disbelief at Wallander, who realised that Hansson thought they were going to have to lift the dead man out themselves.

A large crowd had gathered outside the cordon. Wallander remembered what he had sensed in connection with Carlman's murder. He took Norén aside and asked him to borrow a camera from Nyberg and take pictures, as discreetly as possible, of the people standing outside the cordon. Meanwhile the emergency van from the fire department had arrived on the scene. Nyberg was directing his crew around the pit. Wallander went over to him, trying to avoid looking at the corpse.

"Once again," said Nyberg. He wasn't being cynical. Their eyes met.

"We've got to catch him," said Wallander.

"As soon as possible, I hope," said Nyberg. He lay down on his stomach so he could study the dead man's face. When he straightened up again he called to Wallander, who was just heading off to talk to Svedberg. He came back.

"Did you see his eyes?" asked Nyberg.

Wallander shook his head.

"What about them?"

Nyberg grimaced.

"Apparently the murderer wasn't content with taking a scalp this time," said Nyberg. "It looks like he poked his eyes out too."

"What do you mean?"

"The man in the pit doesn't have any eyes," said Nyberg. "There are two holes where they used to be."

It took them two hours to get the body out. Wallander talked to the workman who had lifted the tarpaulin and the ticket agent who had stood by the steps of the station dreaming of Greece. He noted the times that they had seen the body. He asked Nyberg to search the dead man's pockets to see if they could establish his identity, but they were empty.

"Nothing at all?" asked Wallander in surprise.

"Not a thing," said Nyberg. "But something may have fallen out. We'll look around down there."

They hauled him up in a sling. Wallander forced himself to look at his face. Nyberg was right. The man had no eyes. The torn-off hair made it seem that it was a dead animal, not a human being lying on the plastic sheet at his feet.

Wallander sat down on the steps of the station. He studied his notes. He called Martinsson, who was talking to a doctor.

"We know he hasn't been here long," he said. "I talked to the workmen replacing the sewerage pipes. They put the tarpaulin down at 4 p.m. yesterday. So the body was put there between then and 7 a.m. this morning."

"There are a lot of people around here in the evenings," said Martinsson. "People taking a walk, traffic to and from the station and the ferry terminal. It must have happened during the night."

"How long has he been dead?" asked Wallander. "That's what I want to know. And who he is."

Nyberg hadn't found a wallet. They had nothing to help establish the man's identity. Höglund came over and sat down next to them.

"Hansson's talking about requesting reinforcements from the National Criminal Bureau," she said.

"I know," said Wallander. "But he won't do anything until I tell him to. What did the doctor say?"

She looked at her notes.

"About 45 years old," she said. "Strong, well-built."

"That makes him the youngest one so far," said Wallander.

"Strange place to hide the body," said Martinsson. "Did he think that work would stop during the summer holiday?"

"Maybe he just wanted to get rid of it," said Höglund.

"Then why did he pick this pit?" asked Martinsson. "It must have been a lot of trouble to get him into it. And there was the risk that someone might see him."

"Maybe he wanted the body to be found," Wallander said thoughtfully. "We can't rule out that possibility."

They looked at him in astonishment, waiting for him to explain, but he remained silent.

The body was taken away to Malmö. They left for the police station. Norén had been taking pictures of the large crowd milling around outside the cordoned-off area.

Mats Ekholm had shown up earlier that morning, and stared at the corpse for a long time. Wallander had gone over to him.

"You got your wish," he said. "Another victim."

"I didn't wish for this," replied Ekholm, shaking his head.

Now Wallander regretted his remark. He would have to explain to Ekholm what he'd meant.

Just after 10 a.m. they closed the door to the conference room, Hansson again giving instructions that calls weren't to be put through. But they had barely started the meeting when the phone rang. Hansson snatched the receiver and barked into it, red with anger. But he sank slowly back in his chair. Wallander knew at once that someone very important was on the line. Hansson adopted Björk's obsequiousness. He made some brief comments, answered questions, but mostly listened. When the call was over he placed the receiver back as if it were a fragile antique.

"Let me guess – the national police board," said Wallander. "Or the chief public prosecutor. Or a TV reporter."

"The commissioner of the national police," replied Hansson. "He expressed as much dissatisfaction as encouragement."

"Sounds like a strange combination," Höglund said drily.

"He's welcome to come down here and help," said Svedberg.

"What does he know about police work?" Martinsson spluttered. "Absolutely nothing."

Wallander tapped his pen on the table. Everyone was upset and uncertain of what to do next, and he knew they had very little time before they would be subjected to a barrage of criticism. They would never be totally immune from outside pressure. They could only counteract it by focusing their attention inward on the shifting centre of the search. He tried to collect his thoughts, knowing that they didn't have a thing to go on.

"What do we know?" Wallander began, looking around the table. He felt like a vicar who had lost his faith. But he had to say something to spur them on again as a unit.

"The man wound up in that pit sometime last night. Let's assume that it took place in the early hours. We can assume that he wasn't murdered there. There would have been a lot of blood at the place where he was killed. Nyberg hadn't found a thing by the time we left, so he must have been transported there in a vehicle. Maybe the people working at the hot dog stand next to the railway crossing noticed something. It appears that he was killed by a powerful blow from the front that went all the way through his skull."

Martinsson turned completely white. He got up and left the room without a word. Wallander decided to carry on without him.

"He was scalped like the others. And he had his eyes put out. The doctor wasn't sure how, but there were some spots near the eyes that might indicate a corrosive agent. Maybe our specialist has some opinion on what this indicates."

Wallander turned to Ekholm.

"Not yet," said Ekholm. "It's too soon."

"We don't need a comprehensive analysis," said Wallander firmly. "At this stage we have to think out loud. Maybe we'll uncover the truth. We don't believe in miracles. But we don't have much else to go on."

"I think the fact that the eyes were put out means something," said Ekholm. "We can assume that the same man is involved. This victim was younger than the other two. And he suffered the loss of his sight, presumably while he was still alive. It must have been excruciating. The murderer took scalps from the first two he killed, and this time too. But he also blinded his victim. Why? What kind of revenge was he exacting this time?"

"The man must be a psychopath," said Hansson suddenly. "A serial killer of the kind I thought existed only in the United States. But here? In Ystad? In Skåne?"

"There's still something controlled about him," said Ekholm. "He knows what he wants. He kills and scalps. He pokes out or dissolves the eyes. There's nothing to indicate unbridled rage. Psychopath, yes. But one in control of his actions."

"Are there instances of something like this having happened before?" asked Höglund.

"Not that I can recall," replied Ekholm. "At least not here in Sweden. In America studies have been done on the role that eyes have played in psychopathic killings. I'll read about it today."

Wallander had been half-listening to the conversation. A thought that he couldn't quite yet grasp had popped into his head. It was something about eyes. Something somebody had said about eyes. What was it? He turned his attention to the meeting. But the thought lingered like an uneasy ache.

"Anything else?" he asked Ekholm.

"Not at the moment."

Martinsson came back into the room. He was still very pale.

"I've got an idea," said Wallander. "After hearing Mats I'm convinced that the murder took place elsewhere. The man must have screamed. Someone would have seen or heard something if it happened outside the railway station. We'll have to confirm this. But for the time being let's say I'm right. Why then did he pick that pit to hide the body? I talked to one of the workmen. Persson was his name, Erik Persson. He said that the pit had been excavated on Monday afternoon. Less than two days ago. The killer could have stumbled on it by chance, of course. But that doesn't fit with the fact that he seems to plan everything he does carefully. The killer must have been outside the railway station at some time after Monday afternoon. He must have looked into the pit to see if it was deep enough. We'll need to interview all the workmen. Did they notice anybody hanging around? And did the staff at the railway station notice anything?"

Everyone around the table was listening intently, making him feel that his ideas weren't completely off track.

"I also think the question of whether it was meant as a hiding place is crucial," he went on. "He must have known that the body would be found the next morning. So why did he choose the pit? So it would be discovered? Or is there another explanation?"

Everyone in the room waited for him to continue.

"Is he taunting us?" said Wallander. "Does he want to help us? Or is he trying to fool us? Does he want to trick me into thinking exactly the way I'm thinking now? What would the alternative be?"

No-one answered him.

"The timing is also important," said Wallander. "This murder was very recent. That might assist us."

"For that we need help," said Hansson. Clearly he'd been waiting for an opportunity to bring up the question of reinforcements.

"Not yet," said Wallander. "Let's decide later on today. Or maybe tomorrow. As far as I know, no-one in this room is going on holiday soon. Let's keep it to this group for a few more days. Then we can seek reinforcements if necessary."

"What about the connection?" said Wallander in conclusion. "Now there's one more person to fit into the puzzle we're trying to piece together."

He looked around the table once more.

"We have to realise that he could strike again," he said. "In fact, we should assume that he will."

The meeting was over. They all knew what they had to do. Wallander remained sitting at the table while the others filed out of the door. He was trying to recapture that thought. He was sure that it was something someone had said in relation to the investigation. Somebody had mentioned eyes. He thought back to the day he'd first heard that Wetterstedt had been found murdered. He searched his memory, but found nothing. Irritated, he tossed his pen aside and went out to the canteen for a cup of coffee. When he got back to his office he set the coffee cup on his desk and was about to shut the door when he saw Svedberg coming down the hall. Svedberg was walking fast. He only did that when something important had happened. Wallander instantly got a knot in his stomach. Not another one, he thought. We just can't cope.

"I think we've found the scene of the crime," said Svedberg.

"Where?"

"Our colleagues at Sturup found a delivery van soaked in blood in the airport car park."

A van. That would fit.

A few minutes later they left the station. Wallander couldn't remember ever in his life feeling that he had so little time. When they reached the edge of town he told Svedberg to turn on the police lights. In the fields beside the road a farmer was harvesting his rape.

CHAPTER 21

They arrived at Sturup Airport. The air felt stagnant in the oppressive heat of the late morning. In a very short period of time they determined that the murder had very likely taken place in the van. They also thought they knew who the dead man was.

The van was a late-1960s Ford, with sliding side doors, and painted black sloppily, the original grey showing through in patches. The body was dented in many places. Parked in an isolated spot, it resembled an old prizefighter who had just been counted out, hanging on the ropes in his corner.

Wallander knew some of the officers at Sturup. He also knew that he wasn't particularly popular after an incident that had occurred the year before. The side doors of the Ford were standing open. Some forensic technicians were already inspecting it. An officer named Waldemarsson came to meet them. Even though they had driven like madmen from Ystad, Wallander tried to appear totally nonchalant.

"It's not a pretty sight," said Waldemarsson as they shook hands.

Wallander and Svedberg went over to the Ford and looked in. Waldemarsson shone a torch inside. The floor of the van was covered with blood.

"We heard on the morning news that he had struck again," said Waldemarsson. "I called and talked to a woman detective whose name I can't remember."

"Ann-Britt Höglund," said Svedberg.

"Whatever her name is, she said you were looking for a crime scene," Waldemarsson went on. "And a vehicle."

Wallander nodded.

"When did you find the van?" he asked.

"We check the car park every day. We've had a number of car thefts here. But you know all about that."

Wallander nodded again. During the investigation into the export of stolen cars to Poland he had been in contact with the airport police several times.

"The van wasn't here yesterday afternoon," said Waldemarsson. "It couldn't have been here more than 18 hours."

"Who's the owner?" asked Wallander.

Waldemarsson took a notebook out of his pocket.

"Björn Fredman," he said. "He lives in Malmö. We called his number but didn't get an answer."

"Could he be the one we found in the pit?"

"We know something about Fredman," said Waldemarsson. "Malmö has given us information. He was known as a fence, and has done time on several occasions."

"A fence," said Wallander, feeling a flash of excitement. "For works of art?"

"They didn't say. You'll have to talk with our colleagues."

"Who should I ask for?" he demanded, taking his mobile phone out of his pocket.

"An Inspector Sten Forsfält."

Wallander got hold of Forsfält. He explained who he was. For a few seconds the conversation was drowned out by the noise of a plane. Wallander thought of the trip to Italy he planned to take with his father.

"First of all, we have to identify the man," said Wallander when the plane had climbed away in the direction of Stockholm.

"What did he look like?" asked Forsfält. "I met Fredman several times."

Wallander gave as accurate a description as he could.

"It might be him," said Forsfält. "He was big, at any rate."

Wallander thought for a moment.

"Can you drive to the hospital?" he asked. "We need a positive identification as quickly as possible."

"Sure, I can do that," said Forsfält.

"Prepare yourself, because it's a hideous sight," said Wallander. "He had his eyes poked out. Or burnt away."

Forsfält didn't reply.

"We're coming to Malmö," said Wallander. "We need some help getting into his flat. Did he have any family?"

"He was divorced," said Forsfält. "Last time he was in, it was for battery."

"I thought it was for fencing stolen property."

"That too. Fredman kept busy. But not doing anything legal. He was consistent on that score."

Wallander said goodbye and called Hansson to give him a brief run-down.

"Good," said Hansson. "Let me know as soon as you have more information. By the way, do you know who called?"

"The national commissioner again?"

"Almost. Lisa Holgersson. Björk's successor. She wished us luck. Said she just wanted to check on the situation."

"It's great that people are wishing us luck," said Wallander, who couldn't understand why Hansson was telling him about the call in such an ironic tone.

Wallander borrowed Waldemarsson's torch and shone it inside the van. He saw a footprint in the blood. He leaned forward.

"That's not a shoe print. It's a left foot."

"A bare foot?" said Svedberg. "So he wades around barefoot in the blood of the people he kills?"

"We don't know that it's a he," said Wallander dubiously.

They said goodbye to Waldemarsson and his colleagues. Wallander waited in the car while Svedberg ran to the airport café and bought some sandwiches.

"The prices are outrageous," he complained when he returned. Wallander didn't bother answering.

"Just drive," was all he said.

It was past midday when they stopped outside the police station in

Malmö. As he stepped out of the car Wallander saw Björk heading towards him. Björk stopped and stared, as if he had caught Wallander doing something he shouldn't.

"You, here?" he said.

"We need you back," said Wallander in an attempt at a joke. Then he explained what had happened.

"It's appalling what's going on," said Björk, and Wallander could hear that his anxious tone was genuine. It hadn't occurred to him before that Björk might miss the people he worked with for so many years in Ystad.

"Nothing is quite the same," said Wallander.

"How's Hansson doing?"

"I don't think he's enjoying his role."

"He can call if he needs any help."

"I'll tell him."

Björk left and they went into the station. Forsfält still wasn't back from the hospital. They drank coffee in the canteen while they waited.

"I wonder what it would be like to work here," said Svedberg, looking around at all the policemen eating lunch.

"One day we may all wind up here," said Wallander. "If they close down the district. One police station per county."

"That would never work."

"No, but it could happen. The national police board and those bureaucrats have one thing in common. They always try to do the impossible."

Forsfält appeared. They stood up, shook hands, and followed him to his office. Wallander had a favourable impression of him. He reminded him of Rydberg. Forsfält was at least 60, with a friendly face. He had a slight limp. Wallander sat down and looked at some pictures of laughing children tacked up on the wall. He guessed that they were Forsfält's grandchildren.

"Björn Fredman," said Forsfält. "It's him, all right. He looked appalling. Who would do such a thing?"

"If we only knew," said Wallander. "Who was Fredman?"

"A man of about 45 who never had an honest job in his life," Forsfält began. "I don't have all of the details. But I've asked the computer people for his records. He was a fence and he did time for battery. Quite violent attacks, as I recall."

"Was he involved in fencing stolen art?"

"Not that I can remember."

"That's a pity," said Wallander. "That would have linked him to Wetterstedt and Carlman."

"I have a hard time imagining that Fredman and Wetterstedt could have had much use for each other," said Forsfält.

"Why not?"

"Let me put it bluntly," said Forsfält. "Björn Fredman was what used to be called a rough customer. He drank a lot and got into fights. His education was nearly nonexistent, although he could read, write, and do arithmetic tolerably well. His interests could hardly be called sophisticated. And he was a brutal man. I interrogated him myself a number of times. His vocabulary consisted almost exclusively of swear words."

Wallander listened. When Forsfält stopped he looked at Svedberg.

"We're back to square one again," Wallander said slowly. "If there's no connection between Fredman and the other two."

"There could be things I don't know about," said Forsfält.

"I'm just thinking out loud," said Wallander.

"What about his family?" said Svedberg. "Do they live here in Malmö?"

"He's been divorced for a number of years," said Forsfält. "I'm sure of that."

He picked up the phone and made a call. After a few minutes a secretary came in with a file on Fredman and handed it to Forsfält. He took a quick look and then put it down on the table.

"He got divorced in 1991. His wife stayed in their flat with the children. It's in Rosengård. There are three children. The youngest was just a baby when they split up. Fredman moved back to a flat on Stenbrottsgatan that he'd kept for many years. He used it mostly as an office and storeroom. I don't think his wife knew about it. That's where he also took his other women."

"We'll start with his flat," said Wallander. "The family can wait. You'll see that they're notified of his death?"

Forsfält nodded. Svedberg had gone out to the hall to call Ystad. Wallander stood by the window, trying to decide what was most important. There seemed to be no link between the first two victims and Fredman. For the first time he had a premonition that they were following a false lead. Was there a completely different explanation for the murders? He decided he would go over all the investigative material that evening with an open mind. Svedberg came back and stood next to him.

"Hansson was relieved," he said.

Wallander nodded. But he didn't say a word.

"According to Martinsson an important message came from Interpol about the girl," Svedberg went on.

Wallander hadn't been paying attention. He had to ask Svedberg to repeat himself. The girl seemed to be part of something that had happened a long time ago. And yet he knew that sooner or later he'd have to take up her case again. They stood in silence.

"I don't like it in Malmö," said Svedberg suddenly. "I only feel happy when I'm home in Ystad."

Svedberg hated to leave the town of his birth. At the station it had become a running joke. Wallander wondered when he himself ever really felt happy. But then he remembered the last time. When Linda appeared at his door so early on Sunday morning.

Forsfält came to get them. They took the lift down to the car park and then drove out towards an industrial area north of the city. The wind had started to blow. The sky was still cloudless. Wallander sat next to Forsfält in the front seat.

"Did you know Rydberg?" he asked.

"Did I know Rydberg?" he replied slowly. "I certainly did. Quite well. He used to come to Malmö sometimes."

Wallander was surprised at his answer. He'd always thought that

Rydberg had discarded everything to do with the job, including his friends.

"He was the one who taught me everything I know," said Wallander.

"It was tragic that he left us so soon," said Forsfält. "He should have lived longer. He'd always dreamed of going to Iceland."

"Iceland?"

Forsfält nodded.

"That was his big dream. To go to Iceland. But it didn't happen."

Wallander was struck by the realisation that Rydberg had kept something from him. He wouldn't have guessed that Rydberg dreamt of a pilgrimage to Iceland. He hadn't imagined that Rydberg had any dreams at all, or indeed any secrets.

Forsfält pulled up outside a three-storey block of flats. He pointed to a row of windows on the ground floor with the curtains drawn. The building was old and poorly maintained. The glass on the main door was boarded up with a piece of wood. Wallander had a feeling that he was walking into a building that should no longer exist. Isn't this building's existence in defiance of the constitution? he thought sarcastically. There was a stench of urine in the stairwell.

Forsfält unlocked the door. Wallander wondered where he'd got the keys. They walked into the hall and turned on the light. Some junk mail lay on the floor. Wallander let Forsfält lead the way. They walked through the flat. It consisted of three rooms and a tiny, cramped kitchen that looked out on a warehouse. Apart from the bed, which appeared new, the flat seemed neglected. The furniture was strewn haphazardly around the rooms. Some dusty, cheap porcelain figures stood on a 1950s-style bookshelf in the living-room. In one corner was a stack of magazines and some dumbbells. To his great surprise Wallander noticed a CD of Turkish folk music on the sofa. The curtains were drawn.

Forsfält went around turning on all the lights. Wallander followed him, while Svedberg took a seat on a chair in the kitchen and called Hansson. Wallander pushed open the door to the pantry with his foot. Inside were several unopened boxes of Grant's whisky. They had been shipped from the Scottish distillery to a wine merchant in Belgium. He wondered how they had ended up in Fredman's flat.

Forsfält came into the kitchen with a couple of photographs of the owner. Wallander nodded. There was no doubt that it was him they'd found. He went back to the living-room and tried to decide what he really hoped to discover. Fredman's flat was the exact opposite of Wetterstedt's and Carlman's houses. This is what Sweden is like, he thought. The differences between people are just as great now as they were when some lived in manor houses and others in hovels.

He noticed a desk piled with magazines about antiques. They must be related to Fredman's activities as a fence. There was only one drawer in the desk. Inside was a stack of receipts, broken pens, a cigarette case, and a framed photograph. It was of Fredman and his family. He was smiling broadly at the camera. Next to him sat his wife, holding a newborn baby in her arms. Behind the mother stood a girl in her early teens. She was staring into the camera, a look of terror in her eyes. Next to her, directly behind the mother, stood a boy a few years younger. His face was pinched, as if he was resisting something. Wallander took the photo over to the window and pulled back the curtain. He stared at it for a long time. An unhappy family? A family that hadn't yet encountered unhappiness? A newborn child who had no idea what awaited him? There was something in the picture that disturbed him, but he couldn't put his finger on it. He took it into the bedroom, where Forsfält was looking under the bed.

"You said that he did time for battery," said Wallander.

Forsfält got up and looked at the photo.

"He beat his wife senseless," he said. "He beat her up when she was pregnant. He beat her when the child was a baby. But strangely enough, he never went to prison for it. Once he broke a cab driver's nose. He beat a former partner half to death when he suspected him of cheating."

They continued searching the flat. Svedberg had finished talking to Hansson. He shook his head when Wallander asked him if anything had happened. It took them two hours to search the place. Wallander's flat was idyllic compared to Fredman's. They found nothing but a travel bag with antique candlesticks in it. Wallander understood why Fredman's language was peppered with swear words. The flat was just as empty and inarticulate as his vocabulary.

Finally they left the flat. The wind had picked up. Forsfält called the station and got word that Fredman's family had been informed of his death.

"I'd like to talk to them," said Wallander when they got into the car. "But it's probably better to wait until tomorrow."

He knew he wasn't being honest. He hated disturbing a family whose relative had suffered a violent death. Above all, he couldn't bear talking to children who had just lost a parent. Waiting until the next day would make no difference to them. But it gave Wallander breathing space.

They said goodbye outside the station. Forsfält would get hold of Hansson to clear up formalities between the two police districts. He made an appointment to meet with Wallander the next morning.

Wallander and Svedberg drove back towards Ystad. Wallander's mind was swarming with ideas. They remained silent.

CHAPTER 22

Copenhagen's skyline was just visible across the Sound in the hazy sunlight.

Wallander wondered whether he'd get to meet Baiba there or whether the killer they sought – about whom they seemed to know less, if that were possible – would force him to postpone his holiday.

He stood waiting outside the hovercraft terminal in Malmö. It was the morning of the last day of June. Wallander had decided the night before to take Höglund rather than Svedberg when he returned to Malmö to talk to Fredman's family. She'd asked whether they could leave early enough for her to do an errand on the way. Svedberg hadn't complained in the least at being left behind. His relief at not having to leave Ystad two days in a row was unmistakable. While Höglund took care of her errand in the terminal – Wallander hadn't asked what it was – he'd walked along the pier. A hydrofoil, the *Runner*, he thought it said, was on its way out of the harbour. It was hot. He took off his jacket and slung it over his shoulder, yawning.

After they'd returned from Malmö the night before, he'd called a meeting with the investigative team, since they were all still there. He and Hansson had also held an impromptu press conference. Ekholm had attended the meeting. He was still working on a psychological profile of the killer. But they had agreed that Wallander should inform the press that they were looking for someone who wasn't considered dangerous to the public, but who was certainly extremely dangerous to his victims.

There had been differing opinions on whether it would be wise to take this action. But Wallander had insisted that they couldn't ignore the possibility that someone might come forward out of sheer self-preservation. The press were delighted with this information, but Wallander felt uncomfortable, knowing that they were giving the public the best possible news, since the nation was about to close down for the summer holiday. Afterwards, when both the meeting and the press conference were over, he was exhausted.

He still hadn't gone over the telex from Interpol with Martinsson. The girl had vanished from Santiago de los Treinta Caballeros in December. Her father, Pedro Santana, a farm worker, had reported her disappearance to the police on 14 January. Dolores María, who was then 16 years old, but who had turned 17 on 18 February – a fact that made Wallander particularly depressed – had been in Santiago looking for work as a housekeeper. Before then she had lived with her father in a little village 70 kilometres outside the city. She had been staying with a distant relative when she had disappeared. Judging by the scanty report, the Dominican police had not taken much interest in her case, though her father had hounded them to keep looking for her, managing to get a journalist involved, but eventually the police decided that she had probably left the country.

The trail ended there. Interpol's comments were brief. Dolores María Santana hadn't been seen in any of the countries belonging to the international police network. Until now.

"She disappears in a city called Santiago," said Wallander. "About six months later she pops up in farmer Salomonsson's rape field, where she burns herself to death. What does that mean?"

Martinsson shook his head dejectedly. Wallander was so tired he could hardly think, but he roused himself. Martinsson's apathy made him furious.

"We know that she didn't vanish from the face of the earth," he said with determination. "We know that she had been in Helsingborg and got a lift from a man from Smedstorp. She seemed to be fleeing something. And we know she's dead. We should send a message back to Interpol telling them all this. And I want you to make a special request that the girl's father be properly informed of her death. When this other nightmare is over, we'll have to find out what terrified her in Helsingborg. I suggest you make contact with our colleagues there tomorrow. They might have some idea what happened."

After this muted outburst, Wallander drove home. He stopped and ordered a hamburger. Newspaper placards were posted everywhere, proclaiming the latest news on the World Cup. He had a powerful urge to rip them down and scream that enough was enough. But instead he waited patiently in line, paid, picked up his hamburger, and went back to his car.

When he got home he sat down at the kitchen table, tore open the bag and ate. He drank a glass of water with the hamburger. Then he made some strong coffee and cleared the table, forcing himself to go over all the investigative material again. The feeling that they had been sidetracked was still with him. Wallander hadn't laid the clues they were following. But he *was* the one who was leading the investigative group, and determining the course that they took. He tried to see where they should have paid more attention, whether the link between Wetterstedt and Carlman was already clearly visible, but unnoticed.

He went over all the evidence that they had gathered, sometimes solid, sometimes not. Next to him he had a notebook in which he listed all the unanswered questions. It troubled him that the results from many of the forensic tests still weren't available. Although it was past midnight, he was sorely tempted to call up Nyberg and ask him whether the laboratory in Linköping had closed for the summer. But he refrained. He sat bent over his papers until his back hurt and the letters began blurring on the page.

He didn't give up until after 2 a.m., when he'd concluded that they couldn't do anything but continue on the path that they had chosen. There must be a connection between the murdered men. Perhaps the fact that Björn Fredman didn't seem to fit with the others might point to the solution.

The pile of dirty laundry was still on the floor, reminding him of the chaos inside his own head. Once again he had forgotten to get an appointment for his car. Would they have to request reinforcements from the National Criminal Bureau? He decided to talk to Hansson about it first thing, after a few hours' sleep.

But by the time he got up at 6 a.m., he'd changed his mind. He wanted to wait one more day. Instead he called Nyberg and complained about the laboratory. He had expected Nyberg to be angry, but to Wallander's great surprise he had agreed that it was taking an unusually long time and promised to follow the matter up. They'd discussed Nyberg's examination of the pit where they'd found Fredman. Traces of blood indicated that the killer had parked his car right next to it. Nyberg had also managed to get out to Sturup Airport and look at Fredman's van. There was no doubt that it had been used to transport the body. But Nyberg didn't think that the murder could have taken place in it.

"Fredman was big and strong," he said. "I can't see how he could have been killed inside the van. I think the murder happened somewhere else."

"So we must find out who drove the van," said Wallander, "and where the murder occurred."

Wallander had arrived at the station just after 7 a.m. He'd called Ekholm at his hotel and found him in the breakfast room.

"I want you to concentrate on the eyes," he said. "I don't know why. But I'm convinced they're important. Maybe crucial. Why would he do that to Fredman and not to the others? That's what I want to know."

"The whole thing has to be viewed in its entirety," said Ekholm. "A psychopath almost always creates rituals, which he then follows as if they were written in a sacred book. The eyes have to fit into that framework."

"Whatever," Wallander said curtly. "But I want to know why only Fredman had his eyes put out. Framework or no framework."

"It was probably acid," said Ekholm.

Wallander had forgotten to ask Nyberg about that.

"Can we assume that's the case?" he asked.

"It seems so. Someone poured acid in Fredman's eyes."

Wallander grimaced.

"We'll talk this afternoon," he said and hung up.

Soon afterwards he had left Ystad with Höglund. It was a relief to get out of the station. Reporters were calling all the time. And now the public had started calling too. The hunt for the killer had become a national concern. Wallander knew that this was inevitable, and also useful. But it was an enormous task to record and check on all the information that was flooding in.

Höglund emerged from the terminal and caught up with him on the pier.

"I wonder what kind of summer it'll be this year," he said.

"My grandmother in Älmhult predicts the weather," said Höglund. "She says it's going to be long, hot and dry."

"Is she usually right?"

"Almost always."

"I think it'll be the opposite. Rainy and cold and crappy."

"Can you predict the weather too?"

"No."

They walked back to the car. Wallander wondered what she'd been doing in the terminal. But he didn't ask.

They pulled up in front of the Malmö police station at 9.30 a.m. Forsfält was waiting on the footpath. He got into the back seat and gave Wallander directions, talking to Höglund about the weather at the same time. When they stopped outside the block of flats in Rosengård he told them what had happened the day before.

"The ex-wife took the news of Fredman's death calmly. One of my colleagues smelt alcohol on her breath. The place was a mess. The younger boy is only four. He probably won't comprehend that his father, whom he almost never saw, is dead. But the older son understood. The daughter wasn't home."

"What's her name?" asked Wallander.

"The daughter?"

"The wife. The ex-wife."

"Anette Fredman."

"Does she have a job?"

"Not that I know of."

"How does she make a living?"

"No idea. But I doubt that Fredman was very generous to his family."

They got out of the car and went inside, taking the lift up to the fifth floor. Someone had smashed a bottle on the floor of the lift. Wallander glanced at Höglund and shook his head. Forsfält rang the doorbell. After a while the door opened. The woman standing before them was very thin and pale, and dressed all in black. She looked with terror at the two unfamiliar faces. As they hung up their coats in the hall, Wallander saw someone peer quickly through the doorway to the flat and then disappear. He guessed it was the older son or the daughter.

Forsfält introduced them, speaking gently and calmly. There was nothing hurried in his demeanour. Wallander could see he might be able to learn from Forsfält as he once had from Rydberg.

They went into the living-room. It looked as though she had cleaned up. The living-room had a sofa and chairs that looked almost unused. There was a stereo, a video, and a Bang & Olufsen TV, a Danish brand Wallander had had his eye on but couldn't afford. She had set out cups and saucers. Wallander listened. There was a four-year-old boy in the family. Children that age weren't quiet. They sat down.

"Let me say how sorry I am for the inconvenience," he said, trying to be as friendly as Forsfält.

"Thank you," she replied in a low, fragile voice, that sounded as if it might break at any moment.

"Unfortunately I have to ask you some questions," continued Wallander. "I wish they could wait."

She nodded but said nothing. At that moment the door into the living-room opened. A well-built boy of about 14 entered. He had an open, friendly face, but his eyes were wary.

"This is my son," she said. "His name is Stefan."

The boy was very polite, Wallander noticed. He came and shook hands with each of them. Then he sat down next to his mother on the sofa.

"I'd like him to hear this too," she said.

"That's fine," said Wallander. "I'm sorry about what happened to your father."

"We didn't see each other very much," replied the boy. "But thank you."

Wallander was impressed. He seemed mature for his age, perhaps because he'd had to fill the void left by his father.

"You have another son, don't you?" Wallander went on.

"He's with a friend of mine, playing with her son," said Anette Fredman. "I thought it would be better. His name is Jens."

Wallander nodded to Höglund, who was taking notes.

"And a daughter too?"

"Her name is Louise."

"But she's not here?"

"She's away for a few days, resting."

It was the boy who'd answered. He took over from his mother, as if he wanted to spare her a heavy burden. His answer had been calm and polite. But something wasn't quite right. It had come a little too quickly. Or was it that the boy had hesitated before replying? Wallander was immediately on the alert.

"I understand that this must be trying for her," he continued cautiously.

"She's very sensitive," replied her brother.

Something doesn't add up here, Wallander thought again. He knew he shouldn't press this now. It would be better to come back to the girl later. He glanced at Höglund, but she didn't seem to have noticed.

"I won't have to repeat the questions you've already answered," said Wallander, pouring himself a cup of coffee, to show that everything was normal. The boy had his eyes fixed on him. There was a wariness in his eyes that reminded Wallander of a bird, as though he'd been forced to take on responsibility too soon. The thought depressed him.

Nothing troubled Wallander more than seeing children and young people damaged.

"I know that you hadn't seen Mr Fredman in several weeks," he went on. "Was that true of Louise too?"

This time it was the mother who answered.

"The last time he was home, Louise was out," she said. "It's been several months since she saw him."

Wallander approached the most difficult questions gingerly. He knew that he would provoke painful memories, but he tried to move as gently as he could.

"He was murdered," he said. "Do either of you have any idea who might have done it?"

Anette Fredman looked at him with a surprised expression on her face. Her reply was shrill, her previous reticence gone.

"You ought to be asking who wouldn't have killed him. I don't know how many times I wished I'd had the strength to do it myself."

Her son put his arm around her.

"I don't think that's what the detective meant," he said soothingly.

She quickly pulled herself together after her outburst.

"I don't know," she said. "And I don't want to know. But I don't feel guilty for being relieved that he won't be walking through this door again."

She stood up abruptly and left the room. Wallander could tell that Höglund couldn't decide whether she should follow. But she remained seated as the boy began to speak.

"Mummy is extremely upset," he said.

"We understand that," said Wallander with sympathy. "But you seem to be calm. Maybe you have some thoughts. I know this must be unpleasant for you."

"I don't think it could be anybody except one of Dad's friends. My Dad was a thief," he added. "He also used to beat people up. I'm not sure, but I think he was what people call an enforcer. He collected debts, he threatened people."

"How do you know that?"

"I don't know."

"Are you thinking about somebody in particular?"

"No."

Wallander let him think.

"No," he repeated. "I don't know."

Anette Fredman returned.

"Can either of you recall whether he had any contact with a man named Gustaf Wetterstedt? He was the minister of justice for a time. Or an art dealer named Arne Carlman?"

After looking at each other for confirmation, they both shook their heads. The interview limped along. Wallander tried to help them remember details. Now and then Forsfält interjected. Finally Wallander could see that they weren't going to get any further. He decided not to ask about the daughter again. Instead he nodded to Höglund and Forsfält that he was finished. But as they said goodbye out in the hall he told them he would have to call on them again, probably quite soon. He gave them his phone numbers at the station and at home.

Out on the street he saw Anette Fredman standing in the window looking down at them.

"The daughter," said Wallander. "Louise Fredman. What do we know about her?"

"She wasn't here yesterday either," said Forsfält. "She may have left home, of course. She's 17."

Wallander stood for a moment in thought.

"I want to talk to her," he said.

The others didn't react. He knew that he was the only one who had noticed the rapid change when he asked about her. He thought about the boy, Stefan, with his wary eyes. He felt sorry for him.

"That'll be all for now," said Wallander when they parted outside the Malmö police station. "But let's keep in touch."

They shook hands with Forsfält and said goodbye.

They drove back towards Ystad, through the countryside of Skåne during the most beautiful time of the year. Höglund leaned back in her seat and closed her eyes. Wallander could hear her humming.

He wished he could share her ability to switch off from the investigation, which made him so anxious. Rydberg had said many times that a police officer was never completely free. For once, Wallander wished that Rydberg was wrong.

Just after they passed the exit to Skurup he noticed that Höglund had fallen asleep. He drove as smoothly as he could, not wanting to wake her. She didn't open her eyes until he had to stop at the roundabout on the outskirts of Ystad. At that moment the phone rang. He nodded to her to answer it. He couldn't tell who it was, but he saw at once that something serious had happened. She listened in silence. They were almost at the station when she hung up.

"That was Svedberg," she said. "Carlman's daughter is on a respirator at the hospital. She tried to commit suicide."

Wallander was silent until he had parked and switched off the engine. Then he turned to her. He knew she hadn't told him everything yet.

"What else?"

"She's probably not going to live."

Wallander stared out of the window. He thought about how she had slapped him. He got out of the car without a word.

CHAPTER 23

It was hot. Wallander was sweating as he walked down the hill from the station towards the hospital.

He hadn't even gone to the front desk to see whether he had any messages. He had stood motionless by the car, as if he'd lost his bearings, and then slowly, almost drawling, he told Höglund that she would have to report on their interview while he went to the hospital where Carlman's daughter lay dying. He hadn't waited for an answer, but simply turned and left. It was then, on the hill, that he realised that the summer might indeed be long, hot and dry.

He didn't notice when Svedberg drove past and waved. As always when he was preoccupied, he walked looking down at the footpath. He was trying to follow a train of thought. The starting point was quite simple. In less than ten days, a girl had burned herself to death, another had tried to commit suicide after her father was murdered, and a third, whose father had also been murdered, had perhaps disappeared or was being hidden. They were of different ages; Carlman's daughter was the oldest, but all of them were young. Two of the girls had been affected by the same killer, while the third had killed herself. On the face of it, the third had no connection to the other two. But Wallander felt as if he had once again assumed personal responsibility for all three on behalf of his own generation, and especially as the bad father he felt he had been himself. Wallander had a tendency to self-criticise, growing gloomy, filled with melancholy. Often this led to a string of sleepless nights. But since he was now forced to carry on working in spite of everything, as a policeman in a tiny corner of the world, and as the head of a team, he did his best to shake off his unease and clear his head by taking a walk.

What kind of a world was he living in? A world in which young people burned themselves to death or tried to kill themselves by some other means. They were living in what could be called the Age of Failure. Something the Swedish people had believed in and built had turned out to be less solid than expected. All they had done was raise a monument to a forgotten ideal. Now society seemed to collapse around him, as if the political system was about to tip over, and no-one knew which architects were waiting to put a new one in place, or what that system would be. It was terrifying, even in the beautiful summertime. Young people took their own lives. People lived to forget, not remember. Houses were hiding places rather than cosy homes. And the police stood by helpless, waiting for the time when their jails would be guarded by men in other uniforms, men from private security companies.

This was enough, thought Wallander, wiping the sweat from his brow. He couldn't take any more. A mental picture of the boy with the wary eyes sitting next to his mother became muddled with an image of Linda.

He reached the hospital. Svedberg was standing on the steps waiting for him. Wallander staggered, as if about to fall, suddenly dizzy. Svedberg took a step towards him, reaching out his hand. But Wallander waved him away and continued up the hospital steps. To protect himself from the sun, Svedberg was wearing a ridiculous cap that was much too big for him. Wallander muttered something unintelligible, and dragged him into the cafeteria to the right of the entrance. Pale people in wheelchairs, some connected to intravenous drips sat with friends and relatives, who probably wanted nothing more than to be out in the sunshine, and forget hospitals, death and misery. Wallander bought coffee and a sandwich, while Svedberg settled for a glass of water.

"Carlman's widow phoned," said Svedberg. "She was hysterical."

"What did the girl do?" asked Wallander.

"She took pills. She was discovered quite by chance, in a deep coma. Her heart stopped just as they got to the hospital. She's in very bad shape. You won't be able to talk to her."

Wallander nodded. This walk to the hospital had been more for his own state of mind than for any investigative reason.

"What did her mother say?" he asked. "Was there a letter? Any explanation?"

"No. Apparently it was quite unexpected."

Wallander recalled how the girl had slapped him.

"She seemed unbalanced when I met her," he said. "She really didn't leave a note?"

"If she did, the mother didn't mention it."

Wallander thought for a moment.

"Do me a favour," he said. "Drive there and find out if there was a note or not. If there *is* something, you'll have to check it carefully."

They left the cafeteria. Wallander went back to the station with Svedberg. He might as well get hold of a doctor by phone to hear how the girl was.

"I put a few reports on your desk," said Svedberg. "I did a phone interview with the reporter and photographer who visited Wetterstedt the day he died."

"Anything new?"

"Only a confirmation of what we already know. That Wetterstedt was his usual self. There didn't seem to be anything threatening him. Nothing he was aware of, anyway."

"So I don't need to read the report?"

Svedberg shrugged.

"It's always better to have four eyes look at something than two."

"I'm not so sure about that," said Wallander distractedly.

"Ekholm is busy putting the finishing touches to his psychological profile," said Svedberg.

Wallander muttered something in reply. Svedberg dropped him off outside the station and drove on to talk to Carlman's widow. Wallander picked up his messages at the front desk. A new girl was there again. He asked about Ebba and was told that she was at the hospital having the cast taken off her wrist. I could have stopped in and said hello to her, thought Wallander. Since I was over there anyway. If it was possible to say hello to someone who was just having a cast removed.

He went to his office and opened the window wide. Without sitting down he riffled through the reports Svedberg had mentioned. Then he remembered that he had also asked to see the photographs taken by the magazine. Where were they? Unable to control his impatience, he found Svedberg's mobile number and called him.

"The photos," he asked. "Where are they?"

"Aren't they on your desk?" Svedberg replied, surprised.

"There's nothing here."

"Then they're in my office. I must have forgotten them. They were in today's post."

They were in a brown envelope on Svedberg's tidy desk. Wallander spread them out and sat in Svedberg's chair. Wetterstedt posing in his home, in the garden, and on the beach. In one of the pictures the overturned rowing boat could be seen in the background. Wetterstedt was smiling at the camera. The grey hair which would soon be torn from his head was ruffled by the wind. The photos showed a man who seemed at peace with his old age. Nothing in the pictures hinted at what was to happen. Wetterstedt had less than 15 hours left to live when the pictures were taken. The photos lying before him showed how he'd looked on the last day of his life. Wallander studied the pictures for a few minutes more before stuffing them back in the envelope. He started towards his office but changed his mind and stopped outside Höglund's door, which was always open.

She was bent over some papers.

"Am I interrupting you?" he asked.

"Not at all."

He went in and sat down. They exchanged a few words about Carlman's daughter.

"Svedberg is out at the farmhouse hunting for a suicide note," said Wallander. "If there is one."

"She must have been very close to her father," said Höglund.

Wallander didn't reply. He changed the subject.

"Did you notice anything strange when we were visiting the Fredman family?"

"Strange?"

"A chill that settled over the room?"

He immediately regretted his description. Höglund wrinkled her brow as if he had said something out of line.

"I mean that they seemed evasive when I asked questions about Louise," he explained.

"No, I didn't," she replied. "But I did notice that you acted differently."

He told her of the feeling he'd had. She thought before she answered.

"You might be right," she said. "Now that you mention it, they did seem to be on their guard. That chill you were talking about."

"The question is whether they both were, or only one of them," said Wallander.

"Was that the case?"

"I'm not sure. It's just a feeling I had."

"Didn't the boy start answering the questions you were actually asking his mother?"

Wallander nodded.

"That's it," he said. "And I wonder why."

"Still, you have to ask yourself whether it's really important," she said.

"Of course," he admitted. "Sometimes I have a tendency to get hung up on unimportant details. But I still want to have a talk with that girl."

This time she was the one who changed the subject.

"It frightens me to think about what Anette Fredman said. That she felt relief that her husband would never walk through their door again. I can't imagine what it means to live like that."

"He was abusing her," said Wallander. "Maybe he beat the children too. But none of them filed a complaint."

"The boy seemed quite normal," she said. "And well brought up, too."

"Children learn to survive," said Wallander, reflecting for a moment on his own childhood and Linda's. He stood up.

"I'm going to try and get hold of Louise Fredman. Tomorrow if I can. I've got a hunch that she hasn't gone away at all."

He got a cup of coffee and headed towards his room. He almost collided with Norén and remembered the photos he had asked to have taken of the crowd standing outside the cordon watching the police work.

"I gave the film to Nyberg," said Norén. "But I don't think I'm much of a photographer."

"Who the hell is?" said Wallander, in a kindly tone. He went into his room and closed the door. He sat staring at his telephone, collecting his thoughts before he called the M.O.T. garage and asked for a new appointment for his car. The slot they offered him was during the time he had intended to spend at Skagen with Baiba. When he angrily informed them of the atrocities he was trying to solve, a time that had been reserved inexplicably became free. He wondered who that slot had been assigned to. After he hung up he decided to do his laundry that evening.

The phone rang. It was Nyberg.

"You were right," he said. "The fingerprints on that piece of paper you found behind the road workers' hut match the ones we found on the pages from the comic book. So there's no doubt that the same person is involved. In a couple of hours we'll also know whether we can tie him to the van at Sturup. We're also going to try and get some prints from Fredman's face."

"Is that possible?"

"To pour acid into Fredman's eyes the killer must have used one hand to hold his eyelids open," said Nyberg. "It's unpleasant, but if we're lucky we'll find prints on the lids themselves."

"It's a good thing people can't hear the way we talk to each other," said Wallander. "How about that bulb? The light at Wetterstedt's garden gate."

"I was just getting to that," said Nyberg. "You were right about that too. We found fingerprints."

Wallander sat up straight in his chair. His bad mood was gone. He could feel his excitement rising. The investigation was showing signs of breaking wide open.

"Have we got the prints in the archives?" he asked.

"I'm afraid not," said Nyberg. "But I've asked central records to double check."

"Let's assume for a moment that we don't. That means we're dealing with someone without a record."

"Could be," Nyberg replied.

"Run the prints through Interpol too," said Wallander. "And Europol. Ask for highest priority. Tell them it concerns a serial killer."

Wallander hung up and asked the girl at the switchboard to find Ekholm. In a few minutes she called back and said he'd gone out for lunch.

"Where?" asked Wallander.

"I think he said the Continental."

"Get hold of him there," said Wallander. "Tell him to get over here right away."

A while later Ekholm knocked on the door. Wallander was talking to Per Åkeson. He pointed to a chair. Wallander was busy trying to convince a sceptical Åkeson that the investigation wouldn't be aided by a larger team, at least in the short term. Åkeson finally gave in, and they postponed the decision for a few more days.

Wallander leaned back in his chair and clasped his hands behind his head. He told Ekholm about the fingerprints.

"The prints we're going to find on Björn Fredman's body will be the same ones too," he said. "We know for certain that we're dealing with the same killer. The only question is: who is he?"

"I've been thinking about the eyes," said Ekholm. "All available information tells us that aside from the genitals, the eyes are the part of the body most often subjected to a final revenge."

"What does that mean?"

"That killers seldom begin by putting out someone's eyes. They save that for last."

Wallander nodded for him to continue.

"We can approach it from two directions," said Ekholm. "We might ask why Fredman was the one to have his eyes put out. We could also turn the whole thing around and ask why the eyes of the other two men weren't violated."

"What's your conclusion?"

"I don't have one," Ekholm said. "When we're talking about someone's psyche, especially that of a disturbed or sick person, we're getting into territory in which there are no absolute answers."

Ekholm looked as if he was waiting for a comment. But Wallander just shook his head.

"I see a pattern," Ekholm went on. "The person who did this selected his victims in advance. He has some kind of relationship with these men. It's not necessary for him to have known the first two personally. It might be a symbolic relationship. But I'm fairly certain that the mutilation of Fredman's eyes reveals that the killer knew his victim. And knew him well."

Wallander leaned forward and gave Ekholm a penetrating look.

"How well?" he asked.

"They might have been friends. Colleagues. Rivals."

"And something happened?"

"Something happened, yes. In reality or in the killer's imagination."

Wallander tried to see the implications of Ekholm's words. At the same time he asked himself whether he accepted his theory.

"So we ought to concentrate on Björn Fredman," he said after he had thought carefully.

"That's one possibility."

Wallander was irritated by Ekholm's tendency to avoid taking a decisive view. It bothered him, even though he knew that it was right to keep their options open.

"Let's say you were in my place," said Wallander. "I promise not to quote you. Or blame you if you're wrong. But what would you do?"

"I would concentrate on retracing Fredman's life," he said. "But I'd keep my eyes open."

Wallander nodded. He understood.

"What *kind* of person are we looking for?" he asked.

Ekholm batted at a bee that had flown in through the window.

"The basic conclusions you can draw yourself," he said. "That it's a man. That he's strong. That he's practical, meticulous and not squeamish."

"And his prints aren't in the criminal records," Wallander added. "He's a first-timer."

"This reinforces my belief that he leads a quite normal life," said Ekholm. "The psychotic side to his nature, the mental collapse, is well hidden. He could sit down at the dinner table with the scalps in his pocket and eat his meal with a healthy appetite."

"In other words, there are two ways we can set about catching him," Wallander said. "Either in the act, or by gathering a body of evidence that spells out his name in big neon letters."

"That's right. It's not an easy task that we have ahead of us."

Just as Ekholm was about to leave, Wallander asked one more question.

"Will he strike again?"

"It might be over," said Ekholm. "Björn Fredman as the grand finale."

"Is that what you think?"

"No. He'll strike again. What we've seen so far is the beginning of a long series of murders."

When Wallander was alone he shooed the bee out of the window with his jacket. He sat quite still with his eyes closed, thinking through everything Ekholm had said. At 4 p.m. he went to get some more coffee. Then he went to the conference room, where the rest of the team were waiting for him.

He began by asking Ekholm to repeat his theory. When Ekholm had finished the room was quiet for a long time. Wallander waited out the silence, knowing that each of them was trying to grasp the significance of what they had just heard. They're each absorbing this information, he thought. Then we'll work on determining the collective opinion of the team.

They agreed with Ekholm. They would make Björn Fredman's life the prime focus. Having settled the next steps in the investigation, they ended the meeting at around 6 p.m. Martinsson was the only one who left the station, to go and collect his children. The rest of them went back to work.

Wallander stood by his window looking out at the summer evening. The thought that they were still on the wrong track gnawed at him. *What was he missing?* He turned and looked around the room, as if an invisible visitor had come in.

So that's how things are, he thought. I'm chasing a ghost when I ought to be searching for a living human being. He sat there pondering the case until midnight. Only when he left the station did he remember the dirty laundry still heaped on the floor.

CHAPTER 24

Next morning at dawn Wallander went downstairs to the laundry room, still half asleep, and discovered to his dismay that someone had got there first. The washing machine was in use, and he had to sign up for a slot that afternoon. He kept trying to recapture the dream he'd had during the night. It had been erotic, frenzied, and passionate, and Wallander had watched himself from a distance, participating in a drama he never would have come close to in his waking life. But the woman in his dream wasn't Baiba. Not until he was on his way back upstairs did he realise that the woman reminded him of the female vicar he had met at Smedstorp. At first it surprised him, and then he felt a little ashamed. Later, when he got back to his flat, it dissolved into what it actually was, something beyond his control.

He sat at the kitchen table and drank coffee, the heat already coming through the half-open window. Maybe Ann-Britt's grandmother was right: they were in for a truly beautiful summer. He thought of his father. Often, especially in the morning, his thoughts would wander back in time, to the era of the "silk knights", when he woke each morning knowing he was a child loved by his father. Now, more than 40 years later, he found it hard to remember what his father had been like as a young man. His paintings were just the same even then: he had painted that landscape with or without the grouse with total determination not to change a thing from one painting to the next. His father had only painted one single picture in his whole life. He never tried to improve on it. The result had been perfect from the first attempt.

He drank the last of his coffee and tried to imagine a world without his father. He wondered what he would do when his constant feelings of guilt were gone. The trip to Italy would probably be their last chance to understand each other, maybe even to reconcile. He didn't want his good memories to end at the time when he had helped his father to cart out the paintings and place them in a huge American car, and then stood by his side, both of them waving to the silk knight driving off in a cloud of dust, on his way to sell them for three or four times what he had just paid for them.

At 6.30 a.m. he became a policeman again, sweeping the memories aside. As he dressed he tried to decide how he'd go about all the tasks he had set himself that day. At 7 a.m. he walked through the door of the station, exchanging a few words with Norén, who arrived at the same time. Norén was actually supposed to be on holiday, but he had postponed it, just as many of the others had.

"No doubt it'll start raining as soon as we catch the killer," he said. "What does a weather god care about a simple policeman when there's a serial killer on the loose?"

Wallander muttered something in reply, but he did not discount the possibility that there might be some grim truth in Norén's words.

He went in to see Hansson, who seemed now to spend all his time at the station, weighed down by anxiety. His face was as grey as concrete. He was shaving with an ancient electric razor. His shirt was wrinkled and his eyes bloodshot.

"You've got to try and get a few hours' sleep once in a while," said Wallander. "Your responsibility isn't any greater than anyone else's."

Hansson turned off the shaver and gloomily observed the result in a pocket mirror.

"I took a sleeping pill yesterday," he said. "But I still didn't get any sleep. All I got was a headache."

Wallander looked at Hansson in silence. He felt sorry for him. Being chief had never been one of Hansson's dreams.

"I'm going back to Malmö," he said. "I want to talk to the members of Fredman's family again. Especially the ones who weren't there yesterday."

Hansson gave him a quizzical look.

"Are you going to interrogate a four-year-old boy? That's not legally permitted."

"I was thinking of the daughter," said Wallander. "She's 17. And I don't intend to 'interrogate' anyone."

Hansson nodded and got up slowly. He pointed to a book lying open on the desk.

"I got this from Ekholm," he said. "Behavioural science based on a number of case studies of serial killers. It's unbelievable the things people will do if they're sufficiently deranged."

"Is there anything about scalping?" asked Wallander.

"That's one of the milder forms of trophy collecting. If you only knew the things that have been found in people's homes, it would make you sick."

"I feel sick enough already," said Wallander. "I'll leave the rest to my imagination."

"Ordinary human beings," said Hansson in dismay. "Completely normal on the surface. Underneath, mentally ill beasts of prey. A man in France, the foreman of a coal depot, used to cut open the stomachs of his victims and stick his head inside to try and suffocate himself. That's one example."

"That'll do," said Wallander, trying to discourage him.

"Ekholm wanted me to give you the book when I've read it," said Hansson.

"I bet he did," said Wallander. "But I really don't have the time. Or the inclination."

Wallander made himself a sandwich in the canteen and took it with him. As he ate it in the car, he wondered whether he should call Linda. But he decided not to. It was still too early.

He arrived in Malmö at around 8.30 a.m. The summer calm had already started to descend on the countryside. The traffic on the roads that intersected the motorway into Malmö was lighter than usual. He headed towards Rosengård and pulled up outside the block of flats he had visited the day before. He turned off the engine, wondering why he had come back so soon. They had decided to investigate Björn Fredman's life. Besides, it was necessary that he meet the absent daughter. The little boy was less important.

He found a dirty petrol receipt in the glove compartment and took out a pen. To his great irritation he saw that it had leaked ink around the breast pocket where he kept it. The spot was half the size of his hand. On the white shirt it looked as if he'd been shot through the heart. The shirt was almost new. Baiba had bought it for him at Christmas after she'd been through his wardrobe and cleaned out the old, worn-out clothes.

His immediate impulse was to return to Ystad and go back to bed. He didn't know how many shirts he'd had to throw away because he forgot to cap the pen properly before he put it in his pocket. Perhaps he should go and buy a new shirt. But he'd have to wait at least an hour until the shops opened, so he decided against it. He tossed the leaking pen out the window and then looked for another one in the messy glove compartment. He wrote down some key words on the back of the receipt. *BF's friends. Then and now. Unexpected events.* He crumpled up the note and was just about to stuff it in his breast pocket when he stopped himself. He got out of the car and took off his jacket. The ink from his shirt pocket hadn't reached the jacket lining. He went into the building and pushed open the lift door. The broken glass was still there. He got out on the fifth floor and rang the doorbell. There was no sound from inside the flat. Maybe they were still asleep. He waited more than a minute. Then he rang again. The door opened. It was the boy, Stefan. He seemed surprised to see Wallander. He smiled, but his eyes were wary.

"I hope I haven't come too early," said Wallander. "I should have called first, of course. But I was in Malmö anyway. I thought I'd pop in."

It was a flimsy lie, but it was the best he could come up with. The boy let him into the hall. He was dressed in a cut-off T-shirt and a pair of jeans. He was barefoot.

"I'm here by myself," he said. "My mother went out with my little brother. They were going to Copenhagen."

"It's a great day for a trip to Copenhagen," said Wallander warmly.

"Yes, she likes going there a lot. To get away from it all."

His words echoed disconsolately in the hall. Wallander thought the boy had sounded strangely unmoved last time when he mentioned the death of his father. They went into the living-room. Wallander laid his jacket on a chair and pointed at the ink spot.

"This happens all the time," he said.

"It never happens to me," said the boy, smiling. "I can make some coffee if you want."

"No thanks."

They sat down at opposite ends of the table. A blanket and pillow on the sofa indicated that someone had slept there. Wallander glimpsed the neck of an empty wine bottle under a chair. The boy noticed at once that he had seen it. His attention didn't flag for an instant. Wallander hastily asked himself whether he had the right to question a minor about his father's death without a relative present. But he didn't want to pass up this opportunity. And the boy was incredibly mature for 14. Wallander felt as though he was talking to someone his own age. Even Linda, who was several years older, seemed childish in comparison.

"What are you going to do this summer?" asked Wallander. "We've got fine weather."

The boy smiled. "I've got plenty to do," he replied.

Wallander waited for more, but he didn't continue.

"What class are you going to be in this autumn?"

"Eighth."

"Is school going well?"

"Yes."

"What's your favourite subject?"

"None of them. But maths is the easiest. We've started a club to study numerology."

"I'm not sure I know what that is."

"The Holy Trinity. The seven lean years. Trying to predict your future by combining the numbers in your life."

"That sounds interesting."

"It is."

Wallander could feel himself becoming fascinated by the boy sitting across from him. His strong body contrasted sharply with his childish face, but there was obviously nothing wrong with his mind.

Wallander took the crumpled gas receipt out of his jacket. His house keys dropped out of the pocket. He put them back and sat down again.

"I have a few questions," he said. "But this is not an interrogation, by any means. If you want to wait until your mother comes home, just say so."

"That's not necessary. I'll answer if I can."

"Your sister," said Wallander. "When is she coming back?"

"I don't know."

The boy looked at him. The question didn't seem to bother him. He had answered without hesitation. Wallander began to wonder if he had been mistaken the day before.

"I assume that you're in contact with her? That you know where she is?"

"She just took off. It's not the first time. She'll come home when she feels like it."

"I hope you understand that I think that sounds a little unusual."

"Not for us."

Wallander was convinced that the boy knew where his sister was. But he wouldn't be able to force an answer out of him. Nor could he disregard the possibility that the girl was so upset that she really had run away.

"Isn't it true that she's in Copenhagen?" he asked cautiously. "And that your mother went there today to see her?"

"She went over to buy some shoes."

Wallander nodded. "Well, let's talk about something else," he went on. "You've had time to think now. Do you have any idea who might have killed your father?"

"No."

"Do you agree with your mother, that a lot of people might have wanted to?"

"Yes."

"Why's that?"

For the first time it seemed as though the boy's polite exterior was about to crack. He replied with unexpected vehemence.

"My father was an evil man," he said. "He lost the right to live a long time ago."

Wallander was shaken. How could a young person be so full of hatred?

"That's not something you ought to say," he replied. "That a person has lost his right to live. No matter what he did."

The boy was unmoved.

"What did he do that was so bad?" Wallander asked. "Lots of people are thieves. Lots of them sell stolen goods. They don't have to be monsters because of that."

"He scared us."

"How'd he do that?"

"We were all afraid of him."

"Even you?"

"Yes. But not for the past year."

"Why not?"

"The fear went away."

"And your mother?"

"She was scared."

"Your brother?"

"He'd run and hide when he thought Dad was coming home."

"Your sister?"

"She was more afraid than any of us."

Wallander heard an almost imperceptible shift in the boy's voice. There had been an instant of hesitation, he was sure of it.

"Why?" he asked cautiously.

"She was the most sensitive."

Wallander quickly decided to take a chance.

"Did your Dad touch her?"

"What do you mean?"

"I think you know what I mean."

"Yes, I do. But he never touched her."

There it is, thought Wallander, and tried to avoid revealing his reaction. He may have abused his own daughter. Maybe the younger brother too. Maybe even Stefan. Wallander didn't want to go any further. The question of where the sister was and what may have been done to her was something he didn't want to deal with alone. The thought of abuse upset him.

"Did your Dad have any good friends?" he asked.

"He hung around with a lot of people. But whether any of them were real friends, I don't know."

"Who do you think that I should talk to?"

The boy smiled involuntarily but then regained his composure at once.

"Peter Hjelm," he replied.

Wallander wrote down the name.

"Why did you smile?"

"I don't know."

"Do you know Peter Hjelm?"

"I've met him."

"Where can I find him?"

"He's in the phone book under 'Handyman'. He lives on Kungsgatan."

"How did they know each other?"

"They used to drink together. I know that. What else they did, I can't say."

Wallander looked around the room. "Did your Dad have any of his things here in the flat?"

"No."

"Nothing at all?"

"Not a thing."

Wallander stuffed the paper into his trouser pocket. He had no more questions.

"What's it like to be a policeman?" the boy asked.

Wallander could tell that he was really interested. His eyes gleamed.

"It's a little of this, a little of that," said Wallander, unsure of what he thought about his profession at that moment.

"What's it like to catch a murderer?"

"Cold and grey and miserable," he replied, thinking with distaste of all the TV shows the boy must have seen.

"What are you going to do when you catch the person who killed my Dad?"

"I don't know," said Wallander. "That depends."

"He must be dangerous. Since he's already killed several other people."

Wallander found the boy's curiosity annoying.

"We'll catch him," he said firmly, to put an end to the conversation. "Sooner or later we'll catch him."

He got up from the chair and asked where the bathroom was. The boy pointed to a door in the hall leading to the bedroom. Wallander closed the door behind him. He looked at his face in the mirror. What he needed most was some sunshine. After he'd had a pee he opened the medicine cabinet. There were a few bottles of pills in it. One of them had Louise Fredman's name on it. He saw that she was born on November 9th. He memorised the name of the medicine and the doctor who had prescribed it. *Saroten*. He had never heard of this drug before. He would have to look it up when he got back to Ystad.

In the living-room the boy was sitting in the same position. Wallander wondered whether he was normal after all. His precociousness and self-control made a strange impression. But then Stefan turned towards him and smiled, and for a moment the wariness in his eyes seemed to vanish. Wallander pushed away the thought, and picked up his jacket.

"I'll be calling you again," he said. "Don't forget to tell your mother that I was here. It would be good if you told her what we talked about."

"Can I come and visit you some time?" asked the boy.

Wallander was surprised by the question. It was like having a ball tossed at you and not being able to catch it.

"You mean you want to come to the station in Ystad?"

"Yes."

"Of course," said Wallander. "But call ahead of time. I'm often out. And sometimes it's not convenient."

Wallander went out to the landing and pressed the lift button. They nodded to each other. The boy closed the door. Wallander rode down and walked out into the sunshine.

It had turned into the hottest day yet. He stood for a moment, enjoying the heat, deciding what to do next, then drove down to the Malmö police station. Forsfält was in. Wallander told him about his talk with the boy. He gave Forsfält the name of the doctor, Gunnar Bergdahl, and asked him to get hold of him as soon as possible. Then he told him about his suspicions that Fredman might have abused his daughter and possibly the two boys as well. Forsfält couldn't recall that allegations of that nature had ever been directed at Fredman, but he promised to look into the matter.

Wallander moved on to Peter Hjelm. Forsfält told him that he was a man who resembled Björn Fredman in many ways. He'd been in and out of prison. Once he was arrested with Fredman for taking part in a joint fencing operation. Forsfält was of the opinion that Hjelm was the one who supplied the stolen goods, and Fredman then resold them. Wallander wondered whether Forsfält would mind if he talked to Hjelm alone.

"I'm happy to get out of it," said Forsfält.

Wallander looked up Hjelm's address in Forsfält's phone book. He also gave Forsfält his mobile number. They decided to have lunch together. Forsfält hoped that by then he would have copied all the material the Malmö police had on Björn Fredman.

Wallander left his car outside the station and walked towards Kungsgatan. He went into a clothing shop and bought a shirt, which he put on. Reluctantly he threw away the ruined one Baiba had given him. He went back out into the sunshine. For a few minutes he sat on a bench. Then he walked over to the building where Hjelm lived. The door had an entry code, but Wallander was lucky. After a few minutes an elderly man came out with his dog. Wallander gave him a friendly nod and stepped in the main door. He saw that Hjelm lived on the fourth floor. Just as he was about to open the lift door, his phone rang. It was Forsfält.

"Where are you?" he asked.

"I'm standing outside the lift in Hjelm's building."

"I was hoping you hadn't got there yet."

"Has something happened?"

"I got hold of the doctor. We know each other. I'd totally forgotten about it."

"What'd he say?"

"Something he probably shouldn't have. I promised I wouldn't mention his name. So you can't either."

"I promise."

"He thought that the person we're talking about – I won't mention the name since we're on mobile phones – was admitted to a psychiatric clinic."

Wallander held his breath.

"That explains why she left," he said.

"No, it doesn't," said Forsfält. "She's been there for three years."

Wallander stood there in silence. Someone pressed the button for the lift and it rumbled upwards.

"We'll talk later," Forsfält said. "Good luck with Hjelm."

He hung up. Wallander thought for a long time about what he had just heard. Then he started up the stairs to the fourth floor.

CHAPTER 25

Wallander knew that he'd heard the music coming from Hjelm's flat before. He listened with one ear pressed against the door, and remembered that Linda had played it, and that the band was called the Grateful Dead. He rang the doorbell and took a step back. The music was very loud. He rang again, and then banged hard on the door. Finally the music was turned down. He heard footsteps and then the door was opened wide, and Wallander took a step back so as not to be hit in the face. The man who opened it was completely naked. Wallander also saw that he was under the influence of something. His large body was swaying imperceptibly. Wallander introduced himself and showed his badge. The man didn't bother looking at it. He kept staring at Wallander.

"I've seen you," he said. "On the telly. And in the papers. I never actually read the papers, so I must have seen you on the front page. The policeman they were looking for. The one who shoots people without asking permission. What did you say your name was? Wahlgren?"

"Wallander. Are you Peter Hjelm?"

"Yeah."

"I want to talk to you."

The naked man made a suggestive gesture inside the flat. Wallander assumed this meant he had female company.

"It can't be helped," said Wallander. "It probably won't take very long anyway."

Hjelm reluctantly let him into the hall.

"Put some clothes on," Wallander said firmly.

Hjelm shrugged, pulled an overcoat from a hanger, and put it on. As if at Wallander's request, he also jammed an old hat down over his ears. Wallander followed him down a long hall. Hjelm lived in an old-fashioned, spacious flat. Wallander sometimes dreamed of finding one like it in Ystad. Once he inquired about the flats above the bookshop in the red building on the square, but was shocked at how high the rent was.

When they reached the living-room, Wallander was astonished to discover another man wrapping a sheet around himself. Wallander wasn't prepared for this. A naked man who gestured suggestively had a woman with him, not a man. To conceal his embarrassment, Wallander assumed a formal tone. He sat down in a chair and waved Hjelm to a seat facing him.

"Who are you?" he asked the other man, who was much younger than Hjelm.

"Geert doesn't understand Swedish," said Hjelm. "He's from Amsterdam. He's just visiting."

"Tell him I want to see some identification," said Wallander. "Now."

Hjelm spoke very poor English, worse than Wallander's. The man in the sheet disappeared and came back with a Dutch driver's licence. As usual, Wallander had nothing to write with. He memorised the man's last name, Van Loenen, and handed back the driver's licence. Then he asked a few brief questions in English. Van Loenen said that he was a waiter in a café in Amsterdam and that he had met Hjelm there. This was the third time he'd been to Malmö. He was going back to Amsterdam on the train in a couple of days. When he'd finished, Wallander asked him to leave the room. Hjelm was sitting on the floor, dressed in his overcoat with the hat pulled low over his forehead. Wallander felt himself getting angry.

"Take off that damned hat!" he shouted. "And sit in a chair. Otherwise I'll call a squad car and have you taken in."

Hjelm did as he was told. He tossed the hat in a wide arc so that it landed between two flowerpots on one of the windowsills. Wallander's anger made him start to sweat.

"Björn Fredman is dead," he said brutally. "But I suppose you already know that."

Hjelm's smile disappeared. He didn't know, Wallander realised.

"He was murdered," Wallander continued. "Someone poured acid in his eyes. And cut off part of his scalp. This happened three days ago. Now we're looking for the person who did it. The killer has already murdered two other people. A former politician by the name of Gustaf Wetterstedt and an art dealer named Arne Carlman. But maybe you knew this."

Hjelm nodded slowly. Wallander tried without success to interpret his reactions.

"Now I understand why Björn didn't answer his phone," he said after a while. "I tried to call him all day yesterday. And this morning I tried again."

"What did you want from him?"

"I was thinking of inviting him over for dinner."

Wallander saw at once that this was a lie. Since he was still furious at Hjelm's arrogant attitude, it was easy for him to tighten his grip. In all his years as a police officer Wallander had only lost control twice and struck individuals he was interrogating. He could usually control his rage.

"Don't lie to me," he said. "The only way you're going to see me walk out that door is if you give me clear, truthful answers to my questions. If you don't, all hell will break loose. We're dealing with a serial killer. Which means the police have special powers."

The last part wasn't true, of course. But it made an impression on Hjelm.

"I was calling him about a gig we had together."

"What sort of gig?"

"A little import and export. He owed me money."

"How much?"

"A little. A hundred thousand, maybe. No more than that."

This "little" sum of money was equivalent to many months' wages for Wallander. This made him even angrier.

"We can get back to your business with Fredman later," he said. "That's something the Malmö police will deal with. What I want "to know is whether you can tell me who killed him."

"Not me, that's for sure."

"I wasn't suggesting you did. Anyone else?"

Wallander saw that Hjelm was trying to concentrate.

"I don't know," he said finally.

"You seem hesitant."

"Björn was into a lot of things I didn't know about."

"Such as?"

"I don't know."

"Give me a straight answer!"

"Well, shit! I just don't know. We did some deals. What Fredman did with the rest of his time I can't tell you. In this business you're not supposed to know too much. You can't know too little either. But that's something else again."

"What do you think Fredman might have been into?"

"I think he was doing collections quite a bit."

"He was an enforcer, you mean?"

"Something like that."

"Who was his boss?"

"Dunno."

"Don't lie to me."

"I'm not lying. I just don't know."

Wallander almost believed him.

"What else?"

"He was a pretty secretive type. He travelled a lot. And when he came back he was always sunburnt. And he brought back souvenirs."

"Where from?"

"He never said. But after his trips he usually had plenty of money."

Björn Fredman's passport, Wallander thought. We haven't found it.

"Who else knew Fredman besides you?"

"Lots of people."

"Who knew him as well as you do?"

"Nobody."

"Did he have a woman?"

"What a question! Of course he had women!"

"Was there anyone special?"

"He switched around a lot."

"Why did he switch?"

"Why does anyone switch? Why do I switch? Because I meet somebody from Amsterdam one day and somebody from Bjärred the next."

"Bjärred?"

"It's just an example, damn it! Halmstad, if that's any better!"

Wallander stopped asking questions. He frowned at Hjelm. He felt an instinctive animosity towards him. Towards a thief who regarded a hundred thousand kronor as "a little money".

"Gustaf Wetterstedt," he said finally. "And Arne Carlman. You knew they had been killed."

"I watch TV."

"Did Fredman ever mention their names?"

"No."

"Do you think you may have forgotten? Is it possible he did know them?"

Hjelm sat in silence for more than a minute. Wallander waited.

"I'm positive," he said finally. "But he might not have told me about it."

"This man who's on the loose is dangerous," said Wallander. "He's ice-cold and calculating. And crazy. He poured acid in Fredman's eyes. It must have been incredibly painful. Do you get my point?"

"Yes, I do."

"I want you to do some work for me. Spread it around that the police are looking for a connection between these three men. I assume you agree that we have to get this lunatic off the streets. A man who pours acid in somebody's eyes."

Hjelm grimaced.

"OK."

Wallander got up.

"Call Detective Forsfält," he said. "Or give me a call. In Ystad. Anything you can come up with might be important."

"Björn had a girlfriend named Marianne," said Hjelm. "She lives over by the Triangle."

"What's her last name?"

"Eriksson, I think."

"What kind of work does she do?"

"I don't know."

"Have you got her phone number?"

"I can look it up."

"Do it."

Wallander waited while Hjelm left the room. He could hear whispering voices, at least one of which sounded annoyed. Hjelm came back and handed Wallander a piece of paper. Then he followed him out to the hall.

Hjelm had sobered up, but he still seemed completely unfazed by what had happened to his friend. Wallander felt a great uneasiness at the coldness Hjelm exhibited. It was incomprehensible to him.

"That crazy man . . ." Hjelm began, without finishing his sentence. Wallander understood his unasked question.

"He's after specific individuals. If you can't see yourself in any connection with Wetterstedt, Carlman, and Fredman, you have nothing to worry about."

"Why haven't you caught him?"

Wallander stared at Hjelm, his anger returning.

"One reason is that people like you find it so hard to answer simple questions," he said.

When he got down to the street he stood there facing the sun and closed his eyes. He thought over the conversation with Hjelm, and the anxiety that the investigation was on the wrong track returned. He opened his eyes and walked over to the side of the building, into the shade. He couldn't shake off the feeling that he was steering the whole investigation into a blind alley. He remembered the half-formed idea that he'd had, that something he'd heard was significant. There's something missing, he thought. There's a link between Wetterstedt and Carlman and Fredman that I'm tripping over. The man they were searching for could strike again, and Wallander knew one thing about the case for certain. They had no idea who he was. And they didn't even know where to look. He left the shadow of the wall and hailed a cab.

It was past midday when he got out in front of the Malmö station. When he reached Forsfält's office he got a message to call Ystad. Again he had the terrible feeling that something serious had happened. Ebba answered. She reassured him and then switched him over to Nyberg. They had found a fingerprint on Fredman's left eyelid. It was smudged, but it was still good enough for them to confirm a match with the prints they had found. There was no longer any doubt they were after a single killer. The forensic examination confirmed that Fredman was murdered less than twelve hours before the body was discovered, and that acid had been poured into his eyes while he was alive.

Next Ebba put him through to Martinsson, who had received a positive confirmation from Interpol that Dolores María Santana's father recognised the medallion. It had belonged to her. Martinsson also mentioned that the Swedish embassy in the Dominican Republic was extremely unwilling to pay to transport the girl's remains back to Santiago.

Wallander was listening with half an ear. When Martinsson finished complaining about the embassy, Wallander asked him what Svedberg and Höglund were working on. Martinsson said that neither of them had come up with much. Wallander told him he'd be back in Ystad that afternoon and hung up. Forsfält stood out in the hall sneezing.

"Allergies," he said, blowing his nose. "Summer is the worst."

They walked in the dazzling sunshine to a restaurant where Forsfält liked to eat spaghetti. After Wallander told him about his meeting with Hjelm, Forsfält started talking about his summer house, up near Älmhult. Wallander guessed that he didn't want to spoil their lunch by talking about the investigation. Normally this would have made Wallander impatient, but he listened with growing fascination as the old detective described how he was restoring an old smithy. Only when they were having coffee did they return to the investigation. Forsfält would try to interview Marianne Eriksson that same day. But most important was the revelation that Louise Fredman had been a patient in a psychiatric hospital for the past three years.

"I'm not sure," said Forsfält. "But I'd guess that she's in Lund. At St Lars Hospital. That's where the more serious cases finish up, I think."

"It's hard to bypass all the obstacles when you want to get patient records," said Wallander. "And that's a good thing, of course. But I think we must know everything about Louise Fredman. Especially since the family haven't told the truth."

"Mental illness isn't something people want to talk about," Forsfält reminded him. "I had an aunt who was in and out of institutions her whole life. We almost never talked about her to strangers. It was a disgrace."

"I'll ask one of the prosecutors in Ystad to get in touch with Malmö," said Wallander.

"What reason are you going to give?" asked Forsfält.

Wallander thought for a moment.

"I don't know," he said. "I have a suspicion that Fredman may have abused her."

"That's not good enough," said Forsfält firmly.

"I know," said Wallander. "Somehow I have to show that it's crucial to the whole murder investigation to obtain information on Louise Fredman. About her and from her."

"What do you think she could help you with?"

Wallander threw out his hands.

"I don't know," he said. "Maybe nothing will be cleared up by finding out what it is that's keeping her locked up. Maybe she's incapable of holding a conversation with anyone."

Forsfält nodded, deep in thought. Wallander knew that Forsfält's objections were well-founded, but he couldn't ignore his hunch that Louise Fredman was important. Wallander paid for lunch. When they got back to the station Forsfält went to the reception desk and got a black plastic bag.

"Here are a few kilos of papers on Björn Fredman's troubled life," he said, smiling. But then he turned serious, as if his smile had been inappropriate.

"That poor devil," he said. "The pain must have been incredible. What could he possibly have done to deserve it?"

"That's just it," said Wallander. "What did he do? What did Wetterstedt do? Or Carlman? And to whom?"

"Scalping and acid in the eyes. Where the hell are we headed?"

"According to the national police board, towards a society where a police district like Ystad doesn't need to be manned at all on weekends," said Wallander.

Forsfält stood silent for a moment before he replied. "I hardly think that's the answer," he said.

"Tell the national commissioner."

"What can he do?" Forsfält asked. "He's got a board of directors on his back. And above them are the politicians."

"He could always refuse," said Wallander. "Or he could resign if things get too far out of hand."

"Perhaps," said Forsfält absently.

"Thanks for all your help," said Wallander. "And especially for the story about the smithy."

"You'll have to come up and visit sometime," said Forsfält. "I don't know whether Sweden is as fantastic as all the magazines say it is. But it's a great country all the same. Beautiful. And surprisingly unspoiled. If you take the trouble to look."

"You won't forget Marianne Eriksson?"

"I'm going to see if I can find her right now," replied Forsfält. "I'll call you later."

Wallander unlocked his car and tossed in the plastic bag. Then he drove out of town and onto the E65. He rolled down the window and let the summer wind blow across his face. When he arrived in Ystad he stopped at the supermarket and bought groceries. He was already at the checkout when he discovered he had to go back for washing powder. He drove home and carried the bags up to his flat, but found that he had lost his keys.

He went back downstairs and searched the car without finding them. He called Forsfält and was told that he had gone out. One of his colleagues went into his office and looked to see whether they were on his desk. They weren't there. He called Peter Hjelm, who picked up the phone almost at once. He came back minutes later and said he couldn't find them.

Wallander fished out the piece of paper with the Fredmans' number in Rosengård. The son answered. Wallander waited while he looked for the keys, but he couldn't find them. Wallander wondered whether to tell him that he now knew his sister Louise had been in a hospital for several years, but decided not to.

He thought for a while. He might have dropped his keys at the place where he ate lunch with Forsfält, or in the shop where he had bought the new shirt. Annoyed, he went back to his car and drove to the station. Ebba kept a spare set of keys for him. He told her the name of the clothing shop and the restaurant in Malmö. She said she would check whether they had found them. Wallander left the station and went home without talking to any of his colleagues. He needed to think over all that had happened that day. In particular, he wanted to plan his conversation with Åkeson. He carried in the groceries and put them away. He had missed the laundry time he had signed up for. He took the box of washing powder and gathered up the huge pile of laundry. When he got downstairs, the room was still empty. He sorted the pile, guessing which types of clothes required the same water temperature. With some fumbling he managed to get two machines started. Satisfied, he went back up to his flat.

He had just closed the door when the phone rang. It was Forsfält, who told him that Marianne Eriksson was in Spain. He was going to keep trying to reach her at the hotel where the travel agent said she was staying. Wallander unpacked the contents of the black plastic bag. The files covered his whole kitchen table. He took a beer out of the refrigerator and sat down in the living-room. He listened to Jussi Björling on the stereo. After a while he stretched out on the sofa with the can of beer beside him on the floor. Soon he was asleep.

He woke with a start when the music ended. Lying on the sofa, he finished the can of beer. The phone rang. It was Linda. Could she stay at his place for a few days? Her friend's parents were coming home. Wallander suddenly felt energetic. He gathered up all the papers spread out on the kitchen table and carried them to his bedroom. Then he made up the bed in the room where Linda slept. He opened all the windows and let the warm evening breeze blow through the flat. He went downstairs and got his laundry out of the machines. To his surprise none of the colours had run. He hung the laundry in the drying room. Linda had told him that she wouldn't want any food, so he boiled some potatoes and grilled a piece of meat for his supper. As he ate he wondered whether he should call Baiba. He also thought about his lost keys. About Louise Fredman. About Peter Hjelm. And about the stack of papers waiting for him in his bedroom. And he thought about the man who was out there somewhere in the summer night. The man they would have to catch soon. When he'd finished, he stood by the open window until he saw Linda coming down the street.

"I love you," he said aloud.

He dropped the keys from the window and she caught them with one hand.

CHAPTER 26

Wallander sat up half the night talking with Linda, but he still forced himself to get up at 6 a.m. He stood in the shower for a long time before managing to shake off his weariness. He moved quietly through the flat and thought that it was only when either Baiba or Linda was there that it really felt like home. When he was alone it felt like little more than a temporary roof over his head. He made coffee and went down to the drying room. One of his neighbours pointed out that he hadn't cleaned up after himself the day before. She was an old woman who lived alone, and he greeted her when they ran into each other, but didn't know her name. She showed him a spot on the floor where there was some spilled washing powder. Wallander apologised and promised to do better in the future. What a nag, he thought as he went upstairs. But he knew she was right, he had been too lazy to clean up.

He dumped his laundry on the bed and then carried the papers Forsfält had given him out to the kitchen. He felt guilty because he hadn't read them the night before. But the talk with Linda had been important. They had sat out on the balcony in the warm night. Listening to her, he felt for the first time that she was an adult. She told him that Mona was talking about remarrying. Wallander was depressed at this news. He knew that Linda had been asked to inform him. But for the first time he talked about why he thought the marriage had fallen apart. From her response he could tell that Mona saw it quite differently. Then she asked him about Baiba, and he tried to answer her as honestly as he could, though there was a lot that was still unresolved about their relationship. And when they finally turned in, he felt sure that she didn't blame him for what had happened, and that now she could view her parents' divorce as something that had been necessary.

He sat down at the kitchen table and looked at the extensive material describing Björn Fredman's life. It took him two hours just to skim through it all. Once in a while he would jot down notes. By the time he pushed aside the last folder and stretched, it was after 8 a.m. He poured another cup of coffee and stood by the open window. It was going to be a beautiful day. He couldn't remember the last time that it had rained.

He tried to think through what he had read. Björn Fredman had been a sorry character from the outset. He had had a difficult and troubled home life as a child, and his first brush with the police, over a stolen bicycle, occurred when he was seven. He had been in constant trouble ever since. Björn Fredman had struck back at a life that had never given him any pleasure. Wallander thought of how many times during his career he'd read these grey, colourless sagas in which it was clear from the first sentence that the story would end badly.

Sweden had pulled herself out of material poverty, largely under her own steam. When Wallander was a child there had still been desperately poor people, even though they were few in number by then. But the other kind of poverty, he thought, we've never dealt with that. And now that progress seemed to have stopped for the time being, and the welfare state was being eroded, the spiritual poverty that had been there all along was beginning to surface.

Fredman was not the only one. We haven't created a society where people like him could feel at home, Wallander thought. When we got rid of the old society, where families stuck together, we forgot to replace it with something else. The great loneliness that resulted was a price we didn't know we were going to have to pay. Or perhaps we chose to ignore it.

He put the folders back in the black plastic bag and then listened once again outside Linda's door. She was asleep. He couldn't resist the temptation to open the door a crack, and peek in at her. She was sleeping curled up, turned to the wall. He left a note on the kitchen table and wondered what to do about his keys. He called the station. Ebba was at home. He looked up her home number. Neither the restaurant nor the clothing shop had found his keys. He added to the note that Linda should put the house keys under the doormat. Then he drove to the station.

Hansson was sitting in his office, looking greyer than ever. Wallander felt sorry for him, and wondered how long he would last. They went to the canteen and had some coffee. There was little sign that the biggest manhunt in the history of the Ystad police force was under way. Wallander told Hansson that he realised now that they needed reinforcements. And that Hansson needed a break. They had enough manpower to send out in the field, but Hansson needed relief on the home front. He tried to protest, but Wallander refused to back down. Hansson's grey face and harried eyes were evidence enough. Finally Hansson gave in and promised to speak to the county chief of police on Monday. They would have to borrow a sergeant from another district.

The investigative team had a meeting set for 10 a.m. Wallander left Hansson, who already seemed relieved. He went to his office and called Forsfält, who couldn't be located. It took 15 minutes before Forsfält called back. Wallander asked about Björn Fredman's passport.

"It should be in his flat, of course," said Forsfält. "Funny we haven't found it."

"I don't know if this means anything," said Wallander. "But I want to find out more about those trips Peter Hjelm was talking about."

"E.U. countries hardly use entry and exit stamps any more," Forsfält pointed out.

"I think Hjelm was talking about trips further afield," replied Wallander. "But I could be wrong."

Forsfält said that they would start searching for Fredman's passport immediately.

"I spoke with Marianne Eriksson last night," he said. "I thought about calling you, but it was late."

"Where did you find her?"

"In Malaga. She didn't even know that Fredman was dead."

"What did she have to say?"

"Not much, I must say. Obviously she was upset. I couldn't spare her any details, unfortunately. They had met occasionally over the past six months. I got a feeling that she actually liked Fredman."

"In that case, she's the first," said Wallander. "If you don't count Hjelm."

"She thought he was a businessman," Forsfält continued. "She had no idea he had been involved in illegal activities. She also didn't know he was married and had three children. She was quite upset. I smashed the image she had of Fredman to smithereens with one phone call, I'm afraid."

"How could you tell she liked him?"

"She was hurt that he had lied to her."

"Did you learn anything else?"

"Not really. But she's on her way back to Sweden. She's coming home on Friday. I'll talk to her then."

"And then you're going on holiday?"

"I was planning to. Weren't you supposed to start yours soon too?"

"I don't even want to think about it."

"Once they start moving, things could happen quickly."

Wallander didn't respond to Forsfält's last remark. They said goodbye. Wallander dialled the switchboard, and asked the receptionist to track down Åkeson. After more than a minute she told him that Åkeson was at home. Wallander looked at the clock. Just after 9 a.m. He made a quick decision and left his office. He ran into Svedberg in the hall, still wearing his silly cap.

"How is the sunburn?" asked Wallander.

"Better. But I don't dare go out without the cap."

"Do you think locksmiths are open on Saturday?" asked Wallander.

"I doubt it. But there are locksmiths on call."

"I need to get a couple of keys copied."

"Did you lock yourself out?"

"I've lost my house keys."

"Were your name and address on them?"

"Of course not."

"Then at least you don't need to change your lock."

Wallander told Svedberg that he might be a little late for the meeting. He had to see Åkeson about something important. Åkeson lived in a residential neighbourhood near the hospital. Wallander had been to the house before and knew the way. When he arrived and got out of the car, he saw Åkeson mowing his lawn. He stopped when he saw Wallander.

"Has something happened?" he asked when they met at the gate.

"Yes and no," said Wallander. "Something is always happening. But nothing crucial. I need your help with part of the investigation."

They went into the garden. Wallander thought gloomily that it looked like every other garden he'd been in. He turned down an offer of coffee. They sat in the shade of a roofed patio.

"If my wife comes out I'd appreciate it if you didn't mention that I'm going to Africa this autumn. It's still quite a sensitive topic," said Åkeson.

Wallander said he wouldn't. He explained about Louise Fredman and his suspicion that she might have been abused by her father. He was honest and said that this could well be a false trail and might not add anything to the investigation. He outlined the new tack they were trying in the case, which was based around the knowledge that Fredman had been killed by the same person as Wetterstedt and Carlman. "Björn Fredman was the black sheep in the scalped 'family'," he said, realising immediately how inappropriate the description was.

How did he fit into the picture? How didn't he fit? Maybe they could find the connection by starting with Fredman at a place where a link was by no means obvious. Åkeson listened intently.

"I talked to Ekholm," he said when Wallander had finished. "A good man, I thought. Competent. Realistic. The impression I got from him was that the man we're looking for may strike again."

"I'm always thinking about that."

"What about getting reinforcements?" Åkeson asked.

Wallander told him about his conversation with Hansson earlier that morning.

"I think you're mistaken," Åkeson said. "It's not enough for Hansson to have support. I think you have a tendency to overestimate the work that you and your colleagues can handle. This case is big, in fact it's too big. I want to see more people working on it. More manpower means more things can be done at the same time. We're dealing with a man who could kill again. That means we have no time to lose."

"I know," said Wallander. "I keep worrying that we're already too late."

"Reinforcements," Åkeson repeated. "What do you think?"

"For the time being no, that's not the problem."

Tension rose between them.

"Let's say that I, as the leader of the investigation, can't accept that," said Åkeson. "But you don't want more manpower. Where does that leave us?"

"In a difficult situation."

"Very difficult. And unpleasant. If I request more manpower against the wishes of the police, my argument has to be that the present investigative team isn't up to the task. I'd have to declare your team incompetent, even though I'd phrase it in more kindly terms. And I don't want to do that."

"I assume you'll do it if you have to," said Wallander. "And that's when I'll resign from the force."

"God damn it, Kurt!"

"You were the one who started this discussion, not me."

"You've got your regulations. I've got mine. So I regard it as a dereliction of my duty if I don't request that you have more personnel put at your disposal."

"And dogs," said Wallander sarcastically. "I want police dogs. And helicopters."

The discussion was at an end. Wallander regretted flying off the handle. He wasn't sure why he was so opposed to getting reinforcements. He knew that problems in cooperation could damage and delay an investigation. But he couldn't argue with Åkeson's point that more things could be investigated simultaneously with more people.

"Talk to Hansson," Wallander said. "He's the one who makes the decision."

"Hansson doesn't do anything without asking you. And then he does whatever you say."

"I'll refuse to give him my opinion. I'll give you that much help."

Åkeson stood up and turned off a dripping tap with a green hose attached to it. Then he sat down again.

"Let's wait until Monday," he said.

"Let's do that," said Wallander. Then he returned to Louise Fredman. He reiterated that there was no proof that Fredman had abused his daughter. But it might be true; he couldn't rule out anything, and that was why he needed Åkeson's help.

"It's possible I'm making a big mistake," Wallander concluded. "And it wouldn't be the first time. But I can't afford to ignore any leads. I want to know why Louise Fredman is in a psychiatric hospital. And when I find out, we'll decide whether there's any reason to take the next step."

"Which would be?"

"Talking to her."

Åkeson nodded. Wallander was sure he could count on his cooperation. They knew each other well. Åkeson respected Wallander's instincts, even when they lacked solid evidence.

"It can be complicated," said Åkeson. "But I'll try to do something over the weekend."

"I'd appreciate it," said Wallander. "You can call me at the station or at home whenever you like."

Åkeson went inside to make sure he had all of Wallander's phone numbers. The tension between them had evaporated. Åkeson followed him to the gate.

"Summer is off to a good start," he said. "But I'm afraid you haven't had much time to think about that."

Wallander sensed that Åkeson was feeling sympathetic.

"Not much," he replied. "But Ann-Britt's grandmother predicted that the good weather is going to last for a long time."

"Can't she predict where we should be looking for the killer instead?" said Åkeson.

Wallander shook his head in resignation.

"We're getting lots of tip-offs all the time. The usual prophets and psychics have been calling in. There are trainees sorting through the information. Then Höglund and Svedberg go through it, but so far nothing useful has come in. No-one saw a thing, either outside Wetterstedt's house or at Carlman's farm. There aren't many leads about the pit outside the railway station or the van at the airport either."

"The man you're hunting for is careful," said Åkeson.

"Careful, cunning, and totally devoid of human emotions," said Wallander. "I can't imagine how his mind works. Even Ekholm seems dumbstruck. For the first time in my life I've got the feeling that a monster is on the loose."

For a moment Åkeson seemed to be pondering what Wallander had said.

"Ekholm told me he's putting all the data into the computer. He's using the F.B.I. programme. It might produce something."

"Let's hope so," said Wallander.

Wallander said no more. But Åkeson understood what was implied. Before he strikes again.

Wallander drove back to the station. He arrived in the conference room a few minutes late. To cheer up his hard-working detectives, Hansson had driven down to Fridolf's bakery and bought pastries. Wallander sat down in his usual spot and looked around. Martinsson was wearing shorts for the first time that season. Höglund had the first hint of a tan. He wondered enviously how she had had time to sunbathe. The only one dressed appropriately was Ekholm, who had established his base at the far end of the table.

"One of our evening papers had the good taste to provide its readers with historical background on the art of scalping," Svedberg said gloomily. "We can only hope that it won't be the next craze, given all the lunatics we've got running around."

Wallander tapped the table with a pencil.

"Let's get started," he said. "We're searching for the most vicious killer we've ever had to deal with. He has committed all three murders.

But that's all we know. Except for the fact that there's a real risk that he'll strike again."

A hush fell around the table. Wallander hadn't intended to create an oppressive atmosphere. He knew from experience that it was easier if the tone was light, even when the crimes being investigated were brutal. Everyone in the room was just as despondent as he was. The feeling that they were hunting a monster, whose emotional degeneracy was unimaginable, haunted each of them.

It was one of the most demoralising meetings Wallander had ever attended. Outside, the summer was almost unnaturally beautiful, Hansson's pastries were melting and sticky in the heat, and his own revulsion made him feel sick. Although he paid attention to everything said, he was also wondering how he could bear to remain a policeman. Hadn't he reached a point where he ought to realise he had done his share? There had to be more to life. But he also knew that what made him down-hearted was the fact that they couldn't see a single prospect of a break, a chink in the wall that they could squeeze through. They still had a great many leads to pursue, but they lacked a specific direction. In most cases there was an invisible navigation point against which they could correct their course. This time there was no fixed point. They were even starting to doubt that a connection between the murdered men existed.

Three hours later, when the meeting was over, they knew that the only thing to do was keep going. Wallander looked at the exhausted faces around him and told them to try and get some rest. He cancelled all meetings for Sunday. They would meet again on Monday morning. He didn't have to mention the one exception: unless something serious happened. Unless the man who was out there somewhere in the summertime decided to strike again.

Wallander got home in the afternoon and found a note from Linda saying that she would be out that evening. He was tired, and slept for a few hours. When he awoke, he called Baiba twice without success. He talked to Gertrud, who told him everything was fine with his father. He was talking a lot about the trip to Italy. Wallander hoovered the flat and mended a broken window latch. The whole time the thought of the unknown killer occupied his thoughts. At 7 p.m. he made himself a supper of cod fillet and boiled potatoes. Then he sat on the balcony with a cup of coffee and absentmindedly leafed through an old issue of *Ystad Recorder*. When Linda got home they drank tea in the kitchen. The next day Wallander would be allowed to see a rehearsal of the revue she was working on with Kajsa, but Linda was very secretive and didn't want to tell him what it was about. At 11.30 p.m. they both went to bed.

Wallander fell asleep almost at once. Linda lay awake in her room listening to the night birds. Then she fell asleep too, leaving the door to her room ajar.

Neither of them stirred when the front door was opened very slowly at 2 a.m. Hoover was barefoot. He stood motionless in the hall, listening. He could hear a man snoring in a room to the left of the living-room. He stepped into the flat. The door to another room stood ajar. A girl who might have been his sister's age was in there sleeping. He couldn't resist the temptation to go in and stand right next to her. His power over the sleeper was absolute. He went on towards the room where the snoring was coming from. The policeman named Wallander lay on his back and had kicked off all but a small part of the sheet. He was sleeping heavily. His chest heaved with his deep breathing.

Hoover stood utterly still and watched him. He thought about his sister, who would soon be freed from all this evil. Who would soon return to life. He looked at the sleeping man and thought about the girl in the next room, who must be his daughter. He made his decision. In a few days he would return.

He left the flat as soundlessly as he had come, locking the door with the keys he had taken from the policeman's jacket. A few moments later the silence was broken by a moped starting up. Then all was quiet again, except for the night birds singing.

CHAPTER 27

When Wallander awoke on Sunday morning he felt that he had slept enough for the first time in a long while. It was past 8 a.m. Through a gap in the curtains he could see a patch of blue. He stayed in bed and listened for Linda. Then he got up, put on his newly washed dressing gown, and peeked into her room. She was still asleep. He felt transported back to her childhood. He smiled at the memory and went to the kitchen to make coffee. The thermometer outside the kitchen window showed 19°C. When the coffee was ready he laid a breakfast tray for Linda. He remembered what she liked. One three-minute egg, toast, a few slices of cheese, and a sliced-up tomato. Only water to drink.

He drank his coffee and waited a while longer. She was startled out of her sleep when he called her name. When she saw the tray she burst out laughing. He sat at the foot of the bed while she ate. He hadn't thought of the investigation except briefly when he'd woken.

Linda set the tray aside, leaned back in bed, and stretched.

"What were you doing up last night?" she asked. "Did you have trouble sleeping?"

"I slept like a rock," said Wallander. "I didn't even get up to go to the bathroom."

"Then I must have been dreaming," she said, yawning. "I thought you opened my door and came into my room."

"You must have been," he said. "For once I slept the whole night through."

They agreed that they would meet at Österport Square at 7 p.m. Linda asked him if he knew that Sweden would be playing Saudi Arabia in the quarter-finals at that time. Wallander said he didn't give a damn, although he had bet that Sweden would win it 3–1 and advanced Martinsson another hundred kronor. The girls had managed to borrow an empty shop for their rehearsals.

After she left, Wallander took out his ironing board and started ironing his clean shirts. After doing a passable job on two of them, he got bored and called Baiba. She was glad to hear from him, he could tell. He told her that Linda was visiting and that he felt rested for the first time in weeks. Baiba was busy finishing her work at the university before the summer break. She talked about the trip to Skagen with childlike anticipation. After they hung up, Wallander went into the living-room and put on *Aïda*, the volume turned up high.

He felt happy and full of energy. He sat out on the balcony and read through the newspapers from the past few days, skipping reports on the murders. He had granted himself half a day off, total escape until midday. Then he was going to get cracking again. But Åkeson called him at 11.15 a.m. He had been in touch with the chief prosecutor in Malmö and they had discussed Wallander's request. Åkeson thought it would be possible for Wallander to get answers to some of his questions about Louise Fredman within the next few days. But he had one reservation.

"Wouldn't it be simpler to get the girl's mother to give you the answers you need?" he asked.

"I'm not sure I'd get the truth from her," Wallander answered.

"Which is what?"

"The mother is protecting her daughter," said Wallander. "It's only natural. I would do the same. No matter what she told me, it would be coloured by the fact that she's protecting her. Medical records and doctors' reports speak another language."

"You know best," said Åkeson, promising that he'd be in touch again as soon as he had something concrete to tell him.

The talk with Åkeson set Wallander thinking about the case again. He decided to take a notebook and sit on the balcony to go over the plan of the investigation for the coming week. He was getting hungry, though, and thought he'd allow himself to eat out. Just before noon he left the flat, dressed all in white like a tennis player, wearing sandals. He drove east out of town along Österleden, thinking that he could drop in on his father later on. If he hadn't had the investigation hanging over his head, he could have taken Gertrud and his father to lunch somewhere. But right now he needed time to himself. Over the past few weeks he had been constantly surrounded by people, involved in team meetings, and in discussions with others. Now he wanted to be alone.

Hardly aware of where he was going, he drove all the way to Simrishamn. He parked by the marina and took a walk. He found a corner table to himself at the Harbour Inn, and sat watching the holiday makers all around him. One of these people could be the man I'm looking for, he thought. If Ekholm's theories are right – that the killer lives a completely normal life, with no outward signs that he subjects his victims to the worst violence imaginable – then he could be sitting right here eating lunch. And at that instant the summer day slipped out of his hands. He went over everything one more time. He didn't know why, but he began with the girl who died in the rape field. She had nothing to do with the other events; it had been a suicide, prompted by some as yet unknown cause. Still, that's where Wallander began each time he started one of his reviews of the case.

But on this particular Sunday, in the Harbour Inn in Simrishamn, something started churning in his subconscious. It came to him that someone had said something in connection with the girl's death. He sat there with his fork in his hand and tried to coax the thought to the surface. Who had said it? What had been said? Why was it important? After a while he gave up. Sooner or later he'd remember what it was. His subconscious always demanded patience. As if to prove that he actually possessed that patience, he ordered dessert. With satisfaction he noted that the shorts he'd put on for the first time that summer weren't quite as tight as they had been the year before. He ate his apple pie and ordered coffee.

He tried to follow his thoughts the way a discerning actor reads through his part for the first time. Where were the gaps? Where were the faults? Where did he combine fact and circumstance too sloppily and draw a wrong conclusion? He went through Wetterstedt's house again, through the garden, out onto the beach; he imagined Wetterstedt in front of him, and Wallander became the killer stalking Wetterstedt like a silent shadow. He climbed onto the garage roof and read a torn comic book while he waited for Wetterstedt to settle at his desk and maybe leaf through his collection of pornographic photographs.

Then he did the same thing with Carlman; he put a motorcycle behind the road workers' hut and followed the tractor path up to the hill where he had a view over Carlman's farm. Now and then he made a note on his pad. *The garage roof. What did he hope to see? Carlman's hill. Binoculars?* He went over everything that had happened, deaf to the noise around him. He paid another visit to Hugo Sandin, he talked once more with Sara Björklund, and he made a note that he ought to get in touch with her again. Maybe the same questions would provoke different, fuller answers. What would the difference be? He thought for a long time about Carlman's daughter. He thought about Louise Fredman, and her polite brother. He was rested, his fatigue was gone, and his thoughts rose easily and soared on the updraughts inside him.

He glanced at what he had scribbled on his pad, as if it were magic, automatic writing, and left the Harbour Inn. He sat on one of the benches in the park outside the Hotel Svea and looked out over the sea. There was a warm, gentle breeze blowing. The crew of a yacht with a Danish flag was struggling with an unruly spinnaker. Wallander read his notes again.

The connection was always shifting, from parents to children. He thought about Carlman's daughter and Louise Fredman. Was it just a coincidence that one of them had tried to commit suicide after her father died and the other had been in a psychiatric clinic for a long time?

Wetterstedt was the exception. He had two adult children. Wallander recalled something Rydberg had once said. *What happens first is not necessarily the beginning.* Could that be true in this case? He tried to imagine that the killer they were looking for was a woman. But it was impossible. He thought of the physical strength needed for the scalpings, the axe blows, and the acid in Fredman's eyes. It had to be a man. A man who kills men. While women commit suicide or suffer mental illness.

He got up and moved to another bench, as if to register the fact that there were other conceivable explanations. Gustaf Wetterstedt was involved in shady deals. There was a vague but still unexplained connection between him and Carlman. It had to do with art, art theft, maybe forgery. It all had to do with money. It wasn't inconceivable that Björn Fredman could also be involved in the same area. He hadn't found anything useful in the dossier on his life, but he couldn't write it off yet. Nothing could be written off yet; that presented both a problem and an opportunity.

Wallander watched the Danish yacht. The crew had begun folding up the spinnaker. He took out his pad and looked at the last word he had written. *Mystery.* There was a hint of ritual to the murders. He had thought so himself, and Ekholm had pointed it out at the last meeting. The scalps were a ritual, as trophy collecting always was. The significance was the same as that of a moose's head mounted on a hunter's wall. It was the proof. The proof of what? For whom? For the killer alone, or for someone else as well? For a god or a demon conjured up in a sick mind? For someone else, whose demeanour was just as inconspicuous as the killer's?

Wallander thought about what Ekholm had said about invocations and initiation rites. A sacrifice was made so that another could obtain grace. Become rich, make a fortune, get well? There were many possibilities. There were motorcycle gangs with rules about how new members proved themselves worthy. In the United States it wasn't unusual to have to kill someone, whether picked at random or specially chosen, to be deemed worthy of membership. This macabre rite had spread, even to Sweden. Wallander thought of the motorcycle gangs in Skåne, and he remembered the road workers' hut at the bottom of Carlman's hill. The thought was dizzying – that the tracks might lead them to motorcycle gangs. Wallander put aside this idea for the moment, although he knew that nothing could be ruled out.

He walked back to the other bench where he had sat before. He was back at the starting point. He realised that he couldn't go any further without discussing it with someone. He thought of Ann-Britt Höglund. Could he bother her on a Sunday? He got up and went over to his car to call her. She was at home. He was welcome to drop by. Guiltily, he postponed his visit to his father. He had to have someone else confront his ideas, and if he waited, there was a good chance he would get lost among multiple trains of thought. He drove back towards Ystad, keeping just above the speed limit. He hadn't heard about any speed traps planned for this Sunday.

It was 3 p.m. when he pulled up in front of Höglund's house. She was in a light summer dress. Her two children were playing in a neighbour's garden. She offered Wallander the porch swing while she sat in a wicker chair.

"I really didn't want to bother you," he said. "You could have said no."

"Yesterday I was tired," she replied. "As we all were. *Are*, I mean. But today I feel better."

"Last night was definitely the night of the sleeping policemen," said Wallander. "It reaches a point where you can't push yourself any further. All you get is empty, grey fatigue. We'd reached that point."

He told her about his trip to Simrishamn, about how he went back and forth between the benches in the park down by the harbour.

"I went over everything again," he said. "Sometimes it's possible to make unexpected discoveries. But you know that already."

"I'm hoping something will come of Ekholm's work," she said. "Computers that are correctly programmed can cross-reference investigative material and come up with links that you wouldn't have dreamed were there. They don't *think*. But sometimes they *combine* better than we can."

"My distrust of computers is partly because I'm getting old," said Wallander. "But it doesn't mean I don't want Ekholm to succeed with his behavioural method. For me, of course, it's of no importance who sets the snare that catches the killer just as long as it happens. And soon."

She gave him a sombre look.

"Do you think that he will strike again?"

"I do. Without being able to get a handle on why, I think there's something *unfinished* about this murder scenario. If you'll pardon the expression. There's something missing. It scares me. And yes, it makes me think he'll strike again."

"How are we going to find where Fredman was killed?" she asked.

"Unless we're lucky, we won't," said Wallander. "Or unless somebody heard something."

"I've been checking up on whether there have been any calls coming in from people who heard screams," she said. "But I have found nothing."

The unheard scream hung over them. Wallander rocked slowly back and forth on the swing.

"It's rare that a solution comes clean out of the blue," he said when the silence had lasted too long. "I was walking back and forth between the benches in the park, and I wondered whether I had already had the idea that would give me the solution. I might have got something right without being aware of it."

She was thinking about what he had said. Now and then she glanced over at the neighbour's garden.

"We didn't learn anything at the police academy about a man who takes scalps and pours acid into the eyes of his victims," she said. "Life really turns out to be as unpredictable as I imagined."

Wallander nodded without replying. Then he started, unsure whether he could pull it off, and went over what he had been thinking about by the sea. He knew that telling someone else would shed a different light on it. But even though Ann-Britt listened intently, almost like a student at her master's feet, she didn't stop him to say that he had made a mistake or drawn a wrong conclusion. All she said when he had finished was that she was bowled over by his ability to dissect and then summarise the whole investigation, which seemed so overwhelming. But she had nothing to add. Even if Wallander's equations were correct, they lacked the crucial components. Höglund couldn't help him, no-one could.

She went inside and brought out some cups and a thermos of coffee. Her youngest girl came and crept onto the porch swing next to Wallander. She didn't resemble her mother, so he assumed she took after her father, who was in Saudi Arabia. Wallander realised he still hadn't met him.

"Your husband is a puzzle," he said. "I'm starting to wonder if he really exists. Or if he's just someone you dreamed up."

"I sometimes ask myself the same question," she answered, laughing.

The girl went inside.

"What about Carlman's daughter?" asked Wallander, watching the girl. "How is she?"

"Svedberg called the hospital yesterday," she said. "The crisis isn't over. But I had the feeling that the doctors were more hopeful."

"She didn't leave a note?"

"Nothing."

"It matters most that she's a well human being," said Wallander. "But I can't help thinking of her as a witness."

"To what?"

"To something that might have a bearing on her father's death. I don't believe that the timing of the suicide attempt was coincidental."

"What makes me think that you're not convinced of what you're saying?"

"I'm not," said Wallander. "I'm groping and fumbling my way along. There's only one incontrovertible fact in this investigation, and that is that we have no concrete evidence to go on."

"So we have no way of knowing if we're on the right track?"

"Or if we're going in circles."

She hesitated before she asked the next question.

"Do you think that maybe there aren't enough of us?"

"Until now I've dug my heels in on that issue," said Wallander.

"But I'm beginning to have my doubts. The question will come up tomorrow."

"With Per Åkeson?"

Wallander nodded.

"What have we got to lose?"

"Small units move more easily than large ones, but you could also argue that more heads do better thinking. Åkeson's argument is that we can work on a broader front. The infantry is spread out and covers more ground."

"As if we were all sweeping the area."

Wallander nodded. Her image was telling. What was missing was that the sweep they were doing was happening in a terrain where they were only barely able to take their bearings. And they had no idea of whom they were looking for.

"There's something we're all missing," said Wallander. "I'm still searching for something someone said right after Wetterstedt was murdered. I can't remember who said it. I only know that it was important, but it was too soon for me to recognise the significance."

"You like to say that police work is most often a question of patience."

"And it is. But patience has its limits. Someone else could get killed. We can never escape the fact that our investigation is not just a matter of solving crimes that have already been committed. Right now it feels as though our job is to prevent more murders."

"We can't do any more than we're doing already."

"How do we know that?" asked Wallander. "How do we know we're using our resources to their best effect?"

She had no answer.

He sat there for a while longer. At 4.30 p.m. he turned down an invitation to stay and have dinner with them.

"Thanks for coming," she said as she followed him to the gate. "Are you going to watch the game?"

"No. I have to meet my daughter. But I think we're going to win, 3–1."

She gave him a quizzical look.

"That's what I bet, too."

"Then we'll both win or we'll both lose," said Wallander.

"Thanks for coming," she said again.

"Thanks for what?" he asked in surprise. "For disturbing your Sunday?"

"For thinking I might have something worthwhile to say."

"I've said it before and I'll say it again, I think you're a talented policewoman. You believe in the ability of computers not only to make our work easier, but to improve it. I don't, and maybe you can change my mind."

Wallander drove towards town. He stopped at a shop that was open on Sundays and bought groceries. Then he lay back in the deckchair on his balcony. His need for sleep was enormous, and he dozed off. But just before 7 p.m. he was standing on the square at Österport. Linda came to get him and took him to the empty shop nearby. They had rigged up some lights and put out a chair for him. At once he felt self-conscious. He might not understand or might laugh in the wrong place. The girls vanished into an adjoining room. Wallander waited. More than 15 minutes passed. When they finally returned they had changed clothes and now looked exactly alike. After arranging the lights and the simple set, they got started. The hour-long performance was about a pair of twins. Wallander was nervous at being the only audience. Most of all he was fearful that Linda might not be very good. But it wasn't long before he realised that the two girls had written a witty script that presented a critical view of Sweden with dark humour. Sometimes they lost the thread, sometimes he thought that their acting wasn't convincing. But they believed in what they were doing, and that gave him pleasure. When it was over and they asked him what he thought, he told them that he was surprised, that it was funny, that it was thought-provoking. He could see that Linda was watching to see whether he was telling the truth. When she realised he was, she was very happy. She escorted him out.

"I didn't know you could do this sort of thing," he said. "I thought you wanted to be a furniture upholsterer."

"It's never too late," she said. "Let me give it a try."

"Of course you have to," he said. "When you're young you have plenty of time. Not like when you're an old policeman like me."

They were going to rehearse for a few more hours. He would wait for her at home. The summer evening was beautiful. He was walking slowly towards Mariagatan, thinking about the performance, when it dawned on him that cars were driving by, horns honking, people cheering. Sweden must have won. He asked a man he met on the footpath what the score was. 3–1 to Sweden. He burst out laughing. Then his thoughts returned to his daughter, and how little he really knew about her. He still hadn't asked her if she had a boyfriend.

He had just closed the door to his flat when the phone rang. At once he felt a twinge of fear. When he heard Gertrud's voice, he was instantly relieved. But Gertrud was upset. At first he couldn't understand what she was saying. He asked her to slow down.

"You must come over," she said. "Right away."

"What happened?"

"Your father has started burning his paintings. He's burning everything in his studio. And he's locked the door. You've got to come now."

Wallander wrote a quick note to Linda, put it under the doormat, and moments later was on his way to Löderup.

CHAPTER 28

Gertrud met him in the courtyard of the farmhouse. He could see that she'd been crying, but she answered his questions calmly. His father's breakdown, if that was what it was, had come on unexpectedly. They had had their dinner as normal. They hadn't had anything to drink. After the meal his father had gone out to the barn to continue painting, as usual. Suddenly she'd heard a great racket. When she went out on the front steps she'd seen the old man tossing empty paint cans into the yard. At first she thought he was cleaning out his chaotic studio. But when he started throwing out new frames she went and asked what he was doing. He didn't reply. He gave the impression of not being there at all, not hearing her. When she took hold of his arm he pulled himself free and locked himself inside the barn. Through the window, she watched him start a fire in the stove, and when he started tearing up his canvases and stuffing them into the flames she called Kurt.

They crossed the courtyard as she talked. Wallander saw smoke billowing from the chimney. He went up to the window and peered inside. His father looked wild and demented. His hair was on end, he was without his glasses, and the studio was a wreck. He was squishing around barefoot amongst spilled pots of paint, and trampled canvases were strewn everywhere. He was ripping up a canvas and stuffing the pieces into the fire. Wallander thought he saw a shoe burning in the stove. He knocked on the window, but there was no response. He tried the door. Locked. He banged on it and yelled that he had come to visit. There was no answer, but the racket inside continued. Wallander looked around for something to break down the door. But his father kept all his tools in the studio.

Wallander studied the door, which he had helped build. He took off his jacket and handed it to Gertrud. Then he slammed his shoulder against it as hard as he could. The whole doorjamb came away, and Wallander tumbled into the room, banging his head on a wheelbarrow. His father glanced at him vacantly and went on tearing up canvases.

Gertrud wanted to come in, but Wallander warned her away. He had seen his father like this once before, a strange combination of detachment and manic confusion. On that occasion he had found him walking in his pyjamas through a muddy field with a suitcase in his hand. Now he went up to him, took him by the shoulders, and began talking soothingly to him. He asked if there was something wrong. He said the paintings were fine, they were the best he'd ever done, the grouse were beautifully painted. Everything was all right. Anyone could have a bad day once in a while. But he had to stop burning things for no reason. Why should they have a fire in the middle of summer, anyway? They could get cleaned up and talk about the trip to Italy. Wallander kept talking, with a strong grip on his father's shoulders, as the old man squinted myopically at him. While Wallander kept up his reassuring chatter he discovered his glasses trampled to bits on the floor. He asked Gertrud, who was hovering by the door, whether there was a spare pair. She ran to the house to get them and handed them to Wallander, who wiped them on his sleeve and then set them on his father's nose. He continued to speak in a soothing voice, repeating his words as if he were reading the verses of a prayer. His father looked at him in bewilderment at first, then astonishment, and finally it seemed as though he had come to his senses again. Wallander released his grip. His father looked cautiously about him at the destruction.

"What happened here?" he asked. Wallander could see that he had forgotten everything. Gertrud began to weep. Wallander told her firmly to go and make some coffee. They'd be there in a minute. At last the old man seemed to grasp that he had been involved in the havoc.

"Did I do all this?" he asked, looking at Wallander with restless eyes, as if he feared the answer.

"Who doesn't get sick and tired of things?" Wallander said. "But it's all over now. We'll soon get this mess cleaned up."

His father looked at the smashed door.

"Who needs doors in the middle of summer?" said Wallander. "There aren't any closed doors in Rome in the summer. You'll have to get used to that."

His father walked slowly through the debris from the frenzy that neither he nor anyone else could explain. Wallander felt a lump in his throat. There was something helpless about his father, and he didn't know how to deal with it. He lifted the broken door and leaned it against the wall. He began tidying up the room, discovering that many of the canvases had survived. His father sat on a stool at his workbench and watched. Gertrud came in and told them that coffee was ready. Wallander gestured to her to take his father inside. Then he cleaned up the worst of the mess.

Before he went into the kitchen he called home. Linda was there. She wanted to know what had happened; she could barely decipher his quickly scribbled note. Wallander didn't want to worry her, so he said that her grandfather had just been feeling bad, but was fine now. To be on the safe side he'd decided to stay overnight in Löderup. He went in the kitchen. His father was feeling tired and had gone to lie down. Wallander stayed with Gertrud for a couple of hours, sitting at the kitchen table. There was no way to explain what had happened except that it was a symptom of the illness. But when Gertrud said this attack ruled out the trip to Italy in the autumn, Wallander protested. He wasn't afraid of taking responsibility. He would manage. It was going to happen, so long as his father wanted to go and was able to stand on his own two feet.

That night he slept on a fold-out bed in the living-room. He lay staring out into the light summer night for a long time before he fell asleep.

In the morning, over coffee, his father seemed to have forgotten the whole episode. He couldn't understand what had happened to the studio door. Wallander told him the truth, that he was the one who had broken it down. The studio needed a new door, and anyway, he would make it himself.

"When are you going to be able to do that?" asked his father. "You don't even have time to call ahead of time and tell me you're coming to visit."

Wallander knew then that everything was back to normal. He left Löderup just after 7 a.m. It wasn't the last time something like this might happen, he knew, and with a shiver imagined what might have occurred if Gertrud hadn't been there.

Wallander went straight to the station. Everyone was talking about the match. He was surrounded by people in summer clothes. Only the ones who had to wear uniforms looked remotely like police officers. Wallander thought that in his white clothes he could have stepped out of one of the Danish productions of Italian opera he'd been to. As he passed the reception desk Ebba waved to him that he had a call. It was Forsfält. They had found Fredman's passport, well hidden in his flat, along with large sums of foreign currencies. Wallander asked about the stamps in the passport.

"I have to disappoint you," Forsfält told him. "He had the passport for four years, and it has stamps from Turkey, Morocco and Brazil. That's all."

Wallander was indeed disappointed, although he wasn't sure what he had expected. Forsfält promised to fax over the details on the passport. Then he said he had something else to tell him that had no direct bearing on the investigation.

"We found some keys to the attic when we were looking for the passport. Among all the junk up there we found a box containing some antique icons. We were able to determine pretty quickly that they were stolen. Guess where from."

Wallander thought for a moment but couldn't come up with anything. "I give up."

"About a year ago there was a burglary at a house near Ystad. The house was under the administration of an executor, because it was part of the estate of a deceased lawyer named Gustaf Torstensson."

Wallander remembered him. One of two lawyers murdered the year before. Wallander had seen the collection of icons in the basement that belonged to the older of the two lawyers. He even had one of them hanging on the wall of his bedroom, a present he'd received from the dead lawyer's secretary. Now he also recalled the break-in; it was Svedberg's case.

"So now we know," said Wallander.

"You'll be getting the follow-up report," Forsfält told him.

"Not me," said Wallander. "Svedberg."

Forsfält asked how it was going with Louise Fredman.

"With a little luck we'll know something later today," said Wallander, and told him about his last conversation with Åkeson.

"Keep me informed."

After they hung up he checked his list of unanswered questions. He could cross out some of them, while others he would have to bring up at the team meeting. But first he had to see the two trainees who were keeping track of the tip-offs coming in from the public. Had anything come in that might indicate exactly where Fredman was murdered? Wallander knew this could be highly significant for the investigation.

One of the trainees had close-cropped hair and was named Tyrén. He had intelligent eyes and was thought of as competent. Wallander quickly explained what he was looking for.

"Someone who heard screams?" asked Tyrén. "And saw a Ford van? On the night of Tuesday, 28 June?"

"That's right."

Tyrén shook his head.

"I would have remembered that," he said. "A woman screamed in a flat in Rydsgård. But that was on Wednesday. And she was drunk."

"Let me know immediately if anything comes in," said Wallander. He left Tyrén and went down to the meeting room. Hansson was talking to a reporter in reception. Wallander remembered seeing him before. He was a stringer for one or other of the big national evening papers. They waited a few minutes until Hansson got rid of the reporter, and then closed the door. Hansson sat down and gave Wallander the floor at once. Just as he was about to start, Åkeson came in and sat at the far end of the table, next to Ekholm. Wallander raised his eyebrows and gave him an inquiring look. Åkeson nodded. Wallander knew that meant there was news about Louise Fredman. With difficulty, he contained his curiosity, and called on Höglund. She reported the news from the hospital. Carlman's daughter was in a stable condition. It would be possible to talk to her within 24 hours. No-one could see an objection to Höglund and Wallander visiting the hospital.

Wallander went quickly down the list of unanswered questions. Nyberg was well prepared, as usual, able to fill in many of the gaps with laboratory results. But nothing was significant enough to provoke long discussion. Mostly they had confirmation of conclusions they had already drawn. The only new information was that there were faint traces of kelp on Fredman's clothes. This could be an indication that Fredman had been near the sea on the last day of his life. Wallander thought for a moment.

"Where are the traces of kelp?" he asked.

Nyberg checked his notes.

"On the back of his jacket."

"He could have been killed near the sea," said Wallander. "As far as I can recall, there was a slight breeze that night. If the surf was loud enough, it might explain why no-one heard screams."

"If it happened on the beach we would have found traces of sand," said Nyberg.

"Maybe it was on a boat," Svedberg suggested.

"Or a dock," said Höglund.

The question hung in the air. It would be impossible to check the thousands of pleasure boats and docks. Wallander noted that they should watch out for tip-offs from people who lived near the sea. Then he gave the floor to Åkeson.

"I succeeded in gathering some information about Louise Fredman," he said. "I remind you that this is highly confidential and cannot be mentioned to anyone outside the investigative team."

"We understand this," Wallander said.

"Louise Fredman is at St Lars Hospital in Lund," Åkeson continued. "She has been there for more than three years. The diagnosis is severe psychosis. She has stopped talking, sometimes has to be force-fed, and there is no sign of improvement. She's 17 years old. Judging from a photograph I saw she's quite pretty."

The group was silent.

"Psychosis is usually caused by something," said Ekholm.

"She was admitted on 9 January 1991," said Åkeson, after looking through his papers. "Her illness seems to have struck like a bolt from the blue. She had been missing from home for a week. She was having serious problems at school and was often truant. There were signs of drug abuse. Not heavy narcotics, mostly amphetamines and possibly cocaine. She was found in Pildamm Park, completely irrational."

"Were there signs of external injuries?" asked Wallander, who was listening intently.

"Not according to the material I've received."

Wallander thought about this.

"Well, we can't talk to her," he said finally. "But I want to know whether she had any injuries. And I want to talk to the person who found her."

"It was three years ago," said Åkeson. "But the people involved could probably be traced."

"I'll talk to Forsfält in Malmö," said Wallander. "Uniformed officers most probably found her. There will be a report on it."

"Why do you wonder if she had any injuries?" Hansson asked.

"I just want to fill in the picture as completely as possible," Wallander replied.

They left Louise Fredman and went on to other topics. Since Ekholm was still waiting for the F.B.I. programme to finish cross-referencing all the investigative material, Wallander turned the discussion to the question of reinforcements. Hansson had already received a positive response from the county chief of police as to the possibility of a sergeant from Malmö. He would be in Ystad by lunchtime.

"Who is it?" asked Martinsson, who had so far been silent.

"His name is Sture Holmström," said Hansson.

"Do we know anything about him?" Martinsson asked.

No-one knew him. Wallander promised to call Forsfält to check on him.

Then Wallander turned to Åkeson.

"The question now is whether we should ask for additional reinforcements," Wallander began. "What's the general view? I want everyone's opinion. I also undertake to bow to the will of the majority. Even though I'm not convinced that extra personnel will improve the quality of our work. I'm afraid we might lose the pace of our investigation. At least in the short run. But I want to hear your views."

Martinsson and Svedberg were in favour of requesting extra personnel. Höglund sided with Wallander, and Hansson and Ekholm didn't offer an opinion. Wallander saw that another burdensome mantle of responsibility had been draped around his shoulders. Åkeson proposed that they postpone the decision for a few more days.

"If there's another murder, it'll be unavoidable," he said. "But for the time being let's keep going the way we have been."

The meeting finished just before 10 a.m. Wallander went to his room. It had been a good meeting, much better than the last, even though they hadn't made any progress. They had shown one another that their energy and will were still strong.

Wallander was about to call Forsfält when Martinsson appeared in his doorway.

"There's one more thing that's occurred to me," he said, leaning against the doorframe. "Louise Fredman was found wandering around on a path in the park. There's a similarity to the girl running in the rape field."

Martinsson was right. There was a similarity, albeit a remote one.

"I agree," he said. "It's a shame that there's no connection."

"Still, it's weird," said Martinsson.

He remained in the doorway.

"You bet right this time."

Wallander nodded.

"I know," he said. "So did Ann-Britt."

"You'll have to split a thousand."

"When's the next match?"

"I'll let you know," said Martinsson and left.

Wallander called Malmö. While he waited, he looked out of the open window. Another beautiful day. Then Forsfält came on the line, and he pushed all thoughts of summer aside.

He took a long time selecting the right axe from the ones lying polished on the black silk cloth. Finally he chose the smallest one, the one he hadn't used yet. He stuck it in his wide leather belt and pulled the helmet over his head.

As before, he was barefoot when he locked the door behind him. The evening was warm. He rode along side roads that he had selected on the map. It would take him almost two hours. He would get there a little before 11 p.m.

He'd had to change his plans. The man who had gone abroad suddenly had returned. He decided not to risk his taking off again. He had listened to Geronimo's heart. The rhythmic thumping of the drums inside his chest had delivered their message to him. He must not wait. He would seize the opportunity.

The summer landscape seen from inside his helmet took on a bluish tinge. He could see the sea to his left, the blinking lights of ships, and the coast of Denmark. He felt elated and happy. It wouldn't be long now before he could bring his sister the last sacrifice that would liberate her from the fog that surrounded her. She would return to life in the loveliest part of the summer.

He got to the city just after 11 p.m., and 15 minutes later stopped on a street next to the large villa, hidden away in a garden full of tall, sheltering trees. He chained his moped to a lamppost and locked it. On the opposite footpath an old couple were walking their dog. He waited until they disappeared before he pulled off his helmet and stuffed it into his backpack. In the shadows he ran to the back of the property, which looked out over a football pitch. He hid his backpack in the long grass and crept through the hedge, at a point where he had long ago prepared an opening. The hedge scratched his bare arms and feet. But he steeled himself against all pain. Geronimo would not stand for weakness. He had a sacred mission, as written in the book he had received from his sister. The mission required all his strength, which he was prepared to sacrifice with devotion.

He was inside the garden now, closer to the beast than he had ever been. The entire ground floor was in darkness, but there was a light on upstairs. He remembered with anger how his sister had been here before him. She had described the house, and one day he would burn it to the ground. But not yet. Cautiously he ran up to the wall of the house and prised open the basement window from which he had earlier removed the latch. It was easy to crawl inside. He knew that he was in an apple cellar, surrounded by the faint aroma of sour apples. He listened. All quiet. He crept up the cellar stairs, into the big kitchen. Still quiet. The only thing he heard was the faint sound of water pipes. He turned on the oven and opened the door. Then he made his way upstairs. He had taken the axe out of his belt. He was completely calm.

The door to the bathroom was ajar. In the darkness of the hall he caught a glimpse of the man he was going to kill. He was standing in front of the bathroom mirror rubbing cream onto his face. Hoover slipped in behind the bathroom door, waiting. When the man turned off the light in the bathroom he raised the axe. He struck only once. The man fell to the floor without a sound. With the axe he sliced off a piece of the man's hair from the top of his head. He stuffed the scalp into his pocket. Then he dragged the man down the stairs. He was in pyjamas. The bottoms slipped off the body and were dragged along by one foot. He avoided looking at him.

He pulled the man into the kitchen and leaned the body against the oven door. Then he shoved the man's head inside. Almost at once he smelled the face cream starting to melt. He left the house the way he had come in.

He buried the scalp beneath his sister's window in the dawn light. Now all that was left was the extra sacrifice he would offer her. He would bury one last scalp. Then it would be over.

He thought about the man he had watched sleeping. The man who had sat across from him on the sofa, understanding nothing of the sacred mission he had to perform. He still hadn't decided whether he should also take the girl sleeping in the next room. He would make his final decision the next day, but now he had to rest.

Skåne

5–8 July 1994

CHAPTER 29

Waldemar Sjösten was a criminal detective in Helsingborg who devoted all his free time during the summer to a 1930s mahogany boat he had found by accident. And this was just what he planned to do on Tuesday morning, 5 July, when he let the shade on his bedroom window roll up with a snap just before 6 a.m. He lived in a newly renovated block of flats at the centre of town. One street, the railway line and the docks were all that separated him from the Sound. The weather was as beautiful as the weather reports had promised. His holiday didn't start until the end of July, but whenever he could he spent a few early mornings on his boat, docked at the marina a short bike ride away. Sjösten was going to celebrate his 50th birthday this autumn. He had been married three times, had six children and was planning his fourth marriage. The woman shared his love of the boat, *Sea King II*. He had taken the name from the beautiful boat that he'd spent his childhood summers on board with his parents, *Sea King I*. His father had sold it to a man from Norway when he was ten, and he had never forgotten it. He often wondered whether the boat still existed, or whether it had sunk or rotted away.

He had finished a cup of coffee and was getting ready to leave when the telephone rang. He was surprised to hear it at such an early hour. He picked up the receiver.

"Waldemar?" It was Detective Sergeant Birgersson.

"Yes."

"I hope I didn't wake you."

"I was just on my way out."

"Lucky I caught you then. You'd better get down here right away." Birgersson wouldn't have called unless it was something serious.

"I'll be right there," he said. "What is it?"

"There was smoke coming out of one of those old villas up in Tågaborg. When the fire brigade got there they found a man in the kitchen."

"Dead?"

"Murdered. You'll understand why I called you when you see him."

Sjösten could see his morning disappearing, but he was a dutiful policeman, so he had no trouble changing his plans. Instead of the key to his bicycle lock he grabbed his car keys and left at once. It took him only a few minutes to drive to the station. Birgersson was on the steps waiting. He got in the car and gave him directions.

"Who's dead?" Sjösten asked.

"Åke Liljegren."

Sjösten whistled. Åke Liljegren was well known, not just in the city but all over Sweden. He called himself "the Auditor" and had gained his notoriety as the *éminence grise* behind some extensive shell company dealing done during the 1980s. Apart from one six-month suspended sentence, the police had had no success in prosecuting the illegal operation he ran. Liljegren had become a by-word for the worst type of financial scams, and the fact that he got off scot-free demonstrated how ill-equipped the justice system was to handle criminals like him. He was from Båstad, but in recent years had lived in Helsingborg when he was in Sweden. Sjösten recalled a newspaper article that had set out to uncover how many houses Liljegren owned across the world.

"Can you give me a time frame?" asked Sjösten.

"A jogger out early this morning saw smoke coming out of the house. He raised the alarm. The fire department got there at 5.15 a.m."

"Where was the fire?"

"There was no fire."

Sjösten gave Birgersson a puzzled look.

"Liljegren was leaning into the oven," Birgersson explained. "His head was in the oven, which was on full blast. He was literally being roasted."

Sjösten grimaced. He was beginning to get an idea what he was going to have to look at.

"Did he commit suicide?"

"No. Someone stuck an axe in his head."

Sjösten stomped involuntarily on the brake. He looked at Birgersson, who nodded.

"His face and hair were almost completely burnt off. But the doctor thought he could tell that someone had sliced off part of his scalp."

Sjösten said nothing. He was thinking about what had happened in Ystad. That was this summer's big news. A serial killer who axed people to death and then took their scalps.

They arrived at Liljegren's villa on Aschebergsgatan. A fire engine was parked outside the gates along with a few police cars and an ambulance. The huge property was cordoned off. Sjösten got out of the car and waved off a reporter. He and Birgersson ducked under the cordon and walked up to the villa. When they entered the house Sjösten noticed a sickly smell, and realised that it was Liljegren's burnt corpse. He borrowed a handkerchief from Birgersson and held it to his nose and mouth. Birgersson nodded towards the kitchen. A very pale uniformed officer stood guard at the door. Sjösten peered inside. The sight that greeted him was grotesque. The half-naked man was on his knees. His body was bent over the oven door. His head and neck were out of sight inside the oven. With disgust Sjösten recalled the fairy tale of Hänsel and Gretel and the witch. A doctor was kneeling down beside the body, shining a torch into the oven. Sjösten tried to breathe through his mouth. The doctor nodded at him. Sjösten leaned forward and looked into the oven. He was reminded of a charred steak.

"Jesus," he said.

"He took a blow to the back of the head," said the doctor.

"Here in the kitchen?"

"No, upstairs," said Birgersson, standing behind him.

Sjösten straightened up.

"Take him out of the oven," he said. "Has the photographer finished?"

Birgersson nodded. Sjösten followed him upstairs, avoiding the traces of blood. Birgersson stopped outside the bathroom door.

"As you saw, he was wearing pyjamas," said Birgersson. "Here's how it probably happened: Liljegren was in the bathroom. The killer was waiting for him. He struck Liljegren with an axe in the back of the head and then dragged the body to the kitchen. That could explain why the pyjama bottoms were hanging from one leg. Then he put the body in front of the oven, turned it on, and left. We don't know yet how he got into the house and out again. I thought you might be able to take care of that."

Sjösten said nothing. He was thinking. He went back down to the kitchen. The body was on a plastic sheet on the floor.

"Is it him?" asked Sjösten.

"It's Liljegren," said the doctor. "Even though he doesn't have much face left."

"That's not what I meant. Is it the man who takes scalps?"

The doctor pulled back the plastic sheet covering the blackened face.

"I'm convinced that he cut or tore off the hair at the front of his head," said the doctor.

Sjösten nodded. Then he turned to Birgersson.

"I want you to call the Ystad police. Get hold of Kurt Wallander. I want to talk to him. Now."

For once Wallander had fixed a proper breakfast. He had fried some eggs and was just sitting down at the table with his newspaper when the telephone rang. The caller introduced himself as Detective Sergeant Sture Birgersson of the Helsingborg police. What he had feared had finally happened. The killer had struck again. He swore under his breath, an oath that contained equal parts rage and horror. Waldemar Sjösten came to the phone. In the early 1980s they had collaborated on the investigation of a drugs ring extending all over Skåne. Although they were very different people, they had had an easy time working together and had formed the beginnings of a friendship.

"Kurt?"

"Yes, it's me."

"It's been a long time."

"So what's happened? Is what I hear true?"

"Unfortunately it is. Your killer has turned up here in Helsingborg."

"Is it confirmed?"

"There's nothing to indicate otherwise. An axe blow to the head. Then he cut off the victim's scalp."

"Who was it?"

"Åke Liljegren. Does that name ring a bell?"

Wallander thought for a moment. "The one they call 'the Auditor'?"

"Precisely. A former minister of justice, an art dealer and now a white-collar criminal."

"And a fence too," said Wallander. "Don't forget him."

"You should come up here. Our superiors can sort out the red tape so that we can cross into each other's jurisdictions."

"I'll come right away," said Wallander. "It might be a good idea if I bring Sven Nyberg, our head forensic technician."

"Bring whoever you want. I won't stand in your way. I just don't like it that the killer has shown up here."

"I'll be in Helsingborg in two hours," said Wallander. "If you can tell me whether there's some connection between Liljegren and the others who were killed, we'll be ahead of the game. Did the killer leave any clues?"

"Not directly, although we can see how it happened. This time he didn't pour acid into his victim's eyes. He roasted him. His head and half his neck, at least."

"Roasted?"

"In an oven. Be glad you won't have to look at it."

"What else?"

"I just got here, so nothing really."

After Wallander hung up he looked at his watch. It was very early. He called Nyberg, who answered at once. Wallander told him what had happened, and Nyberg promised to be outside Wallander's building in 15 minutes. Then Wallander dialled Hansson's number, but changed his mind and called Martinsson instead. As always, Martinsson's wife answered. It took a couple of minutes before her husband came to the phone.

"He's killed again," said Wallander. "This time in Helsingborg. A crook named Åke Liljegren. They call him 'the Auditor.'"

"The corporate raider?" asked Martinsson.

"That's him."

"The murderer has taste."

"Bullshit," Wallander said. "I'm driving up there with Nyberg. They've asked us to come. I want you to tell Hansson. I'll give you a call as soon as I know more."

"This means that the National Criminal Bureau will be called in," Martinsson said. "Maybe it's the best thing."

"The best thing would be if we caught this killer," Wallander replied. "I'll call you later."

He was outside when Nyberg drove up in his old Amazon. It was a beautiful morning. Nyberg drove fast. At Sturup they turned off towards Lund and reached the motorway to Helsingborg. Wallander told him what he knew. After they had passed Lund, Hansson called. He was out of breath. He's been even more afraid of this than I have, Wallander thought.

"It's terrible," said Hansson. "This changes everything."

"For the time being it doesn't change a thing," Wallander replied. "It depends entirely on what actually happened."

"It's time for the National Criminal Bureau to take over," said Hansson. Wallander could tell from Hansson's voice that to be relieved of his responsibility was what he wanted most of all. Wallander was annoyed. He couldn't ignore the hint of disparagement of the work of the investigative team.

"That's your responsibility – yours and Åkeson's," Wallander said tersely. "What occurred in Helsingborg is their problem. But they've asked me to go up there. We'll talk about what we're going to do later."

Wallander hung up. Nyberg didn't say a word. But Wallander knew he had been listening carefully.

They were met by a squad car at the exit to Helsingborg. Wallander realised that it must have been somewhere nearby that Sven Andersson had stopped to give Dolores María Santana a lift on her last journey. They followed the car up to Tågaborg and stopped outside Liljegren's villa. Wallander and Nyberg passed through the police cordon and were met by Sjösten at the bottom of the steps to the villa, which Wallander guessed had been built around the turn of the century. They said hello and exchanged a few words. Sjösten introduced Nyberg to the forensic technician from Helsingborg. The two of them went inside.

Sjösten put out his cigarette and buried the butt in the gravel with his heel.

"It's your man who did this," he said.

"What do you know about the victim?"

"Åke Liljegren was famous."

"Infamous, you mean."

Sjösten nodded. "There are probably plenty of people who have dreamt of killing him," he said. "With a criminal justice system that worked better, with fewer loopholes in the laws on financial fraud, he would have been locked up."

Sjösten took Wallander into the house. The air was thick with the stench of burnt flesh. Sjösten gave Wallander a mask, which he put on reluctantly. They went into the kitchen where the body still lay under the plastic sheet. Wallander nodded to Sjösten to let him see, thinking that he might as well get it over with. He didn't know what he had expected, but he flinched involuntarily. Liljegren's face was gone. The skin was burnt away and large sections of the skull were clearly visible. There were just two holes where the eyes had been. The hair and ears were also burnt off. Wallander nodded to Sjösten to put back the sheet. Sjösten quickly described how Liljegren had been found leaning into the oven. Wallander got some Polaroids from the photographer. It was almost worse to see the pictures. Wallander shook his head with a grimace and handed them back. Sjösten took him upstairs, pointing out the blood, and describing the apparent sequence of events. Wallander occasionally asked a question about a detail, but Sjösten's scenario seemed convincing.

"Were there any witnesses?" asked Wallander. "Clues left by the murderer? How did he get into the house?"

"Through a basement window."

They returned to the kitchen and went down to the basement that extended under the whole house. A little window stood ajar in a room where Wallander smelt the faint aroma of apples stored for the winter.

"We think he got in this way," said Sjösten. "And left that way too. Even though he could have walked straight out the front door. Liljegren lived alone."

"Did he leave anything behind?" Wallander wondered. "So far he has been careful to leave no clues. On the other hand, he hasn't been excessively meticulous. We have a whole set of fingerprints. According to Nyberg, we're missing only the left little finger."

"Fingerprints he knows the police don't have on file," said Sjösten. Wallander nodded. Sjösten was right.

"We found a footprint in the kitchen next to the stove," said Sjösten.

"So he was barefoot again," said Wallander.

"Barefoot?"

Wallander told him about the footprint they had found in the blood in Fredman's van. He would have to provide Sjösten and his colleagues with all the material they had on the first three murders.

Wallander inspected the basement window. He thought he could see faint scrape marks near one of the latches, which had been broken off. When he bent down he found it, although it was hard to see against the dark floor. He didn't touch it.

"It looks as though it might have been loosened in advance," he said.

"You think he prepared for his visit?"

"It's conceivable. It fits with his pattern. He puts his victims under surveillance. He stakes them out. Why, and for how long, we have no idea. Our psychologist from Stockholm, Mats Ekholm, claims this is characteristic of serial killers."

They went into the next room. The windows were the same. The latches were intact.

"We should probably search for footprints in the grass outside that window," Wallander said. He regretted his words immediately. He had no right to tell an experienced investigator like Sjösten what to do. They returned to the kitchen. Liljegren's body was being removed.

"What I've been looking for the whole time is the connection," said Wallander. "First I looked for one between Gustaf Wetterstedt and Arne Carlman. I finally found it. Then I looked for one between Björn Fredman and the two others. We haven't been able to find a link yet, but I'm convinced there is one. Perhaps this is one of the first things we should do here. Is it possible to find some connection between Åke Liljegren and the other three? Preferably to all of them, but at least to any one of them."

"In a way we already have a very clear connection," said Sjösten quietly.

Wallander gave him a questioning glance.

"What I mean is, the killer is an identifiable link," Sjösten went on. "Even if we don't know who he is."

Sjösten nodded towards the door to the garden. Wallander realised that Sjösten wanted to speak privately. Outside in the garden, they both squinted in the bright light. It was going to be another hot day. Sjösten lit a cigarette and led Wallander over to a table and chairs a little way from the house. They moved the chairs into the shade.

"There are plenty of rumours about Åke Liljegren," Sjösten began. "His shell companies are only a part of his operations. Here in Helsingborg we've heard about a lot of other things. Low-flying Cessnas making drops of cocaine, heroin and marijuana. Pretty hard to prove, and I have difficulty associating this type of activity with Liljegren. It may just be my limited imagination, of course. I go on thinking that it's possible to sort crimes into categories. Criminals are supposed to stay within those boundaries and not encroach on other people's territory, which messes up our classifications."

"I've sometimes thought along those same lines," Wallander admitted. "But those days are gone. The world we live in is becoming more comprehensible and more chaotic at the same time."

Sjösten waved his cigarette at the huge villa.

"There have been other rumours too," he said. "These ones more concrete. About wild parties in this house. Women, prostitution."

"Wild?" asked Wallander. "Have you ever had to get involved?"

"Never," said Sjösten. "Actually I don't know why I called the parties wild. But people used to come here a lot. And disappear just as quickly as they came."

Wallander didn't answer. A dizzying image flitted through his mind. He saw Dolores María Santana standing at the southern motorway entrance from Helsingborg. Could there be a connection? Prostitution? But he pushed the thought away. There was no evidence for this, he was confusing two different investigations.

"We're going to have to work together," Sjösten said. "You and your colleagues have several weeks on us. Now that we add Liljegren to the picture, how does it look? What's changed? What seems clearer?"

"The National Criminal Bureau will certainly get involved now," Wallander answered. "That's good, of course. But I'm afraid that we'll have problems working together, that information won't get to the right person."

"I have the same concern," Sjösten agreed. "That's why I want to suggest something. That you and I become an informal team, so we can step aside for discussion when we need to."

"That's fine by me," Wallander said.

"We both remember the days of the old national homicide commission," Sjösten said. "Something that worked very efficiently was dismantled. And things have never really been the same since."

"Times were different. Violence had a different face, and there were fewer murders. Criminals operated in patterns that were recognisable in a way that they aren't today. I'm not sure that the commission would have been as effective now."

Sjösten stood up. "But we're in agreement?"

"Of course," Wallander replied. "Whenever we think it's necessary, we'll talk."

"You can stay with me," Sjösten said, "if you have to be here overnight. It's no pleasure to have to stay at a hotel."

"I'd like that," Wallander thanked him. But he didn't mind staying at a hotel when he was away. He needed to have at least a few hours to himself every day.

They walked back to the house. To the left was a large garage with two doors. While Sjösten went inside, Wallander decided to take a look in the garage. With difficulty he lifted one of the doors. Inside was a black Mercedes. The windows were tinted. He stood there thinking.

Then he went into the house, called Ystad, and asked to speak with Höglund. He told her briefly what had happened.

"I want you to contact Sara Björklund," he said. "Do you remember her?"

"Wetterstedt's housekeeper?"

"Right. I want you to bring her here to Helsingborg. As soon as you can."

"Why?"

"I want her to take a look at a car. And I'll be standing next to her hoping that she recognises it."

Höglund asked no more questions.

CHAPTER 30

Sara Björklund stood for a long time looking at the black car. Wallander stayed in the background. He wanted his presence to give her confidence, but didn't want to stand so close to her that he would be a disturbing factor. He could tell that she was doing her best to be absolutely certain. Was this the car she had seen on the Friday morning that she'd come to Wetterstedt's house, thinking it was a Thursday? Had it looked like this one, could it even be the very same car she had seen drive away from the house where the old minister of justice lived?

Sjösten agreed with Wallander when he explained his idea. Even if the "charwoman" held in such contempt by Wetterstedt said that it could have been a car of the same make, that wouldn't prove a thing. All they would get was an indication, a possibility. But it was important even so; they both realised that.

Sara Björklund hesitated. Since there were keys in the ignition, Wallander asked Sjösten to drive it once round the block. If she closed her eyes and listened, did she recognise the sound of the engine? Cars had different sounds. She listened.

"Maybe," she said afterwards. "It looks like the car I saw that morning. But whether it was the same one I can't say. I didn't see the number plate."

Wallander nodded.

"I didn't expect you to," he said. "I'm sorry I had to ask you to come all the way here."

Höglund had brought Norén with her, who would now drive Sara Björklund back to Ystad. Höglund wanted to stay. It was barely midday, yet the whole country seemed to know already what had happened. Sjösten held an impromptu press conference out on the street, while Wallander and Höglund drove down to the ferry terminal and had lunch. He told her all that he had learned.

"Åke Liljegren appeared in our investigative material on Alfred Harderberg," she said when he'd finished. "Do you remember?"

Wallander let his mind travel back to the year before. He remembered the businessman and art patron who lived behind the walls of Farnholm Castle with distaste. The man they had eventually prevented from leaving the country in a dramatic scene at Sturup Airport. Liljegren's name had indeed come up in the investigation, but he had been on the periphery. They had never considered questioning him.

Wallander sat with his third cup of coffee and gazed out over the Sound, filled with yachts and ferries.

"We didn't want this, but we've got it," he said. "Another dead, scalped man. According to Ekholm our chances of identifying the killer will now increase dramatically. That's according to the F.B.I. models. Now the similarities and differences should be much clearer."

"I think somehow the level of violence has increased," she said hesitantly. "If you can grade axe murders and scalpings."

Wallander waited with interest for her to continue. Her hesitation often meant that she was on the trail of something important.

"Wetterstedt was lying underneath a rowing boat," she went on. "He had been hit once from behind. His scalp was sliced off, as if the killer had taken the time to do it carefully. Or maybe there was some uncertainty. The first scalp. Carlman was killed from the front. He must have seen his killer. His hair was torn off, not sliced. That seems to indicate more frenzy, or maybe rage, almost uncontrolled. Then Fredman. He apparently lay on his back. Probably tied up, or he'd have resisted. He had acid poured in his eyes. The killer forced open his eyelids. The blow to the head was tremendous. And now Liljegren, with his head stuck in an oven. Something is getting worse. Is it hatred? Or a sick person's thrill at demonstrating his power?"

"Outline this to Ekholm," Wallander suggested. "Let him put it into his computer. I agree with you. Certain changes in his behaviour are evident. Something is shifting. But what does it tell us? Sometimes it seems as though we're trying to interpret footprints that are millions of years old. What I worry about most is the chronology, which is based on the fact that we found the victims in a certain order, since they were killed in a certain order. So for us a natural chronology is created. But the question is whether there's some other order among them that we can't see. Are some of the murders more important than others?"

She thought for a moment. "Was one of them closer to the killer than the others?"

"Yes, that's it," said Wallander. "Was Liljegren closer to the heart of it than Carlman, for example? And which of them is furthest away? Or do they all have the same relationship to him?"

"A relationship which may only exist in his mind?"

Wallander pushed aside his empty cup. "At least we can be certain that these men were not chosen at random," he said.

"Fredman is different," she said as they got up.

"Yes, he is," said Wallander. "But you can also turn it around and say that it's the other three who are different."

They returned to Tågaborg, where they were given the message that Hansson was on his way to meet with the chief of police in Helsingborg.

"Tomorrow the National Criminal Bureau will be here," said Sjösten.

"Has anyone talked to Ekholm?" asked Wallander. "He should come up here as soon as possible."

Höglund went to see to this, and Wallander made an examination of the house again with Sjösten. Nyberg was on his knees in the kitchen with the other technicians. When they were heading up the stairs to the top floor, Höglund caught up with them, saying that Ekholm was on his way with Hansson. They continued their inspection. None of them spoke. They were each following their own train of thought.

Wallander was trying to feel the killer's presence, as he had done at Wetterstedt's house, and in Carlman's garden. Not twelve hours ago the man had climbed these same stairs. Wallander moved more slowly than the others. He stopped often, sometimes sitting down to stare at a wall or a rug or a door, as if he were in a museum, deeply engrossed in the objects on display. Occasionally he would retrace his steps.

Watching him, Höglund had the sense that Wallander was acting as though he were walking on ice. And in a sense, he was. Each step involved a risk, a new way of seeing things, a re-examination of a thought he'd just had. He moved as much in his mind as through the rooms. Wallander had never sensed the presence of the man he was hunting in Wetterstedt's house. It had convinced him that the killer had never been inside. He had not been closer than the garage roof where he had waited, reading *The Phantom* and then ripping it to pieces. But here, in Liljegren's house, it was different.

Wallander went back to the stairs and looked down the hall towards the bathroom. From here he could see the man he was about to kill. If the bathroom door was open, that is. And why would it have been closed if Liljegren was alone in the house? He walked towards the bathroom door and stood against the wall. Then he went into the bathroom and assumed the role of Liljegren. He walked out of the door, imagining the axe blow strike him with full force from behind, at an angle. He saw himself fall to the floor. Then he switched to the other role, the man holding an axe in his right hand. Not in his left; they had determined in examining Wetterstedt's body that the man was right-handed. Wallander walked slowly down the stairs, dragging the invisible corpse behind him. Into the kitchen, to the stove. He continued down to the basement and stopped at the window, which was too narrow for him to squeeze through. Only a slight man could use that window as a way of getting into Liljegren's house. The killer must be thin.

He went back to the kitchen and out into the garden. Near the basement window at the back of the house the technicians were looking for footprints. Wallander could have told them in advance that they wouldn't find anything. The man had been barefoot, as before. He looked towards the hedge, the shortest distance between the basement window and the street, pondering why the killer had been barefoot.

He'd asked Ekholm about it several times, but still didn't have a satisfactory answer. Going barefoot meant taking a risk of injury. Of slipping, puncturing his foot, getting cut. And yet he still did it. Why did he go barefoot? Why choose to remove his shoes? This was another of the inexplicable details he had to keep in mind. He took scalps. He used an axe. He was barefoot. Wallander stopped in his tracks. It came to him in a flash. His subconscious had drawn a conclusion and relayed the message.

An American Indian, he said to himself. A warrior. He knew he was right. The man they were looking for was a lone warrior moving along an invisible path. He was an impersonator. Used an axe to kill, cut off scalps, went barefoot. But why would an American Indian go around in the Swedish summertime killing people? Who was really committing these murders? An Indian or someone playing the role?

Wallander held on tight to the thought so he wouldn't lose it before he had followed it through. He travelled over great distances, he thought. He must have a horse. A motorcycle. Which had leant against the road workers' hut. You drive in a car, but you *ride* a motorcycle.

He walked back to the house. For the first time he'd caught a glimpse of the man he sought. The excitement of the discovery was immediate. His alertness sharpened. For the time being, however, he would keep his idea to himself.

A window on the top floor opened. Sjösten leaned out.

"Come up here," he shouted.

Wallander went in, wondering what they had found. Sjösten and Höglund were standing in front of a bookcase in a room that must have been Liljegren's office. Sjösten had a plastic bag in his hand.

"I'm guessing cocaine," he said. "Could be heroin."

"Where was it?" Wallander asked.

Sjösten pointed to an open drawer.

"There may be more," Wallander said.

"I'll see about getting a dog in here," said Sjösten.

"I wonder whether you shouldn't send out a few people to talk to the neighbours," said Wallander. "Ask if they noticed a man on a motorcycle. Not just last night, but earlier too. Over the last few weeks."

"Did he come on a motorcycle?"

"I think so. It seems to be his means of getting around. You'll find it in the investigative material."

Sjösten left the room.

"There's nothing about a motorcycle in the investigative material," said Höglund, surprised.

"There should be," said Wallander, sounding distracted. "Didn't we confirm that it was a motorcycle that stood behind the road workers' hut?"

Wallander looked out the window. Ekholm and Hansson were on their way up the path, with another man whom Wallander assumed was the Helsingborg chief of police. Birgersson met them halfway.

"We'd better go down," he said. "Did you find anything?"

"The house reminds me of Wetterstedt's," she replied. "The same gloomy bourgeois respectability. But at least here there are some family photos. Whether they make it more cheerful I don't know. Liljegren seems to have had cavalry officers in his family, Scanian Dragoons if you can believe it."

"I haven't looked at them," Wallander apologised. "But I believe you. His scams undoubtedly had much in common with primitive warfare."

"There's a photo of an old couple outside a cottage," she said. "If I understood what was written on the back, the picture was of his maternal grandparents on the island of Öland."

They went down. Parts of the stairs were cordoned off to protect the blood traces.

"Old bachelors," said Wallander. "Their houses resemble each other's because they were alike. How old was Åke Liljegren, anyway? Was he over 70?"

Höglund didn't know.

A conference room was set up in the dining room. Ekholm, who didn't have to attend, was assigned an officer to fill him in. When they had all introduced themselves and sat down, Hansson surprised Wallander by being quite clear-cut about what should happen. During the trip up from Ystad he had spoken with both Åkeson and the National Criminal Bureau in Stockholm.

"It would be a mistake to state that our situation has changed significantly because of this murder," Hansson began. "The situation has been dramatic enough ever since we realised that we were dealing with a serial killer. Now we might say that we have crossed a sort of boundary. There's nothing to indicate that we will actually crack these murders. But we have to hope. As far as the Bureau is concerned, they are prepared to give us whatever help we request. The formalities involved shouldn't present any serious difficulties either. I assume no-one has anything against Kurt being assigned leader of the new cross-boundary investigative team?"

No-one had any objections. Sjösten nodded approval from his side of the table.

"Kurt has a certain notoriety," Hansson said, without a trace of irony. "The chief of the National Criminal Bureau regarded it as obvious that he should continue to lead the investigation."

"I agree," said the chief of the Helsingborg police. That was the only thing he said during the meeting.

"Guidelines have been drawn on how a collaboration such as this can be implemented as quickly as possible," Hansson continued. "The prosecutors have their own procedures to follow. The key thing is to agree what type of assistance from Stockholm we actually require."

Wallander had been listening to what Hansson was saying with a mixture of pride and anxiety. At the same time he was self-assured enough to realise that no-one else was more suitable to lead the investigation.

"Has anything resembling this series of murders ever occurred in Sweden?" asked Sjösten.

"Not according to Ekholm," said Wallander.

"It's just that it would be good to have some colleagues who have experience with this type of crime," said Sjösten.

"We'd have to get them from the continent, or the United States," said Wallander. "And I don't think that's such a good idea. Not yet, at any rate. What we need, obviously, is experienced homicide investigators, who can add to our overall expertise."

It took them less than 20 minutes to make the necessary decisions. When they'd finished, Wallander hastily left the room in search of Ekholm. He found him upstairs and took him into a guest room that smelt musty. Wallander opened the window to air the stuffy room. He sat on the edge of the bed and told Ekholm what had occurred to him that morning.

"You could be right," Ekholm said. "A person with serious psychosis who has taken on the role of a lone warrior. There are many examples of that, though not in Sweden. Such a person generally metamorphoses into another before they go out to exact a revenge. The disguise frees them from guilt. The actor doesn't feel the pangs of conscience for actions performed by his character. But don't forget that there's a type of psychopath who kills with no motive other than for his own intense enjoyment."

"That's doesn't seem to fit this case," said Wallander.

"The difficulty lies in the fact that the role the killer has adopted doesn't tell us anything about the motive for the murder. If we assume that you're right – a barefoot warrior who has chosen his disguise for reasons unknown to us – then he could just as easily have chosen to turn himself into a Japanese samurai or a *tonton macoute* from Haiti. There's only one person who knows the reasons for the choice. The killer himself."

Wallander recalled one of the earliest conversations he had had with Ekholm.

"That would mean that the scalps are a red herring," he said. "That he's taking them as a ritual act in the performance of the role he's selected for himself. Not that he's collecting trophies to reach some objective that serves as the basis for all the murders he has committed."

"That's possible."

"Which means that we're back to square one."

"The combinations have to be tested over and over," said Ekholm. "We never return to the starting point once we have left it. We have to move the same way the killer does. He doesn't stand still. What happened last night confirms what I'm saying."

"Have you formed any opinion?"

"The oven is interesting."

Wallander flinched at Ekholm's choice of words.

"In what way?"

"The difference between the acid and the oven is striking. In one case he uses a chemical agent to torture a man who's still alive. It's an element of the killing itself. In the second case it serves more as a greeting to us."

Wallander looked at Ekholm intently. He tried to interpret what he'd just heard.

"A greeting to the police?"

"It doesn't really surprise me. The murderer is not unaffected by his actions. His self-image is growing. It may reach a point where he has to start looking for contact. He's terribly pleased with himself. He has to seek confirmation of how clever he is from the outside world. The victim can't applaud him. Sometimes he turns to the very ones who are hunting him. This can take various forms. Anonymous telephone calls or letters. Or why not a dead man arranged in a grotesque position?"

"He's taunting us?"

"I don't think he sees it that way. He sees himself as invulnerable. If it's true that he selected the role of a barefoot warrior, the invulnerability might be one of the reasons. Warrior peoples traditionally smear themselves with salves to make themselves immune from swords and arrows. In our day and age the police might symbolise those swords."

Wallander sat silently for a while.

"What's our next move?" he asked. "He's challenging us by stuffing Liljegren's head in the oven. What about next time? If there is one."

"There are many possibilities. Psychopathic killers sometimes seek contact with individuals within the police force."

"Why is that?"

Ekholm hesitated. "Policemen have been killed, you know."

"You mean this madman has his eye on us?"

"It's possible. Without our knowing it, he might be amusing himself by getting very close to us. And then vanishing again. One day this may not be enough of a thrill."

Wallander remembered the sensation that he'd had outside the cordon at Carlman's farm, when he thought he'd recognised one of the faces among the onlookers. Someone who had also been on the beach beyond the cordon when they'd turned over the boat and revealed Wetterstedt.

Ekholm looked at him gravely.

"You most of all should be aware of this," he said. "I was thinking of talking to you about it anyway."

"Why me?"

"You're the most visible one of us. The search for the man who committed these four murders involves a lot of people. But the name and face that are most regularly seen are yours."

Wallander grimaced. "You can't expect me to take this seriously?"

"That's for you to decide."

When Ekholm had left, Wallander stayed behind, trying to gauge his true reaction to Ekholm's warning. It was like a cold wind blowing through the room, he thought. But nothing more.

That afternoon Wallander drove back to Ystad with the others. It was decided that the investigation would continue to be directed from Ystad. Wallander sat in silence for the whole trip, giving only terse replies when Hansson asked him something. When they arrived they held a short briefing with Svedberg, Martinsson and Åkeson. Svedberg told them that it was now possible to speak with Carlman's daughter. They decided that Wallander and Höglund would pay a visit to the hospital the next morning. When the meeting was over, Wallander called his father. Gertrud answered. All was back to normal. His father had no recollection of what had happened.

Wallander also called home. No answer. Linda wasn't there. On his way out of the station he asked Ebba whether there was any word on his keys. Nothing. He drove down to the harbour and walked along the pier, then sat down in the harbour café and had a beer. He sat and watched the people passing by. Depressed, he got up and went back out on the pier, and sat on a bench next to the sea rescue hut.

It was a warm, windless evening. Someone was playing a concertina on a boat. One of the ferries from Poland was coming in. Without actually being conscious of it, he started to make a connection in his mind. He sat perfectly still and let his thoughts work. He was beginning to discern the contours of the drama. There were a lot of gaps still, but he could see where they should concentrate their investigation.

He didn't think that the way they had been working so far was to blame. The problem was with the conclusions he had made. He drove home and wrote down a summary at his kitchen table. Linda arrived back just before midnight. She had seen the papers.

"Who is doing this? What is someone like this made of?" she asked.

Wallander thought for a while before he replied.

"He's like you and me," he said at last. "By and large, just like you and me."

CHAPTER 31

Wallander woke with a start.

His eyes flew open and he lay completely still. The light of the summer night was grey. Someone was moving around in the flat. He glanced quickly at the clock on the bedside table. It was 2.15 a.m. His terror was instantaneous. He knew it wasn't Linda. Once she fell asleep, she didn't get up again until morning. He held his breath and listened. The sound was very faint.

The person moving around was barefoot.

Wallander got out of bed noiselessly. He looked for something to defend himself with. He had locked his service revolver in his desk at the station. The only thing in the bedroom he could use was the broken arm of a chair. He picked it up and listened again. The sound seemed to be coming from the kitchen. He came out of the bedroom and looked towards the living-room. He passed the door to Linda's room. It was closed. She was asleep. Now he was very scared. The sounds *were* coming from the kitchen. He stood in the doorway of the living-room and listened. Ekholm was right after all. He prepared himself to meet someone who was very strong. The chair arm wouldn't be much help. He remembered that he had a replica of a pair of old-fashioned brass knuckles in one of the drawers in the bookshelf. They had been the prize in a police lottery. He decided that his fists were better protection than the chair arm. He could still hear sounds in the kitchen. He moved cautiously across the parquet floor and opened the drawer. The brass knuckles were underneath a copy of his tax return. He put them on his right hand. At the same instant he realised that the sounds in the kitchen had stopped. He spun round and raised his arms.

Linda was in the doorway looking at him with a mixture of amazement and fear. He stared back at her.

"What are you doing?" she said. "What's that on your hand?"

"I thought it was somebody breaking in," he said, taking off the brass knuckles.

She could see that he was shaken.

"It was me. I couldn't sleep."

"The door to your room was closed."

"I must have shut it behind me. I needed a drink of water."

"But you never wake up in the night."

"Those days are long gone. Sometimes I don't sleep well. When I've got a lot on my mind."

Wallander knew he ought to feel foolish. But his relief was too great. His reaction had confirmed something. He had taken Ekholm much more seriously than he thought. He sat down. Linda was still standing there staring at him.

"I've often wondered how you can sleep as well as you do," she said. "When I think of the things you have to look at, the things you're forced to do."

"You get used to it," said Wallander, knowing that wasn't true at all.

She sat down next to him.

"I was looking through an evening paper while Kajsa was buying cigarettes," she went on. "There was quite a bit about what happened in Helsingborg. I don't know how you stand it."

"The papers exaggerate."

"How do you exaggerate somebody getting their head stuffed into an oven?"

Wallander tried to avoid her questions. He didn't know whether it was for his sake or for hers.

"That's a matter for the doctor," he said. "I examine the scene and try to work out what happened."

She shook her head, resigned.

"You never could lie to me. To Mama, maybe, but never to me."

314

"I never lied to Mona, did I?"

"You never told her how much you loved her. What you don't say can be a false affirmation."

He looked at her in surprise. Her choice of words astonished him.

"When I was little I used to sneak looks at all the papers you brought home at night. I invited my friends too, sometimes, when you were working on something we thought was exciting. We would sit in my room and read transcripts of witness testimonies."

"I had no idea."

"You weren't supposed to. So who did you think was in the flat?"

He decided to tell her at least part of the truth. He explained that sometimes, but very rarely, policemen in his position who had their pictures in the paper a lot or were on TV, might catch the attention of criminals who then became fixated on them. Perhaps "fascinated" was a better term. Normally there was nothing to worry about. But it was a good idea to acknowledge the phenomenon and to stay alert.

She didn't believe him for a second.

"That wasn't somebody standing there with brass knuckles on, showing how aware he was," she said at last. "What I saw was my Dad who's a policeman. And he was scared."

"Maybe I had a nightmare," he said unconvincingly. "Tell me why you can't sleep."

"I'm worried about what to do with my life," she said.

"You and Kajsa were very good in the revue."

"Not as good as we ought to be."

"You've got time to feel your way."

"But what if I want to do something else entirely?"

"Like what?"

"That's what I think about when I wake up in the middle of the night. I open my eyes and think that I still don't know."

"You can always wake me up," he said. "As a policeman at least I've learned how to listen, even if you can get better answers from someone else."

She leaned her head on his shoulder.

"You're a good listener. A lot better than Mama. But I have to find the answers for myself."

They talked for a long time. Not until it was light outside did they go back to bed. Something Linda said made Wallander feel good: he listened better than Mona did. In some future life he wouldn't mind doing everything better than Mona. But not now, when there was Baiba.

Wallander got up a little before 7 a.m. Linda was still asleep. He had a quick cup of coffee and left. The weather was beautiful, but the wind had started to blow. When he got to the station he ran into an agitated Martinsson, who told him that the whole holiday schedule had been thrown into chaos. Most holidays had been postponed indefinitely.

"Now I probably won't be able to get time off until September," he said angrily. "Who the hell wants a holiday at that time of year?"

"Me," said Wallander. "I can go to Italy with my father."

It was already Wednesday, 6 July. He was supposed to meet Baiba at Kastrup Airport in three days. For the first time he faced up to the fact that their holiday would have to be cancelled, or at least postponed. He had avoided thinking about it during the last hectic weeks, but he couldn't continue to do so. He would have to cancel flights and the hotel reservations. He dreaded Baiba's reaction. He sat at his desk feeling his stomach begin to ache with the stress. There must be some alternative, he thought. Baiba can come here. Maybe we could still catch this damned killer soon. This man who kills people and then scalps them.

He was terrified of her disappointment. Even though she had been married to a policeman, she probably imagined that everything was different in Sweden. But he couldn't wait any longer to tell her that they wouldn't be going to Skagen. He should pick up the phone and call Riga straight away. But he put off the unpleasant conversation. He wasn't ready yet. He took his notebook and listed all the calls he'd have to make.

Then he turned into a policeman again. He put the summary he had written the day before on the desk in front of him and read it through.

The notes made sense. He picked up the phone and asked Ebba to get hold of Sjösten in Helsingborg. A few minutes later she called back.

"He seems to spend his mornings scraping barnacles off a boat," she said. "But he was on his way in. He'll call you in the next ten minutes."

When Sjösten called back, he told Wallander that they'd located some witnesses, a couple, who claimed to have seen a motorcycle on Aschebergsgatan on the evening Liljegren was murdered.

"Check carefully," said Wallander. "It could be very important."

"I thought I'd do it myself."

Wallander leaned forward over his desk, as if he had to brace himself before tackling the next question.

"I'd like to ask you to do one more thing," he said. "Something that should take the highest priority. I want you to find some of the women who worked at the parties that were held at Liljegren's villa."

"Why?"

"I think it's important. We have to find out who was at those parties. You'll understand when you go through the investigative material."

Wallander knew very well that his question wouldn't be answered in the material they had assembled for the other three murders. But he needed to hunt alone for a while longer.

"So you want me to pick out a whore," said Sjösten.

"I do. If there were any at those parties."

"It was rumoured that there were."

"I want you to get back in touch with me as soon as possible. Then I'll come up to Helsingborg."

"If I find one, should I bring her in?"

"I just want to talk to her, that's all. Make it clear she has nothing to worry about. Someone who's afraid and says what she thinks I want to hear won't help at all."

"I'll try," said Sjösten. "Interesting assignment in the middle of summer."

They hung up. Wallander concentrated on his notes from the night before until Höglund called. They met in reception and walked down to the hospital so they could plan what they would say to Carlman's daughter. Wallander didn't even know the name of this young woman who had slapped his face.

"Erika," said Höglund. "Which doesn't suit her."

"Why not?" asked Wallander, surprised.

"I get the impression of a robust sort when I hear that name," she said. "The manager of a hotel smörgåsbord or a crane operator."

"Is it OK that my name is Kurt?" he asked.

She nodded cheerfully.

"It's nonsense that you can match a personality to a name of course," she said. "But it amuses me. And you could hardly imagine a cat called Fido. Or a dog called Kitty."

"There probably are some," said Wallander. "So what do we know about Erika Carlman?"

They had the wind at their backs as they walked towards the hospital. Höglund told him that Erika Carlman was 27 years old. That for a while she had been a stewardess for a small British charter airline. That she had dabbled in many different things without ever sticking to them for long. She had travelled all over the world, no doubt supported by her father. A marriage with a Peruvian football player had been quickly dissolved.

"A normal rich girl," said Wallander. "One who had everything on a silver platter from the start."

"Her mother says she was hysterical as a teenager. That's the word she used, hysterical. It would probably be more accurate to describe it as a neurotic predisposition."

"Has she attempted suicide before?"

"Not that anyone knows of, and I didn't think the mother was lying."

"She really wanted to die," Wallander said.

"That's my impression too."

Wallander knew that he had to tell Ann-Britt that Erika had slapped him. It was very possible that she might mention the incident. And there wouldn't be any explanation for his not having done so, other than masculine vanity, perhaps. As they reached the hospital,

Wallander stopped and told her. He could see that she was surprised.

"I don't think it was more than a manifestation of the hysteria her mother spoke of," he said.

"This might cause a problem," Ann-Britt said. "She may be in bad shape. She must know that she nearly died. We don't even know if she regrets the fact that she didn't manage to kill herself. If you walk into the room, her fragile ego might collapse. Or it might make her aggressive, scared, unreceptive."

Wallander knew she was right. "You should speak to her alone. I'll wait in the cafeteria."

"First we'll have to go over what we actually want to learn from her."

Wallander pointed to a bench by the taxi rank. They sat down.

"We always hope that the answers will be more interesting than the questions," he said. "What did her suicide attempt have to do with her father's death? How you get to that question is up to you. You'll have to draw your own map. Her answers will prompt more questions."

"Let's assume that she says she was so crushed by grief that she didn't want to go on living."

"Then we'll know that much."

"But what else do we actually know?"

"That's where you have to ask other questions, which we can't predict. Was it a normal loving relationship between father and daughter? Or was it something else?"

"And if she denies it was something else?"

"Then you have to start by not believing her. Without telling her so."

"In other words," said Höglund slowly, "a denial would mean that I should be interested in the reasons she might have for not telling the truth?"

"More or less." Wallander answered. "But there's a third possibility, of course. That she tried to commit suicide because she knew something about her father's death that she couldn't deal with in any other way except by taking the information with her to the grave."

"Could she have seen the killer?"

"It's possible."

"And doesn't want him to be caught?"

"Also conceivable."

"Why not?"

"Once again, there are at least two possibilities. She wants to protect him. Or she wants to protect her father's memory."

Höglund sighed hopelessly. "I don't know if I can handle this."

"Of course you can. I'll be in the cafeteria. Or out here. Take as long as you need."

Wallander accompanied her to the front desk. A few weeks earlier he had been here and found out that Salomonsson had died. How could he have imagined then what havoc was in store for him? Höglund disappeared down the hall. Wallander went towards the cafeteria, but changed his mind and went back outside to the bench. Once again he went over his thoughts from the night before. He was interrupted by his mobile phone ringing in his jacket pocket. It was Hansson, and he sounded harried.

"Two investigators from the National Criminal Bureau are arriving at Sturup this afternoon. Ludwigsson and Hamrén. Do you know them?"

"Only by name. They're supposed to be good. Hamrén was involved in solving that case with the laser man, wasn't he?"

"Could you possibly pick them up?"

"I don't think that I can," said Wallander. "I have to go back to Helsingborg."

"Birgersson didn't mention that. I spoke to him a little while ago."

"They probably have the same communication problems that we do," Wallander said patiently. "I think it would be a nice gesture if you went to pick them up yourself."

"What do you mean by gesture?"

"Of respect. When I went to Riga I was picked up in a limousine. An old Russian one, but even so. It's important for people to feel that they're being welcomed and taken care of."

"All right," said Hansson. "I'll do it. Where are you now?"

"At the hospital."

"Are you sick?"

"Carlman's daughter. Did you forget about her?"

"To tell you the truth, I did."

"We should be glad we don't all forget the same things," Wallander said. He didn't know whether Hansson had recognised that he was being ironic. He put the phone down on the bench and watched a sparrow perched on the edge of a rubbish bin. Ann-Britt had been gone for almost half an hour. He closed his eyes and raised his face to the sun, rehearsing what he would say to Baiba. A man with his leg in a cast sat down with a thud next to him. After five minutes a taxi arrived. The man with the cast left. Wallander paced back and forth in front of the hospital entrance. Then he sat down again.

After more than an hour Ann-Britt came out and sat down next to him. He couldn't tell from the expression on her face how it had gone.

"I think we missed one reason why a person would want to commit suicide," she said. "Being tired of life."

"Was that her answer?"

"I didn't even have to ask. She was sitting in a white room, in a hospital gown, her hair uncombed, pale, out of it. Still immersed in a mixture of her own crisis and heavy medication. 'Why go on living?' That was her greeting. To be honest, I think she'll try to kill herself again. Out of sheer loathing."

Wallander had overlooked the most common motive for committing suicide. Simply not wanting to go on living.

"But did you talk about her father?"

"She despised him, but I'm quite sure that she wasn't abused by him."

"Did she say so?"

"Some things don't have to be actually said."

"What about the murder?"

"She was strangely uninterested in it. She wondered why I had come. I told her the truth. We're searching for the killer. She said there were probably plenty of people who wanted her father dead. Because of his ruthlessness in business. Because of the way he was."

"She didn't say anything about him having another woman?"

"No."

Wallander watched the sparrow despondently.

"Well, at least we know that much," he said. "We know that we don't know anything else."

When they were halfway back to the station, Wallander's phone rang. He turned away from the wind to answer it. It was Svedberg.

"We think we found the place where Fredman was killed," he said. "At a dock just west of town."

Wallander felt his spirits rise.

"Great news," he said.

"A tip-off," Svedberg continued. "The person who called mentioned blood stains. It could have been somebody cleaning fish, of course. But I don't think so. The caller was a laboratory technician. He's worked with blood samples for 35 years. And he said that there were tyre tracks nearby. A vehicle had been parked there. Why not a Ford van?"

"We can drive over there and work it out very shortly," said Wallander.

They continued up the hill, much more quickly now. Wallander told Höglund the news. Neither of them was thinking about Erika Carlman any more.

Hoover got off the train in Ystad just after 11 a.m. He had decided to leave his moped at home today. When he came out of the railway station and saw that the cordon around the pit where he had dumped his father was gone, he felt a twinge of disappointment and anger. The policemen who were hunting him were much too weak. They would never have passed the easiest entrance exam to the F.B.I.'s academy. He felt Geronimo's heart start to drum inside him. He understood the message, simple and clear. He was going to fulfil the mission he had been chosen for. He would bring his sister two final sacrifices before she returned to life. Two scalps beneath her window. And the girl's heart. As a gift. Then he would walk into the hospital to get her and they would leave together. Life would be very different. One day they might even read her diary together, remembering the events that had led her back, out of the darkness.

He walked into Ystad. He was wearing shoes so as not to attract attention, but his feet didn't like it. He turned right at the square and went to the house where the policeman lived with the girl who must be his daughter. He had come to take a closer look. The action itself he was planning for the next evening. Or at the latest, one day later. Not more. His sister shouldn't have to stay in that hospital any longer. He sat down on the steps of one of the neighbouring buildings. He practised forgetting time. Just sitting, empty of thought, until he again took hold of his mission. He still had a lot to learn before he mastered the art to perfection, but he had no doubt that one day he would succeed.

His wait lasted for two hours. Then she came out of the front door, obviously in a hurry, and set off towards the town centre. He followed her and never let her out of his sight.

CHAPTER 32

When they got to the dock, ten kilometres west of Ystad, Wallander was immediately sure that it was the right place. It was just as he had imagined it. They had driven along the coast road and stopped where a man in shorts and a T-shirt advertising the golf course in Malmberget waved them down and directed them to a barely visible dirt road. They stopped just short of the dock, so they wouldn't disturb the tyre marks.

The laboratory technician, Erik Wiberg, told them that in the summer he lived in a cabin on the north side of the coast road. He often came down to this dock to read his morning paper, as he had on 29 June. He'd noticed the tyre tracks and the dark spots on the brown wood, but thought nothing of it. He left that same day for Germany with his family, and it wasn't until he saw in the paper on his return that the police were looking for a murder site, probably near the sea, that he remembered those dark spots. Since he worked in a laboratory, he knew that what was on the dock at least looked like blood. Nyberg, who had arrived just after Wallander and the others, was on his knees by the tyre tracks. He had toothache and was more irritable than ever. Wallander was the only one he could bear to talk to.

"It could be Fredman's van," he said, "but we'll have to do a proper examination."

They walked out on the dock together. Wallander knew they had been lucky. The dry summer helped. If it had rained there wouldn't have been tracks. He looked for confirmation from Martinsson, who had the best memory for the weather.

"Has it rained since 28 June?" he asked.

"It drizzled on the morning of Midsummer Eve," he said. "Ever since then it's been fine."

"Arrange to cordon off the whole place," said Wallander, nodding to Höglund. "And be careful where you put your feet."

He stood near the land end of the dock and looked at the patches of blood. They were concentrated in the middle of the dock, which was four metres long. He turned around and looked up towards the road. He could hear the noise, but he couldn't see the cars, just the roof of a tall lorry flashing by. He had an idea. Höglund was on the phone to Ystad.

"And tell them to bring me a map," he said. "One that includes Ystad, Malmö, and Helsingborg." Then he walked to the end of the dock and looked into the water. The bottom was rocky. Wiberg was standing on the beach.

"Where's the nearest house?" asked Wallander.

"A couple of hundred metres from here," replied Wiberg. "Across the road."

Nyberg had come out onto the dock.

"Should we call in divers?" he asked.

"Yes," said Wallander. "Start with a radius of 25 metres around the dock."

Then he pointed at the rings set into the wood.

"Prints," he said. "If Fredman was killed here he must have been tied down. Our killer goes barefoot and doesn't wear gloves."

"What are the divers looking for?"

Wallander thought.

"I don't know," he said. "Let's see if they come up with anything. But I think you're going to find traces of kelp on the slope, from the place where the tyre tracks stop all the way down to the dock."

"The van didn't turn around," said Nyberg. "He backed it all the way up to the road. He couldn't have seen whether any cars were coming. So there are only two possibilities. Unless he's totally crazy."

Wallander raised his eyebrows.

"He *is* crazy," he said.

"Not in that way," said Nyberg.

Wallander understood what he meant. He wouldn't have been able to back up onto the road unless he had an accomplice who signalled when the road was clear. Or else it happened at night. When he'd see headlights and know when it was safe to back out onto the road.

"He doesn't have an accomplice," said Wallander. "And we know that it must have happened at night. The only question is why did he drive Fredman's body to the pit outside the railway station in Ystad?"

"He's crazy," said Nyberg. "You said so yourself."

When a car arrived with the map, Wallander asked Martinsson for a pen and then sat on a rock next to the dock. He drew circles around Ystad, Bjäresjö and Helsingborg. Then he marked the dock. He wrote numbers next to his marks. He waved over Höglund, Martinsson and Svedberg, who had arrived last, wearing a dirty sun hat instead of his cap for a change. He pointed at the map on his knee.

"Here we have his movements," he said. "And the murder sites. Like everything else they form a pattern."

"A road," Svedberg said. "With Ystad and Helsingborg as the end points. The scalp murderer on the southern plain."

"That isn't funny," Martinsson snapped.

"I'm not trying to be funny," Svedberg protested. "It's how it is."

"Looking at the big picture, you're probably right," said Wallander. "The area is limited. One murder takes place in Ystad. One murder occurs here, perhaps, we aren't sure yet, and the body is taken to Ystad. One murder happens just outside Ystad, in Bjäresjö, where the body is also discovered. And then we have Helsingborg."

"Most of them are concentrated around Ystad," said Höglund. "Does that mean that the man we're looking for lives here?"

"With the exception of Fredman the victims were found close to or inside their homes," said Wallander. "This is the map of the victims, not the murderer."

"Then Malmö should be marked too," said Svedberg. "That's where Fredman lived."

Wallander circled Malmö. The breeze tugged at the map.

"Now the picture is different," said Höglund. "We get an angle, not a straight line. Malmö is in the middle."

"It's always Fredman who's different," said Wallander.

"Maybe we should draw another circle," said Martinsson. "Around the airport. What do we get then?"

"An area of movement," said Wallander. "Revolving around Fredman's murder."

He knew that they were on their way towards a crucial conclusion.

"Correct me if I'm wrong," he said. "Fredman lives in Malmö. Together with the man who kills him, either held captive or not, he is driven east in the van. They come here, where Fredman dies. The journey continues to Ystad. The body is dumped in a hole under a tarpaulin in Ystad. Later the van returns west. It's parked at the airport, about halfway between Malmö and Ystad. There the tracks vanish."

"There are plenty of ways to get away from Sturup," said Svedberg. "Taxis, airport buses, rental cars. Another vehicle parked there earlier."

"So the murderer probably doesn't live in Ystad," Wallander said. "Malmö's a good possibility. But it could just as well be Lund. Or Helsingborg. Or why not Copenhagen?"

"Unless he's leading us on a wild-goose chase," Höglund said. "And he really does live in Ystad."

"That's possible, of course," said Wallander, "but I don't buy it."

"Which means that we ought to concentrate on Sturup more than we have so far," Martinsson said.

Wallander nodded. "I believe that the man we're looking for uses a motorcycle," he said. "We talked about this before. Witnesses may have seen one outside the house in Helsingborg. Sjösten is working on that right now. Since we're getting reinforcements this afternoon, we can afford to do a careful examination of the transport options from Sturup. We're looking for a man who parked the van there on the night of 28 June. And somehow left. Unless he works at the airport."

"There's one question we can't yet answer," said Svedberg. "And that is: what does this monster look like?"

"We know nothing about his face," Wallander said. "But we know he's strong, and a basement window in Helsingborg tells us that he's thin. We're dealing with someone in good shape, who goes barefoot."

"You mentioned Copenhagen just now," Martinsson said. "Do you think he's a foreigner?"

"I doubt it," Wallander replied. "I think we're dealing with a 100 per cent Swedish serial killer."

"That's not much to go on," said Svedberg. "Haven't we found a single hair? Does he have light or dark hair?"

"We don't know. According to Ekholm he probably tries not to attract attention. And we can't say anything about the way he's dressed when he commits the murders."

"What about his age?" asked Höglund.

"His victims have been men in their 70s, except for Fredman. But he's in good shape, goes barefoot, and may ride a motorcycle, and these facts don't imply an older man. We just can't guess."

"Over 18," said Svedberg. "If he rides a motorcycle."

"Can't we start with Fredman?" asked Höglund. "He differs from the other men, who are considerably older. Maybe we can assume that Fredman and the man who killed him are the same age. Then we're talking about a man who's under 50. And there are quite a few of them who are in good shape."

Wallander gave his colleagues a gloomy look. They were all under 50; Martinsson, the youngest, was barely 30. None of them was in particularly good shape.

"Ekholm is working on the psychological profile," said Wallander, getting to his feet. "It's important that we all read through it every day. It might give us some ideas."

Norén came towards Wallander with a telephone in his hand. Wallander squatted down out of the wind. It was Sjösten.

"I think I've got someone for you," he said. "A woman who was at parties at Liljegren's villa."

"Well done," Wallander said. "When can I meet her?"

"Any time."

Wallander looked at his watch. "I'll be there no later than 3 p.m.," he said. "By the way, we think we've found the place where Fredman died."

"I heard about it," Sjösten said. "I also heard that Ludwigsson and Hamrén are on their way from Stockholm. They're good men, both of them."

"How's it going with the witnesses who saw a man on a motorcycle?"

"They didn't see a man," Sjösten answered. "But they did see a motorcycle. We're trying to establish what kind it was. But it's not easy. Both the witnesses are old. They're also passionate health nuts who despise all petrol-powered vehicles. In the end it may turn out to be a lawnmower they saw."

A scratchy noise came from the phone. The conversation sputtered out in the wind. Nyberg was looking at the dock, rubbing his swollen cheek.

"How's it going?" Wallander asked him cheerily.

"I'm waiting for the divers."

"Are you in a lot of pain?"

"It's a wisdom tooth."

"Get it removed."

"I will. But first I want those divers here."

"Is it blood on the dock?"

"Almost certainly. Tonight you'll know whether it ever ran around inside Fredman's body."

On his way to the car Wallander remembered something. He went back.

"Louise Fredman," he said to Svedberg. "Did Åkeson come up with anything else on her?"

Svedberg didn't know, but said he'd talk to Åkeson.

Wallander turned off at Charlottenlund, thinking that if they'd found the place where Fredman was murdered, it was chosen with great care. The closest house was too far away for screams to be heard. He drove to the E65 and headed towards Malmö. The wind was buffeting the car, but the sky was still totally clear. He thought about the map. There were a lot of reasons to think the killer lived in Malmö. He didn't live in Ystad, that seemed certain. But why did he go to the trouble of dumping Fredman's body in a pit at the railway station? Was Ekholm right, that he was taunting the police? Wallander took the road to Sturup and briefly considered stopping at the airport. But what good would that do? The interview in Helsingborg was more important.

Her name was Elisabeth Carlén. They were in the Helsingborg police station in Sjösten's office. As Wallander shook hands with her he thought of the female vicar he had met the week before. Maybe it was because she was dressed in black and wore heavy make-up. She was about 30. Sjösten's description of her was quite apt. Sjösten had said that she was attractive because she looked at the world with a cold, disparaging expression. To Wallander it seemed as if she had decided to challenge any man who came near her. He'd never seen eyes like hers before. They blazed contempt and interest at the same time. He went over Sjösten's account of her as she lit a cigarette.

"Elisabeth Carlén is a whore," he had said. "I doubt she's been anything else since she was 20. She left middle school and then worked as a waitress on one of the ferries crossing the Sound. Got tired of that and opened a boutique with a girlfriend. That was a flop. Her parents had guaranteed a loan she took out for the business. After the money was gone, she did nothing but fight with them, and she drifted around a lot. Copenhagen for a while, then Amsterdam. When she was 17 she went there as a courier with a haul of amphetamines. Probably she was a user herself, but she seemed to be able to control it. That was the first time I met her. Then she was away for a few years, a black hole I don't know anything about, before she popped up in Malmö, working in a chain of brothels."

Wallander had to interrupt. "Are there still brothels?" he asked in surprise.

"Whorehouses, then," said Sjösten. "Call them what you like. But yes, there are still plenty of them. Don't you have them in Ystad? Just wait."

Wallander didn't interrupt again.

"She never walked the streets, of course. She built up an exclusive clientele. She had something that was attractive and raised her market value to the skies. She didn't even need to put those classified ads in the porn magazines. You can ask her what it is that makes her so special. It might be interesting to find out. During the last few years she's turned up in certain circles that are connected to Liljegren. She's been seen at restaurants with a number of his directors. Stockholm has a record of quite a few occasions when the police were interested in the man who happened to be escorting her. That's Elisabeth Carlén in a nutshell. Quite a successful Swedish prostitute."

"Why did you choose her?"

"She's fun. I've spoken with her many times. She isn't timid. If I tell her she isn't suspected of anything, she believes me. Also I imagine that she has a whore's sense of self-preservation. She notices things. She doesn't like the police. A good way to keep us out of the way is to stay on good terms with us."

Wallander hung up his jacket and shifted a heap of papers on the table. Elisabeth Carlén followed all his movements with her eyes. Wallander was reminded of a wary bird.

"You know that you aren't suspected of anything," he began.

"Åke Liljegren was roasted in his kitchen," she said. "I've seen his oven. Quite fancy. But I wasn't the one who turned it on."

"Nor do we think you were," said Wallander. "What I'm looking for is information. I'm trying to build a picture. I've got an empty frame. I'd like to put a photo in it. Taken at a party at Liljegren's. I want you to point out his guests."

"No," she said, "that's not what you want. You want me to tell you who killed him. And I can't."

"What did you think when you heard Liljegren was dead?"

"I didn't think anything. I burst out laughing."

"Why? No-one's death should be funny."

"He had plans other than winding up the way he did. The mausoleum in the cemetery outside Madrid? That's where he was going to be buried. A virtual fortress built according to his own sketches. Out of Italian marble. But he fetched up dying in his own oven. I think he would have laughed himself."

"His parties," said Wallander. "Let's get back to them. I've heard they were wild."

"They sure were."

"In what way?"

"In every way."

"Can you be a little more specific?"

She took a couple of deep drags on her cigarette while she thought about this, all the time looking Wallander in the eye.

"Liljegren liked to bring people together who lived life to the fullest," she said. "Let's say they were insatiable. Insatiable with regard to power, wealth and sex. And Liljegren had a reputation for being discreet. He created a safety zone around his guests. No hidden cameras, no spies. Nothing ever leaked out about his parties. He also knew which women he could invite."

"Women like you?"

"Yes, women like me."

"And who else?"

She didn't seem to understand his question at first.

"What other women were there?"

"That depended on their desires."

"Whose desires?"

"The desires of the guests. The men."

"And what might they be?"

"Some wanted *me* to be there."

"I understood that. Who else?"

"You won't get any names."

"Who were they?"

"Young girls, some very young, blonde, brown, black. Older ones sometimes, some of them hefty. It varied."

"You knew them?"

"Not always. Not often."

"How did he get hold of them?"

332

She put out her cigarette and lit a new one before she answered. She didn't release his gaze even when she was stubbing it out.

"How does a person like Liljegren get what he wants? He had unlimited money. He had helpers. He had contacts. He could fly in a girl from Florida to attend a party. She probably had no idea she was going all the way to Sweden. Not to mention Helsingborg."

"You say he had helpers. Who were they?"

"His chauffeurs. His assistant. He often had a butler with him. English, of course."

"What was his name?"

"No names."

"We'll find out about them anyway."

"You probably will. But that doesn't mean the names are going to come from me."

"What would happen if you gave me some names?"

She seemed utterly unmoved when she replied.

"Then I might be killed. Maybe not with my head in an oven, but in an equally unpleasant manner, I'm sure."

"Were many of his guests public figures?"

"Many."

"Politicians?"

"Yes."

"Gustaf Wetterstedt?"

"I said no names."

Suddenly he realised that she was sending him a message. Her answers had a subtext. She knew who Wetterstedt was, but he had not been at the parties.

"Businessmen?"

"Yes."

"Arne Carlman, the art dealer?"

"Did he have almost the same name as me?"

"Yes."

"I'll say it one last time. Don't push me for names, or I'll get up and go."

333

Not him either, thought Wallander. Her signals were very clear.

"Artists? Celebrities?"

"Once in a while. But seldom. I don't think Åke trusted them. Probably with good reason."

"You talked about young girls. Brown girls. Did you mean brunettes, or girls with brown skin?"

"Brown skin."

"Do you remember ever meeting a girl named Dolores María?"

"No."

"A girl from the Dominican Republic?"

"I don't even know where that is."

"Do you remember a girl named Louise Fredman? A teenager. A blonde."

"No."

Wallander turned the conversation in another direction. She still seemed willing to continue.

"You say that the parties were wild."

"Yes, they were."

"Tell me about wild."

"Do you want details?"

"Please."

"Descriptions of naked bodies?"

"Not necessarily."

"They were orgies. You can imagine the rest."

"Can I?" said Wallander. "I'm not so sure."

"If I undressed and lay down on your desk it would be completely unexpected," she said. "Something like that."

"Unexpected events?"

"That's what happens when insatiable people get together, isn't it?"

"Insatiable men?"

"Exactly."

Wallander made a hasty outline in his head. He was still scratching the surface.

"I've got a proposal," he said. "And another question."

"I'm still here."

"My proposal is that you give me the opportunity to meet you one more time. Soon, within a few days."

She nodded her assent. Wallander got an unpleasant feeling that he was entering into some sort of agreement.

"My question is simple," he said. "You were speaking of Liljegren's chauffeurs. And his butlers. But you said that he had an assistant. Not plural. Is that correct?"

He saw a faint change in her expression. She knew she had said too much even without providing names.

"This conversation is strictly for my memoirs," said Wallander. "Did I hear correctly or not?"

"You heard wrong," she said. "Of course he had more than one assistant."

So, I was right, thought Wallander. "That'll be all this time, then," he said, getting up.

"I'll leave when I finish my cigarette," she said. For the first time in the conversation she released him from her gaze.

Wallander opened the door. Sjösten was sitting outside reading a sailing magazine. Wallander nodded. She put out her cigarette, stood up, and shook his hand. When Sjösten had shown her out and returned, Wallander was by the window, watching her get into her car.

"Did it go well?" Sjösten asked.

"Maybe," said Wallander. "She agreed to meet me again."

"What did she say?"

"Nothing, actually."

"And you think that was good?"

"It was what she didn't know that interested me," Wallander said. "I want 24-hour surveillance of Liljegren's house, and I want you to put a tail on Carlén. Sooner or later somebody will show up who we'll want to talk to."

"That sounds like an inadequate reason for surveillance," said Sjösten.

"I'll take responsibility for that decision," said Wallander kindly, "as the chosen leader of this investigation."

"I'm glad it wasn't me," replied Sjösten. "Are you staying overnight?"

"No, I'll drive home."

They went down the steps to the ground floor.

"Did you read about a girl who burned herself to death in a field near here?" Wallander asked just before they said goodbye.

"Yes. Terrible story."

"She had hitchhiked from Helsingborg," Wallander went on. "And she was scared. I'm just wondering whether she might have had something to do with Liljegren's fun and games. Although it's a long shot."

"There were rumours about Liljegren trading in girls," said Sjösten. "Among a thousand other rumours."

Wallander looked at him intently. "Trading girls?"

"There were rumours that Sweden was being used as a transit country for poor girls from South America, on their way to brothels in southern Europe and the former Eastern bloc countries. We've found a couple of girls who have managed to escape but we've never caught the ones running the business. And we haven't been able to build a proper case."

Wallander stared at Sjösten.

"And you waited until now to tell me this?"

Sjösten shook his head, surprised.

"You never asked me about this before now."

Wallander stood stock still. The girl had started running through his head again.

"I've changed my mind," he said. "I'll stay the night."

They took the lift back up to Sjösten's office.

CHAPTER 33

On that lovely summer evening Wallander and Sjösten took the ferry to Helsingør on the Danish side and had dinner at a restaurant Sjösten liked. He entertained Wallander while they ate with stories about the boat he was restoring, his numerous marriages and his yet more numerous children. They didn't begin talking about the investigation until they were having coffee. Wallander listened gratefully to Sjösten, who was a charming storyteller. He was very tired. After the excellent dinner he was feeling drowsy, but his mind was rested. Sjösten had drunk a few shots of aquavit with beer, while Wallander stuck to mineral water.

When the coffee came they exchanged roles. Sjösten listened while Wallander talked. He went over everything that had happened. He talked to Sjösten in a way that forced him to clarify things for himself as well. For the first time he let the girl who had burned herself to death serve as the prelude to the murders. It had seemed improbable to him before that her death might be connected to them. Now he admitted that it had been careless to draw this conclusion. Sjösten was an attentive listener who pounced on him whenever he was vague.

Wallander would think of that evening in Helsingør later as the point when the investigation sloughed off its skin. The pattern he thought he had discovered as he'd sat on the bench on the pier was confirmed. Gaps were filled, holes sealed; questions found their answers, or at least were formulated more clearly and arranged in order. He marched back and forth through the landscape of the case and for the first time felt that he had an overview. But he also had a nagging, guilty feeling that he should have seen it all sooner, that he had been sidetracked, instead of realising that he must go in an entirely different direction. Although he avoided mentioning it to Sjösten, there was one question always on his mind. Could any of the murders have been prevented? Or at least the last one – if it was the last one – Liljegren's? He couldn't help but ask. And he knew that it would haunt him for a very long time; maybe he'd never get an answer that he could live with.

The problem was that they didn't have a suspect, not even a group of people among whom they could cast their net. Nor were there any solid clues that led in a specific direction.

Earlier in the day, when Sjösten had mentioned in passing that it was suspected that Sweden, and especially Helsingborg, served as a transit point for girls destined for brothels, Wallander's reaction had been immediate. Sjösten was amazed at Wallander's sudden burst of energy. Without thinking, Wallander had sat down behind the desk, so Sjösten had to take the visitor's chair in his own office. Wallander told him all he knew about Dolores María Santana, that she seemed to be running away when she hitchhiked from Helsingborg.

"A black car came once a week to Gustaf Wetterstedt's house," Wallander said. "By chance the housekeeper noticed it. She thought she might recognise the car in Liljegren's garage. What conclusion can you draw from that?"

"None," said Sjösten. "There are plenty of black Mercedes with tinted windows."

"Put it together with the rumours about Liljegren. The rumours of the trade in girls. Is there anything that would prevent him from having parties somewhere else besides his house? Why couldn't he also run a home delivery service?"

"No reason at all," said Sjösten. "But there doesn't seem to be any basis for believing it."

"I want to know whether that car left Liljegren's house on Thursdays," said Wallander. "And came back on Fridays."

"How can we find that out?"

"There are neighbours. Who drove the car? There seems to be such a vacuum around Liljegren. He had personal employees. He had an assistant. Where are all these people?"

"We're working on that," said Sjösten.

"Let's set our priorities," said Wallander. "The motorcycle is important. Liljegren's assistant is too. And the car on Thursdays. Start there. Assign all your available people to look into these areas."

Sjösten went to set this in train. He told Wallander when he came back that the surveillance of Elisabeth Carlén had begun.

"What's she doing?"

"She's in her flat," Sjösten said. "Alone."

Wallander called Ystad and talked to Åkeson.

"I must talk with Louise Fredman now," he said.

"You'll have to come up with a strong case for doing so," Åkeson said, "or I can't help you."

"It might be crucial."

"It has to be something concrete, Kurt."

"There's always a way round this bureaucratic crap."

"What do you think she can tell you?"

"Whether she ever had the soles of her feet cut with a knife, for instance."

"Good Lord. Why would that have happened to her?"

Wallander didn't feel like telling him.

"Can't her mother give me permission?" he said. "Fredman's widow?"

"That's what I was wondering," said Åkeson. "That's the way we'll have to proceed."

"I'll drive to Malmö tomorrow," Wallander said. "Do I need any kind of papers from you?"

"Not if she gives you her permission," said Åkeson. "But you mustn't put pressure on her."

"Do I do that?" Wallander asked, surprised. "I didn't realise."

"I'm just telling you the rules. That's all."

Sjösten had suggested they take a ferry across to Denmark and have dinner, so they could talk, and Wallander had agreed. It was still too early to call Baiba. Maybe not too early for her, but certainly too early for him. It occurred to him that Sjösten, with all his marriages behind him, might be able to give him some advice on how to present his dilemma to Baiba. They took the ferry across the Sound, with Wallander wishing the journey was longer. They had dinner, which Sjösten insisted on paying for. Then they strolled back through Helsingør towards the terminal. Sjösten stopped at a doorway.

"In here lives a man who appreciates Swedes," he said, smiling.

Wallander read on a brass plate that a doctor had his practice here.

"He writes prescriptions for diet drugs that are banned in Sweden," said Sjösten. "Every day there's a long line of overweight Swedes outside."

They were on their way up the stairs to the terminal when Sjösten's mobile phone rang. He kept walking as he listened.

"That was Larsson, one of my colleagues. He's found what may be a real gold mine," Sjösten said, putting away his phone. "A neighbour of Liljegren's who saw a number of things."

"What did he see?"

"Black cars, motorcycles. We'll talk to him tomorrow."

"We'll talk to him tonight," Wallander said. "It'll only be 10 p.m. by the time we get back to Helsingborg."

Sjösten nodded without replying. Then he called the station and asked Larsson to meet them at the terminal. The young police officer waiting for them reminded Wallander of Martinsson. They got into his car and drove to Tågaborg. Wallander noticed a banner from the local football team hanging from his rear-view mirror. Larsson filled them in.

"His name is Lennart Heineman, and he's a retired diplomat," he said, in a Skåne accent so broad that Wallander had to strain to understand him. "He's almost 80, but quite sharp. His wife seems to be away. Heineman's garden is just across from the main entrance to Liljegren's grounds. He's observed a number of things."

"Does he know we're coming?" asked Sjösten.

"I called," said Larsson. "He said it was fine. He says he rarely goes to bed before 3 a.m. He told me he was writing a critical study of the Swedish foreign office's administration."

Wallander remembered with distaste an officious woman from the foreign office who had visited them in Ystad some years earlier, in connection with the investigation that led him to Latvia to meet Baiba. He tried to think of her name. Something to do with roses. He pushed the thought aside as they pulled up outside Heineman's house. A police car was parked outside Liljegren's villa across the street. A tall man with short white hair came walking towards them. He had a firm handshake, and Wallander trusted him instantly. The handsome villa he ushered them into was from the same period as Liljegren's, but this house had an air of vitality about it, a reflection of the energetic old man who lived there. He asked them to have a seat and offered them a drink. They all declined. Wallander sensed that he was used to receiving people he hadn't met before.

"Terrible things going on," said Heineman.

Sjösten gave Wallander an almost imperceptible nod to lead the interview.

"That's why we couldn't postpone this conversation until tomorrow," Wallander replied.

"Why postpone it?" said Heineman. "I've never understood why Swedes go to bed so early. The continental habit of taking a siesta is much healthier. If I'd gone to bed early I'd have been dead long ago."

Wallander pondered Heineman's strong criticism of Swedish bed-time hours for a moment.

"We're interested in any observations you may have made of the traffic in and out of Liljegren's villa," he said. "But there are some things that are of particular interest to us. Let's begin by asking about Liljegren's black Mercedes."

"He must have had at least two," said Heineman.

Wallander was surprised at the answer. He hadn't imagined more than one car, even though Liljegren's big garage could have held two or three.

"What makes you think he had more than one?"

"I don't just think so," said Heineman, "I know. Sometimes two cars left the house at the same time. Or returned at the same time.

When Liljegren was away the cars remained here. From my upper floor I can see part of his grounds. There were two cars over there."

One is missing, Wallander thought. Where is it now?

Sjösten took out a notebook.

"Can you recall whether one or perhaps both cars regularly left Liljegren's villa late in the afternoon or evening on Thursdays?" Wallander said. "And returned during the night or in the next morning?"

"I'm not much for remembering dates," said Heineman. "But it's true that one of the cars used to leave the villa in the evening. And return the next morning."

"It's crucial that we ascertain that it was on Thursdays," Wallander said.

"My wife and I have never observed the idiotic Swedish tradition of eating pea soup on Thursdays," Heineman said. Wallander waited while Heineman tried to remember. Larsson sat looking at the ceiling, and Sjösten tapped his notebook lightly on one knee.

"It's possible," said Heineman all of a sudden. "Perhaps I can piece together an answer. I recall definitely that my wife's sister was here on one occasion last year when the car left on one of its regular trips. Why I'm so certain of this I don't know. But I'm positive. She lives in Bonn and doesn't visit very often."

"Why do you think it was a Thursday?" asked Wallander. "Did you write it down on the calendar?"

"I've never had much use for calendars," Heineman said with distaste. "In all my years at the foreign office I never wrote down a single meeting. But during 40 years of service I never missed one either, unlike people who did nothing but write notes on their calendars."

"Why Thursday?" Wallander repeated.

"I don't know whether it was a Thursday," said Heineman. "But it was my wife's sister's name day. I know that for sure. Her name is Frida."

"What month?" asked Wallander.

"February or March."

Wallander patted his jacket pocket. His pocket calendar didn't have the previous year in it. Sjösten shook his head. Larsson couldn't help.

"Might there be an old calendar somewhere in the house?" asked Wallander.

"It's possible that one of the grandchildren's Christmas calendars is still in the attic," Heineman said. "My wife has the bad habit of saving a lot of old junk. I'm the opposite. Also a trait I picked up at the ministry. On the first day of each month I threw out everything that didn't need to be saved from the previous one. My rule was, better to throw out too much than too little. I never missed a thing I had discarded."

Wallander turned to Larsson. "Call and find out what day is the name day for Frida," he said. "And what day of the week it was in 1993."

"Who would know that?" Larsson asked.

"Damn it," said Sjösten. "Call the station. You have five minutes to get the answer."

"There's a telephone in the hall," said Heineman.

Larsson left the room.

"I must say that I appreciate it when clear orders are given," Heineman said contentedly. "That ability seems to have been lost."

To fill in time, Sjösten asked where Heineman had been stationed abroad. It turned out that he had been posted to many places.

"It got better towards the end," he said. "But when I started my career, the people who were sent overseas to represent this country were often of a deplorably low calibre."

When Larsson reappeared, almost ten minutes had passed. He was holding a piece of paper.

"Frida has her name day on February 17th," he said. "In 1993 it fell on a Thursday."

Police work was just a matter of refusing to give up until a crucial detail was confirmed in writing, Wallander thought.

He decided to ask Heineman the other questions he had for him later, but for appearances' sake he raised a few more queries: whether Heineman had observed that anything could have indicated a "possible traffic in girls" as Wallander chose to describe it.

"There were parties," Heineman said stiffly. "From our top floor, seeing into some of the rooms was unavoidable. Of course there were women involved."

"Did you ever meet Åke Liljegren?"

"Yes," replied Heineman, "I met him once in Madrid. It was during one of my last years as an active member of the foreign office. He had requested introductions to some large Spanish construction companies. We knew quite well who Liljegren was, of course. His shell company scam was in full swing. We treated him as politely as we could, but he was not a pleasant man to deal with."

"Why not?"

Heineman paused for a moment. "To put it bluntly, he was disagreeable. He treated everyone around him with undisguised contempt."

Wallander brought the interview to an end.

"My colleagues will be contacting you again," he said, getting to his feet.

Heineman followed them to the gate. The police car opposite was still there. The house was dark. After saying goodbye to Heineman, Wallander went across the street. One of the officers in the car got out and saluted. Wallander raised his hand in response to the exaggerated deference.

"Anything going on?" he asked.

"All's calm here. A few curiosity-seekers is about it."

Larsson dropped them off at the station. Wallander started by calling Hansson, who told him that Ludwigsson and Hamrén from the National Criminal Bureau had arrived. He had put them up at the Hotel Sekelgården.

"They seem to be good men," said Hansson. "Not at all as arrogant as I feared."

"Why would they have been arrogant?"

"Stockholmers," said Hansson. "You know how they are. Don't you remember that prosecutor who filled in for Per? What was her name? Bodin?"

"Brolin," said Wallander. "But I don't remember her."

In fact Wallander remembered quite well. Embarrassment crept over him when he recalled totally losing control when drunk and making a pass at her. It was one of the things he was most ashamed of. And it didn't help that she had later spent the night with him in Copenhagen.

"They're going to start working the airport tomorrow," said Hansson.

Wallander told him what had happened at Heineman's house.

"So we've got a break," said Hansson. "So you think that Liljegren sent a prostitute to Wetterstedt in Ystad once a week?"

"I do."

"Could it have been going on with Carlman too?"

"Maybe not in the same way. But I should think that Carlman's and Liljegren's circles have overlapped. We still don't know where."

"And Fredman?"

"He's the exception. He doesn't fit in anywhere. Least of all in Liljegren's circles. Unless he was one of his enforcers. I'm going to go back to Malmö tomorrow to talk to his family. I especially want to meet his daughter."

"Åkeson told me about your conversation. You'll have to tread carefully. We don't want it to end as badly as your meeting with Erika Carlman, do we?"

"Of course not."

"I'll get hold of Höglund and Svedberg tonight," Hansson said. "You've finally found a real lead."

"Don't forget Ludwigsson and Hamrén," Wallander said. "They're also part of the team now."

Wallander hung up. Sjösten had gone to get coffee. Wallander dialled his own number in Ystad. Linda answered at once.

"I just got home," she said. "Where are you?"

"In Helsingborg. I'm staying here overnight."

"Has something happened?"

"We went over to Helsingør and had dinner."

"That's not what I meant."

"We're working."

"We are too," Linda said. "We rehearsed the whole thing again tonight. We had an audience too."

"Who?"

"A boy who asked if he could watch. He was standing outside on the street and said he'd heard we were working on a play. I think the people at the hot dog stand must have told him about it."

"So it wasn't anyone you know?"

"He was just a tourist here in town. He walked home with me afterwards."

Wallander felt a pang of jealousy.

"Is he in the flat now?"

"He walked me home to Mariagatan. Then he went home."

"I was only wondering."

"He had a funny name. He said it was Hoover. But he was very nice. I think he liked what we were doing. He said he'd come back tomorrow if he had time."

"I'm sure he will," Wallander said.

Sjösten came in with two cups of coffee. Wallander asked him for his home number, which he gave to Linda.

"My daughter," he said, after he hung up. "The only child I have. She's going to Visby shortly to take a theatre course."

"One's children give life a glimmer of meaning," Sjösten said, handing the coffee cup to Wallander.

They went over the conversation with Heineman. Wallander could tell that Sjösten was not convinced that Wetterstedt's connection to Liljegren meant they were closer to finding the killer.

"Tomorrow I want you to find all the material about the traffic in girls that mentions Helsingborg. Why here, anyway? How did they get here? There must be an explanation. Besides, this vacuum surrounding Liljegren is unbelievable. I don't get it."

"That stuff about the girls is mostly speculation," said Sjösten. "We've never done an investigation of it. We simply haven't had

346

any reason to. One time Birgersson brought it up with one of the prosecutors, but he said we had more important things to do. He was right too."

"I still want you to check it out," Wallander said. "Do a summary for me tomorrow. Fax it to me in Ystad as soon as you can."

It was late by the time they drove to Sjösten's flat. Wallander knew he had to call Baiba. There was no escaping it. She would be packing. He couldn't postpone telling her the news any longer.

"I have to make a phone call to Latvia," he said. "Just a couple of minutes."

Sjösten showed him where the phone was. Wallander waited until Sjösten had gone into the bathroom before he dialled the number. When it rang the first time he hung up. He had no idea what to say. He didn't dare tell her. He would wait until tomorrow night and then make up a story: that the whole thing had come up suddenly and now he wanted her to come to Ystad instead. He couldn't think of a better solution. At least for himself.

They talked for another half hour over a glass of whisky. Sjösten made a call to check that Elisabeth Carlén was still under surveillance.

"She's asleep," he said. "Maybe we ought to go to bed too."

Sjösten gave him sheets and Wallander made up a bed for himself in a room with children's drawings on the walls. He turned off the light and was asleep immediately.

He woke drenched in sweat. He must have had a nightmare, although he remembered nothing. He had only slept for a couple of hours. He wondered why he'd woken, and turned over to go back to sleep. But he was wide awake. Where the feeling came from he had no idea. He was gripped with panic.

He had left Linda alone in Ystad. She shouldn't be there by herself. He had to go home. Without another thought he got up, dressed, and quickly scribbled a note to Sjösten. He drove out of town. Perhaps he should call her. But what would he say? She'd just be frightened. He drove as fast as he could through the light summer night. He didn't understand where the panic had come from. But it was definitely there, and it wouldn't let go.

It was light when he parked on Mariagatan. He unlocked the door carefully. The terror had not abated. Not until he pushed open Linda's door gently, saw her head on the pillow and heard her breathing, did he calm down.

He sat on the sofa. Now fear had been replaced by embarrassment. He wrote a note to her, which he left on the coffee table in case she got up, saying that his plans had changed and that he'd come home. He set the alarm clock for 5 a.m, knowing that Sjösten got up early to work on his boat. He had no idea how he was going to explain his departure in the middle of the night. He lay in bed and wondered what lay behind his panic, but he couldn't find an answer. It took a long time before he fell asleep.

CHAPTER 34

When the doorbell rang he knew at once that it had to be Baiba. Oddly, he wasn't nervous at all, even though it wasn't going to be much fun explaining to her why he hadn't told her that their holiday had to be postponed. Then he started and sat up in bed. Of course she wasn't there. It was only the alarm clock ringing, the hands positioned like a gaping mouth at 5.03 a.m. The confusion passed, he put his hand over the alarm button and then sat motionless. Reality slowly dawned. The town was quiet. Few sounds other than birdsong penetrated his room. He couldn't remember whether he'd dreamed about Baiba or not. The flight from the child's room in Sjösten's flat now seemed wildly irrational. Not like him at all.

With a yawn he got up and went into the kitchen. On the table he found a note from Linda. I communicate with my daughter through a series of notes, he thought. When she makes one of her occasional stops in Ystad. He read over what she had written and realised that the dream about Baiba, waking up and believing that she was standing outside his door, had contained a warning. Linda's note said that Baiba had called and would he call right away. Baiba's irritation was recognisable from the note.

He couldn't call her, not now. He'd call her tonight, or maybe tomorrow. Or should he have Martinsson do it? He could give her the unfortunate news that the man she was intending to go to Skagen with, the man she assumed would be standing at Kastrup Airport to meet her, was up to his neck in a hunt for a maniac who smashed axes into the heads of his fellow human beings and then cut off their scalps. What he might tell Martinsson to say was true, and yet not true. It could never explain or excuse the fact that he was too weak to do the decent thing and call Baiba himself.

He picked up the phone, not to call Baiba, but Sjösten in Helsingborg, to explain why he had left during the night. What could he possibly say? The truth was one option: sudden concern for his daughter, a concern all parents feel without being able to explain. But when Sjösten answered he said something quite different, that he'd forgotten about a meeting he had arranged with his father for early that morning. It was something that couldn't be revealed by accident, since Sjösten and his father would never cross paths. They agreed to talk later, after Wallander had been to Malmö.

Then everything seemed much easier. It wasn't the first time in his life he had started his day with a bunch of white lies, evasions and self-deceptions. He took a shower, had some coffee, wrote a new note to Linda, and left the flat just after 6.30 a.m. Everything was quiet at the station. It was this early, lonely hour, when the weary graveyard shift was on its way home and it was still too early for the daytime staff, that Wallander took pleasure in. Life took on a special meaning in this solitude. He never understood why this was so, but he could remember the feeling from deep in his past, maybe as far back as 20 years.

Rydberg, his old friend and mentor, had been the same way. *Everyone has small but extremely personal sacred moments*, Rydberg had told him on one of the few occasions when they had sat in either his or Wallander's office and split a small bottle of whisky behind a locked door. No alcohol was permitted in the station. But sometimes they had something to celebrate. Or to grieve over, for that matter. Wallander sorely missed those brief and strangely philosophical times. They had been moments of friendship, of irreplaceable intimacy.

Wallander read quickly through a stack of messages. In a memo he saw that Dolores María Santana's body had been released for burial and now rested in a grave in the same cemetery as Rydberg. This brought him back to the investigation; he rolled up his sleeves as though going out into the world to do battle, and skimmed as fast as he could through the copies of investigative material his colleagues had prepared. There were papers from Nyberg, laboratory reports on which Nyberg had scrawled question marks and comments, and charts of the tip-offs that had come in from the public. Tyrén must be an extraordinarily zealous young man, Wallander thought, without being able to decide whether that meant he would be a good policeman in the field in the future, or whether he was already showing signs that he belonged somewhere in the hunting grounds of the bureaucracy. Wallander read quickly, but nothing of value escaped him. The most important thing seemed to be that they had established that Fredman had indeed been murdered on the dock below the side road to Charlottenlund.

He pushed the stacks of papers aside and leaned back pensively in his chair. What *do* these men have in common? Fredman doesn't fit the picture, but he belongs just the same. A former minister of justice, an art dealer, a criminal fraudster and a petty thief. They're all murdered by the same killer, who takes their scalps. Wetterstedt, the first, is barely hidden, just shoved out of sight. Carlman, the second, is killed in the middle of a summer party in his own arbour. Fredman is kidnapped, taken to an out-of-the-way dock and then dumped in the middle of Ystad, as if being put on display. He lies in a pit with a tarpaulin over his head, like a statue waiting to be unveiled. Finally, the killer moves to Helsingborg and murders Liljegren. Almost immediately we pin down a connection between Wetterstedt and Liljegren. Now we need the links between the others. After we know what connected them, we have to discover who might have had reason to kill them. And why the scalps? Who is the lone warrior?

Wallander sat for a long time thinking about Fredman and Liljegren. There was a similarity there. The kidnapping and the acid in the eyes on the one hand, and the head in the oven on the other. It hadn't been enough to kill these two. Why? He took another step. The water got deeper around him. The bottom was slippery. Easy to lose his footing. There was a difference between Fredman and Liljegren, a very clear one. Fredman had hydrochloric acid poured into his eyes while he was alive. Liljegren was dead before he was stuck in the oven. Wallander tried to conjure up the killer again. Thin, in good condition, barefoot, insane. If he hunts evil men, Fredman must have been the worst. Then Liljegren. Carlman and Wetterstedt in about the same category.

Wallander got up and went to the window. There was something about the sequence that bothered him. Fredman was the third. Why not the first? Or the last – at least so far? The root of evil, the first or the last to be punished, by a killer who was insane but canny and well-organised. The dock must have been chosen because it was handy. *How many docks did he look at before he chose that one?* Is this a man who is always near the sea? A well-behaved man; a fisherman, or someone in the coast guard? Or why not a member of the sea rescue service, which has the best bench for meditating on in Ystad? Someone who also managed to drive Fredman away, in his own van. Why did he go to all that trouble? Because it was his only way to get to him? They met somewhere. They knew each other. Peter Hjelm had been quite clear. Fredman travelled a lot and always had plenty of money afterwards. It was rumoured that he was an enforcer. But Wallander only knew of parts of Fredman's life. They must try to bring the unknown past to light.

Wallander sat down again. The sequence didn't make sense. What could the explanation be? He went to get some coffee. Svedberg and Höglund had arrived. Svedberg had a new cap on. His cheeks were a blotchy red. Höglund was more tanned, and Wallander was paler. Hansson arrived with Mats Ekholm in tow. Even Ekholm had managed to get a tan. Hansson's eyes were bloodshot with fatigue. He looked at Wallander with astonishment, and at the same time he seemed to be searching for some misunderstanding. Hadn't Wallander said he'd be in Helsingborg? It wasn't even 7.30 a.m. yet. Had something happened? Wallander shook his head almost imperceptibly. No-one had misunderstood anything. They hadn't planned to have a meeting of the investigative team. Ludwigsson and Hamrén had already driven out to Sturup, Höglund was going to join them, while Svedberg and Hansson were busy with follow-up work on Wetterstedt and Carlman. Someone stuck in his head and said that Wallander had a phone call from Helsingborg. Wallander took the call on the phone next to the coffee machine. It was Sjösten, who told him that Elisabeth Carlén was still sleeping. No-one had visited her, and no-one except some curiosity-seekers had been seen near Liljegren's villa.

"Did Liljegren have no family?" Martinsson asked angrily, as if he'd behaved inappropriately by not marrying.

"He left behind only a few grieving, plundered companies," Svedberg said.

"They're working on Liljegren in Helsingborg," Wallander said. "We'll get the information in time."

Wallander knew that Hansson had been meticulous about passing on the latest developments. They agreed that it was likely that Liljegren had been supplying women to Wetterstedt on a regular basis.

"He's living up to the old rumour about him," said Svedberg.

"We have to find a similar link to Carlman," Wallander went on. "It's there, I know it is. Forget about Wetterstedt for the time being. Let's concentrate on Carlman."

Everyone was in a hurry. The link that had been established was like a shot in the arm for the team. Wallander took Ekholm to his office. He told him what he had been thinking earlier that morning. Ekholm was an attentive listener, as always.

"The acid and the oven," Wallander said. "I'm trying to interpret the killer's language. He talks to himself and he talks to his victims. What is he actually saying?"

"Your idea about the sequence is interesting," said Ekholm. "Psychopathic killers often have an element of pedantry in their bloody handiwork. Something may have happened to upset his plans."

"Like what?"

"He's the only one who can answer that."

"Still, we have to try."

Ekholm didn't answer. Wallander got the feeling that he didn't have a lot to say at the moment.

"Let's number them," Wallander said. "Wetterstedt is number one.

What do we see if we rearrange them?"

"Fredman first or last," Ekholm said. "Liljegren just before or after, depending on which variant is correct. Wetterstedt and Carlman in positions which tie them to the others."

"Can we assume that he's finished?" asked Wallander.

"I have no idea," Ekholm answered.

"What does your programme say? What combinations has it managed to come up with?"

"Not a thing, actually." Ekholm seemed surprised by his own answer.

"How do you interpret that?" Wallander said.

"We're dealing with a serial killer who differs from his predecessors in crucial ways."

"And what does that tell us?"

"That he'll provide us with totally new data. If we catch him."

"We must," said Wallander, knowing how feeble he sounded.

He got up and they both left the room.

"Criminal psychologists at both the F.B.I. and Scotland Yard have been in touch," said Ekholm. "They're following our work with great interest."

"Have they got any suggestions? We need all the help we can get."

"I'm supposed to let them know if anything comes in."

They parted at the reception desk. Wallander took a moment to exchange a few words with Ebba. Then he drove straight to Sturup. He found Ludwigsson and Hamrén in the office of the airport police. Wallander was disconcerted to meet a young policeman who had fainted the year before when they were arresting a man trying to flee the country. But he shook his hand and tried to pretend that he was sorry about what had happened.

Wallander realised he had met Ludwigsson before, during a visit to Stockholm. He was a large, powerful man with high colour from blood pressure, not the sun. Hamrén was his diametrical opposite: small and wiry, with thick glasses. Wallander greeted them a little offhandedly and asked how it was going.

"There seems to be a lot of rivalry between the different taxi companies out here," Ludwigsson began. "Just like at Arlanda. So far we haven't managed to pin down all the ways he could have left the airport during the hours in question. And nobody noticed a motorcycle. But we've only just begun."

Wallander had a cup of coffee and answered a number of questions the two men had. Then he left them and drove on to Malmö. He parked outside the building in Rosengård. It was very hot. He took the lift up to the fifth floor and rang the doorbell. This time it wasn't the son but Björn Fredman's widow who opened the door. She smelled of wine. At her feet cowering close by was a little boy. He seemed extremely shy. Or afraid, rather. When Wallander bent down to greet him he seemed terrified. A fleeting memory entered Wallander's mind. He couldn't catch it, but filed the thought away. It was something that had happened before, or something someone had said, that had been imprinted on his subconscious.

She asked him to come in. The boy clung to her legs. Her hair wasn't combed and she wore no make-up. The blanket on the sofa told him she had spent the night there. They sat down, Wallander in the same chair for the third time. Stefan, the older son, came in. His eyes were as wary as the last time Wallander had visited. He came forward and shook hands, again with adult manners. He sat down next to his mother on the sofa. Everything was as before. The only difference was the presence of the younger brother, curled up on his mother's lap. Something didn't seem quite right about him. His eyes never left Wallander.

"I came about Louise," Wallander said. "I know it's hard to talk about a family member who's in a psychiatric hospital. But it's necessary."

"Why can't she be left in peace?" the woman said. Her voice sounded tormented and unsure, as if she doubted her ability to defend her daughter.

Wallander would have liked to avoid this conversation more than anything. He was unsure of how to handle it.

"Of course she'll be left in peace," he said. "But unfortunately it's part of the duty of the police to gather all the information we can to help solve a brutal crime."

"She hadn't seen her father in many years," the woman said. "She can't tell you anything important."

"Does Louise know that her father is dead?"

"Why should she?"

"It's not unreasonable, is it?"

Wallander saw that she was about to break down. His distaste at what he was doing increased with each question and answer. Without wanting to, he had put her under a pressure she could hardly endure. Stefan said nothing.

"First of all, you have to understand that Louise no longer has any relationship to reality," the woman said in a voice that was so faint that Wallander had to lean forward to hear her. "She has left everything behind. She's living in her own world. She doesn't speak, she doesn't listen. She's pretending that she doesn't exist."

Wallander thought carefully before he continued.

"Even so, it could be important for the police to know why she became ill. I actually came here to ask for your permission to meet her. Speak to her. I realise now that it may not be appropriate. But then you'll have to answer my questions instead."

"I don't know what to tell you," she said. "She got sick. It came out of nowhere."

"She was found in Pildamm Park," Wallander prompted her.

Both the son and the mother stiffened. Even the little boy on her lap seemed to react, affected by the others.

"How do you know that?" she asked.

"There's a report on how and when she was taken to the hospital," said Wallander. "But that's all I know. Everything to do with her illness is confidential. I understand that she was having some difficulty in school before she got sick."

"She never had any trouble, but she was always very sensitive."

"I'm sure she was. Still, usually specific events trigger acute cases of mental illness."

"How do you know that? Are you a doctor?"

"No, I'm a police officer. But I know what I'm talking about."

"Nothing happened."

"But you must have wondered about it. Night and day."

"I've hardly thought about anything else."

Wallander felt the atmosphere becoming so intolerable that he wished he could break off the conversation and leave. The answers he was getting were leading him nowhere, though he believed they were mostly truthful, or at least partly so.

"Do you have a photograph of her I could look at?"

"Is it necessary?"

"Please."

The boy sitting next to her began to speak, but checked himself instantly. Wallander wondered why. Didn't the boy want him to see his sister? Why not?

The mother got up with the little boy hanging on to her. She opened a drawer and handed him some photographs. Louise was blonde, smiling, and resembled Stefan, but there was nothing of that wariness he sensed now in the room, or that he'd seen in the family photograph in Fredman's flat. She smiled openly and trustingly at the camera. She was pretty.

"A nice-looking girl," he said. "Let's hope she gets better some day."

"I've stopped hoping," the mother said. "Why should I hope any more?"

"Doctors can work wonders these days," Wallander said.

"One day Louise is going to leave that hospital," the boy said suddenly. He smiled at Wallander.

"And it's vital that when she does she has a family to support her," Wallander replied, annoyed that he expressed himself so stiffly.

"We support her in every way," the boy went on. "The police have to search for the person who killed our Dad. Not go bothering her."

"If I visit her at the hospital it's not to bother her," Wallander said. "It's as part of the investigation."

"We'd prefer it if you left her in peace."

Wallander nodded. The boy was quite determined.

"If the prosecutor, the leader of the preliminary investigation, makes the decision, then I'll have to visit her," said Wallander. "And I presume that will happen. Very soon. Either today or tomorrow. But I give you my word that I won't tell her that her father is dead."

"Then why are you going there at all?"

"To see her," said Wallander. "A photograph is still just a photograph. Although I'll have to take this with me."

"Why?" The response was immediate. Wallander was surprised by the animosity in the boy's voice.

"I have to show it to some people," he said. "To see whether they recognise her. That's all."

"You're going to give it to the newspapers," said the boy. "Her face will be plastered all over the country."

"Why would I do that?" asked Wallander.

The boy jumped up from the sofa, leaned over the table, and grabbed the photographs. It happened so fast that Wallander didn't have time to react. He regained his composure, but he was angry.

"I'm going to be forced to come back here with a warrant to make you hand over those pictures," he said, although this wasn't true. "There's a risk that some reporters will hear about it and follow me here. I can't stop them. If I can borrow a picture now, this won't have to happen."

The boy stared at Wallander. His previous wariness had now evolved into something else. Without a word he handed back one of the photos.

"I have only one more question," said Wallander. "Do you know if Louise ever met a man named Gustaf Wetterstedt?"

The mother looked perplexed. The boy got up and stood looking out of the open balcony door with his back to them.

"No," she said.

"Does the name Arne Carlman mean anything to you?"

She shook her head.

"Åke Liljegren?"

"No."

She doesn't read the papers, Wallander thought. Under that blanket there's probably a bottle of wine. And in that bottle is her life. He got up from his chair. The boy by the balcony door turned round.

"Are you going to visit Louise?" he asked again.

"It's a possibility."

Wallander said goodbye and left. When he got to the street he felt relieved. The boy was standing in the fifth-floor window looking down at him. As he got into his car, he decided he would put off visiting Louise Fredman for the time being, but he'd check straight away whether Elisabeth Carlén recognised her. He rolled down his window and called Sjösten. The boy was gone from the window. As the phone rang, he searched for an explanation for the uneasiness he had felt at the sight of the frightened little boy. But he couldn't identify it. Wallander told Sjösten he was on his way to Helsingborg with something that he wanted Elisabeth Carlén to see.

"According to the latest report she's lying on her balcony sun-bathing," Sjösten said.

"How's it going with Liljegren's employees?"

"We're working on locating the one who was supposed to be his right-hand man. Name is Hans Logård."

"Did Liljegren have any family?"

"Apparently not. We spoke with his lawyer. Strangely enough, he left no will, and there's no indication of direct heirs. Liljegren seems to have lived in his own universe."

"That's good," Wallander said. "I'll be in Helsingborg within the hour."

"Should I bring Elisabeth Carlén in?"

"Do that, but be nice to her. I've got a feeling we're going to be needing her for a while. She might stop cooperating if it doesn't suit her any more."

"I'll pick her up myself," said Sjösten. "How's your father?"

"My father?"

"You were going to meet him this morning."

"Oh, he's fine," Wallander said. "But it was very important that I saw him."

He hung up. He glanced up at the window on the fifth floor. No-one was there.

Hoover went into the basement just after 1 p.m. The coolness from the stone floor permeated his whole body. The sunlight shone weakly through some cracks in the paint he had put on the window. He sat down and looked at his face in the mirrors.

He couldn't allow the policeman to visit his sister. They were so close to their goal now, the sacred moment, when the evil spirits in her head would be driven out for good. He couldn't let anyone get near her.

The policeman's visit had been a sign that now was the time to act. He thought about the girl it had been so easy for him to meet. She had reminded him of his sister somehow. That was a good sign, too. Louise would need all the strength he could give her.

He took off his jacket and looked around the room. Everything he needed was there. The axes and knives gleamed, laid out on the black silk cloth. Then he took one of the wide brushes and drew a single line across his forehead.

Time was running out.

CHAPTER 35

Wallander put the photograph of Louise Fredman face down on the desk in front of him. Elisabeth Carlén followed his movements with her eyes. She was dressed in a white summer dress, which Wallander guessed was very expensive. They were in Sjösten's office, Sjösten in the background, leaning against the doorframe, Elisabeth Carlén in the visitor's chair. The summer heat swept in through the open window. Wallander felt himself sweating.

"I'm going to show you a photograph," he said. "And I simply want you to tell me whether you recognise the person in it."

"Why do policemen have to be so dramatic?" she asked.

Her haughty, imperturbable manner irritated Wallander, but he controlled himself.

"We're trying to catch a man who has killed four people," he said. "And he scalps them too. Pours acid into their eyes. And stuffs their heads into ovens."

"Well obviously you can't let a maniac like that run around loose, can you?" she replied calmly. "Shall we look at that photograph?"

Wallander slid it over and watched Elisabeth Carlén's face. She picked it up and seemed to be thinking. Almost half a minute passed, then she shook her head.

"No," she said. "I've never seen her before. At least not that I can remember."

"It's very important," said Wallander.

"I have a good memory for faces," she said. "I'm sure I've never met her. Who is she?"

"That doesn't matter for the time being," Wallander said. "Think carefully."

"Where do you want me to have seen her? At Åke Liljegren's?"

"Yes."

"She may have been there sometime when I wasn't."

"Did that happen a lot?"

"Not recently."

"How many years are we talking about?"

"Maybe four."

"But she could have been there?"

"Young girls are popular with some men. The real creeps."

"What creeps?"

"The ones with a single fantasy. To go to bed with their own daughters."

What she said was true, of course, but her indifference angered him. She was part of this market that sucked in innocent children and wrecked their lives.

"If you can't tell me whether she was ever at any of Liljegren's parties, who could?"

"Somebody else."

"Give me a straight answer. Who? I want a name and address."

"It was always completely anonymous," said Elisabeth Carlén patiently. "That was one of the rules for these parties. You recognised a face now and then. But nobody exchanged cards."

"Where did the girls come from?"

"All over. Denmark, Stockholm, Belgium, Russia."

"They came and then they disappeared?"

"That's about it."

"But you live here in Helsingborg?"

"I was the only one who did."

Wallander looked at Sjösten, as if wanting confirmation that the conversation hadn't completely got off the track before continuing.

"The picture is of a girl called Louise Fredman," he said. "Does the name mean anything to you?"

She gave him a puzzled look.

"Wasn't that *his* name? The one who was murdered? Fredman?"

Wallander nodded. She looked at the photograph again. For a moment she seemed moved by the connection.

"Is this his daughter?"

"Yes."

She shook her head again.

"I've never seen her before."

Wallander knew she was telling the truth, if only because she had nothing to gain by lying. He retrieved the photograph and turned it over again, as if to spare Louise Fredman from further participation.

"Were you ever at the house of a man named Gustaf Wetterstedt?" he asked. "In Ystad?"

"What would I be doing there?"

"The same thing you normally do to make your living. Was he your client?"

"No."

"Are you sure?"

"Yes."

"Completely sure?"

"Yes."

"Were you ever at the house of an art dealer named Arne Carlman?"

"No."

Wallander had an idea. Maybe names weren't used in those cases either.

"I'm going to show you some other photographs," he said, getting to his feet. He took Sjösten outside.

"What do you think?" Wallander asked.

Sjösten shrugged. "She's not lying."

"We need photos of Wetterstedt and Carlman," Wallander said. "Fredman too. They're in the investigative material."

"Birgersson has the folders," said Sjösten. "I'll get them."

Wallander went back into the room and asked whether she'd like coffee.

"I'd rather have a gin and tonic," she said.

"The bar isn't open yet," Wallander answered.

She laughed. His reply appealed to her. Wallander went out into the hall. Elisabeth Carlén was very beautiful. Her body was clearly visible through her dress. Sjösten came of out Birgersson's office with a plastic folder. They went back into the room. Elisabeth Carlén was sitting there smoking. Wallander put a picture of Wetterstedt in front of her.

"I recognise him," she said. "From TV. Wasn't he the one who ran around with whores in Stockholm?"

"He may have still been at it later on."

"Not with me," she replied calmly.

"And you've never been to his house?"

"Never."

"Do you know anyone else who's been there?"

"No."

Wallander replaced the picture with one of Carlman. He was standing next to an abstract painting, smiling broadly at the camera.

"This one I've seen," she said firmly.

"At Liljegren's?"

"Yes."

"When was that?"

Elisabeth Carlén thought for a moment. Wallander surreptitiously studied her body. Sjösten took a notebook out of his pocket.

"About a year ago," she said.

"Are you sure about that?"

"Yes."

Wallander nodded. Another connection, he thought. Now all we have to do is find the right box to put Fredman in.

He showed her Björn Fredman. Fredman was playing guitar. It was a prison photograph, and must have been old. Fredman had long hair and was wearing bell-bottoms; the colours were faded.

She shook her head again. She had never seen him.

Wallander let his hands drop with a smack on the desk.

"That's all I wanted to know for now," he said. "I'll swap places with Sjösten."

Wallander took up the position by the door. He also took over Sjösten's notebook.

"How the hell can you live a life like yours?" Sjösten began, surprisingly. He asked the question with a big smile. He sounded quite friendly, but Elisabeth Carlén didn't let down her façade for a moment.

"What business is that of yours?"

"None. Just curious, that's all. How can you stand to look at yourself in the mirror every morning?"

"What do you think when *you* look in the mirror?"

"That at least I'm not making a living by lying on my back for anyone who happens to have enough cash. Do you take credit cards?"

"Go to hell."

She made a move to get up and leave. Wallander was annoyed at the way he was needling her. She might still be useful.

"Please forgive me," Sjösten said, still just as friendly. "Let's forget about your private life. Hans Logård? Is that name familiar?"

She looked at him without replying. Then she turned and looked at Wallander.

"I asked you a question," Sjösten said.

Wallander understood her glance. She wanted to give only him the answer. He signalled to Sjösten to follow him into the hall. There he explained that Sjösten had destroyed Elisabeth Carlén's trust.

"Then we'll arrest her," said Sjösten. "I'll be damned if I'll let a whore give me trouble."

"Arrest her for what?" asked Wallander. "Wait here, I'll go in and get the answer. Calm down, damn it!"

Sjösten shrugged. Wallander went back in and sat down behind the desk.

"Logård used to hang out with Liljegren," she said.

"Do you know where he lives?"

"In the country somewhere."

"Do you know where?"

"Only that he doesn't live in town."

"What does he do?"

"I don't know that either."

"But he was at the parties?"

"Yes."

"As guest or host?"

"As the host. And as a guest."

"Do you know how I can get hold of him?"

"No."

Wallander still believed she was telling the truth. Probably they wouldn't be able to track down Logård through her.

"How did they get along?"

"Logård always had plenty of money. Whatever he did for Liljegren, he was well paid."

She stubbed out her cigarette. Wallander felt as if he had been granted a private audience with her.

"I'm going," she said, getting to her feet.

"Let me see you out," said Wallander.

Sjösten came sauntering down the hall. She looked straight through him as they passed. Wallander waited on the steps until he saw someone follow her, then went back up to the office.

"Why were you needling her?" he asked.

"She stands for something I despise," Sjösten said.

"We need her. We can despise her later."

They got coffee and sat down to go over what they knew. Sjösten brought in Birgersson to help out.

"The problem is Fredman," said Wallander. "He doesn't fit. Otherwise we now have a number of links that seem to hang together, fragile points of contact."

"Or maybe it just looks that way," Sjösten said thoughtfully.

Wallander could tell that Sjösten was worried about something. He waited for him to continue, but he didn't.

"What are you thinking?" he asked.

Sjösten kept staring out of the window.

"Why couldn't this be possible?" he said. "That he was killed by the same man, but for a completely different reason."

"That doesn't make sense," said Birgersson.

"Nothing makes sense in this case."

"So you mean that we should be looking for two different motives," said Wallander.

"That's about it. But I could be wrong. It was just an idea, that's all."

Wallander nodded. "We shouldn't disregard that possibility"

"It's a sidetrack," said Birgersson. "A blind alley, a dead end. It doesn't seem likely at all."

"We can't rule it out," Wallander said. "We can't rule out anything. But right now we have to find Logård. That's the priority."

"Liljegren's villa is a very strange place," said Sjösten. "There wasn't one piece of paper there. No address book. Nothing. And no-one has had the opportunity to go in and clean up."

"Which means we haven't searched hard enough," Wallander replied. "Without Logård we're not going to get anywhere."

Sjösten and Wallander had a quick lunch at a restaurant next to the station, and drove to Liljegren's villa. The cordons were still up. An officer opened the gates and let them in. Sunlight filtered through the trees. Suddenly the case seemed surreal. Monsters belonged in the cold and dark. Not in a summer like this one. He recalled Rydberg's joke. *It's best to be hunting insane killers in the autumn. In the summer give me a good old-fashioned bomber.* He laughed at the thought. Sjösten gave him a funny look, but he didn't explain.

Inside the huge villa the forensic technicians had finished their work. Wallander took a look in the kitchen. The oven door was closed. He thought of Sjösten's idea about Björn Fredman. A killer with two motives? Did such birds exist? He called Ystad, and Ebba got hold of Ekholm for him. It was almost five minutes before he came to the phone. Wallander watched Sjösten wandering through the rooms on the ground floor, drawing back the curtains from the windows. The sunlight was very bright.

Wallander asked Ekholm his question. It was actually intended for Ekholm's programme. Had there been serial killers who combined very different motives? Did criminal psychology have a collective view

367

on this? As always, Ekholm found Wallander's question interesting. Wallander wondered whether Ekholm really was so charmed by everything he told him. It was beginning to remind him of the satirical songs about the absurd incompetence of the Swedish security police. Recently they relied more and more on various specialists. And no-one could really explain why.

Wallander didn't want to be unfair to Ekholm. During his time in Ystad he had proved to be a good listener. In that sense he had learned something basic about police work. The police had to be able to listen, as well as question. They had to listen for hidden meanings and motives, for the invisible impressions left by offenders. Just like in this house. Something is always left behind after a crime is committed. An experienced detective should be able to listen his way to what it was. Wallander hung up and went to join Sjösten, who was sitting at a desk. Wallander didn't say a thing. Neither did Sjösten. The villa invited silence. Liljegren's spirit, if he had one, hovered restlessly around them.

Wallander went upstairs and wandered through room after room. There were no papers anywhere. Liljegren had lived in a house in which emptiness was the most noticeable characteristic. Wallander thought back to what Liljegren had been famous or infamous for. The shell company scams, the looting of company finances. He had made his way in the world by hiding his money. Did he do the same thing in his private life? He had houses all over the world. The villa was one of his many hide-outs. Wallander stopped by a door up to the attic. When he was a child he had built a hide-out for himself in the attic. He opened the door. The stairs were narrow and steep. He turned the light switch. The main room with its exposed beams was almost empty. There were just some skis and a few pieces of furniture. Wallander smelled the same odour as in the rest of the house. The forensic technicians had been here too. He looked around. No secret doors. It was hot underneath the roof.

He went back down and started a more systematic search. He pulled back the clothes in Liljegren's large wardrobes. Nothing. Wallander sat on the edge of the bed and tried to think. Liljegren couldn't have kept everything in his head. There had to be an address book somewhere. Something else was missing too. At first he couldn't figure out what it was. Who was Åke Liljegren, "the Auditor"? Liljegren was a travelling man, but there were no suitcases in the house. Not even a briefcase. Wallander went downstairs to see Sjösten.

"Liljegren must have had another house," he said. "Or at least an office."

"He has houses all over the world," Sjösten said distractedly.

"I mean here in Helsingborg. This place is too empty"

"We would have known about it."

Wallander nodded without saying any more. He was still sure his hunch was right. He continued his search. But now he was more persistent. He went down to the basement. In one room there was an exercise machine and some barbells. There was a wardrobe down there, too, which contained some exercise clothes and rain gear. Wallander thoughtfully regarded the clothes. Then he went back upstairs to Sjösten.

"Did Liljegren have a boat?"

"I'm sure he did. But not here. I would have known about it."

Wallander nodded mutely. He was just about to leave Sjösten when an idea struck him.

"Maybe it was registered under another name. Why not in Hans Logård's name?"

"Why do you think Liljegren had a boat?"

"There are clothes in the basement that look like they're for sailing."

Sjösten followed Wallander to the basement. They stood in front of the open wardrobe.

"You may be right." Sjösten said.

"It's worth looking into," said Wallander. "This house is too empty to be normal."

They left the basement. Wallander opened the balcony doors and stepped into the sunshine. He thought of Baiba again and felt a knot in his stomach. Why didn't he call her? Did he still think it would be possible for him to meet her? He wasn't happy about asking

Martinsson to lie for him, but now it was his only way out. He went back inside, into the shadows, with a feeling of utter self-loathing. Sjösten was on the phone. Wallander wondered when the killer would strike next. Sjösten hung up and dialled another number. Wallander went into the kitchen and drank some water, trying to avoid looking at the stove. As he came back, Sjösten slammed the phone down.

"You were right," he said. "There's a boat in Logård's name down at the yacht club. The same one I belong to."

"Let's go," said Wallander, feeling the tension rise.

A dock watchman showed them where Logård's boat was berthed. Wallander could see that it was a beautiful, well-maintained boat. The hull was fibreglass, but it had a teak deck.

"A Komfortina," said Sjösten. "Very nice. They handle well, too."

He hopped on board like a sailor. The entrance to the cabin was locked.

"Do you know Hans Logård?" Wallander asked the watchman. He had a weatherbeaten face and wore a T-shirt advertising canned Norwegian fish-balls.

"He's not talkative, but we say hello to each other when he comes down here."

"When was he here last?"

"Last week, I think. But it's high summer, you know, our busiest time, so I might be mistaken."

Sjösten had managed to pick the cabin lock. From inside he opened the two half-doors. Wallander clambered clumsily aboard, as though walking on newly polished ice. He crept down into the cockpit and then into the cabin. Sjösten had had the foresight to bring along a torch. They searched the cabin without finding anything.

"I don't get it," Wallander said when they were back on the dock. "Liljegren must have been running his affairs from somewhere."

"We're checking his mobile phones," said Sjösten. "Maybe that will produce something."

They headed back. The man with the T-shirt followed them.

"I expect that you'll want to take a look at his other boat too," he said as they stepped off the long dock. Wallander and Sjösten reacted as one.

"Logård has another boat?" Wallander asked.

The man pointed towards the furthest pier.

"The white one, all the way at the end. A Storö class. It's called the *Rosmarin*."

"Of course we want to look at it," Wallander said.

They ended up in front of a long, powerful, sleek launch.

"These cost money," said Sjösten. "Lots and lots of money."

They went aboard. The cabin door was locked. The man on the dock was watching them.

"He knows I'm a policeman," Sjösten said.

"We don't have time to wait," said Wallander. "Break the lock. But do it the cheapest way."

Sjösten managed it without breaking off more than a piece of the doorframe. They entered the cabin. Wallander saw at once that they had hit the jackpot. Along one wall was a whole shelf of folders and plastic binders.

"Find an address for Hans Logård," said Wallander. "We can go through the rest later."

In a few minutes they had found a membership card to a golf club outside Ängelholm with Logård's name and address on it.

"Bjuv," Sjösten said. "That's not far from here."

As they were leaving the boat, Wallander opened a cupboard. To his surprise there was women's clothing inside.

"Maybe they had parties on board, too," Sjösten said.

"I'm not so sure." Wallander said pensively.

They left the boat and went back to the dock.

"I want you to call me if Logård shows up," Sjösten told the dock watchman.

He gave him a card with his phone number on it.

"But I shouldn't let on that you're looking for him, right?" the man asked, excitedly.

Sjösten smiled.

"Right in one," he replied. "Pretend that everything's normal. And then call me. No matter what time."

"There's nobody here at night," said the man.

"Then we'll have to hope he comes in the day."

"May I ask what he did?"

"You can," said Sjösten, "but you won't get an answer."

"Should we take more men along?" Sjösten asked.

"Not yet," Wallander replied. "First we have to find his house and see if he's home."

They drove towards Bjuv. They were in a part of Skåne that Wallander didn't know. The weather had turned muggy. There would be a thunderstorm that evening.

"When's the last time it rained?" he asked.

"Around Midsummer," Sjösten said, after thinking for a bit. "And it didn't rain much."

They had just reached the turn-off to Bjuv when Sjösten's mobile phone rang. He slowed down and answered it.

"It's for you," he said, handing it to Wallander.

It was Ann-Britt Höglund. She got straight to the point. "Louise Fredman has escaped from the hospital."

It took a moment before Wallander grasped what she said.

"Could you repeat that?"

"Louise Fredman has escaped from the hospital."

"When?"

"About an hour ago."

"How did you find out?"

"The hospital contacted Åkeson. He called me."

Wallander thought for a moment.

"How did it happen?"

"Someone came and got her."

"Who?"

"No-one saw it happen. Suddenly she was gone."

"God damn it to hell!"

Sjösten hit the brakes.

"I'll call you back in a while," Wallander said. "In the meantime, find out absolutely everything you can. Above all, who it was that picked her up."

"Louise Fredman has escaped from hospital," he told Sjösten.

"How?"

Wallander gave it some thought before he replied.

"I don't know," he said. "But this has something to do with our killer. I'm sure of it."

"Should I go back?"

"No. Let's keep going. Now it's more important than ever to get hold of Logård."

They drove into the village and stopped. Sjösten rolled down the window and asked the way to the street. They asked three people and got the same answer. Not one of them knew the address they were looking for.

CHAPTER 36

They were just on the point of giving up when they finally picked up the trail to Hans Logård and his address. Some scattered showers had started over Bjuv by that time. But the main thunderstorm passed by to the west.

The address they had been looking for was "Hördestigen". It had a Bjuv postal code, but they couldn't find it. Wallander went into the post office himself to check it. Logård didn't have a post office box either, at least not in Bjuv. Finally there was nothing to do but think Logård's address was false. At that point, Wallander walked into the bakery and struck up a conversation with the two ladies behind the counter while he bought a bag of cinnamon rolls. One of them knew the answer. Hördestigen wasn't a road. It was the name of a farm north of the village, a place that was hard to find if you didn't know the way.

"There's a man living there named Hans Logård," Wallander told them. "Do you know him?"

The two women looked at each other as if searching a shared memory, then shook their heads in unison.

"I had a distant cousin who lived at Hördestigen when I was a girl," said one of the women. "When he died it was sold to a stranger. But Hördestigen is the name of the farm, I know that. It must have a different postal address, though."

Wallander asked her to draw him a map. She tore up a bread bag and drew the route on it for him. It was almost 6 p.m. They drove out of town, following the road to Höganäs. Wallander navigated with the bread bag. They reached an area where the farms thinned out. That's where they took the first wrong turn. They ended up in an enchantingly beautiful beech forest, but they were in the wrong place.

Wallander told Sjösten to turn around, and when they got back to the main road they started again. They took the next side road to the left, then to the right, and then left. The road ended in a field. Wallander swore to himself, got out of the car, and looked around for a church spire the ladies had told him about. Out there in the field he felt like someone floating out to sea, searching for a lighthouse to navigate by. He found the church spire and then understood, after a conference with the bread bag, why they had got lost. Sjösten was directed back; they started again, and this time they found it.

Hördestigen was an old farm, not unlike Arne Carlman's, and it was in an isolated spot with no neighbours, surrounded by beech woods on two sides and gently sloping fields on the others. The road ended at the farmhouse. There was no letter box. His post must go elsewhere.

"What can we expect?" asked Wallander.

"You mean is he dangerous?"

"He might be the one who killed Liljegren. Or all of them. We don't know a thing about him."

Sjösten's reply surprised Wallander.

"There's a shotgun in the boot. And ammunition. You take that. I've got my service revolver."

Sjösten reached under the seat.

"Against regulations," he said, smiling. "But if you had to follow all the regulations that exist, police work would have been forbidden long ago by the health and safety watchdogs."

"Forget the shotgun," Wallander said. "Have you got a licence for the revolver?"

"Of course I have a licence," Sjösten said. "What do you think?"

They got out of the car. Sjösten stuffed his revolver in his jacket pocket. They stood and listened. There was thunder in the distance. Around them it was quiet and extremely humid. No sign of a car or a living soul. The farm seemed abandoned. They walked up to the house, shaped like an L.

"The third wing must have burned down," Sjösten said. "Or else it was torn down. But it's a nice house. Well preserved. Just like the boat."

Wallander went and knocked on the door. No answer. Then he banged on it hard. Nothing. He peered in through a window. Sjösten stood in the background with one hand in his jacket pocket. Wallander didn't like being so close to a gun. They walked around the house. Still no sign of life. Wallander stopped, lost in thought.

"There are stickers all over saying that the windows and doors are alarmed," Sjösten said. "But it would take a hell of a long time for anyone to get here if it was set off. We'll have time to go inside and get out of here before then."

"Something doesn't fit here," said Wallander, as if he hadn't heard Sjösten.

"What's that?"

"I don't know."

They went over towards the wing that served as a tool shed. The door was locked with a big padlock. Through the windows they could see all kinds of equipment and rubbish inside.

"There's nobody here," said Sjösten flatly. "We'll have to put the farm under surveillance."

Wallander looked around. Something was wrong, he was sure of it. He walked round the house again and looked in at several of the windows, listening. Sjösten followed. When they had gone round the house for a second time, Wallander stopped by some black rubbish bags next to the house. They were sloppily tied with string. Flies buzzed around them. He opened one of the sacks. Food remains, paper plates. He picked up a plastic bag from the Scan Deli between his thumb and forefinger. Sjösten stood next to him, watching. He looked at the various expiry dates. He could smell the meat. They hadn't been here many hours. Not in this heat. He opened the other sack. It too was filled with frozen food containers. It was a lot of food to eat in a few days.

Sjösten stood next to Wallander looking at the sacks.

"He must have had a party."

Wallander tried to think. The muggy heat was making the pressure build in his head. Soon he would have a headache, he could feel it.

"We're going in," he said. "I want to look around inside the house. Isn't there any way to get around the alarm?"

"Maybe down the chimney."

"Then I guess we'll have to take our chances."

"I've got a crowbar in the car," Sjösten said.

Wallander examined the front door of the house. He thought about the door he had broken down at his father's studio in Löderup. He went to the back of the house with Sjösten carrying the crowbar. The door there seemed less solid. Wallander decided to prise it open. He jammed the crowbar between the hinges. He looked at Sjösten, who glanced at his watch.

"Go," he said.

Wallander braced himself and pushed on the crowbar with all his strength. The hinges broke off, along with some chunks of wall plaster and tile. He jumped to one side so the door wouldn't fall on him.

The house looked even more like Carlman's on the inside, if that were possible. Walls had been torn down, the space opened up. Modern furniture, newly laid hardwood floor. They listened again. Everything was quiet. Too quiet, Wallander thought. As if the house were holding its breath. Sjösten pointed to a telephone and fax machine on a table. The light on the answer machine was blinking. Wallander nodded. Sjösten pushed the play button. It crackled and clicked. Then there was a voice. Wallander saw Sjösten jump. A man's voice asked Hans to call him as soon as possible. Then it was silent again. The tape stopped.

"That was Liljegren," Sjösten said, obviously shaken. "God damn."

"Then we know that message has been here for quite a while," Wallander said.

"So Logård hasn't been here since then."

"Not necessarily," Wallander said. "He might have listened to the message but not erased it. If the power goes off later, the light will start blinking again. They may have had a thunderstorm here. We don't know."

They went through the house. A narrow hall led to the part of the house at the angle of the L. The door there was closed. Wallander suddenly raised his hand. Sjösten stopped short behind him. Wallander heard a sound. At first he couldn't tell what it was. It sounded like a growling animal, then like a muttering. He looked at Sjösten, who'd heard it too. Then he tried the door. It was locked. The muttering had stopped.

"What the hell is going on?" he whispered.

"I don't know," said Wallander. "I can't break this door open with the crowbar."

"We're going to have the security company here in about 15 minutes."

Wallander thought hard. He didn't know what was on the other side, except that it was at least one person, maybe more. He was feeling sick. He knew that he had to get the door open.

"Give me your revolver," he said.

Sjösten took it out of his pocket.

"Get back from the door," Wallander shouted as loud as he could. "I'm going to shoot it open."

He looked at the lock, took a step back, cocked the gun, and fired. The blast was deafening. He shot again, then once more. The ricochets hit the far wall in the hall. He handed the revolver back to Sjösten and kicked open the door, his ears ringing.

The room was large. It had no windows. There were a number of beds and a partition enclosing a toilet. A refrigerator, glasses, cups, some thermoses. Huddled together in a corner of the room, obviously terrified, were four young girls clutching one another. Two of them reminded Wallander of the girl he had seen from 20 metres away in Salomonsson's rape field. For a brief moment, with his ears ringing, Wallander thought he could see it all before him, one event after another, how it all fitted together and how everything suddenly made sense. But in reality he saw nothing at all. There was just a feeling rushing straight through him, like a train going through a tunnel at high speed, leaving behind only a light shaking of the ground.

"What the hell is going on?" Sjösten asked.

"We have to get some back-up from Helsingborg," Wallander said. "As fast as we can."

He knelt down, and Sjösten did the same. Wallander tried to talk to the frightened girls in English. But they didn't seem to understand the language, or at least not the way he spoke it. Some of them couldn't be much older than Dolores María Santana.

"Do you know any Spanish?" he asked Sjösten. "I don't know a word."

"What do you want me to say?"

"Do you know Spanish or not?"

"I can't speak Spanish! Shit! I know a few words. What do you want me to say?"

"Anything! Just tell them to be calm."

"Should I say I'm a policeman?"

"No! Whatever you do, don't say that!"

"*Buenas dias,*" Sjösten said hesitantly.

"Smile," Wallander said. "Can't you see how scared they are?"

"I'm doing the best I can," complained Sjösten.

"Say it again," said Wallander. "Friendly this time."

"*Buenas dias,*" Sjösten repeated.

One of the girls answered. Her voice was unsteady. Wallander felt as if he was now getting the answer he'd been looking for, ever since that day when the girl stood in the field and stared at him with her terrified eyes.

At the same moment they heard a sound behind them in the house, perhaps a door opening. The girls heard it too, and huddled together again.

"It must be the security guards," Sjösten said. "We'd better go and meet them. Otherwise they'll wonder what's going on here and start making a fuss."

Wallander gestured to the girls to stay put. Then the two of them went back down the narrow hall, this time with Sjösten in the lead.

It almost cost him his life. When they stepped into the open room, several shots rang out. They came in such rapid succession that they must have been fired from a semi-automatic weapon. The first bullet slammed into Sjösten's left shoulder, smashing his collarbone. He was thrown backwards by the impact and rammed into Wallander. The second, third and maybe fourth shots landed somewhere above their heads.

"Don't shoot! Police!" Wallander shouted.

Whoever was shooting fired off another burst. Sjösten was hit again, this time in the right ear. Wallander threw himself behind one of the walls. He pulled Sjösten with him, who screamed and passed out. Wallander found Sjösten's revolver and fired it into the room. He knew there must only be two or three shots left.

There was no answer. He waited with his heart pounding, revolver raised and ready to shoot. Then he heard the sound of a car starting. He let Sjösten go and crouching low, ran over to a window. He saw the back end of a black Mercedes disappearing down the farm road, vanishing into the beech woods. He went back to Sjösten, who was bleeding and unconscious. He found a pulse. It was fast. This was good. Better than too slow. Still holding the revolver in his hand, he picked up the phone and dialled 90–000.

"Officer down," he shouted when they answered. Then he managed to calm down, tell them who he was, what had happened, and where they were. He went back to Sjösten, who had regained consciousness.

"It'll be all right," Wallander said, over and over again. "Help is on the way."

"What happened?" Sjösten asked.

"Don't talk," Wallander said. "Everything will be fine."

He searched feverishly for wounds. He'd thought Sjösten had been hit by at least three bullets, finally realised that it was only two. He made two simple pressure bandages, wondering what had happened to the security company and why it was taking so long for help to arrive. He also thought about the Mercedes and knew he wouldn't rest until he caught the man who had shot Sjösten.

Eventually he heard the sirens. He got up and went outside to meet the cars from Helsingborg. First came the ambulance, then Birgersson and two other squad cars and last the fire department. All of them were shocked when they saw Wallander. He hadn't noticed how covered in blood he was. And he still had Sjösten's revolver in his hand.

"How is he?" Birgersson asked.

"He's inside. I think he'll be OK."

"What the hell happened?"

"There are four girls locked up here," said Wallander. "They're probably some of the ones being taken through Helsingborg to brothels in southern Europe."

"Who shot at you?"

"I never saw him. But I assume it was Logård. This house belongs to him."

"A Mercedes crashed into a car from the security company down by the main road," Birgersson said. "No injuries, but the driver of the Mercedes stole the security guards' car."

"Then they saw him," said Wallander. "It must be him. The guards were on their way here. The alarm went off when we broke in."

"You broke in?"

"Never mind that now. Put out the word on that security company car. And get the technicians out here right away. I want them to check for prints. They'll have to be compared to the ones we found at the other murder scenes. Wetterstedt, Carlman, all of them."

Birgersson turned pale. The connection seemed to dawn on him for the first time.

"You mean it was him?"

"It could have been, but we don't know that. Now get going. And don't forget the girls. Take them all in. Treat them nicely. And find some Spanish interpreters."

"It's amazing how much you know already," Birgersson said.

Wallander stared at him. "I don't know a thing," he said. "Now get moving."

Sjösten was carried out. Wallander went into town with him in the ambulance. One of the ambulance drivers gave him a towel. He wiped himself clean with it as best he could. Then he checked in with Ystad.

It was just after 7 p.m. He got hold of Svedberg and explained what had happened.

"Who is this Logård?" Svedberg asked.

"That's what we have to find out. Is Louise Fredman still missing?"

"Yes."

Wallander felt the need to think. What had seemed so clear in his mind a while before was no longer making sense.

"I'll be in touch later," he said. "But you'll have to pass all of this on to the investigative team."

"Ludwigsson and Hamrén have found an interesting witness at Sturup," Svedberg said. "A night watchman. He saw a man on a moped. The timetable fits."

"A moped?"

"Yep."

"You don't think our killer is riding around on a moped, do you? Those are for children, for God's sake."

Wallander felt himself starting to lose his cool. He didn't want to, least of all at Svedberg. He said goodbye quickly and hung up.

Sjösten looked up at him from the stretcher.

Wallander smiled. "It's going to be fine," he said.

"It was like getting kicked by a horse," moaned Sjösten. "Twice."

"Don't talk," said Wallander. "We'll be at the hospital soon."

The night of 7 July was one of the most chaotic Wallander had ever experienced. There was an air of unreality about everything that happened.

He would never forget it. Sjösten was admitted to hospital, and the doctors confirmed that his life was not in danger. Wallander was driven to the station in a squad car.

Sergeant Birgersson had proven to be a good organiser, and he'd understood everything Wallander had said at the farmhouse. He had the presence of mind to establish an area past which all the reporters who had started gathering weren't permitted. Inside, where the actual police were working, no reporters were allowed.

It was 10 p.m. when Wallander arrived from the hospital. Someone had lent him a clean shirt and pair of trousers. They were so tight around the waist that he couldn't zip them up. Birgersson, noticing the problem, called the owners of Helsingborg's most elegant tailor and put Wallander on the line. It was a strange experience to stand in the middle of the chaos and try to remember his waist size, but in an astonishingly swift time, several pairs of trousers were delivered to the station, and one of them fitted.

Höglund, Svedberg, Ludwigsson and Hamrén had already arrived and been briefed on the work that was under way. There was no sighting of the security company's car yet. Interviews were being conducted in different rooms. The Spanish-speaking girls had each been supplied with an interpreter. Höglund was talking to one of them, while three female officers from Helsingborg took care of the others. The guards whose car had collided with the Mercedes had also been interviewed, while forensic technicians were busy cross-checking fingerprints. Finally, several officers were leaning over a number of computers, entering all the information that they had on Hans Logård. The activity was intense. Birgersson concentrated on keeping order so that their work stayed on track.

When Wallander had been briefed, he took his colleagues from Ystad into a room and closed the door. He had obtained Birgersson's approval to do so. Birgersson was an exceptional policeman who performed his job impeccably, and didn't seem to suffer from the jealousy and rivalry that so often degraded the quality of police work. He was interested only in catching the man who had shot Sjösten, working out exactly what had happened and who the killer was.

Wallander told his version of events, but what he wanted to resolve was the reason for his unease. Too many things didn't add up. The man who had shot Sjösten, was he really the same man who had assumed the role of a lone warrior? It was difficult to believe. He would have to do his thinking out loud, with all of them together and just one thin door separating them from the frenzied investigative work. Wallander wanted his colleagues to step aside – and Sjösten would have been there too if he wasn't in hospital – so that they could serve as a kind of counterweight to the work being done. Wallander looked around and wondered why Ekholm wasn't there.

"He left for Stockholm this morning," Svedberg said.

"Just when we need him most," Wallander said, dismayed.

"He's supposed to be back tomorrow morning," Höglund said. "I think one of his children was hit by a car. Nothing serious. But even so . . ."

Wallander nodded. The phone rang. It was Hansson for Wallander.

"Baiba Liepa has called several times from Riga," he said. "She wants you to call her right away."

"I can't right now," said Wallander. "Explain to her if she calls again."

"If I understood her correctly, you're supposed to meet her at Kastrup on Saturday. To go on a holiday together. How were you planning to pull that off?"

"Not now," Wallander said. "I'll call you later."

No-one except Höglund seemed to notice that the conversation with Hansson was over a personal matter. Wallander caught her eye. She smiled, but didn't say a word.

"Let's continue," he said. "We're searching for a man who shot at both Sjösten and me. We find some girls locked up inside a farmhouse in the countryside near Bjuv. We can assume that Dolores María Santana once came from such a group, passing through Sweden on the way to brothels and the devil knows what else in other parts of Europe. Girls lured here by people associated with Liljegren. In particular, a man named Hans Logård, if that's his real name. We think he was the one who shot at us, but we aren't sure. We don't have a picture of him. Maybe the guards can give us a usable description, but they're pretty shaken up. They may have seen nothing but his gun. Now we're hunting for him. But are we actually tracking our killer? The one who killed Wetterstedt, Carlman, Fredman and Liljegren? I'm doubtful. We must catch this man as soon as possible. In the meantime, I think we have to keep working as if this were simply one event on the periphery of the major investigation. I'm just as interested in what has happened to Louise Fredman. And what was discovered at Sturup. But first, of course, I'd like to hear if you have any reactions to my view of the case."

The room was silent, then Hamrén spoke up. "Looking from outside, and not needing to be afraid of causing offence, the whole thing seems like a problem in approach. The police have a tendency to focus on one thing at a time, while the offenders they're hunting are thinking about ten."

Wallander listened approvingly, though he wasn't sure Hamrén meant what he was saying.

"Louise Fredman disappeared without a trace," said Höglund. "She had a visitor. She followed the visitor out. The name written in the visitors' book was illegible. Because there were only summer temps working, the normal system had almost fallen apart."

"Someone must have seen the person who came to get her," Wallander said.

"Someone did," Höglund said. "An assistant nurse named Sara Pettersson."

"Did anyone talk to her?"

"She's left on holiday."

"Where to?"

"She's bought an Interrail card. She could be anywhere."

"Damn!"

"We can trace her through Interpol," Ludwigsson said. "That'll probably work."

"Yes," said Wallander. "I think we should do that. And this time we won't wait. I want someone to contact Åkeson about it tonight."

"This is Malmö's jurisdiction," Svedberg pointed out.

"I don't give a shit whose jurisdiction we're in," Wallander said. "Do it. It'll have to be Åkeson's headache."

Höglund said she would get hold of him. Wallander turned to Ludwigsson and Hamrén.

"I heard rumours about a moped," he said. "A witness who saw something at the airport."

"That's right," Ludwigsson said. "The timing fits. A moped drove off towards the E65 on the night in question."

"Why is that of interest?"

"Because the night watchman is sure that the moped was driven off just about the same time Björn Fredman's van arrived."

Wallander recognised the significance of this.

"We're talking about a time of night when the airport is closed," Ludwigsson went on. "Nothing's happening. No taxis, no traffic. Everything is quiet. A van comes up and stops in the car park. Then a moped drives off."

The room grew still. If there were magic moments in a complex criminal investigation, this was definitely one of them.

"A man on a moped," Svedberg said. "Can this be right?"

"Is there a description?" Höglund asked.

"According to the watchman, the man was wearing a helmet that covered his whole head. He's worked at Sturup for many years. That was the first time a moped left there at night."

"How can he be sure that he headed towards Malmö?"

"He wasn't. And I didn't say that either."

Wallander held his breath. The voices of the others were far away, like the distant, unintelligible noise of the universe. He knew that now they were very, very close.

CHAPTER 37

Somewhere in the distance Hoover could hear thunder. He counted the seconds between the lightning and the thunder. The storm was passing far away. It wouldn't come in over Malmö. He watched his sister sleeping on the mattress. He had wanted to offer her something better, but everything had happened so fast. The policeman whom he now hated, the cavalry colonel with the blue trousers, whom he'd christened "Perkins" and "the Man with the Great Curiosity" when he drummed his message to Geronimo, had demanded pictures of Louise. He had also threatened to visit her.

Hoover had realised that he had to change his plans right away. He would pick up Louise even before the row of scalps and the last gift, the girl's heart, were buried. That's why he had only managed to take a mattress and a blanket down to the basement. He had planned to do something quite different. There was a big empty house in Limhamn. The woman who lived there alone went to Canada every summer to see her family. She had been his teacher and he sometimes ran errands for her, so he knew she was away. He had copied a key to her front door long ago. They could have lived in her building while they planned their future. But now Perkins had got in the way. Until he was dead, and that would be soon, they would have to settle for the mattress in the basement.

She was asleep. He had taken medicine from a cabinet when he went to get her. He had gone there without painting his face, but he had an axe and some knives with him, in case anyone tried to stop him. It had been strangely quiet at the hospital, with almost no-one around. Everything went more smoothly than he could have imagined. Louise hadn't recognised him at first, but when she'd heard his voice she put up no resistance. He had brought some clothes for her. They walked across the hospital grounds and then took a taxi, without any problem. She didn't say a word, never questioning the bare mattress, and she fell asleep almost at once. He had lain down and slept a while beside her. They were closer to the future than ever before. The power from the scalps had already started working. She was on her way back to life again. Soon everything would be changed.

He looked at her. It was evening, past 10 p.m. He had made his decision. At dawn he would return to Ystad for the last time.

In Helsingborg a great crowd of reporters besieged Birgersson's outer perimeter. The chief of police was there. At Wallander's stubborn insistence, Interpol was trying to trace Sara Pettersson. They had contacted the girl's parents and tried to put together a possible itinerary. It was a hectic night at the station.

Back in Ystad, Hansson and Martinsson were handling the incoming calls. They sent over materials when Wallander needed them. Åkeson was at home but was willing to be reached at any time.

Although it was late, Wallander sent Höglund to Malmö to talk to the Fredman family. He wanted to make sure they weren't the ones who had taken Louise from the hospital. He would rather have gone there himself, but he couldn't be in two places at once. She had left at 10.30 p.m., after Wallander had phoned Fredman's widow. He estimated she'd be back by 1 a.m.

"Who's taking care of the children while you're away?" he'd asked.

"Do you remember my neighbour who has children of her own?" she asked. "Without her I couldn't do this job."

Wallander called home. Linda was there. He explained as best he could what had happened. He didn't know when he'd be home, maybe sometime that night, maybe not until dawn.

"Will you get here before I leave?" she asked.

"Leave?"

"Did you forget I'm going to Gotland? Kajsa and I. And you're going to Skagen."

"Of course I didn't forget," he said."

"Did you talk to Baiba?"

"Yes," Wallander said, hoping she couldn't hear that he was lying.

He gave her the number in Helsingborg. Then he wondered whether he ought to call his father, but it was late. They were probably already in bed. He went to the command centre where Birgersson was directing the manhunt. Five hours had passed, and no-one had seen the stolen car. Birgersson agreed with Wallander that it could only mean that Logård, if it was him, had taken the car off the road.

"He had two boats at his disposal," Wallander said. "And a house outside Bjuv that we could barely locate. I'm sure he has other hide-outs."

"We've got a man going over the boats," said Birgersson. "And Hördestigen. I told them to look for other possibilities."

"Who is this damned Logård, anyway?" Wallander said.

"They've started checking the prints," Birgersson said. "If he's ever had a run-in with the police, we'll know very soon."

Wallander went over to where the four girls were being interviewed. It was a laborious process, since everything had to go through interpreters. Besides, the girls were terrified. Wallander had told the officers to explain that they weren't accused of a crime. But he wondered how frightened they were. He thought about Dolores María Santana, about the worst fear he had ever seen. But now, at midnight, a picture had finally begun to take shape.

The girls were all from the Dominican Republic. They had each separately left their villages and gone to the cities to look for work as domestic helps or factory workers. They had been contacted by men, all very friendly, and offered work in Europe. They had been shown pictures of beautiful houses by the Mediterranean, and were promised wages ten times what they could hope to earn at home. They'd all said yes.

They were supplied with passports but were never allowed to keep them. First they were flown to Amsterdam – at least that was what they thought the city was called. Then they were driven to Denmark. A week ago they had been taken across to Sweden at night by boat. There were different men involved at each stage and their friendliness decreased as the girls travelled further from home. The fear had set in in earnest when they were locked up at the farm. They had been given food, and a man had explained in poor Spanish that they would soon be travelling the last stretch of the way. But by now they had begun to understand that nothing would happen as promised. The fear had turned to terror.

Wallander asked the officers to question the girls carefully about the men they had met during the days at the farm. Was there more than one? Could they give a description of the boat that took them to Sweden? What did the captain look like? Was there a crew? He told them to take one of the girls down to the yacht club to see whether she recognised Logård's launch. A lot of questions remained. Wallander needed an empty room where he could lock himself away and think.

He was impatient for Höglund to return. And he was waiting for information on Logård. He tried to connect a moped at Sturup Airport, a man who took scalps and killed with an axe, and another who shot at people with a semi-automatic weapon. The myriad of details swam back and forth in his head. The headache he had felt coming earlier had arrived, and he tried unsuccessfully to fight it off with painkillers. It was very humid. There were thunderstorms over Denmark. In less than 48 hours he was supposed to be at Kastrup Airport.

Wallander was standing by a window, looking out at the light summer night and thinking that the world had dissolved into chaos, when Birgersson came stamping down the hall, triumphantly wielding a piece of paper.

"Do you know who Erik Sturesson is?" he asked.

"No, who?"

"Then do you know who Sture Eriksson is?"

"No."

"They're one and the same. And later he changed his name again. This time he didn't settle for switching his first and last names. He took on a name with a more aristocratic ring to it. Hans Logård."

"Great," he said. "What have we got?"

"The prints we found at Hördestigen and in the boats are in our records, under Erik Sturesson and Sture Eriksson. But not Hans Logård. Erik Sturesson, if we start with him, since that was Hans Logård's real name, is 47. Born in Skövde, father a career soldier, mother a housewife. The father was also an alcoholic. Both died in the late 1960s. Erik wound up in bad company, was first arrested at 14, downhill from there. He's done time in Österåker, Kumla and Hall prisons. And a short stretch at Norrköping. He changed his name for the first time when he got out of Österåker."

"What type of crimes?"

"From simple jobs to specialisation, you might say. Burglaries and con games at first. Occasionally assault. Then more serious crimes. Narcotics. The hard stuff. He seems to have worked for Turkish and Pakistani gangs. This is an overview, mind. We'll have more information through in the night."

"We need a picture of him," Wallander said. "And the fingerprints have to be cross-checked against the ones we found at Wetterstedt's and Carlman's. And the ones on Fredman too. Don't forget the ones we got from the left eyelid."

"Nyberg is onto it," Birgersson said. "But he seems so pissed off all the time."

"That's just the way he is," Wallander replied. "But he's good at his job."

They sat down at a table overflowing with used plastic coffee cups. Telephones rang all around them. They erected an invisible wall around themselves, admitting only Svedberg.

"The interesting thing is that Logård suddenly stopped paying visits to our prisons," Birgersson said. "The last time he was inside was 1989. Since then he's been clean. As if he found salvation."

"That corresponds pretty well with when Liljegren got himself a house here in Helsingborg."

Birgersson nodded. "We're not too clear on that yet. But it seems that Logård bought Hördestigen in 1991. That's a gap of a couple of years. But there's nothing to prevent him from having lived some-where else in the meantime."

"We'll need an answer to that one right away," Wallander said, reaching for the phone. "What's Elisabeth Carlén's number? It's on Sjösten's desk. Have we still got her under surveillance, by the way?"

Birgersson nodded again. Wallander made a quick decision.

"Pull them off," he said.

Someone put a piece of paper in front of him. He dialled the number. She answered almost immediately.

"This is Inspector Wallander," he said.

"I won't come to the station at this time of night," she said.

"I don't want you to. I just have one question: was Hans Logård hanging out with Liljegren as early as 1989? Or 1990?"

He could hear her lighting a cigarette and blowing smoke straight into the receiver.

"Yes," she said, "I think he was there then. In 1990 anyway."

"Good," said Wallander.

"Why are you tailing me?" she asked.

"I was wondering myself," Wallander said. "We don't want anything to happen to you, of course. But we're lifting the surveillance now. Just don't leave town without telling us. I might get mad."

"Fair enough," she said, "I bet you can get mad."

She hung up.

"Logård was there," said Wallander. "It seems he appeared at Liljegren's in 1989 or 1990. Then he acquired Hördestigen. Liljegren seems to have taken care of his salvation."

Wallander tried to fit the different pieces together.

"And about then the rumours of the trade in girls surfaced. Isn't that right?"

Birgersson nodded.

"Does Logård have a violent history?" Wallander asked.

"A few charges of aggravated assault," Birgersson said. "But he's never shot anyone, that we know of."

"No axes?"

"No, nothing like that."

"In any case, we've got to find him," said Wallander, getting up.

"We'll find him," Birgersson said. "Sooner or later he'll crawl out of his hole."

"Why did he shoot at us?" Wallander asked.

"You'll have to ask him that yourself," Birgersson said, as he left the room.

Svedberg had taken off his cap. "Is this really the man we're looking for?" he asked.

"I don't know," said Wallander. "Frankly I doubt it, although I could be wrong. Let's hope I am."

Svedberg left the room. Wallander was alone again. More than ever he missed Rydberg. *There's always another question you can ask.* Rydberg's words, repeated often. So what was the question he hadn't asked yet? He searched and found nothing. All the questions had been asked. Only the answers were missing.

That was why it was a relief when Höglund stepped into the room. It was just before 1 a.m. They sat down together.

"Louise wasn't there," she said. "Her mother was drunk. But her concern about her daughter seemed genuine. She couldn't understand how it had happened. I think she was telling the truth. I felt really sorry for her."

"You mean she actually had no idea?"

"Not a clue. And she'd been worrying about it."

"Had it happened before?"

"Never."

"And her son?"

"The older or the younger one?"

"The older one. Stefan."

"He wasn't there."

"Was he out looking for his sister?"

"If I understood the mother correctly, he stays away occasionally. But there was one thing I did notice. I asked to have a look around. Just in case Louise was there. I went into Stefan's room. The mattress

393

was gone from his bed. There was just a bedspread. No pillow or blanket either."

"Did you ask her where he was?"

"I don't think she would have been able to tell me."

"Did she say how long he'd been gone?"

She thought about it and looked at her notes.

"Since midday."

"Not long before Louise disappeared."

She looked at him in surprise.

"You think he was the one who went and got her? Then where are they now?"

"Two questions, two answers. I don't know. I don't know."

Wallander felt a deep unease creep over him. He couldn't tell what it meant.

"Did you happen to ask her whether Stefan has a moped?"

He saw that she immediately understood where he was heading.

"No."

Wallander gestured towards the phone.

"Call her," he said. "Ask her. She drinks at night. You won't wake her up."

It was a long time before she got an answer. The conversation was very brief. She hung up again.

"He doesn't have a moped," she said. "Besides, Stefan isn't 15 yet, is he?"

"It was just a thought," Wallander said. "We have to know. Anyway, I doubt that young people today pay much attention to what is permitted or not."

"The little boy woke up when I was about to leave," she said. "He was sleeping on the sofa next to his mother. That's what upset me the most."

"That he woke up?"

"I've never seen such frightened eyes in a child before."

Wallander slammed his fist on the table. She jumped.

"I've got it," he cried. "What it was I've been forgetting all this time. Damn it!"

"What?"

"Wait a minute. Wait a minute . . ."

Wallander rubbed his temples to squeeze out the image that had been bothering him for so long. Finally he captured it.

"Do you remember the doctor who did the autopsy of Dolores María Santana in Malmö?"

She tried to remember.

"Wasn't it a woman?"

"Yes, it was. A woman. What was her name? Malm something?"

"Svedberg's got a good memory," she said. "I'll get him."

"That's not necessary," said Wallander. "I remember now. Her name was Malmström. We've got to get hold of her. And we need to get hold of her right now. I'd like you to take care of it. As fast as you can!"

"What is it?"

"I'll explain later."

She got up and left the room. Could the Fredman boy really be mixed up in this? Wallander picked up the phone and called Åkeson. He answered at once.

"I need you to do me a favour," he said. "Now. In the middle of the night. Call the hospital where Louise was a patient. Tell them to copy the page of the visitors' book with the signature of the person who picked her up. And tell them to fax it here to Helsingborg."

"How the hell do you think they can do that?"

"I have no idea," Wallander said. "But it could be important. They can cross out all the other names on the page. I just want to see that one signature."

"Which was illegible?"

"Precisely. I want to see the illegible signature."

Wallander stressed his final words. Åkeson understood that he was after something that might be important.

"Give me the fax number," Åkeson said. "I'll try."

Wallander gave him the number and hung up. The clock on the wall said 2.05 a.m. He was sweating in his new shirt. He wondered vaguely whether the state had paid for the shirt and trousers. Höglund returned and said that Agneta Malmström was on a sailing holiday with her family somewhere between Landsort and Oxelösund.

"What's the name of the boat?"

"It's supposed to be some kind of Maxi class. The name is *Sanborombon*. It also has a number."

"Call Stockholm Radio," Wallander said. "They must have a two-way radio on board. Ask them to call the boat. Tell them it's a police emergency. Talk to Birgersson. I want to get in touch with her right away."

Wallander had his second wind. Höglund left to go and find Birgersson. Svedberg almost collided with her in the doorway as he came in with the security guards' account of the theft of their car.

"You're right," he said. "Basically all they saw was the gun. And it all happened very fast. But he had blond hair, blue eyes and was dressed in some kind of jogging suit. Normal height, spoke with a Stockholm accent. Gave the impression of being high on something."

"What did they mean by that?"

"His eyes."

"I assume the description is on its way out?"

"I'll check."

As Svedberg left, excited voices came from the hall. Wallander guessed that a reporter had tried to cross the boundary that Birgersson had drawn. He found a notebook and quickly wrote a few notes in the sequence he remembered them. He was sweating profusely now, checking the wall clock, and in his mind Baiba was sitting by the phone in her spartan flat in Riga waiting for the call he should have made long ago.

It was close to 3 a.m. The security company's car was still missing. Hans Logård was hiding. The Dominican girl who had been taken to the yacht club couldn't make a positive identification of the boat. Maybe it was the same one, maybe not. A man who had always kept in the shadows had been at the wheel. She couldn't remember any crew. Wallander told Birgersson that the girls had to get some sleep now.

Hotel rooms were arranged. One of the girls smiled shyly at Wallander when they met in the hall. Her smile made him feel good, for a brief moment almost exhilarated. At regular intervals Birgersson would find Wallander and provide information on Logård. At 3.15 a.m. Wallander learned that Logård had been married twice and had two children under 18. One of them, a girl, lived with her mother in Hagfors, the other in Stockholm, a boy of nine. Next Birgersson came back and reported that Logård might have had one other child, but that they hadn't managed to confirm it.

At 3.30 a.m. an exhausted officer came into the room where Wallander was sitting with a coffee cup in his hand and his feet on the desk and told him that Stockholm Radio had contacted the Malmströms' Maxi. Wallander jumped up and followed him to the command centre, where Birgersson stood yelling into a receiver. He handed it to Wallander.

"They're somewhere between two lightships named the *Hävringe* and the *Gustaf Dalén*," he said. "I've got Karl Malmström on the line."

Wallander quickly handed the phone back to Birgersson.

"I've got to talk to his wife. Only the wife."

"I hope you realise that there are hundreds of pleasure boats out there listening to the conversation going out over the coastal radio."

In his haste, Wallander had forgotten that.

"A mobile phone is better," he said. "Ask if they have one on board."

"I've already done that," Birgersson said. "These are people who think you should leave mobile phones at home when you're on holiday."

"Then they'll have to put into shore," Wallander said. "And call me from there."

"How long do you think that will take?" said Birgersson. "Do you have any idea where the *Hävringe* is? Plus, it's the middle of the night. Are they supposed to set sail now?"

"I don't give a shit where the *Hävringe* is," Wallander said. "Besides, they might be sailing at night and not lying at anchor. Maybe there's some other boat nearby with a mobile phone. Just tell them that I have to get in touch with her within an hour. With her. Not him."

Birgersson shook his head. Then he started yelling into the phone again. Half an hour later Agneta Malmström called from a mobile phone borrowed from a boat they'd met out in the channel. Wallander got straight to the point.

"Do you remember the girl who burned herself to death?" he asked. "In a rape field a few weeks ago?"

"Of course I remember."

"Do you also recall a phone conversation we had at that time? I asked you how a young person could do such a thing to herself. I don't remember my exact words."

"I have a vague memory of it," she replied.

"You answered by giving an example of something you had recently experienced. You told me about a boy, a little boy, who was so afraid of his father that he tried to put out his own eyes."

"Yes," she said. "I remember that. But it wasn't something I had experienced myself. One of my colleagues told me about it."

"Who was that?"

"My husband. He's a doctor too."

"Then I'll have to talk to him. Please get him for me."

"It'll take a while. I'll have to row over and get him in the dinghy. We put down a drift anchor some way from here."

Wallander apologised for bothering her.

"Unfortunately, it's necessary," he said.

"It'll take a while," she said.

"Where the hell is the *Hävringe*?" asked Wallander.

"Out in the Baltic," she said. "It's lovely where we are. But just now we're making a night sail to the south. Even though the wind is poor."

It took 20 minutes before the phone rang again. Karl Malmström was on the line. In the meantime Wallander had learnt that he was a paediatrician in Malmö. Wallander reverted to the conversation he had had with his wife.

"I remember the case," he said.

"Can you remember the name of the boy off the top of your head?"

"Yes, I can. But I can't stand here yelling it into a mobile phone."

Wallander understood his point. He thought feverishly.

"Let's do this, then," he said. "I'll ask you a question. You can answer yes or no. Without naming any names."

"We can try," said Malmström.

"Does it have anything to do with Bellman?" asked Wallander.

Malmström instantly understood the reference to *Fredman's Epistles* by the famous Swedish poet.

"Yes, it does."

"Then I thank you for your help," said Wallander. "I hope I won't have to bother you again. Have a good summer."

Karl Malmström didn't seem annoyed. "It's nice to know we have policemen who work hard at all hours," was all he said.

Wallander handed the phone to Birgersson.

"Let's have a meeting in a while," he said. "I need a few minutes to think."

"Take my office," Birgersson said.

Wallander suddenly felt very tired. His sense of revulsion was like a dull ache in his body. He still didn't want to believe that what he was thinking could be true. He had fought against this conclusion for a long time. But he couldn't do that any longer. The truth that confronted him was unbearable. The little boy's terror of his father. A big brother nearby. Who pours hydrochloric acid into his father's eyes as revenge. Who acts out an insane retribution for his sister, who had been abused in some way. It was all very clear. The whole thing made sense and the result was appalling. He also thought that his subconscious had seen it long ago, but he had pushed the realisation aside. Instead he had allowed himself to be sidetracked, distracted from his goal.

A police officer knocked on his door.

"We just got a fax from Lund," he said. "From a hospital."

Wallander took it. Åkeson had acted fast. It was a copy of a page from the visitors' book for the psychiatric ward. All the names but one were crossed out. The signature really was illegible. He took out a magnifying glass from Birgersson's desk drawer and tried to make it out. Illegible. He put the paper on the table. The officer was still standing in the doorway.

"Get Birgersson over here," Wallander said. "And my colleagues from Ystad. How's Sjösten, by the way?"

"He's sleeping. They've removed the bullet from his shoulder."

A few minutes later they were gathered in the room. It was almost 4.30 a.m. Everyone was exhausted. Still no sign of Logård. Still no trace of the security guards' car. Wallander nodded to them to sit down.

The moment of truth, he thought. This is it.

"We're searching for Hans Logård," he began. "We have to keep doing so of course. He shot Sjösten in the shoulder and he's mixed up in the traffic of young girls. But he isn't the one who committed four murders and scalped his victims. That was somebody else entirely."

He paused.

"Stefan Fredman is the person who did this," he said. "We're looking for a 14-year-old boy who killed his father, along with the others."

There was silence in the room. No-one moved. They were all staring at him. When Wallander had finished his explanation, there was no doubt in anyone's mind. The team decided to return to Ystad. The greatest secrecy would have to attach to what they had just discussed. Wallander couldn't tell which feeling was stronger among his colleagues, shock or relief.

Wallander called Åkeson and gave him a brisk précis of his conclusions. As he did so, Svedberg stood next to him, staring at the fax that had come from Lund.

"Strange," he said.

Wallander turned to him.

"What's strange?"

"This signature. It looks as if he's signed himself Geronimo."

Wallander grabbed the fax out of Svedberg's hand. He was right.

CHAPTER 38

They said goodbye in the dawn outside the station in Helsingborg. Everyone looked haggard, but more than anything they were shaken by what they now realised was the truth about the killer they had been hunting for so long. They agreed to meet at 8 a.m. at the Ystad police station. That meant they would have time to get home and shower, but not much else. They had to keep working. Wallander had been blunt in outlining his conclusions. He believed that the murders had happened because of the sick sister. But they couldn't be sure. It was possible that she herself was in danger. There was only one approach to take: to fear the worst.

Svedberg went in Wallander's car. It was going to be another beautiful day. They spoke very little during the trip. Svedberg discovered that he must have left his keys somewhere. It reminded Wallander that his own keys had never shown up. He told Svedberg to come home with him. They reached Mariagatan just before 7 a.m. Linda was asleep. After they had each taken a shower and Wallander had given Svedberg a clean shirt, they sat in the living-room and had coffee.

Neither of them noticed that the door to the cupboard next to Linda's room, which had been closed when they arrived, was ajar.

Hoover had arrived at the flat at 6.50 a.m. He was on his way into the policeman's bedroom with the axe in his hand when he heard a key turn in the lock. He hid in the cupboard. He heard two voices. When he could tell that they were in the living-room, he opened the door a crack. Hoover assumed that the other man was a policeman too. He gripped the axe the whole time, listening to them talking softly. At first Hoover didn't understand what they were talking about. The name

Hans Logård was mentioned repeatedly. The policeman whom he had come to kill was clearly trying to explain something to the other man. He listened carefully and finally understood that it was holy providence, the power of Geronimo, that had started working again. Hans Logård had been Åke Liljegren's right-hand man. He had smuggled girls in from the Dominican Republic, and maybe from other parts of the Caribbean too. He was also the one who probably brought girls to Wetterstedt and maybe even Carlman. He also heard the policeman predict that Logård was on the death list that must exist in Stefan Fredman's mind.

Then the conversation stopped. A few moments later Wallander and Svedberg left the flat. Hoover emerged from the cupboard and stood utterly still. Then he left, as soundlessly as he had come. He had gone to the empty shop where Linda and Kajsa had held their rehearsals. He knew they wouldn't be using it again, so he had left Louise there while he went to the flat on Mariagatan to kill Perkins and his daughter. But as he'd stood in the cupboard, the axe ready in his hand, and heard the conversation he started to have doubts. There was one more person he had to kill. A man he had overlooked. Hans Logård. When the policeman described him, Hoover understood that he must have been the one who had brutally raped and abused his sister. That was before she had been drugged and taken to both Gustaf Wetterstedt and Arne Carlman – events that had forced her into the darkness. All of it was written down in the book he had taken from her. The book that contained the words that controlled him. He had assumed that Hans Logård was someone who didn't live in Sweden. A foreign visitor, an evil man. Now he knew that he had made a mistake.

It was easy to get into the empty shop. Earlier he had seen Kajsa hide the key. Since he was moving around in broad daylight, he hadn't painted his face. He didn't want to frighten Louise, either. When he came back she was sitting on a chair, staring blankly into space. He had already decided to move her. And he knew where. Before he went to Mariagatan he went on the moped to see that the situation was as he'd thought. The house he'd selected was empty. But they weren't going to move there until evening. He sat down on the floor at her side and tried to work out how to find Logård before the police did. He turned inward and asked Geronimo for advice. But his heart was strangely still this morning. The drums were so faint that he couldn't hear their message.

At 8 a.m. they gathered in the conference room. Åkeson was here, as was a sergeant from Malmö. Birgersson was hooked up via speaker phone from Helsingborg. Wallander looked around the table and said they'd start by bringing everyone up to date. The sergeant from Malmö was looking for a hiding place they assumed Stefan Fredman had access to. They still hadn't found it. But one of the neighbours in the building told them that he had seen Stefan Fredman on a moped several times. The building where the family lived was under surveillance. Birgersson told them that Sjösten was doing well, although his ear would be permanently damaged.

"Plastic surgeons can work wonders," Wallander shouted encouragingly. "Say hello to him from all of us."

Birgersson went on to say that they weren't Logård's fingerprints on the comic book, the paper bag, Liljegren's stove or Fredman's left eyelid. This confirmation was crucial. The Malmö police were getting Stefan Fredman's prints from objects taken from his room in the Rosengård flat. Nobody doubted that they would match, now that Logård's didn't.

They talked about Logård. The hunt had to continue. They had to assume he was dangerous, since he had shot at Wallander and Sjösten.

"Stefan Fredman is only 14, but he is dangerous," Wallander said. "He may be crazy, but he's not stupid. He's very strong and he reacts fast. We have to be careful."

"This is all so damned disgusting!" Hansson exploded. "I still can't believe it's true."

"Nor can any of us," Åkeson said. "But what Kurt says is absolutely right. And we need to act accordingly."

"Fredman got his sister Louise out of the hospital," Wallander went on. "We're looking for the nurse who will be able to identify him. Let's assume it'll be a positive identification. We still don't know whether he intends to hurt Louise. It's crucial that we find them. He has a moped and must ride with her on the back. They can't get very far. Besides, the girl is sick."

"A nutcase on a moped with a mentally ill girl on the back," Svedberg said. "It's so macabre."

"He can also drive a car," Ludwigsson pointed out. "He used his father's van. So he may have stolen one by now."

Wallander turned to the detective from Malmö.

"Stolen cars," he said. "Within the past few days. Above all in Rosengård. And near the hospital."

The detective went to a phone.

"Stefan Fredman carries out his actions after careful planning," continued Wallander. "Naturally we have no way of knowing whether the abduction of his sister was also planned. Now we have to try and get into his mind to guess what he plans to do next. Where are they headed? It's a shame Ekholm isn't here when we need him most."

"He'll be here in about an hour," Hansson said, glancing at the clock. "Someone's picking him up at the airport."

"How is his daughter?" asked Höglund.

Wallander was ashamed that he'd forgotten the reason for Ekholm's absence.

"She's OK," said Svedberg. "A broken foot, that's all. She was very lucky."

"This autumn we're going to have a big traffic safety campaign in schools," said Hansson. "Too many children are being killed."

The detective returned to the table.

"I presume you've also looked for Stefan in his father's flat," Wallander said.

"We've already searched there and everywhere else his father usually hung out. And we've picked up Peter Hjelm and asked him to try and think of other hide-outs Fredman may have had access to that his son might know about. Forsfält is taking care of it."

The meeting dragged on, but Wallander knew that they were really just waiting for something to happen. Stefan Fredman was somewhere with his sister. Logård was out there too. A large contingent of police officers were looking for them. They went in and out of the conference room, getting coffee, sending out for sandwiches, dozing in their chairs, drinking more coffee. The German police found Sara Pettersson in Hamburg. She'd been able to identify Stefan Fredman at once. Ekholm arrived from the airport, still shaken and pale.

Around 11 a.m. they got the confirmation they were waiting for. Stefan Fredman's fingerprints had been identified on his father's eyelid, on the comic book, the bloody scrap of paper and Liljegren's stove. The only sound in the conference room was the faint hiss of the speaker phone linked to Birgersson. There was no turning back. All the false leads, especially those they had thought up themselves, had been erased. All that was left was the realisation of the appalling truth: they were searching for a 14-year-old boy who had committed four cold-blooded, premeditated and atrocious murders.

Finally Wallander broke the silence and turned to Ekholm.

"What's he doing? What's he thinking?"

"I know this is very risky," Ekholm said. "But I don't think he intends to hurt his sister. There's a pattern, call it logic if you will, to his behaviour. Revenge for his little brother and his sister is the goal. If he diverges from that goal, then everything he so laboriously built up will collapse."

"Why did he take her from the hospital?" Wallander asked.

"Maybe he was afraid that you would influence her somehow."

"How?" asked Wallander in surprise.

"Picture a confused boy who has taken on the role of a lone warrior. Suppose men have done his sister irreparable harm. That's what drives him. Assuming this theory is correct, that means he'll want to keep all men away from her. He's the only exception. And you can't rule out the fact that he may have suspected you were on his trail. Certainly he knows that you're in charge of the investigation."

Wallander remembered something.

"The pictures that Norén took," he said. "Of the spectators outside the cordons? Where are they?"

Nyberg, who most of the time had sat quiet and meditative at the meeting table, went to get them. Wallander spread them out on the table. Someone got a magnifying glass. They gathered around the pictures. It was Höglund who found him.

"There he is," she said, pointing.

He was almost hidden behind some other onlookers, but part of his moped was visible, along with his head.

"I'll be damned," Hamrén said.

"It should be possible to identify the moped," Nyberg said. "If we blow up the details."

"Do that," Wallander said.

It was obvious now that there had been a good reason for the feeling gnawing at Wallander's subconscious. Grimly he thought that at least he could close the case on his own anxiety.

Save for one thing. Baiba. It was midday. Svedberg was asleep in his chair, and Åkeson was on the phone to so many different people that no-one could keep track of them. Wallander gestured to Höglund to follow him out into the hall. They sat down in his office and closed the door. Without beating around the bush, he told her of the mess he'd made. In doing so he broke his cardinal rule: never to confide a personal problem to a colleague. He had stopped doing that when Rydberg died. Now he was doing it again. He was unsure whether he could develop the same trusting relationship with Ann-Britt Höglund that he had enjoyed with Rydberg, especially since she was a woman. She listened attentively.

"What the hell am I going to do?"

"Nothing," she said. "You're right. It's already too late. But I could talk to her if you like. I assume she speaks English. Give me her number."

Wallander wrote it down, but when she reached for his telephone he asked her to wait.

"A couple more hours," he said.

"Miracles don't happen very often," she said.

At that moment Hansson burst through the door.

"They found his hide-out. A basement in a condemned school building. It's right near the flats where he lives."

"Are they there?" Wallander asked, getting up from his chair.

"No. But they've been there."

They went back to the meeting room. Another speaker phone was hooked up. Wallander heard Forsfält's friendly voice. He described what they had found. Mirrors, brushes, make-up. A cassette player with a tape of drums on it. He played a few seconds of the tape. It echoed spookily in the meeting room. War paint, thought Wallander. How had he signed at the hospital? Geronimo. There were axes on a piece of cloth, and knives too. They could hear that Forsfält was upset.

"We didn't find scalps," he said. "We're still looking."

"Where the hell are they?" said Wallander.

"Either he has them with him, or else he's left them as a sacrifice somewhere," Ekholm said.

"Where? Does he have his own sacrificial grove?"

"Could be."

The waiting continued. Wallander lay down on the floor of his office and managed to sleep for half an hour. When he woke up he felt more tired than before. His body ached all over. Now and then Höglund gave him a questioning look, but he shook his head and felt his self-loathing grow.

At 6 p.m. that evening, there was still no trace of Logård, Fredman or his sister. They had discussed at length whether to put out a nation-wide alert for the Fredmans. Everyone was reluctant to do so. The risk that something would happen to Louise was too great. Åkeson agreed. They kept waiting.

Just after 6 p.m. Hoover took his sister to the house he had chosen. He parked the moped on the beach side. He quickly picked the lock on the gate to the garden. Wetterstedt's villa was deserted. They walked up the path to the main door. Suddenly he stopped and held Louise back.

There was a car in the garage. It hadn't been there this morning. He carefully pushed Louise down to sit on a rock behind the garage wall. He took out an axe and listened. He walked forward and looked at the car. It belonged to a security company. One of the front windows was open. He peered inside. There were some papers lying on the seat. He picked them up and saw that there was a receipt among them, made out to Hans Logård. He put it back and stood still, holding his breath. The drums started to pound. He remembered the conversation he had heard that morning. Hans Logård was on the run too.

So he'd had the same idea about the empty house. He was somewhere inside. Geronimo had not failed him. He had helped him track the monster to his lair. He didn't have to search any further. The cold darkness that had penetrated his sister's soul would soon be gone. He went back to her and told her to stay there for a while, and keep as quiet as she could. He would be back very soon.

He went into the garage. There were some cans of paint, and he opened two of them carefully. With his fingertip he drew two lines across his forehead. One red line, then a black one. He picked up his axe and took off his shoes. Just as he was about to leave he had an idea. He held his breath again, which he had learned from Geronimo. Compressed air in the lungs made thoughts clearer. He knew that his idea was a good one. It would make everything easier. Tonight he would bury the last of the scalps outside the hospital window alongside the others. There would be two of them. And he would bury a heart. Then it would be all over. In the last hole he would bury his weapons. He gripped the axe handle and started walking towards the house and the man he was to kill.

At 6.30 p.m. Wallander suggested to Hansson that they could start sending people home. Everyone was exhausted. They might as well be waiting, and resting, in their own homes. They would remain on call through the night.

"So who should stay here?" asked Hansson.

"Ekholm and Höglund," Wallander answered. "And one more.

Whoever's the least tired."

Ludwigsson and Hamrén both stayed.

They all moved down to one end of the table instead of spreading out as usual.

"The hide-out," Wallander said. "What would be a secret and impregnable fortress? What would an insane boy who transforms himself into a lone warrior seek?"

"I think his plans must have fallen apart," Ekholm said. "Otherwise they would have stayed in the basement room."

"Smart animals dig extra exits," Ludwigsson said thoughtfully.

"You mean that he might have a second hide-out in reserve?"

"Maybe. In all likelihood it's also in Malmö."

The discussion petered out. Hamrén yawned. A phone rang down the hall and someone appeared in the doorway, saying that there was a call for Wallander. He got up, much too tired to ask who it was. It didn't occur to him that it might be Baiba, not until he had picked up the phone in his own office. By then it was too late. But it wasn't Baiba. It was a man who spoke with a broad Skåne accent.

"Who is this?" Wallander asked.

"Hans Logård."

Wallander almost dropped the receiver. "I need to meet with you. Now."

Logård's voice was strained, as if he was having a lot of trouble forming his words. Wallander wondered whether he was on drugs.

"Where are you?"

"First I want a guarantee that you'll come. And that you'll come alone."

"You won't get it. You nearly killed me and Sjösten."

"God damn it! You have to come!"

The last words sounded almost like a shriek. Wallander grew cautious. "What do you want?"

"I can tell you where Stefan Fredman is. And his sister."

"How can I be sure of that?"

"You can't. But you should believe me."

"I'll come. You tell me what you know. And then we'll bring you in."

"All right."

"Where are you?"

"Are you coming?"

"Yes."

"Wetterstedt's villa."

A feeling that he should have thought of that possibility raced through Wallander's mind.

"Do you have a gun?" he asked.

"The car is in the garage. The revolver is in the glove compartment. I'll leave the door to the house open. You'll see me when you come in the door. I'll keep my hands in sight."

"All right, I'm coming."

"Alone?"

"Yes, alone."

Wallander hung up, thinking feverishly. He had no intention of going alone. But he didn't want Hansson to start organising a major strike force. Ann-Britt and Svedberg, he thought. But Svedberg was at home. He called him and told him to meet him outside the hospital in five minutes. With his service revolver. Did he have it? He did. Wallander told him briefly that they were going to arrest Logård. When Svedberg tried to ask questions, Wallander cut him off. Five minutes, he said, outside the hospital. Until then, don't use the phone.

He unlocked a desk drawer and took out his revolver. He detested even holding it. He loaded it and tucked it in his jacket pocket, then went to the conference room and waved Höglund outside. He took her into his office and explained. They would meet in the car park right away. Wallander told her to bring her service revolver. They would take Wallander's car. He told Hansson he was going home to shower. Hansson yawned and waved him goodbye. Svedberg was outside the hospital. He got into the back seat.

"What's going on?" he asked.

Wallander told them about the phone call. If the revolver wasn't in the car they'd call it off. Same thing if the door wasn't open. Or if Wallander suspected something was wrong. The two of them were supposed to stay out of sight but ready.

"He might have another gun," Svedberg said. "He might try to take you hostage. I don't like this. How could he know where Stefan Fredman is? What does he want?"

"Maybe he's stupid enough to try and make a deal with us. People think Sweden is just like the United States."

Wallander thought about Logård's voice. Something told him he really did know where the boy was.

They parked the car out of sight of the house. Svedberg was to watch the beach side. When he got there he was alone, except for a girl sitting on the boat under which they'd found Wetterstedt's dead body. She seemed to be completely entranced by the sea and the black rain cloud bearing down on the land. Höglund took up a position outside the garage. Wallander saw that the front door was open. He moved slowly. The car was in the garage. The revolver was in the glove compartment. He took out his own gun, put the safety catch off, and advanced cautiously to the door. Everything was still.

He stepped up to the door. Hans Logård stood in dark hall. He had his hands on his head. Wallander sensed danger. But he went inside. Logård looked at him. Then everything happened very fast. One of Logård's hands slipped down and Wallander saw a gaping wound in his head. Logård's body fell to the floor. Behind him stood Stefan Fredman. He had lines painted on his face. He threw himself furiously at Wallander, an axe lifted high. Wallander raised his revolver to shoot, but too late. Instinctively he ducked and a rug slipped under him. The axe grazed his shoulder. He fired a shot and an oil painting jumped on one of the walls. At the same instant Höglund, appeared in the doorway. She stood crouched and ready to fire. Fredman saw her just as he was raising the axe to slam it into Wallander's head. He leapt to the left. Wallander was in the line of fire.

Fredman vanished towards the open terrace door. Wallander thought of Svedberg. Slow Svedberg. He yelled to Höglund to shoot. But he was gone. Svedberg, who had heard the first shot, didn't know what to do.

He yelled at the girl sitting on the boat to take cover, but she didn't move. He ran towards the garden gate. It hit him in the head as it flew open. He saw a face he would never forget. He dropped his revolver. The man had an axe in his hand. Svedberg did the only thing he could do, he ran yelling for help. Fredman got his sister, motionless still on the boat, and dragged her to his moped. They rode off just as Wallander and Höglund came running out.

"Call for back-up!" Wallander shouted. "Where the hell is Svedberg? I'll try and follow them in the car."

Heavy rain begain to fall. Wallander ran to his car, trying to work out which way they would have gone. Visibility was poor even with the windscreen wipers on full. He thought he had lost them but suddenly caught sight of the moped again. They were going down the road towards the Saltsjöbad Hotel. Wallander kept a safe distance behind. He didn't want to frighten them. The moped was going very fast. Wallander frantically tried to think how to put an end to the chase. He was just about to call in his location when the moped wobbled. He braked. The moped was heading straight for a tree. The girl was thrown off, right into the tree. Stefan Fredman landed somewhere off to the side.

"Damn!" said Wallander. He stopped the car in the middle of the road and ran towards the moped.

Louise Fredman was dead, he could see that at once. Her white dress seemed strangely bright against the blood streaming from her face. Stefan appeared uninjured. Wallander watched the boy fall to his knees beside his sister. The rain poured down. The boy started to cry. It sounded as if he was howling. Wallander knelt next to him.

"She's dead," he said.

Stefan looked at him, his face distorted. Wallander quickly got up, afraid that the boy would jump on him. But he didn't. He kept howling.

Somewhere behind him in the rain he heard a siren. It wasn't until Hansson was standing next to him that he realised he was crying himself. Wallander left all the work to the others. He told Höglund briefly what had happened. When he saw Åkeson, he took him to his car. The rain was drumming on the roof.

"It's over," Wallander said.

"Yes," said Åkeson, "it's over."

"I'm going on holiday," said Wallander. "I realise there's a pile of reports that have to be written. But I thought I'd go anyway."

Åkeson's reply came without hesitation.

"Do that," he said. "Go."

Åkeson got out of the car. Wallander thought he should have asked him about his trip to the Sudan. Or was it Uganda?

He drove home. Linda wasn't there. He took a bath and was drying himself off when he heard her close the front door. That evening he told her what had really happened. And how he felt.

Then he called Baiba.

"I thought you were never going to call," she said, keeping her anger in check.

"Please forgive me," Wallander said. "I've had so much to do lately."

"I think that's a pretty poor excuse."

"It is, I know. But it's the only one I've got."

Neither of them said anything else. The silence travelled back and forth between Ystad and Riga.

"I'll see you tomorrow," Wallander finally said.

"All right," she said. "I guess so."

They hung up. Wallander felt a knot in his stomach. Maybe she wouldn't come. After supper he and Linda packed their bags. The rain stopped just after midnight. The air smelled fresh as they stood out on the balcony.

"The summer is so beautiful," she said.

"Yes," Wallander said. "It *is* beautiful."

The next day they took the train together to Malmö. Then Wallander took the hydrofoil to Copenhagen. He watched the water racing past the sides of the boat. Distracted, he ordered coffee and cognac. In two hours Baiba's plane would be landing. Something close to panic gripped him. He suddenly wished that the crossing to

413

Copenhagen would take much longer. But when she arrived at the airport he was waiting for her.

Not until then did the image of Louise Fredman, dead and broken, finally disappear from his mind.

Skåne

16–17 September 1994

EPILOGUE

On Friday, 16 September, autumn suddenly rolled in to Skåne. Kurt Wallander woke up early that morning. His eyes flew open in the dark, as if he had been cast violently out of a dream. He lay still and tried to remember. But there was only the echo of something that was gone and would never return. He turned his head and looked at the clock next to the bed. The fluorescent hands showed 4.45 a.m. He turned over on his side to go back to sleep. But the knowledge of what day it was kept him awake.

He got up and went to the kitchen. The streetlight hanging over the street swayed forlornly in the wind. He checked the thermometer and saw that the temperature had dropped. It was 7°C. He smiled at the thought that tomorrow night he would be in Rome where it was still warm. He sat at the kitchen table and had some coffee, going over the preparations for the trip in his mind. A few days earlier he had finally fixed his father's studio door. He had also taken a look at his father's new passport. He had exchanged some money for Italian lire at the bank and had bought traveller's cheques. He was going to leave work early to pick up the tickets.

Now he had to go to work for one last day before his holiday. He left the flat and went down to his car. He zipped up his jacket and shivered when he got into the driver's seat. On the way to the station he thought about this morning's meeting.

It was exactly 8 a.m. when he knocked on the door of Lisa Holgersson's office and opened the door. She nodded and asked him to have a seat. She had been serving as their new chief for only three weeks, but Wallander thought she had already set her stamp on the atmosphere of the department.

Many had been sceptical about a woman who came from a police district in Småland. And Wallander was surrounded by colleagues who still believed that women weren't even suited to be police officers. How could one be their chief? But Lisa Holgersson had soon demonstrated how capable she was. Wallander was impressed by her integrity, her fearlessness and the clear presentations she gave, no matter what the topic.

The day before she had arranged a meeting. Now Wallander sat in her visitor's chair wondering what she wanted.

"You're going on holiday," she said. "I heard you were going to Italy with your father."

"It's his dream," Wallander said. "It may be the last chance we get. He's 80."

"My father is 85," she said. "Sometimes his mind is crystal clear. Sometimes he doesn't recognise me. But I've come to terms with the fact that you never escape your parents. The roles are simply reversed. You become your parents' parent."

"Exactly," Wallander replied.

She moved some papers on her desk.

"I don't have a specific agenda for this meeting," she said. "But I realised that I've never had a proper chance to thank you for your work this summer. It was model detective work."

Wallander gave her a surprised look. Was she serious?

"That's putting it a little strongly," he said. "I made a lot of mistakes. I let the whole investigation be sidetracked. It could have failed miserably."

"The ability to lead an investigation often means knowing when to shift tactics," she said. "To look in a direction you may have just ruled out. The investigation was a model in many ways, especially because of your tenacity and your willingness to think along unconventional lines. I want you to know this. I've heard it said that the national police chief has expressed his satisfaction. I think you'll be receiving an invitation to hold seminars about the investigation at the police academy."

"I can't do that," he said. "Ask someone else. I can't speak to people I don't know."

"We'll take this up again after you get back," she said, smiling. "Right now the most important thing is that I had a chance to tell you what I thought."

She stood to indicate that the meeting was over.

Wallander walked down the hall thinking that she'd meant what she said. He tried to dismiss it, but the appreciation made him feel good. It would be easy to work with her in the future.

He got some coffee from the canteen and exchanged a few words with Martinsson about one of his daughters who had tonsillitis. When he got to his office he made an appointment for a haircut. He had made a list the day before, which was on his desk. He'd planned to leave the station as early as midday so that he could deal with all his errands. But it was 4.15 p.m. by the time he left to go to the travel agency. He also stopped at the state off licence and bought a bottle of whisky. When he got home he called Linda. He promised to send her a postcard from Rome. She was in a hurry, and he didn't ask why. The conversation was over much sooner than he would have liked.

At 6 p.m. he called Löderup and asked Gertrud if everything was in order. She told him that his father had such travel fever that he could hardly sit still. Wallander walked into the centre of town and ate dinner at one of the pizzerias. When he got back to Mariagatan he poured himself a glass of whisky and spread out a map of Rome. He had never been there and didn't know a word of Italian. But there are two of us, he thought. My father has never been there either, except in his dreams. And he doesn't speak Italian either. We're heading into this dream together and will have to guide each other.

On impulse he called the tower at Sturup and asked one of the air traffic controllers, who he knew from an old case, what the weather was like in Rome.

"It's warm. Right now it's 21°C, even though it's evening. Light winds from the southeast. Light fog too. The forecast for the next 24 hours is for more of the same."

Wallander thanked him.

"Are you going away?"

"I'm going on holiday with my father."

"That sounds like a good idea. Are you flying Alitalia?"

"Yes, the 10.45."

"I'll be thinking of you. Have a nice trip."

Wallander went over his packing one more time, checking his money and travel documents. He tried to call Baiba, then remembered that she was visiting relatives.

He sat down with a glass of whisky and listened to *La Traviata*. He thought about the trip he had taken with Baiba in the summer. Tired and dishevelled, he had waited for her in Copenhagen. He stood there at Kastrup Airport like an unshaven ghost. He knew she was disappointed, though she said nothing. Not until they had reached Skagen and he had caught up on his sleep did he tell her everything that had happened. After that their holiday had started in earnest.

On one of the last days he asked her if she would marry him. She had said no. Not yet, at any rate, not now. The past was still too close. Her husband, police captain Karlis, whom Wallander had worked with, was still alive in her memory. His violent death followed her like a shadow. Above all she doubted she could ever consider marrying another policeman. He understood. But he wanted some kind of assurance. How long would she need to think about it? She was fond of him, he knew. But was that enough? What about him? Did he really want to live with someone else? Through Baiba he had escaped the loneliness that haunted him after his divorce from Mona. It was a big step, a great relief. Maybe he should settle for that. At least for the time being.

It was late when he went to sleep, questions swirling in his head. Gertrud picked him up the next morning. It was still raining. His father was in the front, dressed in his best suit. Gertrud had given him a haircut.

"We're off to Rome," his father said happily. "To think we're actually going."

Gertrud dropped them in Malmö at the terminal. On the ferry his father insisted on tottering around the rainswept deck. He pointed to the Swedish mainland, to a spot south of Malmö.

"That's where you grew up. Do you remember?"

"How could I forget?"

"You had a very happy childhood."

"I know."

"You had everything."

"Everything."

Wallander thought about Stefan Fredman. About Louise. About the brother who had tried to put out his own eyes. About all they lacked or had been deprived of. But he pushed the thoughts away. They would still be there, lurking in the back of his mind; they would return. For now, he was on holiday with his father. That was the most important thing. Everything else would have to wait.

The plane took off as scheduled. His father had a window seat, and Wallander sat on the aisle. It was the first time his father had been in a plane. Wallander watched him press his face to the window as the plane gathered speed and slowly lifted off. Wallander could see him smiling, the smile of an old man, who had been granted, one last time in his life, the chance to feel the joy of a child.

Harvill Crime
in
Vintage

Henning Mankell

THE DOGS OF RIGA

'Mankell is in the first division of crime writing'
The Times

Sweden, Winter, 1991. Inspector Wallander and his team
receive an anonymous tip-off. A few days later, a life raft
is washed up on a beach. In it are two men, dressed in
expensive suits, shot dead.

The dead men were criminals, victims of what seems to
have been a gangland hit. But what appears to be an open-
and-shut case soon takes on a far more sinister aspect.
Wallander is plunged into a frozen, alien world of police
surveillance, scarcely veiled threats, and lies. Doomed
always to be one step behind the shadowy figures he
pursues, only Wallander's obstinate desire to see that justice
is done brings the truth to light.

'The real test of thrillers is whether you want to spend more
time in the detective's company. I certainly do.'
Sean French, *Independent*

'Mankell is a powerful writer'
Independent

V

VINTAGE

Harvill Crime
in
Vintage

Henning Mankell

FACELESS KILLERS

'Wallander is among the very best fictional crimebusters'
Daily Telegraph

One frozen January morning at 5am, Inspector Wallander responds to what he expects is a routine call out. When he reaches the isolated farmhouse, he discovers a bloodbath. An old man has been tortured and beaten to death, his wife lies barely alive beside his shattered body, both victims of a violence beyond reason. The woman supplies the only clue: the perpetrators may have been foreign. When this is leaked to the press, it unleashes racial hatred.

Kurt Wallander is a senior police officer. His wife has left him, his daughter refuses to speak to him, and even his ageing father barely tolerates him. He works tirelessly, eats badly and drinks his nights away in a lonely, neglected flat. But now, Wallander must forget his troubles and throw himself into a battle against time and against mounting xenophobia. *Faceless Killers* is the first in a series of Kurt Wallander mysteries.

'Mankell is one of the most ingenious crime writers around. Highly recommended'
Observer

V

VINTAGE

Harvill Crime
in
Vintage

Henning Mankell

THE FIFTH WOMAN

'Mankell could turn you to crime'
Daily Telegraph

Four nuns and a fifth woman, a visitor to Africa, are killed in
a savage night time attack. Months later in Sweden, the news
of the unexplained tragedy sets off a cruel vengeance for these
killings.

Inspector Wallander is home from an idyllic holiday in Rome,
full of energy and plans for the future. Autumn settles in, and
Wallander prays the winter will be peaceful. But when he
investigates the disappearance of an elderly bird-watcher he
discovers a gruesome and meticulously planned murder – a
body impaled in a trap of sharpened bamboo poles.

Once again Wallander's life is on hold as he and his team work
tirelessly to find a link between the series of vicious murders.
Making progress through dogged police work and forever
battling to make sense of the violence of modern Sweden,
Wallander leads a massive investigation to find a killer whose
crimes are the product of new realities that make him despair.

'The real test of thrillers is whether you want to spend more
time in the detective's company. I certainly do.'
Sean French, *Independent*

V

VINTAGE

BoHEART

Claire McKenna is a speculative fiction writer from Melbourne, Australia. Claire grew up in Auckland, New Zealand and came to Australia when she was young. Her stories decided to come with her.

A longtime writer of short fiction with a background in environmental sciences, *Monstrous Heart* is Claire's debut novel.

You can follow her on:

 @mckenna_claire
www.clairelmckenna.weebly.com

MONSTROUS HEART

CLAIRE McKENNA

Book One of the Deepwater Trilogy

HARPER
Voyager

Harper*Voyager*
An imprint of HarperCollins*Publishers* Ltd
1 London Bridge Street
London SE1 9GF

www.harpercollins.co.uk

HarperCollins*Publishers*
1st Floor, Watermarque Building, Ringsend Road
Dublin 4, Ireland

First published by HarperCollins*Publishers* 2020

This paperback edition 2021
1

A catalogue record for this book is available from the British Library

ISBN: 978-0-00-833716-2

Set in Sabon LT Std by Palimpsest Book Production Ltd,
Falkirk, Stirlingshire

Printed and bound in the UK by CPI Group (UK) Ltd, Croydon CR0 4YY

MIX
Paper from
responsible sources
FSC™ C007454

This book is produced from independently certified FSC™ paper
to ensure responsible forest management.

For more information visit: www.harpercollins.co.uk/green

For Mum

Book One: Vigil

1

It was only when the Coastmaster

It was only when the Coastmaster turned to remonstrate the old man struggling to load the Siegfried's voluminous trunk that Arden Beacon seized the moment and made her escape.

She sidled behind the wheels of the automobile — a thing callously ostentatious in this wild country — and walked off with such a laboured pretence of a casual stroll that it could not be seen as anything but. With each step she feared Coastmaster Justinian's realization that she was not waiting patiently for him, but had instead slipped his leash.

A sharp turn at a bluestone wall, and then Arden was free.

Out of his sight she felt overcome with relief, and had to lean against the salt-scored stones and gulp chilly air before she felt remotely whole again.

Had it been so long since she wasn't confined like a criminal under house arrest that she didn't know quite what to do with herself? This was the first time since she'd arrived in Vigil that Mr Justinian had allowed her out of the Manse, his huge family estate that overlooked the small, coarse coastal town. The instinct to make a sudden getaway had come with such an awful slug of panic she'd almost been inclined not to move at all.

Hadn't he told her it was *dangerous*, hadn't he told her . . .?

But he'd spent a month telling her these things about Vigil, and her thudding heart and acid stomach were evidence enough of the contempt she held for Mr Justinian, the man who was both the Master of the Coast and her employer. He had made it clear he wanted to be more to her, still. Arden shuddered.

Still, forced to endure his hospitality, Arden had observed Mr Justinian with a calculating eye and taken his measure. She discovered that foremost her host had a predilection towards causing humiliation. It delighted him to be petty, and mean; and so she had grasped the opportunity to be well away from him while his voice still remained fixated on castigating the poor elderly porter.

'You fool, you'll break every dish in that trunk! Put some backbone into it, guy, or I'll have the Magistrate charge you with the damage . . .!'

Mr Justinian would be occupied for quite a while longer. Arden straightened her jacket and skirts and looked down a street undergoing some kind of market day. Market day was trading day in this town where even the dread sea-serpent, *maris anguis*, could find itself pickled in salt and up for sale with the lumpfish. The siren song of trade brought the coastal dwellers out of their hamlets and huts, hauling with them their spoils of the sea. A row of trestle tables fronted anonymous doorways. Each table was topped with the ocean's produce laid out like a museum of grotesque curiosities. For every recognisable ichthyosaur in a zinc tub filled with ice there bobbed something ghastly and incomprehensible; fish with ten eyes, a barnacle the size of a woman's torso.

Arden set off, searching for the experience that would make her brief sojourn into freedom worthwhile, and instead found to her sinking disappointment that her host had not lied to her. Vigil was both grim and drab in appearance and utility. An oily yellow mist shrouded the slate roofs and slunk about the chimney pots, giving everything a murky air. The cold air had a burned and salty miasma, despite it having drizzled earlier. Arden startled at the tootling of foghorns as the fishing boats came into the harbour. People wore the odd uniform of the shore: salt-country linens dipped in flaxseed oil and fish-tallow, shirt-collars embellished in bleached thread, plain hogwool jumpers knitted thick and warm.

All this strangeness, but no real sense of *blood*. No impression of the power that eddied and washed through her own hot northern country like a tide of whispers, that great sympathetic connectedness with the manifestations of life. No *Sanguis*.

Blood was the great divide that separated the country of Lyonne from the wilder climes of Fiction. The talents that had once been so powerful in this land were now all but forgotten. Once upon a long time ago Arden would have found kin here, talented users of blood like herself.

Arden rubbed her hands, and felt the cut-coins beneath her soft leather fingerless gloves catch and tug from where they'd been newly sewn into her palms. Before the Seamaster's guildsman had come into her Portmaster's salty office with bad-news and orders wrapped up in a vellum scroll, she'd kept respectable employment as a lead signaller upon one of the busiest trading harbours in the world. She had been *Sanguis Ignis,* flame-keeper. Respectable.

But with a single request she had been sent south to this place where no *ignis* had been born for a hundred years. Nobody would share what she was. She would be at best a novelty come from far away. At worst . . . well. There was no bottom to that particular pit.

When Arden walked past one market table, a scarred, bearded man touted her in a foreign language. Old Fictish, the dying tongue of the shorefolk of these cold, grey southern oceans. Then he stopped, and stared.

Arden pulled her fine leather coat about her, feeling as much an outsider as she had at any time in her life. If she thought the Fictish people backwards, then they would see her as inexplicably strange, with her sun-embraced complexion, the bright colours of her clothing, and the waxed cotton of her skirt still creamy and un-stained by the oily coal that heated every rude little home here.

'Roe for sale, madam, sturgeon eggs? Would you like a taste?' he repeated in a passable Lyonnian.

'I'm not buying anything today, I'm sorry,' Arden replied, even though she didn't even know what he was trying to sell her, for the mess in front of him was as unlikely to be caviar as it was anything edible. He shrugged, unconcerned with her disinterest, as she was not quite his usual customer anyway.

There wasn't much of a town centre to be had, and soon she found herself back on the waterfront again, where six feather-footed dray horses provided the counterweight to a pulley and a load bound for an overladen cargo boat. Arden stayed to watch at the marvel of such a thing, for in Lyonne's capital city of Clay Portside a *sanguis pondus* could make a counterweight weigh whatever it had to, ten tonnes if needed, and no effort was required except a simple pulley. Just as she suspected, no blood here in the country of Fiction, no control over elemental forces, just pure labour.

From the waterfront she had her best view yet of Vigil clawing itself from the sea as a hillocky mess of factories and trade offices fronting a sheltering port. The region played host to fish-processing warehouses, one merchant hotel, and a clumping of lonely, ugly little houses with tiny windows. It had not always been so miserable and backwards, perhaps. At one stage in the recent past there had been an effort to modernize the town, for wires still occasionally strung between lamp posts, evidence of *elektrifikation*, that startling new technology. Yet on closer inspection the wires hung lax and broken, the lamps in their curlicued galleries browned out, their internal globes grey with a fine ash from where the filaments had charred away.

A shout and Arden whirled about, expecting to have been discovered by her jailer.

Instead of Mr Justinian however, it was a rotund man with a publican's medallion about his neck, fleeing his own establishment. Vigil's lone merchant inn, the *Black Rosette*, was at three storeys high the largest building in town, ramshackle in stone base and tin cladding. The entirety of the ground floor seemed to have become a cross between a pub and charnel house, for whatever drama was going on inside the Black Rosette tavern, it caused not a few strangled shrieks and cries for mercy.

A man in an oily duffel coat staggered out of the warped saltwood doors, barking for reinforcements. In answer, three men ran in. An intense curiosity made Arden linger a moment. Not more than a breath later, the fight that had begun in the Black Rosette's stifling interior burst its banks and spilled out across the fish-gut cobbles of the Vigil waterfront.

Two men, caught in a savage embrace. It was a hopelessly unequal combat, for one was bearish and older, armed with twelve dangerous inches of boning knife, the other a slighter man blinded by a bloody gash across his forehead.

The boning knife darted towards the younger man's pale chest and snarled itself in the grey linen of its victim's shirt. Tied up in threads the two men fell against a table burdened with a decapitated ichthyosaur head, narrowly missing the row of serrated teeth as the scuffle took them past the carcass, and in doing so they collected Arden, inconveniently in the fight's way.

'Oh!' she cried, and struck the ground with her shoulder, felt her coat tear and a hot pain flower from her elbow.

The fall gave them all only a brief pause. The men were back at each other immediately, locked hand-over-hand around the boning blade while Arden rolled onto her back, stunned and breathless. Beside her the two brutes reached a violent stalemate over control of the knife.

Someone grunted a curse-word in Old Fictish. The older man took higher ground, rolled upon his opponent and pinned him to the cobblestones. The blade-steel blurred in the fringes of her vision before stabbing into a cobble-join inches from Arden's nose.

'Devilment!' she cried out. 'Watch yourselves!'

In that sliver of breath between his living and dying, the younger man's head turned towards Arden. She met a pair of eyes from the distance of a hand span, and all she could see was dark iris in a bloodied face, inhuman almost, and yet . . .

There was there a broken nobility that did not belong on

a monster's face . . . and a suffering too, of the kind one only saw in children, or the carvings of salvagewood saints in poor-man's churches. They were close enough to kiss. A second ago either one of them could have died from a blade through the skull.

The knife lay between them, the white bone handle splatted with blood.

An old dockworker's instinct made Arden snatch the knife out of the cobbles and toss the blade away before either man could retrieve it. Then the demonic face was gone and the brawl was back up again, this time a thankful distance away. Arden picked herself up, chest cavity twanging with pulled ligaments and crushed organs, the fine leather sleeve of her only coat torn to shreds, the skin on her elbow pebbled with rash. The men continued to heave bloody-fisted blows at each other.

How could you have missed a bar fight? Arden scolded herself as she brushed away stringy intestines and grey pebbles. She should have known that dance in three acts all too well; the gust of hot, hop-heavy wind from the flung-open tavern doors, the roil of spilled bodies and flailed fists, and the denouement where someone came close to joining the lamentable list of tavern-deceased.

The younger of the combatants had clearly grown weary of this entertainment, taking only two more hard punches to the torso before turning the fight to his advantage. An upward thrust of hip, and he upended the bearish man onto the cobblestones.

Without a word to yield or surrender, the victor took to pummelling the snarling face of the conquered until a flap of skin sheared clean off the eye socket. Blood across the stones. Blood thundering through Arden's arteries, for suddenly she could feel . . .

Sanguis? No, it was impossible. The talent was gone from here. It must be her panic, making her sense power where there was none.

Something small and wooden escaped the tangle. Not a

weapon this time. A turned black mangrove-wood handle with a screw thread of brass, such as would prime the oil in a ship's pilot-light.

The handle rolled several feet before bumping against the toe of Arden's now woefully scuffed patent leather shoe. She was loath to touch it, for the handle's owner was upright now, a demon-faced man, taller and more brutish than she had thought him at first, his pale chest working like bellows as the blood runnelled from the broken skin of his knuckles. She could not even tell the colour of his hair, for blood from his forehead now coated his scalp with a wave of sheeny black.

How quick the fight had been, how expedient, how unnaturally *silent*.

In Lyonne, police or militia would have crowded around the scene in an instant. Strangers would have pulled the two apart. Shrieks and screams. Accusals might have been shouted and another fight start elsewhere, for in the big city such emotions were as infectious as a plague.

And she would *not* have been left to stand there unassisted in a state of fish-and-cobble-tumbled mess.

The street took on the hush of a sermon. The priest of this hard message spat blood from his mouth and indifferently wiped gore from his beard. He glared about at his witnesses, challenging the other equally bestial fellows ashine in their waxed canvas and fishmongers' overalls to step forward and make their claim.

Nobody spoke. They averted their eyes from him, and went back to what they were doing in the dreary marketplace before the necessary interruption that passed as a trade discussion in this place. A few adjusted the coin they were charging for their bloodied sacks of produce, scrawling higher prices on the slates before facing them outwards again.

Arden sighed at her own hesitations, then with a groan of effort picked up the screw-thread handle, and held it out to its owner.

'I presume yours?'

His attention was upon Arden for less than a second, only long enough for them to acknowledge to each other that she was insignificant and he was grotesque. Despite the muck, she noticed his bearing at once. He was different enough from the locals that she understood why he might attract the ire of fellows naturally suspicious of differences. His body was raw-boned and spare, hewn by necessity. His bloodied beard was a lighter brown than was usual on these shores, and in danger of gingering. There was no sign of the pelt of full-torso hair which appeared to grow abundantly on the Fiction men as if in response to the bitter climate, or the barrel chest built to tackle a fully laden net of monkfish. Though his arms were unmarked, under the tatters of his clothes she spied tattoos blooming across his back and flanks, a pattern of blue fish-scale chevrons, as if he were a selkie interrupted mid-transformation, and had decided to stay on land rather than the sea.

Stayed on land for love, she thought ridiculously, then immediately berated herself, for who could love such a terrifying creature enough that he should return it in kind?

She had thought his eyes dark, but they were Fiction-blue. A common shade. Eyes that averted as he took the handle out of Arden's hands, shoved it back into his belt and returned to the tavern to resume whatever conversations had perpetuated such a disagreement.

Not even a thank-you. His victim lay bleeding on the street, forgotten.

The fight might have been silent, but that did not mean it had gone unnoticed. Mere minutes later the person Arden had been trying to avoid before the fight made his unwelcome reappearance.

He slid in behind her, exhaling a loud indignant rasp of breath in her ear. His voice followed, both sulky and wheedling. 'You saw the fight? It is the way things are settled here in Fiction, in blood and violence. The ignoble creatures of the Darkling Coast do not bargain with words, if they consent to bargain at all.'

Then there it was, the male body pressing insistently against her back, pretending support, but hoping for the other thing too. A sharp stab of irritation made Arden grimace. She pulled away from him and affected a smile of bewildered relief, as if his appearance baffled her utterly.

'Coastmaster Justinian, I'd wondered where you'd gotten to.'

'What happened? I said explicitly for you to remain close.'

'I'd thought you were following me, when I said I was going to look at the market. Then I was lost in the crowd. I didn't realize you were only instructing the old man, and not exactly helping him.'

His eyes narrowed. Peacock he might have been, but Mr Justinian was not stupid. There was hardly a crowd on a Vigil market day. Arden had evaded him. No mere accident had made her slip away while his back was turned.

'You do understand you may call me Vernon, now? We are not strangers to each other.'

His hand slithered about her waist. The flinch was instinctive. Handsome he might have been, with his coif of pomaded hair and smooth chin, his height six foot by the old measure, grey eyes the colour of an institutional slate, perhaps some hint of a tan to his skin that a distant and more noble ancestor had begrudgingly gifted.

But something in the Coastmaster's features was small and bitter. *Snivelling*. As if the world owed him more than the sizable portion he'd been given, and he resented any other soul who merely received a fraction of his advantages.

For a woman newly arrived at this town under the employ of the powerful Seamaster's Guild, Coastmaster Justinian was the only thing close to an equal associate she had. Even though she was *sanguis* and he was not, they were both of them isolated aristocrats in a way, graduated from Northern technical academies, degree-holders beholden to the great service Guilds that linked the two countries into one fraternal parliament. It made a sort of sense that they should cultivate a professional partnership.

The man's constant touching, well, that was merely a Fiction trait, was it not? Certainly, the cold weather made even bare acquaintances huddle.

'. . . now you have made a fool of yourself by running off unaccompanied.' Mr Justinian continued to scold Arden while steering her towards the row of trestles that made up the last of the marketplace stalls. 'Fortunately you must only contend with appearing slovenly in public.'

She held the sharp tongue in her head that would have corrected him, *I have seen more and bloodier dock fights than this one, and I'd prefer a hundred of them rather than one more day with you.*

These things she would have said, if her position in Vigil was not so dreadfully fraught and insecure. Though she had taken her orders dutifully, coming to Fiction had meant abandoning her secure signaller's position in Clay Portside. If she lost this one, she would be effectively over-specialized and unemployed. This was a bad position for a *sanguis* to be in.

So Arden kept her counsel, and stored the little nuisance in a mental glory box of accumulated offences.

Mr Justinian steered her back towards the main street with its row of trestles while maintaining his lecture.

'. . . the worst of the reprobates operate out of that establishment and upon these streets. See? *This* is why I have kept you in the safety of the Manse all this time, despite your obvious lack of gratitude. I have saved you from the worst outcomes that occur when men gather.'

'They rather seemed more concerned with their own arrangements,' Arden said, pulling away from him, and gladly so, for the Coastmaster's hands were never content to rest upon her middle and had the unfortunate habit of crawling up towards the undersides of her bosom or the smallest part of her back. 'My standing there was completely accidental.'

'Oh, so you think yourself lucky for having escaped their attention?' Mr Justinian said mulishly.

'I do, in fact.'

He picked at the ruined sleeve of her coat. 'Go buy a replacement for your torn coat and charge it to the Guild. Then we can leave this place. But don't wander.'

I'll wander off however I like, you insipid creature, Arden thought ferociously, her anger a physical pain that could not be soothed by her speaking the curse aloud, so remained inside her like a swallowed coal that did not cease to burn.

Arden picked in despondent indecision at the mess of fisherman's clothing with gloves too fine for a village on the edge of nowhere, until her arms smelled of fishwax and linseed oil.

She had wasted so much time shut inside Mr Justinian's decaying baronial estate, and at her first breath of liberty all she'd been allowed to see were street-fights and offal sellers. Despair – always so close and so suffocating – had fermented in her time under curfew. She had heard the domestic staff talk behind closed doors or under stairs. To them, Arden Beacon was not a professional guildswoman sent from the great ports of Clay Portside. She was merely produce fatted up for the eventuality of Mr Justinian's bed.

'A devil's curse upon you, Mr Justinian,' she said beneath her breath, tossing aside a scale-speckled pair of trousers, 'and curse you, Mr Lindsay, for—'

The bronze flash caught her by surprise, stopped at once the bleak train of her thoughts. What imagination was that, her seeing such a thing in all these stained linens and thistle-cottons?

Arden dug in deep again and disinterred her find – an odd, slightly sheened garment – out from the knot of unwashed rags.

She raised to the day a thing that in her hands made no sense.

A coat. A stout, utilitarian coat cut for a female worker of hard ocean climates. Not too long in the hem though; no loose fabric to foul a hurried journey up stone steps in a high storm. A thing rightly made of old canvas and felted wool, worn on a body until it fell to pieces.

But the fabric . . .

Arden had to rub the collar with her fingers, make certain her earlier fall was not causing her to see wonders. There was only one creature alive that could supply such a hide. Leather as bright as an idol's polished head and with a crust of luminescent cobalt-blue rings across the arms and yoke. Subtle grading to black when it hit the light just so.

She turned the coat around and her breath caught. She had not expected the fabled *kraken crucifix*, the terrifying pattern of a sea-monster's crest. By all the devils of sky and blood, you'd have found its likeness only in a Djenne prince's wardrobe in Timbuktu, not a filthy rag pile at the edge of the world, and yet here it was; hidden away with thrice-mended broadcloth trousers and sweaters that were more knots than knits.

Before Arden could inquire about the article, her benefactor already had his hand about the coat's collar.

'Let me put that aside for you,' Mr Justinian said and, without asking, slid in between her and the table, ready to yank Arden's prize away. 'This is not suitable.'

Despite her relatively short stature, and the dark, fragile air of over-breeding about her, Arden was no pushover. Growing up within the labyrinthine map of the capital city docks, one learned in the hardest of ways those streetwise traits anybody needed to survive. She saw the snatch coming in Mr Justinian's beady eyes before he made his move, and quickly secured the coat within her strong lantern-turner's hands.

'No, Mr Justinian. I wish to buy it for myself.'

'These wares are filthy. Look at them. Fish-guts and giblets. You are required to own a new coat to work the lighthouse, not cast-offs. As Coastmaster of Vigil I will have a fine plesiosaur leather coat made for you and sent from Clay Capital.'

'I am not fulfilling your list by this purchase, Coastmaster Justinian. This coat is for my –' she doubled down on her grip '– *personal* use.'

'I'm telling you, you do not *want* it!'

He yanked harder, with enough force to pull Arden off her feet had the trestle corner not caught her thigh. She wedged herself deep into the splintering wood and hung on for grim life. Her ribcage groaned from the earlier trauma, sent sharp currents of pain through her chest, but still she held on.

'No.'

'Let . . . it . . .'

'No, sir, no!'

They struggled for a while in stalemate, before he gave in with a hissed curse.

'Keep the disgusting thing if you must,' he said, tossing his end of the coat down. Arden heard the snarl under his disdainful words. 'It is only a murdered *whore's* garment anyway.'

2

A whore clothed herself

'A *whore* clothed herself in this rag,' he concluded with caustic passion. 'A *bitch* who lay down with an *animal* and got herself killed for it.'

His curse words spoken, and with God having not struck him from the face of the earth for saying them, Mr Justinian shoved the trestle table once for emphasis, then stalked off across the town square towards the Black Rosette.

Arden exhaled, prickling with both triumph and remorse. She had won something over Mr Justinian, but at what cost?

The jumble seller, a stout grey-haired woman with the pale vulpine features of a Fictish native, remained cheery in the face of Arden's dismissal.

'You'll get used to the muck and bother here, love. Once our Coastmaster gets a pint of rot into him, all will be back to normal.'

'I must apologize,' Arden said with forced brightness to the jumble seller. 'Ours was not a disagreement we should have made you witness to.'

'The young Baron is correct about the krakenskin, I'm afraid.' The woman shook the violet threads of ragfish intestines off a pair of trousers that looked identical to the ones she herself wore. 'The coat is a cast-off and completely unsuitable for any purpose.'

'But it's hardly used. I need a wet-coat to work the lighthouse. Only krakenskin could reliably stand all the weather that the ocean might throw at it.'

'The lighthouse? You mean Jorgen's lighthouse?' The woman shifted her now-nervous attention over Arden's shoulder. The horizon behind the town was mostly obscured by fog, but a good five or ten miles away as the crow flew the land curved into a hooked finger of stone. At the very tip of the promontory a granite tower stood erect as a broken thumb, a single grey digit topped with a weakly flashing light.

'I am Arden Beacon, Lightmistress, Associate Guildswoman and *Sanguis Ignis* from Clay Portside, the traders' city of Lyonne,' Arden recited, still unfamiliar with her official titles. She held out her gloved hand. 'I have come from Clay Portside in Lyonne to take over the lighthouse operation from my late uncle, Jorgen Beacon.'

'A sanguinem?' The woman frowned at the offered hand. 'All the way out here?'

'It's all right,' Arden said. 'Touch doesn't hurt me.'

Still cautious, the woman shook Arden's hand timidly, her eyes still on the pony-plantskin gloves, so fine compared to the ubiquitous bonefish leather of the coast. Was not the gloves she minded, but what lay *under* the gloves that gave the woman pause. The coins. The little metal spigots that were both symbol and necessity of her trade.

Arden did not take offence. The reaction would be the same in Lyonne, among the commonfolk. The woman was gentle, and released her quickly.

'Oh, I wasn't minding your hands, dear. I was surprised that Jorgen was replaced so quickly when we could have well put a distillate lamp in there and be done with all the sadness.'

'The Guild is very protective of its properties. That flame has been kept alive by *sanguis* for centuries, and they'd not likely stop now. Anyhow, what is the price of the c —'

'Now that you say it,' the woman interrupted, 'I see the resemblance to Jorgen in you, that Lyonne high breeding, so *elegant.*' She simpered a little, trying to curry favour with a rich woman from the hot North country. A rich sanguis woman, possessed of esoteric skills. 'I am Mrs Sage. My husband is both apothecary and doctor in our town centre.' Mrs Sage waved towards a rude row of wood and brick that even in Clay Portside would have been considered little more than ballast shacks. 'We were told of Lightmaster Beacon's passing, and that a blood-talented relative would soon replace him from the North, but . . . We expected a *brother.*'

'All my uncle's brothers have permanent Lightmaster positions in Clay Portside,' Arden explained, annoyed that she would now have to have this conversation, and justify her sex, again. In Lyonne there would have been no question of her capabilities – labour was labour, regardless of the source. 'I was the only one not contracted to any gazetted navigation post, and the Guild requires a sanguinem to crew their stations, so . . .' She shrugged. 'The Seamaster's Guild requested that the Portmaster of Lyonne provide someone of the talent to take his place. So here I am. Buying a coat—'

'Just like that?'

'Well, the Seamaster's Guild does have to administrate a lot of coastline. I cannot shirk a duty.'

Mrs Sage shook her head that Arden had not questioned such a direction. 'It's not right, a woman sent out to those rocks alone . . .'

'The Portmaster of Clay is also my father,' Arden said with a theatrical display of generous patience at Mrs Sage's concern, so desperate was she to conclude this sale. 'He understands more than anyone what my abilities are. He also understands that if there is not a Beacon at that lighthouse, it will go to a Lumiere or, God forbid, a Pharos, and,' she stopped to give the most forced of smiles, '*ignis* families are very competitive for those positions offered us. It would break his heart for our family to lose another lighthouse post.'

'Still. It pains me to sell you this coat, Lightmistress Beacon. I must refuse.'

Arden saw the coat sliding away in the manner of a barely glimpsed dream. She clutched it tighter.

'Then why have it for sale if you won't accept my purchase?'

Mrs Sage smoothed a sou'wester out upon its pile. Her red, chapped hands rubbed the linseedy surface of the rain hat. 'I was hoping one of the ambergris merchants from Morningvale might buy it today, and take it far away from here. Sell this garment for a profit in a city where nobody knows its source. The young Baron was correct. The woman who owned this coat is dead.'

Murdered whore. Coastmaster Justinian had delivered the words with such venom, meant to hurt with all the force of a slap. Why had it concerned a Coastmaster so much, this discard on a rag-trader's table?

'Poor girl. The wife of the brute who killed her,' Mrs Sage continued. 'When her corpse was at last recovered from the water over yonder, all that remained was her scalp of golden hair and this coat, washed up upon the harbour shore.' She tilted her chin towards Vigil's small, pebbled waterfront, lying a short way down the rotting boardwalk. 'Perhaps it was merciful, after all those months she suffered in the bed of a monster, that death should claim her so she might not suffer any more. But still, what an end. Slaughtered, and your meat used as a fisherman's bait.'

Mrs Sage sounded so resignedly matter-of-fact at such an ignominious and unlikely method of dying that Arden couldn't help but snort a laugh at her story.

The woman glared at Arden with brittle offence. 'How else do you think the fisherman calls a sea-devil up from the deep by its own volition, to harvest it for such a fine leather, eh?'

And Arden saw then, the true price of the coat would be in her providing Mrs Sage an audience for a tale, a story that by the aggressive delight in her rheumy eyes was a particularly unpleasant one.

Mrs Sage dipped in close to Arden. Her breath stank of fish chowder and dandelion root.

'These abyssal monstrosities, the kraken, the *maris anguis* and *monstrom mare*, they can only be compelled to surface by human meat. The fresher the better. They are drawn by gross desires and mutilations. There's only so much of a slaughterman's own body he can give. A toe, a finger, a slice of tongue or a testicle, hmm?' Mrs Sage sucked her lined lips in thought, imagining the kind of man that would take a blade to himself for his profession. 'An eye, a hand, a penis most probably, for in what world would anyone fornicate in consent with such an unholy creature as a man who feeds himself in fragments to the sea?'

'I don't—'

'Yes, was him that killed his poor young wife for profit, slice by agonizing slice, and the coat made to clothe her, and remind her just what her sacrifice brought. What other worth was she to him? He had not the tool with which to *fuck*, and from that lamentable position her life was foreshortened indeed.'

Arden recoiled, taken aback by the salacious details of Mrs Sage's story. 'Ah, all right then, thank you for the, um . . . providential lesson.'

'Was no lesson. Was *caution*, Lightmistress.' Her eyes widened. 'Was *warning*.'

Having exhausted her social resilience, Arden hurriedly dug into her purse and took out every note inside it, a wad of Lyonne cotton-paper bills that were not legal tender in Fiction, but all she had. Shoved them at Mrs Sage.

'Here, here, take this money. I'll make sure I give this coat a proper new life.'

Mrs Sage smiled and made motions of pious refusal, then took the money anyway. Her tongue pushed through the gaps in her teeth. Both pity and triumph she showed, as she made her announcement.

'But you are still in the *old life*, Lightmistress. T'was for that reason I hoped you'd be male. If you are bound for the old lighthouse, then see that murderous hybrid of man and monster over there?'

Mrs Sage pointed past the grey haggle-hordes of the market plaza. Beyond the ice-baskets, one figure walked apart from the fishermen, shrugging into the same copper-black-coloured garment that Arden held in her hand. The man from the tavern fight. The demon. The victor.

Next to him, a handcart without a horse. Upon it was laden the raw, bleeding tail of a leviathan.

'See that one? *Mr Riven*, he goes by, the monster of Vigil. That, my poor dear, is your new neighbour.'

3

Oh dear

'Oh dear,' Dowager Justinian said, her thin mouth drooping further once she saw Arden Beacon on the afternoon of her market adventure. 'I didn't quite believe my son when he told me of what happened this morning. You got the Riven-wife's coat.'

Arden brushed the perpetual wet from her dress. 'Was Mr Justinian terribly upset? I rather let him go his own way afterwards.'

'I had not the chance to ask my son his full opinion,' the Dowager said. Her eyes darted evasively behind her black gossamer veil. Dead a full decade her husband had been, and yet she still wore the same silks as for a planned funeral march. 'I have been busy today.'

The Dowager was a thin, regal woman who may have once been warm in her beauty and generosity. Years on Fiction's bleak coast had turned her sallow. The jewellery which she wore upon her constant uniform of black mourning had more in common with dull chunks of quartzite than the diamonds their settings suggested.

'Well, there's not much that can be helped, you weren't to know about the histories of our town. I'll have tea brought to your room.'

'Thank you. I'd like tea.' Arden noticed a small pile of correspondence on the sideboard. 'Are there any letters from my family?'

'Not since the ones from last week. The mail is slow, here.'

There were however some postcards from some old academy friends, mostly of mountains and chalets in daisy-meadows, for the summers were hot in Clay and those who could afford to escape to alpine hostels, did. Arden read the brief messages with a combined muddle of gladness and envy, and doubted finding any similar image to encapsulate Vigil when she wrote in return. Maybe a heavy-set fisherman in gumboots, waxed overalls and a gigantic cable-knit sweater, standing by a wicker basket of headless eels.

The Dowager followed Arden up the creaking stairs of Manse Justinian. The estate house had been built on an escarpment of basalt, and by its position looked down upon the town and much of the shaggy scrub of the Fiction peninsula. The family occupied less than a quarter of its space. In her first days, Arden had found herself easily lost in entire abandoned wings, stripped of furniture and fittings. Swallows nested in the faded walls, flitted through empty corridors. A cold wind moaned through broken windows. Powdered mortar fell from the brickwork at each strong gust, and if one day the house would fall, it would not be a day far distant.

Behind Arden, the woman's black skirt hem whispered ill-gossip against the bare floorboards. By the bleach on the wood Arden suspected the stairs had worn carpet runners once, such as that found in a Bedouin tent-palace, but such valuable things rarely survived the harsh, damp climates south of Lyonne.

Besides, barony or no barony, a Coastmaster's salary could not afford to deck even a quarter of a country estate out in the manner of its Northern equivalents. The house rested on a precipice of decay, the way a family mausoleum will crumble after the last casket is interred. The men in each candle-smoked portrait lining the walls had all long since passed on. Any other images were daguerreotypes and tinplate prints, things one could obtain with half an hour of a photographer's time.

Strangely, no women's faces had been seen fit to add to the cheerless décor. The Justinian line seemed to have sprung like gods, each generation from the other's forehead without need of a woman at all. Going by the profiles she saw as she squinted in the candlelight, the line had grown a little less vital with each passing iteration, until only Mr Justinian was left at the far corner, his photographed face dilute and chinless.

A little like the blood talent that had drained from Fiction itself, Arden thought.

The Dowager did not leave when Arden laid the krakenskin coat out on her small, slender guest bed.

On first arriving at the house twenty-five days previously, Arden had asked the Dowager privately for a room with a lockable door. A request she could not make of the son.

Dowager Justinian had been surprised at Arden's wishes, for the Coastmaster's Manse was patrolled by dogs and a quartet of retired soldiers in her employ. She had granted Arden the room with its hard, narrow bed and a window little bigger than a postage stamp, despite it being hardly a fifth of the size of the guest house Mr Justinian had first expectantly offered.

Still, for three nights in a row Arden had heard footsteps on the landing, the sound of the knob being turned until the lock snapped tight in the jamb. Those nights she drew her bedclothes to her chin and clutched hard the small knife of her profession.

The night visitor never tried to defeat the lock. With entry thwarted, the footsteps would only linger for a moment before moving on.

Now in the dim light of the small room, the blue kraken-cross glowed, an entirely different kind of uninvited visitor. A sullen phosphorescence in each mottled spot, unearthly and benthic. The cut came from the head of the beast, where the fabled *kraken crucifix* graced the cranium of a bull male at full maturity, one of the few places upon that immense, strange body that could be preserved and tanned. Rarely would any one animal produce enough usable leather for half a garment, let alone the panels for a complete coat. Those pieces never even made it to Clay Capital, Lyonne's largest city. They were sold to foreign princes or corporate scions, displayed in glass cabinets and only worn during coronations or lying-in-states. A strange call had drawn Arden to this coat in the market.

A murdered whore's garment.

Arden stroked the decorative leather tooling at the jacket's sleeve. Pretty, but not stamped in deeply enough for permanency. A too-tentative hand had struck the die on these clumsy patterns. A woman's hand, she guessed, one unused to those sharp instruments that her brothers all their lives had been allowed access to. Probably sewn the leather as well, judging by the tiny, precise stitches that suited a formal dress better than a coat. A woman's labour in the threads. Places such as Fiction did not tend towards providing their sons a fully rounded education. Despite an innate skill at leather-work, Clay Portside tailors did a roaring trade in repairing breeches that clueless southernmost men could not repair themselves.

'It's such a beautiful thing,' Arden said. 'I can't imagine anyone just throwing it away, no matter how it came into their possession.'

'I can imagine the beast it once was.' The Dowager's black mourning-dress hushed against the cold hearthstones as she went to the miserly fireplace, where the embers of the night before still collected under the ash. She agitated them with an iron poker, adjusted the flue so they would have air to last them into the evening.

Arden wondered if she would see one, at least once, and if it would be as magnificent and terrifying as her books, and beautiful as the coat upon her bed. An entire mountain of copper-body, sinuous beneath the ocean, with arms as long as a steam train of twenty carriages, a pupil so large she could stumble through.

The Dowager seemed to have heard an inkling of her thoughts and said, 'By the time any specimen makes it into town, it is already cut up for processing. And thank goodness for that. They are hideous. Such arms and legs. Those cold eyes, such unholy thoughts. I've heard they grow large enough to consume a whale, or a bull plesiosaur.' She shuddered. 'A plesiosaur can grow as big as two elephants, so you can make your own decision as to exactly how much monster we are speaking of.'

'You've actually seen one, Madame Justinian? *Monstrom mare*? Or is it *mostri marino* here?'

The Dowager's poker thrust hard into the ash and disinterred a still-flaming coal.

'*Monstrom mare*,' she said. 'Once, when I was a girl in Manhattan, I saw a kraken chick washed up upon an oyster-shell beach. Very immature, just a baby really, but each leg was twenty paces long. The old Emperor Krakens never approached so close to shore, there. It is different in Fiction. The creatures are indigenous to Vigil, and in these waters they breed and die.'

A silence descended upon the small, chill room. Though she was mostly Lyonne by blood, Dowager Justinian hailed from that great country far west of the Summerland Sea, in a small village between two rivers called Manhattan, at the province's south border. Her mother tongue was Lyonne-Algonquian, that great trader's language that most spoke with some measure of fluency. However had a Vinlander ended up on this windswept Fiction coast, presiding over an immense family estate with a husband who seemingly, based on his portraits, had never aged?

Breeding and death perhaps. That was always the way.

Arden pushed aside the lace curtain at the small window, where beyond the sad patches of lawn and holly oak trees – stunted by the wind and salt – the patient expanse of Vigil's shallow bay lurked. Giants lived in that place, creatures that had endured the aeons that had made extinct their ancestors. Every dream or terror that existed in a sailor's lonely night moved and surfaced in those waters. *Here be dragons.*

And somewhere in the fog was her lighthouse, waiting for her.

She had not entirely been truthful with Mrs Sage today, when she had said the Seamaster's Guild had requested she to go to

Vigil – and that her father approved. They had merely relayed the instruction. The request came from altogether another, deeper branch of government, and one not entirely known for sincerity.

Her Portmaster father had not been pleased at the Guild orders. Had begged her not to go. But she had gone anyway, because of what had been promised. It was worth risking everything. Before she'd departed for Vigil, Portmaster Beacon had taken Arden aside. This post was an unlikely request from them, he'd cautioned her. He'd fought hard for her to receive her little signaller position after she'd matured so late and so weak in her talent. The Seamaster's Guild had been reluctant in even that small concession. Now here she was, being offered a prime flame-keeper's position . . . in Fiction granted, but still a full-degree holder posting.

Refuse the post, Daughter. I fear you are in the sight of Lions. If you agree to go to Fiction you will be a puppet. It's not for Fire they've called you. Just give me the word, and I won't sign your release papers.

She should have taken his advice, but an odd, resentful stubbornness had made Arden disagree with her father.

And yet . . .

It's not for Fire they've called you.

The Dowager spoke then, interupting Arden's thoughts. 'The season is too early for kraken, they come in deep winter, most of the time. If the fisherfolk can bring in at least one or two small hens, it will certainly stave off the hungry months.'

'That's good,' Arden replied absently, her mind still on her father's reproach. Had he been right and her wrong? What if the Lyonne Order only wanted her to stay in this mansion for a Coastmaster who desires to have a high-bred wife?

'Yes the kraken are important to our economy, and that's why the Riven man is tolerated here, despite what he did to his wife.'

'*Suspected* to have done, I assume, given that he's still living among you.'

'Suspected.' The Dowager nodded at the coat. 'Because he can bring the giants to shore in the winter time.'

'They're worth covering up a murder?'

'Krakenskin is precious. Not just for leather.' The Dowager picked up the coat and stroked it reverently. 'Keep the skin wet, put it on the deepest burn and there will be no scar. The ground-up beak is medicinal against all sorts of tumours and growths. Kraken eye-jelly dissolves cataracts, can make the blind see. The oil is health tonic for a heart, and fuel and perfume, and is far more expensive than either jasmine, civet or ambergris.' She nodded. 'The flesh makes for a fine meal, if the fishermen butcher it early enough.' The Dowager counted the treasures off as if they were the accounts of a banker.

'I heard the monsters are worshipped as gods, here.'

'Yes. They once were. The old religion is gone now, but we still host many tourists in this Manse during Deepwater season, the winter time. There is even a masque on the longest night, where men dress up like a sea-serpent and rampage through the town until a king is crowned among them, for a day. More than one child owes their beginning to the Deepwater Night. More than one dispute finds its permanent end as well.'

'It sounds very, ah . . . primitive.'

'They love their brutalities, do our Vigil folk. And with its history, and that devotion, are you sure you want to keep that odd coat? It would fit no sea dog of course, but a good tailor could unpick the seams and marry the panels with a dress suit. I could get you an entire bonefish wardrobe for the price of the leather.'

Arden shook her head. 'I could never destroy such a beautiful thing. It would be a desecration. More to the point, this coat is equipment I need. I will be able to attend my duties at the lighthouse and relieve Mr Harris sooner, especially now that I don't have to worry about freezing to death.'

'I am surprised you are not out there already.'

Arden bundled up the coat so that it might fit into the steamer trunk she kept under the bed.

'Mr Justinian has such concern for my wellbeing, you see.' Her irritation prickled her tongue. 'He will not sign a certificate for the interim Lightkeeper's release until he is certain I am *ready*. He has undertaken to prepare an extensive list of equipment.'

She didn't add that she'd never heard of a keeper charged with such a list, full of items not so easy to obtain and that required delivery via a postal network that worked only when certain people felt that it should. Poultices for exotic ailments and shipping encyclopaedias for irrelevantly distant shores. Hot-water heaters and a strange pachyderm-fibre blanket rather than the goat-hair one that suited just as well. Three kinds of leather shoe, the manufacture of which could be carried out only in Portside. An expensive coil of Mi'kmaq coal-ether rope, for no purpose whatsoever. What was wrong with Lyonne-laid coir?

'My son has been a Vigil Coastmaster and proxy for the Lyonne Seamaster's Guild for quite some time too, Mx Beacon. You have a dangerous position out there, literally between the devil and the deep blue sea. I'm sure he knows what he is doing.'

'I need to start my *job*, Madame Justinian. *Soon*. The chemistry of the perpetual flame requires tending by a sanguinem, and if it goes out, the Lyonne Navy will be down here in a flash wondering why half their marine fleet is littering the rocks of the promontory.' She widened her eyes for emphasis. 'I can't imagine what the Seamaster's Guild will say if they start getting invoices for fuelling a regular lamp.'

The Dowager muttered words in a Manhattanite tongue, gave a little hiss between her teeth. She frowned up at the dusty lamp-covers. 'Ah, it reminds me. Best I light the house lamps for the night. It comes quickly on these shores.'

Arden was being dismissed. The staff could very well have lit the fifty lamps within the Manse themselves and the Dowager could have made a promise to convince her son to hurry up and release Arden to her lighthouse. Instead, even the black-veiled woman seemed complicit in Arden's extended stay.

'I'll give you time to freshen up,' the Dowager concluded, as she lit the first lamp in Arden's room. 'Supper will be in an hour.'

Arden waited impatiently until the Dowager was gone before she opened up the flame-embossed lid of her steamer trunk. Though Mr Justinian's mother was harmless, she was just as guilty of familial designs as her son, and possibly just as curious as to what was stopping Arden from falling into Mr Justinian's arms.

Arden's trunk was her life reduced to a painted tin box, four foot by two. It contained all the certificates of her career as a signaller, ten years as a Lady of the Lights upon the Clay Portside docks. It was an odd paradox that she was both nobility and labourer in a country where there was such a deep and unfathomable division between commonblood folk and the sanguinem with their precious and valuable labours.

She paused before the trunk and studied her gloves before sliding one off. Her hands were strong as any common worker's, with calluses from the endless winding mechanisms of signal-work and canal locks.

But the new coins in her palms made her weak.

A metal disk in the centre of each inflamed hand – a silver moon stitched in between the heart and head-line. They were protective grommets for the act of blood-spilling required to keep the lighthouse fire burning.

The small fires of the signal lights she had tended before had needed far less blood. She hadn't needed the disks before now.

With a hiss of discomfort she pulled the gloves back on and shifted books and papers aside.

'Only a few months,' she said herself. 'Then you'll have everything you ever wanted.' All her shuffling of the contents of the trunk to make way for the coat ended up uncovering a small trinket-chest carved of bone. A small noise escaped Arden's throat.

'Don't open it,' she said to herself sternly. 'Don't open it, Beacon.'

But she couldn't help herself. The enchantment within was too great. Love was venomous, its toxin poisoned you forever. Arden opened the box and the past fell out.

A silver-print on paper floated onto the bedspread, no bigger than her palm. A clean-cut man in an airship officer's uniform looked out at her, his black hair grown long from a military shave, rakishly tilted cap, twinkling, good-natured eyes.

On the back, a blue-ink cursive. *Thinking of you always – Richard.*

The regret hit her hard. A bitter memory came, of a stolen kiss at the Guild Ball a year before. *I'll come back for you,* Richard Castile had said to her. *I will be a Captain at last. We will be married in the winter. Wait for me.*

She had wanted to spirit him away to her apartments that night. But Richard had been evasive, preoccupied. Danced with other women. She'd tried not to be upset. Their love was forbidden, so of course he wouldn't risk affections in public. He'd told her that he had already bought a ring for their upcoming elopement. All she had to do was wait. Fretting would only be foolish.

The cracks in their relationship, so easily ignored, could not be ignored forever.

That Guild Ball was the last time she saw him. He left before dawn on his packet-ship to Vinland. Arden didn't arrive in time to catch him, but had caught instead the girl coming out of his apartment, the one wearing Vinland pearl earrings and the rose-gold stag-brooch of the Castile family crest. Perhaps Richard had told her about Arden, for upon seeing a frantic sanguis marching in her direction the girl had blushed ferociously and ran off, dropping the silver-print in the gutter. Arden was about to call after her when she'd seen the face staring up from the cigarette butts and orange peels.

Richard's face.

Thinking of you always – dr.

The pain had been an assassin's dagger, slid between her ribs. She had always wanted a picture of him, but Richard had constantly refused. Too risky, he said. If an Order agent found an image of a common-blood man in a sanguis trousseau, then he would be demoted, if not worse. Arden was a *Beacon*, that oldest and most ancestrally fortified of sanguine genealogies. She would need to wait for Richard to catch up. Until he was a Petty Officer. Flight Lieutenant. Captain. Or the god-damned King of Lyonne, it seemed. Ten years of waiting, with no end in sight.

She snapped the opal box shut. No. He would never change his mind and she'd not lock the damn krakenskin coat away with her other failures. She would wear it, defiantly and proudly. She shared something with Mr Riven's wife, after all. She too had been betrayed by someone she loved.

Arden stood up from the steamer trunk, the photograph still in her hand. Walked woodenly to the fireplace and threw it in. The flame leapt green, the paper crisped black. His eyes, twinkling and knowing. Eyes saying, *do what you like, lantern girl. It's really because of me that you are out here.*

The eyes were the last to burn.

4

As was the custom

As was the custom in the old aristocratic families, she changed clothes for the main meal. Wore a grey linen shirt with no ruffles, a narrow dress that finished in a fishtail at the top of her boots. Bound her hair in severe knots upon her head. She headed down the bare wooden stairs towards the shabby velvets of the Justinian dining room, quite prepared to continue the argument about her new coat. Despite Mrs Sage's pronouncements and the Dowager's warning, she was feeling combative.

Mr Justinian arrived back from his Coastmaster meetings in the languid sort of mood that comes when one has had those meetings in the Black Rosette tavern over seaweed spirit cocktails, and in the presence of somebody generous with their affections.

He took off his coat – a slate-grey plesiosaur leather he could still ill afford on both a Coastmaster stipend and the dregs of a faded title. He sat at the table with a flourish. Arden huffed an understated disapproval. Mr Justinian knew what he was doing. A war of garments. His coat was an affectation that in Lyonne would have been vulgar, like something a slumlord crime boss would wear to impress the poor tenants. The tanned material had the tough grain of a shark or a ray. Less unfinished versions tended to take away a layer of skin against the poor soul unfortunate enough to brush against it.

Her fellow guests, a man and his wife from South Lyonne, glanced at the plesiosaur coat and kept their own counsel.

To pay running costs, the old Manse ran as a guest house for other important merchants and businesspeople who might wish to make profit off the Darkling Sea. Perhaps it did not make as much of a profit as was required, for to save on fuel not every lamp was lit, so instead of bright, cheery galleries, the large rooms became crepuscular, full of shadows and damp. The old tablecloths, laundered to transparency, were held together by little more than browning claret stains. The silverware would have better been called *mottled nickel with silver-plate patches*, and a century of cigar smoke now blackened the plaster ceiling roses with a dour velvet. In more than one corner, water-rot frayed the plaster walls and caused a drooping of the faded stripe wallpaper. There were not quite enough glasses to fill the display cupboards, and none of the tableware arrangements ever quite made a full set.

Altogether, a house in decline. The guests, already unsettled by the Baron's mobster coat, glanced awkwardly at Arden's fingerless gloves. She rubbed her hands. The bloodletting coins snagged in the oblique arches on the side of her palms. Twanged each time she closed her fist.

'New gloves, Madame?' the husband asked her quietly when Mr Justinian left the table in search of a better wine than the cloudy vinegar they'd been served.

He showed her his Guild pin as he spoke, a railroad degree. Though he himself was not gifted with any endowments, the Permanent Way required many sanguis disciplines, from *ferrum* to *pondus* and *vaporis*. A genteel way of telling Arden that even though he was commonblooded he was familiar and sympathetic to her kind. It had been the reason the trade guilds had originated, to unite their labours into one brotherhood, a fraternity of workers despite their wildly different means.

'I've had my coins about a month,' Arden admitted. 'I'm only now getting used to having them in my skin.' She recalled the little Guildsman who had watched with a clear, genial gaze as the nervous phlebotomist inserted the tools of her new position into her hands. *Mr Lindsay*, his name was. He had been a small, delicate fellow in the tweedy suit of a clerk, and wore a golden pin in the shape of a rose. He'd also been the one to bring the orders to her father.

For the railwayman's benefit, and because she did not want to treat them as shameful or remarkable, she rolled her gloves up slightly and showed him the silver buttons set between the heart and the head lines. Her skin was still a little tender at the edges, and she suspected would not ever truly heal.

'Why in the hands?' asked his wife. 'Isn't it dreadfully more painful to cut your hands?'

Arden nodded. 'I suspect they want us to feel pain. To remind us that power doesn't come without a cost. Hands . . . well they are symbolic in a way no other body part is.'

'I could think of one other symbolic body part,' the wife giggled, before hiccupping wine. Arden saw that in anticipation of another awkward dinner the woman had pre-emptively gotten rather drunk. 'The body part they always mention in those funny little Deepwater rituals, ha! I had that strange Mrs. Sage tell me all the stories of what goes on among those deviant brutes . . .'

The railroad man patted his wife's hand and took the glass off her, before returning to Arden and attempting conversation again.

'You must miss Clay Portside, Lightmistress. I've been there many a times, seen the air-harbours stretch out as far as the eye can see, *sanguis zephyrim* making the aerostats fly and the *pondus* who anchor them to the ground. Produce and trade from all over the world, the menagerie of animals, the babel of tongues! Of all those wonders, this place must seem like the colour has been taken from your eyes.'

She nodded, relieved at the admission. She could have never said such a thing to her hosts. 'I do miss home. One does whatever the Guild asks. Especially if you're sanguis, and there's duty involved.'

'Ah,' he said, as if she had confirmed a suspicion. 'I wondered why a grown sanguis woman should be getting such protection on her flesh when it's the preserve of children. Isn't eleven the most usual age?'

She gave them both a tight smile. 'My blood tithings never required much from me before.' She slid up her dress-sleeve to show the calluses on the back of her arm. 'A cut here would last the better part of a week, and I had no symbolic act required of me.'

'But now your work requires more blood, I see. Hence the disks to protect your skin from the knife.'

'Yes.'

'Did the Lions follow you here, Mx Beacon?' he asked.

A sudden question. His wife pretended to sip her thistledown wine, but Arden could feel her listening on with harp-string tension.

'Lions?'

In her mind she saw the little Guildsman Mr Lindsay smile. Arden took a swallow of her claret, to buy seconds and still the sudden shake of her hand.

'I don't quite know what you mean.'

'The Lyonne Order. The Eugenics Society's attack-dogs.' With his fingers the railwayman made the sign of teeth. 'Did they follow you to Fiction?'

Arden went for her claret again and found she had finished the glass. She knew exactly what he meant. Businessmen in Fiction were not at all keen on coming across Lions of the human kind. She was a sanguis invested late into her profession. Such a thing had the stink of Order activity, their skulking and investigations and sudden disappearances. One would think the powerful Eugenics Society would concern themselves only with policing sanguis folk, but they frequently expanded their purview into the citizenry as well. The guests viewed her with no small suspicion.

'No, was on instruction of the Seamaster's Guild that I take up position here,' Arden replied.

'All the way out here? In Fiction, where the blood has faded?'

'Well, the lighthouse is under the navigation chain of the Lyonne sea-road. It's still a blood light, so it needs a *sanguis ignis* to maintain the flame.'

The wife spoke next, and despite her high spirits she was not as generous with her trust. 'Why not install a petrolactose lamp in that tower? Or a natural gas, which is plentiful here. Why deal with such esoteric chemistries as yours? Whenever there are *sanguis*, there are always Lions. The blood attracts them.'

'See, it is . . .' she drifted off, and paused, for she didn't know either. 'I'm sure it's very mundane,' she capitulated. 'Keeping the trade and Guilds of our two countries aligned through the sea-road navigation chain. My family has always maintained the Vigil light. It would be a loss to lose a station from sheer neglect, even an unimportant one.'

The wife pondered, then visibly relaxed. Arden's explanation seemed sound. If her posting was just a matter of navigation, then there were no Lions about.

The husband drained his wine in one gulp.

'Ah then, let us drink to the trade Guilds, the great fraternities of Lyonne.'

They might have been at ease, but there was already an ill cast to the night. *Did the Lions follow you here?* The Order worked in the shadows and bore no oversight. They should not be meddling in the mere business of keeping a navigation road safe.

It's not for Fire they've called you, warned the father in her mind. And Arden shivered, even though the room pressed in oppressively close and far too warm.

A fourth guest joined them then, a man of middle years and a certain overbearing pomposity. His voice came before him, echoing from the foyer, a complaint about the condition of the roads, the driver who did not give him deference of title.

Mr Justinian called Arden's attention as he re-entered, guest in tow.

'Mx Beacon,' he said. 'I'd like you to meet Mr Alasdair Harrow, the Postmaster and Magistrate of Vigil.'

Despite the size of his voice, Mr Harrow was not particularly tall, had fallen into middle-aged stoutness, yet still possessed the domineering characteristics of his youth. The broad, heavy shoulders of a brawler, a pug nose, a cauliflowered ear. She thought his hair was white, but on closer examination in the gloomy light he was a faded blond.

'A shared title, Postmaster *and* Magistrate?' Arden inquired as she shook the new guest's meaty hand. She wondered that Mr Justinian should be so keen as to introduce her to this fellow when he had never presented Arden to anybody else. The day's excursion to town notwithstanding, Mr Justinian had kept Arden all to himself in the same manner as a dragon might sit jealous upon its hoard. If he could not have her for a night in his bed, then she should be walled up within brickwork isolations of his own making.

'It is difficult to find men suited to all the offices of authority,' Mr Harrow said in a barking pronouncement, not talking to Arden but rather a central place in the room where a silk arrangement of artificial flowers collected dust. 'Especially here, in this town. So, I must fulfil my duties by occupying both roles.'

And drawing a double stipend from the Coast Office, Arden added silently. She gave Mr Harrow a nod and returned to her meal, busied herself in chewing the most inoffensive slice of potted meat, so she would not have to fight for her place in the conversation.

'*Miss* Beacon here intends to take over the lighthouse operations that old Jorgen abandoned,' Mr Justinian said, dragging her back in. 'A request from the Seamaster's Guild themselves.'

Caught drinking, Mr Harrow coughed mid-swallow. 'What's that you say?'

'Jorgen Beacon. This is his niece, a Beacon scion and *sanguis ignis* from Clay Portside, sent all the way from our air-harboured capital city to bring some culture to our humble hamlet, and to keep the old promontory flame alive.'

Mr Harrow stabbed a pink cube of fish. 'I'd not allow it, if it were up to me.'

'Well, it is not up to you,' Arden said.

Mr Harrow did not respond to her. She might have been an empty chair for all that she had spoken. 'More fools in the world than there are decent ideas, Vernon,' he grumbled.

'I have my opinions too,' Mr Justinian said, flicking a look Arden's way. At least he recognized that they were speaking as if she were not there, though presumably because a woman *angry* was not a woman who would be *amenable* later. 'But the Guild was adamant she fill the position.'

'She'll be dead within the week, her corpse twice-ravished, mark my words.' Mr Harrow shoved a grape-melon in his mouth, and the juice ran down his chin. 'Give her a rifle and make sure she knows how to use it. I'll not be called out to the promontory to pick up her body like a damned fool.'

Arden stood with a crash, rattling the tableware. 'Gentlemen, I can manage my own business. I've worked harder docks than this pissant bit of rock!'

Mr Harrow started laughing, barks of laughter. 'They served her up for the slaughter Vernon. To the fucking *slaughter*. Wasn't for her blood they wanted a woman out there. The Guild pimped her to the monster on the promontory, and Riven will rape her bloody and thank them for it.'

The house staff came in at that very moment bearing plates of a flavourless broth that would never have been conscionable to serve in Portside, and in the meantime Arden fumed. The gall of these men. The unmitigated dreadfulness of their words.

A server-girl came by with nothing but cow-eyes for Mr Justinian, and spilled claret on Arden's sleeve with a smirk. Between her jealousy, Mr Harrow's gleeful predictions and Mr Justinian's knavish gloating, Arden was twisted up into a knot of frustration so painful it made her want to scream.

'Excuse me,' she said through a rage-strangled throat. 'I'm not feeling well. I need to get some air.'

She fled the crushing mood of the dining room and ran down the murky corridor, finished in what was either a large study or a small ballroom, a gloomy expanse of sapwood parquetry and mildewed corners.

Past the curtain-rags, a cold moonlight spilled across the polished floor. Arden hauled open the double doors, fell out onto the balcony where the frost clawed her face and her breath steamed. All the menace the night could give was immensely preferable to the atmosphere inside, the terrible delight of men savouring that she be in harm's way.

She sucked down salt air until the tremor in her limbs stopped and her breathing slowed. Gooseflesh sprang on her bare arms, and she welcomed that clean discomfort.

Someone stepped into the room behind her, and imagining it one of the guests who had watched on in deep disquiet at Mr Harrow's performance she said, 'I can't stand it, those uncouth —'

'Then I apologize. It was not my intent to harm.'

Arden startled. If she had gained a modicum of relief by going outside, the feeling was gone. Mr Justinian stood behind her.

Had Arden been of a more histrionic nature she might have considered throwing herself off the balcony, only this balcony was at ground level and the act probably lost much of its meaning when one landed safely on the other side.

'Perhaps I'd prefer ravishment by this Mr Riven than being subjected to your snide gossip upon my sense and my work. At least he's honest in his dreadfulness!'

Mr Justinian huffed. 'All right then. You're welcome to him, and him to you, just please come inside. These chills might not seem so much, but they can kill a man.' He tilted his head towards her. 'Or a woman.'

'One may be surprised how resilient I am.'

'But I am not quite as cold-blooded as you. Allow me to explain our trespasses inside. Please. Please.'

Mr Justinian gestured beside him. She shook her head. They were at an impasse. He threw his crumb.

'Postmaster Harrow's her father.'

'Her?'

'The woman whose coat you now own. Let me explain.'

Truth be told, the night was infernally cold, and she wanted to know about this Harrow daughter; in the same way hearing of another's misfortune made one's own life easier to bear. She stepped into the warmer surrounds of the study and closed the doors behind her. On cue, a servant ran in bearing a jug of tea, deposited the tableware and departed as silkily as a shadow.

The large, dark study had the air of a mausoleum viewing area, the books in the shelves gone dusty and unread. When she had first attempted to pass the time in this neglected library, most of the tomes were reference manuals of one permutation or another, lists of shipping indexes, dry histories. If there had been any books read for pleasure, they were sequestered elsewhere, or never existed at all.

Trapped by circumstance, Arden circled a daybed and a chaise longue as big as a small skiff before her attention was caught by a wrinkle of light in the shadows. A gallon-sized specimen jar, containing the formaldehyde-pickled coils of something aquatic and otherworldly – something octopoid somehow. She tapped the glass, experiencing equally the suffocations and convolutions of the poor beast inside.

'My ancestor kept a *Wunderkammer* before he died. A collection of oddities,' Mr Justinian said. 'If you would believe it, a *woman* gave birth to that thing. Nobody but Great-grandfather Alexander wanted that abomination in here, but we were rather forced to keep it.'

She left the pickled monster and returned to him.

'Don't change the subject, Vernon. You say Mr Riven's wife was Postmaster Harrow's daughter.'

'Yes. Mr Harrow is a man grieving.'

'I'm sure he is.'

'He is a wellspring of bitterness. He is too keenly aware what lies in wait for you upon that promontory, having seen it up close, and to someone he loved.' Mr Justinian poured himself a snifter of brandy, but did not offer the same to Arden. The liqueur left runnels upon the glass in the firelight. 'We also must talk of what happened today, else it will always fester in our minds.'

Arden exhaled. 'You were quite adamant I should not have the coat. *Murdered whore*, you said.'

'I acknowledge that.'

'Marrying a monster does not make one a harlot, Mr Justinian. If what you say is true, then it was her husband's fault that she was trapped in the marriage, not hers. You disgrace the dead by your blame. What you said today towards me was unconscionable.'

Mr Justinian stared at his shoes, affected a hangdog expression. 'It upset me to lose such a fine young lady to such a miserly end, that is all.'

'So she is *fine*, now?'

'She was beautiful, and fierce and somewhat intelligent in her own way, and did not deserve what became of her. Reduced from vibrancy to a *shade*. My guilt at not stepping up to save her, my cowardice, is constant. I chose the pejorative out of my own grief.' He glanced about, clearly hoping a voice might pipe up and rescue him, as it usually did when the servants were about. 'But Bellis made her decision to help her father by prostituting herself to Riven when there were other ways out of her predicament.'

'Bellis Harrow,' Arden said. 'So she has a name of her own, then.'

The brandy displeased Mr Justinian. He threw the liquor into the fire, causing a blue spirit to rise from the coals. It reminded Arden of her own arcane fire, starving in its glass in a far lighthouse, waiting to be fed.

Mr Justinian spoke to the fire, and not to her.

'A hundred years ago a family was procured from the

Sainted Isles. The Rivens, they were called. Or at least they received the name because they were shorefolk, sea-savages, not sophisticated enough to understand the concept of familial lineage. It didn't matter that they were brutes and inbreeds. Alexander Justinian, my great-grandfather, needed hands to process kraken-flesh and saurians in his factories upon the promontory. Who minded if the Rivens were illiterates and barely human? Thankfully they were not suited to the modicum of civilization Vigil provided and mostly remained upon the promontory, away from town. Within the span of a century the Rivens fought and sliced and incestually pared themselves down to one disgusting remnant individual.'

Mr Justinian made the sign of the krakenskin crucifix upon his chest before adding, 'Your lighthouse neighbour. T'was he that killed his family in an orgy of ritual and violence nearly twenty years ago. Slaughtered every man, woman and child on that promontory in one night. His own blood, gone.'

'I see,' Arden said. 'But if all this brutality did happen, shouldn't he have been hanged in punishment?'

'Oh, Riven was punished indeed. Charged and pleaded guilty to killing his family, sent away to the hulk prisons of Lyonne. Rotting boats on Harbinger Bay, converted to hold the worst reprobates and degenerates ever disinterred from the social sewage.

'But then some syphilitic judge had a weak-minded moment, and over a decade later returned the animal to this town. That is not the tragedy. Fifteen years of imprisonment merely sharpened the criminal's hunger, made his sexual urges tend to the obscene. Riven was ill-content in wallowing out on the promontory among his factory ruins. He came into town, forced a local girl to wife. Mr Harrow's daughter.'

'Forced?'

'Yes.'

'Now there,' Arden said tartly. 'There is the strange part.

The heart wants what it wants and it takes two to marry. If he wanted to marry anyone, then they would have had to at some stage *consent* to it, to *allow* it. Before witnesses.'

'Allow? Allow? You speak about request and consent upon this brutal shore?' Mr Justinian laughed with an adult's condescension towards a child. 'The woman was stolen, just as you would steal a hog or an unsupervised cure of meat. Dragged her screaming to the Sainted Isles, where illegal unions can be effected as easily as an attack in the dead of night. She came back with both eyes blackened, and never spoke for nearly a year afterwards. Not even to her father.

'Her last year alive she spent in abject horror and torment inside those factories and in his stinking bed. Escaped only once, whittled down to skin and bone and scar. Wanted an abortifacient for the monster curled in her womb, and Mr Sage gave her a tea that . . .'

'I have had experience with such a tea,' Arden snapped. 'You do not need to explain in detail what Mrs Sage already has. Continue, if you decide this salacious horror is what I must hear to make my informed decision.'

'Riven came back for Bellis that night, threatened Mr Harrow. Assaulted him, even as he tried to protect his daughter. A month later she was dead. All that was left was her coat, washed onto the beach. The Rector of our church was to make a statement to the magistrate about her death, for it was to him that she had confided. Our Rector himself went to Riven, to beg that he confess for the salvation of his holy soul. He never returned, his body was never found. Without evidence of death, the mongrel could not be charged or convicted. Two deaths within days. But let us merely agree as to who did both.'

'Circumstantial, still . . .'

'The Rector was your *cousin*, Arden Beacon. Rector John Stefan, the son of Jorgen Beacon, the Lightkeeper.'

Arden's heartbeat quickened in her chest, the rush of panic that any thought of unfair violence brought. Her cousin she remembered only vaguely, for their meetings had been so long ago, a slender, dark youth with the same soft-smoky hair as Arden and soulful eyes. He had been her age, Stefan Beacon, ungifted in blood but touched in other ways – deeply sensitive, accepted into a religious seminary and visiting his family in the North. Arden remembered more her step-mother's exclamation. Stefan and Arden could have been brother and sister, how similar their looks!

Her cousin, murdered, along with the woman.

She needed to keep calm, for such tales were not just for her safety. Her fear was a coin that could buy Mr Justinian several more weeks of her time.

'Surely such a performance as a literal kidnapping by the bogeyman of Vigil would have risen one or two men to heroics. You say all this happened to her, and to Mr Harrow, that you yourself stood by and watched?'

'You don't understand. Riven cannot be killed. The devils of the sea keep him safe, for all that he cut off his cock and fed it to them for his protection.' In the candlelight Mr Justinian's face darkened, and pearls of sweat sprang up from his brow. 'And he makes money! Money for foreign businessmen who purchase his kraken hides and will not allow harm to come to him.'

He snatched at the mantelpiece, held himself there shaking, before the brandy decanter called to him once more. 'I am sorry. For you. For her.'

'Are we done in the telling? Is this all I must know?'

Mr Justinian nodded. 'It is what you must know.'

'Coastmaster, regardless of whatever went before you must sign my release papers. I must go to my lighthouse.'

'You need not hurry. Mr Harris can—'

'Mr Harris is not qualified to keep a lucent flame alive and the season of summer storms will be upon us. A perpetually burning flame is still vulnerable to going out, and a *sanguis ignis* needs to maintain the light.'

'You cannot yet go,' Mr Justinian insisted. 'Not so soon. Not while Riven still lives out on that accursed promontory! He will come to you in the night, come prowling with lust in his black heart!'

Arden sniffed. 'It will not be the first time I've been in situations with lustful men. Anyway, didn't you say he fed his manhood to the devils for his protection? What is he meant to do to me without it?'

He did not take her scoffing bait. 'I cannot release you! My guilt over Bellis' fate prevents me.'

Arden had one play left to her. Such a play could only be used but once, and she had to take a deep breath before she deployed it.

'If you do not sign the papers, Mr Justinian, I will have no recourse but to return to Portside with your so-called essential list. I will present such evidence to the Seamaster's Guild and there will be an investigation. They may do more than investigate me, and cast their eyes on other parts of your business. Good night to you.'

As she turned to leave, Mr Justinian grabbed her arm. His fingers dug hard into the muscle, with the clear intent of leaving an imprint of himself upon her.

'It is not safe.'

'Safer than here, perhaps.' She pulled free. 'You cannot keep me from my lighthouse.'

'All right then, damn you.'

He strode to the desk, unlocked it and pulled out a sheaf of papers from a leather binder, the certificates that completed the Guild transfer. 'I have tried to warn you of the creature who will be no further from your doorstep than the east wing of this Manse from the right. This thing I do will condemn you to danger.'

'The danger is mine to face,' Arden said. 'Otherwise what good am I as a Lightkeeper anywhere?'

He met her steady gaze with something approaching panic. His nostrils flared like a horse sensing the harness.

She held the gaze, until he broke first, picked up his heavy fountain pen from the inkwell and signed both copies with such violence that Arden winced for the paper and the wood of the table beneath.

He held up the certificate. She held out her hand.

'Thank you, sir.'

Perhaps she was too subtle. The certificate never went her way.

'One condition.'

Arden frowned. 'I am not happy with conditions.'

'Allow me to court you.'

'Excuse me?'

'I am a Coastmaster with a barony to my name. You are an interim member of the Seamaster's Guild, the youngest ever. By winter you yourself would hold a full Guild degree, marry whom you wish. A good couple we would make. Our mating would be well-matched. The Eugenics Society will allow it, for we may yet breed some as yet unheard of talent.'

Unbidden, Richard Castile stepped into the halls of her mind. His smart uniform. His rakish cap. His handsome face taking her breath away with yearning. To touch him. To wrap herself up in a body that was not her own.

She shook her head firmly to rid herself of the association.

'I have no interest in eugenics or breeding. Besides, in the interest of fleeting pleasure – which I am quite forbidden to pursue openly – I barely know you.'

'Then come to know me. Allow me the chance to court you and present my case. The Society is favourable to a high lineage such as mine. You could receive a marriage dispensation at the very least. Non-breeding of course, but the operation to remove womb-horns is often quite successful.'

Arden exhaled. She shouldn't shout. Would be unprofessional, but still, the gall of the man!

'Mr . . .'

He moved to the fire, the certificate still in his hand. She saw the leaping flames, the devouring of her freedoms, the going home, the censure of the Guildmaster who might have to come out here and mediate this mess. Maybe even Mr Lindsay, whose owners even the Portmaster of Clay feared.

They would find in her favour, but the taint of being a Lightkeeper who could not handle their own business would remain. She would not keep her degree, not even the associate one. Her signal post had already been reassigned. She would be . . .

'Stop!'

'Well? What say you, Mx Beacon?' He shook the paper. 'I am a man alone in this cursed, misbegotten peninsula courtesy of my great-grandfather's sentimentality. How am I to meet any woman of my equal among these inbreds of the coast? How will my family be redeemed if I marry into worthless muck?'

She wanted to say words in their defence, for the girls of the town were quite the hardworking, straight-talking type. She was no eugenicist, but something of the stoic Vigil seaworthiness in the Justinian line might be a bit more welcome than Mr Justinian thought.

The flames leapt, hungry for paper. She let out a sigh.

'You may come to my lighthouse once a week and court me in the interests of social engagement,' Arden said through gritted teeth. 'I will need regular supplies brought to me anyhow. Your driver can make himself useful at least.'

'Yes. Very good.' Mr Justinian's smile showed his incisors.

She wondered just what shame had sent him packing back here from Clay Portside, a cur with a tail between its legs. Arden reached for the paper again. He pulled the paper away, put the certificate back in the leather binder, then returned the binder to its locked drawer.

'It is still much safer to keep items here,' he said. 'The tower structure is in poor condition. You would not want an inundation or damp to destroy your Certificate of Work. The best place for it is in the safety of the Coastmaster's office. Any high-ranking Seamaster judge would agree with me, if there were ever – as you say – an investigation.'

'Fine,' she said. 'Just make sure that I am paid on time. Certificates on fragile paper are one thing, but Djenne coins survive a sunken ship.'

With that, she swallowed her brandy-laced tea in one gulp, and stomped up the stairs to her room, and made damn sure she both locked the door and shoved a chair under the handle before retiring for the night.

5

Her uncle had left her a boat

Her uncle had left her a boat.

More correctly, Arden thought, putting her hands on her hips in unconscious imitation of her Portmaster father, he had left a boat to whomever the Guild appointed as Lightkeeper after him. No doubt the bad news would have sunk through the layers of missives and post-rumours, that Lucian Beacon's eldest child was *malorum* and dim of blood.

Such a condition reflected badly on a family who made their name in fire. The great genetic and ancestral ledgers of the Eugenics Society would be opened in the inner sanctum of the legendary Clay Library. An accusing cross scrawled in blood-red ink next to the name of *Beacon*. Their partnerships and progeny would be scrutinized for generations to come. Jorgen would have suspected that no Beacon-born would follow after him.

Perhaps he'd made peace with the passing of the baton to a Pharos man, maybe accepted that a lesser Lumiere would take up the fire he had once tended. One of the other *ignis*-gifted families, just not a Beacon. Jorgen wouldn't have ever thought little Arden here, even if he had still remembered her.

Oh, Uncle. If only I could tell you I made it. Like her cousin Stefan, Uncle Jorgen had appeared in her life only in blinks and snatches, a thin, slighter version of his four brothers, timid around adults, but with a rare patience when it came to children. She remembered his peculiarities most clearly, the shine of his nails, his moustache severely waxed at the ends, the precisely polished brass hobs in his shoes. His face was a smudge. They said that the Beacon brothers might have been handsome youths, but only Jorgen was beautiful.

She imagined he looked like her father.

An unspoken trouble had early on separated Jorgen from his Clay Portside brothers. For all that he had died only weeks ago, he had long since passed over in Arden's life. He'd stopped making his annual pilgrimages. He'd refused contact with his family. He became a memory, and then a corpse.

And yet she wondered if he would have been pleased that his niece would be the one to have *Fine Breeze*. It was not the sort of craft she had expected her dour, exiled uncle to own. Instead of the faded blues and greens of those few fishing vessels that dotted the harbour, *Fine Breeze* was as red as a polished lacquer cabinet from the Middle Country.

'Lightmaster Beacon loved that boat,' the Harbourmistress said with a sour expression, as if such an emotion were peculiar and unwelcome. Her accent was pure Lyonnian, as if she'd only come from Clay City yesterday.

Mx Modhi, the Harbourmistress of Vigil, if that was what one could call the position of watching over a miserly pier for most hours of the day, was a tall, stout woman of grandmasterly years and an ancestry that went beyond the small pale folk of Fiction. The shipyard domain she beheld and no doubt ruled, from a sturdy, leather-upholstered rocking chair in the primo position to watch all the comings and goings from the bay. She wore waxed canvas trousers, not a skirt, and her legs were as broad as ship-masts, and her arms suggested the same strength of clipper ship cross-beams. She still had in her oaken face the shades of the beauty she must have been when she was younger.

A curved pipe in her mouth bobbed as the Harbourmistress

watched Arden gingerly put a foot out to test the red boat's wallow. A city girl's apprehension made for fine entertainment.

'Don't fall in,' the Harbourmistress said. 'I'll not get out of this chair to rescue you.'

'Jorgen couldn't have had the boat built here.'

'No, she belonged to a traveller through these parts. Lost her in a game of cards – Beggar's Blight of all things. Ended up in Jorgen's hands – your uncle might have been slight, but he was fiery. Would take on a shorefolk brawler twice his size if he felt an injustice had been done.'

Arden smiled. 'Oh, he was definitely a Beacon, then. We are all about correctness and balance.' She indicated her gloves. 'But if there was fire in him, he kept it under a bushel for the most part. This boat is very unlike him.'

'Sometimes the most austere folk will have a weakness for rare and beautiful things.'

With that said, Mx Modhi nodded at Arden's blue-spotted coat and, grinning, puffed a smoke-halo from her plesiosaur-ivory pipe.

'Well, beautiful things can be useful. And utility is beautiful too.'

'And you're off to the promontory now. Our sea-washed sunset gates.'

'I am.'

'I shan't have to tell you all the local histories then. Nearly twenty years of them I've learned. No doubt every cock-eyed Billie-and-Bob has fallen over each other to breathlessly fill you in about the tale of poor Mrs Riven and her awful comeuppance.' The ivory stem clicked against her teeth as she spoke, and Arden once again was amazed at the Harbourmistress having been here for so long. She could have stepped off a Clay City boat yesterday. 'Frankly, the people in this country can be disgusting.'

Arden picked up a loose end of rope dangling from an arterial-blooded bow. As she coiled it, she asked as casually as she could, 'You've been here twenty years. Did you ever meet Mrs Riven yourself?'

'I did,' the Harbourmistress said. 'Knew her well.' She chewed on the pipe, and a long moment of appraisal followed, as she decided what to tell Arden, and what to leave out. 'Watched her as a child from this very post, coming down here among the fishing boats and yearning out towards the sea. Her father was not a marine-affiliated gentleman, but the girl . . . something was in her. The tide, perhaps. All the fishermen were besotted with their little queen, brought her whelk shells and sea-dollars, mermaid teeth on a string. She would sing them a song for a penny.'

'Sounds like a bit of a sea-sprite, then.' Arden flung the wrapped coil into the boat. 'Very romantic.'

'Oh, no romance there, not our Bellis. Cunning little thing, she was. Never missed a trick. A little gang of orphans and illegitimates used to run riot through the village then as they do now, and Bellis Harrow was their ringleader. Their tiny Genghis Khan, but certainly a benevolent one.' The chewing stopped. 'Then she grew up. Things are different for women around these parts, although one cannot say she didn't fight harder than most to keep from being crushed by the conditions of femininity.'

Arden blinked at the sudden fellow feeling, a rush of warmth to her skin. 'I know what that is like,' she said with deep sincerity. 'I've fought those battles myself. I still wear the scars on my heart.'

The Harbourmistress remained aloof, but her countenance gentled.

'You take care out there now, Lightmistress. There's more powers and prejudices in these sainted waters than you'll hear about in your city towers. Not all the monsters have twelve arms and live in the sea. Some have two legs; you can be sure of it.'

There followed from her a brief instruction on how messages would pass from lighthouse to harbour. Fiction had no reliable telegraph radio infrastructure, nor cable out to the promontory. Arden would need to use a mirror heliograph each morning on the tenth hour, and each evening on the third. Emergency messages to flash on the hour, if required, but anything less than the tower having fallen over was not an emergency, so she was not to bother Mx Modhi with it.

How different from the constant flurry of communication in the signal house! Arden agreed to every instruction the Harbourmistress made, and realized she would need to relearn the mirror code she had forgotten a decade ago.

The Harbourmistress returned to her scanning of the ocean, and Arden went to her uncle's boat, wondering if she should have asked more about her Riven neighbour. Nobody was quite telling the same story. Was it fey and vulnerable Bellis Riven, anchored in a terrible state of marital imprisonment, or was it fighting Bellis Riven, the tough little girl who could make coarse fishermen do her bidding with just a song?

Was there a true story at all?

In contrast to her father, Jorgen Beacon had not been a tall fellow, so he had made the rudder and sail adjustments to suit his height. Conveniently they suited Arden as well. *Fine Breeze* had a small cabin for sheltering in, and batten sails that were cut in a square style. The forward sail was the largest, with a smaller sail behind the rudder.

The waves were not so rough that morning, so after Arden familiarized herself with the craft, she unfurled the mainsail and put Vigil behind her.

The cold bay held as much of a sparkle as the climate would ever allow, and the promontory, as always, was barely visible in the constant mist. Yet each slosh and roll took the days of strain and worry away. Arden had not entirely grasped how tense she had held herself, until the moment she tied off the rigging and relaxed at the rudder. A brisk wind filled the canvas, and she manoeuvred *Fine Breeze* out into the open water for her first proper, clear view of Fiction's last sanguis lighthouse. Her heart skipped a beat, and Arden smiled. There it was, the sense of blood, powerful as homesickness and yearning. Her hands tingled in anticipation.

Eyes upon the promontory spotted Arden long before she made it to the pier.

As the boat danced close to the weatherworn bollards of the tiny sheltered inlet the familiar figure of another Portside guildsman appeared. Friendly Mr Harris from the nomadic Sea Guilds, a man round and bushy with his great blond beard and shipwright's shoulders that could seat both child and full-grown woman on each. He kept his hair short, a custom of the fisher-folk here. Far better to have it under a waxed woollen cap rather than getting caught in all the sea-spray, though Arden suspected hair-locks often ended in the water in superstition before a good catch. There was a parallel to the sanguis giving of blood, though anyone around here would have argued bitterly that it was not the same thing at all.

'Hoy!' he cried out, waving an arm as thick as a ham. 'Hoy, Lightmistress!'

'Hoy,' she shouted in delight. 'You have turned wild since I saw you last in Clay, Mr Harris!'

'We have merely moved up in the world, you and myself both! I'll throw a rope, let me tie you off.'

The journey of a month was ended. At last she saw her light-house up close. It stood at the end of a long, thin natural mole of basalt blocks, squat and wide rather than the tremendously high spire of the Clay Mouth. Whitewash might have daubed the granite once, but neglect had scored the paint down to bare stone, leaving only a thin crust on the lee side. Some of the glass panes in the lantern room were broken. Not much of an attempt had been made to fix the missing panes other than a ragged piece of wood hoarding, to stop the flame from blowing out. A weathercock at the very top leaned at a forlorn angle.

Desolation shrouded the tower. Mr Justinian had been telling the truth about its decay, at least.

Mr Harris lumbered to the end of the pier and tossed out a rope hitch that had to weigh as much as she did. Once she made *Fine Breeze* fast, he reached down and pulled her out with a mighty yank.

'I am glad to see a friendly face!' she said breathlessly. 'And to find the coast hasn't taken the might from you.'

'Little Ardie!' He put her back down onto the pier, his own red cheeks growing redder as he blushed furiously at forgetting his manners. 'I'm sorry, you must be properly called Madam Lightmistress now.' He took off his battered fisherman's hat and gave a quick bow.

'I'm still getting used to the name too, Gerard.'

'Ah, but you're all grown up. You'll need some meat on those bones of yours, girl. The wind would blow you away.'

Arden waved him off good-naturedly. She could not call herself slender, not from all the hard work on the wharves to fill her out. No wasp-waist for her, not if you wanted the strength to haul a Fresnel element up a hundred feet of lighthouse stairs.

'Don't you worry, I'm strong enough.'

'I'm sure you are.' He stood back to measure her with his eye. 'A fine coat you're wearing.'

'It's real krakenskin, before you ask, Mr Harris.'

'I noted that. How did you manage to afford such clothing? Did your father give you your inheritance early, and throw into the bargain that of the rest of the Beacon brothers?'

'Hardly,' she said fondly, even though the mention of her father made her wince with regret. 'I bought it from a rag-trader's table. Apparently, it belonged to a dead woman, as everyone is so keen to remind me.' Arden paused and added, 'The wife of a brutal murderer, apparently.'

Mr Harris' face clouded. 'Ah, you mean Mr Riven.'

'Yes. The Coastmaster of Vigil had certain other titles for him, though.'

'I think most people take care not to mention them aloud. He has a habit of appearing when people speak his name.'

Mr Harris pointed down the ridge. A mile away, three large wooden buildings crabbed the rocky beach as barnacles might cling to rock. They were as large as the workhouses back in Clay Portside, almost wharf-sized. A saltwater lichen frowsed off the grey iron roof. They had been there for a long time and suffered much the same aura of neglect as her lighthouse.

Her sharp eyes caught gulls and cormorants gathered on one corner of the compound, a congregation of devil birds drawn by the promise of a feed.

'Mr Riven lives in those buildings yonder. Does his business on the shore. Once quite an industry in the slaughter of sea-monsters here in Vigil. Serpents. Leviathans. Krakens when they could be called up. A whole family of butchers, I heard, blood-tied to the ocean, but this coast can be hungry, and the political machinations of men hungrier still, so now only one Riven remains.'

The Mr Justinian in her memory hissed, *'twas he that killed his family.*

'Blood-tied? You mean like *sanguis* talent?'

'Not quite, Ardie. Perhaps an earlier, more ah . . . *fundamental* version of the trait, eh? The talent first appeared in this country, remember. Occasionally a sanguis jumps out of the gene pool, though if they have any sense they keep quiet about it and don't let the Lions know.'

'Has Mr Riven caused you much trouble out here?'

Mr Harris shook his head. 'We've had no need for business. He goes his way, and I mine. Whether Jorgen had dealings with Mr Riven previously, that trouble lay between themselves. I would say it's hard to avoid the man if you were here any longer than a month.'

She must have made a face, for he continued, 'He won't be a problem Ardie. Come now, there's talk in town about you, but these towns would talk if a fellow wore the wrong clothes on a Sunday.'

Mr Harris had kept the tower for six weeks, not long enough to attract a maintenance stipend. There would have been next to nothing he could have done to fix the place up. The small lower floor might have had the potential for cosiness, had not the walls been so slimed with sea-damp. Anything resembling home-comforts had been knocked together from desultory driftwood scaffolding. The rude bed might have suited Mr Harris, a man used to sleeping out in the open on a wharf, but for a Guildswoman Lightmistress it seemed little better than the floor. The internal stairs were constructed – if one could consider a spiral of protrusions as crooked as a brawler's teeth a construction – from keystones in the wall. The banisters needed replacing, else Arden could foresee the very real outcome of falling to her death.

On reaching the topmost lantern house, the vastness of the promontory view struck Arden like a bell-hammer. The sea surrounded them in a smothering slab of grey, and the thunderclouds might have been the white-rimmed backs of behemoths, fallen in a heavenly grave.

Behind her, the ruins scattered along the coast. Old monks and hermits had first built impractical monasteries upon this shore, hoping to win the unsophisticated inhabitants of Fiction to the church and to save their immortal souls. Perhaps the stone and glass had stood for a generation, maybe ten, but only rubble remained, slowly dissolving back into the earth.

From up high she observed the one remaining cathedral wall, one that had held a stained-glass rose window, now only a perfect empty circle of mortar and rock. The window stared out to sea with a single, sightless eye.

Old magic here, she thought. Old superstitions. The ancient saints were canny enough not to replace the cold abyssal gods of the sea-folk with the warm, dignified artifices of their own religions. She wondered if her cousin Stefan had grown into his spirituality among these old stones, if he'd felt the Almighty murmur in the drowned lands below the wind and waves and knew that he belonged to a power greater than that of his name, and blood.

Then she inspected the perpetual lamp with growing concern.

The ratio of blood was important to the chemical articulations within a sanguine lantern. A typical lamp required *fuel* to burn, the way metal required *force* to bend, force to control the weather, force to hold the vapour inside a container to give weight and mass and velocity. All things that were finite, exhaustible, subject to the grinding momentum of God's creation. What Arden had, what all sanguinem had, was a catalyst within her veins that turned mass and force in upon itself so that energy in an element (for her, fire), could be sustained and intensified beyond what should be possible.

The pain and danger of blood letting was nature's warning – lest the wielder grow too arrogant in their contortion of the natural order.

Arden remembered an Academy tutor drawing a broad circle with her finger over her heart while explaining. Sanguis blood was an alchemical ouroboros, the snake biting its own tail. *You can change the physical property of a thing. A regenerative cycle outside of time. But eventually entropy sets in. The cycle weakens. The iron remembers it is strong, and becomes hard. The flame remembers it needs to burn fuel, finds none, and extinguishes. So something must make it right. A gifting, an exchange. Blood we use, but it was not always so. In older, less enlightened days, entire bodies would be the sacrament that the cycle of labour required . . .*

Arden frowned, both piqued by the memory and the sense that something was very wrong with Jorgen's orphaned light. In the daytime, the flame should still have burned as bright as a summer's morning, but it had the cast of a midwinter afternoon. The offering funnel, through which Jorgen would have made his blood-tithe each week, was filthy. Dried blood crusted the entrance until barely a channel remained for the offering to run through.

Unthinkingly, Arden thumbed the curve of her arm. As she had shown the guest the previous night, dozens of small scars laddered there. When Arden maintained her small signal light upon the Parrot Wharf, the compact lantern's cold flame had required only a smear of blood, once a week, to stay bright. Grommets had been unnecessary in her previous life. But a lighthouse keeper needed to give so much more blood than a lamp-turning signaller did, to maintain the ratio of instruction, to make those sacrifices. The scar tissue could cause her hands permanent damage, if not for a coin to protect the skin.

Mr Harris joined her at the top of the stairs, puffing and panting. He'd never been tested for talent, but like any associate labour guildsman he had familiarity with the blood tithing of the docks. She did not have to hide the trade tools from him.

'Do you know why my uncle died, Mr Harris?'

'Heartbreak, Lightmistress. Plain and simple heartbreak.'

'Maybe the motivation, but by what mechanism? We cannot easily take our lives.'

'Not take, but certainly neglect.' Mr Harris said evasively, not quite looking at Arden. 'Anyone with implanted silver in their skin must regularly return. Return to Clay annually and have them cleaned, replaced. You think the Lyonne Order would permit their sanguineous guildsmen to live in freedom so easily?'

She tucked her hands under her arms, feigning a chill from an open window. 'It seems odd, that he should not return, or at least, find an illegal phlebotomist to take the grommets out.'

Those great shoulders of Mr Harris gave a slow shrug. 'After Stefan died – was killed, if you ask certain people – Jorgen stopped going back to Clay. No reason to, in his mind. Estranged from his family, his son lost to bad dealings. When an infection set into his hands, the Guild sent me to see what was going on. By the time I arrived, the sepsis had set in. Made him deathly ill, his blood poisoned. I could not convince him to go home. He did not last much longer after that.'

Arden moved through to Jorgen's possessions, trying to marry these crude items, this filthy degradation, with the gentle man in her memory. The knife he'd used to cut away the layer of callused skin from his decaying coins lay encrusted upon a similarly disgusting table. A whetstone nearby explained why the blade had a shapeless edge, the metal pared down paper-thin.

'Could you not have imposed upon him some *penicillium*, and some powdered kraken beak Mr Harris? Of all the places, those medicines would be most available here.'

'Oh, I tried. But it was too late, and the coins belong to the Order, the way the sanguineous do. Only Order-sanctioned phlebotomists can be relied upon to take them out. He would have had to go out to the Sainted Isles to find himself a man who could remove such invasiveness.' Mr Harris tilted his head towards the horizon, straight as a carpenter's plumb. 'People go to the Isles to die, Mx. Beacon. They don't often come back.'

'Thank you for telling me this, Gerry. I shall endeavour to have my coins removed when I finish here and return to Lyonne. A puppet string is one thing, but they shall not put a leash on me. I shall not turn into my uncle. At least . . . at least unlike him I have nobody to lose.'

The Clayman's face became so dour, he might have been dipped in shadow. He motioned her to silence. The walls could be listening. Those bodiless spirits of fate and irony in the old stones were deeply aligned to secrets. They inflicted their own bad luck.

Then quieter, 'Your cousin the Rector was a witness to all that Mr Riven did. All of it. Everything. Took the confessions of both man and wife. Knew secrets in the confessional terrible enough that he would face church censure by testifying in the magistrate's court.'

The wave-bellows echoed through the tower. Words spoken in the confession box were sacred. For a priest to bring such testimony into the open . . .

'Stefan was going to testify against Mr Riven?'

Mr Harris continued solemnly. 'He was the prosecution's only reliable witness and Mr Riven killed him. Look, Jorgen didn't take it lying down. Had it in mind that he would have Mr Riven experience the same fate. If not by an accident, then by some misfortune. He joined forces with Mr Harrow, put aside the feud the men had shared previously. Did the fellow some real damage, but only enough to rile him up, not blunt his teeth.'

'I have had the misfortune to meet Mr Harrow. Surely Mr Riven would have left this place, if he knew the townsfolk hated him so much.'

'The Rivens have populated these shores for centuries, Arden. The man would have no more left his home than call up a storm and cast the promontory into the sea. No, it has been a mighty war of subtle violence here these past few years. Jorgen succeeded in having Riven drowned once, only to have him haul himself in from the ocean as if he'd made a pact with the devil to return. The man can't be killed easily. Something in his nature.'

'I did not come here expecting duty as a foot soldier in a war.'

'Nobody ever does.' Mr Harris pointed at her coat. 'That coat on your shoulders is weighted with bad news. If he sees you in it, only the sea-devils can tell what he will do.'

She collected her resolve. A possession of the dead it might be, but the coat was *her* possession now. Salvaged, the way a shipwreck returned to shore has no owner except the one who reports it. How many times as a signalmistress and lanternkeeper in Portside had she taken up the position others would not, them fearing the dead man who had once rung the shipping bell or worked the signal stick? Accidents were common on the wharves. Every light and buoy had a ghost attached.

'No, I shall keep my coat, and if the maker wants its return, he shall do the gentlemanly thing and ask for it, with an offer of a suitable replacement. I will speak to him face to face, and we shall see if there cannot be some kind of arrangement.'

Mr Harris exhaled, nodded, knowing better than to challenge a woman whose mind was made up.

'You are your father's daughter through and through. And your poor late mother, bless her soul and curse the pirates who took her.'

Once Arden had finished her tour, she shared a lunch with Mr Harris outside the tower. Thick sourdough bread, the hard cheese that travels well, pickles and a runny syrup trying hard to be a chutney. They sat in the ruins of a rowboat that made for a rustic table, an *Owl and the Pussycat* kind of boat, as her favourite Uncle Nicolai would say. Uncle Nicolai had husbanded the great lighthouse at the Mouth, that mighty entrance to Clay Capital, the golden door to the country of Lyonne. Was to him that she had whispered her dream of keeping not just a signal flame, but the Spire at Clay's centre, the one her grandmother used to keep in the old days, before Arden had tested late, *malorum*, and dim.

No Spire for her then. A wharf-light and the associated administrations of signalling at most, but if a Beacon child might return their family's honour by winning the Spire post, it would not be Arden who would do it.

Mr Harris brought out some brown glass bottles containing a yeasty ale. She cast her attention westward, to where the first of the noon clouds had begun to build on the blank slate of the ocean. *Fine Breeze* sensed the storm before she did. The oncoming currents buffeted the boat against the pier.

'I shall move in tomorrow morning,' she said at last. 'There's no point delaying the handover any longer.'

'Very well. I'll signal for the Coastmaster's driver to collect you, first thing. Your lamphouse assistant will be here by then.'

'Male or female?'

'Female. A real stormbride of a lass, did her post out of Harbinger Bay, where the prison ships moor. A real competent sort.'

Mr Harris stood up and collected the scraps, which he threw to the motley collection of seagulls, auks and white ibis that had gathered to watch them eat. Another gust of wind warned her not to dally, and Mr Harris walked her down the cliff path to *Fine Breeze*.

'Aye, I enjoyed sharing your first day, Ardie. Those souls out there are yours to keep, now.'

He pointed at the horizon, then passed over a pair of brass spyglasses from his satchel to Arden. She peered into their eyepieces so as not to embarrass him, for her Beacon-sharp eyes had already seen what lay in the distance.

A flotilla of boats in the distance, moving in and out of encroaching fog. At least fifteen of them, and their crooked, uneven builds had not a single uniform style. Hulks and wrecks, not fit to work a canal, let alone the open water.

'They've bypassed both bays. Where are they going?'

'Sainted Isles lie out there beyond the horizon.'

'The petroleum islands? With the pumps . . . with the perpetual mechanica?' She recalled the maps in her father's Portmaster offices. A broken scatter of atolls and archipelagos surrounding three land masses in the middle of the Darkling Sea. Dashed lines where the cartographer was uncertain of the landscape. They'd seemed so lonely and far away. An exile's islands, where one went to be forgotten, and to die.

'Yes. Even the perpetual arbours and escapements or the rockblood machines need a conduit of labour to wind the springs. The Isles require hands to work. What better labourers than those folk already displaced by sanguine talents?'

Arden pretended to look through the brass again so as not to show Mr Harris her uncomfortable face. She'd seen one *sanguis pondus* replace a dozen longshoremen on a wharf. She'd seen the union riots light up Clay Portside so for a week not one ship left nor entered. 'Surely they aren't attempting an ocean journey in those vessels. Those boats don't look like they could even survive a river crossing.'

'They all of them believe there's nothing else for them in Lyonne.'

'Goodness, who would put such an idea in their heads? We can't do everything with blood.'

Mr Harris stroked his beard with sorrowful dignity. 'The idea of perpetual rockblood wells and their untapped bounty drives men to flights of madness. In Portside I hear of entire congregations afflicted with the idea . . . the dream of a place where *human* labour has real value, not sanguis labour, not machine. But the conduit of *hand* to *work* and no mystical power in between. Aye, a disease of greed and wealth grows in the minds of people who've previously known neither. Where they once sang hymns of the Holy Land and the One Who Walks the Way, they have now started to plan pilgrimages to the petroleum shores.'

Arden returned Mr Harris his brass spyglasses. 'I must not

judge. There's nothing anyone can do about them. Even the Lyonne Parliament cannot stop people from leaving. Free movement is a right enshrined by God.'

He nodded, put his spyglasses away with the finality of a man who has seen all he requires. 'Your sanguinity protects you now, Ardie, but this is the truth of it, eventually whatever privations the poorfolk suffer, the rich will suffer as well. And the rich pay sanguinem wages. *Your* wages. And keep your safety. Whatever cruel siren-song sung on those Islands will not be so easily contained there. Eventually the doctrine must make its way back to the mainland. Aye, coin or no coin, you would be safer at home.'

The wind kicked up, and they had to move again, else be tumbled from the high ground. Arden took Mr Harris' stout elbow and tried to put his troublesome words aside.

'You mustn't fret about my safety,' she said as they walked. 'The Guildsman said I'd only have to work the light until the start of winter. They'll call me back and give me my full degree.' She raised her hands. 'I'll have my coins taken out too, and there will be no leash upon me.'

He raised his eyebrows. 'All this before winter? If you leave then, you'll miss the midwinter crowning of the Deepwater King!' His excursion into dour prophecy quickly returned to jolly banter. 'It's quite a memorable festival, even in Vigil. They barely celebrate anything else.' Mr Harris grinned then, his eyes alight with mischief. Nudged her elbow. 'Could make Deepwater Bride for a day . . . and if you find yourself a suitable husband there's nothing the Order can do about it.'

She felt her cheeks grow hot. Goodness, how could she even consider tumbling into the greasy bed of a coarse Fiction man? He would make love like an animal, all grunts and snuffles, paw her bare flesh thoughtlessly, grow aroused and perhaps he would be coarse down there too . . .

Then her cheeks burned again, for it had been a year since she'd had such a dalliance after Richard Castile had left her, and she had made a firm vow. No more men, or thoughts of love.

She let go of Mr Harris' warm, strong arm and navigated the final rocky stairs down to the pier by herself.

Once there, she turned to him and jutted her chin obstinately. 'It is the ocean I·shall love, not men. Besides, I'm not my uncle. I bear no ill-will or history to anyone.'

Mr Harris flicked a glance towards the old kraken-processing factories and made a disapproving grumble deep in his throat. 'Arden Beacon, I can tell you're planning to work some trader's charisma upon this neighbour of yours, but Riven is more beast than man. The monsters he battles upon the ocean, they are his brethren, not us.'

'I am not going to battle him, Mr Harris,' she said, untying *Fine Breeze*'s lashings. 'I will pay him a visit, like a civilized person. I intend to visit many on this coast by the time the storm season is upon us.'

'He may try and poke you with his harpoon rather than let you onto his property.'

'You cannot make me afraid,' Arden retorted. 'If I am to execute my functions as a proper Lightmistress, I must be at peace with all my *beloved* ocean gives me.'

'Well, you might love the ocean, but a woman with fire in her blood cannot win such love back,' Mr Harris said. 'You talk of power? In two centuries no child alive has displayed a blood-alignment for cryptobiological specimens the way the Rivens have constantly done. Aye, even the human race is closing ranks about such a damn travesty of inheritance. He is incompatible with you. He is incompatible with everybody.'

6

The tides had a certain

The tides had a certain personality in the dusk that they did not have during the day. The waters passed that stage where one would call them *frolicsome* and instead become *malicious*, and active in wanting harm.

After an hour of fighting the steadily swelling sea, the *Fine Breeze*'s bow relievedly turned towards the Vigil pier. Arden would have no trouble in securing mooring, for another boat had just left the small, rickety marina.

Within minutes she saw the shape entirely, huge and dark, an oil-powered side-paddle wheeler that didn't float upon the restless water but rather compelled it to submission. The plume of smoke had a curiously luminous blue tinge. Only one kind of oil produced such luminous particulates.

Kraken oil.

So then. Her neighbour. She adjusted her sails and continued in a straight line towards the docks. Mr Riven's giant sea-barge approached *Fine Breeze* with frightening speed. The bow wave rose on either side with the power of waves breaking against rocks.

'Sir, a sail ship heading into port on this bearing has right of way,' she muttered to the wind. If one of them didn't turn soon, they were going to collide. She wouldn't stand a chance. The barge kept coming and if it did not turn soon, she would be crushed under the threshing wheels.

At the last moment Arden wrenched her rudder sideways. *Fine Breeze*'s sail boom swung around, and had she not had her wits about her, it would have knocked Arden off her feet and into the water.

'Come on, come on!' She cursed. 'If you old gods have any power here, give me wind!' Disturbed, the gusts roiled about her but had little success in filling the sail. And that massive vessel was so close now that she saw the hooded figure in the wheelhouse, resolutely steering his juggernaut onwards.

The chopping wheels powered closer and closer still until finally the ship bore down upon her wake, missing a collision by less than an arm span. She could have reached over and touched the black boat, so close were they. *Fine Breeze* keeled over to near-capsize in the great bow wave, the hammering engine so cacophonous in her ears it made her head ring. For an awful moment a name filled her sight. A name scored upon the black side in an unadorned script. *Saudade*.

'You monster!' Arden screamed, shaking her fist. 'You could have killed me!'

The figure in the wheelhouse did not turn back to see if she was all right. She could be in pieces, drowning, and he would have cared not one whit.

Finally her boat righted itself, the wind returned in somewhat of a constant direction, and Arden could return to the rude little harbour, shaken up but in one piece.

'How did the boat go, Lightmistress?' Harbourmistress Modhi called out as soon as she butted into the buoys lining the lone pontoon that made up the marina.

'Fine,' Arden said, still angry from her near-drowning. In rebellion against her brief imprisonment she had for a little while felt somewhat of a sympathetic warmth towards the mysterious fellow Mr Justinian had spoken so rudely about. She had not wanted the odious Coastmaster to be *right*.

'Wasn't an accident, that. He'd have seen you from a mile away.' Mx Modhi grinned and puffed victoriously on her pipe. 'I had an inkling he'd take uncomfortably to your get-up.'

Arden clutched her coat about her with defiance. One thing said for Beacons, they were known for their stubbornness. The ship moves for the signal light, not the other way around.

'I bought this salvage garment fair and square. If Mr Riven wants it back, he can be the gentleman and ask.'

The pipe smoke surrounded the Harbourmistress in wreaths of grey silk.

'He won't *ask*. He'll just *take*.' Her voice rose in timbre. 'Isn't that right, David, my boy?'

A black-haired lad ran from another pontoon pier, all gangly adolescent limbs yet to settle into adulthood, to fasten *Fine Breeze* on Arden's behalf. He was perhaps seventeen years old, and Arden noted the marks on the youth's hands, pale scars from the required testmoots he'd have taken on his eleventh birthday. Fiction children were still tested, despite sanguinity being uncommon in the south. It was not a duty shirked. A ledgered talent popping up out of nowhere could bring a sudden unexpected wealth to a poor family.

She said her thank-yous to the boy, uttered some words to draw him into a conversation, but he barely met her eye. A fine black down on his upper lip trembled. He hovered in that strange halfway world between child and man He'd be a child far longer yet at this rate under his mother's shadow.

'Don't mind my fool son,' the Harbourmistress said once David scuttled away. 'He's just out of sorts because I won't let him on board that dirty black boat. Doesn't understand I'm protecting him the way a mother should. Lord knows what perversions that fellow gets up to out there.'

'Oh, is your son friends with Mr Riven?' Arden asked, tossing her head. 'I thought him quite the hermit when not trying to run people down in his boat.'

Mx. Modhi chewed on her pipe for a weighty second before gruffly admitting, 'Guild stipend won't cover good tobacco and a proper Lyonnian education for my son. Your neighbour was the only one to give him the time of day. Fisherfolk around here don't take kindly to anyone who can't count ten generations wasting away on these shores.'

'I'll take your word for it, Harbourmistress. I haven't had much contact with the locals.'

'No, you wouldn't have, would you? Ensconced with Mr Justinian up in the Manse, I gather.'

Something in the winking way Mx Modhi spoke made Arden indignant. 'Only until I get myself ready for my lighthouse duties. And we are not *ensconced*. Our relationship is purely professional. He is a member of a professional Guild, as am I. He is bound by vow to help me set up.'

'Indeed. These things take time, do they not? And my boy David here, he's been paid already to ferry Mr Justinian to your doorstep once a week for trysts in case his car won't make it. He thinks of all possibilities, our Baron.'

Arden would wonder later why her mouth hurt. At Mx Modhi's assertion, she had clenched her jaw so hard that bright sparks of pain prickled her cheeks.

'He is Coastmaster, and Mr Justinian has to have his briefings. I would prefer them once a month, myself, but these are unfamiliar waters, and I need supplies brought to me.'

Harbourmistress Modhi sucked on her pipe, blew more smoke for her airy spirit. 'If that is the case, then I welcome the correction. Excuse my misunderstandings, there has been more than one lady here who has fancied herself the *second* Mrs Justinian, and they'll not take kindly to a stranger whisking his affections away.'

'The second?' Arden asked, although she would more prefer that she never speak his name again. 'Nobody spoke of Mr Justinian being married before.'

'Well, nearly married. So far as the priest had not blessed the union in public. They were practically at the altar.'

'What happened to her?' Arden asked, even though her deep suspicions already told her the answer. Who else could it be, to arouse such a passion in him?

'Goodness, we only just spoke of her before. Miss Bellis Harrow was her name, but she died as Bellis Riven.'

Evening fell with all the finality of a closing funeral casket. The Manse's few lights battled the darkness and in the most case failed miserably. Arden retired to the mouldering study, desperate to pass time before the morning, and her final freedom. She had quite expected another argument with Mr Justinian, but the previous day's clash had made him sulk, and there was no better sulking place than in Garfish Point, a hundred miles north, far and away from Vigil and the duties of his home.

That didn't mean he'd taken with him the constant sense of unease that haunted the mansion's main rooms. The uneasiness worked its way though the corridors like a low fog. From a proud position on the library's sideboard, the octopus-thing in the glass bell jar gave a subtle shudder, its liquid tomb sensitive to atmosphere, the barometric shifts in air pressure. Arden stopped to peer in close. Not an octopus, perhaps. No mottled hide, or suckers. Just smooth, human-like skin.

A woman gave birth to that thing.

'Oh, goodness, I'm certain our circus-find will curse you if you look at it too much,' Dowager Justinian scolded as she came in with a cup of tea. She picked up one of the large napkins and threw it over the jar. 'I have nightmares of it breaking out and crawling about the house.'

Startled, Arden stepped away. 'I wondered if it were indeed true.' She kept her voice sceptical. 'That it came from a woman.'

Dowager Justinian's lips vanished inside the disapproving line of her mouth. 'Sadly true. One of the shorefolk worked here as a domestic. They are frivolous with their affections. A child, fourteen years old when she declared herself. In the end we had to supply our own doctor to assist in the delivery.' She shuddered at the memory, twisted her wedding ring. 'The Baron was delighted. The old Baron, I mean. My late husband's grandfather, Alexander Justinian, not my son. Such things reflect badly on the House.'

'Shouldn't the Eugenics Society have been called to report the birth?' Arden asked. 'They get fussy over an extra finger . . .' She waved at the jar, not altogether concealed by the napkin. 'This would make the Society have hysterics.'

'Baron Alexander Justinian had friends high up in the Society during his life,' the Dowager sighed. 'You are right, if it were up to a reasonable person the creature and the wench both would have been investigated. But they didn't seem much to care, and the Baron did like his curios.'

'What happened to the girl? Her family?'

The older woman fiddled with her earring. The marcasite chips caught the lantern glow. 'Oh, I think they're all gone now. Nomadic folk, islanders. They come and go, and the fish are bad, lately. What are you working on?'

She showed the Dowager her map. 'Finding my way. Learning the geography of Vigil.'

According to Arden's maps, which in the last few weeks she had spent most of her time studying in lieu of actually going out to sea, the shore where the Rivens' old factory buildings clung was not particularly accessible by watercraft. The wash and tempest on the rocks made it difficult to bring a small boat close, and the remains of a pier, broken at the root, showed just how dangerous the waves could be.

However on the other side of the promontory, on a circlet helpfully named Dead Man's Bay, a divot in the cliffs provided a few natural shelters and a small pebbled beach that was spared the tumult of the ocean waves. There were more ruins here, old fortifications of a Neolithic tribal folk, made before their more enlightened current era. The map illustrated them with helpful asterisks and the word *ruins* in the key.

To access the Riven factory, she could make her way on foot through the ruins.

Dowager Justinian raised the wick on the lamp. 'It's so dim in here, Lightmistress. How on earth are you seeing?'

'Beacons are good with little light and long distances,' Arden said. 'Blood aside, they're part of our small endowments, the mark of our family.'

'The Eugenics Society must think highly of such a trait.'

'There's always someone who will. It's not just lamps and signals. There's many shipping companies who pay handsomely for the distance-skill alone.'

The Dowager squinted in the lamplight, composed a sentence carefully in her thoughts before speaking. 'My son tells me you are in your twenty-seventh year. Unless you have made a vow to God or the Sapphic orders, I'm surprised someone of your genetic value is not yet married.'

Arden pointed at the risen lamp. 'It becomes complicated when one comes from old ledgered families. The Eugenics Society must approve any union I make. For now, I am forbidden anyone until my full degree.' She closed her eyes briefly, remembering the Guildsman clerk in her father's offices. His sly winking expression. *With a full degree you could certainly choose who you would like to marry, for one thing.*

How pathetic, that Richard Castile feared discovery by Lions, when they had known about the relationship all along.

'You are of a good age,' the Dowager continued, and Arden realized at once what the Madam of the house was leading in to.

She put her fountain pen down. 'Dowager, you never told me your son was going to marry Bellis Riven.'

'Didn't I?' The Dowager's fingers dappled upon a cameo brooch at her throat. 'I could never quite keep up with Vernon's dalliances when he was a young man.'

'A proposed marriage is hardly a dalliance.'

'I suppose not.' Her eyes became hard in the lamplight, knowing that Arden had foiled an ill-considered matchmaking. 'One could never be certain if he'd only suffered a youthful fantasy. Without meaning to, Bellis could be quite the coquette.'

'My concern is,' Arden continued, 'although I have an assistant, there will be times when I'll be on the promontory alone with Miss Harrow's suspected killer nearby. I cannot have unresolved issues between him and your son making my job difficult. Mr Riven is my closest neighbour, and regardless of what he has done, or whatever rumours swirl, I may come to depend on him for assistance out there.'

A little part of her laughed at the thought of seeking assistance from someone who had tried to run her down as casually as a cur in the middle of the road. But she had committed herself to signal-keeper business, and that meant business with the other person who shared her territory.

'Miss Bellis Harrow and Vernon – I mean my son, Mr Justinian – may have made plain their intention to marry, but my son never wasted his youth on adult responsibilities.' The Dowager adjusted the wick on one lamp, for the brightness illuminated an alarming patch of swelling damp on one wall. 'By my count ten girls in all Fiction have considered themselves the next Madame Justinian. I dare not think about Lyonne. But she was the best of them, Bellis. A good, sweet-natured girl. Always had a kind word for me. They were friends from their first year. My son courted her when he still had baby-cheeks, before the city called him away.'

'So they must have been of similar age, then.'

'Yes, yes they were. Quite a few children in town were. They formed quite a cadre. Vernon and Bellis exchanged rings in promise before he left. Being a hopeful mother, I'd hoped that *meant* they would one day marry. But you see, friendships from the cradle rarely survive the storms of adulthood.'

She fiddled with the wick up on a third lamp, this one to chase away the spirits of the gathering night. The only effect was to make the shadows darker, and harshen those lights already in the room.

'Strange,' Arden said. 'With all those tales of a forced marriage to Mr Riven, it led me to believe Miss Harrow a literal child. If she shared Vernon's age she must have been in her late twenties at least. My age, then. An independent adult.'

'Age is relative, you see. Her father, Mr Harrow, is a firm

man. Very firm. Owns the general store in Vigil, and is Postmaster into the bargain. Does duties as Magistrate when we have cause to hold a criminal court. So he rather preserved his child in a state of innocence longer than most.'

'I take it he approved of the union between Mr Justinian and Bellis?'

'Of course. Not a better match could a Vigil girl make, not even the daughter of a Magistrate Postmaster. Perhaps this made Mr Harrow blind to his daughter's beauty and friendly nature, how such a thing is a flame in the night-time, and attractive to night-flying things. Bellis loved my son. What a terrible, tragic surprise that she should marry Mr Riven so very suddenly.'

'Something must have happened to have spoiled this gilded cage that Mr Harrow kept her in. People don't flee comfort lightly.'

'No they do not,' Dowager Justinian said. 'She did not flee. Mr Riven desired that he should have her. An unseemly lust overcame him upon seeing Bellis in the town one day. He is blood-bound to the wild things of the sea, you understand. No doubt his urges are similarly wild.' Her hand went to her throat, appalled at what such an indecorous affinity meant.

Arden shook her head. 'Any magistrate could have granted divorce immediately had there been any true element of non-consent or violence.'

'The economy of Vigil needs kraken—'

'Goodness, morals go beyond that!'

'Well, people tried! Once Vernon attempted to visit Bellis out on the promontory and inquire about her welfare. Mr Riven fired at him with a Middle Country musket. And then a month later the girl was dead.' Dowager Justinian heaved a breath, fiddled nervously with a lace handkerchief wedged up her dark sleeve, then went to close the curtains for the night as if the act, more suited to servant-staff, assuaged a deeper trouble of which she had yet to speak.

'Hers is a wretched tragedy, I agree,' Arden said. 'But it's more tragic that I hear everyone's voice on the matter excepting Bellis Harrow-Riven's. What was her truth? What was her reason?'

'It doesn't need a truth or reason. She is dead. I have cried enough tears.'

With her duties done, Dowager Justinian went from the study with a rustle of skirts, and left Arden in the gloom with her maps.

A storm had come upon the shoreline, whistling mournfully across the barren black cliffs of Vigil's bay. When the oil lamps burned low, Arden put away her ocean-current almanacs and headed to her bed. The embers from the fire cast orange highlights across the room, made them move with an uneven flicker. The krakenskin's thousand eye-rings watched her with abyssal coldness, wiser than any holy stone. The black ship forever bore down upon Arden in her memory.

A dead woman had worn this coat. A dead woman stolen away, as in the fairy stories, where the King of the Sea would take a fair maiden from the beach and ravish her upon his oyster-pearl bed for a thousand nights.

An innocent tale, yet Bellis Harrow's life was just that story, whisked off by a lord of the sea and ravished in a crude bed in a decaying factory-shack. For her the reality had been a story of violence and despair.

The coat, though. The puzzle piece that did not fit.

Months, it would have taken to craft such a garment, to cut and cure and fit and sew. The tremulous leather-work at the sleeves had increased in confidence at the collar and yoke. A teacher had been patient, and their student enthusiastic. The patterns were exultant and joyful. A woman in pain could not have made this garment.

Arden's Portside stubbornness returned. During her duties as lantern mistress she had seen illegal ships enter the harbour through the Parrot Wharf turning bowl, filled with the spoils of piracy and illegal gains. Her job concerned the safe passage of boats through the locks and wharves. If she had no evidence of wrongdoing, it was not for her to judge the misbegotten contents they held. That task she would leave for the sheriffs and the inspectors

She had a lighthouse to manage, and a future far from here.

Whatever the locals got up to in the meantime, that was their business alone.

7

The Vernon Justinian who went to Garfish Point

The Vernon Justinian who went to Garfish Point the day before, and the one who woke up the next morning could hardly be considered the same person. He moaned piteously through the breakfast table and collapsed on the daybed afterwards with a damp napkin over his eyes. The sound of morning rain on the windows made him whimper. The house staff were obliged to tiptoe around, for the shuffle of their feet on the worn parquetry made him yell in a manner most unbecoming to a man of his station.

Everyone from the butler to the pretty girl of the scullery found themselves bludgeoned with his wrathful tongue. The girl's darting, angry eyes found Arden, and blamed her silently for Mr Justinian's foul condition.

Only Dowager Justinian received permission to come close, to bring the opium tea laced with cannabis oil which only served to make him delirious. Within minutes of his dashing the bitter drink to the carpet, Mr Justinian fell into a daze from which he could not be roused.

Arden could not find it in herself to be very upset at the

Coastmaster's complaint. It meant she would get easy escape from the grey confines of the Manse, and an unhurried excursion through the lands she would temporarily call home. Mr Quill, the old, tweedy fellow who did double duty as groundskeeper and Justinian driver, agreed to take Arden to the lighthouse by the long-route. He too feared his employer's temper, and relievedly accepted the excuse of a road trip.

The car rattled and coughed its way along the inland lanes that led past the racelakes and the ethanol-spirit farms that brought Fiction's economy a little coin by feeding the hungry country to the north. The coastal scrub was dominated by an aromatic bush, and the air through the open window smelled of menthol as well as salt.

Through most of the morning Arden hid her gloves under her bag politely until Mr Quill told her that he was not at all troubled by her presence.

'My second cousin twice-removed went to Lyonne after he was tested, near on fifty years ago,' he said. 'I saw the coins in his hands.'

'Oh? Would I know him?'

'Would you?'

'A Fiction blood-worker quite stands out these days. They're so rare.'

Mr Quill shook his head and his mouth fell into long, sad lines. 'Lass, you were not alive when he died. Fool didn't last a week. Got roaring drunk one night. Struck his head on a low beam, fell into a Clay Portside canal.'

'Oh, that is a shame,' Arden said, and felt her hands prickle awfully. 'The city can be quite disorienting to newcomers.'

He gave a phlegmy, dismissive cough. 'Disorienting! We aren't that lumpen, or grain-pickled. I know my cousin never touched alcohol. No, it was the Eugenics Society that had him killed.'

It was such a shockingly open pronouncement that Arden wound the window down a little more and silently turned to the menthol gust and the clattering engine rather than reply. Such conversations were never had in Lyonne, where a Lion might be lurking about every corner. 'The Eugenics Society wouldn't just murder people. They're a little more subtle than that.'

The skin under his eyes had a little nervous tic.

By now the vehicle had crested an uplift in the land and they came upon a great forest of silver and rubber piping, of vessels as large as airship bladders, and tall chambers as high as her lighthouse. If Arden wanted to talk to Mr Quill more about the economies of Lyonne and blood, her thoughts were gone in an instant.

'Goodness,' Arden exclaimed. 'These are automatic rockblood refineries, are they not?'

'Yes, Sainted Isle crude rockblood, straight from the wound.'

'I've never seen one so large before.'

'You don't use petralactose in that big Clay city?'

'All the time. We get petroleum distillates transported to Lyonne, but never in the crude form.'

A giant copper distillation tank towered above the scrub, bristling with walkways and transoms. From their distance, the refinery had the appearance of a malign castle built by madmen, except no man had made this terrible feat of automatic engineering. Arden spotted a puddle of iridescent petralactose pooling at the bottom of one tank, the old edifice leaking through aged valves no living being had the knowledge to fix. It was there that she caught her first view of human figures, oily workers scuttling about the old refinery with patches and seals, trying to keep it alive the way ants might attend at the swollen belly of their great, gravid queen.

'One of them damn grey ships is at dock,' Mr Quill said, pointing. 'Can you see the godforsaken thing? Have you not in your life witnessed such a travesty of nature?'

The ship was more barge than anything, a grey vessel without windows, berthed on the far shore of the peninsula. Arden knew little about the logistical workings of the Sainted Isles, only that the grey ship was a watch-worked craft with a single purpose, obligated to ferry itself to the Islands and return with a bellyful of raw petrolactose. Compelled by old bloodworked commands, it cruised back and forth between the Island wells and the mainland refineries as thoughtless as the gears in her lantern house.

'Is that a *lich-ship*? I saw one beached at the Clay Mouth when I was a girl.'

'Really? I didn't think the lich-ships went that far north.'

She shook her head. 'Usually they don't. A storm forced one off course. The internal mechanisms were confused and it ran aground in Lyonne. The Clay Mouth swampfolk weren't impressed by their clockwork visitor.'

'What did they do?'

'Burned it. They thought it was evil.'

'Perhaps they were not wrong. What manner of sanguinity could make such a machine?'

'Ones lost to us now, thank goodness. *Ferrum perpetua, mandari, orientis* . . . the old talents. Though one would need the entire compliment to control something like *that*.' She tilted her chin towards the grey ship and its empty dock.

Mr Quill drove on, relieved to be away from the unholy automata. The copper forests faded along with the relentlessly aromatic fermented-pine smell of petroleum fractions. Some of the acrid scent clung to Arden's skin, a dreadfully bitter perfume. It made her recall the petroleum dens of Clay, where debauched scions might inhale distillations of rockblood from crystal decanters. The euphoria was brief and terrible, and long-term partakers often lost control of their faculties, became confused, and died.

Perpetua, procuro, orientis. Her intonation of the old talents to Mr Quill had made her uneasy, a feeling that carried even after the refinery was out of view. There were some sanguineous symmetries that were not inheritable, even by a Society who knew more about coaxing heritable traits out of a bloodline than any scholarly system in existence. She knew only of the old talents as one knew all general trivia, something learned to pass an Academy mid-term exam and then forgotten forever.

Out on the ocean, more boats dotted the grey slate water. More desperate, hopeful souls heading to the source of the refinery's awful contents. A land torn open and dying, like a wound. Imagine breathing that kind of air all the time, she thought with a shudder. Imagine such a place.

They stopped at a sugar-beet farm for midday refreshments, and the family were pleased to offer Arden provisions in exchange for Lyonne coin. She needed a little smear of her blood to restore antique bloodlight lanterns extinguished for over a century. They had last been lit only in those days when blood was strong in Fiction.

'These instruments are of a good design,' Arden said to her hosts, pleased at the steady glow. 'They'll not need feeding for two years, maybe three.'

And I'll be far away from here.

The children gawped at the strange, cold blue flame behind glass that had always resisted a normal fire. Their parents, as expected, were a little less enthusiastic.

Arden did not begrudge the farmers their caution around her. In Fiction, more so than in Lyonne even, there were bad stories of northern industries casting out a thousand workers after company had hired a lone bloodworker.

The one man who could replace a thousand men is dangerous to you.

How could they not be guarded against her and her talents when they see the lich-ships on the horizon, or the automatic refineries and see themselves replaced and redundant? Great powers had walked the earth in the time of their legends but it had not stopped the tide of industry. It may not have been by pure neglect that the Fiction folk had abandoned the power that ran in their veins.

The day matured and chased away the rainclouds.

Mr Quill turned the car towards the shore again, and that long, elegant spit that would lead back to her lighthouse.

Arden folded back the roof and stood up at seeing the Riven factory ruins crabbing to the rocky cliffs in a precarious embrace. She had yet to view the compound from this angle, crooked upon the old foundations of Neolithic ruins.

'Wait,' she said. 'Stop here.'

'Are you certain?' Mr Quill slowed to a crawl but did not apply the brake. 'This is the Riven ground.'

'I'm not going to waste a single night here worrying about what my neighbour might be up to,' Arden said. 'I need to speak to him. You can stay with the car.'

Mr Quill was in no way in agreement, but he pulled the vehicle over to a roadside shoulder.

'This part of the promontory is frequently covered by winter surge,' he warned her. 'It will only be you and him on the island for great stretches of time.'

'Then it is fortunate I'm only here until autumn's end.' She held up her gloves and made a face at them. 'My coins won't hold within my hands much longer than that. They'll need replacing.'

'Still. I have a powder-pistol in the trunk. It's not much but . . .'

'If I am not back on the hour, then you may commence my rescue.'

She left Mr Quill to fret in the car and gladly got out, her legs cramping and stiff from the hours bracing against the rough terrain. The road had overgrown with dandelion and salt-sedge, but under her boots she saw plaques of tar and stone, the remnants of a fairly civilized road.

Though it crossed her mind to leave the krakenskin coat with the rest of her belongings, another stubborn instinct had her wear the coat instead. Best they quarrel about this now, rather than later, when she would not have a man with a powder-pistol and a car waiting in the wings.

Now that she could make her up-close observations, Arden noted how many of the factory houses visible from the lighthouse grounds had fallen into disrepair. The environment had gnawed and savaged the metal as a shark might a corpse, reducing it to warped rust and wood splinters. Despite her coat's warmth, Arden wrapped her arms around her. An odd caul of melancholy draped over this place. Great leviathans of the deep had been processed on these shores, their meat harvested, their ambergris and oil packed into barrels, their skins tanned to leather. How odd that such an important industry be reduced to a lone man and his cart?

The squally wind tore and jostled about her. Mr Riven's black wood boat had since parked below his factory ports, louring and waiting.

I will be strong, she decided. I will be strong. So, the man had merely attempted to run her down with his boat like a coward. Let him be a coward now to her face. She had experienced worse manner of trials. A scar upon her throat remained from when a hapless dockside mutineer once took her as a hostage before taking his own life. She had worked the docks during the False Unionist war, the War of the Wharves, and the Battle of the Tea Leaves. She had seen the worst of people.

At the end of a double-rutted track, the processing compound emerged from the scrub in fits and starts of abandoned engineering, gears and old machines. If any paint had ever graced the processing bunkers and the icehouses, the sea-wind had scoured it away in a century of furious assault. Some telegraph poles leaned in the wind, their wires stripped away by time and storm.

A lone insulated cable flapped against a tilting trunk and left a dissonant image that made Arden ponder. If the Riven clan were savages fit only to play with knives, why would they have such technology as telegraphs and electricity?

She continued through the grounds, found stables for at least ten heavy horses. A printing press turning to rust, with three fonts of lead type crystallizing in their cases. The foundations of a fireplace of the massive kind that heats a great hall. Pipes and spigots, an aqueduct for grey water so it would not contaminate the small freshwater streams. Easily fifty people could have lived and worked here with the home comforts one could expect in a well-serviced Lyonnian town. And a dozen more would have been required to provide support services. The administration of an electrical and communications system by itself would have employed at least four, five trained workers.

This was no savage shore. This was an industry, ceased abruptly and without reason.

She passed a sad patch of dirt, the only thing that looked halfway cared for in recent years, and seven wooden crosses, scored and faded by storm.

Then she caught the smell of krakenhides.

A strange quirk of cryptozoology made the rot and decay of animals despised by God and embraced by the devil so different in their decomposition. The sweet smell reminded Arden of a heavy Koutoubian spice. She'd heard tell of the learned sultans of the desert kingdoms using krakenmusk to bring a garden to the senses while their eyes viewed only sand and ancient books. A Djenne mathematician might burn the oil in incense, to aid her mental acuity. Arden had smelled kraken perfume oftentimes on the collar of a sharply suited Khanate merchant as he passed by with a trolley of legal agreement documents.

But those memories belonged to her bustling trader's home, not a desolate hamlet on the coldest end of the Darkling Coast.

'Hello? Mr Riven?'

Nobody answered. The smell of the curing hides wafted stronger here. Somebody was nearby, for nobody left their catch unattended to either elements or seabirds. A ragged pair of cormorants sat on the roof of a nearby ruin, their attention longingly fixed on the source of the smell.

She walked past a pile of massive cuttlefish bones, each one as big as her torso. The tusks of a short-necked saurian made an unusual entry passage. Her meanderings took her by one of the few houses left standing, a country-style lodge decorated in the gingerbread-style that only a woman of Vigil could have appreciated.

If the lodge had made it through the disaster that claimed the rest of the compound, the years were already taking their toll. The decorative architraves and wind-icons showed the ragged edges of warp and decay. Whoever had built their home here and given the stark place such a gentle touch had long vacated it. Already the garden beds were piles of dirt, any hope of flowers long gone.

She had already made up her mind about what the lodge would look like inside. Rotted floorboards, walls leaking horsehair insulation. A bare, stained mattress would be on the floor where a man might sleep, if he slept at all.

Beyond the house lay the vats and curing tables for krakenskin, shining bright brass in the dull day.

Then at last she saw Mr Riven.

He had not altered since the day when she had first lain eyes upon him. If she were pressed to admit it, then he was more appalling than before. A male, shirtless figure, almost entirely encrusted in dirt, trudging up the pier. A heavy object lay floppy in his arms, a slimy thing as big as a small woman. As she watched, he dumped it upon the curing table. A coiled rope and flabby sack followed. Plesiosaur foetus with the placenta still attached, torn viciously from its mother's womb. Though they were reptilian by family, plesiosaur were warm-blooded and viviparous, same as mammals. They birthed live, had a maternal sense. Arden ached at seeing the baby's wretched limpness, would have cried out if she could.

Mr Riven was every bit the monster Mr Justinian proclaimed him. Dried plaques of blood smeared him from beard to bare belly. His body echoed the decay of his compound, flesh harrowed and scarred by sea and storm. A recent trauma had made a mutilation of his face, swelling eyes into blue puffs, his lip split, jaw disfigured under his facial hair.

She forced down her odium and approached the wicked scene.

'Excuse me, sir?'

He ignored Arden at first, too busy arranging the dead foetus lengthways on the table, more gently than one would expect given the violence he must have used to procure the poor thing. Did not glance up, and that gladdened her, for she did not have to witness his grotesque face any more than she needed to.

At last he spoke.

'What do you want?'

No asking her name, no giving of his own. No acknowledgement that she were stranger or enemy or friend. She would not have been surprised if he spoke in animal grunts.

'I am Arden Beacon from Clay Portside and now Vigil,' she said, infuriated by the tremble in her voice. Why should she be so distracted by his filthy nakedness, the way an Old Master might have painted him in a hellscape triptych, minus the trident and the pale sinner for poking?

'I am the Lighthouse—'

'I know who you are.' He fixed her then with those ferocious blue eyes, blue like the horizon that mocks the castaway sailor. 'You are Jorgen's niece, and you are not welcome here.'

'What business my uncle had with you, that was his own,' Arden said, light-headed with revulsion. 'I came to ask that whatever bad blood you two had with each other, stays in the grave. I do not intend to bother you, merely conduct my lighthouse business.'

'Then go conduct your business. I will not interfere, if you give me the same respect.'

She stood for a moment, strangely unfulfilled, having expected more, and less from him. Yelling and curses she could have borne. But not this quiet horror.

'Thank you.' She turned to leave, and paused. 'It has not escaped your notice, sir, that I am wearing this coat. I bought it off a jumble seller in town. I need this coat to work the flame during a storm. I want to wear it with your blessing.'

'You don't need my blessing.'

'But it is your wife's coat. That is what people tell me.'

'My wife is dead. Wear whatever you want. Just don't come back here again.'

He returned to the table, and his terrible face stared at the plesiosaur's murdered child as if it had materialized, like an awful magic trick, in front of him.

8

Mr Quill was dreadfully curious

Mr Quill was dreadfully curious, but far too polite to pry. He had seen enough to presume, from Arden rushing back to the automobile before climbing inside and taking several gulping dry sobs, to her wiping her eyes with a handkerchief and saying, 'Let's leave this place. I have seen enough.'

They drove the last mile in silence, and he watched her twist the handkerchief to knots within the tangle of her fingers.

Her composure had not quite returned by the time they reached the lighthouse, and when she saw Mr Harris she hugged him for longer than was necessary to hug a friend.

'Oof, Ardie, what is that in aid of?'

'I'm a touch vulnerable today, that's all. And dismayed by all men. Except you. And Mr Quill of course, who remains a delightful travelling companion.'

She blew her nose on her handkerchief and the tears prickled her eyes again, but every time she tried to think about something else, the poor tiny puppy-face of the foetus came back to her, a little animal that would only know the cold butcher's table and never its mother.

'And I shall refuse to eat meat ever again.'

'Ah, all right, then. Now if you have finished with your

discussions on pitiful humankind, come and meet your new assistant. She's from Lyonne originally but has since been working in—'

'Harbinger Bay. With the Lightkeeper there. Morningvale before that.'

Arden stood back cautiously as Mr Harris introduced a young, strong-boned woman as Miss Chalice Quarry, the Lightkeeper's assistant. 'Miss' and not 'Mx' of course – for she lacked the higher guild degrees for that title. Miss Quarry, pale, freckled skin and auburn plaits dusted with sea-salt, had a sturdiness to her frame that made her what the signallers called a *stormbride*, for only the stoutest among them could survive the hard weather and relight an extinguished lamp or tie a giant mooring howser after it has snapped at the pier. Such folk were married to the storm, their equal. She wore a Guild-associate coin on a chain about her neck, a chunky pewter triangle.

After Mr Quill had unpacked Arden's belongings, he left with Mr Harris, and Arden, quite unexpectedly, had to share her surroundings with a stranger. This assistant would not always be in Arden's company, but she would be around enough that if they did not get along, the next few months would be miserable indeed.

They sized each other up with the wariness of fighters in a wharf-house pit-ring. Arden decided this red-haired Chalice Quarry suffered no nonsense. In their day together she had quickly made a home among the rocks and scrub of the promontory and the gruff company of Mr Harris. The arrival of an actual sanguis Lightkeeper, and a startlingly young one at that, would not have been altogether welcome.

'Um, are your hours here long, Miss Quarry?' Arden asked as politely as she could.

'Most days I will be of help,' Chalice said. 'Other days David Modhi ferries me by boat from Vigil. I have a small business in town, to keep my mind off this desolate place. Oh, and before our greetings become too long in the tooth, you shall call me Chalice and I shall call you Arden. There are no standards to uphold here except expedience.'

'Of course, Miss . . . I mean, Chalice. Mr Harris said you toured Harbinger Bay. That's a hard inlet. Are you from Clay Portside?'

'No. My hometown is Shinlock, far west of Clay Riverina. I trained in Portside for a while. T'was Mr Harris who hired me to work at Morningvale, so I did not mind joining him here when they made him an interim keeper.'

The woman picked up Arden's entire shipping trunk as casually as she might have hefted a linen basket, set it inside the tower's ground floor with an effortless grunt. 'David Modhi will come by tomorrow. We'll sail back and retrieve your boat.'

'That would be appreciated, but perhaps he could do that today.'

'Not with this place a pigsty and a squall coming. By the time we're finished here it will be almost dark.'

'Finished?'

'Cleaning, of course. Come now. Hop to it.'

A little flustered at being bossed around in her own signal post, Arden took off her coat, rolled up her sleeves, and followed Chalice's lead. They got a fire started in an iron coal-pit outside, and Chalice unearthed a large rusted kettle from a mound of rubbish. A prior attack on the lighthouse's poor condition by herself and Mr Harris had unearthed several treasures. A mercury barometer, a storm glass, a radio-electrograph that inscribed approaching objects with a needle on carbon paper. She hauled some seawater up from a blowhole, and boiled it with an oily soap.

Arden stared with dismay at the salt-encrusted remnants of a valve-telegraph, the earpiece now a home to a family of tiny spiders. A ticker tape rained a miserable confetti on the floor. She imagined composing a letter in her mind to her friends, and having to pretend everything fine and dandy, when it completely was not.

'How am I meant to report the conditions if none of the communications are working?'

Chalice hauled open a large journal, the leaves a sturdy drab green. Mr Harris' penmanship had always been atrocious, and Arden noticed he'd missed a few entries. Of Jorgen Beacon's entries, there were none.

'You'll need to make the weather observations by hand, four during the day, two at night. I will post them weekly, on a Sunday, to the Meteorological Society,' Chalice said. 'I will maintain the barometers, and we shall share the work of collecting the measurements from both bays. Any storm or adverse conditions, one of us must immediately take a boat across to Vigil and have Mr Harrow send a telegraph to the Garfish Point station.'

Arden nodded, trying to keep the dismay from her face. 'I have met Mr Harrow.'

'I can do that errand if you like,' Chalice said, kindly now. 'If you prefer to watch your light.'

At least one duty was hers alone. 'Yes, I'd feel better, staying close to my lantern.'

So, into the kettle went all Uncle Jorgen's implements of his talent. His knives and bloodletting equipment, the dishes and vials, the collectors and extractors and refiners.

They stood about the fire and watched the water bubble. The old clots floated up with the detergent.

'Well,' Arden said at last. 'This is all very rustic.'

Chalice agitated the pot with a paddle, sent some miserly soap bubbles skidding across the surface.

'We cannot waste the water here on the peninsula. There is a spring, but it is barely enough for drinking and bathing, and besides, the rain is mostly sea-spray. The streams are further down the promontory, near the pilgrim ruins. Their water must be carted by hand.' Chalice continued to stir the kettle until the blood tools lost their noxious crust.

'There,' she said after a few minutes. 'You can use them now.'

'You're familiar with bloodworking?'

Surprisingly, Chalice pointed to an old scar upon her hand. 'Went to a testmoot on my tenth birthday. Shinlock fell under the auspices of Clay Capital despite the distance between the town and the city, so of course we all had to go and get ourselves tested.'

'Did you test positive for a talent?' Arden blurted out, and instantly regretted it. Of course the woman hadn't tested positive. Children with talent were given stipends and scholarships, went to school in Clay Capital. The best of them stayed on, were utilized for their precious labour. The rest went home, often subtly neutered so they might not sully their family lines further.

To Arden's further surprise, Chalice nodded. 'Not positive, but some latencies for trace minerals. The salt of the ocean appeals to my sense of sodium chloride, but that's about it.'

'Oh, what a shame, to not have a talent.'

'Trust me darling, I wouldn't wish to be sanguine. Far too much trouble, and the Society breathing down your neck like an overly invested uncle during St Stephens dinner? Ugh, not for me.'

Over the bubbling kettle Arden admitted her own failings, of her late blooming at seventeen rather than eleven, of a half-brother with *sanguis ferro* talent. 'Between me and him, our family is not particularly healthy in the eyes of the eugenicists right now. Our ledger page is all red crosses and angry notations.'

She waited for Chalice to enquire incredulously how, with all that against her, Arden had managed such an important signal post.

To her credit, the stormbride kept her counsel and only said with genuine feeling, 'Then I hope this small sojourn to these shores works out well for you, Arden Beacon.'

'Thank you. I do hope it works out.'

'What happens once you are done here?'

'Home awaits. I'll have a full Guild membership then and dispensation to—' she faded off, worrying she might be too personal with this woman she'd only just met.

'Dispensation?' Chalice said with a chortle. 'To marry, you mean?' Her eyes sparkled wickedly.

Arden's cheeks grew hot. 'It would be nice, I suppose.'

Chalice wagged a finger at Arden. 'Then make this time quick, and marry your fellow. It will make a fitting end.'

'What do you mean, a fitting end?'

'This is the last of the blood-kept lights, and the Guild has decided to keep it no more. The light will be de-registered at your departure, and I will return to Clay and take another posting.' She picked up the triangular Guild assistant coin from about her neck and kissed it. 'God willing it be an easy one this time.'

'Oh, that's a shame,' Arden said, crestfallen. She couldn't bear thinking of her uncle's light extinguished like the beet-farmer's lanterns. A Beacon could not let a fire lapse, it was against their code.

'It's *politics* darling. The Fiction Guild folk would prefer one of their own in this tower. And since they don't lean to blood, its only fair this should be a common fire.'

Then another worrisome thought came over her, and it showed on her face long enough for Chalice to ask, 'What troubles you?'

'I think it *is* peculiar.'

'Losing a lighthouse?'

'No, that the Fiction Seamaster's Guild should wait until winter to decommission the light. It would have been better to replace the lamp now, when the days are long.'

Chalice silently stirred the pot until the tools clunked, and Arden felt bad for dumping her cares upon a stormbride whom she'd decided was quite nice after all.

'Oh, don't mind me, Chalice. I'm just glad for the opportunity. I'd never have gotten this chance in Lyonne. Maybe they're even expecting a *sanguinem ignis* from Fiction? Maybe that is the delay.'

An odd expression made Chalice's freckles wrinkle. 'Darling, there hasn't been a Fiction-born sanguinem for . . . goodness, well over a decade.'

'Who was the last?' Arden asked, wondering if she should know of a foreign-born sanguinem in the academies. The ladies of the Guild would have talked forever and a day of such a person.

Chalice seemed to pause, as if deciding whether or not to tell Arden, then pointed her chin down the promontory.

'*His* wife, for one.'

Mr Justinian's voice hissed in her mind, as it always did, as if he had infected her with a hateful memory. *Murdered whore*, he'd said.

'Bellis *Riven*? Chalice, I don't remember her being in the Clay Academies at all.'

'She never went to Clay,' Chalice continued, 'She was tested positive for sanguinity, but stayed at home.'

'And the Eugenics Society *let* her?'

'They did indeed. Looks like our over-invested Society is capable of some empathy. Bellis had a sick mother. A father with connections. You know that tale, how it goes.'

'Goodness. Well, then. I would be curious to know of her endowment, if you remember so well.'

Chalice Quarry checked for the unlikely eavesdroppers on this desolate promontory, then leaned in close.

'When the test masters applied the assessment, her blood drew powerfully to the black oil from the Islands,' Chalice replied with a fine hint of condescension sprinkled with the slightest salt of jealousy.

'Rockblood? *Sanguinem petrae?* But, Chalice, a petroleum symmetry is a golden talent!'

Chalice sat back, still as nonplussed by the fact of Bellis' result as she must have been the first time she heard it. 'Gold, and *old*! The *petrolactose* bloodline is almost extinct! Every big-city technical academy and Guild tower clamoured for her presence. She chose to stay here.'

'Chalice, come now. The Eugenics Society would not have allowed her to stay here. Much less the Lions.'

'They may not allow it, but this is Fiction, not Lyonne. There are no Lions here. Wished only to stay with her loving father, her poorly mother. Be a dutiful daughter, unlike all the other greedy little shits who run away to Lyonne at their first chance at a golden dollar and sanguis coins.' Chalice clasped her hands dramatically to her breast and affected a swoon. 'Poor Bellis. So they let her.'

'Put me in the camp of undutiful peasant then,' Arden sighed, twitching with envy. 'My father wasn't too pleased at my coming to Vigil. We had quite a row over it.'

'Quite frankly, the rockblood talent was wasted on her. What's a little innocent creature like Bellis going to do with *sanguinem petrae* anyway? Go out to the Sainted Isles and start digging around for old pipes so the prospectors can bunker them? Live with the machines? I think not.'

With that, Chalice gave the steaming kettle a kick, and they retrieved the now passably clean blood apparatus from the bowl. Arden wrapped the copper parts up into one of Dowager Justinian's towels, and they headed up – gingerly on account of the corroding staircase – to the lamp room.

Chalice watched with interest as Arden reaffixed all the bloodletting devices to the fading flame wick. When it came to Uncle Jorgen's knife, she declined the uneven blade and pulled from one of her corset-bones a small stiletto knife. It made a fine cut in the centre of the button, and the blood welled up like a cabochon ruby.

'Like stigmata,' Chalice opined, which prompted a huff from Arden.

'Coins,' she corrected.

At the touch of the blood, the white flame kicked and roared up, making both women stand back with a gasp.

'Ah, so bright!' Chalice exclaimed, her hand over her eyes. Then she put her hand in the fire and waved her fingers about so that the blue flame hissed through her fingers. 'So bright and so *cold*. I'll never get over how strange a sanguine flame is.'

Arden nodded. 'Of course it will be brighter than usual. The ratio hasn't been correct for a long time.' She wound the wick down and closed the fresnel lenses. 'My uncle suffered illness long before he came out here, I think. His blood was fading. My blood is hardly strong, either. Like I said, I came into it too late.'

'Would it have been different if you had come into your talent earlier?'

'Very much. You should have seen my Uncle Nicolai's blood-light, Chalice. You could wear welder's goggles with your eyes shut, and you would still see the flame though your eyelids. I used to love going to the Clay Mouth signal tower, helping him on my vacation days.' She stood back and sighed. 'I never thought I'd have a signal tower. It's almost a dream too good to be true.'

Chalice pressed her palms to the lens and fussed over the cold light. Arden was pleased that her stormbride had not been fearful. Hard enough to convince any commonfolk with little experience that the sanguis talents were not always dangerous, and almost never if one took the proper precautions.

Arden finished the rest of her light business, lowering the mantle so the flame burned incandescent against the knitted hood, and wound the revolving mechanica to last the night. Chalice made her final observations for the journal. They descended the spiral stairs, and Arden decided that she would like this Chalice Quarry. The woman was clearly a little older than her, past thirty years at least. Had an easy experience about her, as if she were a sturdy, trustworthy boat, unlikely to sink.

Chalice put a kettle upon the coals outside. 'You are a hard worker, and helpful,' she acknowledged Arden with grudging good humour. 'Not like Lightkeeper Pharos in my previous posting, who could barely raise a fork to his lips if he thought I could be around to do it for him!'

'I think we will make a good team,' Arden replied, shy with her new friendship. 'My light and your—'

'Well, I'm no witch, but with my chemical latencies I can make a *very* good medicinal tea. Come sit now, Lightmistress, and you may show yourself as better company than Mr Harris.'

Arden sat inside the rowboat and watched Chalice work her

botanical magicks. When the steeped brew came to her she clutched the enamel mug of tea for warmth.

The setting sun skimmed the grey sea with a scar of gold. Chalice pointed towards the horizon. A plume of luminous smoke rose against a backdrop of red sky. This time it was not a sainted flotilla, but a boat Arden knew only too well, having survived those chopping wheels the day before.

'Mr Riven's heading out to sea,' Chalice said. 'Thank the Redeemer, we won't have to think of him prowling around tonight.'

'He prowls?'

Chalice shrugged. 'Personally, I don't think he cares about us one whit. He wants to know what's happening on the promontory though. Most fishermen keep stock of their surroundings, and he does the same.'

'I came to discover what manner of man Mr Riven is this afternoon,' Arden said darkly. 'I had Mr Quill stop his car so I might make my acquaintance and beg of him not to come kill us in the night.' Arden dry-laughed without humour at her own joke, which was not amusing, was true and terrifying.

'And? Was he monstrous? Did he have giant eyes on the side of his head and the arms of a squid and a cuttlefish beak between his legs?'

Arden *tsk*ed at Chalice's bleak wit. 'A tattoo of that, perhaps. I could not look. He had his kill in his arms. A baby plesiosaur, a little helpless thing torn from its mother's body. I came upon him laying it out upon his slaughter table.'

'The devil's damnation, then. The sea will not forgive such a travesty.' Chalice studied the tea leaves skimming the top of her mug. 'Hunting plesiosaur is illegal in spawning waters. The locals say bad luck follows anyone harming an unborn pup. Once they get word of it you know there'll be misfortune upon the waters. Perhaps you could advise the Captain of the Coast, who I understand you have spent a month with . . .?'

'Ha!' Arden cried. 'And who then will Mr Riven have to blame for the accusation? The one person who saw him in the act! If Postmaster Harrow and Coastmaster Justinian could not protect a man's own daughter, what chance do I have?'

Chalice shrugged, topped up the tea, put a third mug aside for the *Old Guy* – a wharf superstition that had made its way from lighthouses and docks and to the edges of the world – before joining Arden in her rowboat throne.

'People in these parts had many envies in their hearts towards pretty little Bellis Harrow with her rockblood talent, Arden, but marrying a man who slaughters monsters, being forced into sexual slavery, neither of those was bloody one of them. Forget about what you saw in those factories. Every place needs a monster, and you won't do anybody any favours by trying to find anything redeemable in Vigil's own.'

'I wasn't trying to redeem him . . .' Arden protested, burning with that furious heat of shame because she had been, in a way, wanting to prove Mr Justinian wrong.

'You went to his doorstep, did you not? What did you think, that by your gracious, unprejudiced Clay Capital ways and your generosities and over-bred face you might tame Mr Riven the way Biblical Daniel tamed the Lions?' Chalice then softened, knowing her words harsh. 'I don't intend cruelty. Mr Riven has been implacable since the day he returned from his captivity in the worst Lyonne prison hulks the Parliament administers. Arden, you remember my posting before this one?'

'Mr Harris said it was the Harbinger Bay lighthouse.'

'Yes, and I've seen the degradations these men are put through on those floating hell-ships, what scarred abominations it creates of them. Why, the Harbinger hulks make the Sainted Isles a paradise in comparison.'

'I can't listen to the opinions of others,' Arden protested, 'I needed to confirm this for myself. Not from Mr Justinian, who has been controlling every whisper and conversation since I arrived here last month. From people I trust. From my own eyes.'

'And you found out. Congratulations, you're still alive. Now leave Mr Riven be and maybe he'll leave us.'

Dejected by the failures of the day, Arden carried the last of her belongings into the lighthouse. She rolled out a Mi'kmaq mat – repurposed from airship battens and lighter than a mattress – on the stone floor, and finished it with a cosy mammoth-wool blanket. The set-up made Chalice's eyes widen appreciatively, and Arden decided she would give the bed to the woman as a present once she left.

The appreciation did not extend to the krakenskin coat.

'I know it's hers,' Arden said after Chalice had another round of conniptions over the death-shawl of Bellis Riven so obviously on display. 'But I hadn't the heart to let it be picked apart for rags, and Mr Riven gave me his blessing.' She paused. 'Or something similar to one.'

'So who is the favourite one now? I wouldn't give you a blessing. Regardless of whose fault, it must be a dreadful thing to see again, and to remember.'

Arden thought about Mr Riven trying to run the *Breeze* down. Perhaps she was being foolish, taunting him with his wife's coat. Foolish, and cruel, and deserving of any misfortune that came in return.

9

When she'd first met

When she'd first met Mr Richard Castile they had both been young. He had just joined the Friesland Corps as an air cadet, and it was in uniform that she'd noticed him, standing near a rainbow buffet of shaved-ice sorbets. She remembered the epaulets winking gold at his shoulders, his black hair glistening in bud-lights, as beautiful as a dream. Arden had failed two testmoots by then and was unlikely to make her third, so she'd been invited to the Guild Ball only out of her father's influence. For that she was in her secret heart not at all upset. Life as a sanguinem was a roster of proscribed affection and arranged marriages and she was glad to escape such boundaries. She had made commonblood friends, and had not begrudged her old companions from her potential days, so she walked the world a popular girl without too many cares, and a curiously protected future.

Until that night.

They grew them handsome and dashing out on the north Summerland seas, and the night Arden saw Mr Castile was the moment she fell in love. Until then she had not quite known if her desires would be towards either men or women, or both, or neither, for at such an age one was little different from the other. But Mr Castile in his navy blue dress uniform and tilted sky-pilot cap could have been a character lifted out of a penny-printed chapbook. She remembered his hair black as a raven's wing, nestled under her chin after they had shared a kiss. Up close his eyes were an impish hazel, and there was a sweet curl to his full lips that would have suited a stage player of Arabian princes. Language danced easy upon his tongue, jokes and stories. Women loved him, men enjoyed his company, and then, for nearly ten years on and off, each meeting achingly brief and deeply regretful, he had been Arden's lover.

Lover. How small a word for all the importance of him.

For all that she promised to forget Richard each time he sailed away, Arden lost her senses upon each return to Clay, and maybe for the most fleeting of moments he had done the same, for there had been a time when he had spun tales of their escape by land and air and sea, away from the Guilds and the Eugenics Society and on to lands where sanguinity meant no more than a name.

But always, the sense of something between them, for each time he put off their escape for another year an invisible hand reached up and lay upon the back of her neck, said: *this man does not have the strength to fight Lions.*

Her blood was not her own. Its labour belonged to the Seamaster's Guild, and its inheritance to the Eugenics Society, and very quietly, her body to the Lyonne Order and Nomenclatures. She would always do what they told her to do.

So she had waited for Richard Castile to become strong. Not always in celibacy, for sometimes the nights grew hot, and the yearnings fierce, and there were always others with coins in their hands and regret in their words who might tangle in darkness for a few hours. Make her forget that once she loved a man, and once a man loved her back.

The months became years, and Richard could never commit to taking a chance. His fear of discovery tangled up about his affections like a choking vine. Her love ossified into a quiet despair. Their reunions were punctuated by her doubts. Until it had all become too much, and he'd flown away for good.

Tonight the winds brought back his memory. She recalled the same sharp pangs of excitement as Mr Castile made love to her, the old familiar way her heart overflowed as he shuddered and spent. The soft kisses from his sweet lips afterwards.

Arden sat up, blinking in the half-light. Her breath made steaming curlicues in the lantern's gleam.

My heart, she thought. *Why are you awake? Why are you hungering now, when you have been asleep for so long?*

Arden greeted the late morning with a stiff back, a stiff neck, and a vague ache in her lower belly, as if she had been aroused by passion in remembering her intimate moments, then left hanging in a confusing state of demi-desire.

In the manner of any good stormbride, Chalice had risen early to stoke the outside fire in the misty drizzle. The smoke from the wet logs had a slithering, seething quality, the kind witches loved.

'Pity your small combinations of minor chemical talents didn't end up with fire-lighting,' Arden said as she joined Chalice.

'Pity *sanguis ignis* coldfire gives no heat, likewise,' Chalice grumped. 'How did you fare in the night, before I took over?'

'Quietly. There were ships out there, but they never came close.'

'The same with my watch. The season is still young. Besides, you sleep well.' Chalice grinned wickedly at Arden. 'Some moaning and groaning and calling of a man's name. I hope yours was a good dream.'

Arden felt herself blushing furiously. 'I did not!'

'Maybe only a little whimper, but you were certainly stoking a mightier fire than this one.'

Her mortification must have been so great that Chalice took pity upon her and gave her knee a playful shove. 'Ease up, Lightmistress, you're hardly the first I've seen to lose their decorum when sleep comes. The air here is bracing, and the sea has the most gloomy of qualities. I know what it is like for a sanguinem, held so rigidly to task in protecting those precious genes of yours.'

'What about you, Chalice Quarry, huh? You and your latencies.'

'Huh indeed, I stick with lovers of a female persuasion and all is well.' She grinned at Arden, and then the fire gave a little skip, finally lighting the pine-cones. Chalice hurriedly threw on some kindling, and at last they had something worthy of a blaze.

Chalice put the kettle on the embers and turned back to Arden. 'What was his name, this man who drove you to remember him so all of a sudden?'

Arden could not have been more solemn if she had been a priest giving last rites. 'Richard Castile. A Frislander. Airship pilot in training. We were going to elope together. Then my talent came in late, almost to the day of our planned escape. After that, well. He didn't quite seem so keen any more.'

'Ah,' Chalice said. 'Farewell is such a sorrow.'

Arden sat on the damp log and rubbed warmth into her shins. 'I wish he had said farewell that day. He kept on orbiting like a rather uncommitted comet.'

'Taunted you with promises, did he? Swore to work towards some great application to the Society for you to marry a common-blooded man like him, but not yet? Wait, wait, wait, for the right time which never came?'

Arden stared, open-mouthed. 'How did you know?'

'Oh, you think you're the first? As soon as you said *airship*, I completely deduced what kind of philanderer he was.'

Somewhere in the smoke the flame that was desperately trying to keep hold, faded. A rain shower threatened, fat blobs of chilled water on her cheek. Arden stood to collect more dried tinder, tried to help the fire along with kindling that wasn't already sopping wet. An excuse, she decided, to talk no more about Mr Castile.

'Didn't my uncle perceive of a kitchen?' she scolded, desperate not to think of him, and irritated by the fact she needed to kneel in the rain just to have a meal going. 'Why is everything so relentlessly *difficult*?'

Her carefully constructed personality of staunchness broke down and Arden wept into her hands. Not for Richard, for she had cried those tears a year ago, or even that she was cold and sore. It was a cathartic, miserable and ugly cry, as selfish as a rich woman who has to wear a lesser golden brooch upon her breast for a party, when people outside are starving for bread.

Chalice hugged her shoulders and rubbed her back.

'There you go, dear, let it out. It's not the plesiosaur child weighing on your mind, is it? Because nature is red in tooth and claw.'

'It's not the pup. Or maybe it is. I don't know. I shouldn't have come here,' Arden said in between gasps and swallows. 'Here, this town, this place. I don't know what came over me to come.'

'But wasn't your post voluntary?' Chalice handed Arden the linen cloth she had been using to handle the hot kettle. The teacloth was damp from rain, and grubby from ash, but better than wiping her nose on her sleeve. 'The Guild never forces people to go anywhere too far from Clay City, even the sanguineous.'

Arden desperately wanted to tell Chalice about Mr Lindsay and her father's suspicions that the Guildsman clerk had really been a messenger of the Lyonne Order, then remembered how frightened the Manse's guests had been, her father, the phlebotomist that put in her coins. Even Richard Castile. All fearing the Lions. She liked her assistant too much to make the rest of their assignment a worrisome chore.

'The Seamasters offered me a full Guild degree if I came here until the start of winter. Such a title would be almost impossible to come by working a mere blood-lantern, and I'd never be permitted an independent navigation post without one.' She looked at her dirty, tear-stained napkin. 'I'm tired of being scared.'

Chalice kissed her on the cheek. 'Buck up, love. I was myself weepy when I first came to this place. The isolation, you see.

The way the waters just never let the fog go. There's ghosts in the ruins, and the sadness has soaked right through.'

'And Mr Riven down there, the beast that might one day break his chain.'

'Yes, him too. Now, if we can keep this *real* fire going, perhaps after eating we can pry through your late uncle's garbage pile. I'm sure I saw a pot-belly stove in that mess. Something remotely salvageable.'

For all the crude surrounds, Chalice managed to get a pot of porridge upon the boil, sweetened with wild honey. After Arden ate, the burden of an interrupted life lightened a little. Only a few months to go before freedom, and then the autumn testmoot, and if God and the Old Guy should both allow it by granting some sullen coastal child blood-talent, then she could go home sooner and not have to mourn being the last flame-keeper to hold this old tower's post.

The sea hissed and shushed at her mood, and the wind whispered about the lighthouse spire, and slowly she began to feel a little better. Arden reminded herself once again, and this time sternly, that it had been her childhood dream to work a lighthouse signal. So it wasn't exactly the Clay City Spire, but this was still the tallest signal in the country, which had to count for something.

True to Chalice's words, their inspection of the old lantern gears discarded behind the outhouse uncovered a rusted stove, of which its only failing was a firebox door missing a hinge. Arden repurposed some barrel hoops that would do as a gusset about the stove's belly until they could employ the services of a proper blacksmith.

They had just finished setting up the stove inside the tower, with a chimney spout through a window stopped with rags, when a distant squawk of a car horn sounded.

Arden wiped her hands on a rag. 'That not Mr Quill's automobile. The rockblood makes the engine clatter.'

The two women stepped outside. Arden's assessment was correct. It was not the Justinian Siegfried. Instead, a large black sedan that had seen better days nosed its way through the rough roads. An older-model Maybach of the kind popular in Lyonne when she was a girl, with an electrical engine that made it slink in a predatory and dangerous silence. Arden felt her hands prickle with anxiety. If strange vehicles were making their way out to the tower, it was not due to fine tidings.

The Maybach braked suddenly, its wheels leaving dark gouges in the white quartz crust. A short Fictish man in a grey damask waistcoat and a bowler hat exited the driver's seat.

Could there have been anyone less welcome at her door than Mr Justinian? Yesterday she would have said *no*, having erased the unpleasantness of Alasdair Harrow from her mind the way a body pushes out a splinter. Today however, Mr Justinian seemed as benign as a summer shower compared to the stormy presence of her visitor.

Chalice whispered out of the side of her mouth. 'What does the Postmaster Magistrate want with you?'

'It can't be good,' Arden whispered back. 'I had a dreadful dinner with him three nights ago. Best get this over with.'

Postmaster Harrow came with three others of similar pale ethnicity, two large strapping youths with ruddy pink cheeks and full yellow beards, and one sea-bitten fellow who had obviously been on the losing side of a fight.

'Mr Harrow,' she said with assumed brightness. 'What brings you here?'

Mr Harrow did not at first return Arden's greeting. He cast his judgmental gaze over the lighthouse, and his lips thinned over his gravestone teeth.

'Um, can I help you? Is this Postmaster business, sir?'

'I am Magistrate Harrow today,' he said brusquely, then grunted towards his two deputies, made them walk off around the tower grounds to scout the area. Only the sea-bitten fellow that they had brought with them remained, scowling under his drooping canvas fisherman's hat. The cant of the brim did not quite hide a purple bruise on the side of his face as big as a birthmark. Alone among them, he acknowledged Arden and Chalice with the briefest of nods.

Chalice ran after one of the large lads, scolding them for kicking over the porridge pot. Arden stayed before the door, ready to not permit entry if they tried to come in.

Fortunately they merely did a cursory if destructive patrol of the outer grounds, before returning to slouch by the electric Maybach, and smoke a sour-smelling tobacco.

Mr Harrow returned last, one of Jorgen Beacon's blood-knives in his fist.

'Yours, I presume.'

Arden took the knife back. 'Thank you,' she said grudgingly. 'I meant to throw it out, though. This tool has reached the end of its life.'

'Still, not a good thing to leave lying around outside. Not in your circumstances.'

'My circumstances were fine, up until now. Whatever is your reason for coming here?'

She may have spoken to the wind. He took off his spectacles, polished them with a cloth, then did the same to a pewter star upon his breast pocket.

'I note you have settled in well to your new abode,' Mr Harrow said. 'Not so secure, but some people have different requirements when it comes to that.'

'If you needed to do an inspection, you could have asked me for an appointment rather than barging on in.'

He put his spectacles back on his face. 'My apologies, Lightmistress, but there were chances you were already being held hostage, maybe dead.'

'Excuse me?' Chalice interjected, returning from righting the mess the deputies had made. 'Who's saying we were dead?'

Mr Harrow did not immediately recognize Chalice as a person different from any other Vigil woman in his orbit. What was one more in coastal drab? He was the sort of man that decided all women invisible, and then became startled by their speaking, as if a ghost had rapped on a spiritualist's table in the middle of dinner.

'I am Alasdair Harrow, the Postmaster and Magistrate of

Vigil. You two ladies are adjacent to my investigation of a violent act and attempted murder that happened yesterday. Thank you for speaking with me.'

He came forward and shook Arden's hand. A damp and indifferent grip. *Were you a good father to Bellis Riven?* She envisioned asking, before a deeper caution warned her to silence.

'Then sir, if this is an investigation, how may we help you?'

He stood aside. 'These fellows are Giles and Pieter Haas, brothers and peacekeeping deputies of mine.'

The two lads moved almost imperceptibly but obviously, so that their oil coats parted to reveal the long-guns they carried.

'We have come with Captain-Guide Mr Georges Cormack, who as you can see had a crime committed against him and his clients.'

'A crime, sir?'

Mr Harrow paused briefly, noting that Arden had refused to use his title yet, before he continued, 'I am investigating a theft and an assault, as a Marshal of Vigil and the Eastern Fictish Coast.' He puffed himself up, a bantam cock certain that investigating the concerns of sea dogs in far-flung coastal hamlets were equivalent to a Clay High Court.

'My livelihood,' Captain Georges Cormack barked. 'My client refuses to pay since he din' get what he wanted. I am out almost five hundred guineas! Real Djenne Bank currency, not that rubbish Lyonne rag-paper. A year's wages worth to a man here!'

'I don't quite understand how I am involved . . .' Arden started, before Mr Harrow held up his hands.

'As a witness, my dear Lightmistress, a witness.'

Chalice jumped in. 'We didn't see anything.'

'But I understand you have been to visit your *neighbour*,' Mr Harrow said. His face twisted as he enunciated the word. He could not bear to say Mr Riven's name. 'Mr Justinian's driver told me you went to converse with him at an opportune time yesterday, perhaps observed something that could assist in my inquiry.'

'But into what, exactly, sir? You haven't yet explained why you've turned up here.'

'Like I said, grievous *assault* and a *theft*. Details would only worry you, but what did you see of him when you visited him in his compound?'

Something about the four men and their half-explanations aggrieved Arden in a way that made her hackles rise. She had experienced much the same behaviour in merchants at the docks pushing her to let a ship laden with contraband through a backwater lock when they knew she could not allow them. Oh, they would not specifically *say* there were *illegal wares* aboard, but they would give the same sly half-answers to her questions.

'I saw many things in the Riven compound. But if you can narrow down your request to a specific thing, then I can say yay or nay. Otherwise, we had a deal, Mr Riven and I, to stay out of each other's business. I cannot help you Mr Harrow and you are wasting my valuable time.'

She went to move off, when Captain Cormack shouted out, 'A hunter's longboat and a plesiosaur corpse.'

'Plesiosaur?'

She exchanged a glance with Chalice, who bit her lower lip and kissed her Guild assistant triangle nervously.

'Hush,' Mr Harrow said, but the Captain had his dander up now and snapped, 'I will not hush! A longboat that wretched bastard stole from me, after he dashed a rich man called Mr Landwin into the water with an oar, assaulted another with his fists. Rich men, blood-bound men from Morningvale, who had paid me good money to hunt plesiosaur!'

'But why hunt here? These are *breeding* grounds, sir. There is no licence to hunt gravid females south of Garfish Point.'

All four men swayed in an uneasy quorum. Now they would have to tell the truth. Was not adult males the Captain's clients had been hunting.

'I issued them a local dispensation,' Mr Harrow said. 'To do some limited winnowing for the good of the species.'

'Mr Harrow, you of all people should know it is an Act of Parliament that the breeding females not be touched,' Arden said. 'A local Magistrate cannot grant such things.'

Georges Cormack came close, and he smelled of fish oil and old tallow. 'Then you saw it? Saw the bounty that my clients paid me good money to procure?'

He turned back to Mr Harrow. 'Sir Magistrate, the bastard twice interfered with us and let the quarry flee. We shot him out of his ship with a stunning cannon. A face-full of cotton ballast he took, and fell straight into the water as good as dead. A godly man would have been killed instantly. The thug rose out of the waves as the devilspawn he is and pursued us for a night. An *entire night*. He boarded just as we cut out the pup from the plesiosaur bitch.'

'You cut out a foetus,' Arden said. 'You . . .'

'T'was not a foetus. It wriggled and cried, fresh enough that we could skin the caul from it's face and have it take a breath. A thousand gold coins that runt's skin was worth to them and to me, and a thousand more for the egg case!'

Mr Harrow caught the Captain's arm before he could advance more on Arden. 'Easy now, friend. We will get your property back. Plesiosaur veal does not degrade so quickly as beef-meat.'

The Captain continued in a frenzy now, his grievances storming about him. 'And then he assaulted us again, a madman possessed by all the devils of the deep, beat this bruise upon my face and broke the arm of Mr Landwin who wants compensation for his lost property!'

Arden felt a tightness in her chest that made it hard to breathe. Hunting and fishing was a way of life on the sea, that was true, but there were laws and morals attached to procuring bounty from the ocean. This Captain had allowed a barbarism to occur on his watch, and worse than that, had people pay him for the privilege.

'I am sorry, but I cannot help you.' Her voice came out in a rasp, her tongue felt like an iron filing, her throat sand. Her fists clenched to think of the little beast squirming and crying on the bloodied deck of the longboat, a dead mother nearby. At least with Mr Riven there had been a sense of a lone sailor hunting for sustenance, but these men had done so for *sport*.

Why, if she were certain her punch carried the weight required, she would have struck the Captain herself.

'Lightmistress, you can tell us what you saw. Give your testimony to me in my capacity as Magistrate and it will go no further,' Mr Harrow said.

If he had promised this Captain a quick fix to his complaint, Mr Harrow was about to find out that he was not the only authority on this coast. Arden set her jaw and shook her head. 'If you have an issue with Mr Riven, then take it up with him.'

'He has assaulted men. The plesiosaur cow was dead already, he had no cause. Is that not enough of a reason for you to assist us in his arrest and prosecution?'

'Go home, all of you. Go home and school yourself on moral equivalence,' she said. She shook now, sick to her stomach with the sheer effort of keeping a calm countenance. 'Away with you.'

Mr Harrow's face grew as red as a fresh-harvested beet. 'This is not the end of it, *Miss* Beacon. You do yourself no favours helping that *nephilim* over yonder.'

'If he is a fallen man, then your complainants are doubly fallen. A beast has nobody to speak for them. Good day, sirs.'

Muttering to themselves, three climbed back into the Maybach. Only Mr Harrow remained, bloodless as a ghoul.

'Your safety is dependent on us, you know this? You won't be the first woman to disappear from this coast because of him.'

'You use your dead daughter as part of a threat to my life?'

His nostrils flared. 'I use her as *everything*, for she meant *everything* to me before she was taken, raped and discarded.'

Would be a wretched life, she thought, as the sole orient of existence for this man. To be on a pedestal was much the same as a prison.

She remained at the transom of her lighthouse, refusing entry and Mr Harrow returned to the sedan with failure naked on him as a burn, spun the vulcanized rubber wheels in the soft road, and left angry gouges behind.

The waves fretted along the promontory. The gulls screamed at each other.

'Sea slime,' Chalice said. 'Miscreants.' She pursed her lips. 'That Captain Cormack. Heard a few stories about him, oh yes. On the off-seasons when there are no wealthy game hunters for him to escort, he ferries poor, unlicensed folk to the Sainted Isles. If there is not enough room on the boat, or if he runs into trouble, he is known to dump his motley cargo into the ocean. Entire families, murdered by drowning.'

'I'm not at all upset about Mr Harrow,' Arden said as gamely as she could, given that her hands were still trembling. 'They'll not be the first and last men to threaten me.' A strange concern made her nod towards the factory sheds in the fog. 'Do you think they'll go to Mr Riven's now?'

'No, you could tell they were too scared. Mr Harrow would have to request the Morningvale judge to intervene on a visit, and she won't send anyone here unless they could provide a clear reason for it.'

'Such as the testimony of a former Clay Portside Lightmistress.'

'Exactly. If Mr Harrow were to ask for vexatious help too often, then the Lyonne courts might decide the region cannot manage its own affairs. Both Magistrate and Coastmaster could lose their positions.'

With that, Chalice headed off to the ratcheting log-splitter, a contraption that resembled a torture device from the oldest times.

Arden hurried after Chalice. 'Go on. Tell me. I'm an *idiot*.'

'What are you on about, Arden Beacon? If you're coming to that conclusion now, you are quite behind the times.' Chalice hefted a log into the cradle and pumped the handle with the enthusiasm of winching a garrotte.

'I was completely wrong about what I saw in the compound. I jumped to all the wrong conclusions. Mr Riven hadn't killed the plesiosaur pup. He had rescued the animal from Cormack and his hunters, and I had . . . in my rush to agree with everyone . . . *failed* to entertain that possibility!'

Chalice only gave a snort at Arden's crisis. 'Just because Mr

Cormack is a devil, it does not make Mr Riven a saint. I have known many a bad man to show kindness to animals. It is something of a perversion that they appreciate a beast for keeping its place in the scheme of things, that is, lower than low.'

'Yet, the other way is just as true. If you have no compassion for animals, hard to extend it to humankind.'

'Then consider this,' Chalice said, giving the splitter a few final hefts. 'It takes two boats to hunt plesiosaur comfortably. Far better for a lone rogue to attack a couple of milksop dandies in the company of an old man than single-handedly attempt a giant beast about to whelp. Our neighbour wasn't being compassionate. He was being expedient.'

She turned away from Arden and with a sharp kick, the log was torn asunder.

10

Mr Harrow

Mr Harrow did not return. If he'd found any other proof of the crime he had accused his former son-in-law of, the balance could not have been enough to send his men to arrest Mr Riven. Arden worried for her mail, her tenuous links with her family. It would not be unheard of for a malicious Postmaster to withhold her correspondences.

But the letters from her former life still came, albeit with some crinkled evidence of steaming and re-gluing. A riotous scrawl from her Uncle Nicolai, speaking of lighthouse matters as if she were an equal to him in his great tower at the Mouth. Her father's careful penmanship, reviews of some books he had read and promised would send in the next post. Well wishes from step-mother Nina, and her step-sister Sirena, and her half-brother Odie, who was *sanguis ferro* – his blood trammelled iron – and whose labour contract had been won at auction by Clay's largest steel-works. He quoted a tremendous sum. Arden wrote back to him cautioning that he see a financial adviser at once.

More postcards arrived from desert countries, where the sand moved like a river, and the men wore blue robes. An engagement announcement from a close friend who'd made full Guild on her eleventh birthday, and another letter mourning the end of a brief affair.

Arden read them all with detachment. For all that her name was on the envelopes, they were missives meant for another person. A Guildswoman with her own posting, one obtained honourably.

On the second week, a message came from Mx Modhi across the harbour. The Coastmaster had been called away on business for at least a month. It would be her son David who would bring supplies.

Arden greeted that particular news with relief. Since the dream of Mr Castile, she had agonized over meeting up with the young Baron and his whispered offers. Fretted that she might cast aside her good nature and say *yes*. The nights had been strange to her, aloft in the sea-facing tower while the clockwork motor ground out its constant refrain of escapement and arbour. The wild messenger pigeons in the dome, cousins to the ones Chalice kept in a roost behind the lighthouse to run the daily observations, cooed to each other in the darkness, an avian language, full of augury. The ocean breathed and retreated. The nights held Arden captive, overwhelmed her with a physical hunger of missing – *something*.

But what? Not the blind fumbling of intercourse surely, for she'd experienced enough to know it would only lead to sadness and emptiness upon the sunrise. But something. An experience deep and meaningful, an equivalent revelation about another human being.

The days passed quicker than she could mark them, for an instinct lived within Arden to find joy and purpose in things she could rely on, and in her work. The rising of the sun, the clock-chime advising the keeping of records, the morning and afternoon flash of mirrors to Mx Modhi signifying that all was well. In the afternoons a lich-ship might grind towards the horizon, and in the morning another would return. She logged them studiously in the journal, along with the records of flotillas, single boats, patchworked barges, all heading in one direction and these ones never returning.

Over those first days of her seasoning, she emptied the last of the old furniture and rubbish from the house's interior. On Chalice's first return to Vigil, she came back with buckets of whitewash paint, and for a while they slept in the upper convolutions of the tower with every window open, just to escape from the drying paint-fumes below.

Chalice made good company during her waking hours. She collected many stories of her time in Shinlock a mining town not so different from Vigil, where the fibrous asbestos from the mines would turn the air smoky-blue, and the men chewed kraken-beak pills so as not to get tumours in their lungs, though sometimes unscrupulous doctors sold squid beak instead, and they died anyway.

She gossiped too, about her Harbinger Bay assignment with the sanguinem Lightkeeper Stephen Pharos, of the rotting ships lashed together to make the floating prisons in the small bay, for the laws on the sea were different from on land, and a man could be disappeared into the prison hulks without legal recourse or trial. A prisoner had escaped once, found shelter in the lighthouse. Chalice had cared for him three days, until he had died of his injuries. He had not said much, Chalice recalled, but his ruined eyes and terrified silence spoke volumes.

In the afternoons, when Chalice slept and took her stories with her, Arden subsumed herself into her hermit's life. In between blood-letting and record-keeping she walked through the missionary ruins and down to the rocky shore. Occasionally she saw a plesiosaur pod rise their necks, swan-like, above the waves, and once found a sea-cow sunning itself on the pebbles, all glistening bulk with a sharkskin hide. Each rhomboid flipper was the size of Arden's torso.

Arden dared not come any closer, but the saurian was not at all comfortable with the added human presence, and humped back into the wave-wash with agitated hissing.

Near the sea-caves she disturbed trilobites and anemones in the rockpools. Fossicked small relics clearly discarded from the older settlements, small icons of religious protection. A pottery kraken missing most of its glazed arms. A small tooth of nephrite jade. Her favourite was a blanket-ring featuring a tiny cast iron man straddling a coiled *maris anguis* – a giant sea-serpent.

'That's the Deepwater King,' David Modhi would tell her later, when she showed him her find upon his weekly visits to the lighthouse.

The young man rubbed the crust of red oxide from the small figure's face and gazed at it. 'The King lives in a cathedral under the ocean, and all men who drown must serve Him.'

'He must be a fierce regent, if he rides a serpent like a horse.' she quipped, keeping the tone light, for she knew belief systems were inscribed deep upon Fiction hearts, and the Harbourmistress' son might take offence to mocking.

'Oh no, He's killing the serpent here, see? Bringing the meat to feed those people who keep His laws. It is His gift for those who believe and still follow His ways. He won't ever let them starve or go hungry . . .'

'Does your mother know you're familiar with such legends, young David?'

He blushed, and shook his head.

'I won't tell her,' she said. 'It can be our secret.'

David Modhi smiled, before gazing at the ring fondly. 'This will bring you luck. It reminds me of Mr Riven, don't you think?'

She smiled with kindness, for love and worship tangled painfully in the young. 'I wouldn't know Mr Riven well enough to say.' She paused and then said, 'Would you like to have it?' She offered the blanket-ring to him.

He shook his head again. 'The King made you find his image, so it's yours to keep Lightmistress.'

The youth looked over her other finds, then picked up the legless ceramic kraken. 'And this is the King's enemy, the Old Emperor, whom He must battle on the Last Day. The sea belongs to the Deepwater King. Everything upon the shore and under the waves.'

He leaned in close as if whispering a secret.

'And in the midwinter He takes a wife.'

'Goodness,' Arden said, laughing. 'That's quite a thing to say.'

'It's true,' he said flaming with offence. 'He's given you His ring, Lightmistress. He's seen your face.'

11

Mr Quill's car

Mr Quill's car chattered out of a fog bank the same way the devil might greet lost travellers, appearing from nowhere while trailing malice and shady agreements. The Siegfried's patched-up wheels churned through the thin, sandy slip of soil that made for the lighthouse road. The skids from Mr Harrow's arrival in the month before still scarred the top layer of stones.

Arden, in the challenging middle portion of throwing a seldom-laundered bedsheet up over a rusted washing line her uncle had probably never used, watched the car's arrival with all the sinking dread of a condemned criminal. Well, so much for her peace. Reality had arrived over the walls of her austere garden.

She raised her hand in greeting to Mr Quill, who did not leave his seat. Instead the rear door of the car opened, and a pinstriped trouser leg emerged, shining shoes, that spotted plesiosaur leather coat.

'Mr Justinian? I thought you were away on business until next week. I'd have made an effort otherwise.' She pointed at the sheet with arms as raw as pork skin in an icebox.

'I cut it short, after news came to me.'

'What news?'

'I was concerned for your safety,' he said. 'You left without saying farewell, and Mr Quill said you did something rather rash a few weeks ago when he first took you here.'

'I can't quite—'

'Of course, he neglected to tell me all this, so he'll get his pay-packet lightened.'

Arden sighed and looked in sympathy at Mr Quill, cowering behind the steering wheel. 'Coastmaster, please don't blame him. We were quite safe. As for yourself, you were in no fair condition that day. I needed to act in haste, to save my uncle's light.'

Mr Justinian dropped his pleasant-face for a brief moment. 'Those Garfish Point ingrates should tackle that particular blame. Will cheat a man out of honest money and sell contaminated liquor to boot.'

She returned as much of a smile as she could without it being forced. 'See? Mr Quill did excellent work. He must be rewarded, as an example, otherwise your staff might lose their sense of pride.'

'Hmm,' Mr Justinian said, unable to figure if he was being manipulated or her request genuine. In the afternoon light Mr Justinian stepped towards Arden. She had to admit his dress was impeccable. He wore an expensive cologne, touches of gold upon his eyelids, carmine on his lips. Handsome in any part of the world, and here among the 'lumpen inbreds', as he so dismissively called his Fiction counterparts, beautiful.

The only man of any worth available to her, if she were to choose that path.

'Anyhow, where is your Miss Quarry? I thought your storm-bride should be out doing the hard domestic work, not a Lightmistress.' He sniffed disapprovingly at the flapping sheets.

'She has taken the boat into Vigil,' Arden said. 'She must deliver the tide observations to the Postmaster.'

'Why do you not do it yourself? I seem to recall you had a desire to meet the good people of our town.'

She shrugged, and pushed a damp tendril of hair from her

brow. 'I like it out here. I can see why the missionaries chose to build their first church upon this site.'

'For all the good it did. The loneliness killed them, in the end.'

'Yes,' she said, then berated herself for agreeing with him.

Mr Justinian blinked, not missing that tenuous connection. 'Have you felt it, Lightmistress, the noonday demon? What the climate of the Darkling Sea does to those newcomers unused to our great melancholy sink?'

He took another step closer, and the heat from the Siegfried's internal heaters still radiated off him.

With an inward sigh, Arden suspected that Mr Justinian might not have gone away on business at all, and waited for the isolation to do its work. He would know her alone with only the waves and wind. Her defences could be breached now.

'I dare say one could get used to it. Under the right conditions.'

'There were no right conditions. Those missionaries, they were constantly at *war*, my dear. With the old religions who worshipped the kraken and the spawning monsters of our coast and the abominable King in his abyss. Built their first church they might have done, but they could not stay. More than one massacre has left behind a choir-load of bones.'

She shivered, not from cold. Ghosts perhaps. His closeness, so unwanted, but piquing her memory. Coldfire in her blood, but still, her needs had always burned hot.

He saw the shiver, and her response pleased him.

'Go on then. Clean yourself up. We shall go for a walk, you and I. A sortie of your assigned portions. I shall tell you more history, if you wish.'

Arden searched for excuses, found none. Why should a Lightmistress not patrol grounds that a Coastmaster controlled?

And walks tended to turn into much more.

'I'll meet you out here,' Arden said brusquely. 'I won't be long.'

* * *

She closed the driftwood door and leaned hard against it. This had to be a test, surely. What would she endure for that full Guild degree? She had invited Mr Justinian to her lighthouse, and he would be unlikely to leave without his pound of flesh. Arden knew his kind. Too much refusal would make an enemy out of him. Trapped in a cage of possible disasters, Arden lingered over Bellis Riven's krakenskin by her bed, the blue eye-marks bright in the dim light.

'Why not just once, scratch the itch, get it over and done with? It's not like he's the kind that makes a habit of it,' she said to the empty room. Squeezed her fists until her coins hurt. He had dressed well, at least. It would not be distasteful.

In Lyonne, Arden's position and her family protected her. Here, she would need to put all the morals of the North aside. Why not spend a few uncomfortable minutes with Mr Justinian and consider her duty done? The act would put a firm boundary between the woman who used to believe in love, and the one who saw it only as expedience. She would be gone before the winter and he would be forgotten.

As she had promised, Arden changed quickly. At the last minute she decided to forgo her utilitarian cotton undergarments for a particular gold silk lingerie set purchased from an old traveller-folk merchant back in the days of Richard Castile. Maybe they would make her think romantic and sensual thoughts, yes? She still remembered the old woman's shrewd sales pitch. *An old magic in these gold threads. Wear this before your beloved and he will be overwhelmed with desire.*

Not that they worked, for she'd had no chance to disrobe in front of Richard when she last wore them. The garments had most likely been fenced from a pirate haul, and were possibly not altogether made of sea-silk either. Yet for the story the old woman wove Arden had bought an overpriced courtesan's corset, cut far too low about the neck and boned such that her upper half would be forever in danger of falling out.

Such an ignominy to waste their prettiness on Mr Justinian. Quite the opposite of the krakenskin coat, which bore such a disagreeable tale. What better way to discard a memory that had also become disagreeable?

Her best dress was a blue broadcloth, warm enough against the wind but not too dowdy. She fixed her hair and stained her lips with crimson.

Mr Justinian smirked when at last he saw Arden again. His fingers and thumbs made small circles, already envisioning her skin between them.

His back is straight and his voice is well spoken, Arden thought to herself in a desperate catalogue of positive things. *He has the kind of style that serves a man well in high company. He is a Baron by blood.*

None of her silent declarations eased the antipathy that kept intruding on her desperate attempt to feel remotely interested in her companion. Instead Mr Justinian's little annoying traits amplified into ugliness. He complained most of the time he walked, and when his discussions were not negative, they were aggrandizing monologues on his own advantages over other lesser folk. The wind snickered through the scrub, blowing her dress sideways, and making her regret she had not chosen to wear a decent pair of woollen long johns instead.

They trekked along the old coastal path, following the limestone and shale pavements that led to the other side of the promontory, where the larger and more windswept cliffs of Dead Man's Bay battered the cliffside ruins.

The wind whipped up with angry little teeth and got underneath Arden's skirts, and at one stage she shivered enough for Mr Justinian to sidle close with the offer of a warm embrace, his move fouled only by the narrow path. On the old trail they could only walk in single file and not two abreast, a situation that Arden preferred, for the silky rustle of her golden lingerie made her anxious with impending unpleasantness.

A sea-spray spangled Arden's lips with salt kisses, caused Mr Justinian's hat to blow away and a careful coif of hair to droop sadly over one eye.

'Ugh, this blasted climate. I could have driven you back to

town, my dear. I know I said a *walk*, I can offer something more civilized. Such as, the promenade.'

The idea of the pair of them strolling the fishy-smelling, sad little boardwalk had even less appeal. 'No, this is nice,' Arden replied. 'I prefer the wildness.'

'Don't prefer it too much,' Mr Justinian cautioned. 'It drove your uncle mad in the end.'

'We are entirely different people, Mr Justinian. You must not worry.'

At one cliffside Arden stopped at a pile of stones that were newer-hewn than the ruins, a careful little cairn in the shape of a rotunda. A flat piece of stone at the base bore chisel marks. A crude *Bellis* pitted there. Someone had added underneath – and this with a different hand and including the Beacon family mark – *Stefan*. Her cousin, who had disappeared along with Bellis before he could testify against Mr Riven.

Mr Justinian *tsk*ed. 'Such a rude little cenotaph. She deserves better than that pile of rubble. I should have it knocked down.'

He shoved it with his foot, swept a few stones from the surface with the dismissal of clearing a table of crumbs. The cairn held fast, mostly. The sea grumbled through caverns below them, as if upset at the interference.

'Perhaps you could build her one.'

'Out of what, dear? She deserves better than rubble.'

'I saw much hidden statuary mouldering in the Manse gardens. Maybe the little mer-girl that sits at the edge of the south fountain. Put her on the promenade. Have a brass plaque made in Bellis Harrow's memory.'

Mr Justinian laughed, and did not bother to hide his ridicule. 'Arden, the Coastmaster budget would never extend so far as to encompass such fripperies as statue moving and random emplacement.'

'What about your own money, Vernon? Doesn't Bellis deserve that?'

His laughter stopped. Arden cast her eyes over his wormsilk suit, his plesiosaur coat, the pink diamond on his index finger in a recent gaudy style. There might not have been a lot of money left, but that did not mean he couldn't liquefy old baronial assets for his own *fripperies*.

Annoyed now, he changed the subject abruptly. 'We must talk about you visiting Mr Riven.'

'I made my introductions on the first day, yes.'

'You are brave, I give you that.'

'I doubt Mr Harrow would say the same thing.'

Mr Justinian shrugged. 'His job is his job. The wretch did assault three people the day before. You could easily have been the fourth.'

'I find that unlikely.'

'Unlikely, you say?' With barely restrained glee, Mr Justinian launched into a story, told her of the corpses that might wash ashore from the Sainted Isles, bloated with seawater and lungs black with congealed rockblood. He described the white bone poking through paper skin, the scars upon their flesh that suggested shackles, or worse. Purposeful mutilations, bodies hurt beyond measure.

'. . . not long after the man returned from prison, myself and Stefan Beacon came to this very spot. We saw Mr Riven down here trying to carry away one of the bodies. A woman, I think. He ran away when he saw us. No doubt he intended to use the corpse for his own pleasures. Eventually he became tired of such easy pickings and turned his attention to the living.'

The disgusting descriptions excited him. His face flushed, his breath quickened. Vaguely nauseated now, Arden hurried on ahead, down the rough stone steps that gave access to the inlet. The steps were slippery from the sea mist, so she capitulated to take Mr Justinian's hand to help her down.

'Arden, my dear, this is hardly a beach. Come up and we might rest in the old ruins. You can have my jacket for warmth.'

She ignored the lingering squeeze his hand left upon her fingers, and concentrated on making her descent in a halfway vertical fashion. She would succumb to his invitations eventually, but the mood had not taken her quite yet.

'I'll scout around down here, first.'

Realizing she wasn't yet ready to submit, Mr Justinian resentfully followed Arden to beach level.

The rocky shelf had a sharply uninviting atmosphere where it met the waves. The monastery ruins above fell away at the eroded cliff and into a jumble of slime-shiny basalt blocks. Spars of grey shale occluded coarse yellow sand, and the remains of anchors, winches and other rust-smeared equipment littered the shoreline.

'Ah, your cousin's boat is still on the rocks.' He pointed to the sea-battered remains of a small oak and steel dinghy wedged in the granite, several winters' worth of storms melting it into the earth. 'I remember that day too well,' he added. 'No sea-sense in Stefan Beacon. Twelve years old and pretending himself a master sailor.'

'Did you know him very well before he became a Rector?'

'We were youthful friends, but adult responsibilities are what they are. Years in a seminary and he never lost the . . .' Mr Justinian picked up a sea-stone, worn smooth from the waves. '*Impulsiveness*. A certain rash wanderlust. His mother came from the Sainted Isles, and she lived with Jorgen for a time. Only a time, mind. The blood of the rock has a call on certain people. She abandoned her child to go back to the Islands, left him to live with a half-mad Lightkeeper. In the end, they both went mad together.'

'It would be a sad story, though my account is a little different.'

'Is it now? Who have you been talking to?'

Arden rolled her eyes. 'Stefan was already six years old by the time he came here. I knew his mother. She was a Lyonne *sanguinem*. Jorgen and her divorced amicably, and sometimes she visited during Festival.'

Mr Justinian's face went scarlet. 'So, my memory is rusty. It was a long time ago.'

'Which leads me to think that maybe memories can't be that reliable.'

Mr Justinian waved her away. 'Perhaps his early years are shrouded in mystery, but I can recall crystal clear when our Rector started stealing back here for trysts. When he began his affair with Bellis Riven.'

Arden shook her head, not understanding.

'Excuse me? Stefan was a priest. He had taken vows. Would only have been out of friendship that he spent time with her.'

'The idiot abandoned his vows. Oh, did you not know? He had an affair with Bellis in the last month of her life. He would meet her here in the ruins when Riven was away, hunting. He brought her medicines for her injuries, sympathies from when her treatment had been rough. Then he gave her his body, and you know where that leads.'

As much as she tried, Arden couldn't visualize Stefan Beacon having such a rash affair. He'd seemed so deliberately fey and insular whenever they'd met, even now she could not quite imagine him having an affair with any human being, much less a woman.

'Are you sure, Vernon? Or is it another bit of fishmonger gossip ill-remembered?'

'He confessed to me his sin,' Mr Justinian said. 'In confidence.'

'The local Coastmaster seems an odd choice for a holy man to reveal such a dangerous relationship to.'

'It may be gauche to say this, but I called Stefan my best friend, once. We grew together as boys. Brothers, almost. Yes.' He nodded to himself. 'Confessed to me. Wanted my blessing since Bellis and I were once engaged and the guilt weighted his brow.'

'Blessing for what, exactly?'

'To run away. Bellis' brutish husband suspected something afoot.'

Arden exhaled. 'Running away. Of course. The one idea always doomed to failure.'

'Devil curse him, that Riven.' He threw the stone at the distant horizon with an almighty heave. 'If he never existed, Bellis would still be here.'

'Mr Justinian, look out—'

A wave broke upon the rocks, so close that they were spattered with foam. Mr Justinian turned upon Arden and seized her up by her waist and pressed himself close. His wet lips caught the side of her mouth. His tongue, foiled by her clenched teeth, trailed damp upon her wincing cheek before turning wet slug-trail circles under her ear.

'Arden, don't fight me.'

She attempted to squirm away. 'Wait a minute, Vernon, this is rather sudden.'

'Why must we tease each other?' he whined. 'All these games of love are for children.' He fumbled his hand on her breast. 'Ah, your heart beats fast with passion.'

Was not passion that moved her so. Her loins could have been a desert, for all that she responded to Mr Justinian. His fingers folded over into the corset of her dress, his heavily manicured nails sharp as a scratch upon her delicate skin.

'Vernon . . .'

She froze the way a watch-escapement that has danced out of synchronicity will stop the whole clock, her prior thoughts of giving in to Mr Justinian's lusts evaporating.

I cannot go through with it. He disgusts me. In the distance of miles felt him seize the neck of her corset with a frantic grip while with the other hand yanked up her dress hem. 'It's all right if you are a virgin, it will not hurt but a prick.'

A terrible antipathy came over her as the ruffled silk tore. She had not thought this thing through, not thought how the touch of Mr Justinian upon her intimate places would cause her such distress.

She was a spring wound too tight. The escapement tore free of the tooth. 'I said *no*, Mr Justinian!'

Shoved him away with her lantern-turner's strength and with a wide, swinging blow slapped him hard across his face.

The contact sent a shockwave of pain through her elbow and shoulder, sent him spinning. She lost her foot upon the wet rock. Mr Justinian lunged for her as another wave breached the rocks and suddenly the world went cold and white, yet all she could think of was to dart away from Mr Justinian's grip.

She fell into the foamy tumult, half by accident and half – the worst and most dreadful half – by the same instinct as that of an animal that will gnaw its leg to escape a trap.

Her legs tangled up in the cotton of her skirts. The wave dragged her out with an almighty surging, sucking power, casting her perilously close to the sharpest rocks before she reached the becalmed straits of deeper water.

Reeling from both water-dumping and Mr Justinian's assault, she drifted as the waves gathered for another battering. She was gone and gone.

Don't try to make it back in. The rocks will kill you.

A jolt of anoxic raptures forced her hands and she tugged on the release-strings of her dress. With a tug, suddenly freed herself from the billowing fabric. Her head cleared the water and she gasped for air, rode over the swell as it headed back to the rock where Mr Justinian, drenched and horrified, watched his lighthouse keeper drift helplessly out to sea.

12

She swam with the surge

She swam with the surge, and the further she went from the rocks, the more the sea-rip lost its power. By now her jaws ached from her clattering teeth, and she had overshot the small stony bay by far too much of a distance to consider swimming back. Another inlet appeared, this time one sheltered from much of the waves. Gathering the last of her strength, Arden over-armed herself through the slosh, half-blind with salt water. When her boots touched gravel, she wanted to weep with joy.

The cold had numbed her completely now, and she staggered chill-drunkenly out of the foam. Her torn undergarments stuck to her in membranous translucent flesh, made her a sea-monster half in the process of shedding skin. She limped across the sand, only half-believing that she'd survived and not lost herself within the rapture of drowning.

Before Arden could fall upon the dry beach a dark shape flopped towards her, as large as a mastiff but not a dog, not a seal, a thing with a long neck and a sharp head, and a toothed reptilian mouth that let out a chatter of sharp hissing coughs.

Arden braced for impact, received none. The beast swung wide at the last moment, entered the water to her left instead.

It splashed on past in a riot of flipper and barking, before diving under a small wave. A scar on the pebbled grey back, like that left by a flensing blade . . .

'Plesiosaur,' she said to herself as if the speaking would make it seem less perplexing. 'That's the baby plesiosaur.'

She turned back to the shore. A man stood there on the sand, watching her with dumb surprise.

Only then did Arden notice the glowing blue rings of kraken-hide and the tall figure made spare and severe by the ocean's trials. Wasn't an ordinary man. She was in front of Mr Riven.

Naked, in front of Mr Riven.

Three Djennes'-worth of the gold silk she'd intended for her only love, and now her promise-night garb hung in tatters. The sight that should have greeted Mr Castile was given instead to a bearded, swollen-eyed brute. She didn't bother to cross her hands about her chest. It wouldn't make much of a difference to what he saw anyway.

'Well then,' she said to any devils that might be listening. 'This day cannot possibly get any worse.'

He did not stare, not long at any rate. The expression on his face amounted to dumbfounded shock, then to another, firmer and more decisive gaze. He dropped the bucket of fish-guts held in one hand, and shrugged out of his coat.

So, she thought with frozen, and exhausted inevitability. *This is the place where I will be ravished, and if I'm fortunate he might not finish me off with my head upon a rock.*

Mr Riven took off his woollen sweater and revealed a tattered shirt. Another chill wind gusted against her wax-cold skin. She huffed with impatience. *Get on with it so I can get back somewhere warm. I'm not going to put up a fight.*

The plesiosaur child lumbered past her again. The sharp, beaky nose plunged into its bucket of disgusting meal.

Instead of disrobing completely, Mr Riven placed his sweater on a basalt spar and shrugged back into his coat. He nodded once, before leaving. In all that time he did not say a word.

Arden, stupefied by surprise and cold, merely watched him

go. She should have spoken to him, acknowledged this odd meeting, but her nakedness made her so self-conscious she could not bring herself to speak to the man. His back gave communication enough and she welcomed it.

When the fear drained away, the shivers came. She dived for the dry, warm sweater, would not have cared if the wool were filthy and crawling with maggots and prepared herself that it would be, that she would retch from the stink of unwashed flesh from this man who lay with the dead, and yet . . .

And yet . . .

A whiff of a clean, warm, masculine scent filled her senses as she tugged the knitted cables over her head. The yarn startled her with softness, but lay heavy across her shoulders, arms and bosom in a gentle embrace. Along with the smell of a young, healthy man, there came the dusky smell of kraken oil, that exotic perfume that always lingered in the air of the more important Clay Portside offices. The purled hem brushed her knees.

Relief dizzied Arden. She had expected horror and received the opposite. She might have collapsed and rolled herself up in a warm knitted cocoon if she had not heard someone calling her name.

Mr Justinian appeared, ashen, at the top of the cliffside track. 'You're all right! Oh, by the Gods! When I saw that Riven character heading for the likely deposit of your body, I was certain you'd be lost.' He stopped, realizing that from the ragged fronds of her bloomers and her waterlogged boots, she'd ended up quite naked below the knees. 'And what are you *wearing*?'

'Shut up, Vernon,' she said harshly. 'Was your fault I ended up in this mess. I told you to stop!'

'I'm sorry,' he cried. 'I'm sorry, forgive me! My desires overcame my senses, I thought they were reciprocated! I don't know what came over me!'

He crawled towards her feet, prostrating himself. Arden jumped back, not knowing how to take this sudden change in character.

'You should have asked! Presented your case, but instead you speak filth about a dead woman and her husband, then grab at me as an animal in heat!'

'I'm a goddamn fool, it's true. I was impassioned in my concern for your safety around the Riven creature!'

A font of disgust flowered in her, a sudden bloom of sympathy for her wretched, broken neighbour.

'Nothing you say about Mr Riven assists me in any way. No repetitions of my neighbour's monstrous appetites, no gloating appeals to my sanity! You relish speaking of your fiancée's ordeal with a pleasure and not a shame. You revel in her torments. In fact, I don't know who I should despise most, Mr Riven or you.'

Mr Justinian stood up, rubbed his cheek, affected an aspect of sheer misery.

'The fault is mine! I never learned how to properly romance a woman in anything other than the coarse ways of Fiction. My background has been emotional poverty and stolen, pleasureless embraces. I've never had a teacher to show me how to make love.' Mr Justinian raised his eyes hopefully to her. 'Arden Beacon, please help me become this man.'

Arden laughed, incredulous. 'Enough, Vernon. I'm not blind. The ladies of the Black Rosette have had plenty of opportunities to show you how to make bloody love. You are a disgrace to your profession, trying to use it to seduce and bully me. I won't stand for it.'

She stomped on up the beach-track stairs as best she could without toppling off them in the wind, reached the cliff-top before he did.

'Then what do you want from me?' Mr Justinian whined behind her. 'Shall I prove my newfound desire to improve myself? Do you want me celibate, and swearing off all pleasures before you will acquiesce to my devotion? Is that what it will take to win your affection?'

'Whatever you want, Vernon Justinian,' she snapped. 'Bind yourself up in thistles and itching-ivy if you must, but keep your impure thoughts to yourself. I could have died this afternoon.'

His face was furious, but he capitulated to her anger. Bowed his head. 'It is done. It is done!'

He kept his silence as they returned from their walk. Chalice had returned, and had since coaxed Mr Quill out of the car with a cup of one of her bitter teas.

'What happened to your dress?' Chalice asked, then caught sight of Mr Justinian's hangdog appearance, Arden's dishevelled rage. 'Ah,' she concluded. This required a more private interrogation.

'Come, Mr Quill,' Mr Justinian barked. 'I'm not paying you for laziness. We must be back in town before nightfall.'

The driver gave up his tea to the ashes, and quickly returned to his duties.

Once the car disappeared from sight, Chalice followed Arden inside the lighthouse.

'You cannot keep me in suspense. I return to your absence and the driver waiting, only to discover you were gallivanting with the second last person in the world I'd expect you gallivanting with.'

'And the last person being Mr Riven?'

'By God, no. I saw the expression on your face when you heard he gave a whipping to those foppish plesiosaur hunters. If I know your weaknesses yet, it would be an overwrought sense of moral justice if you gave our besmirched neighbour the portion just to say you were sorry.'

Outside with the bowl of warm water and a sponge, Arden pulled off the sweater. Chalice gasped at what she had revealed.

'Dear me, trying to make yourself a tasty morsel for Mr Justinian? By your appearance I'd wager he ravished you *both* ways.'

Arden scoffed, but had to admit she had become a sight. Getting dragged out over the rocks by the waves had knocked her bruised and bloody.

'Just be a help and get me some soap. I couldn't be worse if I tangled with Poseidon himself.'

'You need more than soap. Clean yourself off and I'll put some iodine on those cuts. Damn the devils, which man must I kill today?'

'It's not what you think. I fell into the water, on one of the shipwreck bays. Blame the rocks for my injuries.'

'*Just* them?'

'Just them.'

'All right. It is a relief. The ground around here is quite unsuitable for graves. So hard to dig and I'd rather not be breaking my back for anyone.'

Arden washed the salt out of her skin and hair, and in the fading evening light deigned to sit on a stool in her cotton nightdress while Chalice dabbed reddish balm over her cuts.

As Chalice tended to her, Arden told her stormbride about Mr Justinian's actions, the desperate swim, and the beach with Mr Riven. 'He was feeding a plesiosaur today. A juvenile.'

'I thought the man could only call kraken?' Chalice asked, mid-dab.

'Let's just say my perilous position did not allow me to ask him. But I could have sworn the creature was the same one he carried from his boat weeks ago, except it was healed and very much alive.'

Chalice shook her head, sceptical. 'Are you sure?'

'Very certain. There was a scar on its back, the exact same one.'

'An interesting talent. Truth, I couldn't tell the difference between one plesiosaur and another, myself.' She finished her dabbing, stood back and admired her handiwork. 'There you go, spotted as a leopard. Now I'll throw this old rag out.'

She had barely lifted the sweater before Arden took it out of her hands.

'I have to clean it and give it back to him.'

She hadn't managed to inspect this gifted garment of Mr Riven's until then. Unlike the immaculate coat, the uneven knots in the woollen sweater very much told a sad tale by their own selves. Songs of rending and patching at least a hundred times, pale scours from repeated washing, and threadbare where sand soap had not quite rinsed out the ichor of kraken calling. Now the sleeves from the elbows down were sticky with blood.

'Are you trying to scry the future in those woollen entrails?' Chalice commented as Arden gently laid out the sweater on the slab table and touched the fibres as one might touch a sacred object for luck. 'Because I can imagine scabies, and a furious genital itching.'

'It was clean before I bled on it. I don't want to bring it back in such a condition.'

'Just think of it as an excuse for him to change clothes for once.'

Arden tutted at Chalice's uncharitable thoughts. 'I'm just fascinated. See, its old, but the quality of the work is wonderful. You'd struggle to get similar in a Clay Capital high street.'

'I never realized the fashion tends to wearing big Fiction sweaters.'

'Chalice, you know what I mean.'

She shrugged. 'So the natives know their way around a needle.'

'Don't you think this is odd how the collar is embroidered so, with all these fun little decorations?' Arden's fingers stroked busy needlework of blue waves, black kraken-arms, a sun and moon. One read in the threads affectionate gestures, a shared memory between old friends.

'What are you trying to say, dear?' Chalice asked, droll. She dumped a load of firewood by the brazier and slapped sawdust from her hands. 'How pretty the stitches, what delight in her patterns?'

'If Bellis sewed these, she was not a woman in pain.'

'Perhaps you should offer your services as a detective to Magistrate Harrow. Devils know how useless his lumpen deputies are.'

'I don't recognize abuse, though. The sweater and the coat were both made with affection. There is love here.'

Chalice sniffed, lit up her pipe, took a long dismissive drag.

'There are *spells* here, Arden. Old Fictish magic, binding up the monster in thread so it may not harm the maker.'

Arden wanted to argue with Chalice. She saw fondness, adoration in the threads. Ill-fated, eternal, storybook love, not the brutality of the local gossips, and a twist of envy towards Bellis, small and bitter, pricked Arden's heart. She'd have made such clothes for Richard, given the chance, were it part of their culture.

Chalice sat next to Arden wrapped her arm about her waist, lay her fiery head upon Arden's shoulder. The smoke curled about them.

'I'm just glad you're alive, darling.'

'It feel so strange, though. Like I cannot trust anything I'm being told.'

The arm squeezed harder. 'Arden, the gods loved you today. Are you certain you've not got a shadow talent for enchanting wild men?'

Arden wriggled free. 'Chalice, you mustn't joke about shadow talents. They're a terrible thing for a child to be afflicted with.'

Chalice held up her hand. 'My apologies. But I can see your jealousy for Bellis Riven.'

'I am not jealous, either!'

'You are jealous. It's plain as day. You want what Bellis had, to be both *sanguis* and free of the Guild, to be blessed with such a thing as a man's tender devotion.' She shrugged. 'Even if it is Mr Riven's. And it killed her in the end.'

Much to the displeasure of Chalice Quarry and her proclamations on the dangers of lice-borne diseases, Arden washed the blood from the sleeves, and brought the sweater indoors where it might dry by the fire. It splayed out cruciform upon the washing line, a winged shadow.

In the morning's dark early hours, when her shift ended and weariness made her maudlin, she fell back into her old physical longings, walked those worlds as she hovered between waking and dream.

You are jealous.

But this time, the princes and airshipmen and dockworkers of her night-time fantasies were cast aside, and a man with swollen eyes and damaged features beheld her as she emerged from the sea, her body a gold-fronded nakedness, his expression a raw wound, and a terrible longing upon his face.

13

Something in the quality of her life

Something in the quality of her life. Something had changed. She no longer worried about her real worth on the signal tower, or her tending of a dying flame. As the weather cooled from the summer mildness Arden oriented now to the old factories down the promontory, the way a creature in pain will be drawn towards its own destruction. She had to return Mr Riven's sweater. Soon, she promised, for tardiness would raise questions.

But each hour she spent thinking about visiting Mr Riven and thanking him for the use of the garment made the act take on far more import than it should. She was not foolish enough to consider any neighbourly relationship more than casual politeness – he would never be a comrade or friend, not a Chalice Quarry or a Gerry Harris. Her imagination couldn't extend to talking with him about anything other than the best way to slaughter a thing ten times larger than yourself.

More dangerously, her isolation from any human companionship other than Chalice made her assign fictional qualities to Mr Riven that had no true bearing on his unknown character.

He had battled poachers, he was a man of moral standing.

He had nursed an orphan water-pup to health (perhaps it had not been so dead), he was patient.

He had given her a garment, was kind, he had not taken advantage, he was polite, he was this and he was that.

See, all those things make Mr Riven not at all those things that Mr Justinian accuses him of. See? See?

Afterwards, she would become angry at herself for her wool-gathering. She needed to maintain the discipline of the lighthouse, to identify and catalogue the ships that passed, the movement of air within the barometer, the variances in the tide. Her attention was required seawards, not behind her.

I must nor contrive, she told herself. *I must not.* She must not wander into a fork in the road where he had taken her upon the beach, tearing the silks from her body, doing everything the traveller woman had promised. Mr Riven existed only as a cipher for her own loneliness and worry. Arden had come here to shake herself free of a demon, not pick up another one.

Her pronouncements were only playthings for a capricious God. Her solitude made her vulnerable, to the long days of watching the coast, listening to Chalice snore and snuffle in her sleep, the low hissing roar of the wind through the sea-caves, long walks along the promontory on top of gravestones and crumbled walls.

The nights were worse, and she hid Mr Riven's sweater in a pillowcase so that Chalice might not see it unreturned. An object of veneration and suffering, to take out and press her face into the thick cables, catch a remnant of a man's scent, regardless of who it belonged to. A life not hers, but was promised, once.

She was wise enough to know the depressive condition of *acedia*, how it affected isolated Lightkeepers and signallers just as it affected monks and aesthetes. Knew how close she risked falling into that dark well-pit, and could not find any way to stop herself from sliding.

14

Wake up!

Arden startled awake, alert and in a panic. The grinding of the lens motors a level above made a sound as familiar as the whoosh of blood in a womb. Light-shadow crawled over the white-washed stone. The cold-flame burned and bright from when she had last supplied it. Devilment! How long had she been napping? To fall asleep was an unforgivable transgression in signal keeping.

'Chalice?' she asked the darkness, waiting for the returning scold of her assistant.

No reply from either the doorway or downstairs. Arden quickly checked the luminous hands of the clock against her last time-measurement. The shipwright's clock pointed to a three, the devil's number, and Arden calmed down a little. Three o'clock wasn't too bad. She had started her shift at two o'clock, already taken the half-hour measurements, noting the low pressure and high wind of a Darkling Sea storm. She could not have been subsumed by storm morphia for more than twenty minutes.

She took her pen and notated in her log book: *Atmospheric Pressure – Barometric Event?* Some exotic storm conditions caused the air pressure to plunge so suddenly that entire townships would fall into unconsciousness. The pale-skinned among them would turn blue with hypoxia. *Enchantment tempests*, the locals called such catastrophes, invoking fairy stories of princesses asleep for a hundred years, except in these ones they never woke up.

She crossed out her notation with a shake of her head. An enchantment tempest would have dimmed the beacon flame. Perpetual it might have been, it still required oxygen. The cold-fire still glowed bright.

Arden opened her glove and touched her coin to a small lantern-wick she kept for the purpose, and in the blood-light inspected her fingernails. They were bitten and split from weeks of hard work, but did not show the cyanotic darkness of a low barometric event. Something else had sapped her strength.

She replaced her notation with *Absent*, before cat-footing down the tower stairs, not wanting to wake Chalice. The bride's gentle breath stuttered, and then she too woke up. Chalice hoisted herself onto her elbow, blinked in the dim glow of the brazier, then at her own small clock.

'I'm sorry,' Arden said. 'I hoped some brew still remained in the pot.'

'Was not that soft footfall of yours that woke me.' The stormbride's eyes shone in the gloom, her distance unseeing. Arden remembered that Chalice had tested positive for chemicals and salts at a testmoot. Theirs was a shared language. 'You fell asleep.'

'Something in the weather. Can you feel it?' Arden said. 'Not a barometric event. Powerful, but distant.'

A blink again. 'Yes,' Chalice church-whispered. 'There's blood on this storm. It's almost suffocating. I can take another watch, if you want. I can't see myself going back to sleep.'

The wind whiffled at the glass of the lamphouse. 'I'd best go back up and check on the light. I wouldn't be able to sleep either.'

'I'll have the fire going. This storm's only going to get worse.'

Arden quickly slipped into her krakenskin while Chalice

141

changed back into her clothes. The stone staircase vibrated under her feet as gales battered the column.

The glass in the lamp room had held strong. The tower might have been left to weather, but mere squalls would not topple her. Arden remained behind the light-shade as her beam shot out into the wild night.

Blood on this storm, Chalice had said. Yes, there definitely *was* a wrinkle in the wind out there. If she were in Lyonne it would not have meant much, but in Fiction the sense filled her like the vibration from a tuning fork, struck and held.

'We'll have to run the foghorn!' Arden shouted down the tower. 'There's no visibility up here!'

'I'm on my way,' the stormbride called back, and a gust of wind came up from below as Chalice opened the driftwood door to exit.

Barely half a minute passed before Chalice came back.

'Arden!' Chalice screamed up the staircase. 'Arden, get down here!'

'What is it?' Arden tried to navigate down the staircase as best she could. 'Is it the horn?'

'There's people in the water outside,' Chalice panted. The rain had soaked her utterly. 'Down at where promontory meets the water. One of them has a flare . . .'

'For goodness' sakes, get your oil coat on,' Arden scolded. 'I'm going outside.'

She snatched up a lantern, pushed her glove aside and squeezed blood into the reservoir until her hand burned and the flame inside sprang up white as burning magnesium. The wind pounced as soon as she stepped into the night, but it could not get past the krakenskin.

She battled her way down to the promontory point. Chalice had seen true. There were people in the water, at least four of them, staggering out of the swell. The phosphor flare in the hand of their leader illuminated them in a ghastly pink.

'Hoy! This way!' she cried.

The strongest of them, an older man clad only in a sopping

waistcoat and breeches, stumbled to Arden and grabbed her shoulders as if he were still drowning. 'My family,' he said between coughs. 'The boat . . . the storm . . .' He was cold as death, and his lips blue-black in the lantern light. He was a Lyonnian, but it was not his blood she had sensed.

'A shipwreck?'

The man nodded, and ran back to help another shadowy figure who waded out of the phosphor-pink foam. A hot fork of lightning illuminated the wreckage of a prospector's boat, a spindly flat-bottomed thing lashed together from river-barges that should never have approached open water.

From the darkness a woman's voice wailed, amplified by the cliffs and rain.

'My babies! My children!'

A roar of horror came from the second castaway, a cry of excoriated anguish. He dived back into the surf, screaming incoherently.

Arden could not move, paralysed by empathy. Chalice ran past her and with the first survivor pulled the grieving parents out of the sea.

The woman fell to her knees and wailed. She shouted at the sky, and the dark ocean, before falling, insensible, into the sand.

'You'll all die out here,' Chalice shouted at them through the tumult. 'There's nothing you can do.'

The wind had in the space of minutes increased. Devouring the children had given the storm strength. Chalice hauled up the woman, and Arden likewise, and in a darkness crackling with sorrow and electricity they shuffled up the lighthouse entrance in the way of a blind rat king, a creature with tails snarled together in one unbreakable knot.

Then inside, to the silence.

The woman, once she was let go, fell to the floor in a puddle of seawater and spume. Arden felt nauseous from despair. At once she had seen that the soggy group were all Clay Hillsiders from the villages in the country of Lyonne, simple folk who had no sanguis endowments and no knowledge of the water except for the expanse of Clay Portside's distant Mouth. From what little she had seen of their boat, it had most likely been assembled in an aqueduct, a house-barge pulled by Clydesdale horses in summer.

Chalice, in her tough Shinlock way, went to work immediately, stoking the brazier with coal until it burned insolently against the cold. The kettle already rocked with boiling water. For the first time, Arden allowed some gratitude for Mr Justinian and his long list of equipment. On the list had been a stack of ten woollen blankets, more than she would ever need. Now, faced with these dripping strangers, the blankets became very handy. She ordered them to strip so she could hang their clothes to dry on a length of oil rope. The clothes, even after a washing in the salt, were stained and musty. The poverty of these poor folk clung to them like ship-salvager's pitch.

At a loss of something authoritarian to do, the patriarch of the family handed out dented cups of tea to the three shivering others before accepting one for himself.

'Thank you,' he said to Arden and Chalice at last. He fell into the rote of greetings. His face was waxen with the effort it took to remain stoic. 'My name is Leyland Tallwater, this is my son Gregor, his wife Helena, and her brother Sean Ironcup.' He frowned, and added in a way that Arden found disrespectful, 'Sean is a cripple. He cannot use his body properly.'

The one called Sean affected nonchalance through his shivering, but she could tell by his young face that the words cut him to the quick.

'You are Hillsiders?' Arden asked. 'From outer Clay?'

'In the lands of the plateau. We are farmers.' Leyland Tallwater bent his head to tea-mug, attempted to scry the past from the present. 'Until the land soured in the last season. My grandchildren grew sickly. I lost my younger son when we could not afford to buy him the medicine.' His face collapsed, and Arden felt sorry for him despite his crudeness, and covered his rough, cold farmer's hand with her own. She felt in him something that did not entirely sit right however. As if this journey had been his idea, and he had buffaloed the others into coming along . . .

If she thought it, she did not say it. She patted his hand again. 'My sympathies, sir. This is the worst pain a human can bear.'

'I have killed all of them. All our babies, on a folly.'

The woman, Helena Tallwater, silently watched as the patriarch spoke. In the brazier's glow her face had no expression. Her spirit had vacated her eyes. Relentless, the storm ground against the tower stones, sent deep and disquiet harmonics through the empty space of the lighthouse.

'You'd best get some rest,' Arden said. 'There's nothing we can do until first light. Maybe that will bring some good news.'

Immediately Arden regretted her thoughtless words. There was no good news in a shipwreck. There would be bodies. There would be death.

Arden excused herself. She retired to the motor-room, where her mouth might do the least damage, only to find that Chalice had claimed the space before her. She wound the clockwork with vicious yanks.

'Are you all right?' Arden asked. 'It's cold up here.'

'Can't bear being among them,' Chalice said mid-yank. 'I lost a little brother to the sea when I was a child. It destroyed my mother, made a ghost of her.'

The winder seized as tight as it would go.

'This journey was their decision,' Arden said.

'You think so? I saw your face when you patted that fellow's hand.'

Arden frowned, and Chalice waved her away. 'Forgive me. I'm in a mood, is all.'

Chalice was reliving her own tragedy. As gently as she could, Arden said, 'I remember a child pulled from the freezing waters of Clay Mouth during their coldest winter, and surviving. The sea is sometimes kinder to the young.'

'Their children are dead.' Chalice was harsh. 'Their bodies are shoring up the Sainted Island platforms amid the Sargasso strands as we speak.'

Arden took the last blanket and wrapped it about the storm-bride's shoulder and her own. She took off her damp glove and held Chalice's hand.

'Was he very young, your brother?'

'Yes.'

'I am truly sorry.'

'He lives in the halls of the Deepwater King now,' Chalice said, inexplicably, for she was not one to make a mockery of others' religion, or replace her own arid Shinlock catechisms for the old gods of the coast.

Though what was Chalice's religion? She had worked this ocean for a long time. What strange instructions had she been exposed to?

'The King will keep him well and forever,' Arden replied. 'And the children too. They belong to Him now.'

With their backs to the old dovetailed joint of the stone they huddled, and waited for the blood-soaked storm to dwindle and die.

15

A delicate pattern of daylight fell

A delicate pattern of daylight fell on her face, disturbing her through the thin veil of sleep, and Arden stirred. The previously incessant wind had stopped so suddenly, Arden's ears still rang from the absence. She would rather not have moved out from under the blanket, but a pressing urge to relieve herself put all other necessities aside. She rubbed the crook of pain out of her neck, before descending the stairway to where their rescued prospectors huddled together by the brazier.

The belly of the stove received one of their precious coal briquettes rather than a log of scrub wood. Arden quietly left the lighthouse to survey what damage had been caused outside.

The morning sun hovered low behind filmy clouds, a baleful yellow eye. A blood morning, full of portents. The sea had becalmed, but only so much that it didn't surge, merely roll as if it were the scanty covering over a gigantic resting form. Arden rubbed her damp gloves, the silver coins itching beneath the leather. Where had the blood come from, she wondered. Why was she feeling it so strongly? She'd always been burdened with a particularly powerful nose for sanguinity in others, but it never had disturbed her so much as it did this morning.

After she had paid a visit to their new outhouse, she walked around to the cliffside, and sucked in an uncomprehending breath—

Three Lyonne Hillsider children wandered down by the scanty sand of the point, dazed and lost and grey with cold, but not in the least bit drowned.

'Oh!' she cried to nobody and everybody. 'Come quick, come quick!'

Her shouts roused the prospectors, who dashed out of the door in half-dressed shambles. Arden had already made her muddy slide down the cliff-slope and was running for the children.

She reached a little girl who could be no more than four years old. Fell to her knees in front of the child, placed her hands upon the child's face, her arms, touching a miracle. Understandably clammy skin, but the girl showed no sign of chill-sickness yet. How could this be? Such a Lyonne Hillchild could not have spent the night in the ocean, on the storm, and survived it. This phenomenon was of a kind Arden had never witnessed.

The eldest girl saw Arden and walked over with a casual air. 'Excuse me, ma'am,' she asked in the polite way of Hillfolk when they come upon sanguis nobility. 'Have you seen my parents?'

'Lissa! Tomas, Deborah!' came the screams. The prospector woman ran across the cold sand and fell about with her children tangled in her arms. 'It's a miracle, a miracle! Oh, my babies!'

Arden stood back to watch the family reunion, delighted and puzzled at the same time. The children shook their heads to their mother's impassioned questions as to their survival. They didn't know how they'd bested the storm. All that had happened between the breaking up of their ship and their arrival on the beach was a blank canvas upon which no memory had been painted.

Unless . . .

Arden turned around. In the panic of finding the children she had missed seeing the boat floating at the old pier.

Not just any boat. A longboat, a hunting craft with *CORMACK* daubed on the side. Captain Georges' stolen plesiosaur boat.

And there, walking away from the commotion of the shore. A man in a wet krakenskin coat.

Arden felt her breath fall out of her, as it all suddenly made sense.

'Mr Riven?'

He turned about stiffly. It obviously hurt him to do anything more than walk upright. He wore no shirt underneath his coat save for rags. Great weeping cuts scored diagonally along the pale span of his chest.

In the weeks since their first introduction, Mr Riven's face had yet to lose all its discoloration from his battle with the game hunters. The water straggled his gingering beard into serpentine twists. He took a step towards her, and she immediately took one back, feeling by the lurch of her blood in her chest the wildness rampant beneath his bruise-mottled skin. The power had come from him.

'What do you want?'

Not a threat. Only a deep weariness, the kind that blood-loss brings.

'I wanted to say thank you,' she blurted, cotton-mouthed and quite suddenly shy. 'For rescuing the children.'

'Those fools took their children to the mouth of death.'

'But still . . .'

He made to turn away but had given so much blood to the sea. One knee failed to take his weight, and he went down onto the other as if making obeisance to an angry god.

Arden stumbled through the sand up to Mr Riven, torn between giving comfort and keeping distance. 'Are you all right?'

Not only his chest, but also one corded forearm was laid open to blade-cuts. It was a desecration of talent to bleed so profusely and openly, and she *tsk*ed in indignant concern.

'Do you even know how to use your blood endowments, sir?'

Despite the strength in his lean, raw-boned body, the clumsy cuts almost made him fragile. A creature infinitely wounded, not just physically, but spiritually too. Forgetting her concern, she reached out a hand.

He recoiled as her fingers grazed his shoulder. 'Don't touch me.' Salt-rasped, his accent falling into an odd lilting place between Fiction and Lyonne. 'Don't . . .' he said again, before staggering upright with the ungainliness of a newborn foal. 'I don't need your help.'

'Come now,' Arden scolded. 'There's only so much blood in a man before he empties himself out.' She held out her hand again. 'Do you want my support or not? Your boat is not going anywhere ever again.'

His boat – and obviously not *his* property but the longboat of Captain Cormack – had wedged high in the spar of rock at the promontory. Another improbable artefact of the rescue, along with the babes who should have been dead.

He muttered some curse word at her, something filthy learned in a prison hulk no doubt, but she had heard worse on the docks and he still leaned on her so that he might stand upright. Arden grunted in quite an unladylike way as she heaved his arm across her shoulders. Despite his clamminess, he radiated warmth where his skin met hers. Hale enough to walk.

'This way,' she said. 'And for heaven's sake, don't bleed over my dress.'

Mr Riven ate the leftover stew in starving, bestial gulps, and halfway through his second bowl fell asleep sitting upright, head thrown back against the wall, his mouth open and gurgling. For the first time she was able to look at him unconstrained. Once it dried out, his hair lightened, and had the distinct unevenness of having been chopped off with a knife blade at moments when it suited him. His nose was long and straight, aristocratic almost, and would have made him appear weak, among these people. His cheekbones high and his skin translucent, blueing where his eye sockets deepened. Long blond lashes, such as one might find on a child. A contradiction of toughness and utter vulnerability.

'So, there's the blood I sensed upon the storm.' Chalice nodded at his wounds. 'There's your Fiction sanguinem, Lightmistress.'

'It's not just a monstercalling trait,' Arden said, and the surprise she felt was a little glow of solidarity with this wild creature. 'That's proper bloodwielding he's gone and done. I never would have guessed.'

'Well, in times past, Fiction had more genetic lines of sanguine endowment than Lyonne,' Chalice said. 'The folks here were quite diverse.'

'Yes, before they thought themselves better off without blood talents.'

'Oh rats,' Chalice said. 'The lumpen out here couldn't keep a guinea in their pocket let alone talent in their blood. They lost it all in ten generations. Your fellow here's probably the last of them, along with Bellis. What a sorry pair they probably were.'

It turned out that Helena had some Hillside folk medicine about her, and she packed Mr Riven's chest wounds with spider webs procured from the rafters. Though Arden was uncertain about touching him, nursing duties required a certain intimacy. She followed Helena's lead and tugged off her neighbour's wet krakenskin coat. His breath surged warm in her ear. His ginger-blond beard tickled her neck, but did not arouse the shudders of revulsion she expected from such an encounter. There was no threat to him, only an exhaustion beyond measure.

'Webs will stop the bleeding,' Helena Tallwater instructed Arden, as the woman passed a linen bandage about the sleeping man's chest. 'A well-known cure.'

'Thank you. I don't have enough clotting powder for anything bigger than a scratch at the moment.'

'Brew up some fruit-mould tea if you have it, soak the bandage in some. It tastes terrible to drink, but the wounds are less likely to go bad under the dressings.'

'I do have some spore-powder, and the tea sounds like a good interim.'

Helena had not, however, anything to stop the deep, physical pain that came from a sanguis losing so much blood, and Mr Riven's sleep was a deep pit from which he could not be roused. Arden took the spoon and bowl from his slack hands, and tipped him sideways onto her makeshift bed, where he could sleep off the blood-loss hangover.

'Will he be all right, wife?' Gregor Tallwater asked once Helena had finished her ministrations. 'This man saved my children. I cannot leave without thanking him.'

'I cannot say,' Helena said. 'I have no experience for these sorts of people.' Her eyes swung nervously between Arden and Mr Riven's uncouth drunk-sleep. 'No offence, Lightmistress, but your kind is different from ours in body and mind.'

'Sanguine folk have a slightly different physiology, it is true,' Arden said gently. 'But there is much in us that is similar. Let him sleep off his blood intoxication, and you may thank him later.'

The patriarch of the rescued family appeared less than impressed by their saviour. Leyland Tallwater sat at a remove near the brazier, his craggy Hillfolk features not hiding his deep discomfort. In Clay he would rarely have spoken to anyone blood-bound, and only if he had known them before a testmoot, and then only as a child. Unlike in Fiction, Lyonne society stratified through the existence of sanguine talent, and in such social separations, superstitions took root. Arden had known of Hillfolk to tell their children night-creeping stories. Tales of how the sanguinem sometimes needed the blood of others to replenish their own.

Considering it took only a drop of blood to execute one's phlebotomous labour, it did not bode well to see Mr Riven so pale and lifeless. In his blood-loss frailty one could halfway believe such stories of vampiric hunger. Arden wished she hadn't been so quick to send Chalice with Sean Ironcup to Vigil earlier.

It had very much been Chalice's idea that they report the castaways to the Coastmaster at once. She'd chosen to take the Ironcup lad with her, a slim, delicate youth of perhaps twenty-two years, who had a palsy of his left side. 'Not to offend, but the more wretchedly vulnerable you people appear to the Coastmaster, the more he'll likely let you come ashore with only a warning and not a penalty,' Chalice had said. 'The Baron Justinian has a distaste for deformities. So, Master Ironcup, you come with me.'

'I'll have you know,' Sean Ironcup had said, deeply affronted, 'I can handle a boat with one hand better than most men with two. And it's *Mister* Ironcup.'

'It's true,' Helena had added. 'He's the only one of us who knows his way around a ship.'

A vegetable barge is certainly not a ship, Arden thought. From her wincing face, Chalice thought exactly the same thing. Still, it was those two who did the honours of reporting, and left Arden with six wary strangers.

'Come, children,' she said to the two eldest. 'I'll show you how I keep the lighthouse fire alive.'

'Go,' Helena urged, when they looked at their mother.

'All right then,' replied the girl. 'Come now, Tomas.'

They followed Arden up the twisting stairs to the lamp room. She showed them the disks that she kept under her gloves, and how she cut into each one in turn to feed the flame.

'How does it work,' asked the girl, Lissa. 'Your blood?'

'Well now,' Arden said, and launched into a familiar explanation. 'It is said that when God made Man, He also made angels, and demons. Demons feast on angel blood, you see. And angels are argumentative, easily offended. The angels formed a union against God for allowing such powers to exist, and there was a war in heaven. An agreement was made that He should cast them down to live with humankind. And so they do, hid in every nook and cranny of the earth. Even our blood.'

There was no response from the children, and Arden, flustered, barrelled on.

'In time, some angels rebelled and fell in love and came to mate with Men. The descendants can feed the demons not only of flame, but demons of mathematics, of memory and storm and iron and physics, make them do their bidding.'

The tale satisfied most Clay city children, but the two Hillsiders glared at her with darkly sceptical eyes. 'That is not the truth.'

'Of course it is.'

'It's not. Don't lie to us.'

Arden sighed, refastened her gloves. 'All right then. I don't believe it either. To tell you the truth, the real truth, nobody quite knows where the genetic talent comes from. There was indeed a war at some time, one that nearly destroyed the entire human race. There weren't pretend things like gods or angels involved. It was us. A war of spirit perhaps, a whispered war. And there may have been some contamination introduced into our bodies that is passed on through the family line. Men of science have speculated on many things. Morphic resonance. Machines smaller than the smallest microscope can see. Magic even, although any science advanced enough can appear like magic.'

Their mother called them from downstairs. 'Children,' she cried, 'Uncle Sean is back.'

'I don't think it's science or magic inside you,' said the boy. 'I think it is *sin*.'

Mr Riven groaned bearishly and rolled over. He had yet to fully wake, but that was to be expected. The sanguis comedown could be gruelling on those untrained in the nuances of the sacrament; Mr Riven now wallowed at the tail end of a hard bleed, where a man might flutter in and out of consciousness, the waking body quite nonplussed by the agony of the bright new day and retreating to the insensate safety of dreams.

No thank-yous for him, then. Leyland showed himself only too happy to board the recovery boat to Vigil when the Harbourmistress came. His gratitude was tempered by preconceptions and prejudices. This wild man had returned Mr Tallwater's family entire, yes, however the methods of rescue filled the Hillsider with deep dread.

Arden reluctantly left Mr Riven sleeping on her now-ruined bed, before retreating to the pier.

Mx Modhi in her usual foul temper, barked at her boy to help the children into the dinghy. 'David, lad, they've had enough trouble with the sea, they don't need it from you,' she said between furious puffs of her pipe. While she sat on the tiller of her recovery boat, the youth wrestled with the waterlogged pieces of Tallwater possessions that the afternoon swell had seen fit to deposit on the rocks.

Satisfied that her son had done his part, she returned to Arden.

'Won't be the first survivors you'll haul from the drink. Jorgen Beacon would average five a year. Bodes well that you got the whole family alive, Lightmistress. Perhaps we should rub you for luck.'

'The rescue wasn't just my doing. Mr Riven helped.'

Mx Modhi blew pipe-smoke towards the longboat. 'Best you not let that be known in these parts. Between you and me, Captain Cormack's stolen longboat got onto the rocks itself.'

She whistled over to Leyland Tallwater.

'Ma'am?' he responded.

'We'll attend the office of Postmaster Harrow and Coastmaster Justinian, fill out the papers advising of a wreck and rescue, friend. There are debts and charges attached to a rescue in these waters, and the licensing board of Clay will require contacting.'

The Hillsider jammed his hands into his pockets. 'We ain't had no papers nor funds for this journey.'

'No papers? No funds? You had your eyes on Sainted Island stars with no penny for the Old Guy, eh?' Mx Modhi cackled.

'We bring our hands, and the willingness to do hard work.'

She laughed again, before exploding into a coughing fit. 'Journeyman, your journey has ended. You don't know the Islands. They'll not accept prospectors to their shores unless you come with assets. They have all the labour they want over there.'

Leyland bristled and yanked his hands out of his pockets. 'And how would you know this, huh? Sunning yourself on a stinking little harbour?'

Gregor, perhaps sensing that his father might be drawn into a fight, stood up and announced, 'Well, that's it, then. All packed. In the boat, children. And wherever has Helena gone?'

Leyland gave a grunt and went to sit in the boat, sulking. Mx Modhi looked at him with a deep suspicion, and her tongue moved agitatedly about her ivory pipe-stem. She left the tiller on the pretence of bending to check a rope tie, but instead leaned in close to Arden's ear.

'You sure plucked a good one out of the sea, Lightmistress,' she gruffed at Arden. 'I don't like him.'

With her sharp Beacon eyes, Arden spotted the woman standing on the furthest tip of the promontory, staring out to sea.

'Wait, I'll get her,' Arden said. 'Make the children comfortable, Harbourmistress. The water can be rough, and another trip may traumatize them.'

She glanced at the boy, who only glared back, untraumatized and full of accusation.

The wind blew strong on the promontory. Helena stood there motionless, her shawl pulled back and her raw face rimed with salt and tears. Arden approached her with care.

'They are ready to go,' Arden said gently.

'You cannot see the Sainted Isles from here.'

'No, they are over the horizon. That cloud line to the southeast is only *Tempestas*, which you might know as the Tempest, the permanent storm. There is another route north, on which you would have gone, had your boat not wrecked.'

'You have been there, yourself?'

Arden shook her head. 'Sometimes I spot the ships heading out. They turn at this lighthouse. I make notations for the Navigation Council. But maybe it is best that you are going home, because despite what they say, I've never seen anyone returning from the Islands. Only the lich-ships heading for the refineries and distillation forests of Dead Man's Bay, never people.'

Helena turned to Arden then. A desperate faith in her. 'We will not go home. Leyland says we are going to the Islands, and he means it. He will buy us passage on a fishing boat, a smuggler's boat, anything that floats.' She tilted her chin at the lighthouse. 'That cut-up fellow in there seems to know his way around a craft. Perhaps Leyland will make a deal with him.'

'Think about your children, Helena. If you had made it to the Isles, what sort of life would it be for them? They say nothing lives out there, any more. They say that Hell would be a better place to go.'

'I know.' The woman returned to her constant scanning of the grey horizon. 'When I thought they had drowned, you know what I felt? *Relief.* Relief that my babies are gone, that they will suffer no more. All the way here I have had my heart pricked by the demons of anxiety and worry. I thought: now my children are dead, I can be wounded no more. But your wild fellow brought them back to me, and the torture begins anew. So then. Damn you both to that Hell over the horizon.'

She pulled up her shawl and wrapped the coarse wool around her, swept past Arden with a hiss of resentment.

Arden watched the Tallwaters leave the pier upon Mx Modhi's boat, all of them stiff-backed and nursing their secret determinations. Arden could not stop the dread gathering her bones. Chalice had gone with them, ostensibly to help, but in actuality to provide more muscle in case Mr Leyland Tallwater, in a fit of storm-addled courage, might steal the Harbourmistress' boat for another shot at the Isles.

Would not have been the first time it had happened, given the way Chalice merely stepped into the boat with nary a word.

Leaving Arden alone with—

'Heavens!' she exclaimed, and ran back into the lighthouse. 'Oh no!'

She burst through the door into the tower's lower floor. To her dismay, apart from the blood-stained sheets the bed lay empty.

'Mr Riven?' she called tremulously. Maybe he had gone home. Or at least she hoped he had.

The metal stairs creaked in the rock. A body moved about in the upper reaches of the tower.

In a fit of panic Arden reached for one of Uncle Jorgen's old butchering knives that hung from iron hooks in the walls, hefted it, then put it down with a groan.

What was she expecting? She had invited Mr Riven as a guest. He had not sought to harm her in all the times they had met.

With her heart in her mouth she climbed the stairwell.

Mr Riven stood in the engine room, peering out of one of the narrow windows. In the low light he seemed more beast than human, his back marked by scars, swirls and spirals lain in with squid-ink and broken shell, patterns that outlined each vertebra before flaring out across his hips to disappear into the waist of his canvas strides.

He did not startle when she came in. The bones of his shoulder blades moved beneath the flesh of his back as he shifted his point of view to another window.

'I've never been up here,' he said. 'Always wondered what kind of fire got the light flashing.'

'It's not really the light that flashes,' Arden said. 'The battens turn. The light is always lit.'

She heard the Tallwater boy's voice in her head. *It is sin.* She briefly closed her eyes. From this moment on she could either send Mr Riven on his way, or invite him into her life, and all the problems such people bring. His woman he had killed, his family he had murdered. The plesiosaur baby he had laid gentle upon the table when he had fought three men to save the mother, and the sweater he had given her when she was close to death and vulnerable to attack. The mottled, bearded face pressed against the glass.

She took a breath, took the dive.

'There's a better view in the lamp room. I'll bring the battens down over the coldfire, and you can discover for yourself.'

Those horizon-blue eyes on her again, almost unnaturally bright in the engine room. She unhooked the gate and went up first, let him make his own path as if he were an untamed creature she had fed but did not expect to follow.

He shadowed her at a silent, respectable distance. She heard the catch of his breath as he beheld the view from the height, the wide sea and the scrubby, desolate land in a thousand different directions.

Mr Riven walked about the lamp room. He touched the blood collection chamber. He studied the horizon maps over the windows, the semaphore codes, the shipping signals. Arden stayed by and watched him. Despite his height, he didn't strike her as a particularly threatening sort of gentleman, carrying his lean strength with a certain economy and his power under a bushel. As far as he was concerned there might have been nobody in the room other than him.

Arden had a strange, unbidden recollection from her childhood, of her half-sister Sirena rescuing a stray dog from the streets. The mutt had shown no interest in its new surroundings, only paced the walls of their bedroom for a day before their step-mother came upon them with exclamations of *responsibility* and *ownership*.

Nina Beacon had allowed her daughter to keep the pup on strict orders that it be fed and cared for by Sirena herself. A week later it returned to the streets, having never bonded to anyone, and fleeing the room at the first moment of freedom it got.

Maybe Mr Riven would flee, after he'd exhausted his curiosity about his old nemesis' home. Perhaps it was better if he did.

'I must excuse the slovenliness of downstairs,' Arden said nervously. 'My uncle never left it in very much of a good condition. In fact, the only thing he was good at was reminding an eternal flame to keep eternal. Whichever way, this might be the last time you ever see it. The Seamaster's Guild intends to replace it with a regular light come winter time.'

Mr Riven didn't answer. Arden found herself looking skyward for a modicum of heavenly help with these taciturn men and boys.

He rubbed one of the window panes. Mx Modhi's boat was well on its way to Vigil with the other equally conversational guests. The bandage about his chest had soaked entirely black with blood. It runnelled over his abdominal muscles, stained the waistband of his waxed-canvas breeches and to Arden's dismay spattered the lamp room's finally clean floor.

'. . . which is why you should really consider getting some stitches in those deep cuts. The skin is likely to damage if you let it gape around in the open with just a rag bandage.' She pointed to her own hands. 'Even *I* required disks sewn into my skin when I was deployed to the lighthouse so I wouldn't destroy my hands.'

'I'll stitch it myself when I get back.'

His rebuff annoyed her. This was not charity. This was necessity. Was he being obnoxious out of spite?

'If you doubt my skill, I have my minor surgeon's certificate. It's a requirement of dock working. Lest I forget to remind you, Gregor Tallwater also wanted to pass on his thanks that you rescued his children, but he doesn't have a penny to his name, now. He owes you. I owe you.'

Mr Riven was not entirely incapable of reading the mood in the room. Sensing he had crossed a line of social grace, the man nodded, though from his expression he was not pleased.

'Do what you must.'

She encouraged him, dripping blood all the while, down to the engine-room, where there was space and light enough for her to do her work. Directed him to a driftwood stool and pulled her surgical case from the trunk. A blood-worker always had boiled needles nearby, pre-threaded in glass so they might be used at once. One can never tell when a knife will cut too deep.

Then, feeling somewhat awkward for the intimacy it presented, knelt between his knees and released the bandages.

She knew soon after that she needn't have worried about his reaction to her nearness. Only a moment where a brief apprehension crossed his face – not so easy to hide when their breaths were on each other and his leather-clad thighs spanned her waist – and Arden huffed, 'I won't hurt you.'

As if a light had gone out behind his eyes, Mr Riven became still and absent. Only the slight rise and fall of his chest made it certain he was alive. One could envisage her touch turning him to stone, like the curses of old. She looked over him, and wondered what hand had carved this clay, what had flensed this man so brute and lean? His skin was warm and pale under her fingers, pale russet hairs upon each pectoral and the thin, dark blond line to his belly, the dip of skin at his throat where his heartbeat raced.

He neither startled nor acknowledged her contact, nor the cold tincture across his chest, but she could feel a deep nervous tremble in the long muscles, a prey-animal finally caught. She wondered about his prison time as a child, and how he'd survived. About what the sea required of him. Shamefully, looked between his legs, to see if he had cut off his maleness to catch his sea-monsters, and was assured, with a flush of heat to her cheeks, that he had most certainly not.

Strange thoughts came to her. Had anyone ever touched him in love, and tenderness? Had Bellis? Or had all his human interactions been in cruelty and convenience? It seemed so odd, that he not react at all when she pierced the lip of one wound and drew through a thread, yet that he tremble so when she placed her hand upon his knee so she might draw closer.

'So, what is your kinship to blood then, Mr Riven?' she said, wanting to fill the silence lest it grow too deep. 'Storm caller? Searcher, *sanguis appellandi*?'

'I should have left the children in the water.'

Arden had not expected him to speak, and the Lyonnish lilt to his flat Fiction vowels caught her by surprise. His eyes were still elsewhere. She only sighed in reply, did not scold him for making such a comment, and tied off her stitches. 'Their mother said much the same thing. Oh, they'll find their way to the Isles, one way or another. You may have a visit from Leyland, pleading for transport.'

'He'll not have to go so far. Would be a score of fishermen

161

who would take him over for a bag of pennies. Or a night with the daughter.'

'Mr Riven, that's rather mean-minded of—'

He looked down at her, cold as the ocean. 'Why do you think he's taken the children, the family? Why has he gone to such trouble to drag such baggage, when it would have been more expedient to go to the Islands on his own? The Old Guy doesn't take anyone without payment, everyone knows that.'

Arden's face burned, realizing that in her wilful ignorance she had seen Mr Tallwater as equally innocent to the cost of prospecting. The family was even more abject than the crowd of hopefuls she had seen on the Firth crossing, when she had first come to Lyonne. No paddle-steamer cruise for them. They would find themselves on a boat of rot and driftwood, and be half-dead when they reached one corpse-pontoon shore.

'He'll sell the children?'

'You know it.'

'Then I'll have to warn Helena, and the Harbourmistress!'

Mr Riven stood awkwardly up from the stool. Winced at the stitching. 'Yes, warn the women. Warn the Coastmaster and the Magistrate. Flash it coded in this devil's light. Shout it to the wind, Lightmistress. Do what you must so that you may sleep at night. It will make no difference. You think I do not know this from experience?'

She bowed her head in surrender. 'By God in his heaven, this world is cruel.' She repacked the bandages. 'Every time I think that it tilts towards miracles, I am dismayed by the awfulness of it.'

'You're a fool if you thought any different.'

He went to go past her, and she shot out a hand to grab his arm.

'Did you kill your wife, Mr Riven? Am I the same fool for having invited you in here so you know that I spend most of my hours vulnerable, and alone?'

She shocked him with her directness. She wanted him shocked, not dismissive, not regarding her as a mere annoyance. If this man wanted to kill her, he could kill her now and be done with it. She stood up to him in defiance but *oh*, a part of her, a beaten, cast-off and love-scarred demon inside Arden imagined – in a wrench of forbidden and sordid joy – him doing to her what they whispered he did to Bellis; his rope-burned hands about her neck, her air-starved convulsions as he took her life, took without thought to Guild laws or eugenics or the portion of the blood that gave talent.

Her breath came fast and heavy. Her heart moved in her with the anxious fear of a bird caged in bone. Her body became an object of disgust and deceit, wanting an awful thing because it felt better that way. Better than the nothingness forced upon her by her duties as a Fiction lighthouse keeper, tending a lantern destined to die.

He did have some measure of sensitivity. Sensing the repellent desires in her, Mr Riven scowled and jerked back.

'No,' Mr Riven growled, harsh with reproach. 'I did not kill my wife. I love her and love her still. All these things you wish to do to save the Tallwater children, I have done for Bellis, and no difference has it made. Good day to you.'

Then he was gone, down the stairs in a rush, snatched up his coat and slammed the door as he left.

It is sin.

The terrible compulsion drained from Arden, leaving her wrung-out and weak. What demon had compelled her to such disrespect? She returned to the lamp room, pressed her cheek to the salt-crusted span of glass. In the dreary afternoon light watched Mr Riven's small, distant figure exit the lighthouse, throwing the coat over his bare torso before striding down the old coast road.

Until he came to the cenotaph of Bellis Riven and Stefan Beacon.

There he knelt by the cairn, placed a stone upon its peak, but not before he'd pressed his lips to the stone with all the tenderness of one whose beloved is before him. Arden knew him weeping then, this scraggled, tattooed man beaten by sand and storm, mourning a woman gone from him.

Oh, to be loved and missed so. Arden had experience aplenty with family and the embraces of itinerant lovers, wisps of passions. She considered them only temporary. When they left, she did not mourn them. Nor they, her. Not even Richard. She'd made her peace with the transitory and shallow nature of the love she inspired.

This, though. This made the bitter demon of Envy stir in her breast. She had invoked spells against loneliness with the garments of both this man and his wife, and she was now tied to them in primitive, hungry ways.

That. Give me the kind of love they had.

In her whirl of emotions, a more sensible self whispered in her ear.

Calm yourself, it said in the voice of an old signal instructor whose name she had forgotten. *You are tired and traumatized from the night and the rescue. This widowed husband might pay all the respects to the wife now, but acts in grief and regret never mirror the treatment of a real flesh and blood woman. Witnesses called him cruel. Bellis is still dead.*

I love her and love her still.

The tenses he used. He had not spoken of the past. No stumble of words, no excuse or explanation for a dead wife.

What truth is it? she wondered. Who did Bellis marry, a monster or a man? Had the Justinians and the Harrows spread a twisted story as false as the one with the plesiosaur game hunters? Had Bellis just sailed off and fallen afoul of the weather, died by accident, an adulteress punished by God?

There was nobody who could say for certain. Except him. Still shaken by the ghastliness of her body's lunge towards defilement, she watched Mr Riven place one more kiss upon the stone, then set off down the coast road in the waning afternoon sun, back to his decaying house and stained mattress, his krakenskin coat-tails snapping in the wind like bronze wings.

Book Two: The Lion

16

The invitation came

The invitation came on one of David Modhi's deliveries on the day of autumn equinox, a time when the migratory seabirds became restless from their nesting, and the fluffy chicks shed the last of their down, leaving a storm of white fluff blowing out across the sedge-grass and catching in any exposed laundry as if it were thistle seeds.

At once she saw that she had not received an onionskin letter from Lyonne, but a missive of an entirely different sort.

Arden rubbed the ivory card with its edges of gold scallop. The neat cursive hand requested that the Lightmistress of Vigil join an assortment of Guildsmen and Allied Persons for an evening at Manse Justinian.

She flipped the card back and forth, barely trusting the date, the words. Intellectually she had known it a year since the last Guild Ball, and that Fiction would have a ball just as its northern counterpart did, but it had not *felt* like a year. More like a deep geological moment, her life changed so utterly from that moment to this.

'I'm not going.'

'Say what, darling?' Chalice asked when she snatched the letter out of Arden's grasp. The delivery had come at that brief window when they were both awake, otherwise Arden would have fed the invite to the brazier's belly.

'Oh, Chalice, I'm not interested in going to a Guildmaster's Ball.'

'A *ball*? This is a surprise! It's not always the young David brings us anything except sausages and evaporated milk, now.'

Chalice read the invitation aloud in her most toffee-nosed Lyonne accent: 'The Masters of Fiction Annual Ball will be held at the Manse Justinian two weeks from now, and the combined Guilds of Fiction and Lyonne request your presence.'

'A request,' Arden repeated. 'Not an order. I don't need to go. Besides, the last one in Lyonne was such a disaster I've sworn off the things altogether.'

The stormbride gave Arden a snagging grin. 'Our servant of the flame gets to go to the Guild Ball. A real Guild Ball, not one of those piddling cattle-calls they hold in Portside. You know who will be there, don't you?'

Arden snorted. 'Mr Justinian.'

Chalice slapped Arden's hand with the paper. 'We *know* that useless heel will be creeping about his mouldering old mansion. I mean *men*! Real live men. Unmarried Lyonnian bachelors with their names in the Eugenics Society's ledgers, signed and underlined.'

At the mention of men, David Modhi swayed from one gangly foot to the other and blushed mightily.

Arden batted her away. 'I told you, I've put that idea aside, Chalice. I only have, oh, less than three months left of my time here.'

'Three months! Why, you've gone spare enough in the first two!'

'Look, I'll say I never got the invitation. Mr Modhi will dissemble for me.'

'Uhh . . .' David Modhi started.

Chalice mock-slapped her again. 'Fool! You know what I mean. You've been moping and pining about, and even Mr Riven is starting to look good.'

Arden's cheeks grew hot. Had Chalice suspected the methods

in which her mind betrayed her in the deep night? Since she had carried out the small intimate act of tending to Mr Riven's wounds, she had tried and failed not to linger upon her neighbour. Cast away the thought of that abraded, tattooed body forcing itself upon her, and inside her. A mere interaction would not have been enough, anyway.

No, when Arden invented Mr Riven with her, she experienced an inexplicable act of transference. She became Bellis Harrow, taken away to the Sainted Isles to marry the Deepwater King. In her conjurations Arden was swept away by a power stronger than she could articulate, wrapped up in her own obsessions of class betrayal and self-immolation. Had concocted a fantasy that could not possibly be true, but she wanted to be true, for it filled her with a forbidden delight.

In that miserable matrimonial year that followed their elopement, Bellis had not left her husband, though all the others in her life had clamoured to help.

Only one reason could fully explain why the two had stayed together. Bellis had loved Mr Riven back. Somehow she must have had to, to stay with him. In the dark, secret ways she must have loved her husband. Yearned for what he gave her, be it wrapped up in jealousy or sexual violence, or the brutishness of a man obsessed.

Such a terrible, fearful thing. It should have repelled Arden, but she was not repelled, only drawn towards it as if an inevitable outcome.

The King has seen your face.

Arden, bound to fire and light, could not comprehend such an affection, but wanted it for herself all the same. *Chalice is right. I am jealous, and I am glad she is dead.*

Alarmed that her vices should be so obvious to Chalice, Arden protested with a croak. 'That is so unfair, and a smite on my preferences. He appeals to me less than . . . less than Mr Justinian.'

'Come on now. It has been weeks since we rescued those miserable Tallwaters and not a day has passed when you don't watch entirely the wrong section of coast and bite your finger-nails down to rags. You still haven't brought back the jumper to him.' Chalice's eyes narrowed. 'Don't think I haven't seen you wadding it up and cradling it to your heart. You intend to make a pillow for a man's head.'

'I haven't had the chance to return it! I appreciate nice woollen things, ever since I was a child. Allow me some credit for taking simple pleasures.'

'Empty sweaters and make-believe are not a man. What you need is a friendly gentleman who will – without commitments – ease the aches and pains of solitude. Must I explain that in detail as well?'

David Modhi had not moved from his spot at the doorway where he had delivered his message, and after a confused silence at the back-and-forth argument of these older women, bright-ened up. 'My mother has a good liniment for removing aches and pains. She's been testing it on Sean Ironcup, the man we rescued last month.'

'I'm not talking about those pains, lad,' Chalice said airily. 'Women's pains, which are never spoken aloud because we are far too high on our perfect pedestals, aren't we? Anyhow, were you being a sneak, David Modhi? It hasn't escaped my notice the envelope to our Lightmistress' fairy-tale ball found itself opened upon your delivery.'

'Mr Harrow gave it to me opened.'

'Of *course* he did,' Arden snapped. 'He opens everything of mine.'

With a snatch she retrieved the letter from David and the card from Chalice. 'Check the date. It came to Vigil a fortnight ago. Let me add the corollary to all fairy-tale gatherings. I am unprepared, I have nothing to wear. Will you be the godmother to force me into something from Mrs Sage's rag-table then?'

'Goodness, no. But wear your waxen keeper's uniform, love, because if you need something solid to weather a storm, you'll be needing it on that night.'

* * *

Another letter came one day before the Master's Ball, this time a missive from the Coastmaster. Mr Justinian grandly proposed that Mr Quill would collect her upon sundown on the day of the ball, and that she would be welcome to stay in the guest room overnight. There was something else too. A package wrapped in brown paper, with a shape and give so obvious Arden knew exactly what it was.

This letter ended up finding itself shoved into the brazier's belly, and the package would have too, had Chalice, awakened by the noise of Arden's exclamation of offence, snatched it out of her hands.

'Oh Chalice, could you stop doing that? Is anything I own not sacred to you?'

'Darling, if I didn't, you'd never allow me to read anything. I am your stormbride and protector, and you are my little innocent babe who has received—'

She ripped the paper and gasped. 'A dress! Oh Arden, the most beautiful dress!'

Arden averted her head from a billow of peacock blue. 'I shan't look at it.'

'Your fairy godmother has indeed come. Did she mention a pumpkin too?'

'*She* . . . wants me to stay in his damned house on the night of the ball.'

'Well, why not? A lady can't possibly sleep on the streets, and there is no way you could pilot *Fine Breeze* home on a bellyful of wine and a half-moon night. You'd end up whisked into the Tempest in an instant.'

Arden paced the tower's base, before sitting on her bed as she did as a child in a temper, confined to her room and with nowhere else to go. 'He's still trying to seduce me in exchange for signing the damned Guild degree document. I might as well offer myself up on a plate.'

'I thought you told me he's made a vow of celibacy? On his knees, you said he was. You'll stay in Vigil overnight,' Chalice said firmly. 'You're not coming back here.'

Arden glared in mock-horror at Chalice.

Chalice *tsk*ed. 'I meant overnight *in general*, not the Manse overnight specific, sweetheart. Let me send one of my pigeons to the Black Rosette. I have an acquaintance there, Fionna La Grange, whom I used to know from my posting at Harbinger Bay.'

'A lady at the Black Rosette? Dare I suppose that my storm-bride has a lover?'

Chalice rolled her eyes, then returned the smirk, for what could she hide?

'We are intimate occasionally, yes, but friends more, having weathered historical storms of the human kind. Miss La Grange has an apartment behind the tavern. There is a chaise longue in her front room which does solid work as an emergency bed. Now, let's look at your dress.'

She led it up to the coldflame lantern. Blue silk, the colour of a summer's sky at the highest point, a shade so deep that to Arden's eyes it became almost violet. Seed-pearl fronds across the waist and under the bust, flowing in tendrils. A peplum of cormorant feathers, and the rest of the dress subtly hooped so it did not fall straight down but billowed as if caught by a stray breeze.

In the glittering lights of a Clay Capital soiree the dress would be beautiful, if one were hoping to win the attention of several suitors. But for a professional gathering in the cold recesses of Vigil? Beyond inappropriate.

'So, the Baron has sent you his message,' Chalice said. 'His enforced celibacy is over.'

'I'll refuse to wear it.'

Chalice shook her head. 'That kind of principle works well in story books, but rarely in practice. Just go, get it over and done with, Arden. Turn up to the stupid ball. Be as ungainly in that dress as if Mr Justinian had clad a bearded wharfman in spider silks, and you will never be asked to wear such things again.'

* . * . *

Unfortunately, when Arden put on the flowing layers of fabric the next day, they had the opposite effect to the one she hoped for. The dress wrapped her up in an illusion of pearls and iridescence, and her bare skin was so warmed with those adjacent hues that she might have been as beautiful as a spice-island princess. Each time she moved, the faceted glass beads on her shoulders caught the sunlight, cast rainbows on the opposite wall.

'Heavens, this is not me at all,' Arden said weakly as her chest threatened to fall out of the neckline of the dress. 'I'm a ham dressed for a Yuletide dinner.'

'I'm certain that is the point.'

She rubbed the fabric between her fingers and thought wistfully of the kraken coat – warm and protecting. She thought of Mr Justinian's hissed *murdered whore's garment*. This dress seemed a more likely clothing for bad decisions and unfortunate trades.

'Yes, but I would rather it not be.'

'Just make sure he signs your document first,' Chalice said. 'I have not had much use for a man, but Fionna tells me it's much easier if one is drunk.'

'Chalice!'

'All right. I take it back.'

'Now what other wicked magicks does my fairy godmother have for me? My glass slippers? My pumpkin coach that doesn't involve Mr Quill driving? A silver hatpin to prick him if Mr Justinian comes too close?'

'The slippers I cannot do. The hatpin you'll have to supply yourself. But the coach, well, let's just say there will be some mode of transport outside the Manse this evening at the stroke of midnight.'

'Make it ten o'clock,' Arden said. 'I don't intend to stick around for the sorry end of this little enchantment.'

The evening came upon Vigil with the sea-fog, and the Manse turned on its lights for the two hundred guests that descended upon the granite doorstep.

In Fiction's harsh austerity, there were very few opportunities for the few aristocrats of the country to show off. Arden quickly decided that the Guild had not been aiming low when they sent the invitations for a ball at the Manse. There were at least fifty North Fictish and South Lyonnian here of sanguis endowment, and three hundred of non-blood Grandmaster degree. She could smell the blood-endowed in the mingling crowd, taste metal on her tongue. The people wore garments that might have seemed restrained and severe were they at a Clay Capital ball, the men's dinner coats never moving from tones of gorse-brown and stone, their shirts plain and unruffled.

Dowager Justinian greeted her warmly. 'It's been a pleasure, and a long time,' she said, grasping at Arden's hands so hard that her coins twanged in discomfort. 'I had rather hoped you would visit more.'

'I am kept busy enough at the flame. The weather seems to change every hour – I do believe I spend more time running between the window and the record ledger than I do going outside.'

'It is the autumn, come hard winter, every day will be dreary. Let me take your coat.'

Arden didn't particularly want to pass over her krakenskin coat, but truth to tell, if the men were drab then the women exhibited for both, were unrestrained in their chiffons, their silks and satins. Arden's blue-sky dress didn't seem so outrageous in their company.

She handed the coat over to a wait-servant she did not recognize – one of the new young men from the coast, still gauche in unfamiliar fine clothes – and accepted a tall glass of champagne. Divested of her travelling garments, she headed for the ballroom, where she might hide in the crowd from the mansion's owner.

If she were eager to leave, the others were not. The guests had gathered with a view to eat and drink as merrily as they could, given that the other days of the year rarely provided opportunities for either. Rows of tables at either end of the room were illuminated with one hundred branching candle-sticks and piled with food expressly bought from the far ports of Lyonne and Vinland. Candied plums dripping with cinnamon paste, plates of artichokes and marinated octopus arranged in swirls, breadsticks cradling dodo-liver pâté, messenger pigeons baked in holy-land clay and stuffed with alpine pine seeds from Gaul and Lebanon. Shrimp crusted with sourdough bread-crumbs, cannabis-infused chocolates rolled in gold leaf, gelatine squares soaked in sugarcane brandy, a roasted boar still bearing a ridge of bristles, the crisped skin glistening with an oily craquelure, potatoes dusted with sumac-spice . . .

Arden had not seen such a feast since her father had brought her to a Guild event in Clay Portside. She could hardly have pictured that the Manse, with all its frowsy, hard-worn appearance and that low-lying detergent smell, could have put on such a civilized cloak and attain such a sense of opulence.

To add to the air of decadent consumption, more wine than was strictly required for a professional gathering flowed from the great demijohns of sparkling Clay Riverina *cuvée*. The waitstaff pushed glass upon glass of spritzing sweet liquor at her. She thought them innocuous and realized at her third glass that they were anything but. Her head spun. Another one would only make her intoxicated.

Yet even with the goldware and the glistening food, and the candles and the lanterns and the gas lamps turned to full, a dour cast fell about the Justinian residence, for the surroundings were bleached of contrast and colour. A desperate undercurrent flowed through the conversations, and it did not take too many minutes of eavesdropping upon small-talk for Arden to work out that they were talking of Clay Portside.

'Trouble on the docks in Lyonne,' said the one wharfmaster from Garfish Point she managed to capture in a proper conver-sation. 'Talk of commonfolk unions and other nonsense.'

Another young man, Fiction-pale, dark hair and craggy, weatherworn features, wore fingerless gloves upon his hands the same as Arden. 'I myself have narrowly escaped their acts of violence and sabotage. They attacked me at my very post, not more than two months ago. Called me a *scab*, an affront to good morals, a stealer of food from the mouths of children. Can you believe it? I'm like them, I have to work off my employment fees too. It's not as if I'm getting showered in banknotes. I'm paid just the same.' He held his fingers in such a way they suggested an encroaching paralysis. 'I was glad to get a post at Garfish Point,' he concluded. 'I only hope I can get my coins changed soon.'

Nervously, Arden touched her own gloves. He saw her action, and nodded. He wore a pin upon his lapel, the shape of a box. Had it in him, the pin suggested, to divest some mass from an object to make it more easily manoeuvrable. Perhaps not *sanguis pondus*, a manipulator of inert mass, but something adjacent. A useful skill on the wharves, though not so useful that he'd been carted off to Fiction.

'Many a commonblood family had their fortunes increased when a member tested positive for endowments,' Arden said. 'But there are jobs that require no sanguis talent at all. So even though I have these,' she held up her gloves, 'I can understand a mature worker's concern. How would you like it, sirs, to be replaced by a child thirty years your junior, purely due to an *inferred* and irrelevant skill?'

'Oh, you sound like a unionist,' the wharfmaster guffawed. Unlike his companion, the wharfmaster was physically impressive, a tall, heavy fellow of elderly years with an abundant grey beard made yellow with pipe-smoke. 'Malcontents and the like. Sanguine folk *enable* trade. The commonbloods should be happy enough with a job, and not starving in the hills or shoring up the Sainted Isles.' He nodded knowingly at Arden. 'Men chance the attention of Lions if they knock heads with industrial progress.'

Arden looked down at her near-empty wine glass, and debated another. This night would be less annoying if she saw it to the end in a drunken haze.

Before the others could ask further of her opinions, a hand came from nowhere, seized her elbow and whisked her away.

'No need to speak to them, Lightmistress. The anti-unionists drink to excess and make up stories of persecutions that are only the push and shove of a busy city.'

'Mr Justinian,' Arden said, nonplussed. 'I'm certain I could have worked that out for myself without having a sudden rescue.'

'You don't want sudden rescues, huh? I'll have to remember that.' His gaze scraped her up and down. He was quicksilver. 'See, the dress makes you attractive for a plain girl.'

So, all his promises of restraint upon the cliffside had indeed flittered away. She bit back the sharp retort on her tongue. *Concentrate on the signature for your Guild degree, Arden. Make that the goal you must endure trials to achieve.*

A pair of Morningvale Guilders passed them, smiling. They'd never been this far South before, and though he couldn't sense their veiled derision of his rotting house and his poorly chosen décor that was a shade too gauche, Mr Justinian still greeted them with such oily charisma he practically gleamed. With the practice born of a thousand false relationships, he introduced Arden to most of the room, spoke of her highly, made the subtlest insinuations that he was physically intimate with her on a regular basis.

The social gauntlet never showed an end, and Arden became a mess, internally quivering with a breathless rage, her hands balled into sweaty fists. She could reveal no outward sign of her distress, and that perhaps was the worst pain of all.

At last the great room cleared for dancing. Mr Justinian took her by waist and hand. She wanted to shy away from his touch. A death-moth's poisonous dust could be no less welcome than the scrape of his fingers. Her stomach churned. The wine spritzer bubbled into the back of her throat.

'Dance with me,' he said. 'It is the Guild Dance. They are expecting the Coastmaster and the Lightmistress of Vigil to lead the waltz.'

'I am not much of a dancer.'

'I insist. Just follow my lead.'

Halfway mortified by circumstance, she allowed him to take her out onto the floor while the string quartet played a lively Lyonnese Waltz, with its racing fiddle and steps that were complicated enough that Mr Justinian stood on her feet more than twice despite him claiming to know these moves. Arden began to suspect he was doing it on purpose.

'Yes, you are not quite so unattractive in this light.' Mr Justinian shuffled closer, until his hot breath steamed on her forehead. With a thumping shock she realized that it was not a belt buckle but the covert press of his erection into her lower stomach. His cologne had a noxiousness about it, a too-strong mix of civet and ambergris, but without the pleasing ratio of either.

I shall either faint or purge, she thought.

'I shall make love to you tonight,' Mr Justinian murmured in her ear. 'You have teased me long enough.'

She could have pulled away then. Should have, only they were waltzing in the centre of the crowd and all the Guildmasters were smiling and clapping and watching. *Devilment*, she thought again. *Devilment!* If she were to pull away and leave him obviously aroused, it would be a most embarrassing situation. Better she should let him extricate himself in relative dignity against a wall at least, before slapping him in private.

'What say you, Lightmistress? After this dance ends?'

'Is this your blackmail attempt?'

His unctuous voice in her ear. The bulge in his crotch grazed her hip as she attempted to thwart his unsophisticated flirtation. 'You will never be a true guildswoman let alone a Master degree-holder, Arden Beacon. Your blood is as weak as pisswater and you have no real endowment to speak of. I know you are not allowed Lyonne lovers because your dirty blood will despoil the line of *sanguis ignis*. I may be the only man you are allowed. Conversely, there are some who say I should not sign your Guild form because of your genetic failures. I am in a bind. I need convincing, you see.'

'May the devils *fuck* you, Mr Justinian.'

He tightened his hands on hers. Hard, and the coin beneath snagged hot against the skin.

'No, I don't think they will, tonight. But you shall certainly do so . . .'

He pressed closer, reeking of civet-glands and ammoniac soap. She despaired that in her isolation she might have once thought him passably handsome, for up close he was tiny-eyed and snivelly-chinned and stank with bitterness. She stared at an ill thread on his suit, swallowed the urge to scream.

'We were interrupted by the sea-waves, before. But the sea cannot extend so far. What say you? I can release you right now, Arden my dear. Just say the word.'

What would Chalice have advised, or any of her Clay Portside friends? Their ghosts whispered their practical advice. A cock in and of itself was a minor thing, despite the pronouncements of men who talked about their *lances* and *swords* and *weapons*.

The music slowed down to a more traditional waltz of the Vinland style, a dance slow and seductive. Others came onto the ballroom floor. Just as Mr Justinian pulled her towards the door, a plainly dressed boy ran up to them, bearing a folded parchment envelope affixed with a candlewax seal.

'Lightmistress,' the boy said, 'I have a message. It's quite urgent.'

'Get away from here,' Mr Justinian rasped. 'What kind of fool are you, boy?'

The boy ignored Mr Justinian's anger. 'It's urgent, Mistress.' The boy pulled a chain of tarnished brass from about his neck, and showed a small golden coin.

Arden could not make out the markings upon the coin's surface, but Mr Justinian may as well have been struck across the cheek with it. Instantly his awakening drained out of him as effectively as a slap.

'You little shit,' he said. 'You little disgraceful shit. Give her your message, cub, and be quick about it.'

Both the reprieve and the lingering after-effects of the wine conspired to make her dizzy again. With mounting unease Arden took the envelope and edged away from Mr Justinian. She need not have worried about him, for he stalked off, adjusting the buttons of his fly with angry yanks.

'Who sent you?' she asked the boy. He was a child from town, obviously. A gold coin could buy any sort of labour, especially a pretty gold coin on a chain. She saw it close now, and the stamping had the appearance of a flower. A rose, crossed with thorns.

'He said you were a friend of his.'

Curious to see what had occasioned this reversal of fortune, Arden tore open the envelope and read the message quickly. The penmanship was neat, but severe.

If you wish to save Mr Riven, follow the boy.

She glared at him. The youth only stared back at her with his guileless child's eyes.

'No friend of mine gave you this.'

'He is a Lyonne guildsman, Lightmistress,' the boy said. 'You are to come with me to the Orangery.'

A Lyonne Guildsman? There were many here, but none that should have had the necessity to be calling her away in the night using the name of her neighbour. A cold feeling touched her neck, a whisper of angel's caution. Arden glanced about her. Nobody watched this little drama, or appeared inquisitive about this sudden interruption of ceremonies. Mr Justinian had since retired to a place to lick his wounds, a corner conveniently adjacent to the liquor cabinet. He poured a dark splash the colour of treacle into a crystal glass as a pasty young lady sidled towards him, her tongue painting a wet, hungry trail about her lips at the thought of having the Coastmaster of Vigil all to herself.

'A Guildsman, you say? Who?'

The boy only thrust the rose-coin forward again.

A rose upon thorns, she thought. *You know this symbol. You've seen it before.*

The child only shrugged, knowing she would get nothing out of him. Arden nodded.

'I'll come with you, lad. Just let me get my coat.'

17

The night took on a different feeling

The night took on a different feeling upon the Manse's uplands than it did closer to the water. For all that Fiction bunkered in the southern chill from low latitudes, the coastal climate remained blunted by the great temperate sink of the nearby ocean.

But in the higher altitudes of the Justinian property the air sharpened, and Arden was glad to have her krakenskin coat. Still unsteady from the wine, she paused at the mud room to light one of the spare oil lamps before following the boy down the gravel boulevard of the mansion grounds.

A coin, the boy had shown Mr Justinian. A rose with a thorned cross. She recognized the symbol, but its meaning fluttered out of reach.

Instead of taking her outside the walls, the child led her further into the gardens. They hurried past the dry Poseidon fountain with sea-horse hippocampi and once-naked gods sporting their new clothing – a dark mossy verdigris that would one day smother them – through the domed grottoes and overgrown night gardens to where a cast-iron and glass conservatory stood among the shadows of unkempt box hedges and overgrown bougainvillea.

The moonlight sheened off the conservatory glass, made the walls white. The boy gestured to the door.

'In there, Lightmistress.'

Another light source shone inside the leafy bowers. A cold yellow glow, from that new power of electrification.

'Mr Riven wanted to meet me here?'

The child only gave a vacant, angelic smile, made his gesture again.

Her better sense would have told her to leave, but then again, her better sense would have told her not to come to Fiction in the first place. She slowed her racing heart with a deep breath, then with a ginger caution stepped into the fecund warmth.

The Orangery in the night was as gloomy as the day, same smell of moss and dirt, perfume of camellias, and a tart citrus rot from the few runty orange trees that still grew from the planting of nearly a century before.

She winced at the light. Almost as bright as coldfire, the glow came from an unfamiliar pear-shaped tube as round as her head. A yellow arc light too bright to properly look at. Electric light was rare in Lyonne, especially when a few members from the Lumiere *ignis* family could blood-light a whole city with their delicate talents. The charged atoms in the globe made her hands itch.

'The former Baron had the sodium lamp installed to show off to his friends.'

Arden turned at the familiar voice. A figure stepped out from shadows where he had been waiting. Short and slender, a pretty face with the stillness of a wax figurine, gold spectacles as round as marbles, and a gold pocket-watch chain hanging from his waistcoat.

'Do you remember me? Three months can seem like three years in this country.'

She swallowed as the wine threatened to rise in her throat. It was the Guildsman who had given Arden her coins and her instructions to come to Fiction.

'Mr Lindsay? What are you doing here?'

'Working, same as you.'

The small man's beautiful smile was duplicitous, as only a man who has turned up unexpectedly in a different country can be. He wore the same suit as he had in her father's Portside offices, a dull camel woven through with emerald threads. In the orange light, they glittered with a strange enchantment.

Lastly upon his lapel, the same image that had been on the boy's coin. A rose, and black enamel thorns. Arden felt her strength leave her as she realized at last what it meant. The Eugenics Society rose, and the controlling thorns of the Lyonne Order. Symbol of the garden, forever tended and protected from the weeds that might encroach upon it.

Mr Lindsay had come to give her the coin of instruction. This was the thing she had been dreading for months, the truth of her coming here.

It is not for Fire they want you.

'Excuse me.' Mr Lindsay stretched up to the electric tube. 'Let me turn this off. I assume your body can sense the charged atoms in the atmosphere. Electrical fields create quite a physical reaction for the blood-endowed, I am told.'

With a twist, the light was gone. Green afterimages jumped behind Arden's eyes. Her hands still ached. The man's cunning attention never left her.

No, decided Arden. Not a man. Lyonne Order and Nomenclatures. A Lion.

Have the Lions followed you here, Mx Beacon?

'Now then,' Mr Lindsay continued, 'my boy tells me that Mr Justinian is being difficult with endorsing your final degree. Well, if he does not sign the forms, there are other options.'

'You come all this way and through all this covert behaviour just to tell me this?' Arden pressed her still-cramping wrists against her cormorant-feathered hips. 'If you required a private meeting, not a soul would have seen you upon the promontory.'

Mr Lindsay held his hand out towards her oil lantern. 'More light, please. My eyes are not as dark-keen as yours.' Upon receiving the handle, he turned the wick up and gestured towards a marble bench. 'I apologize for being so clandestine. I assure you, there are reasons. Come, sit.'

Though her entire instinct protested, she gathered up kraken-hide and silks, and sat beside him.

'So, what more is required of me?'

'What makes you think more is required?' Mr Lindsay asked, his eyes amiably perplexed past his spectacles.

'You are Lyonne Order and Nomenclatures. My father saw it instantly, the moment you stepped into his offices.'

'A perceptive man, Lucian Beacon. He always had a special *sense*, one might say. His daughter too.'

'All right, sir. Enough banter. I am here, and minding my uncle's light, as I agreed. What is this note about helping Mr Riven?'

'I hear you had some meetings with the man.'

She frowned. What business was her neighbour to the Lion? 'We have had occasion to meet, certainly.'

'And he was *proper* to you?'

The words were loaded. She chose her reply with care. 'I did not intend to come here to fight with my neighbours, and that is exactly what I haven't done.'

'No,' he mused. 'You have not fought with him at all.' He took his spectacles off his face, polished each lens slowly and deliberately with a silk handkerchief. 'How close are you to Riven, Mx Beacon? Close enough to leave a warm house in the middle of the night and flee to his assistance, certainly.'

'I would have run from that disgusting lech in that decayed mansion on the flimsiest excuse. Even to save you, if it were your life in danger.'

'Yet still. You came for an ex-convict with a history of kidnapping and murder, and rape-within-marriage, that most grievous sin?'

'I understand what has been said about him, sir.'

'And you do not believe? Such accusations are not made lightly.'

She took her breath and prepared for a speech. 'Mr Lindsay, all my life I have grown up and worked on the docks as a minor sanguis lanternkeeper. I saw more of human existence by my tenth birthday than many a person at the prime of their life. My senses do not recoil from him as they would . . .' She clenched her teeth. '*You*, perhaps. Or Mr Justinian. I suspect that far too much energy has been spent on cultivating an overt brand of monstrosity in him without him taking on a monstrous charisma in return.'

'Yes, true evil is seductive, and beautiful.'

The Lion rose, went to one of the oranges still on the tree, brought the wrinkled fruit to his nose but did not pluck it.

'I share your suspicion,' he continued. 'Let me tell another story, Mx Beacon, an inverse of the one more familiar to you. It is of a girl named Bellis Harrow, a pretty and outwardly unremarkable girl born in a far-flung fishing village whose only importance is illegal plesiosaur trade and a promontory known for shipwrecks. The lass is testmooted late, as many of her generation are on this coast where talent is faded and the moots may only happen once every five years. Children mature slowly here, the genes are dim, and the tests are limited to those laborious endowments more useful to us in the North.

'Whatever the reason for the delay, she is over sixteen years old when she tests positive for rockblood. Rockblood! *Sanguinem petrae!* A talent as golden as her hair! A goddess of the black liquor! Well, there is a commotion. Regardless of her rough Fictish heritage, such golden talents automatically make her eligible for a full degree and Master's certification in the craft or trade Guild of her choosing – sight-unseen – as you are well aware.'

'But she stayed here, though.'

'Sadly, her father refused to let her go.'

'Hmmm, he seemed like the sort of fellow who would welcome Industrialist money.' Arden pretended mild interest, even as talk of Bellis made her uneasy. This story was as relevant to her as the ships passing her lighthouse on the sea-road. But a Lion had come north and was pulling her into the lives of these troubled people.

Mr Lindsay shrugged. 'The mother was poorly, and Bellis an only child. She was a good daughter. It was curious, but we don't interfere.'

'That's not like Lions *at all*.'

'Scoff all you like Mx Beacon, but talent can be ruined by too much meddling, and as you know, the Fiction-born sanguinem rarely survive long in Lyonne – the city disorients them, makes them vulnerable to misadventure and accidents.'

Like falling into Portside canals, Arden silently added.

Mr Lindsay made a moue of regret. 'For a while all was at peace. She matured into a sweet young woman, no sanguis psychosis, no nervous conditions. Then all of a sudden, this beautiful, filial child abandons her Baron fiancé and marries Mr Jonah Riven, a criminal convicted of a heinous crime and recently returned to the coast. Marries, if one might say, under extreme duress in the Sainted Isles, where such unions can be coerced. A year later, she disappears, with only this krakenskin coat and a lock of her golden hair recovered.'

In the garden, a Middle Country firecracker went up, burst into the sky. Only a lone ordinance, a star-sparkling omen, and not a good one. It reflected as a smear upon the salt-scored glass.

'Some believed in the forlorn tale of her death, for a while,' Mr Lindsay said. 'Me, I was rather baffled when I heard what came of her. Why all the degradation and despair? Bellis and Jonah were best childhood friends before he was sent away to Harbinger Bay for killing his family. She was a filial daughter to her father, why should she not be equally as devoted a wife to her husband? All extremely odd. Then all of a sudden the affair. Another old friend. A priest, as pious as they come.'

The answer arrived to Arden at once, for hadn't she spent ten years planning and wishing for such a thing herself?

'She *escaped* you!' Arden drew a shuddering breath. Bellis Harrow, golden-talented and clever. Cleverer than the Lions themselves. *Oh*, Arden's envy sharpened. *That clever girl!*

Mr Lindsay threw up his hands in gracious surrender.

'You seem rather thrilled, Mx Beacon.'

'I won't lie to you, sir. There's not a sanguinem alive who hasn't dreamed of escaping the Eugenics Society and the Order, and leading their own lives.'

A nerve in his cheek jumped. One eye at a squint. 'Yes, the three of them, Jonah Riven, Stefan Beacon and Bellis Harrow. Concocted a little ruse of a disastrous and violent marriage, an affair and a death. But let me tell you the truth of foolish, immature girls with golden talent who think they can run away from their own blood. There is no place for them outside of Clay Capital's sanctuary. Fiction folk don't know how to take care of its sanguineous, the attention and delicacy that must be taken. Your uncle Jorgen Beacon found that out in the hardest of ways, immolated by grief and despair. He had the *psychosis*. Became the extinguished flame, just like his talent.'

A starfield of rockets followed the first, and their pink-hued explosions cast garish lights across the Orangery glass. Some cheering in the distance. Arden's hands hurt.

'Mr Lindsay, why share the story of a stranger?'

'Because Bellis Harrow-Riven disappeared and Riven refuses to confirm what happened. He's impenetrable but for his weakness.' Here the Lion smiled, 'Love.'

'It can be, if it seems the more gentle way. However Bellis Harrow-Riven still disappeared and Riven refuses to confirm what happened to her. He's impenetrable. But his weakness is his love for the woman he married. Despite his tricky little theatre of sadism, we quickly found out what Bellis had done. Slipped her collar. Run out with a blood talent she had no training for. She's in hiding, and Riven knows where she is.'

'Oh, Mr Lindsay,' she said, dripping scorn. 'I'm not about to seduce Bellis' whereabouts from him, I barely know the man.'

'We would not ask such a thing of you.'

'Then what will you ask?'

'Your assistance. A different kind of labour, but labour all the same. You are to help Bellis survive this exile she has chosen until she is ready to return. We don't want her back. She will come back when she is ready. A bird will always *orient* itself to home. And eventually she will come to Lyonne. That is a given. But if she has sought refuge among the indigenes of the Sainted Isles, because she is sanguineous and unsupported, then her existence is right now fraught and tenuous, and forever in danger.

'You have always helped your fellow comrades on the wharves. You've had a sense of supportiveness about you, they say, a brace against bad accidents. Every *sanguis pondus, transverto* and *vaporum* who have ever worked under your instruction all tell us they trust you implicitly. They say they trust *themselves* more when their reliable *sanguis ignis* Arden Beacon is around. We need you to use that goodwill. Help *her* now, Mx Beacon. Help Bellis Riven survive, as you have helped those around you survive.'

His words were a cadence, a seductive song. She pressed her burning hands together. Trapped them between her knees. Why were they hurting so? There was no cold-flame lantern needing ignition, and even then her endowments were so dim the sense should have been little more than an itch.

'I earned that trust, over years. I don't know Bellis at all. Why would she be in any danger? She is *sanguis petrae*. She'll be useful to Islanders. They can exploit her labour.'

'The autochthonous Islanders worship strange gods, Mx Beacon, gods that pre-date the prospecting of rockblood. She will be anathema to them. A reminder of Northern conquerors and defeat has no place among those brutal shores. Bellis may be fine now, but at some stage she will require Jonah Riven to show his face, and protect her with his dreadful reputation.'

He made the sign of the circle upon his chest, the sea-serpent, and Arden recognized it at once for the blanket ring back at her lighthouse. *The Deepwater King*. The old religion of the Sainted Isles, and the Riven ancestral home.

He continued, 'We cannot force Mr Riven to join his wife, but perhaps you can *remind* him of what he misses. The trust you engender in your associates? Foster the same in him. He may confide in you, Lightmistress, of his loneliness. From what my advisers tell me, you yourself know what it is to hold a torch for a love, for years and lonely years. Yes, Mx Arden Beacon knows what it is like they say, to grow old waiting while her friends marry, have children of their own. She may consider herself trapped by circumstance, but Mr Jonah Riven is not. Give him the permission of a woman with regrets, Arden my dear. Tell him not to end up lonely, and despairing. Tell him he can go to Bellis, and be blessed.'

Each of Mr Lindsay's words lashed her heart with a switch of thornwood. Yes, she knew those shackles as a sanguinem under the rule of the Order. Yes, these were the freedoms she had wished for, and had them taken away.

Arden spoke through a throat tight with resentment.

'This was your intent all along, for me to abandon my home and my family to come here? This is why you didn't decommission the flame on the day Jorgen died?'

'Is it a bad motive? You're saving a woman's life.'

Arden closed her eyes briefly, and let an old grief wash over her. A sanguinem was always a tool and conduit for greater powers, but this request made her bereft of true meaning. The Guild had not wanted her here as Lightkeeper at all. The Lions had made them use Arden, not for the direction of her blood, but an entity to effect another purpose. Bellis Riven was the objective, and Arden was just a source of labour.

She said wearily, 'I don't feel right, instructing Mr Riven about his wife's peril just so he can be beholden to you. He probably has his reasons to stay behind. I'm sorry. I can't . . . I can't impose myself on a private matter and do what you ask.'

Mr Lindsay rubbed his knees as if preparing to rise. 'Oh, well. It's a shame you are unable to help. That's that, then. I'm sure you'll encourage some other official to sign the Guild-membership form, of course.'

'What?' Arden exclaimed. 'Is this you reneging on my contract?'

'Well, your work contract implicitly stated you are required to carry out your duties as instructed before you can receive a full Guild degree,' Mr Lindsay said with such a smugly genuine apology Arden almost wanted to slap him. He stood up with an old man's effort despite the youth of his face. Offhandedly said, 'Oh, and another thing. I was to advise you about a . . .' He fetched a paper square from his waistcoat and opened it. 'Captain Richard Castile? Yes, the Order tells me he has *suffered* quite a bit after you broke off your illicit relationship with him. Has lived quite the monkish existence since, grieving the woman he left in Lyonne.'

As he spoke he plucked the small orange he'd sniffed earlier, and peeled it with a sympathetic nonchalance. She glared at him, feeling the manipulations tighten furiously.

'There's no harm in delivering our message in the sweet requests of a lady.'

'He'll not listen to the sweet requests of a lady either, you fool!' Arden scolded him. 'If the folk down in that town were to give their opinions, Mr Riven is a lustful fiend more likely to forget his wife *at once* and have *me* take her place in squalor.'

'Ah, rather than making him *forget* Bellis, you would *elevate* that memory, I think. I would posit that a strong woman up against the world would in fact be a powerful reminder of his woman over the waves.'

Mr Lindsay held out the peeled orange, and she slapped his hand away.

'I don't want it.'

'But I know what you do want. Mr Castile waits for you.' He leaned forward. 'Give your service to Lyonne,' he pressed. 'Inform Mr Riven of his wife's jeopardy, get him out to her and you may have the chance to have an independent life. You'll still have partial Guild membership whether you assist us or not. This patriotic act would take you all the way there. Full degree. Permission to marry.'

With that, he popped the orange into his mouth, and chewed.

'I have no reason to visit him,' Arden said, low and mutinously. 'We are not likely to share a cup of tea and a heart-to-heart soon. I *posit* you will be waiting a long time for our intimate conversation.'

'Such was my thought at first. So we devised a meet, another message sent by my boy-cub to the Black Rosette tavern a mere hour ago. A message for a Mr Jonah Riven, who patronizes the merchants' bar.'

Cold, invisible fingers pressed upon the back of Arden's neck. 'What sort of message?'

'An urgent one, from Mx Arden Beacon, just like the one you received this evening, pleading that Mr Riven should come help his neighbour who is trapped in the guest house of the Manse Justinian.'

She gasped at Mr Lindsay's forwardness and stood up. 'He would not waste his time coming to rescue me!'

'One would hope not, because the guest house is currently occupied by Mr Alasdair Harrow's deputies, a pair who will have no compunction in . . .' He lingered, savouring the moment. '*Hurting* Mr Riven if he were to stumble upon them.'

Arden ran from the Orangery, and in the dark stumbled towards the guest wing, a semi-detached building linked by stone colonnade. Mr Riven couldn't be so foolish as to heed the boy's message. Her dress snagged under her feet as she struggled up an incline in her ridiculous shoes.

'Devilment!' Frustration stung her eyes with hot, angry tears. She had fallen into the Lion's den. Once their eyes were upon prey, there would be no escape.

Midway along a retaining wall, a pair of the Manse's hired guards waved at her as she passed.

'Hoy!' one cried out.

She skidded to a stop. Beyond them, the leafy walkway beckoned, the doors of the guest house.

'Gentlemen,' Arden said breathlessly, and gave a high strangled laugh. 'Can't be late for the party!'

Her tardiness did not concern them, and they sauntered up, hands on muskets, their broadcloth uniform as dark as the night.

'What brings you outside, Lightmistress?'

Devilment, they recognized her. A layer of sweat glossed her face and she was certain her carefully applied cosmetics would have now turned her face into a circus-tumbler's mask.

'Oh,' she said with such forced gaiety that her voice came at a screech, 'enjoying private company. You understand.'

With that she gave a suggestive wink. They did not smirk back.

'Your friend, where is he now?'

'A separate way. For the sake of his . . . standing.'

'Best you enjoy such breaches of standing indoors, madam,' the first guard gruffed. 'There is an intruder afoot. The grounds are under alert until he is found.'

Arden had never fainted, but decided if she did, it might begin with a feeling very much like this: her blood rushing from her head, and her fingers tingling hot as if a match had been lit under each one.

'Of course, of course. Best . . . best be getting back.'

With the gait of a wounded soldier she stumbled on to the guest wing, and entered through the side door, which she knew the Dowager Justinian often kept unlocked. Slid her way along the dim foyer and immediately realized she had arrived too late; a gross commotion echoed from deep within the bedroom, and a Middle Country porcelain pot lay strewn in pieces across the parquetry floor. A picture of the elderly patriarch Baron Alexander Justinian lay crossways over a chaise longue, a buffet was over-turned, and the entire contents of the fireplace littered the rug.

A yelp of alarm, more grunting, and then a muffled bang which could only have been a silenced musket.

Terrified for Mr Riven, Arden picked up from the floor the only slightly wieldy thing in sight: a small paperweight bust of Sir Alexander Justinian the Elder. Small it might be, the bust was still a heavy chunk of bronze. She ran into the bedroom only to nearly trip over one fallen body. A deputy. The other one stood with his musket in hand, seemingly aimed at a third heap behind the bed.

She did not wait to see his reaction. With all her strength she swung the bust and caught the oafish fellow by the temple. The contact shock jolted up her elbow, twanging her tendons with electric pain. He collapsed like a felled log.

'I'm sorry,' she cried, 'I'm sorry! Oh, heavens . . .'

A blow to the head could kill a man. What had she been thinking? She should have yelled at him, negotiated surrender. But the sight of Mr Riven, that foolish love-struck imbecile lying dead out of misbegotten heroics, had made her panic.

The deputy's chest rose and fell. Thank all the sea gods, then, she'd merely stunned him. She ran over to Mr Riven, sprawled out across the coverlet of the bed. He appeared as if he had left the hot interior of the Black Rosette in some kind of a rush. Beneath his coat wore only his high-waisted trousers and suspenders.

'Mr Riven?' she ventured.

By his groaning, he was conscious. The musket shot, slowed by the silencing device, had slammed into the krakenskin coat hard but had not penetrated the leather.

She picked up the damaged wing of coat to push it aside. A bullet could still cause a man to bleed into his cavities, perhaps a more dangerous scenario than a penetrating wound. When he tried to slap her away, she seized a tiller-roughened hand.

'I've seen you shirtless, fool,' she hissed. 'Are you hurt?'

'*Oof.* I'm not sure.'

'Do I have your permission to find out?'

He opened the coat, and Arden prodded about at the bruises coming up on the serrations of his abdomen. His skin had rapidly discoloured from the force of the projectile but showed no break or blood. The scars of his Tallwater rescue attempts were flat pink marks across his broad chest, and a sharp want took her, to touch them, and him. Not in desire, not quite. But the need to touch capstones and cairns in places where great battles have been fought, to feel the history beneath and become a part of it somehow.

'Where the hell were you?' he gruffed as his breath returned. 'That message said you were here . . .'

'I never sent a message.'

'Excuse me?' He glared at her as if insulted.

She went to the window. Closed and double-glazed, and the curtains had been drawn. No light or sound to attract the guards. 'I didn't send that message, Mr Riven. It was meant to lure you here.'

'Why?'

'We have become ensnared in things bigger than us.' She put her hands on her hips and looked at him as if he were the aftermath of a disaster that she would have to clean up. 'You've been ensnared in this thing from the beginning, I think.'

Mr Riven sat up with a wince and surveyed the two fallen men. 'I believe you, Lightmistress. As soon as I saw they were Mr Harrow's lads, I knew the message was a lure. They intended this as a convenient killing.'

'They don't want you dead. Not while Bellis is alive.'

His terrible blue stare fell upon her then, questioning.

'Bellis? How did you—'

She shook her head. 'No time to explain. I must get you out of here first. *Damn it*. There's guards all over the Manse tonight.'

'I will go out the way I came.' He nodded towards the window, and the wall beyond.

'You can't do that either. Mr Justinian's security detail saw you come in, you enormous fool. The grounds are lousy with staff and mercenaries.'

One of the deputies let out a groan, fighting his unconsciousness. He would not be indisposed for long.

Mr Riven dragged a hand over his rough head. 'They might not want me dead, but they'll kill me if I stay here.' He tried to stand up and only ended up rattling the bedside bureau, overturning the porcelain toilette bottles and hairbrushes. Somebody so completely out of place among the frills and fripperies of the guest room would be equally incongruous outside it. As far as concealing him beyond these walls, it would be easier to hide an elephant that had wandered into the town square. Mr Riven was no stranger to the people of Vigil.

'Wait now,' Arden said. 'We'll make these goons sleep a little longer.'

The adjoining bathroom was, as she had earlier discovered in previous sorties of the Manse, stocked with all kinds of chemicals and potions. Clearly the deputies had noticed this too. Open bottles and pillboxes lay scattered across the dresser: laudanum, the cocaine drops, the heroin tinctures, the opium tobacco and the ergotine.

Mr Riven must have stumbled in while they were both as mad as hatters. They would not remember much of this night.

She found what she wanted, a bottle of ether, and with a handkerchief and an averted head, managed to roll the pair on their sides and send them into a deeper sleep.

'They'll be asleep for a good few minutes,' she said, and pointed at the scars on Mr Riven's chest with a broken, wry smile. 'I was always better at administering sleep-ether than I was at stitching when I completed my minor surgeon's certificate.'

Mr Riven watched her warily. 'Why treat them with such kindness?'

'These men are addled with pharmaceuticals. If we are fortunate, they may awaken to think they themselves caused this situation. But you, sir. You are my biggest problem.'

'Let me pass, and I will be a problem no longer.'

'No longer?' she retorted. 'Mr Riven, have you heard of Lions?'

He snorted at her question. 'The animals or the Investigatory Order of Lyonne? I have dealt with both.'

'The worst of the two have their eyes on you, sir, and now on me. Our problems are entwined. With Bellis at its centre.'

Under the wiry fur of his face she saw wretched hope and concern spring forth. A familiar envy moved in her heart, to see a man with such naked affection for his beloved. No

Clay detachment. No cool appraisals. This was a man who loved fiercely.

'What has happened with Bellis?' he demanded. 'Why are they circling her now? She's gone. From them, from this country altogether!'

'There's no time to explain. We need to hide your escape.'

Arden quickly took stock of the guest-house room. Even an elephant might be disguised, given enough of a garment. She settled on the patriarch's painting. Take away his finery, and the elder Justinian had a hard and angular Fictish face that his three scions, in their unions with soft Northern women, had not managed to keep.

She went to the wardrobe and threw open the doors. The miasma of cedarwood and camphor swelled into the room. Those garments within, completely the wrong size for Mr Justinian and therefore unworn, showed themselves untouched by moth or beetle, fabric as intact as if they were new.

'Get out of your clothes,' she said to Mr Riven.

'Excuse me?'

'The party. There are hundreds of people here, and nobody can possibly know every guest. We can get out through the Manse. There is transport waiting in the forecourt. I already have my exit strategy from this place taken care of, so to speak.'

She pulled a suit from the closet. Its dull faded colours made it seem conservative in aspect, the sort of thing old money might wear. Fashions did not change much among the rich.

'You call me fool, but this is a foolish idea.'

'Your coming here was a foolish idea, Mr Riven, so that makes two!'

'I came for you, neighbour.' He reached for the suit. She pulled it out of his reach and sighed.

'Thank you for your chivalry, sir. Now get the beard off your face. Make it so you belong among those people.' She frowned. 'Do you even know how to groom?'

'I am *not* fully a barbarian,' Mr Riven countered. He yanked off his shirt and alarmingly was already freeing himself of his trousers as he went into the bathroom. The tattoos on his back dipped into his sacrum and the curve of his buttocks.

He closed the door. She heard the water run. She paced the room, casting worried glances at both the sleeping men and the foyer.

Whatever experience of Mr Riven's past had taught him quick grooming, it worked upon him now. Within ten minutes of the mantel clock, the door opened.

A sorcery, perhaps. She had sent Mr Riven in there, but a much younger man than him stepped out. A stranger, with an unevenly handsome face that still needed another decade to settle into mature nobility, the pale Fictish features softened by a cautious, almost shy expression. He might have turned into a creature shorn of his fearsome mane, but something more interesting lay beneath. A bed sheet about his waist gave him the appearance of a statue from antiquity.

In silence, she handed him the clothes of the patriarch, and he let the sheet drop as he began to dress. She kept her eyes low.

He had seen her entire, so perhaps they no longer required false modesty, she thought, and then stole another glance before she could stop herself. His maleness nestled in russet curls, and he unselfconsciously tucked himself into the mossy green of Sir Alexander Justinian's trousers. Despite the urgency of the moment, her cheeks flamed.

Dressed, he could have passed for any low-bred noble master. The tawny suit fitted him perfectly. The boots still held their shine. The narrow waist accentuated the hard work that had formed the clay of Mr Riven into flesh. Only his hair was shorter than fashionable. Hard to disguise the fisherman's habit of cutting a lock from his scalp every time he wished to bless the catch, giving sacraments, the way the sanguis did with their blood.

'It will do,' Arden said, and wondered why her mouth was dry. 'But quick.' She swept a pomade off the dresser. 'Fix your head.'

He beheld the pomade tin the same way a scholar might, if

faced with a Sumerian tablet written with indecipherable code. Mr Riven may not have been a barbarian, but he was not entirely tamed, either. With a *tsk* of impatience she scooped out a wad of cream and ran it over his hair, tried not to think about the mind that lay beyond the assorted lumps and bumps on the skull beneath her hand. The skull of a life hard-lived. He smelled of kraken oil, far too fresh and deeply luxurious for comfort. The higher-priced dock girls used the essential ingredient in their alluring scents, to woo potential customers from the decks of their ships. The smell always had a sense of illicitness about it.

He pulled away sharply.

'My coat.'

She wiped her hand on a towel, mortified that she had allowed herself such a distraction.

'The coat is the most obvious part of you, sir. If you wish to take it, it must be smuggled.'

Grateful for the diversion, she rummaged in the cedar wardrobe, retrieved a carpet bag that wasn't too shabby, and stuffed Mr Riven's krakenskin coat into the satin-lined depths.

The two deputies started to stir. No choice but to leave now. She took Mr Riven's elbow and dragged him through the litter of the guest-house foyer.

Perhaps the enormous import of what had happened here had struck him insensibly mute. Especially since now he was not fighting for his life. He became passive in his caution, Well, so should he be. Mr Jonah Riven would have to trust a Beacon now, put his safety in her hands.

Out in the cool colonnade that connected the house to the Manse she grasped his elbow to her side, forced him to slow down to saunter, an arm-in-arm-with-a-lady kind of stroll, and not fleeing-the-scene-of-the-crime kind of stroll. Her heart beat far too fast. Ahead of them, another pair of hired guards moved into position. They were not the first she had seen.

'Calm yourself,' she murmured, 'or they'll know something is afoot.'

'I am calm. You're the one shaking.'

Small candles lit each column, put in place by the staff to ensure an atmosphere of romance, but instead it had the air of a prison walk. Mr Riven's arm went about her waist and propped her upright to stop her stumbling. The guardians ignored the two lovebirds as they passed. One pulled out a pipe and spoke to the other in a Low Fictish dialect. Arden held her breath so fiercely, her vision started to tunnel.

Once in the portico, a butler opened the door, and they stepped into the Manse. The dull lights, that previous irritation, were now a blessing. She hurried Mr Riven through the dusky rooms, getting closer and closer to the entry foyer until—

'Mx Beacon?'

Arden froze, then turned about with a fixed rictus of a smile.

The Dowager Justinian stood there, in one of the drawing rooms, a glass of sherry in her hand. She had clearly had one too many, and she came up from the chaise longue on unsteady feet.

'Were you leaving? I thought you would want to stay in the guest house.'

'I have an apartment in town.'

'Nonsense. There are no apartments in town, only hovels and front rooms for the harlots.'

The Dowager turned her attention to Mr Riven. 'You,' the Dowager said faintly. 'You wear a familiar face. The old Baron's face, and yet you are young. How can that be so?'

In all her fussing Arden had not seen what she should have seen from the outset. The old man who graced all the paintings about the Manse had been young once. For a reason unknown, they'd confined the patriarch's youthful image to the drawing room of the women – a delicate floral abode in the daytime, but in the night all the crochets and doilies turned to spider webs and crypt moulder.

That youth, Alexander Justinian. The first Baron who had taken the Rivens from their ancestral home in the Sainted Isles and put them to work in his factory. As she glanced up at Mr Riven it became clear to her that Alexander Justinian had taken more than labour from the family, perhaps. Replaced a genetic line with one of his own.

'My dear Dowager Justinian, this is Mr Castile,' Arden said desperately. 'An old friend from Clay.'

Mr Riven dipped his head, and if Arden had not held his muscular arm close, he would have retreated into the gloom.

The Dowager frowned. 'And what do you do, Mr Castile?'

'I work leather and bone.'

Dowager Justinian darted forward, seized his arm and turned it, revealing the scars of rope-work on the palm and knife-work upon the meat below his thumb. 'It is dangerous to cut there.' She threw the hand down in disgust. 'You are sanguis.'

'Somewhat,' he said, yearning towards the door.

The woman wouldn't let them go. 'Alexander and his son were stormtellers. Common enough round these parts once, but bred out of their line, thank the Lord. My son doesn't have a modicum of that heinous trait. Good memory for figures, and his blood clean. He is human.'

Arden gently patted the woman's arm in an anxious farewell. 'Dowager Justinian, I must leave, my ride is waiting for me.'

The Dowager grabbed Arden's wrist, hard, and peered into her face.

'My son will miss you in his bed tonight. He hasn't quite been the same after he lost Bellis to the monster on the promontory. She was much prettier than you though,' Dowager Justinian slurred, the sherry at last taking hold. 'Fairer of skin and face. Wheaten hair, as straight as a waterfall. *Don't trust Bellis*, I said to my boy. Don't trust anyone who cleaves to the dank emissions of the underworld. These are sinful things, *sin* . . .'

Her hand released. She fell off the precipice of consciousness, slid back against the wall and sank into dark, morphiated sleep.

Mr Riven stared down at the Dowager. Her words had enchanted the will out of him entirely.

'Mr Riven,' Arden said. 'She's had too much to drink.'

'She is more than just drunk,' Mr Riven said. 'She never has more than a sherry-glass on an evening. There is something else going on here tonight.'

'Drugged?'

'Absolutely.'

Arden thought of the Lion, Mr Lindsay, making certain all the pieces were in their place. Making sure they were not disturbed. 'There always has been something going on, Jonah Riven, since your wife went to the Sainted Isles and disappeared.'

He turned his attention to Arden, bewildered and angry. 'You must explain what this has to do with me. With Bellis.'

'I have no idea if what the Lion says is true,' she said, tugging him towards the exit. 'But we must go at once or we could find out in the worst of ways.'

18

Half an hour I waited in this freezing cold

'Half an hour I waited in this freezing cold,' the buggyman grumbled. 'Was told ten o'clock. *Specifically* ten o'clock. I could have had other passengers.'

He huffed and tutted at the two bodies who had climbed in his little coach, expecting them to give him the same drunken noise as his previous customers, perhaps offer him a penny or two extra with a slap on the back and a chortle about needing to attend a bed post-haste.

Instead, a pall of deep disquiet bound them.

The pale Fictish man had the fine, raw bearing that would have garnered the attention of any lady, but the guildswoman barely gave him an inch of her attention. She had the cast of severe and purposeful breeding about her, from her diluted features, jet eyes and indifferent curls pinned upon her head. She wore a krakenskin coat, something he'd only seen the wealthiest office-holders wear. She must be a woman of some standing indeed. She couldn't have been unattractive to her companion, but he sat stiffly in his preoccupation, arms folded, head turned to the coach glass.

Fair enough, the buggyman thought. This night brought quarrels too. He did not continue to debate the mysteries of his passengers long, and *tsk*ed the horses down the pebbled curve of the driveway and out upon the crushed-rock road.

A deep, uncomfortable silence filled the coach. A boundary had been crossed in their relationship. An irrevocable binding between two strangers with nothing in common.

Mr Riven spoke first.

'She lied back there,' Mr Riven said, as they left the gates of the Manse. The lantern swung shadows into the cabin. 'The Dowager.'

'About sanguinity being sinful? Of course, it's just the sherry and the drugs speaking.'

'No. About Bellis being prettier than you.'

Surprised, Arden snorted a short laugh. A quick, wretched feeling akin to embarrassment came over her. She didn't need mollifying with faint praise. She knew Bellis had been extraordinary.

'Anyone can appreciate beauty. It is the most common of denominators.'

'So, Mr Justinian is your lover. I think he suits.'

'Heavens, does everybody conspire for me to have relations with this man? I have no interest in Mr Justinian. I have no interest in anyone! The only thing I need to do is navigate the terrible hand tonight has dealt. The Lyonne Order has me in their employ now, body and blood!'

Mr Riven sat like a wraith in the dark seat, with the look of a cur-dog kicked to the gutter. By the way his arms wrapped about his stomach, the bruise about his midsection troubled him. She breathed and tempered her words. He'd proven himself a gentleman.

'Still, thank you for coming to my rescue, false as it was,' she added ruefully.

'So. Tell me why we are here, together like this.'

'I—' she started, and he interrupted her again.

'If you intend to lie to me, say nothing. Look out the window and hold your tongue. I am not interested in a story.'

She looked into the darkness, not knowing what she should reveal, and what she should keep.

'All right then. The truth. In the early summer the Seamaster's Guild invited me to manage my uncle's lighthouse. Because I was *malorum*, and dim of blood, I'd never ever have such an opportunity. I jumped too quickly at the chance. I didn't think about who else might be involved. Tonight they came to me, and spoke of you.'

Mr Riven's breath fogged up the cabin glass.

'Not about me. They came about Bellis. It's always been about her. The Lions have been watching Bellis since she broke a rockblood glass during a testmoot,' Mr Riven said quietly. '*Sanguis petrae.*'

'They are concerned for her safety in her Island exile. The Lyonne Order even desire her fearsome husband to go back out there and protect her, and I must be the one to relay the instruction. All this, for a girl with *sanguis petrae*! I mean, certainly it's a golden talent, but why all this fuss over rockblood? We have several *sanguis petrae* members in Lyonne. It's rare, but not exceptional.'

She stopped her rant as she saw his pained expression. 'I'm sorry,' she concluded miserably. 'It's been quite a night. I just found out my true value. I am not a Lightkeeper to them, just *sanguis malorum*. I am a puppet, a pawn in their game. It was not for Fire they wanted me, and I'm a fool for even entertaining that they did.'

He returned to the window, and there was such a deep, infinite sadness in him she wanted to lean across and take him in her arms and say, *I am sorry she left you, Mr Riven. I'm sorry for all this, and what was done.*

'You think me fearsome?'

'You must be to someone.'

'Then they are wrong. Bellis doesn't need me. She thrives out there, she has a strength and a will . . .' He stole a look at Arden, as if it had only just occurred to him. 'As much as you remind me of Stefan, Bellis is like you, Lightmistress. Very much so. Strong and gentle at once. I never thought so much and so often of Bellis since I saw you on the beach that day, in gold sea-silk.'

His words should have been a delightful compliment, yet Arden felt herself wallow further into the pit of despair. Mr Lindsay had said much the same thing.

'I was *meant* to remind you of her. To *elevate* your memory of her. It was my only purpose. Otherwise they'd have let the sanguine coldfire extinguish, and replaced the lighthouse with a common gas.'

He was silent for a little while, before nodding.

'Then thank you. For your honesty.'

'Not much of a point in keeping it secret.' She wrapped the coat tighter about her. 'So are you going to go to her? If the Lions are saying she's in danger, she may very well be.'

A muscle in his jaw popped. 'It would be against her explicit instructions. You see, when she left . . . she told me not to follow her, not until she called for me. It's complicated. Hard to explain, but I'm more use to her hidden.' He grimaced, as if a bad thought crossed his mind. 'My name is shored up by the many men who once held it. Riven, the monster caller. Riven, who walked upon the islands and fought even the Deepwater King for His crown, and His Bride. You are right, about being fearsome. I'm more fear-inspiring as a myth than as a man. It keeps her alive. Keeps her protected. Even though Stefan Beacon, your cousin is with her, he's not much of a fighter I'm afraid.'

'Can I still be honest?'

'Do. Please.'

'Don't go. Even if she is in danger. Stay here. We have dealings with the Order all the time in Lyonne. If the Lions are trying to move a minor chess piece on their board, it means they have decided to sacrifice it for the bigger play.'

'You think me a minor chess piece?'

She wondered if he was offended, and she stammered apologies, and he put his hand on hers, silencing her, and his touch seemed to bring a calmness over her all at once. She sought out his eyes in the darkness.

'You are not minor,' she said.

'Coming from you, I believe it.'

'But be careful, please. They dangle me as a bait for your wife's memory, but I am the poison to make you obey, and they haven't told me everything.'

'What bait did they use to move *you* on the board, little rook?'

'Only,' she sighed, 'only my deepest and most impossible dreams.'

'What were they?'

'Guild membership, and the return of a man I'd loved for a long time, who was forbidden to me, because I am sanguine, and he is not.'

'Guild membership,' he repeated. 'Dreams. And love. All the treasures of the world.'

'Yes.'

His hand squeezed once, then withdrew. She felt the acknowledgement of her sacrifice in her words. Understood that he knew she could have stayed silent, and those promised rewards would have been secured.

'Again, thank you, Lightmistress.'

A strangeness stirred inside her, as she beheld his crookedly handsome face in the lantern light. What is this, she thought with alarm. Not affection, of course, she barely knew him. Barely. *Barely*. Her night-time fantasies of the brute who might ravish her against all the Society orders had passed away. Another man, another feeling had taken their place. An enigma and cipher, but no less attractive.

She felt dazed by her epiphany. Chalice had been correct. Arden had been too long without desire in her life, and her body had, in starvation, reached greedily for the first bright and beautiful thing out of her reach. She had seen Mr Riven and his passion for his beloved, talented, troubled wife and now she yearned to have such a thing. *I want that, I want that.*

When he spoke, he held a note of uncertainty. 'Release me at the docks. I should get back to the lodge tonight.'

'The lodge? On the *promontory*?' Arden shook her head. 'If I were the Justinian guardsmen, I'd have already deployed out there. If you trust me now, then you can trust me until morning. There is a bed available at the house of Fionna La Grange, I will be quite happy with a couch.'

'Fionna La Grange?'

'Well, of course. She is my stormbride's friend.' Arden noted then the tone of his question. 'Have . . . have you met?'

'In passing. She is the madam of the Black Rosette, a lady of the night.'

Arden gasped. 'Chalice never told me her profession!'

'Don't fret. It's a good choice. She's handy with bar-fight injuries.' Mr Riven winced as he moved about. 'Better her services than Mr Sage's. His wife has not much time for me, and the man cannot keep his mouth shut.'

After half an hour, the cab stopped at a small townhouse at the rear of the Black Rosette. The cobbles shone in the lamplight from the rank run-off from cesspits. A row of duck-boards kept feet from the worst of the night-soil. A pair of drunks in an alley wrestled each other over the last few fingers in a bottle of potato liquor. Overhead, pigeons cooed in their roosts.

From her own roost in a dimly lit doorway, a lady in shabby dress approached them. Her face had the powdery appearance of a moth, and the kohl around her eyes flaked, leaving black spots about her white cheeks. From her fingers a stiletto cigarette-holder dangled precariously.

'Jonah?' she asked in the breathless craquelure of age and lung disease. 'Jonah, is that you?'

'It is, Betsey.'

She stopped short when he came into the lantern light. 'By the devils, lad, but you are dressed in finery. Has the old man of the Manse relented and brought you home?'

Arden sensed Mr Riven's tension beside her. His origins were a secret he did not wish to share, and yet it seemed more people knew than he let on.

'The night has demanded things of me, that is all.'

Betsey sucked at the stiletto. A sweet smell of cigar smoke rose up in lazy curlicues, a pinch of morningflower with it. A subtle madness coiled about the woman, prophecies and spirits.

'Demanded, as the night demands things of us all. Who is this beside you? Not Bellis. Too tall, too dark, and not a ghost.' She sucked on her stiletto again. 'No plain Fictish daisy. A fragile flower from the North, eh?'

Arden spoke up. 'I am a friend of Fionna's.'

A male voice called from the doorway, a plaintive wheedle, 'Betsey, Betsey, come away, my sweet.'

The woman waved towards an alley and the pink-hued light. 'She's in there. Up the stairs.'

Betsey retreated, and they made their way across the duck-boards.

Arden turned to Mr Riven. Twice this night she had heard his name. 'So, *Jonah* she calls you? The Dowager seems to know you with some intimacy.'

'My mother, Thalie Riven, she worked in the Justinian Manse as one of the domestic staff. Betsey knew me as a child, as the Dowager knew me then too.'

Hard to see him a child. She pondered over the scraps of his life, of the mother who had worked at the Manse, and the aristocratic elder who wore Mr Riven's face. They added up to a great deal of inferred history.

At the doorway to Fionna La Grange's apartments, a red Arabesque lantern dangled high over the lintel as a symbol of her profession. The occupant, roused by Betsey's voice, came out of her doorway clad only in a basque and semi-sheer black peignoir gown, the edges tatty with wilting black feathers. Both garments would have come from far and distant shores. Nothing so beautiful originated in Vigil, or Fiction.

Neither, did it appear, did Miss La Grange. She presented as tall and slim, hair bobbed and as shiny as an oil slick.

'Well then, Jonah Riven, I never thought I'd see you cleaned up and at my door any time soon.' Fionna nodded at Arden. 'About time too. He'd been too long pining over poor dead Bellis who loved the boy but never the man.'

Mr Riven bristled and Arden stepped forward. 'Thank you for taking us in, Miss La Grange.'

The woman gave a knowing wink, as if Bellis' mortal fate were not quite the secret the Lions thought. 'Come forth, my dears. Chalice said you would be unaccompanied, Mx Beacon, but I am always prepared for any eventuality.'

Fionna La Grange's rooms were dressed in sateen and fraying trim, and the perfumes could not hide the musk of Miss La Grange's profession. Sex and male sweat. The parlour had the chaos of a theatrical backstage, with haphazard stacks of gaudy showgirl clothing and room dividers, velvet ottomans, crystal-frilled lampshades.

Mr Riven seemed both unconcerned and familiar with the surroundings. He collapsed into one of the ornate leather chairs with a grunt of exertion.

They had arrived at the tail end of a client's time. By the odd and possibly intentional placement of a mirror over the hearth, Arden's line of sight went directly from the cluttered front room and into the equally busy pink-hued boudoir. A man, hairy as a bear from chest to groin, casually released a rag-paper note from a billfold and gave it to Fionna. They spoke in a friendly manner as he struggled back into his workday clothes, before Fionna kissed him on the cheek and sent him out through the rear door.

'Gracious,' Fionna exclaimed once he had left. 'I thought Albert would never make his exit.' She tossed a stray hair out of her face. 'Now, Jonah, what have you done to yourself?'

'Took a musket blast to my side. Coat stopped it.'

'Yes, that glorious krakenskin coat. You should sell it, buy a ticket to Vinland. Less liable to get shot, there.' As he opened his mouth to protest, she waved him to silence. 'I know, I know. You cannot bear to leave your precious Darkling Sea, and are mourning Bel—'

'Fionna, *please* look at my *injuries*,' Mr Riven interrupted. He took off the jacket and shirt, showed his injury to Fionna, who touched him with a confident hand.

'Ah, breathe in, and out, no ribs broken? May have a bruise in the muscle but you will live. Not the first injury you've had recently, either.'

She thumbed the shiny scar where Arden had stitched him before returning to Arden.

'I know you. You are the Lightmistress who replaced poor Jorgen,' Fionna said at last. 'My lovely Chalice tells me of you out there. Exiled on your promontory with only this gormless fellow for company.'

Buffeted by the hormonal fug in the room, dizzy from her sharpened senses, Arden took a few seconds longer than necessary to reply. 'It is a fine and temporary existence,' she said. 'The isolation strengthens spirits.'

'And whets longings, I would say. People gossip that this poor boy killed his wife—'

'Fionna—' he protested.

'They say it, but it is not true. She was a smart girl, much smarter than you, Jonah Riven, and her boat would not have overturned unless she *told* it to do so, ha!' Miss La Grange gesticulated with a half-full wine glass. 'Personally, Lightmistress, I don't think she's dead at all. Everything in its time and place for Miss Harrow. Even staying in Vigil and marrying Jonah here, when the Eugenics Society quite forbade such a thing. Having a Postmaster for a father would make her stubborn like that.'

Mr Riven shared a glance with Arden, an odd, indecipherable expression. Reminding him of Bellis, she thought.

After Miss La Grange applied upon Mr Riven an unguent meant for both bruises and showgirl-wrinkles, she deposited a carafe of cloudy wild-grape wine with two glasses upon a scrolled lacquer side table.

'Now, you know your way around, Jonah, love. You may show Mx Beacon the facilities. Avail yourself of the wine. I understand you are not much of a drinker, but it may soothe inflamed muscles, help you sleep. I unfortunately must bathe and rest. The Manse and all her visitors have kept me busy this evening!'

She nodded at Arden and gave Mr Riven a sly crimson grin.

'Don't make too much noise when you make love to the girl, dear. No wild howling. You're not on the promontory and the neighbours will talk if she is too vocal in her delight.'

'Um . . .?' Arden started.

'Darling, if you were drooling over your neighbour any more I'd need to get you a bib. I'm sure he will be gentle. Goodnight!'

When she left, Mr Riven dropped his impassiveness and visibly blushed. 'I'm sorry, she makes assumptions.'

'Best be quiet about it, then.'

'Huh.' He huffed good-naturedly. 'She suspects Bellis is still alive and I'm still married.'

Of course Fionna La Grange knew. Love-struck fool.

'Do many people know Bellis' true fate?'

'If they think she fled me with Rector John Stefan's help,' he replied, 'then they keep their mouths shut.'

As Mr Riven struggled with the unfamiliar buttons, Arden tried to put her mind off his proximity by examining the oddities of the parlour. The angled mirror and the position of the seats were clearly set up for seductive purposes, and a collection of garments in black patent leather lay draped across a side table. Over the cluttered mantelpiece, a row of glass phalluses marched like pink soldiers heading for battle.

Arden went to touch the largest one, then caught herself at the last minute, for Mr Riven was watching her again.

'Strange, seeing you wear that coat. Bellis last wore it during our wedding.'

'Oh, I didn't realize,' Arden said, burning with embarrassment for not realizing. She shrugged out of the leather. 'It's so fine I didn't even feel myself getting too hot.' She swallowed and said, 'I suppose it's strange seeing me wear it, and not Bellis.'

Mr Riven gave an unexpected smile. 'Although it was her wedding coat, Bellis never wore it much either. She was so little, she'd swim in it. No, that coat belonged to my mother.' He nodded. 'It did it's duty as evidence of Bellis' *death*, but she was never fond if the texture enough to make it a daily thing.'

'It is an unusual feel,' Arden agreed, quietly experiencing a stab of delight. 'Your mother's coat! Goodness.'

Arden picked up a nearby matchbook instead of letting him see her dizzy grin. *Not Bellis' at all!* She composed herself and returned to him. As a coincidence, a Justinian crest was embossed on the paper fold, and Arden remembered what he'd said about his mother's background.

'Since we are speaking of her, how long did your mother work at the Manse Justinian?'

'A while. When the kraken got harder to hunt, Justinian money kept my family alive until some of us showed up with monstercalling talents.'

Some of you. Until you killed them. The thought came like a contamination in her joy, and she worried at its source. Would they ever be able to talk about it? Looking at Mr Riven now, he could not have been anywhere near an adult when the crime happened. Younger than David Modhi, even. A child, accused of a massacre? It made no sense.

Then she thought of the old Baron Alexander Justinian, whose face was so much like Mr Riven's. 'And your father? Who was he?'

He shook his head. 'My mother never said.'

She did not pry further. It could not have been any more obvious that he was not altogether a deepwater man.

'I never knew my birth mother long,' Arden admitted. 'She died when I could count four years old. Old enough to remember, and not completely forget.'

'Was she a Lightmistress too?'

'No. Had good neutral standing in the Eugenics ledger, good family, but my talent comes from the Beacon, the paternal, side. She was an airship pilot. The best that God could deliver without resorting to endowments, they used to say. Not good enough to survive a Vinland Crossing, though.'

'I've been through a Vinland Crossing storm, on a convict ship. They are vicious.'

'As are the pirates who patrol the air.'

'Yes. Them too.'

Arden poured the wine and took a huge gulp from her glass, needing the wine to still her nerves. 'My father tried to keep the unfortunate details from me, but no storm brought down my mother's craft. The crew made contact with a rogue inflatable corsair from the Summerlands. Her ship suffered a pirate seizure and . . . well. They tell me it was quick.'

'Summerlanders are not known for taking prisoners. I met some during my time in bondage. They'd rather kill a man quickly than torment them. If it is any consolation, they have no patience for torture.'

'It is a consolation, in its own strange way.'

They were quiet then. She wanted so much to interrogate Mr Riven about his history, about his time in the prison hulks, about his Lyonne accent and the people who gave him those rounded Northern vowels. About his journey, from child to man. He had travelled while in captivity. What had he come to know? Did he ever love before Bellis? Could there be love after? What did each scar mean, and when had he received each one? What was the taste of his skin, his response to a kiss?

'You'd have liked her.'

'Who?'

But she knew who.

The squeak of a gramophone winding came from Fionna's room, and then the piano tinkle of a song popular twenty years ago slid out from under a gap in the door.

'Mr Riven, *Jonah*.' She lingered, not knowing quite how to put the words, but needed to say them. 'Were you really married, or was it all an act to fool the Lyonne Order? Why did Bellis not take her golden talent and go to Lyonne and live like a Queen?'

He winced, and Arden felt quite suddenly she had opened a wound.

'We are married. It was no pretence.'

Now it was her turn to sigh from disappointment, but he went on, 'When I was released from my imprisonment, I had nowhere to go. I came back here. Stefan was a Rector in Garfish Point at the time, a hundred miles away and yet to take his post here. The only friend I had was Bellis. When I would have been flogged in the town square on my first day back, it was Bellis who stood in front of the crowd and stopped them. My best friend. The talent she had, it was a hard burden to carry. *Sanguis petrae* is a Sainted Isle trait, but she was not a Sainted Islander. Unless you've been there . . . it's hard to explain what the Islands are like to an outsider. The rituals. The superstitions. The deepwater folk worship the monsters as kin, and gods.'

'David told me about the Deepwater King,' Arden said, and wished she had the little iron figurine upon his serpent with her, so then she could really see if David was right, if it did look like Mr Riven. 'That he's still worshipped. Like God.'

'Yes, the one, who takes a wife and no man shall sunder them. His word is law.' He looked down at his hands, and the scars across his knuckles. Sighed, and continued with his story. 'So, four, five years ago, Bellis decides she's going to escape the Order once and for all. Went out unprotected, and on her own. She thought that the deepwater folk might more likely accept her on the night of the King.'

Arden recalled Mr Justinian's tale, of the woman dragged out to the islands and wedded in the terrible, brutal ways. Of her return to Vigil bloodied, bruised . . . and married. Suddenly a piece of the puzzle fell in to place.

'I take it the deepwater folk didn't accept her at all.'

'If I hadn't wedded Bellis, they'd have *killed* her. Fed her to the sea and *maris anguis*, the great serpent. But I meant my vows when I gave Bellis my name. I didn't take them lightly. But though she is protected now, like I said, I cannot be with her. Since my family . . . since they died I am no longer welcome back to my ancestral lands. I am a Riven in name only. It is a strong name, but I wear it in sufferance.'

So something had happened out there beyond the storm and in the islands where the monstrosities were venerated as gods, but of it Mr Riven would not elaborate further. Some horror on the Deepwater Night, when the abyssal King of the Abyss came up and stole away a woman for a wife.

'I'm sorry if the rumours about our marriage were troublesome, Mx Beacon.'

'Oh, I tried not to listen to them.'

'We never consummated our wedding,' he continued hesitantly, as if the reality needed softening, and evidence of him not doing Bellis harm.

Arden stilled again. Jealousy and envy only worked had it the scaffold of a coveted thing. In a blink Mr Riven had changed the rules. 'Not consummated . . . you mean, you and Bellis . . . not ever?'

Mr Riven shook his head. 'Our marriage was so sudden. The time was not right so soon after the ritual – we never discussed making it a union of the flesh and in the end, the time never came for us. She was, she was poorly in spirit. The threat of the Order was a great strain on her.'

'I'm quite . . . I'm quite stunned.'

'Why?'

Arden struggled to reply. How could she articulate loneliness and monkish yearnings, the flesh which burned through her fire-aligned blood, the whisper of flame in her mind? How could she tell this man that he'd provided the face for her ruminations in the bleak and endless nights, and even now if he was to ask, she would say yes, *yes*, and take him into her embrace at once?

'I thought you might have been with her that way. Because you loved her.'

He lay down, adjusted his head on the tassel-fringed cushion, looked up at the ceiling. 'She no longer needs me. Nobody will dare touch her, and that is why I can confidently say I will not do as the Lions ask tonight.'

'I'm still worried, Mr Riven.'

'Of what?'

'That I might have stumbled into a bigger theatre than just encouraging the pair of you to sail off to your happy ending. The Eugenics Society never lets any endowed child stay in Fiction. Mr Lindsay spoke words of *care* and *gentleness*, letting her *mature at home*, but I don't believe him, not one inch! The moment her talent was revealed, she'd have been sent to Lyonne, sick mother needing care or Mr Harrow forbidding her or not.'

The wounded look came back, and this time interlaced with fear. 'There are always exceptions.'

'What exceptions? Tell me! I am completely jealous.'

The gramophone stilled. The room grew quiet, and the perfumes stifling.

'You would not want what Bellis had.'

'What do you mean, *sanguis petrae* is a golden – oh!'

In her distraction she'd let the wine glass fall out of her hand. Without waiting, Mr Riven rolled off the couch and picked the goblet from the floor, wiped the rug and the hem of Arden's dress with the old Baron's silk handkerchief – and then stilled as he realized where he was, looking up at her, his hot blue eyes darkening the same way they had when he'd seen her on that pebble beach, clothed in scraps of gold.

With an anxious swallow, he stood up and put the glass away. 'Enough wine for you tonight, perhaps. Now you need not worry about the Lions, Mx Beacon. Bellis certainly would not.'

The room was warm. Arden stood up and examined her skirts. The feathered dress beneath, all silks and softness, remained intact, despite the night they'd spent.

Mr Riven watched her all the while. Another expression came over him now, and this one not so rigid and disciplined. If Bellis was an object of worship, then Arden was some other inarticulate manifestation altogether – something unfamiliar and intriguing.

She blurted, 'You speak pretty words of friendship and duty and risking your life to marry her before she got turned into serpent food . . . but did you ever desire her like a grown man?'

'I don't know,' he said hesitantly. 'It would be demeaning to think of her in that way.'

An odd rebellion came over her then, against the Lions who would have her chase the jewel of love and an independent life. She wanted to remove the dress, have Mr Riven behold her naked body, invite him to touch her. This man, who belonged to another, was a man more forbidden than Mr Castile ever had been. Oh, but the room was hot, or maybe she was hot, a furnace banked and under pressure. She fleetingly imagined him aroused, wanting her, and the relief he would bring in all his maleness, his scent, his body tender and coarse at the same time.

If he noticed her mood he made no sign of it, turning over on the chaise. 'If I snore,' Mr Riven gruffed, 'you are welcome to throw a shoe in my direction.'

He grabbed the end of a crocheted throw, rolled over and turned away. Arden, abandoned, watched the coke-flame flicker in the grate, and took far longer to sleep.

19

Vigil in the morning

Vigil in the morning became an exceptionally sorry place, dank and dreary, with the sulphurous smell of coal and the odour of the night-soilman's cart. Mr Riven woke early, at the first ray of light though a tiny window set into the sloping ceiling.

'How are you getting home?' he asked, as she stirred on the bed. Arden squinted into the grey dawn, pulled the coverlet to her chin.

'Heavens. I hadn't thought. I'll need to hire David Modhi to take me back.'

'Don't bother. I'm heading in your direction. I can pull my boat up to the pier if you don't mind the walk.'

'Well, that makes you handy indeed.'

That made him smile, and his face, normally so hard and flinty, softened about his eyes.

Arden dressed behind the room divider and despaired at the stained satin of her formerly pretty blue shoes. She had not slept well. Mr Riven had not snored, but the thought of him nearby had been a terrible distraction. She had hoped to escape and dream of anyone else – if not Richard, then maybe one of her first sweethearts – but Mr Riven had persistently slid into that place.

How disrespectful you should think this way, her heart whispered. *He is both married and a gentleman. A hero even, assisting his wife in escaping from the Lions and the deep-water savages.*

'We should thank Fionna for her hospitality,' Arden said when she emerged from behind the screen. 'I hate taking off without a polite gesture.'

'That guinea you left on the mantelpiece will be the best thanks you can give her, along with the extra hour sleeping in,' Mr Riven said. He opened the door and ushered Arden out onto the landing, before walking down the stairs first so he might help her over the two missing ones at the bottom. At the courtyard he added, 'Better than rag-paper dollars. Anyhow, she won't be up until noon. We'll be back on the promontory before—'

'So, the old bitch Betsey was *right*.'

Mr Riven halted suddenly at the male voice. Trapped behind him, Arden had only the view of his shoulder blades, but previous meetings had made her more than familiar with the voice's owner.

'Well, what do you know, lads? The mongrel had time to stop at the whores to wet his pecker before leaving. Shaved, too.'

'Let me pass, Alasdair,' Mr Riven said. 'I do not wish to argue with you.'

Arden squeezed out from behind Mr Riven. Mr Harrow stood in front of them, grinning broadly. His two deputies, very much the worse for wear. A third deputy lingered nearby, this one newly minted by the shiny pewter star on his shabby coat lapel. Gregor Tallwater, probably trying to earn an honest coin. Altogether, they made a crowd of the little outside yard. The skull-grin on Mr Harrow's face faded as soon as he saw Arden.

'Lightmistress? What are you doing here?'

'I might ask you the same thing, *Post*master.'

'I have come to arrest this reprobate for assaulting my men. Best you step aside now, Guildswoman.'

'No,' Arden said. 'Best you step aside. I do not take kindly to threats upon my person or the people of my acquaintance.'

With that she took Mr Riven's hand in her own.

He resisted for a few seconds, but she squeezed hard with caution until her coin hurt. Flicked out with a little finger so it might touch the heel of his hand. An obscure signal of the docks, but if he'd had any experience in prison hulks and other places of ill-repute, he would know what such a secret sign meant.

Trust me. Follow my lead.

'Why do you come here with false accusations?' she continued. 'Mr Riven was never at the Justinian residence, and has been with me all night.'

'You left the Manse with him. Witnesses saw you leave. Which means he consorted at the Manse with you during the Master's Ball.'

'I certainly did not leave or consort with Mr Riven in the Manse. I left with Mr Castile, a friend and chaperone. Then I came here to the Black Rosette to spend time with my . . . lover.'

Beside her, Mr Riven tensed. Mr Harrow swallowed, affected disgust.

'Lies. My men arrested this fellow in the guest house. He got away. Clearly with your help.'

'You mean, Mr Justinian's pleasure house. A room stocked with all manner of drugs and recreational pharmaceuticals? These men here, still so inebriated they can barely see as much as when I stumbled across them last night, now concoct a story so they may excuse whatever general shambles they may have caused in their carousing? Why, you can ask any of these so-called "whores" to vouch for our presence here all night.'

Mr Harrow bared his teeth like a cremelo highland ape, and his wispy yellow hair crackled with his rage. The sorry deputies cowered.

'You think you can cover for this monster, Lightmistress? You think your succumbing to his depravity without hurt is a privileged game for you blooded folk?'

Mr Riven squeezed Arden's hand so hard she nearly cried out from it. But she knew what Riven meant. The Postmaster's invective was mere talk: Mr Harrow was a man grieving, lashing out. Let him vent, let him direct his anger to her, and then be on his way. If Mr Riven fought them, he would go to prison, and to the hulks and to his death.

In a tempest of bitterness Mr Harrow ranted at Arden, his eyes wild when he saw her silent. 'Does it give you perverted pleasure, when he ploughs your furrows with the same tool he used to rape my daughter and take her maidenhood? Does it excite you to think of how she would cry and try to fight him every devil-damned night? How she came to my house, her undergarments rent, stinking of kraken oil inside her and this creature's sexual odours, begging me to dissolve the marriage? My only joy is that his rotted seed could not infect her with child!'

He continued for a solid minute. Behind him, only Mr Gregor Tallwater had the grace to seem embarrassed by the foulness that emerged from Mr Harrow's mouth. The other two deputies had clearly heard it all before, glad enough that Arden should be the target of Mr Harrow's displeasure instead of them.

Mr Riven lurched close to an anger-induced fit. His neck turned near-purple in his effort to keep calm.

At last Mr Harrow took a breath. He had no more to say.

'Are you done, Mr Harrow?' Arden asked, flatly.

'I am done.'

'Then can we pass?'

He jerked his head sideways. 'Get out of my sight.'

'Gladly.'

She dragged Mr Riven across the courtyard duckboards. Only Gregor shared with her an apologetic glance, and it appeared he would not have argued if Arden had dragged him away from this unholy indictment as well.

As soon as they were in the streets and had made their way in silence across the town square to the salty fog of the harbour, she seized Mr Riven's chin so that he would meet her eyes, not go to dark places in his mind.

'Jonah,' she said, using his first name as if he were a hurt child. 'It's for the best that Mr Harrow exhaust himself on his own illusions. If he had truly loved his daughter, she would never have got into her mess. She'd have gone to Lyonne a golden talent princess and eaten honey sweets and sat on velvet chairs and grown fat among silks for the rest of her life.'

He turned on her, despair making his blue eyes gleam almost incandescent. 'You think me a dupe, for helping her and not getting real love in return?'

'No. I think everyone is a dupe, for putting so much stock in sanguinity. The damned Sainted Isles and their unmanned rockblood wells. This cursed town. Bellis' fool idea of using you to escape the Lions and secure her place in the Islands by putting fear in the hearts of other men. The devil knows there are enough women in the world who live in a marriage of such abjectness for real. They cannot be whisked away to some mysterious islands with a lover when it all becomes too much. Bellis did not need to add her story to theirs, however the end may have been justified in her mind. You may have been the only good thing she had while she was here. She didn't deserve you, Mr Riven.'

He let Arden go. Her hand smarted from where he had held her hard. She rubbed it with a wince.

'I'm sorry,' he said of her aching hand, and perhaps for more. 'I have kept to myself for too many years. I know there are stories. Bellis encouraged them. I suspect she knew it would make her eventual disappearance more legitimate, and send a message to the people over the waves that she was not to be trifled with, and neither was I. But what Mr Harrow said . . . sometimes it's difficult to maintain that image without feeling ashamed of it.'

She huffed a breath. 'She wove her protective deception well. You are quite the scoundrel, as everyone was at pains to tell me in no less detail than Mr Harrow did just now.'

'Yet not knowing the truth, you still came to me as a neighbour, and with dignity.' He briefly touched the end of Arden's coat sleeve. Patterns his mother had made, not Bellis. 'It says much for your character, Mx Beacon.'

'Does it earn me some credit towards being your friend?'

'You have earned every right to be my friend.'

She took off her glove and held out her hand for him to shake. Her left hand. Blood to blood. Would he know?

He did. 'Ooh, and gently,' she said, as his fingers closed around her palm. His hand was calloused with work and bloodletting, deliberate, but gentle too. She need not have worried.

He gave a crooked smile, and that same tightness budded in the centre of her chest. In Clay Capital he would not be at all handsome, too angular and Fictish, his nose too thin and his smile too crooked and his skin kissed by shades of sea foam, not sun.

But still. He was not hers to love.

Somewhere over the waves a woman had asked her best friend to *wait*. Asked him to protect her by his unseen presence until she was ready to call him back. Like the lich-ship gears, this love of Bellis and Mr Riven's had been set into place long before Arden had arrived. It would continue upon her departure. She was merely a stowaway upon this journey.

They went to the harbour, where Mx Modhi had already taken her Harbourmistress position in her rocking chair, and her first pipe of the day. She saw them coming, Arden Beacon and a groomed Mr Riven, and did not recognize him at first. Only when he spoke to her did her eyes turn into hard squints.

'People have been seeking you,' she said through a cloud of tobacco smoke. 'Magistrate Harrow especially.'

'I am aware of this.'

'You'd best not be up to nonsense, Jonah Riven. My position here does not allow for illegal activities.'

Arden quickly interjected, sensing tensions rise. 'I assure you, anything that Mr Harrow may have said is all down to mistaken identity. I can vouch for Mr Riven.'

Mx Modhi obviously had opinions on Arden's vouching, but chewed on her pipe to stop the words from coming out and costing her the coin of her harbour fee. David Modhi scrambled to prepare Mr Riven's boat ready for departure, and beamed in joy when Mr Riven thanked him for taking such care. The youth's wispy moustache trembled with delight. 'Anything for you, Mr Riven!'

Compared to the pleasure boats of the visiting Masters, Mr Riven's craft was a shadow coated in pitch. The boat's name on the black wood became apparent as Arden came close. *Saudade*.

Now that she could see her without danger of being run down, Arden noted that all her trimmings were the same oily black wood. Mangrove-ebony, a prized timber for shipbuilders if they could ever harvest enough to construct a craft more sizable than a dinghy. The mangrove stands formed floating islands that travelled piecemeal across the Darkling Sea. The largest stands were rumoured to be found in Sainted waters, where the sea monsters sported. It was a monster-hunting ship, down to its bones. *Saudade* had all the solidity of an ocean transport barge.

Other than the high wheelhouse, the bulk of her was mostly below decks, to resist tipping in hard swells. She had side wheels to keep her hunting-craft nimble and enable her to plough through Sargasso fronds without fouling, but given her speed Arden suspected a screw-propeller under the water too.

Propped up by a winch at *Saudade*'s stern was a smaller craft, a tender boat made in the same black wood. The little dinghy had a brass motor of some oil-burning type, perhaps kraken or rock distillate.

Mr Riven helped Arden aboard over a mist-slippery gangway. Arden ran her hand along the rail. Intuited that bloodwork had been used aboard her, powerful sacraments.

Inside the wheelhouse, things both antique and modern. He owned both spyglass and spectrograph, but also a near-new and extremely expensive echo box, technology only the principal signallers had.

He noticed her staring at the box.

'Echo box. Traces shoals, floating pumice, stalker ships. It is a cunning little machine. It uses electric signals, the same as a Sumerian-Congolese wireless device, and traces them upon this paper roll.'

'I never took you for a technological fellow.'

'I prefer *pragmatic*, myself,' he said. 'If I had the time and the necessity I could refit her in all the latest inventions.'

'Mr Riven,' David Modhi called up at that most inopportune time, 'I've taken down the gangway!'

'Good lad,' he said back, throwing him a wave. 'Say thank you to your mother for me.'

'I will, Mr Riven!'

Arden smiled as they cast away. 'I think he has a little crush on you.'

'Poor devil,' Mr Riven said, after the youth had run back to the harbour shed to once more be in thrall to his mother's commands. 'He deserves a better life than this.'

'I've seen his test scars. At least he's tried.'

Mr Riven nodded. 'He's falsified his name and gone to at least six more moots, up and down the Fiction coast. I took him each time, the optimistic whelp.' Mr Riven shrugged. 'Even if he was positive for something, it would be a risk if he tested for the wrong thing.'

'What would be a wrong thing?'

She saw his jaws clench, and realized he'd not meant to speak.

Arden sighed, and nodded. 'Well, he looks like he's nearly of age. A sanguis shadow would have shown up long before now. The best he can hope for is that he is *malorum*, a late bloomer, I suppose. The Society isn't too fussy with *sanguis malorum*.'

'From your voice I'd assume you have familiarity with the condition.'

She nodded. 'I failed my eleventh- and thirteenth-year tests, tested just positive at seventeen. The only reason I was allowed a third test was because of my father, and my name. He is Portmaster for Clay Portside, and he is a Beacon.'

'Then you know what it is, to have a name that precedes you.'

'When did you test?' Arden asked. 'Prior to your, uh, prison term? You obviously have *something*.'

To her alarm Mr Riven gestured for Arden to take the wheel. 'Never tested,' he said. With a yelp, Arden grabbed the paddle wheeler's mechanism. Alarmingly, Mr Riven intended to show her how to drive *Saudade* out of the marina.

'Never . . . never tested?' she stammered, trying to navigate both a powerful steamer and her own tongue at the same time. She had served her assigned duty on slow dockside tugboats, but this craft exceeded anything in her experience.

'Our family has always had endowments,' Mr Riven said as she steered, half-terrified and half-exhilarated. 'Why test for something I already know I have?'

'But you could have left this place. Got away from everyone who wished you and your family harm . . . oh, a buoy, is that a buoy? Did I just run over the signal buoy?'

'Keep going. You're fine.'

'My Lord, she's a powerful craft. You could get all the way to Clay Portside in your boat.'

He walked to the window. '*Saudade* was never my boat. She belonged to my family. And kraken-calling is a fisherman's talent. Specific to a region. It is not a talent of any importance outside of here.' A light rain fell across the glass. 'My blood is tied up with this ocean. The devils that live beneath the waves, the leviathan, the *monstrom mare*. This is what my blood trammels. If I'd left for Clay, what could I do there?'

He turned to Arden, who had committed to a grip on the wheel and relaxed into the engine's power.

'Was the same with Bellis. The Sainted Isles lie east, not north, not in Clay. That's where the rockblood flows. It's where she yearned for. When she needed to go, I let her go.'

'I can't say I've ever experienced any geographical under-pinnings to my sanguinity myself.'

'There's fire everywhere in this world. Everywhere and in

everything. Besides,' he turned back to the rain-lashed glass, 'even if I was not tested for endowments, they came for me in the end. Took me to the prison hulks. Tried to make sure I died. Which I did not.'

'You must have been barely a child.'

'I was fourteen.'

'Fourteen! How could they have pinned a slaughter on a child?'

'Huh, so, Vernon spared no grisly detail about my crime.'

She sighed. 'Some nonsense about you having killed your family in a night. Everyone on the promontory.'

'Then that is what I did.'

'I will not believe you. I know what lies Lions are capable of.'

'Sometimes they don't lie.'

The side wheels ground through the slosh. Arden wondered what she could say. Words of comfort? Too late now, such things were behind him. He stared out beyond the horizon, where the cloudbank grew, undoubtedly thinking of Bellis beyond that straight edge, under that self-same cloud, needing him.

The waves slapped *Saudade*'s bows and sheeted across her forecastle. The forward rock became pronounced as they hit deeper water, making the brass crossbar at her feet a great necessity in keeping her upright.

'See,' he said once they had left Vigil harbour, 'you're a natural skipper.'

'Is she the only boat your family owned?' Arden asked, once she found her balance.

'There were several in my grandfather's time. And my father had two more, *Sonder* and *Sehnsucht*.'

'What happened . . . after . . . after, you know. They died?'

'*Sonder*, I've no idea where it went. *Sehnsucht* I gave to Bellis and your cousin Stefan, to pay for passage to the Sainted Isles. The penny for the Old Guy. Somebody else has her now, or she was long ago made firewood.' Then, unexpectedly he asked, 'Who was Mr Castile?'

She started. 'Excuse me?'

'When you said you had a chaperone. And to the Dowager. Nobody can lie properly when put on the spot. Ergo, there was a Castile of your acquaintance.'

'A man of my social circle when I lived in Clay Portside.' Then, emboldened by their newfound familiarity, 'He was my lover.'

'Your first?'

'My first *important* one.'

'The one the Lion bribed you with.'

'The very one. I'm no fool, Mr Riven, he's probably on the other side of the world by now and living quite high on the hog. I've not spoken to him since the day he left, a year ago.'

Mr Riven frowned, entirely confused. 'Why would a man do something so unfathomably absurd as leave you?'

She let herself smile at his compliment. 'It's so political when endowments and genetics are concerned. Not everyone is as noble as you, Mr Riven. He wouldn't run away with me, and I was quite terrified to do it myself. My cowardice, you see.'

'I cannot see you a coward.'

'You would be surprised.'

She must have telegraphed a need for distraction, for he pointed to a rope on top of a rivet. 'Lash the wheel, slow the engine. Let me show you something.'

Arden did as Mr Riven requested and followed him down to the deck. He pulled off his jacket, rolled up his shirt, held out a tanned and lean arm. With a knife blade from his pocket, he put a nick in the side of his hand, where a coin might be if he were a Lyonnian sanguinem. A callus pinched there, from a hundred cuts. Once he let a few drops fly he withdrew from the railing.

'Come see.'

She held fast to a post, for the wheels were still going at a chop. The intermittent sunlight caught the cloud of water vapour from the wheels, gave the spray a corona of rainbow colour. As she waited, the wheels slowed to a gentle turn.

'What am I looking for?'

He gave a sly smile, and suddenly, she didn't care, only wanted to admire Mr Riven's face. Unsymmetrical, too pale, his hair too dark-dun a shade of brown to mark him as kin to the yellow-crowned longboaters of the Estotilian winterlands. Yet in all ways he was beautiful. As she surveyed him, she had a sense of coolness, for the flume of the waves had risen from the stilled wheels and surrounded her, the light refracting as in the very path of a rainbow. Down below . . .

Arden's breath stilled. The water turned to moving glass.

No, not glass. A thousand moving, twisting shapes of luminescent transparency, for the colours had turned to life.

'Are they cuttlefish?' she shouted over the threshing waves.

'Krakenspawn,' Mr Riven shouted back with unconcealed delight. 'A hen has managed to lay before dying. It's a good sign.'

The kraken had taken up the propulsion that the wheels had abandoned, and *Saudade* picked up speed, moving with the slightest side-to-side yaw until they came in sight of the dark rocks of the Riven Promontory. The churning bodies of the new-hatched little monsters threw off flashes of electric brilliance. She could not tell if it were them or the running tide that caused such speed.

With a dismissive gesture, Mr Riven flung out his hand and with a rainbow flash, the krakenspawn were gone. The boat coasted on the residual momentum.

Arden stayed on the deck while he returned to the tower, to reverse the wheels and gently drift in to the pier.

The morning had taken on a delicious strangeness now, shiny-new with possibilities and responsibilities.

'What happens from here?' she asked when Mr Riven came down out of the cabin. 'Because I'm obliged to report to the Lions if you decide to go anywhere.'

'You'll be waiting a long time to make that report.'

It was not her place to opine on his decision. But she could not help her feelings. Found herself sneaking looks in his direction, and finding herself gladdened by his sight.

'You're still not going back to Bellis? I know you said it last night, but feared the wine might be talking.'

He shook his head with a half-grin. 'If the Lyonne Order has taken interest in her after all these years, they've left it too late. They have no influence over there. Why do you think she kept heading to the Isles?'

Mr Riven tied the boat off and helped Arden onto land. His work-roughened hand warm in hers. Making her brave. She could easily have broached the gap herself, but she appreciated the concern, and besides, a sense of safety strengthened those hands of his, an impression that he could pluck a person out of the wildest seas.

The wind roused up, and the sun came out a little, and the golden bloom on his cheeks made him seem otherworldly, an ancient idol carved from an occluded marble. She internally debated furiously about how to say goodbye, about how to steal a few more minutes with Mr Riven.

They were disturbed by a feeble *yip* from the pier's landing. A brown and white terrier dog, grey at the muzzle, trotted down the wooden jetty.

'Ah, Lightmistress, the boss has arrived. Come and meet Chief.'

'Hello, Chief,' Arden said to the little dog. She squatted down to scratch him under his salty jaw and patted his wiry back. 'Hello, old pup.'

The dog gazed up at her with eyes blued from cataracts, then put his paw on her knee. Mr Riven's critical attention was upon her. The dog's opinion was a great test.

'Dogs are keen judges of human character,' Arden said, standing up with bony, scruffy Chief in her arms. He licked her under her chin, tasting krakensalt from their journey.

'They are indeed.' Mr Riven stroked Chief's head. 'I'd only owned him a year when my family was . . . when I was . . .' He stopped. 'Did you know Jorgen Beacon looked after him when I was gone? Took care of the two boats as well. *Saudade* and *Sehnsucht*.'

'Mr Harris never told me. I thought you were at odds, because of Stefan.'

'No, it was not Stefan that made us distant. Well, maybe a little. My uncle Zachariah had quite a friendship with Jorgen. They were stuck on the same promontory, like us.'

He turned to walk away, before stopping to say, 'Well, are you coming? I can't have you stumbling back in those heeled slippers. If you fall off a cliff, Mr Harrow will accuse me of having given you a shove.'

'We can't have that.'

'There should be some boots that might fit you.'

Arden put Chief down and followed Mr Riven up the pier path to the factory sheds.

A selection of wind chimes, some bright, and some ancient with salt-rust, made a symphony as they entered the small quad-rangle afforded by the building shells. A cormorant on a roof watched them, one of the compound's constant birds. Mr Riven disappeared inside the first of the warehouses, came out dragging a shipping trunk banded in iron. The locks were broken, and the hinges almost rusted solid. Inside, under old portside uniforms and shipbuilder's diagrams, the trunk was filled to the brim with boots, some of them barely worn. From the variation of sizes, more than one person had owned the contents.

Arden picked out a pair of general-purpose low heels, brushed off the dust and knocked them out for spiders.

An odd smell wafted out of another open barn door, hot metal and salt water.

'It is the hen,' Mr Riven said at Arden's unspoken question. 'Mother of the spawn you saw earlier.'

'You caught her?'

'Yes.'

'Can I see?'

He nodded. 'But say a prayer on entry, Lightmistress. She has made a hard sacrifice and deserves respect.'

The factory hunkered down low and dim, with a row of lanterns set about a long, broad table that was more a giant chapel altar than a butcher's block. At first, the creature seemed entirely *eye*, a golden disc wider than the reach of Arden's arms, shining in the lamplight. The pupil gleamed wise and cold, having beheld all the mysteries of the devil's abyss with a form beloved only by God. A luminescence was inside her sizable cranium, which Arden figured roomy enough to hold three Clydesdales in an embrace. Yet the kraken turned out smaller than Arden had previously thought. This was not to say the creature was *not* massive, but of a conservative heft that might destroy only the *Breeze* or *Saudade*. Certainly not to tangle up an entire clipper ship as in the woodblock paintings of her old books, or an armada as the old stories suggested.

The hen's long legs were pale, and in the low light had the softness of a child's arms. The chain and canvas harness Mr Riven had used to haul her onto the sacrificial altar from his boat still cradled the head the way fingers might hold a giant egg.

Reverence here, no violence. A lying-in-state, not a slaughter.

Mr Riven watched Arden examine the kraken hen in silence until she had finished her worship.

'I took her yesterday,' he said at last. 'She had laid the last of her eggs. A *monstrom mare* in its natural habitat will prefer to die upon a pontoon of black mangroves, part of the ecology of the creature's natural environment. My boat was the nearest vessel to achieve that end, so she came to me in consent.' He reached out and touched the hen's rubbery flesh. 'Now we wait for her to die so she can be harvested. For the oil in her head, the fabric of her skin.'

'It sounds quite a process.'

'Yes, and there is not much of a window to do either. After she breathes her last, the decay is quick. They bleed ichor, not blood. The mortification is absolute. If she is not prepared, there will be nothing left of her except seawater tomorrow morning.'

Suddenly the creature's siphon, big enough for Arden to have wedged herself in up to her waist, let out a miserable puff of air with a seawater plume. Arden yelped, caught the misty brunt of that last exhale.

'Oh! She's still alive,' Arden said, wiping her face and arms. 'And now I smell of salt-rust.'

Mr Riven grinned and pulled a pony-plant chamois off a rail, held it out. 'I'm sorry, I should have warned you not to get too close.'

'Getting too close is the ultimate warning for all things,' she replied, meaning to say it in grudging humour, but as she took the fine vegetable leather, her hand met Mr Riven's own, and a shock of longing went through her, a feeling beyond desire, for the ground had opened beneath her and all she could do was flail and fall.

He dropped the towel and Arden reached up for him as a vine in darkness might reach for sun. On tip-toes she pressed her mouth to his chapped lips and thought for a moment he would resist her, that she had made a terrible mistake, that she only intended to crash and burn this nascent friendship with an unwanted kiss.

Then he let out a moan so soft it could have been a sigh and wrapped his arms about her, a grip both tight and trembling, and crushed his mouth against her own with such untaught carelessness it could have been the kiss of a child.

What was this? Was it love, or anger, or exultation at stealing this wretched left-behind lover who had been made monstrous to protect a golden queen?

Or was it her own obsession grown beyond its bounds? His entire body stood rigid and humming in her arms, a human tuning fork struck and held, and the raw newness of him when she'd spent so long without made the furious stabs of desire in her belly as painful as glass shards. She kissed him greedy as a thief. He was an illicit feast she'd stumbled on when all her life she'd been content with scraps, wanted to taste the dark mysteries of his mouth, the salt of him, hear his gasp of pleasure when he—

Without warning he pulled away, leaving Arden gasping.

'Bellis,' he said through a tight, hoarse throat. His breath came fast and shallow.

Bellis. Bellis, her shadow, the Woman Who Fled and Lived.

'Jonah.' Arden stepped to him again, not yet ready to relinquish him. He took her shoulders and held her away. His expression was more akin to grieving than passion.

'It's too risky for her, Arden. Her safety depends on our marriage being true.'

'A safety *imposed* upon you by a marriage you had no choice but to comply with! She should never have gone out there if she knew the deepwater people would be so upset.'

He backed off as if she was spitting poison instead of truth, and Arden pursued him no more. Only sat by the table as he shook his head.

'She is still my responsibility.'

'What if she were no longer your responsibility? It's been years, Jonah. She is an adult.'

'And do what? Be with you instead?' he said, and it felt so blunt and emotionless that a frightful thought made her blood run cold as the salt upon her skin.

'Maybe . . . you could. I would not say no,' she stammered. 'I'd like to try.'

'Try. Like an experiment?'

'Not . . .'

He shook his head. 'No further now. Arden, you are beautiful and so wonderful but I could be no more than an amusement to you, something indulgent to pass the time before you go back to Clay Portside and leave me with as much thought as you would discard scrap and spoil.'

'I didn't kiss you for my own *amusement*, Jonah.' Arden's tears prickled her eyes and she hated that he made her feel this way, run headlong into her fears of mistakes and abandonment. The Order saw her desires as dangerous and unwanted. But it hurt so much more when a lone man should come to the same conclusion.

'We are lonely, you and I, and I thought . . .' Her cheeks

were so hot they would burn if she touched them. Humiliation crisped her breath to ash. Where was the lightning to strike her? Where was the ground beneath her feet to open and swallow her into a peaceful oblivion?

He ran his hands through his hair, leaving runnels in the dyed pomade of the night before. An absent, impatient gesture.

'I am not some brief occupation for your spare time. I am not an object for you to use when it suits, or a rag for wounded hearts.'

'Jonah, I didn't mean it that way. I'm completely adrift. Just now it seemed that you were the only real thing that I could be certain of. Jonah Riven. Not even my blood belongs to me!'

And now she was reduced to begging, as if she could not descend any lower. A look of infinite tenderness softened his eyes, as brief as a whisper. He made to move towards her, as if about to hug, and comfort.

The sympathy ended almost as soon as it began, and he caught himself, his expression twisted with anguish.

'I made a promise.'

The spell was broken. She was bested by Bellis. Mr Riven's first and only love. He lived only to provide her protection. She was once again *malorum*, a lightless failure. She could not bear the shame any longer. Ran from him as he stood in the darkened warehouse with his dying beast, fled into the grey, cold day. The seabirds cried above her. The waves fretted against the shorelines. The ache of desire that had come so suddenly to her now twisted into a miserable thud.

As she crested the hill she rolled her ankle upon a loose rock while running in the unfamiliar shoes, and coupled with her exhaustion, she slowed down to a limping walk along the trail.

'Stupid, stupid,' she said to herself, while her smarting ankle brought tears to her eyes.

Her ankle, and the other things. Self-pity was an easy cloak to wrap herself up in.

How awful she was. How greedy.

I will cease to think of him. Let him do what he wishes. I

shall tell the Lions he is angry with me, and by the end of the
month I shall be far from here. I will not have my Guild Degree,
or employment. I shall wear a commonblood *coat.*

But no sooner had she come about the corner bluff than she
saw Chalice standing outside the lighthouse with a stack of
pigeon crates, each one bearing the seal of the Lyonne
Investigatory Order.

20

Arden had expected that she would break

Arden had expected that she would break to Chalice the news of her recruitment into the Order with some delicacy, perhaps over the last of their fig-brandy, because Chalice in her cups was infinitely more agreeable than Chalice in her normal day-to-day. Instead, the admission came with a box of messenger pigeons dumped outside her door.

Each bird was banded about the leg with a metal ring. Engraved on each, a tangle of thorns entangling an open rose.

Now Chalice knew Arden's shameful secret.

'Not every day one is gifted Clay Tipplers owned by Lions,' Chalice said peevishly as Arden approached. She stuck her finger in through the wire, and a yellow beak pecked her. 'Bad-tempered as the bloody delivery driver who dropped them off.' She withdrew her finger. 'I must wonder when I was to be included in this little complication of yours. Lions. Here's me thinking you were just another Seamaster's Guild ingenue.'

'Please understand, I didn't want you to worry, Chalice. You'd have been in a state if I told you what was really going on.'

'What was going *on*?' She turned to Arden, eyes narrowed,

judging every mud-splattered, salt-encrusted, kiss-abraded inch of her. 'What the devil have you been up to, Lightmistress? Don't think I didn't see you coming in on Mr Riven's black boat either.'

Without the gentle preamble she would have preferred, Arden was forced to tell Chalice about her father's suspicions, the work instruction she should never have had, and the constant fear that one day her true function would be revealed.

The admission of Mr Lindsay's appearance as a Lyonne Order agent and her subsequent instruction to befriend Mr Riven raised only an eyebrow. Chalice was truly unflappable, and for that Arden loved her.

The kiss, however, Arden left out.

Chalice, she suspected, already deduced that such a thing had happened between her and Mr Riven. Maybe more. The storm-bride went to place a teapot on the fire pit, dropped in handfuls of pennyroyal and raspberry leaf along with the tea leaves.

'So, you rescued our intimidating neighbour on the words of your Order handler,' Chalice said, stirring the concoction. 'Had a deep and meaningful talk on the duties of a husband. Well then. The puppet master gathers his strings.'

'The Lion made me think I had a choice. A mendacious choice. Either I left Mr Riven to his fate, in which case he might have died, or I went and rescued him and established some sort of connection.'

'And did you establish a connection?' Chalice asked, stirring her witches' brew so hard it sloshed into the fire.'

'Of course I did,' Arden sighed. 'They knew my weaknesses, that I wouldn't let Mr Riven come to harm. They'd have lost their only tenuous link with Bellis Harr . . . *Riven*, I mean. Their runaway sanguinem, taunting them from across the waves.'

Chalice gave her a sideways eye, as if to say: *come on now. You dropped her marriage name on purpose.*

'That's not the kind of connection I'm talking about. Arden, talk to me. How close did you come to that man?'

Arden looked at Chalice's angry face and down at the minty brew so astringent it made her throat sting. 'Chalice why are you making a pennyroyal tea?'

'Did you and him . . .?'

'No, goodness gracious. No! He's married, and he loves his wife. I am merely his neighbour.'

Chalice stopped stirring the tea and gave a relieved exhale at the abortifacient mixture. 'Indeed. At least it hasn't been a night of entirely bad choices. One wouldn't want the daughter of Alasdair Harrow getting upset at you. If she's anything like him, she would be a terror.'

A mutiny stirred in Arden, a resentment towards that loved and perfect woman. 'If Bellis cared about Jonah, she'd not have sailed away without him,' Arden sniped. 'She's given up her vows, as far as I'm concerned.'

The stormbride jutted out her chin in preparation for some harsh truths. The words that came were more measured than Chalice probably wanted them to be. 'Darling, when I said you should think of getting yourself *companionship*, I in no way considered *him*. If you've ever listened to me in our brief time together, keep your wits about you and your emotions cool.'

'Are you telling me to stay away, *Headmistress* Quarry?'

'I'm saying, be convivial and neighbourly all you like, but if Lions are involved, you leave Mr Riven deal with his wife *alone*, do you hear?'

'Goodness. If it's such an importance that I should promise you, then all right. I shan't involve myself in his personal matters. He's really not interested in me . . . that way.'

Mollified somewhat, Chalice left the tea to brew. Arden later drank some, for the menstrual cramps were due in a few days, and the concoction helped women's pains.

In the yellowing light, Chalice prepared the lighthouse's winding mechanism for Arden's shift, but did not, as part of her afternoon ritual, go immediately to bed. Instead Chalice began loading her dry-sack with a change of clothes and her travelling coat.

'I forgot to tell you, in all this morning's strangeness. I have business in town. Mr Sage is harvesting one of his night-flowering herbs for me, and if I'm not around to watch him, he'll do it all wrong.'

'You're leaving?'

'Only a night. I'll take your *Fine Breeze* across to Vigil and return in the morning, if you can cover the first three hours of my shift.' She nodded to the empty earthenware cup in Arden's hands. 'You are not the only one who gets the noonday demons around here. Perhaps some nightflower will be just the cure.'

Arden didn't know why she pained at hearing Chalice would not be around. Chalice always spent the nightshift asleep – it wasn't as if she would miss the stormbride's company. The instruments foretold calm weather, no need for the woman to stay.

And yet, Arden did not want to spend the night-time staring between the Riven compound and the horizon where the Sainted Isles lay. She feared him leaving, and what that meant. Like he'd said, he had not thought much of Bellis until seeing Arden. Now with the memory of a kiss burning his lips, would the night bring urges and pining for the love he'd never consummated? The what might-have-been would crowd his memories. He would board his boat, sail towards the horizon to his woman beyond the waves.

We cannot force Mr Riven to join his wife, but perhaps you can remind him of what he misses.

Jealousy was a sin, a terrible sin. Tonight of all nights she needed company and a friendly ear. Even if it was Chalice.

Fleetingly, Arden debated on telling Chalice to stay, then decided it a mean-spirited request. Was obviously not for the plant-harvesting Arden's stormbride was spending a night in Vigil. She gave Chalice as benevolent a smile as she could. 'Enjoy your night hunting mandrakes and night-blooming things.'

For all her ill timing, Chalice was not ignorant of her Lightmistress' sorrows. 'Now are you sure you will be all right? Last night was a trial for you.'

'I will manage well enough. Oh, and I saw Gregor Tallwater doing Harrow muscle work, behind the Black Rosette. Doing it, but not enjoying it. If you cross his path tell him I don't feel badly towards him for this morning's unfortunate altercation. It can't be the best life, working for Mr Harrow.'

'Not much money in grunt enslavement, if it is a Harrow doing the paying,' Chalice said impishly. 'At least we can put aside our previous concerns of our shipwrecked foundlings making an illegal run to the Sainted Isles. They'd need more than pittance wages to pay for a boat out past the permanent storm.'

'His children have a better chance of surviving here than they would over there.'

Chalice darted forward and kissed Arden on the cheek. She smelled of pennyroyal mints and a herbal liquorice: comfort and authority at once. 'There will be yet a few weeks before the first of the Deepwater festivals, and winter. The ashes and leaves augur well for a fair season, then you can go home to Lyonne. I know this place has been a trial.'

'Made better with you.'

Arden hugged her stormbride back and let her go.

Approaching dusk made her maudlin sometimes, and tonight more than most. As she had told Mr Riven, Arden's mother had been an airship pilot before her death at the sword-hands of Summerland pirates. Arden's understanding of the climes might not have been a blood talent, but her inherited instincts were strong all the same.

There was a storm coming. Arden grumbled to herself and tapped the recalcitrant barometric tubes, which had spuriously committed themselves to fine weather right until the entire sky became overcast. Once they begrudgingly gave correct measurements, she went up upon the lamp-room gantry and checked the glass.

For the first time in years Arden recalled the woman she remembered only in fleeting, sightless moments. A smell of jasmine, a visceral memory of being embraced. Pale blonde hair as soft and billowy as a dandelion flower against her cheek, hair so different from her own. The blurred mother murmured promise of her return, soon, soon.

And the thick scent that came with her mother's departure. *It's only a little rain, my darling, only a few little days. Will you be good and wait for me to come back from Vinland? I'll bring a rubber dolly and diamond ring for my favourite girl.*

It had fallen to Jorgen Beacon to tell Arden, when Lucian was too bound in grief to speak. Her father's visiting younger brother, with his thin, smudged face, moustache so spiky and severe.

Your mother has gone, girl. She will never come home.

The high sea licked over the wooden pier as Arden watched *Fine Breeze* sail away into the aged day. Her instincts for trouble were not Beacon-born. They flitted in and out of her awareness, never quite real, but never completely absent. The cold wind chased her skirts, pressed against her bones like a great friendly animal.

'Calm yourself, Arden Beacon,' Arden said to herself. 'It is only the weather, and the changing seasons.'

She retired inside the lighthouse and prepared her first watch of the evening. Her spyglass showed no flags upon the Vigil message pole, or messages telegraphed in light from the Harbourmistress. There were no flotillas of prospectors, just the lone grey silhouette of a lich-ship, that automatic coffin-vessel forever winding back and forth from the rockblood wells of the Sainted Isles to the refineries of Dead Man's Bay.

By sundown a gale came up, and properly so. The fishing boats did not return to harbour, for they would sail north to miss the worst of the storm cell.

There was, however, *Fine Breeze*, bobbing gamely through the sleety bluster.

'Chalice,' she scolded under her breath. 'It's nearly dark. What are you coming back for in this wind?'

Her stormbride would be cold and wet when she got in.

Arden went to load up the fire, and put a kettle to boil for tea, muttering her practice rant. How could Chalice be so foolish? If she'd had an argument with Mr Sage on the correct way to pull up a weed by lamplight, then she should have stayed in one of the guest rooms at the tavern. No need for Chalice to make her way back here.

'By the graces of all the devils,' she called down the tower as the door opened to let the wet occupant in. 'Chalice, I thought you were more sensible than this.'

She ran down the stairs with a blanket in one hand, a cold-fire lantern in the other. Nearly got to the bottom before a great loom of trouble came over her. She stopped, one foot hovering above the final shadowy landing, watching the light and dark flicker below.

Deep senses, lantern keeper's senses, the ones that told of the shift in a current, or the shape in the fog, now told her that it wasn't Chalice downstairs. Too many people. The lantern-light skipped and swam over the concave walls.

She turned to run, but too late, for the intruders who had come into the lighthouse had secured a head start. In the snuffling twilight where the lit lamps and the dark warred between each other, she did not see them until one seized her about her legs and pulled her down onto a landing. She fell, mere inches from splitting her head open on the iron stair-rise behind her.

She thought, *I will leap up to my feet, I will kick him*, but the caustic smell of ether and the awful nothingness that rose up to greet her were stronger than her will and Arden fell into a whirling, punch-drunken night.

21

I just wish you didn't have to kill them

'. . . I just wish you didn't have to kill them. The boy and the woman.'

'Shut up, Sean. Hold the tube steady.'

'Still. Bad luck taints such a sin, even if the Magistrate himself permitted it . . .'

'Helena, stop that cripple's tattling, or so help me—'

Hushed murmurs, imploring. 'Sean, little brother, it's fine. We'll be long gone, oh my babies will forget us and our evil . . .'

'It's a sin . . .'

A scuffle followed, the sound of a landed punch and a cry in pain.

Then snuffled sobs, a woman's careful soothing.

Arden groaned, and the breath required to make such a sound hurt her. A pain throughout her body, her mouth cottoned, her head whirling still. She tested her arms, and they would not give. The tower was cold, the fire had gone out.

The woman's voice again. 'Leyland . . . She's waking up.'

'Hold her arm, it's hard enough getting the vein.'

A pain jagged sharp and centred now, in the crook of her

arm, which hung over the armrest of Jorgen's rocking chair.
And a face in the centre of her rapidly tunnelling vision, cragged
and pale. Leyland Tallwater. He smelled bad, the vinegar sweat
of a man in high crisis. She recognized the tight bun and Hillsider
features of Helena. The linen bandages that must have been
taken from Arden's kit now bound her tight to the chair. Her
heart beat fast in her chest. *Blood loss*, she thought with an
odd clarity. *I'm losing too much blood.*

Through the veil of her lashes she saw the needle in her arm,
almost black with clots, the metal lying hot and heavy upon
her skin as the snake in the Garden of Eden might do, after
feasting on the blood of . . .

. . . *no, wait, wrong story, why can I not think straight*, she
thought. *Speak to him, Arden. Make him stop.*

'Leyland,' the woman pleaded, 'this isn't right. Magistrate
Harrow was too insistent. It's a bad idea. I don't trust him.'

He ignored her, and strange again, Arden did not much care,
for a lassitude had filled her, a warmth rising and rising, her
eyesight almost vignetted in black clouds, a beautiful way to die.

Lucian Beacon appeared from the gloom of her past,
comforting his young daughter when she first saw a horse put
to sleep on the Cotton Wharf after a crane had snapped and
broken the poor creature's legs. Her father had let Arden press
her face into his chest, smell of clove-spice and lantern oil while
she heard the pitiful whinnying turn to snuffles and silence.

*She is not in pain, my darling. The most humane way to
kill an animal is by bleeding them out*, her father in her mind
told her.

Her heart had not the blood to pump, went into a fluttery
tachycardia, and she imagined herself back in the moot of her
third trial, the rebuilt royal Wharf and the test cubes all lined
up with the thickest glass, each cube as thick as three encyclo-
pedias bound together . . .

She forced herself back into the present, scared of drowning
in the bituminous murk of time. If she disappeared, she would
be gone forever.

Convince them, Arden. Convince them not to take this path . . .

If the patriarch would not speak, then maybe the woman who lingered nearby would.

'Helena,' Arden implored breathlessly, 'tell him to stop.'

Helena, or the blurry shape that was most probably the Tallwater wife, waited for her expressionless father-in-law's approval before saying apologetically, 'We need to buy our way onto the Islands, Lightmistress. It is imperative we do this. A penny for the Old Guy. Your blood . . . They say a pint of incendiary *ignis* blood is worth its weight in gold. The Magistrate said so.'

'But it won't work. My blood . . . I'm *malorum*, not strong . . .'

Leyland did not pause in his work. 'Helena,' he warned. 'Stop talking to her.'

Helena withdrew out of sight. 'She's dying, Leyland. It's wrong to kill, even one of *them*.'

'Do you think I care, woman?' He tightened a belt at Arden's bicep. 'Here. It's full. Put it with the others.'

Arden heard the scratch of a metal lid on a glass thread, saw in the vision-tunnel Helena Tallwater slide the mason jar into a crate of similarly filled containers. In a quirk of reasoning she counted a full crate. Three jars were already dark with congealing blood.

Arden gathered enough spit to say with all the corrosive effort she could muster, 'Were your grandchildren's bodies not enough for coin, Leyland Tallwater?'

Leyland glanced away. Oh, he had tried it, tried it! Had offered all three most probably, and in the Black Rosette they'd have cursed him, and kicked him out.

Then Mr Harrow would have come, pickled with revenge and grieving. *'I have a solution for your problems. Take a boat to the lighthouse. A pint of sanguis blood will get you passage to the rockblood isles.'*

'You people with your contaminated blood, your sin, your

cheap labour,' Leyland Tallwater growled. 'The sins of the world are upon you. It is a good thing, to allow you to die.'

He released the tourniquet. Her blood leapt into the jar.

No

No

No

She might as well have said no to death. The vision-tunnel closed. The pain left her. She was floating now, with the old devil, with death.

Death who smelled of salt and kraken oil, death who said her name through a cave of utter darkness, *Arden, Arden, oh God*.

No.

22

I saw him passing

death

Death, who scooped her up in his arms and took her into the storm.

death

Death, who took her to the water's edge, yelling her name, telling her to wake, to wake, to stay awake by the devil and the deep blue sea.

death

This was not a watery hell, but a tempest surrounding her, this was the water come alive from the monstrous call of blood, this was the story they told of the Rivens on the promontory who were half-kraken, half-man, spawned in unholy congress with the monsters of the deep.

Save her, a voice screamed into the storm. *Save her*.

Mr Justinian saying, *I've seen him take the corpses from the beach. Caught him in the act.*

Her bloodied dress torn off by the ocean. A venom flowing into her, replacing what the Tallwaters had taken, filling her with a brutal vigour, not blood, but something else. She jerked and shuddered in the arms of Jonah Riven.

She gave herself over to wildness, was beset by a hunger that

249

burned through her, and in the tempest of the storm she clawed open Mr Riven's shirt, went to kiss him upon the sparse rough hair of his pale broad chest, the straining cords of his neck, the hollow of his throat, she wanted him with an urgency she had never wanted anything before.

'Arden, it is the storm,' he protested, but could he not feel it, could he not be a part of this terrible ritual that had yanked her back from the precipice of—

death?

And he could not contain himself for they were both awash in the surge and with a cry of despair he gave in to the moment. He returned Arden's kisses with hard, angry, inexperienced kisses of his own, tore away the silk that bound her breasts and sucked electrical sparks of pleasure from her skin and nipples with a mouth that knew nothing of a woman's body except what instinct gave him. They fell against the stony shore in a desperate embrace, riven by inhuman passions, raw ichor, blood and all the combined essence of the ungodly creatures summoned from the benthic horrors below.

Arden tore at the last of her undergarments before pushing down the kraken leather strides of Jonah Riven, clutched him close, ground her quim against the curled hair of him, dizzy with savagery. He was hot and proud, the thing that would bring her such relief, he slid reflexively along the channel of her thighs before pushing inside her with such a rush of sensation she cried out from it and he froze, said her name, his face with desolate surrender.

'*Gods, if you wish for me to stop, I will, I will . . .*'

But she couldn't stop. She wanted to speak. A small horrified part of her wanted to say, Jonah, you are right, this is not us, this is not me. But the monster he had summoned only wanted satiety, wanted the one who had called it from darkness, and he smelled so good and he smelled of blood and salt and skin, and she embraced him among the stones of the beach and each time he plunged into her body the storm-sea heaved about them in turn. He clung to her as a drowning man might fight an ocean for driftwood, thrust clumsily upwards again and again, following an instinct as old as time but no less terrible. His belly slapped against hers as his rhythm increased in urgency. She accepted him in all ways, inside her body, his chest rasping against her own, the heat of his exposed throat. Spent himself, hot, hot, into her cold body. The phosphorescence of the water around them became clear and he beheld her with such a vaulting, desperate emotion.

The moment passed in fits and starts. His strength left him he shuddered and fell away, still gasping for breath. She reached for his hand and he grasped hers.

They lay there in the cold lip of the shore as the rain fell upon their naked bodies and the monster, the old devil himself, withdrew, having done the thing the blood-bound man had asked of him and saved the woman he . . .

Book Three: Blood

23

Sing to me

Sing to me, love
Of all that was
When once we walked upon golden fields
Sing the sky, love
Sing down the stars
My virtue will be your reward.

Silly old song. Arden had never cared for it. The gramophone scratched as the record ended. She could hear it in the next room. A hand wound it up again, and another record of much the same kind of music began playing again.

But maybe Mr Riven considered the song a favourite. In which case, she did not mind. She hadn't considered him romantic before. It didn't quite fit with the brutish idea she had formed of him in those months separated. In a way, she rather welcomed this new material in her patchwork image of the man.

Shadows dabbled across Arden's eyelids, sunlight hitting the surface of water. Through her closed eyelids she sensed dawn light, with all the colour of fire. She could smell kraken oil and aromatic ashes, a pleasant ambergris perfume not so far away, a more utilitarian soap, old wood, and her own body, a crust of blood and organic matter over smouldering embers.

Her senses were more alive then than they had ever been. Her legs slipped in a nightdress of silk, her feet in between cotton sheets. She rolled over and the hedonistic warmth gave way to her injuries. Arden touched herself carefully, explored the abrasions between her legs and the tenderness between her thighs.

Well then, no fever-dream, what had happened the night before. The insides of her thighs smarted terribly, but not as much as the crook of her—

Arm

'Devilment!'

Arden sat up with a gasp, clawing at her memory of tubing and touched nothing except the ghost of a bruise.

She had been deposited into the chintzy surrounds of an unfamiliar room. A feminine room, bedecked in creature comforts and faded pastel colours, patterns that were nearly white where the morning sunlight hit them day in and day out.

Bellis, Arden thought. She had stayed here once. Before that, another woman's room, maybe generations of women, who had knitted the bed covers and crocheted the curtains, had embroidered a tapestry on the wall, where krakens and plesiosaur frolicked about an archipelago of islands.

The Sainted Isles. The birthplace of the Rivens.

The bed was narrow, befitting a girl and not a wife. A single bed, with a *Stella Maris* star above the plain bedhead. Upon the yellowing crochet of the side table, a Fiction Vulgate Bible bound in fish-skin. Her goose-down pillow still felt damp from the towel that must have bound up her salted hair. The simple nightdress clothed her inside out and back-to-front.

Wincing from her bruises she climbed out of bed and moved for the door.

The music came from behind it, and suddenly it made Arden nervous. She had shared something miraculous and dangerous with Jonah Riven. Had known him intimately.

'Jo—'

The door opened, and the Harbourmistress' son, David, stood there with a porcelain water-jug and a string bag full of clothes.

'Oh . . . David,' she corrected herself. 'Mr Modhi. I thought Mr Riven would be the one to greet me.'

'Goodness, Mx Beacon, Lightmistress,' the Harbourmistress' boy stammered, trying to avert his gaze, for the raw silk nightdress was threadbare and tight. 'I didn't mean to wake you up, Mr Riven said you would sleep more and that I should bring you some clothes and a jug of hot water to, *um*. To wash.'

'Give it here,' she said, her early-morning fancies dashed into reality.

'Be careful of the jug, the water's hot. I boiled it only a few minutes ago.'

'I will be careful.'

'There's a bath, but Mr Riven says it takes a long time to stoke the boiler. You'll need to make do with this for now. Call if you need more . . .'

Arden flashed him an impatient smile and closed the door.

She retreated into the room. Sure enough, a small, simple bathroom adjoined the bedroom. It had a claw-footed bath that – from the maker's mark on the enamel – had long been appropriated from a much fancier Clay hotel. To top off the small luxuries there was even a halfway-modern water closet that actually flushed. Arden wanted to weep with the joy of facilities that were not in essence holes in the ground.

All this was here, and she had imagined Mr Riven living in a ruin!

She washed herself as best she could, the salt from under her arms, her throat and hair, between her breasts and legs, tried not to think of Jonah Riven there, his hands his mouth, his yearning body, and found no true pleasure in the thought, for his act wove a coarse thread through the warp and weft of the Tallwaters' attack.

It is the remains of the night, she told herself. *Whatever poison had brought me back from near death, it still courses through me.*

Clean as she could possibly be in the circumstances, Arden emptied out the string bag on her bed.

A never-worn lady's bloomers and chemise, slippery with salmon-coloured silk, still with faded Clay Capital shop-tags tied with string. Not her size, of course, they would fit tight rather than loose as intended. She wondered who they'd been bought for in the beginning? Maybe not Bellis, they seemed last century's fashion. Another woman perhaps, one who had died.

The dress, though, belonged to Arden. The best blue one from her signal-keeper's graduation, torn away by the sea on that day she had come to find Mr Riven with the plesiosaur child. She rubbed the broadcloth against her cheek, before sliding the dress over her head, fastening the release-panels back into their origami of folded fabric, and pulling on her borrowed shoes.

The rest of the lodge was constructed from the same basalt stone as the church ruins, and simple in its layout, so it took Arden very little time to locate Mr Riven in the stone kitchen, shirtless, back to her, trying to sew together a split eyebrow in a slice of morning sun. The piece of silvered mirror before him reflected his face back to her, but was too tarnished for him to see where he should go with the needle. His hands shook with exhaustion.

She considered the mottled skin of his half-tattooed back, the chevrons following his spine. Whatever healing had been done to her, it had taken a toll on him.

'Do you want some help?'

He turned to Arden. Bruise popping in the hollow of his eye, one cheek hard and white.

Arden ran her hands nervously though her thick dark curls, suddenly aware how different she must be to Bellis Harrow, the dissonance she must present to Jonah Riven, and then hated that she should care.

'I'm not being vain with such a tiny injury,' he said, holding the offending needle in front of him. 'I've decided I'd rather not be quite as fearsome as I'm made out.'

'It would take more than a cut to make you fearsome, I'm afraid.'

He poked at his eye with the needle once again, and she sighed.

'Oh, give it here. You'll make yourself blind. I might be rubbish with a needle but at least I can see what I'm doing. Come, sit.'

He did so, and she laid her hand on his warm shoulder, and the night came back to her in flashes of lightning and breath. He trembled beneath her touch, the terror of a wild thing cornered.

'Head back,' she said. 'Careful now, the iodine will sting.'

The crown of his head against her belly, and like it had been when she had tended the wounds at his chest, he did not wince at the needle's entry. Older scars pocked his brow. His lost expression reminded her of a child, a pale craggy child, asleep to fever dreams. She would have caressed the bad thoughts away had their relationship followed such warm currents, but the union had been consummated in violence, and they were in the cool frost now.

A pair of neat stitches in his brow, and ends clipped with a small knife. A daub of antiseptic honey and brown paper.

'There,' she quipped with pathetic humour. 'You are beautiful again.'

'And you've recovered.'

'David is alive too. It's been a busy night for all of us.'

'He's tougher than he seems. From what he said the Tallwaters took both him and your stormbride from the harbour in your boat.'

'Oh! Mr Riven, I didn't realize. He never said . . .'

'The lad's modest, I'll give him that. Escaped them and made his way onto shore to raise the alarm. He might not have blood talent, but he's an excellent swimmer.'

'And Chalice Quarry? They took her too?'

259

Mr Riven shook his head. 'David says she jumped from the boat first. She was bound, hand and foot, and sunk like a stone. I'm sorry.'

Arden twined her fingers together and fought down a wave of anxious illness. Without Chalice she would be utterly alone. 'Oh. Chalice. Oh.'

Upright, he pulled a bubbling kettle from the stove and poured tea into enamel cups. She smelled ginger and coast-sedge, the aroma of the saltwood shavings in the fireplace, and Mr Riven's warm skin. Pleasant smells, yet with the probability of Chalice's death they were perfumes of despair.

'If it helps, when the tide turns *Saudade* will be free of the kraken dock. I can take you to Mx Modhi. I must return her son, anyway. If by chance your stormbride made . . .' he drifted off, not wanting to give her false hope. 'Whatever happened, we will find out for certain.'

'Thank you.' She heaved a breath, to calm herself so she might think usefully rather than all a-jangle. She took the offered cup of tea. 'There's a full story in last night, Mr Riven. They were stealing my blood.'

'*Penny for the Old Guy.* Passage onto one of the islands.'

'I don't remember all of what they said, but it sounded . . . it sounded as if *Mr Harrow* had suggested it.'

Mr Riven would not meet her gaze. 'Then it was not personal. He was trying to hurt me through you. The Tallwaters were merely an opportunity. Incendiary blood is worth more than kraken oil in some places.'

'Not *my* dim blood. They'll find that out soon enough.' She paused. Gathered her thoughts and said shyly, 'Then you put me in the water with the kraken. Or some . . . thing? I felt it. I felt myself dead, and coming back.'

A movement outside the bay window captured his attention more than anything in this kitchen. The delicate light made him fragile, fine-boned. His skin was pale as a cuttlefish skeleton, his body dreadfully vulnerable despite Mr Riven's Fictish vigour and the terrifying ink. The memory of the night wrapped around them in Sargasso strands, strangling them, pulling them into dark, sunless places.

'*Aequor profundum.* My mother called it *the trick*. She used it once, on my uncle when a bar fight nearly killed him, and I heard it rumoured . . . she brought my cousin Jeremiah back from the dead when he was attacked by a *maris anguis* on his initiation day. A sea-serpent bit him almost in half. Many a time I wished it had finished the job.'

Arden pondered on what he's told her. 'Healing someone from that bad an injury . . . it's a sanguinity, Jonah!'

'It's a shadow sanguinity,' he corrected her. 'Monstercalling is our talent.'

'Yes, but an endowment like that on top of what you already have . . . why, something like that would have the Eugenics Society all over it. They'd either collect everyone up to Lyonne or . . .'

She trailed off.

Or.

She did not want to say it, because it was impossible. The *or* that had suddenly come to her was *death*. The *or* was an entire family killed in a night and the blame placed on a child meant to die in a Harbinger Bay hulk prison.

But even that conclusion made no sense to her. A healing talent was harmless. Shadows and permutations were unwanted, but never engendered more than sterilization, at the most. Certainly, shadows spoiled the ledgers, interrupted the inheritance line, but the Eugenics Society were pragmatic about the necessity of evolution. If something new and useful were to appear in the sanguineous lineages, it would come first as a shadow. If it were dangerous in the way most useful talents were, then they'd find ways to manage the risk.

She could think of nothing so hazardous that an entire bloodline should be wiped out.

Mr Riven studied her. 'You're trying to find an excuse.'

'Excuse me?'

'An excuse, for what I did to them. When I killed my family. Hoping the blame is elsewhere, on Lyonne. But it's not, Arden.

The blame is mine. I was young, I had no control over my talent, and they all died. That is what I live with.'

'I wasn't . . .' she started, then took a breath. 'How often have you used this *aequor profundum*?'

He frowned. 'Not often. I never had a skill at it like Thalie did. The biggest thing was the plesiosaur pup.'

'Yes, the pup! I saw it that day, on the beach when I had almost drowned.'

A blush appeared on his neck and cheeks, as he remembered her in her gold silks. 'I'm sorry, what I did last night. It was a violation. But it never felt so strong as last night, when I used it on you.'

'Are you ashamed of saving my life?'

'No. Of course not.'

'Then why speak of it as sin and not miracle? What you did was miraculous, was epic and wonderful and incredible and can I not just thank you for that? Why must it be so difficult?' She laid her hand on his. 'Jonah, I want to thank you.'

He took her hand and gently placed it away.

'You are alive. I need no gratitude. But we cannot deceive ourselves by thinking there was any emotional truth in what happened when I brought you back.'

The moment had passed. Mr Riven had thrown up a wall about himself, and busied himself with his shirt and his boots.

Arden needed to get away. 'I will wait at the dock for the tide to come up. It's too stuffy in here.'

'All right.'

She pretended to leave casually, but once out in the quad-rangle had to sit and gulp deep breaths. Was not love or desire that had moved Mr Riven to take her upon the beach, only an urge in his blood like Bellis towards her petrolactose islands, a deceptive instinct. He felt nothing towards Arden at all.

The morning sun had been but a fleeting apparition of a pleasant day. Outside, the clouds returned in slabby formations, grey and formless as the rock of the promontory, and the wind blustered about with an old crone's natter.

Chief waddled up to her on arthritic legs, snuffling his grey snout at her skirt hem.

'I have nothing for you, pup,' she said. 'If I had known, I'd have waited until your master cooked his breakfast before leaving.'

'Ah, he's already had a feed, the little reprobate.'

She had not noticed David Modhi nearby. The youth wore some cast-off Riven clothes that dangled off his thin shoulders. Behind him, upon a washing line, the dress from last night hung on a recycled line of telegraph cable.

'Earning your keep with the laundry, I see?'

He gave a self-conscious gasp. 'Oh Mx Beacon, I didn't see you naked . . . in any disgraceful way. After Mr Riven took you off the beach he, *um*, tended you with the door shut.'

'It is no concern. It really is not.' She re-tied her belt, and gathered her strength for her conversation ahead. 'So tell me. How did the Tallwaters come to have my boat?'

'Yesterday afternoon,' he said. 'I saw them in the harbour. Just hanging about. I should have known some nefariousness was afoot earlier. I sometimes talk to Sean Ironcup on the eventide, and normally he is a fine conversationalist, but yesterday . . .' David sighed and shrugged. 'Sean seemed distracted. I would even say ashamed almost, as if he did not wish to be seen with me.

'I could not find Mother anywhere, and at the time I was glad of it. She doesn't trust the Tallwaters, and doesn't like me talking to Sean.'

'But she still must have impressed some suspicion on you, David.'

'Yes. I saw the senior Tallwater and Captain Cormack speaking with each other. Deviously. Making a deal. I heard your name. I suspected they were up to no good.' He dipped his head, blushed again. 'I meddled with Captain Cormack's ship. They were going to hire it and I scuppered the engine before anyone could be the wiser.'

'Quick thinking, Mr Modhi.'

'It didn't work. I hadn't thought it through. They saw Miss Quarry come into harbour and decided to take *Fine Breeze* instead. I can't remember much of the rest, only waking in the bilge well of *Fine Breeze,* a prisoner, with Chalice. Sean made apologies, but he is in thrall to Leyland Tallwater. They all do what he says.'

'And Chalice? What happened to her?'

'Um.' He frowned. 'We listened to them talk for a while. They intended to exchange us for some payment in the Isles.' David's eyes shone. 'Blood or enslavement, one or the other. Devils. Miss Quarry jumped into the water fully bound rather than contemplate such a thing as slavery. I was not brave enough at first. Afterwards Sean Ironcup retied my bonds loose enough to slip. I waited until we got close to the promontory shore before I bailed.'

'You were still brave, lad. It is just as brave to wait and get a better sense of the situation. You are alive and Chalice is—'

A ferocious clanging from the waterfront interrupted their talk, and Arden winced. Whatever could have made such an inopportune noise?

A dark shape loomed through the sea-fog. The wrong shape for a boat, and yet familiar all the same.

'What is that coming in to the pier, David Modhi? Even I can't work it out.'

David didn't wait. He took off in a run. The fog congealed and shivered as Arden followed him down the rocky path to the promontory dock. The clanging grew louder, and now Arden could discern the distinct shape of a gable roof and a large whitewashed sign.

A sign bearing the words *VIGIL HARBOUR.*

David reached the dock first. He did not show the same surprise as Arden did, and watched with weary defeat as the entire harbourside of Vigil carved through the water towards the promontory shore.

'Why, Master Modhi, is that your mother's houseboat adrift with half the harbour with it?'

A chorus of signal buoys clanged piteously, having been swept up along the unstoppable force of a hundred feet of pontoons, while decking and glass floaters and at least a dozen skiffs and dinghies dragged along behind in an ignominious bridal train.

His upper lip and baby moustache trembled. 'Mother has come.'

'And she brought her responsibilities with her!' Arden seized up a coil of rope. 'Quick, David, help the juggernaut dock or it'll overshoot us and head into the cliff.'

David ran down the long length of the jetty, stopping only to make certain Arden could keep up, before sprinting off again. The fog came with them, turning the world white. The house-boat bell rang through the pea soup. Arden took the coil from David, tossing it out to the dark-hooded figure leaning out of the window of the houseboat.

'Got it!' a familiar voice barked. 'We're pulling her in.'

Suddenly Arden saw the figure in the window, the red hair, the stout shoulders.

'Chalice!' Arden held out her hand, gasping, and the hood reappeared, with Chalice's dear freckled face beneath it. Their fingers met and clasped.

'You're alive, Arden?' Chalice could not have been more startled if a spectre had made an appearance on the dock. 'Alive and not a ghost? Oh my, I feared the worst!'

'Mr Riven saved me!'

'Ah now, that is good,' she said somewhat uncertainly.

Once David secured the houseboat, Mx Modhi came out of the wheelhouse in a flurry of denim, waxcloth and a sou'wester upon her frowsy grey hair. She grabbed her tall son's head, clutched him down to her massive bosom to rub his back and murmur affectionate things, and David swooned in his mother's love.

'I didn't know our house could move, Mama,' he muffled into Mx Modhi's breast.

'Kraken oil will get anything moving,' the Harbourmistress replied. 'And those reprobates that kidnapped you would have experienced the full extent of my ire had I caught them! After all the liniment I wasted on that brother? Why, they even left their children behind in their rush to get to the Islands. Three little orphans now.'

'I'm so sorry about losing your boat, Arden,' Chalice said as she climbed onto the pier. 'I was rather outnumbered, so fell back on my one useful skill of slipping knots.'

'Boats can be replaced. The priority is that we are all safe and well. And you, Chalice! I am pleased to see you, so very much!'

'Darling, you are whole and untouched! I nearly had conniptions, hearing them talk,' Chalice said. 'How they intended to take your blood. *All of it.*' Chalice took Arden's shoulders and gazed upon her with such fiercely relieved emotion, in any other circumstances Arden would have thought Chalice in love. 'I believed I would come here to find you dead and drained, and my heart was breaking. I didn't know what to do. But look, not a scratch!'

'Chalice, you find me more alive than ever.'

'I've never been so happy to be wrong. By the devils, I hope the Tallwaters meet their maker with an eternal debt.'

Arden shrugged. 'Seems a Tallwater trait. Making bad decisions without thinking it through. Six pints they might have taken from me, but all they'll get is some dim *malorum* blood that will barely feed a flame. The Old Guy won't get a penny.'

Chalice dropped her hands.

'What?'

Arden blinked. 'Six pints . . . Or four. I can't quite remember. It seems a lot, it does! But as I said, Mr Riven rescued me. Some . . . ah, local folk medicine.' She declined to say more, as a protective feeling encouraged her to silence. 'As much as it's uncharitable to wish harm on those wretched fools, the Islanders will punish them well enough when they discover the rotten deal they've made.'

Arden expected Chalice to nod with the same agreement and joy. In fact, she would have expected any other reaction except for Chalice to turn an odd shade of green, open then close her mouth speechlessly. When at last words came out she croaked, 'Devils, did you say they took six *pints*?'

'Chalice, whatever is the matter?'

Chalice gave a grimace, too shocked to be entirely coherent. She grabbed Arden's wrist, hard enough to hurt, and thrust up the sleeves on her dress. The needle marks were still there, faint from her impromptu miracle.

'Oh no . . .'

Arden yanked her arm away from the stormbride's manhandling. 'Stop it! This is most unpleasant.'

Mx Modhi let out a rumble of disapproval. 'The thieves bled her. Well, here is an unmitigated disaster.'

'Why is it a disaster?' Arden snapped. 'It's only *malorum* blood. It's of no danger to anyone except the fools who want to trade it.'

Chalice clutched the hair at her temples, shook out her hands, looked about as if the solution to her crisis could only come in the form of a miracle. 'By God. By *God*. We should *never* have sent you here.'

A familiar loom of disaster came upon Arden. All of a sudden she didn't want to ask what it was that afflicted Chalice so. Her deep familial sense for trouble weighted like stones in her belly.

Mx Modhi dug her pipe out of her dress pocket, packed the bowl with tobacco with the insouciant submission of a deckhand having been told that the ship is about to founder after he has spent the day being ignored about the leak.

'Go on then, Quarry,' the Harbourmistress drawled. 'You might as well tell the woman. Mr Lindsay will tell her himself soon before he has to put his own head on the disciplinary chopping block.'

'Tell me *what*? And how do *you* know Mr Lindsay, either of you?'

Cornered now, Chalice reluctantly pulled the pewter Guild

triangle from around her neck. The metal moved on a hinge. Her coin began as triangular locket, the symbol of her assistant profession.

Once flipped about, the triangle became a rose crucified upon thorns.

A rose on thorns, just like the pin Mr Lindsay wore. Just like the bands on the messenger pigeons in the roost. Symbol of the Lyonne Order and Nomenclatures, forever pruning, forever gardening.

Arden recoiled from Chalice as if she'd been knocked sideways.

'Chalice . . . you're a Lion?'

24

Do they know

Do they know how he healed me? was her first thought. *Have I just said too much about him?*

'All right. I am a Lion. Mx Modhi is a local agent,' Chalice said faintly, not that Arden was in a mood to appreciate the differences. 'She's been here a long time, keeping an eye on things for us.'

'Oh, really now.'

'And well,' Chalice said, distraught and awkward at her sudden unveiling, 'and well, this thing that has happened to you, this blood-theft, it's quite unexpected. It wasn't supposed to happen. We will handle it, of course. It can't be helped. But your placement here is ended, I'm sorry.'

'Excuse me, did you say *ended*?'

'Yes, Mx Modi can take you back to Garfish Point. You can be on a train back to Clay tonight.'

Arden reeled back, stunned from Chalice's unveiling, and the urgency of her. 'I'm not leaving, Chalice. The flame still needs me—'

'It wasn't for flame you were here! You completed your duty, but the blood . . . the missing blood is a complication we must deal with ourselves. It is safer for you to be home while we fix it up.'

'Why?'

'You just are. Safer. Please darling, the more questions you ask, the more at risk you will be.'

Arden's chest squeezed painfully as if enclosed by a mighty fist, and her breath came out in a wheeze. Was this her own leash being tightened? She would not have it.

'I'm not leaving just because you say so, Order Coin or not. The Order doesn't control my lighthouse. It's the Seamaster's Guild who do that, and I see no Guild*master* here.'

Harbourmistress Modhi chewed upon the goat-horn stem of her pipe as if in a pendulum swing between extremely bored and frightfully annoyed. 'Huh, I knew this would happen, Quarry.'

'What?' Arden snapped at her.

'Postmaster Harrow was in a state all day,' the Harbourmistress said. 'You must have riled him up good and proper with your lustful gallivanting with Mr Riven, for him to suggest that the Tallwaters do what they did. The worst possible scenario.'

'Then have the Order send *Mr Harrow* away in punishment!' Arden snapped at them. 'Or does he control the Lions when it comes to murder just like he controlled them when it came to his daughter?'

She pretended to brush a loose strand of hair from her face. Was in reality the tears of frustration and anger. She had probably just condemned Mr Riven to the Lions, all but confirming his shadow sympathies. They'd have him sent for a castration, have him returned to this coast neutered, like a show-dog born with a confirmation defect.

She turned around and stomped away, unable to bear looking at her deceitful stormbride.

Who was not a stormbride at all.

Chalice ran after Arden, her Order medallion clinking around its hinge. 'Arden! Please, darling, listen to me. I meant what I said. It's all gone wrong, we should never have sent you here. But you were the only one who could perhaps break through Mr Riven's defences around Bellis. Others have tried and failed, you were our final chance!'

'You should have sent a *whore*!' Arden shouted back. She tore off the krakenskin coat, threw it on the ground so the eyes winked up at her in the dull day. 'Then Mr Justinian could gloat about *two* murdered whores!'

Chalice stumbled behind in a punch-drunken trot. Arden moved too quickly up the slope to the lighthouse for Chalice to catch up. She remained outside while Arden made a deliberately slow and thorough check on the measuring instruments and the flame of her misbegotten tower, and shed angry tears all over the ledger paper, making the ink run where they fell.

'Please, let me fully explain what is happening here,' Chalice pleaded up the column from the doorway, her voice echoing off the walls.

'You just wait your turn!' Arden yelled back. 'The Lyonne Order can just wait before they prostitute me out for another trick.'

'They are not—'

'Lies! Lies, Chalice, why the Order brought me here like bait-meat for my neighbour's memory. It was worse that you lied about it yourself, for I *trusted* you!'

'I didn't know about that, darling! I didn't know!'

When Arden finished her duties and left her lighthouse, Chalice was not there.

The tattered semaphore flags snapped in the wind. A chain rattled against the flagpole. Arden found her stormbride sitting miserably on the cement base, head in her hands, rocking in her ballooning waxed canvas skirts. Arden's krakenskin lay across Chalice's knees. Against her chalky-white face, Chalice's hair had darkened with sea mist and sweat.

She had cried enough. Only a slow exhaustion upon her, and the cold.

Chalice held out the jacket. Arden put it back on.

'I thought you'd go back to your Lion business,' Arden grumped.

'Go back to what? My heart is broken. I care for you very much.'

'I wonder if you people really care, or just fret over the outcome of your conspiracy.'

'My love, I honestly didn't know what Mr Lindsay planned for you. All my orders were, look after the Lightmistress while she completes her task. You were at the gates of hell and harm here, and I was meant to keep you safe.'

'Well, you didn't do that very well, did you? I was attacked in my own lighthouse by people completely *not* Mr Riven, while you were entertaining Mr Sage and plucking herbs!'

'Was not Mr Riven I was meant to protect you from!' Chalice wailed back. 'I was to protect you from bloody *Bellis Riven*!'

After Chalice followed her unexpected disclosure with a little sob that was less sadness and more relief that she didn't have to pretend any more, the stormbride collected herself. Despite the seeming ridiculousness of her statement Arden felt pity enough towards her contrite traitor that she returned to the outdoor fireplaces and put the kettle on the stove. She bid that Chalice sit near the fire.

'So, if I have a cat-fight and roll around in the dirt with Jonah's wife you're to jump in and rescue me, then? She going to return and gossip about me to Mrs Sage in the market place, hmm?'

Chalice did not take kindly to mockery. 'It is no laughing matter. Bellis is not to be trifled with.'

'Ah, so she can manage herself. Mr Riven is not needed for her protection at all. For a moment Mr Lindsey almost had me fooled.'

Wearily, Chalice shrugged. 'I was not privy to such detail. Mr Lindsay gave me my duties and I did them as he asked,' Arden said bitterly. 'Humiliated myself. Forced by loneliness into love with a man who cannot love me back. But Mr Riven's wife is oblivious to my existence and I am as much concern to her as a butterfly flapping its wings on the other side of the world. So elucidate me on your cry of *protection*.'

Chalice swallowed, and spoke. 'You asked me once why the Eugenics Society allowed Bellis to stay in Vigil after she was tested *sanguis petrae*.'

'I did. Some guff about this being Fiction, and not Lyonne. And Mr Lindsay spun me a tale of gentle nurturing. But that wasn't the reason, was it?' She sucked a breath and recalled the words from Mr Riven's mouth. *There are exceptions.*

'No. It wasn't the reason. The Society didn't know what they wanted to do with Bellis once they realized what talent she *really* had.'

'So. Your golden princess had a good old Fiction shadow.'

'*Sanguis petrae was* the shadow. By her main talent, she trammelled something else.'

Though Arden had been told so much already, a fresh chill came upon her. *Something else.* The thing that made Bellis different. That kept her from going to Lyonne. That made her dangerous to Arden somehow, that she needed a Lion chaperone. 'Spit it out then. What did she have?'

'A thing so awful, that even the Society fears it, but wants very much as well. There have been many mutterings behind closed doors that I am not privy to.'

'A thing so awful,' Arden repeated dryly. She recalled her last witnessed dock accident with the *sanguis inertiae* and the careless worker who had walked into the halo of blood-forced air. Died so suddenly there had been no blood when the *inertia* tore him to pieces a second later. She'd spent an hour chasing off the stray dogs attempting to run off with body parts, while at the same time trying to calm the stunned young man who'd had his first fatality but not his last. 'A thing so awful to keep her here.'

'You think of death, Arden, but there are things that are worse. A thousand times worse! The Society were content for a while to leave her in the Sainted Isles. But a year ago a message came from our deepest agents. Something's happened to her. Something bad. They needed Mr Riven's assistance desperately. That's all I know.'

'Why not send the Lyonne Navy and protect Bellis Riven with a thousand guns and cannons if she's so bloody vulnerable?'

'Because she doesn't *need* protection. She needs *control.*

Because Jonah Riven was able to bring her back under sufferance before, he could do it again. It's not her safety he brings at all, it's her *compliance*.'

Arden breathed in a huge angry lungful of salt air. 'On. *Oh*. So there it is. Bellis is too independent for the puppet master's strings.'

'We will all be puppets, if by chance Bellis gets your blood. Because those jars are heading towards her now, with a bunch of Clay City Hillsiders with not an ounce of sense to call their own.'

Arden waved her off. 'Dim *ignis* blood is of no value to anyone. Why would it be of value to Bellis?'

'You are *sanguis malorum*,' Chalice said flatly.

'Well yes, but—'

'You are *sanguis malorum* in a family who have never, not once, bred without strong sanguine endowments, not even your priestly cousin for all he tried to hide it. Instead, your flame is scant. How does that happen? Whoever heard of a dim Beacon?'

'Stop.' Arden's voice was cold as her fire. 'Hush now, Chalice. I saw your face when you realized my blood had gone away with the Tallwaters. Even pure *ignis* serum would not inspire such terror.'

Chalice's cheeks were almost as red as her hair, and she cast a guilty glance in Arden's direction. 'Am I not allowed to speak?'

'I know what you are going to say. You will suggest to me that I too have a shadow, and this concerns you, as I am now in danger of whatever lies over that horizon. And I will reply, if I did have another endowment, it would have shown up in testing long ago and the Eugenics Society would certainly have put it to laborious use. But they didn't, because what I have is useless.'

Chalice looked at her, bleak. 'Would you like to know what it is you have?'

Arden snatched up a cloth and put the whistling kettle aside. Its strident cry faded to splutters. A heaviness in her. Grief, almost. She had suffered muchly being *sanguis malorum*, dim of light, but at least the little fire she had was a Beacon expression, a pure talent in an honourable ancestral line measured in centuries. She had been content, with her small blue flame, her skerrick of *sanguinem ignis*, she could call it her own.

Now even that confidence was muddied by the threat of a shadow, power cut in half, less than the sum of her parts. Her future dreams of work and meaning were corroding before her eyes. *She* was corroding.

'No, Chalice,' Arden said. 'I don't think I want to know. Because you are saying that my shadow endowment was never of any value to me or the Society, but of great use to another person more cherished than me, more loved and more free. To think my blood will give her freedom, but only commit me further into servitude . . . it hurts beyond meaning.'

'Darling you have . . .'

'No, don't say a single word.'

Chalice's translucent skin crimsoned. 'If Bellis receives your blood, she will want to know its source Arden.'

'The Sainted Islands cover an area as large as Fiction. There would be tens, hundreds of thousands of prospectors and indigenes there right this minute. How in all the wide expanse of ocean is my blood going to land in one missing woman's lap?'

'Postmaster Harrow knows his daughter is out there.'

'Excuse me? Postmaster Harrow yesterday spent ten minutes cursing Jonah for harming her!'

'But not for murdering her, am I right? That man steams open every letter and correspondence that comes in or out of this town. He listens on the telegraph every night. I don't care if Gertrude Modhi says she wrote to the Lyonne Offices in code for twenty years, a child could crack those missives. Everything we know, he knows!'

Chalice stood up, and pointed an accusing finger across the waves towards Vigil. 'Mr Harrow labours under the belief of the dutiful, battered daughter, fleeing from her cruel husband. He will trust that Bellis does not yet dwell in the abyssal court of the Deepwater King. He would have told the Tallwaters how to take your blood and how to find her.'

275

25

No

'No,' said a third voice.

They'd been so wrapped up in their private exchange, they had not heard Mr Riven's arrival at the lighthouse. By his face, he had heard everything. Arden saw his panic. She tried to head him off as he bore down on Chalice, fists balled.

'Jonah, wait.' Arden dashed between him and Chalice. 'She hasn't said she's going to do anything.'

'She's Lyonne Order,' Mr Riven rasped. 'They've experimented and assassinated and ruined lives for centuries. They will not make a sinner of Bellis. I will not allow it.'

'That's not what—'

'Arden,' Chalice said. 'Go back to the lighthouse. Let me deal with him.'

'You don't know Bellis, *Lion*.' Mr Riven's voice dropped to a growl. 'You treat her as a mad thing needing control but you don't know her.'

'Oh, but we *do* know her, Jonah Riven. *We do!*' Chalice shrieked back. 'Jonah Riven, do not imagine for one second we believed Bellis' sweet innocent face, her delicate lies, her mental fortitude against the endowment God cursed her with! From the very beginning we saw her true sympathies and *you*

276

enabled that, you supported her through the flowering of her abominations. *You!*'

'Chalice!' Arden shouted, too late to stop the words coming out of the woman's mouth, but Chalice, once started, could not be stopped.

'Your monstrous wife will not be much longer happy out there shuffling around some deserted island like a castaway!' Chalice continued at a wail. 'She'll not be content forever on the dregs of her power! She will turn her eyes towards Fiction, or Lyonne, and what will happen then? How deeply will her sin go? How deeply will it be your fault? More deaths upon your head, Mr Riven? More slaughter to your name?'

Mr Riven raised his fist, the whites of his eyes rolling in his face gone near-purple with rage.

'I would not strike a woman,' he said quietly, and if not for the cords straining at his neck he could have been giving confession at a church. 'Or a man less my size. But you, Madame Lion, I will say it again. You do not know Bellis. Nobody did. She was a good person and you people treated her like *shit*.'

'She would not have ever been in control of it, Mr Riven. Not ever, not even if she were a *saint*. Even you and your little healing tricks could not ever cure that wound festering in her mind. We kept her safe. We even let you out of prison so you would do your duty, and you still let her go!'

'I want you gone from this promontory, Lion,' Mr Riven said with such abyssal coldness Arden feared for his soul. No man could speak such banked-down fury without immolating on the spot. 'And gone from Vigil. All of you. You have forced this evil upon Bellis.'

'We will go only if you return to your wife and tighten the noose, Mr Riven,' Chalice said. 'Oh, don't whine that you've made a promise to stay here and leave her to her mendacities. Search your heart. You have felt it this last month, haven't you? Felt your longings sharpen, your desire for healing focus. Ever since we brought Arden Beacon here, and have you for once wondered why?'

Mr Riven's harsh gaze landed on Arden. He'd acknowledged much the same to her in Miss La Grange's boudoir.

'I never said anything,' Arden protested. 'I don't know what is going on!'

Mr Riven winced as if she'd betrayed his secret. He was a man in despair. Arden wanted to wrap her arms around him and take him down from that terrible precipice. *I did not mean for this to happen, whatever this is.*

She saw the decision in his face, the making up of his mind. 'No,' she said. 'Jonah, no. Don't go to Bellis, please.'

'I need to warn her. That blood of yours is a poison.'

Bleak and cold, he turned to leave. His strides outmatched hers. It took a while before she could catch up.

'Jonah. It's what the Lions want. To use you.' Her breaths came in short gasps. 'They would make a *slave master* of you.'

'Or will you be the master? You've *influenced* me. Somehow. I heard Miss Quarry say it. A wicked influence in your blood that Bellis must not get. Well, then. Go. Go find your safety. You've done enough damage.'

His rejection struck her as a blow. She wanted to protest her innocence, but he moved too fast to catch up, and she had to stop to catch her breath.

She barely noticed Chalice sliding alongside, speaking low and insistent.

'Arden, it is time. Mx Modhi has a boat ready.'

'No, Chalice. Don't speak to me.'

But the woman spoke despite Arden's insistence. 'Your watch here is ended, darling. We played with the fire of your shadow endowment, but we underestimated the risks of your presence when Bellis Riven was so close. Let us deal with the remains. Go on back to Vigil with Mx Modhi now, and back to Clay. You'll get your Guild degree, I promise. You'll get your airshipman lover, or any other thing you want.'

The words broke the spell. Arden turned to Chalice. 'You knew what was offered?'

'Yes.'

Arden held up a fist, clenched, daring her to come closer.

'Am I so easily manipulated, you Lion *witch*? Are these my strings? Well, I cut them now! They are cut!'

'I—'

'I'm not going home. And her name is Bellis-damn-*Harrow*. She is not a Riven. The marriage was a sham all along, and Jonah's just too damn honourable to realize it.'

Arden broke away and began to run. Chalice struggled to keep up. 'Wait, Arden, where are you going?'

Arden whirled, snarling. 'To stop him from doing something stupid. Whatever mendaciousness is going on here, he doesn't deserve that infliction.'

Arden didn't wait to hear Chalice's blessing. She hefted up her skirt hem and ran after Mr Riven.

'Jonah,' she yelled. 'Jonah, wait.'

The urgency of her footsteps made him slow down.

'What is it now?'

She gasped cold air, her lungs burning. 'Yes, there is something wicked in my blood. It was kept from me too. But we can still get the blood-jars back before they get anywhere close for any Islander to pick up. Whatever is in them, we won't endanger Bellis by letting them near her.'

'The Tallwaters already have an advantage of a day. It's almost enough.'

'If they're trying to get out to the Sainted Isles in *Fine Breeze*, they'll take nearly two days to do a trip that *Saudade* could make in less than one. You can get to them before anyone else does.'

'You'd wager ten hours on your uncle's boat?'

'*Fine Breeze* handles like a bathtub. Lyonne Hillsiders cannot sail from one side of a canal to the other without getting lost. I checked the currents earlier, they'll be pulled around the southern route, the long route along *Tempestas*. We have time.'

'The southern route?' His thoughts were so ferociously deep, even the air stilled around him.

'Check my instruments if you must. They are never wrong.'

279

He released a breath. 'All right. All right then. I trust your instruments.' He ran his hand through his shortened hair. 'We'll bring David Modhi,' he said. 'I need another experienced engineman if I'm going to run *Saudade* at full speed.' He turned and caught Chalice trying to make as unobtrusive an exit as possible. 'And you have a few martial tricks up your sleeve I would wager, Madame Lion. Willing enough to use them on me, before.'

Cornered, she protested vehemently. 'What, I'm not trained for that kind of fighting . . .!'

'I don't want that traitor coming with us,' Arden said.

He was not finished. 'Perhaps it would be best if you stayed behind instead, Mx Beacon.'

Even more untenable. Arden shook her head stubbornly. 'No, three people against four adults is too much. You need my help. I will not stay behind. I'm coming with you.'

Saudade was already stocked from days of kraken fishing, and ready for a good week more. Mr Riven's choice of crew, however, would prove harder to assemble.

Mx Modhi had words to say when she discovered her son had been given an offer to crew on board the black ship. Though most of her argument occurred behind the closed door of her now-floating harbour office, her disagreements rang loudly over the pier.

'I'll not have it, David. You're not going to go with him.'

'You've always hated him, Mother.'

'I'm no fool. Disaster stalks that man the same way it took his family. He'll be the end of you, David. The end!'

Arden swayed from one foot to the other, uncomfortable at hearing a private conversation so openly. Would have felt better if she could have met someone's eye and shared the awkwardness, but she could not bear to look at Chalice, and Mr Riven was in a world of his own, so all she had was the old dog, Chief, gazing expectantly up at her with his milky cataracts.

The rickety door flung open, and David escaped, wound up and fuming.

'Get back here!' Mx Modhi bellowed. 'I'm not done with you.'

The boy turned to Mr Riven, hoping for a word of support. He only shrugged, midway between thrusting a brace of harpoons into a leather quiver. 'You are eighteen years old, and a man. Your family discussion belongs to you, and the conclusion belongs to you.'

'David,' Mx Modhi warned from her doorway.

David turned about to her, panting with exultation. 'I'm eighteen. I'm a man.'

'You'll be a dead man!'

She slammed the door shut.

Chalice rubbed her hands together. 'Well then, now that that is agreed upon, I'll, ah, leave Gertrude Modhi with some instructions on what to tell Mr Lindsay and we can be off.'

'And get her to feed my dog,' Mr Riven added. 'If anything happens to me, her boy gets the boat. I have a will with the Black Rosette tavern keeper.'

Chills in her bones, and Arden tried not to linger on his words. Surely their journey would not come to that.

Once on *Saudade*, Chalice paced the foredeck, twisting her Order medal in her hands so it became a storm-spouse triangle, untwisting it to become the rose of the Order. David remained joyously active with his newfound liberty, running to secure the ship and lay the mooring ropes into neat coils.

After some barked commands to the youth, Mr Riven climbed into the wheelhouse to ignite the kraken oil engine. Blue sparkles coughed from the funnel. The side wheels churned through the water before the screw-propeller foamed up the water beneath. With the same dark, imposing grace of the creatures it hunted, the boat moved away from the dock, and at last they were in pursuit.

Although, thought Arden, it did not feel much like a pursuit. More like a tilt towards the Sainted Isles, and an inexorable slide towards doom.

26

I have come

'I have come to broach the ogre's tower.' She stood at the door to the wheelhouse and held a tin box of biscuits liberated from her own stores. 'And I bring food. It's not much, but better than dried meat and coast-limes.'

Mr Riven stood at his wheel, his attention focused on the late afternoon sea. Long golden rays of sunlight came from behind them, casing the wheelhouse shadow over *Saudade*'s bow. Despite the kicking wind, there was not such a swell on the water when the currents veered south, and *Saudade* was large enough to swallow all but the deepest troughs.

'Set it aside next to there. We'll have them with supper.' He pointed at a shelf below the wheelhouse port window, and a polished ironwood crate that held the echo box. The crate was open.

Arden peered in to watch the carbonized copper drum with its constantly oscillating needle. The needle scrawled a scratchy little line through the carbon upon the drum. At each revolution the line was re-carbonized, and the needle drew again.

'I take it Miss Quarry is not being an adequate conversationalist if you have to come to me,' he said gruffly, yet with enough welcome that Arden knew he harboured no ill will towards her.

Arden adjusted her fingerless gloves. 'I'm not really in the mood to deal with a treasonous assistant right now. I'm feeling a little adrift.' She gestured to her hands. 'These. What are they even for?'

'You didn't know you had a shadow symmetry before today, did you?'

'It seems so unlikely to be true.' Arden shook her head. 'I'm cautious about accepting anything Chalice says. The Order are well-versed in the expedient lie.'

'I did not mean to make a dishonest woman of you, Arden.'

Ah, so he'd heard as well her accusations of harlotry. Arden felt the imps of shame poking her with their tridents. 'I said things out of emotion. I was angry with Chalice. I regret not one second with you, Jonah.'

'Hmm.' Mr Riven pretended to be casual, but she could tell he was both shy and curious, and not altogether comfortable with the questions that now must be asked. 'Has Miss Quarry said what it is you trammel?'

'No. I won't give her the satisfaction. They'll find some way to exploit it! I refuse to be a tool for the Lions to use.' She stopped, and sighed. 'Oh, say it. I'm being irrational and stubborn.'

Mr Riven gave a questioning shrug, easy for him, who had admitted to two sanguinities but probably held more in his wild Fictish blood.

'You're not irrational. And don't pay any attention to anyone on Bellis and her monstrousness. She was no fool. We all made certain to find her sanctuary, and she lives there now. She is safe. You are safe, and God willing we catch up with the Tallwaters by tonight or tomorrow and put this to rest.'

'Jonah,' she started. 'What . . . what other talent did Bellis have? What made the Order so scared that they couldn't bring her to Lyonne?'

'Something very old, I think. Not seen for a long time.' He adjusted the wheel. A muscle popped in his cheek. 'Stefan knew first, before she did. Our Rector learned a lot sneaking around those libraries of prohibited books in Clays Church's catacombs. Learning about the sanguinities the Society had erased from the bloodlines. I only wish he hadn't told her what he suspected. Things only got bad after Bellis found out. Your decision to remain innocent is the right one, Arden Beacon.'

A small, shy warmth bloomed in her chest. 'Thank you. I needed to hear your blessing.'

At the sound of the scratching beside her, Arden glanced at the drum again. The needle continued to scrawl shapes on the enamelled copper. Apart from one or two shadows that might have been whales or megalodons, there was nothing of any size that could be considered her yacht. Her worries mounted. What if they didn't catch up with the Tallwaters? What if they were too late and Bellis was delivered six pints of *sanguis* blood that could . . .

That could do what? A small part of her regretted not asking Chalice for specifics, but at the time it had all been too much.

'Are you still very upset with me? For my poison blood? For my putting Bellis' mortal soul in danger?'

He glanced down, and something about her expression must have stirred his pity. Mr Riven pointed towards the horizon. 'We're still a way out from the main current. You should catch some sleep in the cabins.'

'I couldn't. Not really. It's like a wire is plucked in my mind and keeps humming, and will only get more insistent. Until all this is over. I'm scared if we don't find the Tallwaters, that something terrible will happen.'

'I won't allow it to happen.'

She wanted to kiss his rough mouth and hold him close, and have him tell her that no matter what, everything would be all right. Out there, and between them.

'Come,' he said. 'I need to show you something.'

He set the wheel to due east, then called David up into the wheelhouse from the engine room. When the young man arrived a minute later, Mr Riven gave him brief instructions.

'Keep heading in that direction, lad. Keep the sun at your

back and follow the compass east until you hit fast water, then let it take you south. Lightmistress, follow me.'

Although she'd been introduced to the wheelhouse on the morning after the Guild Ball, she hadn't been down below in *Saudade*'s cabins before. They were decked out in the same dark wood as the hull, so that it took her eyes a while to adjust to the compact, decorative surroundings. Polished brass in an angular rococo style. Lanterns set into the walls with sconces of frosted glass.

Mr Riven gestured towards a great desk, where a huge map printed on silk was rolled out from end to end, with a great thick pane of lead crystal over it. The map looked very old.

'Look,' he invited her.

Not as soon as she would have expected, given her familiarity with the area, she recognized the lands on the western edge, Fiction and Lyonne. Most ocean-current maps had the Sainted Isles well off the chart, among the sporting sea-serpents and the warnings: *Here be dragons.*

In this map of Mr Riven's, the two landmasses of Lyonne and Fiction only skirted the eastern edges. It was the three islands of the Sainted Isles that provided the map's focus, with the whirling *Tempestas* at its centre.

One island had the outline of an animal's head, the other was a system of archipelagos scattered like the pages falling from a book, and the third, the smallest and most southern, was like a woman's face in profile. *Equus, Libro, Maris.*

Equus was the largest and closest of the islands, north of *Tempestas*, with permanent storms. Arden knew Equus, for the island was where the prospectors went, drawn by the siren-song of work and wealth. It was where Bellis would have gone when she first fled, and where the Tallwaters intended to go now.

'I've never seen it in such *detail*. All the maps in Lyonne are drawn second-hand.'

'They've changed since then, with the rockblood drilling.' Mr Riven straightened it out. 'This map came with my great-great-grandfather, in the days before the automata took over Equus.'

Arden nodded. 'Every Hillfolk and street-rat in Clay knows the way into Equus. They talk about the path in taverns and in bedrooms. It's their magical land, the sunset country. The Tallwaters will be expecting the northern passage.'

'Yes, but like you said, the currents favour south this time of year. Alasdair Harrow might have found out about your blood somehow, but the land-bound fool didn't consider the *currents*. They'll flank the *Tempestas* storm wall the entire distance, and come south under it. Arden, now you tell me where it leads.'

She inspected the silk with a dome of optical glass.

'It leads to . . . Maris Proper. The southern island.' Arden read aloud: *volcanic, deserted, uninhabitable*. Grey crosshatches in the water. *Barren. Poisoned water. No Fishing.*

She looked up at Mr Riven, and met his eyes. 'It's a desert. A sea-desert! The Tallwaters won't come across anybody down there.'

Mr Riven leaned back, a sense of calm about him, as if the worry had drained away. 'I trust you now, with Bellis' whereabouts. When we knew she had to hide, Stefan and Bellis didn't go to Equus, as one would assume. They went to one of the Libro refuge islands to the north-east. Up here. There is a secret church he'd seen on his old liturgical maps.'

'That's almost three hundred miles away!'

'Three hundred miles, and safe. She lives in seclusion and solitude at an abandoned religious priory. The Lions can't find her there, and neither can her dammed father.' He nodded. 'And thank the gods, no murderous Hillsiders with six pints of sanguis blood.'

'A secret island,' Arden said. 'But why there instead of Equus?'

Mr Riven pushed the protective crystal and wrinkled the silk a little. 'She burned those bridges the first time she fled. Ran into a lot of trouble with the deepwater folk on the northern shores of Equus. She could never return after our marriage, and neither could I.'

A strange little silence came up between them. A portent of

deeper questions. 'Have you thought about what we'll do once we've got through this, and gone back to Vigil?'

'You told me. You have dreams you've dreamt all your life, Arden. If I stay with you, I fear I might stop them from coming true.'

'I don't know what my dreams are, Jonah. They changed when you put me into the ocean.'

He shook his head. 'I need to explain why I didn't want you to come along on this journey. My motives were utterly selfish. *Aequor profundum* – sometimes it doesn't work and I nearly lost you to it. I lost my family to the evil that's inside me, I . . . I thought I could manage it, and then you nearly died in my arms . . .' Another pause. 'It terrifies me, Arden, these feelings I have come to experience towards you. This loss of myself. This terror. This way that I forget all but you, even Bellis becomes like a faded memory. Would be best if I let you go.'

She took his hand then, intending to tell him to quiet himself and calm down, but as soon as he slid his rope-roughened palm into hers a visceral tremor went through her, unforgiving as a hot desert wind, and Mr Riven's blue eyes darkened in the kraken-lights.

'Arden . . .'

'Yes,' she said, and he fell upon her raised mouth to kiss her then, a moan of effort and surrender escaping him at doing so. She accepted him with a love born of desire and sadness, marvelling how lips so hard upon his face were so soft and hot upon her own, the way his tongue met her own nervously, unsure of intimacy even now, but wanting, wanting.

She wanted him. Arden fumbled for the hem of his knitted top, pulled it up and his pale chest was flushed with this star-tled rush of sexual quickening. She moved her hands on, over shoulders indented with muscle, a back hard with work, the ghosts of scars upon his skin, a living map of the journey he'd taken to get back to his ocean and his monsters. There was a slight ridge to his tattoos, their patterns under her fingers suggesting a sea-snake's scales.

She took his hands, those forearms rope-burned from salt scour and harpoon cable, stroked him into compliance and guided his hands to the waxed cotton covering her breasts. He felt her with silent wonderment, bent to nuzzle sparks of sensation through the cloth, panting with effort and surprise at the way his body had responded so powerfully without permission from his mind. With his busy thoughts preoccupied, she could leave him to unhook the button-eyes at her flanks, let the dress panels fall, the sleeves detach. At her encouragement, his hands slid inside her chemise, outlined her body with his slaughterman's hands, pausing only to bite soft at her lips, her jaw, attend to his own heated desires with his eyes half-shut, for the taste of her skin transported him to other worlds.

Still distracted, his thumbs brushed over Arden's nipples, causing her to murmur at the unruly shocks through her pelvis, between her legs. He pinched harder, she bit his bottom lip. She was wet. On shaking limbs they fell upon the worn carpet.

The seawater sloshed and rocked through the hull outside, growled through the black mangrove wood with the rhythm of blood through an artery. Mr Riven collected Arden up in his powerful arms and his clumsy kisses grew harder now, more confident, his ragged breath increased as the chains of his necessity pulled him so taut that his body quivered the way metal hummed in high wind.

Beyond her rush of insensate wonder, the demons in her mind still whispered. *Will he change his mind and stay?*

Too late to fret, not when her own need was a hunger that could not be slaked by mere gestures of affection alone. She unbuckled the belt at his breeches, tugged the leather tongue and let it fall away. He was already hard.

As she handled him, Mr Riven panted deep in his throat, before gasping aloud, '*By the gods, by the gods.*' Wanted to thrust into her hand, gain a portion of the pleasure denied him as a husband in a convenient marriage. The urgency was up, no time for long meanders.

She pulled aside her undergarments so that the hot length of him might slide inside her.

No gentle explorations now, no murmurs of fealty and of love. Had she not been so ready his hurried, rough entry might have been uncomfortable. She gasped as he took her, as he dug his fingers into her shoulders for support, seeking relief. He was beholden to darker spirits, the ones beneath them, all around them. He surged inside Arden with the passion of his own tide, gasping each time he moved, and each time she dug her fingers into the resisting slabs of his buttocks he cried out. His crisis became too much for him to carry and his body stiffened, the contortion of a man under the lash. He spent himself with a strangled sound, then collapsed upon Arden with a sob.

With a guilty, drunken rush of pleasure Arden climaxed in joy.

The waves whispered and muttered their secret language. The side wheels beat the water. The beams creaked. The last shudders of her own culmination left Arden in fits and starts. She put her nose into the short fuzz of Mr Riven's skull, breathing in the scent of him, sea and spice. His body still shook. Where could she put her emotions? He had not wanted to stay with her, and the devil knew how many men had been content with a roll in the hay before moving on to other lovers.

He softened inside Arden's body and his breath lost its panting rhythm, but otherwise Mr Riven made no movement to detach himself from their embrace. His weight upon her had a comfort she did not expect. By now she'd have tipped her previous lovers off and would be stepping into her dress, one eye firmly upon the exit. Jonah Riven she could not bear to let go.

'So, lost your bones, monster caller?' A little levity she tried, to cover her pinching, nervous heart. She dared not move, lest he slip out entirely, and she lose this tenuous, intimate connection. The lights slipped over the sweat of his pale, flushed skin, and the moment took on a deep gravity.

He did not reply, only rose on his elbows, and his gaze scraped over Arden's face, trying to read her for deceptions, work out why he'd been so easily compromised, why Bellis had been supplanted in his affection by Arden's presence. If she satisfied him, he gave no sense of it.

'What's wrong, Jonah?' she asked.

'*Saudade*,' he said, 'is a word in Old Fictish. There is no equivalent in Lyonne for the feeling of *saudade*. To miss something, to yearn, to remember a moment that might not have existed.'

'I have felt this, though my language could not name it.'

Mr Riven nodded. His thumb caressed her shoulder, her arm, placed a small kiss after it, the kind one might lay upon the body of a saint. She trembled at the juxtaposition there, his rough chin with two days' growth, his lips swollen from kissing and so soft. She envisioned those lips in other places, saying words that she longed to hear.

'If my family had not died, if I had not been sent to prison, perhaps I could have made a little fortune on the coast. Perhaps I might have gone to Clay Portside as a young man, and met the lighthouse keeper there. I hope she might have allowed me to court her.'

Arden touched his face with tenderness, wanting to wipe away the sorrow lines so deep-set within. The people of Fiction always aged beyond their years. There was a coarseness to them, the way a leather might bleach in the sun and become hard. Was that Jonah's fate, if he survived this journey?

'There are many lighthouse keepers in Portside, and I was only good for signals before my uncle died. But I would have gladly allowed the mysterious and handsome man from Fiction to court me.'

Her words only drove him into a deeper despair. Arden reached to kiss him again, and this time there was a bittersweet taste to his kiss-abraded lips, a regret for what they could have shared if the world had not ridden roughshod between all the chances that might have allowed them to meet in earlier, more hopeful times.

He grew hard again within the embrace of her body, and

moved with the aching tenderness of a farewell. Arden held on to him in the silent terror of their eventual parting, but she could not stay motionless, and she jerked and quivered with her second climax. He grasped her hips, her thighs, finished with a final half-dozen grunting, ragged strokes. Oh, Mr Riven, still too inexperienced to maintain those rhythms of love into that moment when desire collapses with all the force of a mountain on the Day of Judgment. He slipped out of her in his zeal and with the clumsy gaucherie of a raw youth, spent his essence in the hollow between Arden's centre and thigh. The sudden expression of abject shame that came over him as he suffered the throes of a too-quick orgasm needed kissing away.

'By the sea, Arden,' he said, his breath hot and hoarse against her cheek. 'If only . . .'

He never got to finish. The engines, previously a background grumble, suddenly screamed. *Saudade* lurched sideways.

Outside, one wheel was beating air. The hull below them screeched in metallic pain.

'Devils!' Mr Riven exclaimed. 'That was a collision!'

Arden fumbled for her dress, still punch-drunk from love-making and her limbs decidedly uncooperative. 'Go. I'll be all right. You check the below deck, I'll check what's going on upstairs.'

He nodded, and as he was halfway into his breeches he dived forward and kissed her. Kissed her twice and had he done so a third time she would have damned the boat and the inrushing sea to tangle once more with Mr Riven on the carpet, would have committed desperate adultery with him as they sank into the deepest oceans.

'Later,' he said, and ran barefoot out into the corridor, heaved open the trapdoor, and descended below.

Arden took longer getting into her own dress. How complicated could it be, wearing women's clothes? But within a matter of seconds she was outside, in the wind, and seeing exactly what they had collided with.

27

A hull, upside down

A hull, upside down, floating in the water. A hull, with a bulbous, broken keel painted as red as lacquer. Chalice Quarry looked down at the wreck as if flummoxed by its sudden appearance.

'*Fine Breeze*.' Chalice Quarry nodded at Arden guardedly as she approached. 'Was already like that when David steered into it.'

Her poor capsized vessel yawed and bobbed in her death-throes. Arden panged with gladness. A terrible accident had occurred, and lives might very well have been lost, but it meant that their troubles were at an end.

Still, it presented a mystery.

'What could tip over a perfectly good boat in flat sea?' Chalice asked. 'We haven't reached *Tempestas* or Sainted waters.'

The large cloud wall of the Tempest boundary was a good ten miles away. Even hopeless Lyonne Hillsiders would have known better than to chance a little vessel like *Fine Breeze* against the storm.

'I'm willing to leave the secret to the Old Guy and never find out,' Arden said, happy enough that she did not want to curse too harshly the sea-devils who'd given her such a gift. 'She was built to come out of a capsize. This was fated.'

David stuck his head out of the wheelhouse window. 'I'm sorry, Lightmistress! I tried to avoid the boat, but she was so low down I didn't catch her until the last minute.'

Arden waved back. 'Nobody could have seen her and there's no damage, David. Don't fret.'

Mr Riven exited the forecastle trapdoor, slimed with kraken oil and pitch. He went to the balustrade to survey the water, and the capsized *Fine Breeze*. Without a word, he cleared the edge of the deck and dived into the water, disappearing beneath the opaque surface.

'What was that in aid of?' Chalice asked. She tilted out over the deck rail, but nothing remained other than whitecaps and *Fine Breeze*'s water-faded hull. 'They'd be dead for hours,' she shouted into the water.

Whatever their fate, Mr Riven had to make sure. The moralities of life upon the sea required such efforts.

Arden called for David to throw down the boarding gear, and David reappeared with a yellow canvas bag. It made a solid thump as it landed on the deck. The crossbars and knots of a rope ladder spilled out of the waxed mouth. Arden tugged on the leading end and motioned Chalice over. 'Help me get it secured to the rail.'

'I doubt there's an air pocket,' Chalice said between puffing, for the wood slats and lengths of sisal made it heavy indeed. Arden ran to help, and they jostled the boarding bag to the edge of the deck. 'We had quite a solid collision.'

They made fast the rope ladder and waited. The ship knocked up against *Fine Breeze*'s wreck.

'Surely Mr Riven should have found what he wanted by now,' Chalice said after several minutes of their watching the impenetrable water.

Chalice was right. He should have. Jorgen's boat contained only one cabin, no *Saudade* rabbit warren. The reconnaissance should have taken seconds. Not this long.

'You go in,' Arden said to David urgently. 'Something's not right.'

The young man nodded and pulled off his boots.

Just as he had set one bare foot on the ladder, Mr Riven cleared the surface with a gasp.

He had not risen empty-handed. He hauled up a body into his arms, a man limp and pale.

'Grab him,' Mr Riven shouted. 'I'm going back in.'

'Jonah—' Arden started, but he was once more gone under the water, and David was struggling with a corpse.

The woven straps that Mr Riven used to pull kraken hens onto his boat still coiled neatly upon the forecastle deck. The thick webbing barely fitted under the corpse's arms, and Arden half-expected the shoulders to detach completely with the slightest force. Dead men rarely lasted in the ocean. The hungry things consumed the flesh of the dying even before they drew their last breath.

To Arden's relieved surprise, the body held together, and with Chalice's assistance, they managed by sheer effort to haul it up onto the black wood. Arms and wrists bounced limply upon the deck. Strands of violet kelp fronded the face and shoulder in a manner more befitting a pagan burial.

She saw at once who Mr Riven had rescued.

'Sean Ironcup,' she said. 'Helena's brother.' A stabbing whirl of disgust and enmity directed towards the dead man. If she didn't have witnesses she might even have kicked him.

Chalice took Arden's arm and pulled her back. 'Easy, sister. He's more than paid for his trespasses towards yourself and God now.'

David loitered about in concern. 'Can we not resuscitate him? I've seen my mother bring back a few.' He mimed pressing down on bellows.

'Be my guest.'

With a dulled impassion she watched David kneel and put several enthusiastic puffs of air into the corpse's lungs. After a minute of compressions upon the blue sternum, the hopelessness became obvious. David sat back, panting from his exertions.

'You've done your moral duty, Mr Modhi. Go help Mr Riven,'

Arden said brusquely, as David attempted a second round of resuscitation.

'I've heard of it taking an hour.'

'He doesn't deserve a minute. Go.'

When David retreated, she knelt to formally acknowledge the thing they had plucked out of the sea. How small he seemed, now that the kick of life had gone from him, how wasted his frame, how young his face. She could almost pity him. 'I suppose we will be charged to give you a sea burial, Sean Ironcup.'

The sound of Mr Riven's voice commanding something of David brought her back to the present. If there was anything more found in her boat, she did not particularly want to discuss it with Chalice around.

'Get some cloth to wrap him,' Arden said to Chalice. 'Like you say, we have to respect the dead, especially if they don't deserve it.'

Chalice, unimpressed about being sent off the deck, returned into the dim interior of *Saudade*. Once the Madame Lion was safely ensconced and out of hearing, Arden ran to the edge of the deck, only to have David throw a glass jar at her.

Arden nearly dropped the slippery object, before clutching the blood-filled mason jar to her chest.

'Devils, David, I'd rather not be sweeping this muck off the deck.'

'Can't climb with one hand, Lightmistress.'

He pulled himself off the ladder, and Mr Riven came after. He'd turned nearly as blue with chill as the dead man. Arden snatched up one of the rough blankets used to protect the wood from rope wear and threw it over Mr Riven's shoulders. He wiped the seawater from his face and head, nodded at the mason jar.

'The Ironcup boy was trying to hide it. Fell out of his grip when I moved his body.'

'Only one jar?'

'Last one. Five broken jars in the crate, blood in the water.'

'I take it the other Tallwaters aren't down there.'

Mr Riven made a sign to the negative, ran the canvas over his torso to dry off. 'Like I said, a lot of blood. These are plesiosaur waters. A pod could easily finish off three adults in a matter of minutes.'

Arden held the jar close to her chest. The blood had jellied since last it flowed through her veins. Soon she would let it fall into the ocean. She knew that she should say a quick prayer for the dead Tallwaters now, but ended up saying one of quiet blessing to herself. It was over. It was over.

On the deck, David still fussed over the dead man. A little sense of guilt wormed into her heart. Had it been Sean Ironcup who had broken the jars? Or had he only condemned his family's share to give himself better options of survival?

They would never know, she thought. They would cast him overboard and go back to Vigil, and she would map out a new life that included Jonah Riven . . .

Mr Riven had not moved from the deck.

'Jonah,' Arden asked gently. 'Aren't you cold?'

'We have a problem.' Mr Riven tilted his chin towards the Tempest boundary. 'There's a ship in there, just beyond the Wall.'

'A boat? Prospectors gone off course maybe? We're too far south for Equus, and Maris is uninhabitable.'

'I don't know. I've not seen a Lyonne-built ship to withstand such weather. Your blood might not have been going north to Bellis, but it was definitely going to someone. Someone still waiting to collect.'

Arden nodded. She did not doubt his hunter's instincts. 'All right. We'll leave *Fine Breeze* for salvage and go. I'll tell Chalice.'

'Tell me what?' Chalice exited the door, closing it solemnly, laid some linens next to Sean Ironcup's body. She sagged with knock-kneed relief when she saw what Arden carried. 'You got the blood! Oh! You got the blood back! Excellent!'

Chalice stopped speaking. Her joy was not shared.

'What?'

Arden grabbed Chalice's arm, offered her excuses to Mr Riven and dragged her away.

'Madame Lion,' Arden hissed once they reached the opposite deck. 'Who else knows . . . about my shadow endowment, about Bellis? Do any of the Islanders know? Would they manipulate Mr Harrow, make him think he was helping his damn golden daughter?'

Chalice's lips pressed together. A wave passed over the boat, drenching them in a spray.

'Not more than ten officials within the Order were allowed that information. It . . . was too sensitive a matter to speak of.'

Arden pointed at *Fine Breeze*'s hull. 'Then pray to the gods and devils this was an accident. Jonah says there is a boat beyond the storm wall and it has not moved. He thinks it might be the ones who intended to rendezvous for my blood.'

A thin blush of pink spread under Chalice's freckles. 'If it was, why would they stay?'

'Let's hope they're just waiting for us to leave.'

'Yes. We've got your blood back now. The last of it. We can toss it over the side and go home.'

'This won't end by throwing away this jar! If someone got Mr Harrow to send the Tallwaters out here, someone, somewhere *knew* there was something more than just *ignis* about me. And if he knew, then others would know.' She pointed accusingly at the storm wall. 'Even *them*. What chance of others knowing our secrets, Chalice? Can you even trust your own people?'

'The Order would never . . .'

Their conversation was punctuated by Mr Riven clearing his throat. 'Ladies,' he said. 'Whatever business demands this privacy needs to wrap up damned quickly. Our guests are coming.'

The sea-fog had slunk upon the ocean. A thin, distant sound headed up the darkening of the sun. Carried through the moist air and still ocean, a threshing of bows against waves.

Arden did not need the spyglass Mr Riven offered her. It would have made no difference. The fog was too think, and even she could not see anything beyond the Wall, but she had her own signal keeper's instincts too. A boat *was* out there. Not by chance, not here where the volcanic island of Maris poisoned the water. The boat lingered there on purpose.

She hefted the jar in her hand. A solid, jellied weight. A sudden panic for what it represented. The shadow that had complicated her life. She needed to be rid of it, and she readied her arm to throw . . .

Only to have Mr Riven's hand firmly placed on top of her own. He nodded at the corpse bound in sheet. 'If worst comes to worst, we will need something to bargain with.'

'You can't possibly consider such a thing, Mr Riven,' Chalice scolded. 'That blood isn't worth anything to anyone except your wife.'

'I can consider bargaining for our lives,' Mr Riven continued. 'The current's pulling us into the Tempest. We might hide there until that ship passes, but if she's any bigger than a fishing boat, we're in no condition to get boarded by pirates.'

'Pirates?' Chalice asked. 'Here?'

'We're in a desert, Madam Lion. There's no living to be had but theft.' He took the jar from Arden, and nestled it inside the lifejacket box, before closing the lid. 'Rather it, than you.'

Arden nodded, and would have kissed him had the situation not been so charged.

David had by then reluctantly abandoned Sean's body, and was halfway through the retrieval of the rope ladder when he paused, head cocked like a sparrow that hears the worm. 'What is that sound?'

He shoved the heel of his hands into his ears as the whistle picked up. A constant harmonic of agony, the cry of atmospheres caught in a perpetual collision.

'Storm wall,' Mr Riven barked. 'It's closing in faster than I thought. Get inside, all of you.'

Mr Riven ran for the wheelhouse ladder and seized the riser. A simple action, enraging the gods, and no sooner had he boosted himself to the first rung than a wave with all the power of a massive fist backhanded *Saudade*, six ways to Sunday.

With a whirl of vertigo Arden was boosted up by the rising deck and tossed into the side of the cabin with such an impact, every tooth in her skull rattled.

Chalice and David went sliding past her in a startled jumble of soaking limbs and open mouths, and if they had been screaming, the roar of the Wall took the sound away.

Another wave, *Saudade* lurched to starboard. This time Arden took off down the end of the deck with the speed of a bottle rocket. In a single, time-frozen moment, the wreckage of *Fine Breeze* tossed up into the air, suspended in spume and wavewash, before descending towards *Saudade*. The little yacht dropped upon the forecastle deck with an unholy chorus of splintering wood before smashing into the railing, opening a gap on one side like broken teeth in a jaw.

Arden slid towards the edge, and slipped. Unable to arrest her long fall, she saw herself as though from above, as if through the longest of spyglass lenses, a small figure in waxen broadcloth sliding across the oil-slicked wood to where the balustrade was broken, to plunge over the side . . .

28

. . . *and stopped.*

Her skirt caught on a hook that jerked her from neck to knee, and Arden spun on an axis of wet broadcloth to discover the corpse, blue with cyanosis, now holding the hem of her dress in the grip of death.

His staring eyes had the shade of granite set in pearl.

The fist tightened harder on her skirt. The stitches crackled. Sean Ironcup, yanking her away from the seething wreckage of *Fine Breeze* as the wood battered and chewed upon the side of *Saudade*.

'Sean,' she shouted. 'Hold on!'

Then just as suddenly Chalice joined him in trying to haul Arden up from the brink, three souls locked against the storm of the Tempest Wall. All the while behind them a man shouted in strangulated harmonics, shouted Arden's name.

The boat pitched forward again and now the three were all in the sea, no air, no breath, no purchase in the roil and thunder. Arden could only dream of fire as she clung to the submerged edge of the boat, her head under the waves and her ears filled with seafoam and water.

Just as suddenly the boat bow flipped upwards once more, propelling them all high into the air with a seabird's vertigo.

Arden snatched at a railing, only to have it tear out of her hands from the inertia of the boat's fall . . .

And then they plunged again.

The storm no longer roiled or roared. Only silence here, and her battering heart in the cavern of her chest, and her dragged down to lightless depths. Fingers clasped and scrabbled. Was that a foot upon her shoulder? A wisp of hair at her hand? All three of them, caught in the wreckage of a floundering ship?

Arms as cold as death reaching about her.

Arms muscular and alien all at once.

Long arms, and bright cobalt rings.

29

Was the dumping that woke her

Was the dumping that woke her, flat on her back on the hard wood of the deck, her head shooting stars. A boneless hand flopped in her face, and she could not be certain if her own or somebody else's. Whatever had happened, wherever afterlife she had ended up in, it was an infinitely less soggy, choppy and very much calmer one than her life of two minutes previously. The Tempest still roared, but at a remove, a distance long passed.

Arden coughed seawater from her lungs and sat up.

'I'm never getting used to—' she started to say, then stopped. Through the haze of rain, a single golden eye beheld her.

One giant golden eye, staring from over *Saudade*'s transom, wider than the full stretch of her arms. Up and up, it loomed overhead, so round it filled the world in concentric circles huge enough to fall into. The double pupil, blacker than the oldest and deepest wisdom, stared down at her with the detachment of kings.

' . . . devils,' she finished.

With equal languid nonchalance, the long arm that had seized them from the water moved about the deck in the manner of a drunken person searching for a door key in the dark. The

302

kraken's limb spanned wider than Arden's own torso and shone with a bright metal iridescence, even in the dwindling storm.

Arden could only bear mute witness as the entire scolex of the monster rose in majesty above the deckline, same as every woodcut and eyewitness account of kraken attack she had ever seen or heard. The blue phosphorescence of a living *kraken crucifix* left afterimages in her vision, so bright was it, putting the colours in her coat to shame.

Oh, she thought. Oh, he was the devil and God as one.

Seven more arms rose up to join the lone limb, lashed at the storm and writhed luminous against a lightless sky, before slipping away into the fog and plume.

Arden clung to the deck in a wreckage of terror and exhaustion, and a pair of arms – a man's arms, not monster's this time – picked her up with infinite tenderness and against the rocking boat helped her below decks. She collapsed upon warm leather, as her lungs expelled an ocean.

He could not stay long. His rope-callused hand caressed her cheek once, making certain she was not mortally injured, before he was gone back into the storm. The snapping doors belonged to the passage of Chalice, limping down the stairs in an over-hand shuffle with the formerly dead Sean Ironcup.

'So we have an unsinkable,' Arden said with some effort. She sat up and peered at the Hillsider. 'You've survived your second capsizing.'

'No thanks to you,' Sean replied, still feisty despite his partially maundered state.

Chalice dumped their revenant in one of the upholstered chairs, then put her hands on her hips, glowered down at him. 'No nonsense, young man. You've caused us a fair bit of trouble. Attempted murder of a Guildswoman, and a sanguinem at that? Stealing a boat? Consider yourself formally under arrest by the authority of the Lyonne Investigatory Order and Nomenclatures.'

'What's that mean?'

'It means you're stuck with us until we can take you to a

decent Magistrate who isn't leading you into iniquity like Mr Harrow. You have a right to be kept alive, but that is quite about the limit of it, I'm afraid.'

'I won't try to run away,' he said, both wretched and defiant at the same time. The chill and sudden dunking had aggravated his palsy. Both sides of him curled up with spasms. 'I know what I did was wrong.'

Chalice clicked her tongue and fetched Arden a blanket from the camphorwood chest. Arden shook her head at the offering. 'I'll change into a dry dress. Give it to the lad before he ties himself into a knot. Maybe get one for yourself too, Chalice.'

'I'm quite all right,' Chalice said, and with a gentleness that belied her mood, she tucked the blanket around Sean's thin shoulders. He watched them both warily through swollen, red-rimmed eyes, but did not complain.

Behind a brass divider all rococo with weed-fronds and clam shells, Arden slid out of her sopping blue uniform and into her spare dress, a dark linseed and wax wet-work garment hardened from the cold. The kraken eye still played behind the curtain of her mind. Jonah had summoned it, that creature. Had given a monster instructions, compelled the thing to save her. Was for a moment, the monster's master.

The *aequor profundum* in her blood moved hot through the chambers of her heart. Every moment that passed, every event that confronted her with her own mortality, she was becoming more tied to Jonah Riven. She had not yet the time to think of it before now, but in this dark panelled room with its moving shadows and winking brass, a future began to congeal. A possible future, with her half-Islander lover, and her coins gone, and the city of her birth forgotten.

I want that.

The thought filled her with triumph and panic. The Lyonne Order would not let her go so easily, but if Bellis had achieved it, then she could too. Maybe there would be room on the secret island for all of them.

'What a performance!' Chalice continued on the other side

of the room divider. 'The menfolk are up in the wheelhouse effecting emergency repairs. We're lucky our hull is intact. The side wheels are completely shot to smithereens, but the screw is still working.'

As she spoke, thunder grumbled outside, and the boat lifted on a great wave before sinking again.

Arden shook her head, dismayed Chalice could court fate so blatantly. One did not count lucky stars until broad daylight, and they were still in the night-time of their crisis.

'Don't thank any deity just yet. We're still not past the Wall, I assume.'

'No.' Chalice steadied herself against a support beam and snorted. 'Anyway, what's the chances of our captain keeping at least a whiskey in this office, hmm? A dram of spirit to ease our conditions, and then we could go about drying our clothes.'

While Chalice went on a hunt for liquor, Arden returned to Sean Ironcup.

'Some gratitude is in order on my behalf,' Arden said to him. 'You grabbed me as I was sliding off the deck.'

'I wasn't much help, my stronger side doesn't feel much different from my leeward. We still fell in.' He gasped then, remembering. 'What manner of monster seized us?'

'Blood-called kraken bull.'

'He was big.'

'He was big. Angry too. Same I was angry when you bound me and bled me, no more than an *animal*. What moral *failing* had you think hurting another fellow human was worth profit?'

Sean's face crumbled. He was not so guilty, she decided, had been dragged on this malarkey out of sheer familial duty, but if he considered himself a man, then he had to take a man's responsibility, whether he was nineteen or ninety.

'I'm sorry! I'm so sorry! Leyland said that there was no way onto the Islands without payment. He wanted to sell the girl, my sister's child! Tried to auction her off to the highest bidder in the Black Rosette when a man arrived.' He made motions of his hands. 'The Magistrate, Gregor's employer. Approached Gregor's father and said he would give all three children a home if he were to do a task on his behalf . . .' Sean heaved a breath, close to tears.

'And your sister did not protest?'

Whatever bulwarks the boy had put up against his family's disintegration, they were swept away on Helena's mention. Sean began to weep. Blubbered some things. Arden caught the gist of his crisis. After the transaction in the Black Rosette turned ugly, Helena had closed down, gradually, like a great house might do for the night. She still had a modicum of function about her when they had come to steal Arden's blood, but that was the last time she had spoken. The children were gone. Her work was ended. Best she die in fractions.

'Leyland, I think, would have been happier for her to die as well. She had the blue fever last year, can bear no more children. Her family had no money and her blood . . .'

'She carries sanguine traits?'

'No traits. Not in the Ironcup line. Leyland never liked her, or me. If Gregor had married well there could have been the chance of sanguinity. It might have meant a reversal in our fortunes, and we would never have needed to come out here.'

The strength sapped from Sean, he fumbled for the blanket's end, curled up in speechless horror at what had been done in the name of Leyland Tallwater's ambition.

The ship lurched again. The sound of shouting, footsteps. A heavy piece of equipment lost balance, slammed into a supporting structure above. Someone cried out in pain. Mr Riven, at battle with the weather.

'Hold on,' Chalice called from the rear of the ship. 'We're back in heavy water again.'

Arden fell onto the floor and clutched the carpet, suffering *Saudade*'s sway on all her axes.

Then, the way a curtain can fall upon a stage play of destruction, the storm abruptly subsided into a desultory scatter of wind and did not resume. The ship's sways eased into a rhythmic bob. Arden waited for another minute before chancing an upright position.

Chalice let go the brass post she'd been clinging to and regarded the black wood ceiling beams as if she could see the sky through them. 'Looks like we are fully out of the wall-storm at last,' she said, with no small measure of relief.

'Yes, but on what side?'

The deckside door slammed again.

Mr Riven was a mess. The tattered remains of his shirt had turned pink from the alarming wound that ran diagonally across his chest, bigger than the ones he'd opened to save Arden with *aequor profundum*. The wound still bled. But his face was alight with indignation, his mouth a grimace, his pupils dilated in rage.

'You,' he said, pointing to Sean Ironcup. 'Explain yourself.'

Sean Ironcup stared at Mr Riven, his eyes bulging with terror. 'I was dead, now I am alive, and the Redeemer provided me with a breath so I can walk the world.'

Sean pulled his knees up. His palsy wrapped him in painful iron bands, for the entire situation had wounded him. Ah, thought Arden, he's going to lose himself.

Swallowing her antipathy towards Sean Ironcup, Arden sat down next to the young man and tried to remember how her father talked to people in distress. Lucian Beacon had been gifted with words as well as fire. He could rouse a fellow to great achievements, talk down an angry fighter, console a grieving widower.

The latter Lucian did best, having been one himself, once.

'Mr Ironcup, breathe in and out, there's a dear. Take that air in like it's a *fine* liquor. And when you exhale . . . yes. Now, begin at the moment you realized the current was taking you south, and not north of the permanent storm.'

Mr Riven remained silent and glaring as Sean did as Arden commanded. His jaw trembled, then steadied.

Shakily, he began to speak.

'We . . . we knew the current would take us south, not north. Mr Harrow said it would. He said someone needed *ignis* blood and they would be prepared to pay passage.'

Arden exchanged a concerned glance with Mr Riven. There was a sense of too much planning going on here, more than the opportunity of some Hillside folks about to be killed in a tavern.

'Why would the Magistrate send you south of the storm? There's nothing here, not even people.'

Not even Bellis, Arden heard him add silently.

'I don't know. It was a different route than the ones they sing of back home. I didn't want to go that way but Leyland said it was what Mr Harrow wanted. We went south until full morning. Leyland let off a signal as he approached the Tempest. A craft approached to meet us.'

'What sort of craft?' Mr Riven pressed. 'Describe it.'

Sean Ironcup blinked. 'Why, it would have been like this one, sir. Ghostwood, though, not black mangrove. It burned rock-blood. I remember the smell, it is on my fingers and in my head. As noxious as ash and a trillion dead things turned to rot and slurry.'

A cold finger of warning traced Arden's spine. Mr Riven had asked such a specific question, knowing what the answer would be.

'Did it have a name? Across the bow, carved in red like a wound?'

Sean shook his head. 'I remember only a difficult word. Not in Lyonnese. *Sen . . .* something.'

'*Sehnsucht.*'

'Yes, that was it.'

Before Arden could stop him, Mr Riven grabbed Sean and hauled him up. 'Who were the people on that boat? Was there a woman there?'

'I don't know, sir,' Sean cried. 'I don't know! They took Leyland off, Helena and Gregor. Beat them up a bit, sir, this I recall. I thought I would be next. Then a man, he boarded first and he broke the jars. He told me . . . *play dead*, he said to me. *Pretend you are dead.* So dark . . . I couldn't see him, but he spoke with a Lyonne accent. Shoved me into the rope box with the last jar and then . . . and then . . . and there was crashing and yelling I don't remember what happened after that. Not until I woke up here.'

'What did this man look like?'

'I cannot say. It was dark, the salt water was everywhere, it blinded me.' A gasp. Stared at Chalice. 'The man had a coin about his neck, like yours. Made me look at it. Told me it was his coin of instruction.'

Chalice clasped her medallion tight. 'There was a Lion aboard?'

No sooner had she spoken, Chalice gasped, as if having spoken out of turn.

Mr Riven dropped Sean Ironcup back on the chair, where he once again folded up in a rumple of limbs and anxious terror. Turned on Chalice 'A Lion there as *well*? Where are you people *not*?'

Chalice effected a stubborn look. 'He couldn't have been one of ours. If he was, he was under deep cover. Despite our efforts, we have next to no influence in the Sainted Isles.'

'Please Chalice . . .' Arden warned. 'Tell him the truth. We're all on our own out here.'

The duplicitous stormbride could have been a criminal in a courtroom under questioning, for all her eyes were wide with truth and horror.

'Mr Ironcup must have misread this coin-wielding fellow's intentions. Lots of people wear coin pendants. It could have been a mutiny, an argument that had him hide you in the closet. Nothing to do with us.'

Mr Riven huffed a breath, went pale. 'The lad told the truth. If there was an Order man on board that ship, then he was there because of Bellis.'

30

So it's true

'So it's true? You really gave her *Sehnsucht*, Jonah Riven?' Chalice scolded.

'Only to get to safety. Only to get away from you. She was meant to get rid of it after reaching sanctuary . . .'

He staggered. Arden went to catch him but it was a blank-faced stranger who shrugged her off.

'I can't think. My mind . . . If I don't get rest, I will pass out on the floor and be useless to anyone. Fix this, Lightmistress. You and David Modhi. Get us away from that boat and out of this storm.'

He blood-drunkenly made his way to the private berth. The door slammed. If it had had a lock, he would have slid it shut.

'What happened?' Sean asked in the blistering silence that followed. 'Um, are we going home now?'

'Shut up,' Chalice shot back. 'You've caused nothing but trouble, boy.'

'But how can the Captain sleep? Right in the hour of our need!'

'Because he sliced himself open to call that kraken bull to save our lives.' Arden squeezed the last of seawater from her braid, feeling herself as exhausted as Jonah had been. 'You give blood to the sea like that, it pulls strength out of you. Do they not teach the conservation of energy and mass in Hillsider schools? When he wakes up, then he can help, but at this minute we are on our own.'

Sean wisely did not reply. Still irritated, Arden bound up the damp locks of hair that had escaped her hairpins and readied herself to go outside again. If they were on the wrong side of the storm wall and floating about in the Tempest's eye, the combined experience of David and herself would not make the crossing without Mr Riven behind the wheel.

They'd barely managed it the first time.

'What was that last little exchange about?' Chalice asked. 'Who did she give the boat to?'

Arden shrugged, felt the bite of anger. 'Not the slightest clue.'

Chalice's eyes narrowed. 'Did he actually think anyone would purposefully give away a damned monster-hunting boat? God and devils, I once saw daguerreotypes of *Sehnsucht* in Mr Lindsay's briefing notes. It's grotesque. More than twice the size of this one.'

'You should be the one to answer who owns *Sehnsucht* now, Miss Quarry. Your being a Lion and all, and your man aboard her.'

Arden's tartness made Chalice huff. 'I told you, if Sean's benefactor was Lyonne Order, he was under the deepest cover.'

'And he will remain that way, Chalice. When Jonah wakes up, we're going back to Vigil.'

Chalice put her palm on the map glass, stroked the *Libro* island archipelago with her thumb. One of those the secret islands, where Bellis and Stefan had taken refuge. Telling Arden without words that she knew more than she was letting on.

'But will *he* want to go back, Arden? Mr Riven might be curious to know what became of his first love, and of the people who still bear his name.'

A quick stab of covetous jealousy went through Arden. A jealousy tinged with guilt, for she was indirectly the cause of his troubles, and he would not love her for that.

'He is not at all curious. His work for you is *done*, Chalice Quarry. And so is mine.'

31

The Harbourmistress' boy yelped at her

The Harbourmistress' boy yelped at her when Arden turned up
unannounced at the wheelhouse.

'Lightmistress, you took me by surprise.'

'Sorry. I was taking advantage of the reprieve with a nap.
How long before the current turns?'

'By the map, the daylight should have us turning west and
back to Fiction,' David said with a nod of certainty.

She didn't have the words to express her relief, but hugged
his shoulders. 'I will be happy to see even Fiction again.'

This was followed by a yawn, for Arden had only managed
a brief but unsatisfying doze in the cabin earlier, but the aches
and pains and anxieties of their return made her restless, and
she finally surrendered to waking.

The moon shone through the clouds. A small kraken-oil
lantern cast a cold blue glow over the instruments.

'Where's Mr Riven?'

'Still sleeping off a blood-hangover, as they would say in my
home country. It will keep him unavailable for a while.'

'Is that all? He didn't look well before, and I worried.'

She patted his arm gently. The boy was hopelessly in love
with Mr Riven, and in that respect she and David were kin;

both bound to the wrong man by troubled emotions and unable to effect any true response from him one way or the other.

'I'm sure he will come out of this syncope by the current's turn, and we can go home, and forget this day like a bad dream.'

'And yourself, Lightmistress?'

'Only a few bruises and scrapes, nothing to measure a casket over,' she said. 'I have tangled with a *monstrom mare* and lived to tell the tale.'

At first he smiled, and then the smile faded, and he slipped back behind the wheel.

'What's wrong, Mr Modhi?'

He pointed ahead of them, over the damaged bow. She tried to peer out of the wheelhouse and failed, for the night and fog were so absolute. 'It's back.'

'The boat's back? I thought it moved on after the monster came.'

Relying on her Beacon-born darksight, Arden scanned the gloom. Through the marbled wisps of fog and sea-plume, there was an outcropping of rock that to call an *island* would be far too generous. Almost as a mere optical illusion, such was the faintness, a column of boiler-lit smoke seemingly rose from one corner.

'Devils!' Arden took the wheel from David. 'Very sneaky of them. Top observation, Mr Modhi.'

'I can see well in the dark.'

'Indeed. Keep those eyes of yours peeled, for I've a feeling you'll see more shortly.'

Once the rudder was under her control, she shoved the engine-order telegraph to stop. *Saudade* was mechanical, and instantly she moved perpendicular to the current. The propeller slowed. The boat began to drift side on, but with much less speed.

The dull, distant roaring of the Tempest Wall continued.

'All right. The storm is loud,' Arden said, counting her blessings. 'It's good. They might not have heard us.'

She went to the crate, and opened it up, inspected the

revolving drum. A shape had taken form on the carbon. The rock, jagged and huge. Behind, a rectangle tapered at one end.

'What are those lines here?' Arden asked, pointing at a riffle of linework between the boat and the rock.

'Thresh-waves.' David said. 'She's not powered down. The island is floating, and they are using it as either pier or cover.'

'We are all drifting at the same speed. No doubt they have an echo box of their own. Waiting to see who will make the first move.'

Down on the deck, Chalice Quarry emerged from the cabin with her hair mussed from sleep, and a wet-battery flashlight in her hands. She frowned up at the wheelhouse. Arden held a finger to her lips, bade her turn off the light, then beckoned her inside.

'They're back,' she said quietly as Chalice entered. 'Our monster didn't scare them off at all.'

Chalice swallowed nervously. 'Oh, I was wondering why the engine stopped.'

'More for your concern, where is Sean Ironcup, Chalice? You're charged with looking after him tonight.'

'Mr Ironcup consented to getting locked in one of the storage rooms. He's worked out it might be safer for him all round if he not appear to take sides if things take a wrong turn.'

'Are they going to take a wrong turn?'

Chalice gestured towards the night before examining the echo-image of the rocky island. '*Sehnsucht*, I presume?'

'We haven't yet seen, but your presumption is likely correct.'

'Darling, if Bellis is on that ship, you need to get Mr Riven awake.'

'No. After blood loss, rousing him is just going to hurt. And if we don't change angles soon, we're going to run into that boat or she'll try and run into us. The current takes us right past that rock. We need to turn *Saudade* off this fast water.'

David suffered a look of pure despair. 'It's too early. If we turn off now we'll hit the storm wall. Besides, we won't outrun *Sehnsucht* against the current,' he said. 'I remember stories about *Sehnsucht*, Mx Beacon. She's a bigger, more powerful craft than *Saudade* ever was. She's made for fighting monsters.'

Arden took a breath. This ship. *Sehnsucht.* This ghost which haunted Mr Riven in blood and love, and now in the childhood he had lost. He would want answers, about what had happened to Bellis after she sailed away. He would not be content with watching her go by like a *memento mori* afloat on the water.

'David,' she said, 'get down below and open all the engine throttles.'

'Mx Beacon?'

'We can't outrun her cross-current, you say? But if we keep going and with a head start, I think *Saudade* can do just that. We are unencumbered, half as small again as that white behemoth.'

'But the water just gets harder to escape the closer we get to Maris!'

'Let me worry about that. Go. Go!'

Chalice waited until the boy had left the wheelhouse to express her complete dissatisfaction. 'He's right, Arden. We'll hit fast, hot water soon. Once that happens we might not be able to turn out so easily.'

'We don't have a choice. That ship is in hunting mode, and she's not waiting for plesiosaur.'

From down below there came a screech and growl as auxiliary boilers filled with kraken oil. The gears started to turn with the slow, massive torque of lower-deck screws, and then they moved, slow at first, then faster still. The propeller grumbled up white water, the remaining vanes fell off her damaged side wheels, but it mattered not. Manoeuvrability was not the issue here.

Saudade thrust forward until the bow wave curved up nearly as high as the deck. The needle on the echo box juddered with such frantic oscillation, it was almost impossible to make out each new picture.

Then the fog parted and the moon cast its cold light. Arden saw Bellis' ship for the first time.

Sean had not been at all creative when he called *Sehnsucht* a ghost ship. The craft could have been constructed out of fog and ice, for all that it stood out from the Tempest mist. Arden ran to the wheelhouse window, watched on with horrified wonder as *Saudade* thundered past that white shadow. She was like *Saudade* in design, but so overwhelmingly larger.

'She's turning,' Chalice yelped. She grabbed Arden's elbow. 'Arden, she's turning.'

'I *know*, Chalice. I'm trying to concentrate.'

'This isn't right. We should be chasing *them*! They tried to steal classified Order secrets!'

Arden debated shouting down the speaking tube for David to give her more oil, but without Mr Riven's intimate knowledge of his boat, she was unsure how much to push.

Chalice pressed herself against the door frame while Arden hugged the wheel with hands and knees. They were on the current, a dun-coloured sluice through the canyon of fog. The *Saudade*'s wheel became capricious and unsettled. The craft failed to aim true, and any moment now it would snicker out of her hands and spin. Had she not the lantern-turner's strength, she would have lost her grip.

A smaller paddle wheeler would have found no purchase in the disturbed water, or kept up with *Saudade*'s screw. They'd have escaped scot-free. From what little she'd seen of *Sehnsucht*, the vessel had vanes that bit deep, so she still kept behind, even if she could not gain without a screw propeller to give her speed.

Behind them, the ghost ship slid into the wash *Saudade* left behind. With each passing minute it receded in their view.

'You know, we could probably lose them completely if we went faster,' Chalice complained. The dawn stained the clouds in sickly yellow, and now there was light enough for even Chalice so see. Every few seconds she would hazard a peek out of the wheelhouse windows to make a disapproving noise.

Though most of the night had gone by without seeing their

pursuer, the echo box told the story of the big threshing ship, slow but inexorable, following them along the dun current. If she lost ground, it was not enough to lose *Saudade* completely. If the white boat had won races against *Saudade*, it must have been in a time before Mr Riven had upgraded her engine to accommodate a propeller.

'Can't you pick up the speed a little?' Chalice asked for at least the fifth time that night.

'This is not my boat to make go faster or to risk,' Arden said. 'We can keep going this speed indefinitely, but if we don't do something drastic, she'll stay on our tail until this ship starts falling apart.'

'Which is how long?'

Arden tapped one of the brass indicators. 'She could run like this for another hour or two maybe. Eventually we're going to overheat the valves.'

'Then do something drastic.'

'What?'

'I needn't be making suggestions to you, darling.'

Arden had words she could have said, but held them all the same. Chalice was not wrong. When she spoke at last to David, she could hear the defeat in her voice.

'Get up here, Mr Modhi. You take the wheel. I need to wake Mr Riven.'

Chalice Quarry tutted. 'Huh. You said he couldn't be woken.'

'I did not say waking was an impossibility, only that it was highly unpleasant.'

Mx Modhi had trained her son well. He did not dally on a command, and was out of the engine room within seconds, taking the wheel so she might do the most solemn of duties.

She went below decks, into the dark halls.

Arden lingered at the cabin door with a vial of ammoniac hartshorn from the surgeon's box, uncertain of what to say to him when he woke. She rested her head upon the wood, breathed deep, and pushed it open.

He lay upon the old night-silk sheets of the bed, shirtless and unconscious in a half-state of undress: he had clearly been trying to undo his waistband buttons when he had succumbed to the malaise of a kraken-calling comedown. Prior to then, he had made some effort to tape up his wounds. Plasters and bandages ran along the length of a crusted blade-track that had been roughly stitched, so he resembled nothing so much as a discarded doll, ill-treated and mended and treated ill again, so many times over that he was no longer fit for anyone except for the one who had loved him first.

Images and memories not hers came unbidden: child Bellis, whispering promises to love him through the storms of life, even though hers would be the worst of them. Child Bellis and child Jonah curling little baby fingers about and making promises to cross their hearts and hope to die, die, die. And elsewhere a small Arden Beacon, a squib of blood that was either useless or mysteriously disastrous with no appreciable in-between.

She would never kiss him properly again, she feared, never experience what it was to kiss him in love, and not ambiguity, or ambivalence, or stolen. Like her coat, second-hand his feelings for her were ill-fitting, made for another.

'Goodbye, Jonah.'

She bent to his lips and kissed him there. He stirred, murmured words in Old Fictish.

Then she broke the hartshorn vial beneath his nose.

The scent of the smelling salts hit her just as they hit him, a urinous punch of searing stench, and Mr Riven inhaled with the gasp of a fist darted into his diaphragm. He sat up, coughing, and frowned, instantly aware of the ship's engines. 'Why are we at full speed?'

'*Sehnsucht*,' Arden said. 'Bellis' ship. It's definitely following us. We've been having a merry slow chase for most of the night.'

She stood back, waited for him to gasp and run to his wife. And for a moment it seemed certain. A leaping agitation in his eyes, then the familiar curtain closed. The chances of Bellis being on the same ship that she and Stefan had sailed to their Island sanctuary, they were slim to none. Two people on their own could not have fought off pirates with a view to a ghostwood vessel. They'd have been like castaways in plesiosaur waters.

'How long away is she?'

'Maybe half a mile. *Saudade* got a head start on propellers. Though *Sehnsucht* is not catching up, she's not slowing down either.'

He shook his head to clear his mind. Tried to stand. Thought otherwise. The blood-hangover making his body tremble. Fell back down with his hand over his eyes.

'Why do you wake me to tell me this, Arden? Could you have not given me another hour asleep?'

'Whether it's your wife or pirates, it's better if you're awake. We need you ready.'

'Just give me a minute.'

Arden shifted uncomfortably, her envy making her speak. 'Do you think Bellis is on that ship?'

'I thought about it. Searched my heart. I don't think she's on board.'

'You don't?'

'Stefan promised me, Arden. Before they left. Whatever happened, Bellis would stay with him. She knew full well how important that was, how her life depended on it.'

'Then why did those people go after my blood, Jonah? Why did they destroy *Fine Breeze*?'

Mr Riven propped himself up on his elbow. 'Is it not obvious now what is happening?'

'No! Explain it to me!'

'The Lyonne Order own *Sehnsucht* now,' he said wearily. 'Probably from the moment Stefan let it go. That's why there is a Lion on board. If your blood is so important, would they have chanced its safety to Madame Quarry alone? Would the all-powerful Lyonne Order not have prepared for something like this to happen, had their agents standing by?'

'I . . . I guess so.'

'*Sehnsucht* could catch up to us easily if they wanted her to. It's an escort. We'll make it past the Wall, head back to Vigil with Mr Ironcup.'

'And you? Will you come back with me, to Vigil?'

He sat up. 'Isn't that the plan?'

'I don't know what the plan is. What is the plan, Jonah?'

He looked as if he were thinking, and she held her breath, terrified of what might come after. Then his eyes crinkled, and when he smiled she had never seen something so beautiful, or that filled her heart with such gladness.

'To run away with the Lightmistress, if she would allow me.'

The days and months of her solitude had done their part in reducing her to a raw nerve, and even his humour could not stop her blurring tears and half-formed syllables.

And Mr Riven swept her up in arms and kissed her with those lips and held her close to his poor wounded body.

Arden pushed him away. 'I am not a thing to mollycoddle. You turn hot and cold, and it is unconscionable to me. Are you staying, or going? What are your intentions?'

He released her, his gaze went to the floor. His voice had a strange thoughtfulness to it. 'It hurts me, the reality of you.'

'Then it's my fault now?'

'Always!' he said. 'You are everything. You filled my head with thoughts of you every day. Every *day*. When I first saw you on the beach in your golden threads I thought you were more beautiful than . . . than any dr*eam*. Even when I look at you I am torn. How could I be anything else for Arden Beacon of Clay Portside but a savage from Fiction? I learned enough from Stefan to know what your posting means. I fear you one day returning to Clay and forgetting the simple creature you dallied with, and I will be twice broken.' His bloodshot eyes were rimed with suffering. 'Twice broken, for I *loved* you.'

'Love? You speak of love when you would not let anyone love you back? You are so infuriating, Mr Riven,' she said between gasping sobs. 'The most infuriating man I have ever met. I don't take lightly my affections. I'm no coquette.'

Her pronouncements confused him so, and he seemed so stricken that she had to kiss him again, and he whimpered at the pain in his chest and when Arden went to pull away he only darted in again, his clumsy, uncouth mouth rough and greedy on her lips.

'Ah,' he said, and his eyes became dark with desire and his lips red and swollen from kissing, and she had to sigh to herself, for how often had she read in her penny presses about women swooning from kisses? Tough, incorrigible Mr Riven, weak and pliant before her. His excitement was evident in the soft leather of his breeches.

He took her hand, a silent query in him, regret and shame and longing at once. Her touch had merely started a cascade. Was perhaps not fully aware of his body's response, only that it came with so many others he could not distinguish.

'Oh, come now? In your condition? We have no time.'

'We must be quick, then,' he said, already unbuttoning himself.

'You are love mad,' she laughed, only the words came out hoarse with her own rapid quickening, and they were fools together, scraping out these hollow minutes from the uncertainty beyond them. She scooped him free of the leather strides and stroked the thick, silken length of Mr Jonah Riven, wanting to own him for the moment when he was so unquestionably certain of his love for her, when he spoke from lust and sexual hunger and yes, maybe yes, the thought of Bellis forever between them.

If her body wanted Mr Riven then, her mind was merely a startled passenger. Desire had the same landscape as pain, and its map – though detailed in familiar places – had lines hastily scrawled where they did not intersect with true trust and true love.

This was one of those places. She went into his lap, and his mouth again claimed hers in insatiable gulps. He wanted to devour her with kisses. His trembling hands moved under her skirts, over her thighs, through the still-damp lace, and was there he touched the centre of her in newfound intimacy, took startled delight in the folds of warmth he'd only experienced so briefly before.

Had they the time Arden would have guided Mr Riven's fingers to where they pleased her most, the creamy folds between her labia, the hard arousal of her clitoris, but the creaking juddering reminder of their rapidly gaining pursuers made her take matters to their conclusion. She mounted his lap, guided his penis into the hot centre of her, and he jerked up with forceful, inelegant thrusts into Arden with the same determined expression of a man committed to a fight.

Once more they heaved together, moved on by the thrum of the levers and their own breaths in the dark room, and their lovemaking was the engine that drove on the ship, an engine bruised and battered in both body and soul. Two people who had been tested and failed in all their dreams and perhaps had little else but one another, and even in that they weren't sure; for to what others had they promised themselves first?

Lost to his crisis, Mr Riven growled Fictish words, and his thrusts shortened and quickened. His arms tightened about her waist, the strength in them elating and terrifying at once. He lingered at the precipice of a terrible, violent act, and although she had consented to his bed, the fear remained that were his mind to change she could not stop him.

Arden was too wrung out and sore to climax again, too overwhelmed by this man's demands upon her body. So she held Mr Riven carefully as he breathed through his final peak. He came inside her, and she let him grow soft within the heated embrace of her.

They held each other with the closeness that only comes with uncertainty. Aftershocks of pleasure still coursed through him. Arden laid her cheek on Mr Riven's sweat-damp shoulder, doubtful if she should stay in this illusion of love or wake up to her place in his affections. Time had stood still in this room. Perhaps only five minutes had passed beyond the doors.

There was magic here, the same as those stories of children who walked through glowing doors into other worlds and remained in timeless stasis as all outside grew old and faded away.

But such stories rarely ended well. They always had to return to the cold, real world to die.

'We need to go,' she murmured. 'We are almost at the Maris waters.'

He pressed a soft kiss to both her eyelids, her mouth. 'Ah, devils, you are lovely, Arden. I wish I could do it again.'

Hard not to smile, so she hid it in his shoulder, then nodded, serious again. 'For the best, we really have to get up top.'

He pulled on his damp clothes and submitted to Arden sticking some more dressings upon his cut. They would have been better served with stitches, but he was flighty under her hands, like a captured animal that could not sit still.

'Right,' he said with a breath as he slid back into his coat. 'Let's evade my father's boat and it will be finished once and for all.'

'About time,' Chalice said to them when they made it to the wheelhouse. 'Ghostie's been gaining on us. What took you so long, anyway?'

Arden murmured non-committal words about trying to patch up wounds which needed a second pair of hands, but Mr Riven ignored Chalice's criticism and moved out onto the balcony with a pair of range-finding binoculars, for calculation, and a telescope, for a closer view.

'She can't be gaining, not while I'm running kraken oil under screw.'

'I'm not guessing,' Chalice said. 'I'm very good at distances.'

'Teach you that at Lion School do they?' Mr Riven jibed. He did not wait for Chalice to respond, only put the glass to his eye. 'Now, lets see who's running this old girl. Maybe old friends of yours Miss Quarry.'

'Well I—'

He was barely looking five seconds before something made him startle, and put the binoculars down. His confidence had whisked away, as if with the wind.

'Jonah?' Arden asked, concerned at the sudden departure of colour from his face. 'What do you see?'

He did not reply, not at first, only to say to David, 'Lad, ease back on the oil.'

Chalice murmured in protest, but for all that, she had read the situation fast and knew when it was time to fuss, and time to commit to silence and caution. 'She'll *definitely* catch up.'

Mr Riven turned to Arden, and whatever was on his lips, it could not be spoken of. He seized her hand.

In the silence she felt the heartbeat in him, his palm gone slick with sweat.

'Jonah?'

'Arden,' he said urgently. 'Get Sean Ironcup. Have David help you all with unhitching the tender dinghy at the back of this ship, lower it quietly and bring the Lion with you.'

'The dinghy? You said we could evade her.'

'Yes, I said that.' He pointed at a fog bank. 'You're all going to float as far back as you can to disappear. Then I'm going to tow you on a spider-web line, an invisible leash. Arden, listen to me. You cannot be here when they board.'

'What do you mean, *board*? Jonah, what's going on?'

A thump sounded overhead.

Mr Riven's hand tightened upon Arden's. His head tilted up. Said in the most grave voice, 'They had a trebuchet on the deck and—'

A voice said, 'Excuse me, I hate to interrupt.'

Chalice squeaked. However it had happened, a man was on the roof of the wheelhouse and his ruddy nose was in the open window, staring upside down at them.

The man was squash-faced and blond, with prison tattoos on each cheek. He looked at them with a pleasant if crooked smile. 'I'm sorry for interrupting your discussion, friends, but there are more important things you must contend with.'

The man's accent was strange, as if he spoke with a stone in his mouth. At his hands a small gas-powered crossbow.

Mr Riven lunged in front of Arden, and in the scuffle all Arden could see were limbs, and Chalice's head striking the wall, and a bronze coat snapping back as the bowman shouted, released a bolt from his crossbow.

It struck Mr Riven in the shoulder with the sound of a mallet to wet meat. With a scream of fury Mr Riven was smashed against the opposite wall, pinned by the five inches of black dart protruding from his collarbone.

He grabbed the bolt with both hands and pulled, and might as well have tried to draw a lance of iron from a rock.

The wail of pain from below came from the bowman, back-broken from having been torn off the roof from the recoil.

Arden ran to Mr Riven, afraid to touch the bolt, but in fear if she stayed. She gingerly placed her hands on the thin shaft and found no purchase there. 'Where's the tool box? I can pull it out.'

'Run,' Mr Riven gasped.

'I can't leave you.'

'He said *run*,' Chalice shouted, yanking Arden up by her collar. 'They have a catapult and glider-men! We must get in the lifeboat before another one lands!'

'But Mr Riven . . .'

Chalice shoved Arden through the wheelhouse door and buffaloed her onto the ladder. 'Move you, fool,' Chalice wailed. 'He's holding them off. You're the prize they . . .'

Chalice never got to finish. With a sickening crunch, the armoured prow of a ship rammed into *Saudade*'s side, nearly throwing Arden from the rungs.

A ship as ghostly as a fog, white as boiled bone, except for the glossy black square of her elaborate nameplate and the letters red as blood.

Sehnsucht.

32

Mr Riven made a sound

Mr Riven made a sound only once, and that was when the smartly dressed man, the first to board, finally snapped off the bolt that had fastened him to his wheelhouse wall. The barbs had proved difficult to prise from the black mangrove panels. Armed with a fearsome hinged tool, the man sweated through his silk shirt, his damask waistcoat and a medic's shawl with several false starts before untying his mustard-coloured cravat and rolling up his sleeves.

Arden, still kneeling in the corner where she had been shoved quite roughly before, watched the removal of Mr Riven's dart with bewildered dread. The man was Lyonnian. His accent did not belong to a Fiction pirate. He was not the only one with such confusing origins. Among the several pirates who had invaded their ship, fully half of them chattered like Claysiders.

The man put the bolt-cutter aside and nodded at the more utilitarian-dressed Sainted Island sailor who had accompanied him. 'All yours, Mr Taufik.'

'Thank you, Mr Absalom,' said the one called Mr Taufik good-humouredly. Opposite to the generous physicality of Mr Absalom, Mr Taufik had the spare, proletarian bearing of a Hillsider with a Pasifica-man's sea-severe face. 'There was a moment where I thought I might have to present our captive to the Queen with half the wall attached.'

'One mustn't upset the Queen.'

'No, one must not.'

'Carry on.'

Now that Mr Riven was free, Arden tried to scoot towards his prone body, only to have Mr Taufik slide himself between them.

'Oh no, your friend is in no condition for touchy-feelies.'

'Sir, he is hurt.'

'Mistress, we are all hurt in one way or another. And if he doesn't survive a bolt to the shoulder, what good is he, as a man, or a Riven?'

He bent down to touch the shiny end of the bolt as it protruded from Mr Riven's shoulder. 'My broken-backed scout downstairs tells me you can be clever when it comes to your freedom. And my Queen wishes to talk to you, sir.' He turned back to Arden. 'Therefore I'm not taking any chances on an upset. You understand. We are all of us beholden to our vows and orders.'

Mr Taufik called a pair of sailors up to the wheelhouse. He pointed at Mr Riven, said some words in a tradesman's cant that Arden vaguely found familiar – the rhythms were as familiar as a dockworker's dialect though the consonants were all wrong – and they hauled him up to his feet.

'Careful,' she pleaded.

Mr Taufik gave a gallant sort of bow. 'They will be careful. The Captain does not wish him harmed. You can stand up now, girl.'

In the midst of it all, Arden rankled. She had not been a girl for nearly a decade, and Mr Taufik was easily her age, but she was hardly in a place to quibble. She stood up on unsteady feet, feeling the weight of the shackles bear down upon her wrists.

'So, you are the lighthouse keeper of Vigil.' Mr Taufik touched the brim of his seaman's cap to nod respectfully. 'The navigational coldfires of Lyonne are legendary all around the world. It is a respect that you have earned well, Guildswoman.'

On the splintered deck, Chalice had not been granted the trial of an innocent. They'd bound her arms securely behind her back and gagged her into the bargain. Clearly these pirates had seen immediately in Chalice what had taken Arden weeks.

Chalice kept flicking her attention to *Sehnsucht*'s deck, willing Arden to focus on the ghost ship.

There was nothing on that high deck, not a person. David and Sean were missing.

One of the crewmen approached Mr Taufik, wearing impatience on his salt-burned face. 'Tauf,' he said. 'There's nobody else on this boat.'

'Have you checked everywhere?'

'The head, the engine rooms, the cabin. There's nobody.'

Mr Taufik frowned. 'There should have been five souls aboard.'

'Aye, if the craft is properly stocked, but there's a tender boat winch at the back of this boat. Whatever was on it, is missing.'

'Hmm, *she* won't like that.' Mr Taufik considered the fog and what it meant. The day was here now, and the sunrise on a distant Island shore gave the permanent storm a jaundiced murk. 'Hard to survive out on these waters with only a small craft. We'll call the other two lost at sea and be done with them. We have what we came for.'

A wretched tingle of hope made Arden perk up. The boys had escaped, though if Mr Riven heard the good news, he gave no notice of it. He looked the part of a man familiar with detention and chains. An excoriated distance overwhelmed his expression, his pale skin gone a driftwood grey. They had taken no chances with their prisoner, bonding him to a yoke-contraption that fixed his wrists on either side of his head, must have caused considerable agony to his wounded shoulder.

She felt his pain. Felt the wound as if it were upon her own flesh.

'Jonah,' Arden whispered when Mr Taufik's attention was averted. 'Are you all right? What do we do?'

Whatever fugue had caught him now slipped. He wobbled his fingers, only just realizing they had bound him in a most specific method, a position that would not allow him to draw his own blood. A way they should not have known, unless . . .

His waxen face turned to her. 'Don't get close to me. Whatever happens, you and I, there is nothing between us . . .'

Mr Taufik returned, and snatched Arden away. 'Ah now, no talking to the merchandise. We must all get on *Sehnsucht*. I fear *Saudade* is taking on water. If anyone is hiding on her, well then. I hope they can swim.'

Shock-numbed, Arden allowed a sailor to help her across the gangway and onto *Sehnsucht*.

The moment she set foot on that bone-white wooden deck, a kick of cold jolted through Arden's body. Dark *Saudade* always had an aura of warmth and intimacy about her, her rich mangrove wood echoing a holy relic. This bleached giant of a sister-ship had the smell of slaughterhouses and desecrated tombs, along with a fungal sediment of decay.

Like criminals they were led onto *Sehnsucht*'s broad open forward deck, an area that could accommodate fifty people if needed be, a hundred at a crush.

Only twelve stood here in the wind apart from them, waiting, along with Mr Absalom, insouciant upon the bow, as if an interesting stage play had come to be acted out in his presence.

The pirates set Arden and Chalice aside, leaned them against the bridge. Mr Riven was placed upon the foredeck to stand bloodied and on display. Arden yearned towards him. If she could have taken his pain upon herself she'd have done so, twice over.

The sound of a door opening made the entourage shuffle to attention. Someone else was on the ship who did not slot so easily into the role of Sainted Island bandit.

A woman.

The Pirate Queen?

She was a girl, younger than Arden, her dark hair bound up in an abalone fork. She wore a flowing yellow sea-silk robe embroidered in black pearls that would have better befitted some royal court than the deck of a ship.

Or at least the dress had been yellow, until the stains of dirt and blood had streaked it orange in places. Many of the pearls had fallen off in the way such decorations will do if they are worn for a very long time and not carefully maintained.

She shared a look with Arden, distress and mortification combined, before concealing her face under a silk shawl of faded yellow.

'I am Persephone Libro, the Queen's lady-in-waiting and spoil of war. You are guests upon *Sehnsucht* of the Maris Island Cluster,' the girl continued, her thin reedy voice fluting in the empty air. 'These are the Marians from Maris Proper who have welcomed you.'

Arden frowned. The girl spoke by rote and a harassed familiarity, but what had she seen and done to make her so desperately dishevelled?

Spoil of war, she had said. Persephone Libro, a Sainted Isle girl and spoil of war. What political upheavals was she referring to? How in danger were they?

Mr Riven, unable to hold himself upright, fell on his knees. The bolt was not bleeding badly, however it did something to him that made him hunch over in ashen pain.

'Listen,' Arden said urgently to the gathered men. 'There is a code among sailors and pirates alike. You cannot leave him like that.'

Mr Taufik winced, then hissed at a pair of bandits. 'Get him to his feet.'

'Captain on deck,' a male voice shouted. 'Her Majesty on deck! Queen of the Islands is present, you louts, you wretches. Bow to your damned Queen!'

The sailor holding Mr Riven quickly snapped to attention again, and the others followed. Released, Mr Riven fell back into a kneeling crouch.

No false alarm this time. Everyone had frozen in place.

Then the twelve men fell to their knees. Arden shared a glance with Chalice, and at the stormbride's nod, they both carefully bobbed.

The dress came first, ruffles and layers of discoloured white. Stained satin slippers stepping across the white wood. Tiny hands in fingerless cream gloves, entwined piously about a wedding ring of black iron worn over the cloth. The ring was too large for her finger, and stained the glove-satin green.

The face, sharp and Fiction-pale, was so deteriorated by an internal, seething rage it was as if she were a porcelain doll left to crackle into decay. Frayed yellow hair touched her thin, bony shoulders. The crown she wore was ship-hull nails dipped in gold. A livery collar of plesiosaur teeth bound up in wire obscured most of the tattered lace of her bodice. A train of fishing net, tangled and worn, followed her along with a brace of glass floats.

Arden found she'd been holding her breath. Who was this woman? Not Bellis, the beautiful girl who Jonah loved.

This had to be someone else.

Two men swept the floor before their Queen with brooms of a bitterbush. The acrid fragrance of the brushes overwhelmed the salt in the air.

Mr Taufik stepped forward. 'We recovered them,' he said. 'One man, two women.'

The husk Queen ignored Mr Taufik and her prisoners to gaze down at Mr Riven's crumpled form. She shook her head. 'Jonah,' she said. 'My God, husband. You shouldn't have come.'

33

When he didn't immediately reply

When he didn't immediately reply, Bellis grabbed the bolt-end in Mr Riven's shoulder and twisted it terribly, forcing Mr Riven out of his daze.

'I said you *promised* me you wouldn't *come*, Jonah.'

He groaned, said her name with a breathless wheeze. 'Bellis, you were in danger . . .'

She cut him off with an impatient gesture. 'When am I always not in danger, in this boat of venomous snakes? I'm told Mr Absalom had to take you off the wall. Well, then. Was a time you would have torn your arm off at the root rather than remain imprisoned so.' A sadness in her soft, fragile voice, as if she had lost something important. 'And now you kneel in submission to pain. The years have diluted you, husband.'

'Wife, this is different. The Lions know where you are, they want to control you, and use you now.'

'Use me? Why would you hold me in such low regard? The Lyonnians and their Order have wanted my labour forever.' She looked around her, smiled benevolently at her gathered silent crew. 'I was doing quite fine, and now you came back to me like this, ruined, by these devils, *ruined*.' She grabbed the bolt again, and she was weeping as she did so, fat milky tears upon her broken-doll face, oblivious to Mr Riven's suffering as she revelled in her own.

'The man I married would have held himself above pain! What stranger wearing my beloved's face are you? These witnesses of mine cannot be fooled by such a despicable disguise!'

Mr Riven was transcendent with agony. A sound of strangulated surrender came from him. Beside his head, his trapped hands balled into fists. Old injuries opened, sending blood pouring down his exposed forearms.

Arden could stand it no longer. 'Stop it, damn you. He's hurt, and he came on your behalf!'

Bellis stopped testing her husband and glared at Arden for the first time.

Mr Riven swallowed deep huffing, shuddering breaths, began urgently trying to capture her attention back.

'The women have nothing to do with this . . .'

Bellis waved the voices away. She was done with him. One of the Islanders shoved a bight of coir between Mr Riven's teeth. Her attention was on Arden now.

Chalice Quarry made murmuring sounds that could have been plea or prayer. The girl in saffron yellow wrapped her arms around her body, brought one fist to her mouth.

Bellis was smaller, up close. A twig would have more strength. The acrid-bush smell was about her, a petrochemical aroma of heated stone and rockblood.

'I know that coat of yours,' she said to Arden.

'Your wedding coat,' Arden replied as steadily as she could. She knew she should have diplomatically added, *and you may have it back*, but could not, for the coat had the importance of a contested trade region. Even now, Arden was not about to give it up.

Bellis wrinkled her nose, drawing sharp lines across her face, highlighting the deep shadows beneath her eyes. 'The hell that ugly thing was my wedding coat.' Tugged at the collar. 'Was forced on me by necessity, but never mine. The Deepwater Queen does not wear the coat of her enemy.'

She circled Arden, inspecting every inch of her. 'So, you're the one the angels talk of, when they sing their songs from the Lion's den.' Bellis pushed up the krakenskin sleeve and touched the inside of Arden's arm. Her thin white finger looked like a chicken bone laid against Arden's skin. 'They sing so sweetly, of something in these veins that entangles and endows. A strange chemistry, bred out of our genetic lines, but still commanding fear, the way mine does.'

Arden wanted to recoil from that dry, hard finger. 'I don't know what—'

'So very, very Lyonne to lose sight of the gold from over-gilding,' Bellis said, sharper now. 'Well, we here in Fiction might not have thousand-year ancestral ledgers, but we know good breeding, and who to *fuck*.'

Bellis' pinched Fictish features turned mean, and she grabbed Arden's arm hard with her fingerless gloves, dug in her bony fingers. Had Bellis still retained fingernails, she'd have broken skin. Instead those tiny fingers were knobs, like the joints at the end of bird bones.

'You have no right to destroy my life's work! Jonah Riven, my *Jonah*, was carved in suffering and restraint, a creature conceived only to inspire terror and protection and one day be a leader to challenge even the dirty *anguis* worshippers on the fucking northern shore, and somehow he ends up back in my lap like this, like *this*, snivelling with a little hurt, for *everyone* to *fucking see*!'

Behind Bellis, Mr Riven tried to stand up. One of the crewmen shoved him by his wounded shoulder, forced him into kneeling again.

No, Jonah, Arden prayed through her terror. *Don't make it worse.*

Chalice moaned. This time she wiggled her fingers, and an outsider would have seen only a woman trying to make comfort of their bonds. But she kept making the same finger sign, over and over again, and Arden recognized the signs she saw on the Clay Portside docks among men who had been imprisoned for crimes or just bad luck, the secret language of captives, made with their hands.

Fire, she was saying, but with emphasis. *Fire.*

Bellis turned on her gathered crew and berated them with a spitting rant that was as familiar to them as breakfast gruel, given their resigned expressions. 'Which one of you will be running back to Miah Anguis, huh? Scurrying back to the slaughterman of Equus with little tales of this evening, of my once-terrifying husband so toothless, so lame? Oh, he'll come to my castle and murder me with a laugh . . . and then I'll fucking kill the lot of you!'

A dozen pairs of eyes turned to their feet in terror, except for Mr Absalom, who viewed them all with the odd benevolent humour of a person secure in his position.

Fire, Chalice repeated hurriedly. *Sacrifice. More. More.*

Bellis spun to Arden, leaned in, her breath a miasma of petrolactose fumes. 'So how did you do it?' she wheedled. 'How did you take what was fierce and brilliant and important to me and soften it to rottenness? Did you fornicate with him like a fine Lyonne *whore*?'

Mr Riven jerked upright on his knees, his body trembling, eyes wide as a hunt-spooked animal that senses danger but cannot articulate its edges. 'Bellis, nothing happened between us,' he started to say through the rope bight, before Mr Taufik tugged the end and silenced him.

'We are all puppets,' Arden protested. 'All of us. You might think you are free now, but Lyonne controls us with words, spreads rumours to make us dance. They wanted you to dance right back into their arms.'

'There was a special dance around you too, was there not?' Bellis mused, tapping her lip with her finger. 'Some odd symmetry, some strange shadow, and they exiled you to Fiction, an experiment. See, I am exiled here too. An experiment. I know. Safe and sound and so very far away from Clay City so I can't cause any trouble.' Bellis simpered and giggled. 'Oh, every once in a while the Order sends a spy or three, but nobody has got me talking yet. It is I who make them talk. And sing. And they sing such a strange song of you, I am very curious, Arden Beacon.'

'If you and I were truly twinned in any kind of special blood chemistry, we would be meeting in the Lyonne Towers as honoured guests, not on this ship,' Arden said urgently. 'All I can do is make *ignis* fire, and that not very well.'

'A fire,' Bellis echoed emptily.

Arden implored her. 'You must believe me. I've no wish to hurt you.'

'Oh, you wouldn't hurt me. Not in the slightest. The songs all alleviated that worry.'

Behind Bellis, Mr Absalom smiled, and even from across the room, Arden could see one tooth was Djenne gold. He reminded her of Uncle Nicolai Beacon, the confidence in him, the way the moving parts of the world operated around him yet affected him not at all.

'We will discover the truth of that music soon enough, Your Majesty,' he promised.

A clatter of activity distracted Arden from her interrogation. The sailors were hauling up tin water buckets from over the side of *Sehnsucht*, placing them in concentric circles about Mr Riven as he knelt in his supplication to those gods of pain. The water sloshed on the deck.

'Now I have an opportunity, see,' Bellis continued. 'Certainly, I have been delivered back something broken, but what is broken can be mended. I can purge the softness and the rot from him. Not enough to kill and maim. But enough pain to remark and remember, and to do it before witnesses.'

One of the *Sehnsucht* sailors ran up to Bellis from outside the door. 'We found the blood our messenger said she'd be carrying. Hidden in the lifejacket crate,' he said breathlessly. He held aloft the mason jar. Beside Arden, Chalice stopped murmuring and became still.

'Your blood?' Bellis asked Arden with a beatific smile. 'In a jar? Well, that will save us the problem of cutting you.'

'Bellis . . .' Arden implored.

'Of course, it wouldn't be unlike the Lyonne Order to try and trick me. This could be poison blood, and if I were to daub it on myself – well then. Would I not be the fool?' She caressed the glass. 'Can I tell you of my experience with fire?'

Arden did not reply. Saw the horror coming.

'I saw a terrible accident once, in an automatic refinery fire on Equus.' Bellis' white fingers fluttered in the air before her. 'A long time ago, in the days before I was married. A man burned alive because they were stealing the rockblood from the mechanica, and forgot the mechanica cannot abide being stolen from. Such a screaming fit he made of it, up in flame, eyes popping in his skull, *pop-pop*. And the heat, like the surface of the sun.

'Oh, I was full of sorrow for him at first, for I was young and did not appreciate that his test was necessary and holy. How someone could survive such an immolation – it is only a question for God and His devils, but afterwards, this previously weak, cowardly man, this man who had not a single quality of leadership, was *transformed* by his pain. Made *anew*. A prophet he became, blind and hideous but powerful, oh yes. People now set themselves alight for him, and I, with my own secret flame burning within my breast and in my heart, know that this is how I will save my Jonah from his own weakness.'

Arden would have risen to her feet were she not held down. 'He can't be saved if he's dead!'

Bellis poked her finger into Arden's cheek. 'You aren't dead. Because I can smell the *aequor profundum* on your skin. He *healed* you. That secret Riven talent. Let's see if he can heal himself.'

Chalice made noises into her gag that sounded like *no no no*.

Gasping, Arden strained against the ropes. 'Bellis Harrow, your soul will be damned forever if you hurt him.'

'*Harrow*, you call me? Harrow, when I was wedded to a Riven before witnesses?' She came close to Arden, tilted her chin in Mr Riven's direction. Bitterbush stench all about her.

Petroleum on her breath. Her teeth blackened with coal. 'Bellis *Riven* I am, protected only by my name. Only two things are feared on our Islands, the threat of fire and the name of *Riven*. I will be both threat and Riven, after today.'

With that, Bellis stood and in a whirl took the mason jar of Arden's blood from the subordinate and up-ended it over Mr Riven's head. The blood had congealed down to gelatinous lumps and smeared him in gore. He shook his head to whip the muck from his eyes. He growled furiously through the rope bight, trapped but not surrendered.

'Oh, look. Nothing happened. That is a shame. You did say your cold flame was weak, so I cannot fault your honesty.'

Bellis smiled down at her husband. Her expression softened to him for the first time and Arden glimpsed what she may have once looked like, as a child. He was suddenly beautiful to her like this. She caressed his bloodied, whiskered face, his shoulders, then ducked down into a squat, caressed his leather-clad thigh as if teasing him, pressed a thin, hard hand between his legs. Whispered something into his blood-smeared ear as she did so.

When he did not react quite so enthusiastically to this, their long-awaited reunion, she slipped her hand past the waistband of his strides, clasped what she found there, stroked him.

Bellis meant to humiliate Jonah further, reduce him to nothing before her men, show him in sexual thrall to the Queen of this death-white ship. And Arden understood with a dreadful clarity what it meant. Maybe . . . maybe if he responded to her gross ministrations, Bellis would spare him. Maybe if he showed Bellis proper deference, this would all be a threat and never carried out.

Arden wanted Mr Riven to look at her, to silently give him courage in this abject act. *Grow hard at her touch*, she implored. *Spend yourself into that hand of bones and skin. Make Bellis believe she is that upon which all your desires hinge, even when there is nothing left outside of promised pain and endless despair. This might save you.*

But his gaze had turned blank and distant, and he shrank in upon himself, encased in a cocoon of his own flesh. Bellis continued to stroke him and whisper her fascinations. Nobody moved, except Mr Absalom, who watched them all with his knowing basilisk gaze.

The fact that Mr Riven didn't – or couldn't – respond clearly vexed Bellis. She gave him one last malicious squeeze and stood up suddenly. 'What's wrong with you? You have lost your vigour. *Impotent.* Neutered. Like a dog.'

She turned back to Arden. Bared her teeth. 'Now we find out what the Lions were talking about. Persephone!'

The yellow-dressed girl fished in the folds of her dress, and pulled out a pint-jar that might have once been a milk-bottle. Bellis discarded the lid. Aromatic fumes washed over them. Distilled petroleum, and flammable as the sun. A man nearby lit a flare, a crimson, phosphorous eye, almost too bright to look at. Laid it between Jonah's knees.

'*Ignis* fire is cold, more's the pity. But my fire is strong.'

Arden saw Mr Riven swallow a breath. The phosphor flare turned his skin an unholy colour. The sailors readied their buckets nervously, ever fearful of a fire upon a wooden ship.

'Healer,' Bellis said. 'Cure this.'

Jonah, Arden breathed.

The liquid fell upon him and the fire ignited.

34

A whump of hot flame

A *whump* of hot flame and a roil of smoke and char that filled the air with embers. Arden might have screamed, if not for the rattle and bang of people falling upon the decks and a lone body stumbling out of the smoke into Bellis' arms.

'*Save me, Holy Maria*,' the burned sailor groaned.

'Get off me, you brute!' Bellis shoved him away into the acrid mist. 'Where is he? Where is my husband?'

The smoke was thicker than the fog, a grey murk swirling with trails of white. A fire had taken hold of the forecastle, flames licking as high as the wheelhouse.

The smoke swallowed Bellis from Arden's view, and in the melee Arden dived for Chalice, tearing off her gag.

'Quick Chalice, move!'

Arden dragged Chalice sideways, down the length of the deck. Anyone would have been blinded by the smoke if they'd not worked all their lives in pea-soupers, could tell by the echo of a footfall where to go.

She got her stormbride about and twisted off the shackle catch, freeing her arms. 'Did you see Jonah, is he dead?'

Without waiting for the obvious answer Arden turned about so Chalice could do the same.

Once Chalice had her bit out, she spat coir and said, 'No, he healed himself, your blood can—'

A man loomed out of the clouds, still in stocks. Mr Riven, his shirt blackened and in tatters, emerged slightly singed but otherwise unharmed. His eyes bright. Arden sobbed in relief. She wrapped him up in her arms, wanted to take the weight of him if she could.

'How? I saw you consumed!'

'I need . . . to get help. To call up . . .' he gasped, and began to cough, each spasm wracking his injured chest. He'd used sanguinity from the blood in his wound, but too much, too much . . .

'Jonah, *dammit*.' Arden seized one bound hand. 'Let me get the stocks off.'

'No time,' he croaked. 'We have to get to the back of the ship before they put the petroleum fire out and regroup.'

Chalice took the other side of Mr Riven and they stumbled through the clearing air.

'These people are mendicants of the highest order!' she protested, as they came across the dinghy lashed to *Sehnsucht*'s side. 'You too, Chalice Quarry.'

Mr Riven shook himself free of their hands. 'You must lower the lifeboat, quickly.'

A throat cleared with a cough. Arden's shoulders wrenched tight. They were too late.

'Ah, I *thought* you would make it back here,' said the deep Lyonne voice. 'My instincts for sensing benightedness are still keen despite repeated exposure.'

Mr Absalom stood on the deck with a harpoon spear in his hand, one long enough to spike a leviathan if he had to. His eyes streamed red from the smoke. His waistcoat was singed from escaping the fire upon the deck.

He nodded at Mr Riven. 'So it's true. The woman is a catalyst. That blood of hers turned your little healing trick into something powerful. You survived immolation.'

Mr Riven made to lunge at him, but Mr Absalom did not

have the clumsiness of a brute fighter from a dock pit, nor was there a chance of Mr Riven defeating him while bound up and close to collapsing. Arden stepped in front of Mr Riven before he could move, caught him about his waist, could feel his heart in his chest, the dread in him.

'Wait, Jonah.'

'Arden,' he said. 'Don't trust this man.'

'Sir,' Arden said to Mr Absalom, 'let us go. We did not deserve this inhumane treatment from your *Queen*. I can see you are different from the others, but there is no help you can give other than letting us go.'

Mr Absalom shook his head. 'At present the others scramble about their Maiden Queen and try to stop *Sehnsucht* from springing a burning leak, but not for much longer. If a lifeboat is to disappear, then they will blame me.'

'Then make up something, damn you! If you consider yourself noble Djenne, or Karakorum or whatever you are! If you wear the embellishments of great people, then live up to them! Just say we struck you from behind or you passed out. Have you no pride?'

Mr Riven sagged behind Arden. She caught his body, and he had seemed so much more solid when she had held him in joy. Now he was a wraith.

'Jonah, I need you awake. Don't falter now . . .'

'Arden, you can't be here.'

Behind them, Chalice struggled with the rearward lifeboat rope.

'The damn thing has an Athenian knot! I can't budge it.' She stared hopelessly out towards the horizon. '*Saudade*'s drifting. We'll never catch her.'

Mr Absalom stood above them, watching with all the pitilessness of a desert. 'They will make a vivisection of you, Lightmistress. Bled and torn limb from limb until you are meat. Your blood has proven itself worth a little parlour trick, but the Queen will want to see it work on herself. She has many shadows that, were they to be increased, well . . . she would be a very powerful creature indeed.'

Shouts echoed from the end of the ship. Angry shouts. They had been spotted. Mr Absalom's eyes widened.

To Chalice he said, '*Is there no help for the Widow's Son?*'

The words meant nothing to Arden, but Chalice stopped yanking on the knots. A strange, almost blank acknowledgement appeared on her face. 'What do you need, brother?'

He pulled a small tablet of polished brass from his waistcoat pocket and shoved it into Chalice's hands. '*Hide it.*'

Arden had only a moment to look upon the rose and thorn crest of the Lyonne Investigatory Order as her stormbride snatched up the shining locket and shoved it in between her bosoms.

'Take Mx Beacon off this ship,' Mr Absalom urged Chalice. 'Now. But the man must stay here.'

He had given an order. Chalice grabbed Arden's hand. 'Arden, we have to jump.'

She pulled herself away. 'No! What has gotten into you, Chalice Quarry? We don't leave without Jonah.'

The footsteps peppered the deck through the smoke. She stood firm, ready to protect him. Mr Riven made a last despairing sound. His chin fell against her face and the words came out raw.

'Go. Go but remember me. Remember your poor fisherman from Vigil. Give him the Deepwater prayer in midwinter and remember him.'

'I don't know the Deepwater prayer.'

'Nor do I, but I will serve the King soon. He will teach it to me in the court of my ancestors.'

'You cannot die. You cannot.'

Jonah Riven kissed her once upon her forehead, something more tender than passion, more marbled with regret.

From the centre deck, Bellis Harrow screamed.

'Don't you dare move!'

Arden looked at Jonah one last time, then she met the woman's eyes in defiance. Glassy as cataracts, with only evil behind them. With a gasp of a desperately committed breath, Arden tipped backwards over *Sehnsucht*'s stern.

The wake of the water swallowed her in a roar of bubbles, and the cold wash penetrated her with the agony of a thousand needles. When her head cleared the surface, Chalice was already floundering alongside, agitating her skirts to make them buoyant.

'By the Cross of the Redeemer we survived the fall,' Chalice gasped. 'If not for that paddle-foam the drop would have killed us.'

'What the devils did you do?' Arden shouted back, spitting salt. Her krakenskin coat ballooned with air, making her bob on the surface of the water. 'And who was that man you just gave up Jonah for?'

'I saved our lives,' Chalice huffed, dog-paddling towards her within a ring of inflated fabric. Her face had taken on a fish-belly shade from the cold water. 'They have a spy from the Order on board. He knows them, so if he says they'll kill us if we stay, they *will*.'

'This *water* will kill us! We'll not last ten minutes!'

A shriek from the boat interrupted them, so high-pitched and commanding that it could only have come from Bellis: *Get her out. Get them out!*

The paddlewheels ceased turning. The ship listed. A rope ladder flung over *Sehnsucht*'s side. Mr Riven did his best to run interference, but from her water-vantage Arden knew he was hopelessly outmatched. A fist from one of Bellis' sailors struck him once, twice. Hauled him halfway over the port railing, where his bound hands grasped open air on either side of his head.

His eyes met Arden's, and she had never seen such a look on a living thing.

Jonah . . .

Little more than a whisper, an entreaty, a farewell.

Mr Riven bit down hard upon his lip and spat blood into the water.

Bellis let out a horrific piercing scream. '*Get him the FUCK devil AWAY from the WATER!*'

The sailors dragged him back and Arden saw him no more.

Bellis ran to the edge of the boat, pointed at Arden, warning and accusing. Nothing she said, for such demons needed to say nothing.

By now the men charged to bring Arden back had descended the ladder and commenced swimming out to meet their two wretched prisoners.

. . . or they would have done if the surface of the water had not turned to glass and rainbows, a thousand translucent bodies writhing around them, and the ocean falling away, preparing their ascent into heaven.

35

Where are they taking us

'Where are they taking us?' Chalice yelled over the slosh and roar of the waves.

'I don't know,' Arden replied breathlessly, her mind whirring as fast as the water that carried her. Magic? Magic was fragile, a phenomenon that could be explained by science eventually. Her dress clung to her but it was not unpleasant. Like a liquid carriage. Arden forced sense on what she could see: from the corner of her eye she could discern the vague shape of an eye, perhaps a hoof on the end of a long leg, forming from the white wash of the waves that lifted them away. They should have frozen in such water, but the water-horses warmed the water to the temperature of blood. Electric flashes darted about them, they were carried aloft on a tide of light. Hard bodies, threshing tails, manes of wet kelp. Arden grabbed one hippocamp mane to find it fall away in her hands and turn to jelly.

Then almost as suddenly as it had come the phenomenon was gone and the two castaway women were floating in empty sea once more.

'Well, that's a fat lot of help,' Chalice gasped once the last of the horse-waves had receded. She rolled about on the puffs of her inflated skirt. The becalmed sea sloshed lazily about them as the night fell and darkness closed in. 'If he was going to summon a herd of hippocampi he could have at least taken us all the way.'

'He might not be conscious any more, Chalice.'

'Oh. All right.'

Arden tested the waters with her hand. With the fading light, another source of illumination came, this time from deep below, faint red, like the afterimage of a bright light on an eye.

'Water's warm.'

'Hot water current. Sea-vent, or an underwater volcano,' Chalice said. 'Ah, to die of exhaustion and thirst rather than chill. That makes all the difference.'

'Wasn't it your idea to jump?'

'It was a spur-of-the-moment decision,' Chalice protested in between spitting out salt water. 'Jumping felt better than being dragged off for Queen Harrow's entertainment.'

Arden paddled vigorously even though the krakenskin coat would not let her sink. 'What happened on the boat, anyway, Chalice?' she gasped, kept aloft by anger more than anything. 'I can put a fire out, is that my damn shadow?'

'No,' Chalice panted in return. 'Not the fire. You only made stronger what Jonah could do. Water is his element. You *increased* that.'

'But still, a fire like that . . . nobody could heal from it.'

'You're not a very strong *sanguis ignis*, but of that other thing . . . you are strong indeed.'

Arden paddled about. 'I think,' she started, raising her chin away from the water, 'I think I know what Bellis has. What shadow made the Society so cautious and you Lions so interested.'

Chalice tilted her head, frowned, swallowed water and coughed. 'Oh?'

'I saw a broken doll of a woman, yet I saw her issue instructions to those frightening men, on a ship that was once slower than *Saudade*, yet which caught us easily.'

A look of guilt passed over Chalice's face. Yet one more thing to hold against her former friend in the short time they probably had left.

'These old talents overlap, Arden. They were never bred to be specific. Nobody can say for certain what Bellis has, or had, or what she may yet develop . . .'

'*Sanguis orientis*,' Arden said. 'Why not? A Sainted Isle trait for a girl in such close proximity? I saw how she made those men jump at her word. She could command legions if she could work it properly. Sure, it's a scrappy bunch of toothless pirates she compels now, but think her with an army.'

'I don't want to think of it,' Chalice said.

'No. I suppose nobody does. It would be awful, wouldn't it. Her, Queen of Lyonne and Fiction. The Society and the Order would have to work to her command. No wonder they wouldn't let her go to Lyonne!' Her exhaustion made her slightly hysterical, and she giggled and wept at once.

Dark things flitted below them. Arden was certain she saw the long neck of a plesiosaur, the bulbous head of an ichthyic whale. Were Jonah unhurt, these creatures would be in his control. But he was, and they were not.

So Bellis was sanguis orientis. The bloodworked command upon the lich-ships that ran between Equus and Vigil, objects that did what they were told, forever.

'There was a chance she could be . . . amenable though,' Chalice said.

'Oh yes, because Mr Lindsay hoped Jonah would tighten her leash!'

'Well, we thought he would! He did it once! How was anyone to know how much of a ruse of hers that idea was!' Chalice wallowed in her inflated dress. 'Damn it, I'm sinking.'

The night, when it came, was so dark. The fog hid the stars. Away from the warm-water upswell, the cold began to seep in, promising pain. They were neither of them brave enough to enter the cold water and freeze, so they remained paddling around in their little thermocline. Arden prayed for one of the monsters to come up, to eat them or save them. But they did neither, oblivious to the pitiful little lives above them, and she felt for the first time the tenuous link between herself and Jonah Riven sever, like a thread pulled tight until it snapped.

'Arden,' Chalice said, and the harsh tone brought her back from her despair.

'What is it?'

'We don't have to do this. This waiting to end in agony, by thirst or frost.' Chalice took Arden's hand with her water-wrinkled own. 'I have a vial,' she said urgently. 'A poison given to all Lions. It is placed under my skin, in my arm here. If you could dig it out, we could share it.'

'I don't . . . I don't know. Let us think a while.'

'All right. A little while.'

The two women clung to each other for comfort, aware of the only path forward left to them.

The water was getting colder. The current was moving them on.

'Chalice,' Arden said after a long silence.

'Yes, darling?'

'You said my blood could *increase* an endowment. Make someone else's stronger?'

'Or your own. You've been riding on a *sanguis ignis* talent that was just about latent anyway. You were never *ignis*, or *malorum*. Just increased the tiny correspondence with fire you naturally had.'

Had she not been so cold, Arden might have mourned such a revelation. Now they were identities stripped away by water.

'You've been tested, Chalice. What did you say you had?'

'Only the slightest symmetry for salts and minerals. Sodium, some lower metals.' She shrugged as best she could with her shoulders half-submerged in the water.

'Sodium is an atomic component of salt . . .' Arden murmured, as if her mouth spoke a memory she could not.

'See. Nothing useful, I'm afraid. Unless you wanted *more* salt.' Chalice said, her teeth now chattering. 'Curse! It could be rock candy and saltwater taffy I trammel, for all I know.'

Arden pulled off her glove, let it float away.

'What are you doing, darling?'

'I saw Mr Lindsay with a sodium light in the Justinian orangery,' Arden said. 'I can't make enough light with *ignis malorum*, but if you helped me . . . if you could control that element, maybe I could increase your interaction with it.'

'To do what?' A note of panic twanged in Chalice's voice.

'Whatever it can do.'

Chalice stared, terrified. For a long moment Arden feared Chalice would refuse. Then she nodded. Pulled her locket out. *A rose upon thorns.* She used the thorn of the Rose Order to dig into the coin in Arden's hand. Arden could not help but hiss at the pain.

Then Chalice inflicted the sharp locket upon her own hand. She had calluses there, from years of work, and Arden wanted to tell her that it was not important, the place.

But Chalice wanted to cut herself in the same place she had cut Arden. It was important to her.

'Ugh, almost, almost.'

Arden senses the blood in the water with a sick lurch, both for the meaning of it, and for the realization that it was her shadow endowment making her so sensitive to sanguinity. She'd always carried that shadow with her, not knowing, oblivious.

Now only if it would work.

The stormbride let the rose locket go. Let it float to the bottom of the ocean. They wrapped their hands together. Arden felt the blood in her grommets prickle and ache. A deep weariness overcame her. *Please*, she thought. *Let something happen, anything, that is not dying on an empty sea.*

Their buoyancy was increasing. They wallowed on the surface of the becalmed water.

'Maybe it is salt. Oh, I could imagine an island of salt,' Chalice murmured, her shivering chin knocking into Arden's ear. Arden's mind was becoming fog. Chalice's voice drifted through it. 'A salt crystal palace.' Their hands squeezed tighter.

'A Kingdom of Salt and we will be Queens upon it.'

'Is anything else happening?' Arden asked. Her hands had gone into a rictus. She was having trouble moving.

'Nothing,' Chalice said. 'Nothing. Is it morning though? It's so light.'

'It's not the sky,' Arden said. 'It's us.' She kicked with all her remaining strength, and the sea might have been a shimmer of yellow light. 'It's you, Chalice, it's you!'

Light all around them, orange as a sunset.

Chalice Quarry's cracked lips split into a grin. She spun around and shrieked into the fog. 'Hey! Hey! Over *here*.'

Through the illuminated yellow mist came the chatter of a small kraken-oil engine, and the prow of a longboat loomed. Same black dinghy the pirates had reported missing from *Saudade*'s stern, with a roof of black canvas. Over the bow, two familiar faces, both incandescent with sodium light and relief.

David Modhi and Sean Ironcup. Still alive.

36

Are you awake

Are you awake, dear? Truly awake?

I have been awakened to something.

Then best get up now. You have been asleep long enough.

Arden sat up suddenly in a bed of soft cotton sheets. She immediately saw the portrait of the senior Justinian staring down at her from the foot of the bed. The Dowager had called him a stormcaller, from old Northern bloodlines. The old baron, Alexander Justinian. He wore shades of Mr Riven's face.

Next to the portrait, the very real figure of a nurse, who gasped and dropped her tray of potions, before running out of the room. Within seconds she was back with the Dowager Justinian and Mr Sage.

'Where . . .' Arden croaked with a voice that sounded as if her throat were lined with sand. 'I need to get up.'

The light through the small, high window seemed altogether too bright. She winced, and the Dowager went to draw the curtains.

'You're safe in our Manse,' she said. 'The Coastmaster decided it would be better for you to recover here than in Mr Sage's hospice. He sent out a search party, you see. Saved your life.'

After all that had happened, the simple thought of being

in such a debt to Mr Justinian was the thing to turn her stomach. A more pressing need took her. 'Bathroom.'

Mr Sage came forward. 'Ah, take your steps easy, then, Mx Beacon. You haven't been on your legs for nearly three days.'

She frowned. 'Three days? But I was halfway to the Sainted Isles a minute ago.'

'Dear, whatever you and your stormbride were doing on the open ocean so close to winter I cannot begin to opine, but you caught yourself a dreadful case of *ichor meritis*.' When Arden remained bewildered the Dowager added, 'It's a disease of the water around here. The creatures from the depths have a wicked venom.'

'Chalice, oh, how is she?'

'Hale as anything. Some people have a natural resistance. Some however, not. Up you get.'

The Dowager Justinian helped her into the bathroom, and afterwards waited with a bowl of lukewarm soup for Arden to teeter back, as weak as a foal taking its first steps.

'If you're up to visitors, there's the young lady here for you.'

Arden nodded. 'Give her permission.'

Chalice ran in before Dowager Justinian had a chance to advise her of Arden's decision, and kissed her messily on both cheeks before seizing up her hands.

'Ah, Arden, you're quite alive! Mr Sage came by twice a day and said all you needed was rest. I snuck David Modhi past the nurse at the door. He was so worried. *Ichor meritis!* It's a death sentence in these parts. I would have sent for a proper doctor but . . .'

'Your work is appreciated,' Arden said, and smiled though every muscle in her face hurt and her heart hurt twice more.

When the Dowager left them alone, Chalice closed the door and came close. The rigours of their castaway journey were still on her peeling skin and sunburned face.

'Mr Lindsay interviewed me,' she said quietly. 'I gave him the locket Mr Absalom gave me.' Arden frowned and Chalice waved her hand in dismissal – for a moment resembling the no-nonsense friend she'd known before.

'Don't fret, a copy was made before I handed it over. It contained a map printed on a square of silk, an up-to-date map of the Islands and their cities more detailed than we had ever yet seen.'

'What else did you tell him?'

'Not about Mr Riven, or that you know of your shadow endowment now, or that you made me stronger, if only for a little while.'

'I can't remember what we did. It's all rather muddy.'

'You increased me, made me *sanguinem*. Only long enough to make a little sodium arc in seawater. I can't say it was the most brilliant talent ever to show itself, but it certainly helped the boys find us. Oh, and I brought you a present.'

Then Chalice took a pair of new leather gloves from her pocket and unwrapped the bandages from Arden's hands. The grommets had been sealed with an antibiotic honey-wax.

'To replace the ones you lost.'

'Thank you, Chalice.'

'The Eugenics Society would use you terribly, if they had real proof of what they suspect you capable of, this *sanguinem evalescendi*.' She pushed the gloves forward, urged Arden to take them.

'Doesn't this silent assistance go beyond your Order vows?'

'Oh, I am loyal to the Lyonne Order. But the Order is made up of mere men, and they will make all the same wrong decisions if they try to use you the same way they tried to use Bellis. You deserve to make your own decisions about your body and your blood.'

Arden turned to face the window, where the salt-stumped gardens of the Manse struggled against the climate.

'You appear to be in the minority,' Arden said. 'For holding that belief.'

Fortunately, Mr Justinian's lechery was not sufficient to induce him to intrude upon a convalescent, and for a long time Arden did not have to contend with him. Besides, according to the whispering gossip of the house staff, sickness and disablement were conditions quite distasteful to the young lord of this salt-water estate.

He did not approach to claim his gratitude from Arden until she took her first steps in the delicate winter sun a few days later. She was in an empire line dress of urchin-blue cream, with her beloved krakenskin coat over the top of it, and her wobbly gait had eased enough to stand upright, unaided. One of the walled gardens provided a natural shelter from the elements, caught rays of the morning sun in that brief period before the afternoon fog came in.

She sat among the moss-covered statuary. Her strength returned in small moments. She would rub her grommets through her new gloves, and her thoughts had no purchase, turning to fog and forgotten memories, losing themselves to the chill air. A true endowment she now had, one that was powerful, but only expressed through the terms and skills of others. She herself was a cypher, without purpose of her own.

She was gifted and depleted at once. Jonah was gone. Her body was numb to his passing. He had been torn out of her, and she was hollow without him.

Time passed both slowly and fast. She'd taken some of the brighter days in the walled garden by herself. Today Mr Justinian intruded on her without apology.

'I rescued you,' he said once he had been given grudging allowance to sit beside her on the wrought-iron garden chair. 'That tugboat of Mr Riven's was floating out past the edge of the world and would have kept going had I not sent out a flotilla to search when it was discovered.'

'You have my appreciation,' she said, suspecting Mx Gertrude Modhi had actually gathered the party together not long after they'd left Vigil. A mother would not give up on her son.

'Your stormbride, your Madame Quarry. She said Mr Riven is dead?'

The rush of grief startled Arden at hearing his name aloud,

after keeping it at bay for so long. The air sucked out of her lungs. She could not take a breath. Mr Justinian took her silence as agreement.

'A shame. I know you pitied him and dallied with him. It behoves you well to lean tenderly towards the lesser among us. It is a virtue after all.'

Emboldened, he continued. 'We the nobility have our right as patriarchs of these folk to take whatever minor pleasures they can give us, but one must move on from fripperies and think seriously about the unions that will benefit us.' He sidled close. 'I have made overtures to the Eugenics Society to make an honest woman of you, so your mark of genetic shame is removed.'

His words cut through the numbness with breathless horror. 'You mean marry *you*, Vernon?'

'I have received a letter back from the Council today. An enthusiastic permission.'

Without warning, Mr Justinian was on his knees in front of her, and had snapped the top off a velvet box so she might see a big, antique diamond ring with a band scratched and thinned from all the women who had worn it before.

Arden fumed. There was audacity, and then there was just ambushed rudeness. Behind Mr Justinian's head a thin-faced statue peered out from the bushes. The stone and shadows were familiar. Alexander Justinian, the old baron. There were ghosts all around.

'Was Jonah Riven your brother, Mr Justinian?'

Mr Justinian paled. He stepped back. 'Whatever makes you think that?'

'No. Not a brother,' Arden said. 'A half-uncle, or a half-great-uncle? His mother worked in this house for your great-grandfather, Alexander Justinian, while the old man was still alive, did she not? It's not uncommon, for the lords of such estates to assault and demean those in their employ. I don't suppose there are many civilizing laws here in Fiction to protect a simple serving woman.'

Mr Justinian's eyes popped, and he made weak, mewling noises. 'My great-grandfather Alexander would nev . . .' He stopped. Started again. 'We don't entertain bastard claims here.'

Arden shook her head. 'In Clay Capital, it is genetics and the laws of eugenics, not marriage, that outline the terms of inheritance. Would be an interesting claim for a Riven to make, that the Manse is his.'

'Riven is dead!'

'Allegedly.'

Mr Justinian grabbed her arm, squeezed hard, and spittle flecked his lips. 'Don't think I can't tell that you have let the brute despoil you utterly, Arden Beacon. I know he spilled his seed inside you and that you may now carry his child.'

He was wrong, of course. She knew her own body and her monthlies had come while she lay recovering Arden tried to pull away, but he hung on with grim determination, intent on having her confess.

The moment became fraught with all the bad luck and poor decisions possible for a man to make. She was weakened from her illness. He could make it so that she never screamed again, and claim that *ichor meritis* had taken her life. Anything could happen.

Then he let her go, blushing furiously.

'I know what the Lions are capable of.'

'Yes, and they will test whatever issue comes from me. Landed titles are granted by Lyonne laws, not Fictish ones, and Lyonne inheritance is through genetics alone. If there's any dispute in ownership the legal vultures will come calling, and your title claim as Lord of the Justinian manse will become very, very weak.'

He backed away. A sneer on his lips. 'You think you have won both child and Lordship, Arden Beacon? Then I'll tell you what that thing in my father's glass jar really was. The cryptid in the study, the bell-jar you were so very much drawn to? That *thing* in the jar was the twin that exited from the Riven woman first, when she birthed your lover. Was the eight-legged monster, the snake-coils in her belly that first tumbled out of her and into the world. A monster twin coiled in the womb. That mutancy lies coiled up in your dear dead Mr. Riven, and who knows if it yet sets root and grows within *you*. Perhaps this is the real thing the Lions wished to have come about.'

Arden viewed Mr Justinian with pity, and no tenderness. Perhaps he did or did not tell the truth about the creature in the jar.

So what, if Mr Riven had been birthed with a poor, sea-creature twin? The Eugenicists of Clay Capital would have considered that a fair sacrifice for the endowment of blood. Mr Justinian had been away from Clay too long. Otherwise he'd have known that—just as the Order had decided with Bellis Harrow—it was considered better to be birthed monstrous than birthed without talent at all.

She squared her shoulders. Faced him with a gaze both limpid in its nonchalance and loathing.

'You do not scare me, Vernon. Give your mother my thanks for her hospitality, but when her duty is done to the Seamaster's Guild I will be on my way.'

37

Mr Justinian had the last word

Mr Justinian had the last word. He would not give her permission to return to her lighthouse on the edge of the Darkling Sea. Another girl took her place at the lighthouse now, a bride from the South, someone who could run a lighthouse on her until the Guild decommissioned the flame.

But Arden, of course, had not yet been given orders to leave. For now, she was effectively homeless, and without employment. Since their last conversation, Chalice had been sent back to Lyonne in disgrace in the dead of night. Without the chance to say goodbye.

In the face of her loss, the loss of Jonah, those blows were inconsequential.

A day later, the Dowager arrived in the guest house foyer as Arden was packing to leave, her hands bound up in an agitated tangle.

'A visitor for you,' she said, a thin note of fear in her announcement. This was not the same disapproving voice that she had used when Chalice had come to visit. The caller's importance was not lost upon the Lady of the Manse. 'He says it is most urgent.'

Mr Lindsay stood behind the Dowager's black-crêpe shadow,

bowler hat in one hand, briefcase in the other. His face was guileless as a child's. Arden nodded her permission. He waited until the mistress of the house was gone and the doors firmly shut before speaking.

'Such a shame you did not find her son worthy a match,' he said. 'We could have used you in domesticating our young Coastmaster. His family name is still starred in our ledger through his great-grandfather. It was a great loss that we could not keep the bloodline strong.'

'I have no emotion for him one way or another.'

'Of course. But I'm certain he'll work on that for as long as Mx Arden Beacon lives in this house, won't he?'

'What do you want, Mr Lindsay?' Arden asked, and did not bother to hide her annoyance.

He sat upon the edge of the daybed, fingered the crochet throw as if admiring the stitch work. He found the small bust of Baron Justinian, picked it up, studied the bronze handiwork. Perhaps he mused upon the likeness between the bust and the man who had lived upon the promontory.

'Miss Quarry also tells me there was an . . . ah . . . interesting electrical phenomenon that led to your being found. The search party saw the glow in the water and naturally came to your assistance.'

'That is correct.' Arden pressed her lips together firmly before speaking. 'A glow. A sea monster glow.'

'Not something else?' He looked at her, sly and knowing. 'Not something that the Order has long hypothesized but has never seen replicated in any individual?'

She took the bust out of his hands and placed it back on the marble side table. 'Tell me why I am entertaining your presence, sir?'

A smile split his thin cheeks. 'Well, you see, after his dereliction of Magistrate duties, Mr Alasdair Harrow has been escorted to Clay City. I thought you would like to be informed.'

'You're going to kill him?'

Mr Lindsay shook his head, as if puzzled. 'For questioning,

no more. If you are wanting someone punished, that other criminal, that Sean Ironcup, will find himself collected by the Constables at the end of the month. It was him that bled you.'

'Was Mr Harrow's idea.'

'Yes it was, and we can't have Order assets be flung about to the wolves without proper advice now, can we? As much as it would have been amusing to see what his fully empowered daughter could do, I fear she would not have shown the correct restraint at finding herself so *potent*.'

'Not without Jonah strong enough to tighten the leash on your behalf.'

'We'd hoped you could have assisted in that regard.'

Arden gave him a long, venomous silence before closing the shipping trunk. 'Well, I couldn't assist. So this little exercise in deception has turned out to be a complete waste of our time.'

'On the contrary. You brought back precious information our spy had so carefully curated for years. Riven may not be able to fully leash his wife, but he can certainly keep her attention focused. With those two in union, the balance of power in that rebellious region will change. Bellis Riven will soon rule the Isles. And though she doesn't know it, Lyonne rules her. Your assistance will not be forgotten.'

She did not trust herself to speak, otherwise she would shout at him to leave. Bellis and Jonah were not in *union*, no more than a broken horse was in union to the brutal owner who wielded the whip.

She will kill him, you little fool, Mr Lindsay. Jonah has no influence over Bellis. Nobody controls a sanguis orientis, *and one day you'll find this out the worst of ways.*

She could not say it. And not saying it made her dizzy with vexation. Mr Lindsay only saw her reeling from her fierce, unspoken emotion, thought it her illness.

'My dear, you are faint. Sit, sit.'

Mr Lindsay fetched Arden a chair. She wanted to recoil from his unctuous touch.

When at last she could govern her tongue, Arden spoke through a strangled throat. 'What happens to me now?'

He made a gesture of surrender. 'Mx Beacon, I know it must have been painful to strike up a friendship with such a dreadfully lonely, long-suffering creature as Jonah Riven. To perhaps . . . come to care for him? And we are not oblivious to what sort of woman Bellis has become. How it must have affected you, to meet her. I can only offer apologies that we could not supply you all the reasons, and give this humble restitution.'

He clipped open the brass hinges of the business satchel, and brought out an oxblood leather diploma roll. A golden tassel swung on the end.

He held the diploma roll out to her.

'Take it.'

She frowned. She had seen such a thing in her father's study, behind glass. The most precious thing he owned. All his status and his professional standing, bound up in whale vellum and a Guild seal stamped in wax.

'What is that?'

'Sanguine Order, Fourth Degree,' he continued. 'Master of Light. Higher than Portmaster, even. Higher than your father could ever hope to attain. You can return to Lyonne, join a lodge and after initiation receive the colours of your Guild Order. You will be Maria of the Unquenched Flame.'

The tassel swung, the golden glints catching the sunlight through the high windows. She shook her head, appalled at the offer. 'Mr Lindsay, a false membership to the associate order is one thing, but if I took that, it would make a *lie* of what the degree represented. I am not so powerful.'

Mr Lindsay came close. With his short stature, he was eye to eye with her as she sat in the chair. His voice was little more than a whisper.

'You and I both know that it is no *lie*, Arden Beacon. You are to return to the city with full honours. No cramped night train for our newest Guildmistress. You will put this time behind you. You shall live in Clay Capital in luxury for the rest of your life and your family's honour will be restored. Your father may regain his status in the Eugenics ledger, the very thing he lost when your *ignis* talent presented so . . . poorly.'

Mr Lindsay's eyes glittered like the tassel. He knew what she was capable of. No stories of quenching fires or sudden salty sanguinities for him. She had been brought to Vigil for a reason, and that reason was bordered on all four sides by Bellis Harrow.

Arden instinctively wrapped her hands over her grommets as he spoke, his words tying her up in chains of honour and filial piety.

'The Coastmaster Justinian still holds *my* leash,' she said. 'Despite your Lion friends and all the laws of Lyonne, that office is still his and he won't let me go so easily. There is no Master of Blood to replace a lighthouse keeper.'

'Perhaps there will be. No doubt you have heard of the test-moot slated for Garfish Point at this month's end, ten days from now. Those charged with tracing the genetics of Fiction say that a *sanguis ignis* is long overdue.'

'You cannot be certain.'

'Mx Beacon, when it comes to sanguinities, we are *always* certain.'

He paused, and smiled, as louche and conniving as ever. 'Oh, and before I forget. Something else for you.'

Mr Lindsay took from his pocket a thin rice paper envelope. Arden's name on the front, in a hand whose familiarity stabbed her with a hot spike of surprise. The wax seal was of the Airshipman's Guild. The postmark was Frieslandish.

'Since you are a guildswoman in full, you may make your own decisions about with whom you may consort. Perhaps even a certain Richard Castile. In fact, he was advised of your new position a week ago, and immediately made his way to Clay Capital.'

'Richard's in Clay?'

Mr Lindsay nodded. 'He composed a letter to you, which I now have pride in delivering. Take it.' He shook his offering as one might try to convince a shy bird to the snare. 'Go on.'

Arden took the envelope. It felt dry and brittle under her fingertips, the way of a newspaper left too long in the sun.

'He misses you, and seeks a reconnection,' Mr Lindsay said with affectionate magnanimity. 'You can reunite with your first love, now. Come. You have *earned* this.'

When it became clear that she would not open the letter in front of him and satisfy his curiosity about the letter's contents – contents he perhaps had a hand in dictating himself – Mr Lindsay shrugged, and touched the brim of his hat.

'Whenever you are ready, then. We will meet again, one week from now, Guildswoman. Remember me on your wedding day.'

The document roll might as well have been dipped in blood. The envelope mocked her with deceit. Richard Castile had not written to her since his departure of the last winter. Would not be writing letters to her *now* unless he'd been forced to do so.

As soon as Mr Lindsay was gone she screwed both desecrated objects up in her hands and shoved them into the deepest recesses of her coat pocket.

38

She could not bear to stay

She could not bear to stay in the guest house. Arden rented some rooms above Mr and Mrs Sage's shop, an apartment that was small but clean. Word had crept out, as all gossip did, that Arden Beacon had suffered trauma at the hands of Mr Riven. Something that had rendered her close to mute and perhaps had put to rest any chances of matrimonial happiness with the handsome young Baron who had once courted her.

Tall tales whispered lasciviously, just as they had done with Bellis.

Mrs Sage, her warnings vindicated, spent the first day fussing about Arden. She was charitable in her pity. Was not Arden's fault she had been harmed so, merely that of the men that had put her upon a rocky promontory with a fiend so close by. Besides, Mr Riven was gone now, no chance of him returning to wreak more damage. She took Arden's silence both as an after-effect of her ordeal and shame that she had not listened to Mrs Sage when they had met all those weeks before.

Arden could not be bothered changing the Vigil woman's mind. What a far more delightful story for a Fictioner to tell, of the ignorant Lyonne guildswoman who had wandered into a monster's lair.

Her life had begun to throw up its walls. The lid was about to close upon her freedom. Mr Lindsay inquired with her every afternoon. If she had dallied with the idea of staying in Vigil, waiting in case Jonah managed to get away from Bellis' clutches and return.

Each day was one more where he did not.

But *Saudade* did return.

She was battered by abandonment and weeks in the Tempest, her central axle broken beyond repair. A fisherman towed her in for the price of a whiskey fifth. As Harbourmistress, Mx Modhi had jurisdiction over who managed the promontory assets while Mr Riven was absent. Some previous instruction of Mr Riven's had granted the craft to David on his death, but since Mr Riven was not confirmed dead, she gave the boat to Arden.

'The salvage is yours to deal with, for now,' Mx Modhi said bitterly on the morning she passed the boat along. 'I don't want my child anywhere near that cursed vessel.'

'It *belongs* to your son, though.'

'Oh? Only upon Riven's confirmed death, and who knows in what form that monster might come back.'

They both knew. There would be nothing left of Mr Riven left to come back, nothing save what Bellis wanted to preserve. If anything, the petrochemical Queen would keep Jonah alive to punish Arden, so that even over the greatest distance she would remember.

Someone suffers in your stead.

Arden walked through the black mangrove boat with her heart in her mouth, bleeding memories. Jonah had had a soldier-prisoner's neatness and austerity about him, all items of necessity stacked and stored with rigid military precision. Being alone in the ship had an intimacy she doubted he would have been comfortable with, were he still here.

Apart from the external damage, Mr Riven had secured

everything well from the storm. Perhaps some glassware fallen across the map-room floor, doors flung open. There was little evidence of heavy seas.

Then she came to his cabin.

She only meant to glance inside, but the pull was too much. She stumbled inside and lay face-down upon his narrow bed, still rumpled from their lovemaking and blotted with the blood spots from the injuries he took to save her life. She did not cry, only allowed herself the fall into a deep, terrible abyss.

The lightless reality of Jonah's loss bore upon her with all the horror of being smothered, and when her third and fourth breaths did not come, she had to tear herself from the room and run to the deck, and dry-retch. *Someone suffers in your stead. Forever, until the end of your days.*

She had no life to go back to, only deceptions, only Mr Richard Castile compelled by Lions – by blackmail no doubt – to be the prize for their new *sanguis evalescendi*. The brief hope she'd shared with Jonah – to be free, to love without chains – had risen and died within the span of a day. Now she was wounded and could not heal.

The crisis only passed when she caught herself, for David and Sean Ironcup were on the newly restored harbour with a third man she did not know.

'Excuse me, Mx Beacon. I hope we weren't interrupting.' The man spoke up, taking off his fisherman's hat and wringing it in his big hands. He wore a huge felted coat of black wool, with epaulets winking silver, and a waistcoat of old Lyonne fashion. Across his chest he wore a sash of a minor craft Guild.

Arden wiped her mouth with the back of her sleeve and resumed her composure. 'I'm sorry. You had me in a moment of weakness.' She stood up tall and took deep breaths before joining them on the floating dock. 'It's been a great trial, you see, to lose a friend.'

'We could return later,' the stranger said politely. 'If that would best enable our conversation.'

'No, get on with it,' Arden replied. 'State your business.'

He stepped forward and shook her hand. 'I am Mr Zander Fulsome. I understand you have both a boat in need of repair and cryptozoological trophies. I was hoping we could come to an arrangement in terms of sale and trade.'

Would not have just been Arden to notice the kraken oil containers were all mostly full, and the cured krakenskin segments, as sweet-smelling as crocus stems, were laid out ready for the sale that Mr Riven had planned. David Modhi had seen them with a trader's eye, and known exactly where to procure a buyer.

'David Modhi, your mother was quite adamant,' she said to him warily. 'You can't have this boat.'

David stood tall. 'My mother might have forbidden *me* to do anything with *Saudade*, but that caveat does not extend to you.'

Mr Fulsome continued, 'For the krakenskin I could install a new axle upon your craft. I am the best boat merchant in all of Morningvale, and I can supply addresses of commendation, here and in the entire Fiction region.'

David was practically hopping out of his skin by Mr Fulsom's side. Arden did not have the heart to deny him.

'Sounds like it's a fair trade,' she said, wrapping herself back up with her Lyonne sanguine aloofness. It was not at all a fair trade. She could have purchased another boat for the hide. Two boats even, sleek and fast. Maybe a small balloon-craft. She added, if only for her guilty benefit, 'Mr Riven would wish *Saudade* fixed.'

A date was agreed upon. Two full days, and a team of men who could do in those hours what would take a regular ship-wright a month. Pleased, the boat-builder Zander Fulsome went on his way.

At a nod from David, Sean followed Mr Fulsome to complete the terms of business.

Arden prepared to walk back to her apartment, and found the young man following her at a close distance.

'So then,' Arden said. 'Out with it. I know you have a vested interest in seeing *Saudade* fixed soon and made the worst bargain in doing it.'

'There is a Eugenics Society testmoot in Garfish Point coming.'

Arden nodded, and remembered Mr Lindsay's confident words. He knew the sanguinem that would replace her.

'There is. Though if you had the slightest sense, David, you would keep your distance from anything to do with them.'

Her advice might have been stolen away by the wind. He pulled out some Fiction coins from a fish-bladder purse.

'Please take me there. In *Saudade*.'

'Oh, put them away, David. My employers won't let me leave this town until they come calling. Besides, would you not want to stay with Sean in these last days? He has not long yet before the Lyonne Constables come calling for him too. I can see you've formed quite a friendship.'

'He can come with us. Mx Beacon, I studied Lyonne law. If he stays on a Vigil-registered boat, he is still in Vigil. On a technicality.'

'Technicalities are not law, David.'

'You could technically still be in Vigil, too.'

She met his hopeful eyes and felt a small rebellion stir in her heart.

'Then I suppose . . . Well. I suppose I could make it up and back to Garfish Point. A newly repaired boat does need settling in.'

39

So, to the testmoot

So, to the testmoot, one last trip on *Saudade*.

Along with David Modhi and Sean, *Saudade* beat a fast course along the inner transit stream to Garfish Point, that busy promontory at Fiction's almost-civilized northern shore. From there, it would be less than six hours to Morningvale, and south Lyonne.

And home.

So strange to think of Lyonne as home, Arden thought, as she looked out over the choppy waters beyond the black boat's bow. She had changed so much. Would her friends even recognize her, after their long lazy summers on cool alpine meadows, a woman carved raw by the sea?

Every time Arden was in danger of feeling gladness at her upcoming return, the undertow of regret and guilt would come to pull her back in. She would go home having left pain and destruction in her wake. Not even the sight of small silver porpoises for much of the journey, and the wheeling gulls, drawn by the stirring of fish shoals, could lighten her mood. There was a Deepwater winter coming, she could smell the strange chill in the air.

Mr Castile's letter stayed in her pocket like a killer's confession. Try as she might, the thought of reading the contents only made her tip into a greater despair. She feared the effect the words would have on her. Feared falling in love again, a diminished, rotten kind of love, decayed by betrayal and time. A love belittled by what she'd felt with Jonah.

She did not want to see Mr Castile. She knew that now. Anything she'd felt for him was gone, leaving only an ugly lesion of experience.

Devilments, she fretted. *There is nothing I want less than to be loved under instruction.*

Garfish Point lay ahead of them, Fiction's largest town. The sails and shadows of a thousand crafts chequered the port waters.

'Is that the Order's boat out there?' David called from the wheelhouse, holding out the spyglass. 'It has a rose upon its sails.'

She needed no instrument. She had already caught the unmistakable silhouette of a Clay-class clipper against the orange of the sinking sun. 'Yes. They will have seen me leave. Doubtless the Order will collect me as I reach the shore, and take me to Lyonne. Hang on, David, I'll have the wheel now.'

He offered to stay on the wheel, having more experience at navigating the Point's demanding harbour. She shook her head.

'I'd rather make them come aboard and take me. One must strike a certain difficult tone of rebellion for the rest of my golden incarceration.'

But David Modhi, normally so tractable, made a face and would not relinquish his position. He appeared to have aged in these last few weeks. A man's face was upon him, not a boy's.

'I want to take the wheel,' he said again.

She let it go, and peered at him. 'What's wrong?'

'I've been talking with Sean Ironcup.'

'Yes, among the other things you two have been doing,' she said with a regretful exhale. She knew a burgeoning romance when she saw one. With Jonah gone, his grieving eye had settled on the next best thing. 'He's a good lad after all. He has a great affection for you, I can see that much. It will be difficult when he must leave. Perhaps the Order will be lenient in his sentencing. Mr Harrow was the true sinner.'

Her words didn't make David nod in agreement. Instead, he jutted out his lower jaw with an odd stubbornness.

'Lightmistress, if I were to test positive this time around—'

'It's very unlikely, David. This final test is merely ceremonial. They already know who their sanguinem is.'

'But if I was, I would have to leave Sean and go to Clay Capital. I will go into seclusion. We might lose each other.'

She shrugged. 'Let's cross that bridge when we come to it. This time tomorrow, the pair of you will be steaming back to Vigil.'

And I will be locked in a cabin with iron on my wrists.

So preoccupied was she with her fate, it took her several seconds before she became aware of the light in the wheelhouse. 'Devils, David, cover that lantern—'

She stopped. That was no light from one of the oil lamps. David Modhi clutched a coldfire lantern, one of the little storm-lights Jorgen had kept in the lighthouse – a miniature version of the lighthouse flame, kept for emergencies. The flame burned without heat. David's face was split by tear tracks in the bright yellow glow. His hand was bleeding.

With a gasp she struck the light out of his grip. The lantern smashed. They were plunged back into a colourless dusk.

'You tested *yourself*?'

'Yes, I know it's forbidden,' he said. 'No need to scold me. But I wanted to see for myself because I *knew*. I knew what I was. And last year, this happened.' He picked up the lantern. 'Mr Riven said I'd probably expressed the trait earlier. I don't know why I wasn't told.'

'The Eugenics Society is careful with Fiction bloodlines,' Arden said, feeling a cold sense of purpose growing in her. 'They know what might come out of such wild genes.'

Bellis. Jonah.

'I didn't come for the test,' David said. 'I came to get us away.'

In the harbour beyond, the clipper unfurled its sails. The Order boat had seen them. The mainsail was the last to hoist itself up. There would be an engine on board the ship as well, something fast, maybe.

She pressed her hands against the wheel spokes. 'David, this is not a choice. You have to go to the test and on to Lyonne. You can't have wild *ignis* endowments. The Order wouldn't let you.' Her breath escaped her as she saw the ship prepare to give chase. 'They won't let you live.'

Arden thought of Bellis, allowed to stay. *Unless they want to use you.*

'I don't want to lose Sean. I want to choose who I love. So drop us in the ocean here. It cannot be more than a mile to shore. We'll find our own way. Find somewhere to go. Just . . . don't tell the Order.'

Their conversation wasn't unwatched. Sean Ironcup stood on the deck with the replacement crutches David had painstakingly carved for him, his face marbled in hope and dread. She understood how David and Sean must have discussed a life on the run. Understood that they had already made up their minds what they were going to do.

All this had happened while she had been too busy with her own preoccupations to notice.

'Once upon a time,' she said, 'I dreamt of such a thing. Running away.'

'What happened?' David asked, knowing instinctively that her answer was wrapped up in her decision from this point forward.

She cut the throttle to the engines. A cloud of blue-sparkling kraken-oil smoke wafted over the forecastle. She pulled out Mr Castile's letter. Brandished it like a warrant of judgment.

'The one I loved was too scared to go through with it. That's what happened. And so our love withered like a flame unfed. But I shall not hold him to an old promise. His life is his own, just the same as mine.'

With a flourish she ripped up the envelope and tossed it out of the side window. *Goodbye, Richard Castile,* she thought. You were a young girl's fleeting lesson, but now lessons are over.

David blinked, as it dawned on him what Arden intended to do. She throttled forward on one wheel. *Saudade* started to turn.

'You're not letting us off here?'

'I'm taking you somewhere the Order can't touch you,' Arden said. 'And I'm going to set things right. I'm either going to rescue a man, or pay homage to a dead one, but whatever I do, the decision is mine. Are you coming with me?'

A huge grin spread across David's face. 'Certainly am, Lightmistress!'

The clipper was in full sail now, but against the current, the waters were far too quick for the large ceremonial ship to reach full speed. Within minutes of turning, *Saudade* had lost their three-mast pursuer. The kraken oil bloomed blue from the smokestacks, and Arden's coat shone in the half-light of the wheelhouse. One could fancy she had taken on the luminescence of the beast herself.

David Modhi went to tell Sean the development, and they embraced upon the forecastle in between bobs and heaves. Well then, she thought. The Order had certainly chosen her well. Wasn't she primed by experience to help lovers find one another? To increase a flame, a fire, a rebellion?

And now she was on her own journey, something not proscribed or ordered or necessary. Nobody pulled her invisible strings.

I'll find you, Jonah.

Maybe she would. Maybe she would not. Maybe Bellis had eviscerated him and replaced him with cogs and machine parts, like they did with the lich-ships on their eternal sea-road. Maybe he believed Arden had forgotten her fisherman from Vigil, thought her returned home with her old lover. But still. She would look. If he was alive she would find him, and if Bellis had transformed him into either corpse or monster, she would remember him in the Deepwater midwinter, and say a prayer so he might enter the cathedral of the King.

I'll find you.

The sun set upon the eastern horizon and the indigo sky spilled with stars. She still felt him: in her blood, and in the hide of the monster's skin she wore, and in the vast, lightless depths of the sea.

Fin

Acknowledgements

A million thank-yous to the usual suspects: my agent Sam Morgan, my editor Vicky Leech, to my family for putting up with all this, particularly Mum and Dad, Linda and Kerry and especially Eric and Xavier. Thanks to all those patient coffee-shop and café staff who kept me hydrated during the entire process.

Shout-out to my friends online, at work and in real life, both the Liminal and Clarion South crews, Axe Creekers, assorted drongos, my Nemesis, the Good Locust and Papa Bear.

And to Paul Haines, never forgotten.